His demons are women. All women. He is compelled to kill...and kill...and kill....

BY REASON OF INSANITY

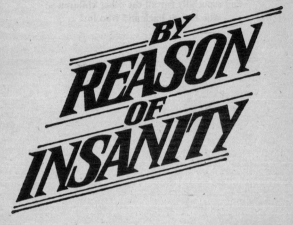

BY REASON OF INSANITY

SHANE STEVENS

A DELL BOOK

For Dr. Cornelia Wilbur
and for all the Sybils everywhere—
and especially for all the other children
who fought back and who lost

Published by
Dell Publishing Co., Inc.
1 Dag Hammarskjold Plaza
New York, New York 10017

Dell ® TM 681510, Dell Publishing Co., Inc.

ISBN: 0-440-11028-9

Reprinted by arrangement with Simon and Schuster, a
division of Gulf & Western Corporation.
Printed in the United States of America
First Dell printing—February 1980
Second Dell printing—March 1980
Third Dell printing—March 1980
Fourth Dell printing—May 1980

History is the story of the world's crime.
—VOLTAIRE

You ask me why you were born into a city of ghouls and murderers . . . I will tell you—it is because your beloved ancestors performed unspeakable crimes in secret and in silence, and now you must pay the hideous price!
—HERMANN HESSE

PROLOGUE

The flames ate at the body ravenously, searing, tearing through flesh and muscle. First flaking, then blackening and charring, the skin disintegrated swiftly. Soon arms, legs and trunk would become flame-flushed down to whitened bone. And in due time the head, stripped of facial features, would come to resemble a skull.

Silent now but for a gurgling singsong moan from somewhere deep in his throat, his eyes maniacal in the red glow of fire, the boy watched his mother's body burn and burn and burn . . .

BOOK ONE

Thomas Bishop

ONE

In the spring of the year, the mist that rolls like silent thunder across the bay seems to bathe San Francisco in quicksilver. Mercurial, it passes through everything, changing nothing, leaving nothing. Yet it shrouds whatever it touches, raising the purely natural to the mystical, however temporarily. Nowhere is this more evident than north of the city, along the coastal fingers of land extending into San Francisco Bay. It is here that the primal mist best works its magic, covering the shimmering towns and fields and inlets. Here lie the threads of a thousand folktales. Here too, an eerie centerpiece, looms San Quentin Prison. Dark-rocked, forbidding, the prison rises out of the earth mist, a landscape in tortured stone. Oftentimes, in the early gloom, San Quentin looks like the lighthouse at the end of the world.

On just such a day, to be exact, on May 2, 1960, a condemned man was led into the gas chamber at San Quentin. He was accompanied by four guards, two of whom quickly strapped him into the right-hand one of two metal chairs in the small steel room. The stethoscope was connected. The guard captain wished him good luck. His face showed no emotion as the guards left and the metal door was sealed from the outside, its spoked wheel given a final turn. He continued to stare at the sixty witnesses assembled outside the octagonal cell, watching him through five thick glass windows. The final prayers had already been said, the last words already spoken for Caryl Chessman. For twelve years he had fought the coming of this day in the courts of California and the Supreme Court of the United States. Now the fight was over. He had lost, and at age thirty-eight Caryl Chessman awaited the penalty of death.

Behind the gas chamber, set into one side of a larger room on the first floor of the death house, a hand opened a valve at a signal from the warden. The time was 10:03 A.M. Instantly cyanide pellets dropped from a container under the death chair into a basin of sulfuric-acid solution. In a matter of seconds the lethal acid fumes reached the condemned man, soon filling the room with the odor of bitter almonds and peach blossoms. His body strained against the straps, his head jerked back. Slowly he slipped into unconsciousness and death, the brain denied oxygen. The official pronouncement, at 10:12, created no stir beyond the necessary clean-up details. And in the rest of San Quentin, above the gas chamber known as the Green Room because of its dark-green walls, life went on much as before.

The killing of Caryl Chessman, the infamous "Red Light Bandit" who had committed a series of robbery-rapes in Los Angeles in the late 1940s—coming as it did in the pivotal year 1960—was thought by some to mark an end to an era of violence in America that stretched from the gangster lawlessness of the twenties, through the violent labor disputes of the thirties and bloodshed of World War II and the Korean war, to the indiscriminate mass killings of a Perry Smith or a Charles Starkweather in the late fifties. The leisurely Eisenhower days were over and soon Kennedy would begin the years of Camelot. The first major stirrings of protest over capital punishment were being heard. The country was in a scientific race with Russia that would create jobs and improve the economy. Everywhere new directions were opening that would require energy and dedication. It was thought to be an exciting time, for America was once again on the move.

Instead, Caryl Chessman's death at the start of the sixties marked the beginning of an age of bloodletting which is not yet over. And, by a strange twist of the fates, Chessman's life and death were also the beginning of a bizarre and savage series of killings that would—more than a decade later—involve law-enforcement officials across the nation, and reach into the highest governmental and communications levels. To see why and how this came about, one must first go back to the early postwar years in Los Angeles. Uniforms were scarcer on the streets now that the war was over, and tract houses were being built by the thousands all over the valley. Food was more plentiful too. Upstate, Henry

Kaiser was forming companies to make everything. In Washington the Truman administration was trying to save Europe from economic collapse. But as usual nobody did anything about the weather. It was hot and humid on this September 3, 1947, and people were glad to see the sun go down. Sometime during the evening a man with dark hair and bushy eyebrows decided that it might be a good night for rape and robbery.

While most of the city played cards or drank beer or went to a movie or even to sleep, others could be found turning off roadways and streets, inching along without lights until a spot was reached where the occupants, usually two, could nuzzle in privacy. Lovers' lanes were still plentiful, though the housing boom was already whittling them down. In these various secluded groves Fords and Chevies and an occasional Cadillac would form a loose daisy chain, with each car a respectful distance from the next, and every nose pointed toward the center so that leaving would cause no disturbance to others.

Inside the cars people would fondle each other, and when the girl got disheveled enough to call a temporary halt the boy would pull out a pack of Camels and they would smoke and listen to the radio and talk in whispers. For those more seriously involved, the idle chatter would soon give way to the language of passion and pleas of eternal love.

In less accessible areas cars would simply park as far from one another as possible. Often this meant virtual seclusion, and couples could then feel they were alone in the world. It was to this kind of lovers' lane that the man came seeking victims. His search was soon rewarded.

The car was a blue Plymouth sedan. The window on the driver's side was down and murmuring could be heard from within. A pool of cigarette butts lay on the soft ground, deposited from a filled ashtray. There were no other parked automobiles to be seen as the man silently crept up, a gun in one hand and a light in the other. At the last step he stiffened and hurriedly flashed the light into the Plymouth.

Behind the wheel the driver turned toward the light, startled. Someone asked him what he was doing there. Before he could answer he was ordered to open the door. Flustered, he did as he was told. Then he was ordered to step out with the car keys, and remove the contents of his pockets. When he saw the gun he quickly complied. He was marched to the rear and told to get in the trunk. "You'll be out in a little while," the voice said to him. "Don't worry." The driver obeyed and heard the trunk being locked.

The next moment the man was beside the girl, flashing the light on her. She was pretty in a plain way, a little too plump perhaps, but rounded and soft. Her light-brown hair was short and done in the fashion of the day, curls framing the face. She wore a yellow dress and green sweater which she had unbuttoned. These the man ordered her to remove in the back seat as he got in after her. He was polite and told her that she would not be hurt if she didn't resist. He asked her twice if she understood.

Sara Bishop, age twenty-one, understood perfectly. At thirteen she had been seduced by her uncle, her dead mother's brother, who had brought her to Oklahoma City from a small town to live with his family. He would sit her on his lap when his wife wasn't home and his aged and cranky mother-in-law was asleep upstairs. She would feel his hands on her, all over her body, until one day it was no longer just his hands. For three years she said nothing, suffering his attentions quietly. She had nowhere else to go. At sixteen she married an oil hand who left her after three months. At seventeen she was attacked by three high school boys behind a luncheonette where she worked. At eighteen she left Oklahoma City for Phoenix and a serviceman who got her a job as a B-girl and took all her money before leaving her one night with a black eye and a few loose teeth.

By age twenty Sara Bishop hated men, all men, with a passion others usually reserved for love. Yet she was intelligent enough to know that they came in handy at times. She didn't care much for sex, though it sometimes could be used to get what was needed. What amazed her was her inability to get pregnant all those years, a mystery for which she was thankful. The following year, after moving to Los Angeles, the mystery was cleared up by a doctor who repositioned her womb during a minor operation. For this she loudly cursed him. When the bill arrived she wrote two words on it and sent it back unpaid. She never received another. But to Sara it was just one more man in a long line that proved her hatred justified.

Now, lying on the back seat of the blue Plymouth, Sara Bishop prayed. She didn't want to die and she didn't want to become pregnant. Yet here she was naked, with her legs open, and this stranger was on top of her having his fun. All because he was a man and had a gun. Goddam men, she thought, goddam them all to hell. Twice she asked him to please not come inside of her but he merely grunted.

To escape the moment Sara thought of the young man in the trunk. She had been seeing him for a month, hoped that he would ask her to marry. She was broke and she was lonely. But mostly she was plain tired. It would be easier with a man, even if he was just a twenty-three-year-old drifter. But he's worked a lot of jobs, she thought grimly. He could work at something to take care of us. She hadn't been intimate with him yet because she wanted to hold his interest until—

The man was getting off her. It was over. She didn't know if he had come inside of her or not. He probably did, she told herself, defeated. But at least one thing he didn't get was feeling. She hadn't moved a muscle, hadn't moaned or groaned or begged or pleaded or even squirmed. All he got was a dead fish, she said to herself. Hope he liked dead fish. She corrected herself. Hope he didn't like dead fish.

He tossed her the car keys. "Let him out after I go," he said softly. Then he thanked her. Just like that. "Thank you." And he was gone.

She lay there quietly in the dark, holding back tears. She felt used up, drained of all energy. What was the sense of fighting? Men always got what they wanted, the bastards. They made promises or gave a few dollars or took by force, it all came to the same thing. They got their fun and then they were gone. If she had her way she would kill every last one of them, the miserable bastards. Miserable bastards, she shrieked to herself. She opened her mouth to shout it, but nothing came out. Suppose he was still around? What did she know of him? He carried a gun and a funny kind of light. He had dark hair and bushy eyebrows. And a big nose. What else? The rest of him was small, she thought with grim satisfaction.

A thump startled her. She quickly threw on her dress, shoving her brassiere and panties and slip under the cushion. She leaned over the front seat and fixed her face in the mirror. Tired or not, scared or mad, she knew what she had to do. Just in case.

Fumbling with the key, she finally got the trunk open. He was wild with anger, running around, wanting to go after the man with a tire iron. But there was no one in sight. Embarrassed, mortified at the blow to his pride, his manhood, he cursed his enemy incessantly as he was slowly led back to the car. In his rage he didn't notice that she had pulled him into the back seat.

Now she snuggled tightly against him, cooing softly, murmuring words of encouragement. She stroked his cheek, his chest, calming his anger little by little. After a while she placed his hand on her ample breast. Her face was ecstatic, her eyes wide and limp with innocence.

In her heart she was cursing him as just another bastard man, so wrapped up in his own feelings that he gave no thought to what she had just been through. Not a word of pity, not a gesture of sorrow, not even a look of interest to see if she had been hurt. Nothing but his own stupid pride, his own hurt feelings. You son of a bitch, she almost screamed at him.

Her face showed nothing as she slid farther down the seat, pulling him on top of her. Her sexual whisperings became frenzied, her breathing heavier. She felt his hand beneath her dress as she wiggled it higher until it was above her hips. Her open mouth found his tongue and held it, working it between her teeth. Now his breathing became charged, his movements more frantic. He suddenly leaned to one side and began fumbling with his pants. As she heard the zipper she silently vowed to give an Academy Award performance right here, this night, on this deserted strip of road. She would, by God or the devil himself, give this bastard man the greatest sex he ever had, the greatest sex any man ever had. She would do it because she had to. She needed him.

Two months later they were married in Las Vegas. The chapel cost twenty dollars, the other eighty they lost at the crap table. With return tickets in hand, they boarded the last bus back to Los Angeles. Sara didn't tell her new husband that she was pregnant.

True to her vow, Sara had given him all the sex

he wanted and any way he wanted it. Shutting off her mind, she performed her act so well that he soon came to believe he couldn't live without her, or at least shouldn't. He hadn't realized women could be so passionate—some women, anyway—so willing to satisfy his every fantasy, yet never demanding anything of him. It was like having a wind-up toy, life-sized and eager to please. He decided that he would play along with it for a while.

After the marriage Sara kept on with her act, though with somewhat diminished fervor, as befits a married woman. She had little use for sex herself since no man had ever brought her to satisfaction. But the emotional security of just being with someone was worth the effort, she believed. And the money helped too. His pay at the gas station was more than she could ever make in the bakery. With two paychecks they even had a bit to spare. Between the sex and the promised good times, she thought she could hold him. And so one day she decided that she would keep the baby when it came.

A month later she told her husband that he would be a father. She was lying for in her heart Sara somehow knew, as only a woman could know, that the real father was a rapist with dark hair and a big nose and a funny light. But he wasn't here and this man was, so of course he was the father. Poetic justice, Sara told herself. Here's at least one time to get back at the bastards.

Her husband was impressed. Dumb as only a twenty-three-year-old can be dumb, he felt that fatherhood made him even more of a man. And when Sara promised him that a baby wouldn't interfere in any way with the sex he was getting, he dropped his pants right there on the kitchen floor and had her make love to him where he stood. Afterward he went out for a few beers.

On January 24, 1948, Sara Bishop, now Sara Owens, read in the Los Angeles papers of the capture of a robber-rapist who preyed on couples in lovers' lanes. She looked at the picture. It was him! She looked again, more closely. Now she wasn't so sure. He was only a man she had once been under for a few minutes, and the father of her child. She read the name of the rapist: Chessman. Caryl Chessman.

When her husband came home she showed him the paper. The man had taken thirty dollars from him, a supreme insult. "I hope they kill the son of a bitch" was all he said. He hadn't seen the face clearly that night. But she had. "I'm not positive," she told him, and threw the paper down in disgust.

For days Sara thought about going to the authorities. But what good would it do? They hadn't reported it at the time because neither wanted to get involved with the police. And of course she had told her future husband that the man was impotent, that he had just played with her a little that night and had then left. She wasn't sure she was believed but she didn't really care, that was her story. Now with the baby coming, it might not be a good idea to bring all that up again. In the end she decided to do nothing about the night. But she followed the case in the papers, and when they started calling Chessman the Red Light Bandit because he had flashed a red light on the occupants of cars, she was almost certain he was her man.

On April 30, 1948, a son was born to Sara Owens. Named Thomas William, his eyes were brown and his hair dark, whereas both Sara and her husband had light-brown hair. At a glance he looked nothing like his father, but a nurse kindly pointed out that physical characteristics often skipped a generation. The father nodded gravely.

On May 18, 1948, Caryl Chessman was convicted on seventeen of eighteen counts of armed robbery, kidnapping and rape. He was subsequently sentenced to death and given a July date of execution. In handcuffs and under heavy guard, he was taken to San Quentin. His appeal delayed the execution, and by summer's end the Chessman case—except for further appeals and various legal actions over the next twelve years—was out of the headlines and the public mind for the moment.

In the Owens household the addition to the family brought about subtle but increasingly disruptive changes over the next several years. Sara lost some of her energy, which had never been vast anyway. The birth had drained her physically and emotionally. She vowed never to have another baby, no matter what. She would die first. Then, too, her great disappointment at not having had a girl could not be contained forever. Unconsciously at first, without willful deliberation, she began to resent the boy. Toward her husband as well she became increasingly remote. After losing the job at the garage he had run through a string of odd jobs that never seemed to bring in enough money. She herself could not work because of the boy, nor did she feel up to it any longer. With alarm she sensed her husband changing, not realizing that she was changing as well. She came to feel that he was careless toward her, that he was no longer accepting his responsibilities. She resented the spiraling amount of time he spent away from home with his friends, whom she saw as drifters and bums. She worried that he might be with other women. In short, Sara gradually began to feel cheated out of whatever it was she should have had, and as always she saw it as a plot directed against her by men.

Harry, for his part, also felt cheated. His wife no longer was the sex toy he had married. She wasn't exciting anymore, she didn't make him feel alive. Now she just nagged him and was sloppy around the house and screamed at the kid all the time. And he resented her wanting him to work night and day, especially when she did no work. He was good with cars and he liked money, sure, but he couldn't see spending his life just working to take care of her and the brat. He never should have tried to settle down, it just wasn't in him. He felt trapped, and somehow he knew it was all her fault. What he would do is figure out a way to get enough money to leave.

By the third year of their marriage Sara and Harry were openly dissatisfied with each other. Yet they remained together in their three-room apartment, each afraid to let go of the old, fearful of the new. She still gave him what sex he wanted, or at least some of the time. He still gave her what money he had, or at least part of it. Sara had taken to drinking wine in the house. Harry, strictly a beer man, didn't think women should drink, at least not married women, and certainly not his wife. The first time Sara got drunk, at least the first time Harry came home to find her drunk, he hit her. After that the beatings became more frequent.

On June 24, 1951, Caryl Chessman again made the Los Angeles papers in one of his many legal actions. Sara, glass in hand, read the account avidly. Over the years Chessman had assumed celebrity status for her because of his notoriety. Everyone seemed to know of him;

why, she had even seen magazines with stories about him. For her, Chessman was no longer just a rapist; he was a name and a face, someone familiar. Of course he was still a man and therefore to be hated and despised. But at least he wasn't around to torture her every day of her life, as others were doing.

By the time Harry got home Sara had had a number of drinks. When the shouting started she turned on him and loudly informed him that he was not the boy's father. He laughed, and Sara, stung by his derision, blurted out that she had lied to him. "It was Chessman in the car that night, Caryl Chessman, you stupid son of a bitch. And he wasn't impotent. He's more of a man than you'll ever be." Now it was Sara's turn to laugh. "You think you're so good. By the time I let you touch me his seed was all the way inside me, keeping me warm. What do you think of that, Mister Big Shot?"

She didn't notice Harry's eyes getting smaller. "You don't believe me, do you?" She stormed into the next room, coming back a moment later dragging the boy by the arm. He had been sleeping and his eyes were half shut. "Look at his hair," she shouted at her husband, "it's dark. Yours is light brown and so is mine. Look at his mouth, his whole face. Nothing like yours. Not even the skin's the same." She grabbed up the paper from the table. "You want to know whose kid he is? You really want to know?" She tossed it at her husband. "There's his picture, right on that page. Look at it, you poor dope. Look at it," she screamed at him.

Harry, deathly still, took the paper and examined the picture. He looked at the boy, who was sniffling now with fright. He looked at the picture again for a long time, then again at the boy. Without a word he gently put the paper back on the table and quietly walked over to his wife and hit her full in the eye. She staggered back and he hit her again with all his strength on the side of the cheek. She fell and lay there. The boy, terrified, stood rooted to the spot. Harry walked up to him and with doubled fist slammed him in the face, knocking him unconscious.

After three days Harry returned home, unshaven, smelling of liquor and perfume. He didn't mention the incident. Neither did Sara, nursing a black eye and puffed cheek. Nobody mentioned the boy, who was still sick in bed from the beating.

Sara knew that her husband would soon be gone for good. But she just didn't care anymore. She wondered only why he had bothered to return at all.

That night Sara dreamed about Caryl Chessman. He was chasing her and she couldn't seem to get away. He was all around her. There were other people in the dream too, crowds of men. But the next morning she could not remember exactly what they were doing. That afternoon she picked up a man in a bar and had illicit sex for the first time since her marriage. It was unsatisfying and she came home tired and defeated. She lay down on her bed and cried bitterly and asked God to grant her wish that all men be horribly killed that very second, all men everywhere, right down to infant males.

Six weeks later her boy was admitted to a hospital with second-degree burns covering his left arm and side. An accident, Sara told the doctor. She had been boiling water for coffee and he crashed into the stove while playing. When it was pointed out that such extensive burns would require a large amount of water, she replied that she always made enough coffee in the morning for a small army. "Saves time later on," she murmured sweetly.

In the afternoon the hospital administrator and resident physician met with the intern who had admitted the burned boy.

"Where is he?"

"I put him in 412."

"How bad is it?"

"Hyperemic and vesicant damage from the neck to the waist. Same for the left arm almost to the wrist. Some plasma leakage already. Could be worse, I guess."

"You're an optimist, Doctor."

"I have to be in cases like this or I'd go nuts."

"We all would."

"Is the mother in the hospital?"

"Home. Or somewhere. I think she got scared."

"The son of a bitch."

"Daughter."

"What's that?"

"Daughter of a bitch. She's a woman, isn't she?"

"She's still a son of a bitch."

A nurse came into the room.

"Joanne, make sure someone stays with him tonight. Just in case."

"Yes, Doctor."

"Christ, he's tiny."

"How old is he?"

"Three."

"Oh my God," said the administrator.

"There are two others worse than this in the burn section downtown."

"The Ames girl?"

The resident physician nodded. "Of course she's older."

"Yeah, she's five."

"What'll happen to him when he gets out of here?"

"Go back home, I guess."

"Back to more of that, you mean."

They stood at the foot of the bed watching the boy, unconscious now. He was wrapped in white.

"Can't he be taken away from her?" asked the nurse, her voice cracking. "I mean, can't somebody—" She stopped, her eyes watery.

The administrator shook his head. "There are cases like this all over the city," he said quietly. "Thousands of them. Parents who burn their children, beat them, starve them. Sometimes they kill them. And if they don't they get scared and come running to a hospital. It's always an accident." He removed his glasses and rubbed his eyes. "The hell of it is you can't prove anything most of the time. The boy *could've* burned himself accidentally."

"Not hardly likely," said the intern.

"Not likely," agreed the administrator wearily. "But without definite proof the hospital can't go to the authorities. No one can." He replaced his glasses.

"And so she gets a second shot at the boy, and then a third."

"Only if he's lucky."

"Lucky?"

"If he's lucky enough to survive the second," whispered the resident physician, walking toward the door.

"You can never tell how these things work out. No one knows for sure."

"I know one thing for sure," said the intern vehemently in the hall. "One thing I know for goddam sure." His voice shook with anger. "That boy in there is doomed. No matter what happens, he's doomed."

The others nodded, their lips tight, their eyes sad.

"Doomed," he repeated.

Doomed or otherwise, the boy was visited every day by his mother, a bundle of concern. When she finally took him home she bought him a pint of chocolate ice cream, his favorite. The next day she banged his head on the side of the bathtub when he accidentally splashed water on her. Screaming, he fainted.

Sara decided that she had better give up drinking in the house. Frightened now, because she still had feeling for the child even though he was a hated male, she sought help from a self-styled minister of the Astrological Church of the Planets, one of the many religious sects that seemed to grow like crabgrass in southern California. He listened politely to her problem, then told her that for a fifty-dollar offering to the church he would study her astrological chart. Two days later he sadly informed her that she labored under a double cosmic cross, "perhaps the gravest sign in the heavens." However—and here he brightened considerably—her planets were such that she would soon enter a peaceful phase, one filled with great opportunities and rich rewards. How soon? He couldn't tell unless he did her horoscope, which would require a further offering of course. Sara thanked him and left, stopping in the bar next door for a glass of wine.

After the third glass she felt better, thinking about the peaceful phase to come. God knows she deserved some peace. When the man came in and sat next to her, she smiled back at him. Later in the motel room, looking at the stranger sleeping alongside her naked body, Sara just knew that her phase had already begun.

By the end of September she also knew that she was pregnant again. Scared now, more scared than she had ever been in her life, and insanely angry at the gods, all males naturally, who somehow conspired to bring this fresh horror on her head, Sara Owens vowed that she would not have another baby. No, never. Whatever else happened she would take, but not that. Never again.

Set in her determination, the helpless fright subsiding, she tried to figure out how such a thing could happen. All those years with her husband produced nothing. Now, the second time she strayed in almost four years of marriage, and she's pregnant again. It wasn't just punishment and it couldn't be mere coincidence. Suddenly the answer seemed clear. Of course. Her husband was sterile, that had to be it. For all his crazy sex urges, he couldn't make a baby if he tried. Sara nearly burst out laughing, the thought was so delicious. He's only half a man, the poor bastard. Wait a minute—if he's sterile, then the boy really is Chessman's. Or the rapist's, whoever he was. Sara shook her head. It was Chessman, all right. She needed to believe that, for it was easier living with a name than a faceless nobody, so over the years she had convinced herself that Chessman was her rapist.

Sara saw what she must do. She would get an abortion. First, somehow, she would get the money. Then she would never again have sex with a man, any man. Not even her husband. Let him go to hell for it, let them all go straight to hell. She didn't need them and didn't want them. All she ever really wanted was to be left alone.

Every afternoon Sara put on her best dress and stockings, her highest-heeled shoes and a freshly made face and sat in elegant cocktail lounges in the best sections of town, smiling at moneyed men with murder in her heart. She could still act, and if she no longer gave Academy Award performances she was nonetheless a better player than many wives waiting at home.

In three weeks she had nine hundred dollars. Fifty of it bought her the name of a doctor who would handle her problem. Eight hundred more bought the doctor. An overnight stay in an elaborage address on Mulholland Drive and she was free to go.

Free! Even the air in this part of town felt better to Sara. She had the cab stop at a plush lounge, where she ordered a glass of very expensive wine. Then another. Though it was early afternoon, several well-dressed men were at the bar. She returned their smiles and when one joined her she engaged him in conversation. She was charming, animated, flirtatious, seductive, everything a man could desire. When he finally asked if he could help make her day profitable as well as pleasurable, Sara turned to him with eyes wide and a sweet smile and told him in graphic language what he could do with his manhood. She delicately put her last fifty-dollar bill on the bar in payment for her drinks and walked out, head held high.

At home she fed the boy, who hadn't eaten since the previous day, and then slept for fifteen hours. She had no intention of telling her husband anything. He wasn't home half the time anymore and she wished he would never come home again.

Harry didn't really want to go home, it was just that he wasn't ready to make the break yet. All he needed was one big score, anything, and it would be goodbye forever. There was nothing more for him at home, not since she had told him about Chessman and the brat. Harry didn't like that, made him feel foolish. What he should do was just pack up and go, he kept telling himself. Sure, it'd serve her right, serve them both right. Her and that damn brat.

For months Harry had been brooding about Chessman and the night in the woods years before. He had never been sure it was Chessman; he didn't remember any flashing red light. But she was so damn sure, at least since the kid came. She probably enjoyed it, the slut. And then lying to him like that, telling him the guy did nothing. Forcing him to make love to her right after someone did a thing like that. He should have hit her and driven away, just he felt sorry for her.

Harry was very certain that his wife would suffer terribly when he finally left her, and for that he was glad. But it was Chessman who really bothered him, laughing at him, taking what was his, insulting him that way. The more Harry thought about it, the angrier he got, until one day he decided that he would kill Caryl Chessman. He would wait for them to bring Chessman to Los Angeles again for something and then he would shoot the bastard, just like that.

Three months later, in January 1952, he got his chance. Chessman was whisked into town for a hearing on a petition filed by his lawyer. Harry bought a stolen gun through a friendly connection and waited across the street from the courthouse. The gun, a Colt .45 army issue, was in his topcoat pocket and Harry fingered it warmly. He had never killed anyone, never even fired a gun in his life. All he knew about guns was what he had seen in the movies. The good guy always killed the bad guy, and he always had more bullets in his gun. Harry knew he was the good guy, so all he had to learn was how to load the bullets. When this was done, he felt ready for anything.

As he sat on a bench in the small park waiting for the bad guy to show, Harry's mind raced through all the war movies he had ever seen. Machine guns, tanks, bombs, grenades, dead bodies everywhere. He remembered Bogart hitting the beach, his trusty .45 in his hand, killing every Jap around him, crawling under barbed wire, racing forward ahead of his men. When the tank rolled over him he just slid between the treads, then leaped on it, opened the turret and dropped a grenade down its throat before diving off. Boom! One dead Jap tank. Only Bogart could've done that. Wait a minute— it was John Wayne. Was it John Wayne? Goddam right it was. So what, same thing. Harry wished he could have been there, he would have shown them a few things. If only his trick knees hadn't kept him out of the army.

Two police cars braked to a halt across the street, one behind the other. A half dozen reporters rushed down the courthouse steps. Harry jumped up, his hand still on the gun in his pocket. The people suddenly looked small across the street, he didn't think he could hit anything. Hesitating, he watched as a wedge of cops hustled somebody up the stairs and into the building. Then they were gone. The whole thing had taken only a few seconds and he had hardly caught a glimpse of Chessman.

Harry was so mad he sat down and cursed his lungs out, vowing to remain there forever if necessary. Staring with grim determination at the court, Harry's mind eventually saw Chessman walk out alone, whereupon he ran over him with a tank, stuck a grenade in his mouth, chopped him to pieces with a machine gun and killed him eighteen times with one clip of his trusty .45, after which he shot him ten times in the groin just to make sure. Satisfied, Harry did it all over again.

After a while the rain started and Harry left the park. When he got home he found the loaded clip in his other pocket. He had indeed learned to load the bullets, but he forgot to insert the clip in the .45. The gun was empty.

That same night Harry sold the gun and made back the fifty he had paid for it. The buyer told Harry that he already knew how to load it. "Don't everybody?" he said.

The very next month Harry Owens got the break he had been waiting for all his life, a shot at a big score, the big money. The bankroll he needed to get away. He was twenty-eight years old and had never really had much of anything. A drifter since his teens, he had come out of the west Texas slums working whatever jobs he could find. Always moving on down the line, he hit Los Angeles at twenty-one and stayed a while. Then he met Sara Bishop and got in over his head. Now was his chance to get out with something, maybe the only one he'd ever get.

Harry was good with cars, driving them, fixing them. His aptitude was quickly noted by a few acquaintances at one of his hangouts, a bar on the city's north side that catered to a rough-and-ready sort. Like him, these men were drifters of little education and limited job potential. They were not criminals in the usual sense of the word; rather, they were blue-collar opportunists who worked at whatever was available while they sought a big killing that would put them on easy street. Dreamers all, they were yet realistic enough to know that such a venture would require a certain risk. War veterans mostly, they had lived with violence and had seen death and destruction, and they were just alienated enough to be willing to gamble their futures on a quick throw of the dice. None had records beyond the misdemeanor stage, and only one was married. When Harry joined the group he made them six. Complete now, they plotted and planned and waited for their turn at the dice.

They did not have long to wait.

February is a bad month in Los Angeles and gets worse toward the end. On this dark February morning the rain had been falling steadily since midnight. The sky was an angry gray and even the sun had trouble finding the city. In the business areas people stumbled into offices and stores soaked to the skin. Everywhere houses leaked, lawns drowned and new foundations settled. It was February 22, 1952, the day six men had picked to rob Overland Pacific, the country's biggest armored-car company, of a million dollars.

While mothers all over the city hurried their children off to school and policemen on the day shift lined up for inspection, a massive black-and-white fortress on wheels lumbered out of Overland's main terminal, eased past the barbed-wire-topped steel fence and slowly turned right into traffic. Built short and stubby, its riveted 12-gauge steel-plated body sprouting concealed air vents and gunports on all four sides, the ten-ton monster gradually picked up speed.

Inside, behind tinted bulletproof windows, the driver and his partner cursed the weather, the world, and the work they were doing. Friday was a "dog day," a day of heavy cash flow and many stops. Their schedule called for seventy-five such stops in the eight hours they would be on duty. The grumbling continued in good-natured fashion until the first stop, a Los Angeles branch of a statewide loan company. From his seat the driver locked the steel door separating the cab from the truck's main compartment. In the back the guard opened the rear door and peered out cautiously. Seeing nothing suspicious, he quickly hopped out with a bag of currency and entered the squat building, his gun in hand, barrel pointed down. In a moment he returned and, after a look from the driver, the electrically operated rear door opened and he reentered the truck.

In the next hour the driver-guard team made nine more stops, mostly to banks and stores. The cash flow was heavy, as expected, and several times required the assistance of a dolly. At some stops money was delivered, at others it was picked up. But always the procedure was the same. The driver would park, with the motor running, in such a way that he could see his partner enter and leave the building. He would then lock the compartment door, which was usually left open for conversation when both men were in the truck. While his partner used the rear door for money handling, the driver would sit safely in the cab, encased in steel and bulletproof glass. If anything went wrong he could set off a siren and quickly radio for help. When a stop was completed the guard would show himself to the driver before the rear door was again opened for him. At no time would the team leave the truck together.

By ten o'clock they had made twenty-one stops and were beginning to feel bored and irritable. Rain still beat rhythmically on the steel roof. Roy Druski, the driver, wished that he were home in bed. Or better yet, with his girlfriend home in her bed. A lewd thought crossed his mind and he laughed.

Druski had never encountered trouble on the job; he didn't really believe that anyone would be dumb enough to try a hijack on his truck. After five years with Overland he didn't think about the money anymore; it could as easily have been toilet tissue. His partner, Fred Stubb, younger and with the company only a year, liked the job and liked the guns. He just wished somebody would try something.

Their twenty-second stop was a shopping center a mile away. Pulling into the lot, the armored car handling ponderously as a Sherman tank, Druski braked it to a squealing halt in front of a long low building. With exaggerated thoroughness he inched it backward and forward until the vehicle was up against the entrance. Satisfied, he shut off the motor. Stubb, unmindful of the breach of regulations, stepped out of the rear and checked both ways for sign of trouble. Finding none, he scurried into the building and disappeared.

In the black sedan that had been waiting for the Overland truck to show, two men peered intently through the rain. The driver, a big man wearing a brown jacket over a service revolver, noted the sudden lack of exhaust fumes from the truck. He shook his head in disgust. The man beside him kept his eyes on the vast parking lot and on each car that splashed by. Without words, they sat there tense and watchful. They were an Overland security team on backup surveillance.

Stubb soon emerged with the store's deposit, two full bags, which he carried past the cab to the rear. Nothing happened. Cursing, he banged on the door until it finally opened. His cursing continued inside. Another moment and the engine roared to life. With heavy gears meshing noisily, Druski pulled away from the entrance, turned left into an exit lane and continued to the roadway, where he turned right. The black sedan followed. It was 10:15 Pacific Coast time.

Eight minutes later, after a frustrating string of red lights, Druski pulled around the rear of a huge supermarket in Highland Park, a suburb of Los Angeles. Again he shut the motor, because he wanted to continue reading the newspaper while Stubb went in for the money—still another breach of company regulations. He was going to take his girl to the movies that evening and he wished to see if a good cops-and-robbers picture was playing anywhere. If not, he told himself, he could always show her his own gun. He laughed again.

Twenty yards away three silent men sat in a stolen Buick watching Stubb enter the hallway behind the market. Business was good even on this rainy day, and the car was lost among hundreds of others in the sprawling shopping center. Inside, the men waited impatiently, knowing that very soon they would be rich. The plan, remarkably simple, was for two members of the group to overpower the guard in the building and hold him while a third put on his jacket, tie and cap and walked out with the money. In the rain the driver wouldn't notice the difference. When the rear door opened, the other two would quickly bring out the guard and jump in the truck. Threatening to kill the guard, they would force the driver to open the compartment door, and Harry Owens would then leap in the cab and drive away. The men in the car would cover the hijack in case of trouble, following it to a barn a mile away, where they would quickly divide the money and disappear in two waiting cars. They had the plan and they had the rain; now all they needed was a little luck.

Carl Hansun, age thirty-six, nervously gripped the steering wheel. He was tall, with iron-gray hair already thinning. A native of Washington, he had worked as a lumberjack until the war took him to a dozen Pacific islands. With one lung all shot up and a steel plate in his head, Hansun figured he didn't have too long, and he wanted to go out in style. Next to him sat Harry Owens, waiting to race over to the armored car. Harry had awakened with a premonition of disaster, which he didn't mention to the others when they met at eight o'clock. Before he left home he had glanced at his wife Sara, asleep in the other room. He didn't expect to see her again.

In the back seat Johnny Messick stared out the window. A drifter with no permanent base or allegiance, Messick was pushing thirty and worked occasionally as a short-order cook. On this day he carried a gun that he hoped would not be needed.

Carl Hansun lit a Camel and immediately coughed. He took a second deep drag and broke into a coughing fit. "Goddam," he muttered hoarsely, "can't even smoke no more." His pack was empty. He crushed the burning end on the window and snapped the cigarette in half and put the good half back in the empty pack.

Across twenty yards of driving rain the armored car stood motionless. Johnny Messick looked at his watch. "What's keeping them?" he asked. No one answered him.

Inside the building, in the darkened hallway, three men wearing butcher's aprons had just seized the guard by surprise. In a matter of seconds one of them, Hank Green, age twenty-eight, was walking toward the exit with the guard's keys and pistol, and the deposit bag in his hand. The other two, Don Solis, thirty-four, and his brother Lester, thirty, covered the guard at the exit door.

When Green walked out the door the three men in the Buick held their breath. In a few moments they would know all about their future. The time was 10:27 and counting.

Carl Hansun had planned the robbery after weeks of careful scrutiny. He had studied the routes of the armored cars, learned the routines of the guards, their timing and techniques. A steal in the central city was quickly ruled out because of traffic and tight security. What was needed was an open spot with minimum protection: a supermarket rather than a bank, a supermarket in a large shopping center. Highland Park seemed the best bet. The inside men could do their job with little chance of interference, while those in the car would go unnoticed unless needed. Everything depended on getting the driver to open the rear door for the phony guard, and Hansun planned on natural carelessness and a heavy rain to take care of that.

In numerous run-throughs while waiting for the right day, Hansun and the others clocked the operation at ninety seconds from the time Hank Green left the building to Harry Owens driving the truck away. One minute thirty seconds.

Roy Druski looked at his watch. What the hell was keeping Stubb? Flicking an eye at the doorway, unable to see anything clearly through the rain, he spotted Stubb coming out with the deposit bag. "About time," he mumbled to himself. He put down the paper and waved his arm to let Stubb know he had been seen this time. Then he pressed the button to open the rear door and went back to his paper.

As Hank Green pulled the door wide he motioned to his companions in the hall. They quickly came out, Stubb between them, each wearing a butcher's apron. To the two men in the black sedan parked nearby, they looked like three supermarket butchers going out for a smoke. Except nobody smokes in the rain. The two men tensed, watched in amazement as the butchers jumped into the truck behind the guard. A hand quickly reached for the two-way radio.

Inside the truck Don Solis shoved Stubb against the compartment door separating them from the driver. "Open it up," he rasped. "Open it or I'll kill him." He forced his gun into Stubb's mouth. Behind the bullet-proof glass Roy Druski heard him, saw the three men, Stubb, the gun. He hesitated. Instead of his whole life flashing before him, he thought only of his being safe in the cab, with the currency bags, the big money, on the jump seat beside him. Then he heard Solis' voice again. "I'll kill him, so help me," Solis screamed. "Open it!" Druski knew the man would pull the trigger. Moving swiftly now, he did as he was told.

Unseen by the two men in the black sedan, their attention riveted on the armored car in front of them, Harry Owens had already left the Buick and was sprinting toward the truck. They spotted him as he jumped in, the rear door slamming behind him. "Where the hell did he come from?" one said irritably and reached for the radio again.

A moment later the Overland truck roared to life, Harry at the wheel. Jamming the gears, he slammed down on the accelerator, and the armored car shuddered— and stalled. Cursing, Harry frantically worked the gears and tried again, the rain muting the sound of the starter. No luck, the motor wouldn't catch. Precious seconds were being lost as the whining continued.

In the Buick Carl Hansun saw his future fall apart. The truck wasn't moving, something was wrong. All he could think of was the driver, that he didn't unlock the compartment door. Hansun started the car. He had hoped there would be no shooting, he had told the Solis brothers not to shoot unless absolutely necessary. He was so damn sure the driver would obey. The next moment he swerved into an open lane and roared the Buick down to the truck, slamming to a stop across the back. He banged on the door, shouting, until it opened. Inside he quickly saw the trouble—Harry Owens. The dumb son of a bitch couldn't even make it move.

"Get the bags," Hansun shouted. "Get all you can in the car." He grabbed one and flung it out of the truck. "Not the coin bags, just the money." For the next few seconds three of them tossed bags of currency into the waiting hands of Johnny Messick while Don Solis covered the driver-guards. "Keep them away from the guns back here," Hansun ordered, picking up a Mossberg pump-action riot gun and a shotgun. In the cab Harry was still kicking the starter.

Nearby the Overland backup team watched anxiously, waiting for reinforcements. If necessary, they would follow the car. What they didn't understand was why the gang didn't just drive off with the truck. "It's dumb," said one. The other agreed. "I hope they're not so dumb they kill the guys in there." The driver's eyes narrowed. "If they don't take any hostages, we won't either."

Up ahead Hansun jumped out of the truck. "There's still bags up here," Don Solis shouted. He was told to leave them. "C'mon, we got enough," said his brother on the way out. Solis looked at all the money still in the cab, then he slowly turned to Harry Owens getting out of the driver's seat. "It's all your fault," he said softly as he shot Harry twice. Racing past the two guards, he banged the rear door shut and followed the others into the car.

"He shot them," whispered the driver of the black sedan in disbelief. He turned the engine. "The bastard shot them," he repeated, zooming out of the space and after the fleeing Buick. "The hell with waiting. We'll take them now."

In and out of busy lanes the two cars weaved in a wet zigzag scramble for the road. Messick spotted the tail. "Cops," he muttered savagely. At the next parking intersection Hansun sped across, braked a sharp left at the first lane and suddenly swerved into an empty double space. "The shotgun," he yelled to Messick as the squealing of tires came closer. Throwing open the door on his side, Messick stepped out as the sedan flashed into view. "Now!" roared Hansun, and Messick let go with both barrels dead on the moving target in a heavy rain at fifteen feet.

The sedan shuddered as the shotgun loaded with sabot blasted away much of the front end. That it kept going at all was due to sheer momentum. With the left front wheel collapsed, the car skidded madly for a moment before flipping over and crashing up against a panel truck. A hubcap sailed crazily in the air.

While the Overland backup team scrambled out of the wreck Hansun gunned the Buick and shot forward through the front row of cars and into the next lane. Turning right on two wheels, he raced the lane all the way to the exit and out of the parking lot. "We done it," Hank Green shouted, holding up one of the money bags from the floor. "We goddam done it."

By the time Overland security and the police arrived, the Buick was being traded for two other cars, which promptly fled into the noonday gloom and disappeared.

In the shopping center lot the driver of the demolished sedan was cursing himself for trying to do the job alone: He was also thanking his gods for still being alive. His partner, equally shaken but unhurt, wondered if they would be fired.

Elsewhere ambulance attendants were lifting the body of Harry Owens onto a stretcher. One bullet had entered his right side, the other his upper right arm. Seriously wounded, he was rushed to nearby Community Hospital. Roy Druski and Fred Stubb were taken to police headquarters to tell their story, and afterward driven to Overland's central Los Angeles office. The armored car was checked for prints after the remaining money was transferred to another team to complete the route.

While reporters were getting details of the robbery for their metropolitan dailies, company investigators were already setting up a file on the operation, a file that would eventually be sent through an industry clearing house to every bonded money carrier and security firm in the country. Included in the report would be each specific detail of the robbery. All that would be missing were the names of the participants.

These too would shortly be known.

Three days after the shooting Harry Owens died in the hospital without regaining consciousness. The more serious of the two entrance wounds had traveled downward, smashing his spleen and liver. His premonition of disaster had been accurate. So was his belief that he would never see his wife Sara again.

Officials were dismayed by Owens' death, for they had hoped that he would lead them to his companions. The investigation settled into the routine but little was immediately learned. The guards could not identify their assailants from mug shots, which meant that the five men had no known criminal records. Nor did fingerprints from the truck and abandoned Buick match any existing ones on file. Owens hadn't belonged to any particular gang known to police. He had been a regular patron of several bars around the city, in which he had always behaved himself well enough. His wife knew none of his friends. The search continued but what was needed was a break.

On March 26 the break came in the form of a man who walked into a showroom in Glendale and bought a new car for three thousand dollars. The man paid cash. Elated, the salesman completed the transaction and afterward routinely reported the matter to the police, as was the custom with all large cash transactions. The man had presented his driver's license on which were his name and address. An investigation determined that he was a drifter with no visible means of support. His name was Hank Green.

The following day Green was taken to Los Angeles police headquarters, where he was questioned about the Overland robbery. At first adamant in his denials, Green relented when the guards made a positive identification. "You got me," he announced finally. "Make a deal and I'll talk."

Within hours the police knew everything about the armored-car hijack, including all the names: Carl Hansun, Don Solis, his younger brother Lester, and Johnny Messick. Harry Owens? "Don shot him. But he deserved it." Why? "He told us he knew all about cars."

Police bulletins quickly went out, and the manhunt was on throughout California and the western states. Within two weeks three of the men were captured, Messick in San Diego and the Solis brothers in Fresno. Police recovered $210,000 of the stolen money.

Only one man escaped. Carl Hansun, 36, a wounded war veteran, got away with one hundred thousand dollars and has never been heard of since that day. Because of his war injuries he is presumed long dead. But the file on the Overland robbery in Highland Park, California, in February 1952 has never been officially closed.

During those long months of the investigation and then the trial of the four men that June, life was pure hell for Sara Owens. She blamed Harry for everything. He married her when she didn't really want to get married, he was the cause of her having the boy when she didn't ever want any children. If he was not the father he was still responsible, for if she hadn't been with him that night she wouldn't have been raped by Caryl Chessman. And now, after four years, almost five years, of nothing but misery and no money her husband had to get mixed up with gangsters and get himself killed. Sara really didn't care anything about that; it was the shame she had to go through every day that his name was in the papers. The neighbors knew, the police knew, everybody knew who she was. The wife of a gangster who was so dumb that he got killed by his own gangster friends. For Sara, it was the last straw. Obviously the gods had abandoned her for good. Hopeless and now alone, she determined to leave Los Angeles forever.

On August 1, 1952, in the midst of one of the worst droughts of the century, Sara Bishop, as she now called herself again, moved out of the city. She got on a bus with her four-year-old boy and traveled north to San Francisco, where she found a small apartment and a job as a waitress. At night she would tell the boy about his two fathers, one a rapist and the other a bank robber. She would jeer him and taunt him and take out all her animosity on the boy. One day she brought home a brown leather strap.

The following year Sara moved to a small rural community two hundred miles above San Francisco. She lived in an old clapboard house at the edge of town, a quiet, secluded existence she found neither lonely nor depressing. True to her vow, she had nothing to do with men. In the daytime she worked as a waitress in a local diner, sleeping with the boss—an old, fat man with greasy hair— once a week in order to keep her job. During those few hours she would simply shut her eyes.

At night she would regale the boy with horror stories about terrible monsters who did bloodthirsty things to people; all the monsters were men and all the people were women. Somehow the monsters were always named Caryl Chessman or Harry Owens. As the years slipped by, all the monsters gradually became one, Caryl Chessman, for Harry Owens was dead and forgotten but Sara would read now and then of Chessman in a new appeal or stay of execution. These things she would read to the boy, always with frightful additions of her own, always about women suffering and men hurting them terribly. After such stories she would always beat the boy with the leather strap. Over the years the stories increased and grew more fearsome.

In 1956 Sara Bishop moved farther out of town to a small farmhouse three miles away. The house had no electricity, but it did have running water and a massive woodburning stove in the kitchen. Her nearest neighbors were a quarter mile away. To get to town she bought a used car with a hundred dollars she had saved. Toward the end of that year she also bought a heavier leather strap.

Sara had quit the waitress job several years earlier, after she burned the old man's private parts with a cigarette one night as he lay sleeping. She then went to work for the town carpenter, answering his phone and minding the tiny shop. When he became strongly amorous one night in a drunken frenzy, she almost severed his left arm with a handy axe. A quick succession of such jobs and incidents gradually brought her the reputation of being a somewhat demented woman. She was finally no longer bothered by the menfolk, much to her relief. She was also no longer employable, for Sara had indeed become strange in her ways. Shrewish and withdrawn, mistrustful of everyone, she made few friends and invited no one to her house. Supporting herself by sewing and an occasional weekend in San Francisco, leaving the boy alone at home, she barely managed to survive. But at least Sara, to her way of thinking, was not being bothered by anyone. That is, except for the boy.

That the boy was growing vexed Sara no end. From four years old to six years to eight years, he was swiftly becoming the hated man. Sara believed she loved him in a motherly way, though she seldom showed it. She also hated what he was, and this she showed more and more. The boy often missed school and would sometimes show up with bruises and welts. He was bright enough but very quiet and given to strange tantrums. Some people worried about the boy whenever they thought of him, but it was in a time when children were the sole property of parents, and in an area where neighbors never interfered in family matters. The boy belonged to his mother and it was all, as people said, in the hands of God.

During the fall of 1957 Caryl Chessman was again in the papers. His third book had been published, one he had reportedly secreted out of prison after he had been ordered to publish no more. On her next trip to San Francisco Sara bought the book, just as she had bought his two earlier books, *Cell 2455 Death Row* and *Trial by Ordeal*. Sara was not much of a reader but she liked to leaf through Chessman's books, thinking of him locked up like an animal and waiting to die. The thought pleased her. She often imagined herself watching the men in San Quentin stalking their tiny cages, alone and helpless. She wished all of them would die.

Sara was also impressed by Chessman's publicity. She saw him as some kind of celebrity, this man who was talked about by famous people all over the world. For a while she even kept a file of those names she recognized in the papers who had stood up for Chessman. Soon the file got so big she either had to throw it away or start a second one. She burned the file in the big wood stove. But she kept the books and the newspaper stories about him. And whenever she thought of it, the one thing she couldn't understand was how a rapist could get all those famous people to say great things about him while no one ever said a word about his victims.

That night when Sara got home from San Francisco she read parts of the book she had just bought. It was called *The Face of Justice* and on the back cover there was a big picture of Caryl Chessman's face. It was smiling. Sara studied the face a long time, with its dark hair and dark eyes and big nose. Then she took some paper and began writing about herself, of the rape ten years earlier and her marriage to Harry Owens, of her early life and its youthful dreams, of her later life with all the fear and hatred of men. For hours she scribbled word after word, painfully, tearfully, on the kitchen table. When she finished she folded all the pages in half and stuck them, unread, into Chessman's book. Then she put the book away in a cardboard box with other things in the closet.

Afterward she beat the boy for a long time with the heavy leather strap. She beat him and cried over him and she beat him and told him horrific stories of men and then she beat him again. For the next week the boy was not seen in school. When he returned his mother reported that he had been ill in bed with a cold.

On May 27, 1958, Caryl Chessman was taken from San Quentin under heavy guard to Sacramento, the state capital, in connection with an appeal to the state's highest court. It was his thirty-seventh birthday. Sara heard about the appearance the night before on the radio and she decided to go see him. Arriving in Sacramento in midmorning she drove directly to the court, where she found pickets demanding an end to capital punishment and the release of Chessman. Flustered by all the activity, she sat in her car, uncertain. Finally gathering her courage she went up the steps to the entrance, where a guard politely informed her that no visitors were allowed in the courthouse that day. She tried to tell him that she was not a visitor, that she knew Chessman—she wanted to scream out the word *"intimately"*—and had to see him. The guard, unmoved, would not listen. He had his orders, and would she please move along.

Defeated, Sara sat on the lawn. Chessman was in the building and she couldn't get to him. Over the years the focal point of all her hatred had been transferred from her husband, long dead, to Chessman. Sara had visions of killing him, of shooting him with a gun and taking a knife and cutting off his private parts and then shooting him again just to make sure he was dead. Harry was dead. Why wasn't Chessman dead? It wasn't fair. They should let women have a gun and teach them how to use it. Then women could get together and kill all the men, and everybody would live happily ever after. It just wasn't fair.

When the commotion started she stiffened. Chessman —he must be coming out. Sara ran back to the entrance as a group of men rushed out of the building. There he was, it had to be him. She stared at the face. After eleven years she was seeing him again, for it was by now firmly fixed in Sara's mind that she had seen him that night so long ago. She kept staring, then she was shouting, she didn't know what. A moment later he was gone, the face was gone, and she was alone again.

An empty feeling gnawed at her all the way home. She felt drained, and desperately weary. She kept telling herself that somehow she should have killed him. She was dead in a way, and he should be dead too. Twice before reaching home she pulled over to the side of the road and cried.

In the months that followed, Sara's horror stories to the boy became more and more fearsome and disjointed: monsters were seen everywhere, hideous, unrelenting monsters in the shape of men destroying women in gruesome sinister detail. Carnage was rampant, pain was normal, death was release. Sara would squeeze the boy's scrawny shoulders as her intensity mounted, clutch his head, pull his hair, pummel him, cuff him, beat him. Horror-filled eyes huge now, mouth foaming, she would scream at him, castigate him, warn him. Monsters! In the house, everywhere. Too late! Shadowy mindless things seeping through the walls. Blood demons pouncing, crushing, wrenching muscle from bone. Insane paws ripping flesh apart, huge gaping mouths gulping whole intestines, heart, liver, kidneys split open strap beating beating screaming both of them screaming now in nameless terror slowly sinking eyes unseeing frenzy-flushed pain-pleased bodies slowly sinking sinking softly into silent sleep.

In September Sara bought a whip. She told the man she was going to buy a horse. He told her she should buy the horse first, but Sara bought only the whip.

Winter came early that year. Sara and the boy stayed in the house most of the time, and the fire in the big wood stove burned brightly. Her mind began to wander a bit; at times she didn't know the boy, sometimes she called him by other names. She grew even more short-tempered with the boy, shouted at him constantly, found fault with everything he did. She began to curse him and to make him the monster in her stories instead of Caryl Chessman. The whippings became more frequent.

One night late in December the boy's mind snapped. He put his mother, still conscious, in the wood stove and watched her burn, watched her body fry and burn to bleached bone.

Three days later a customer came to the house to deliver some cloth and found the boy sitting on the floor in front of the dead fire. He was swaying back and forth and whining in a strange animal language that could not be understood. In his hand was a bit of charred flesh that he had been eating. His upper body was full of cuts, now festering and caked with dried blood.

When the police came they took the boy away.

The killing of Sara Bishop never made the metropolitan dailies and was listed in the local paper only as a woman found dead in her home. But everyone in the small community knew what had happened. The boy was quickly judged to be hopelessly insane, in the fashionable language of the day, and sent to a nearby state mental hospital. The house three miles out of town was closed and left vacant.

In the hospital the boy was among the first to be placed in a new wing, separate from other facilities, for disturbed children who had killed. At the beginning he was isolated, and he would spend his time screaming and falling to the floor as though being dreadfully attacked. At other times he would sit quietly and softly tell himself stories of monsters and demons. If anyone approached he would immediately stop. Sometimes he would just whine for hour after hour, sitting swaying on the cold cement floor.

Often the boy had to be forcibly restrained, for he would attack others, children and adults alike, suddenly and without apparent reason. Eventually he came to be regarded by the attendants as truly crazy and dangerously homicidal. As the decade of the fifties drew to a close, the boy was more alone than he had ever been in his young life.

On February 19, 1960, Governor Edmund Brown of California granted Caryl Chessman a sixty-day reprieve. Some thought it to be politically motivated, since the President of the United States was touring South America, and the government quite naturally didn't want anti-American demonstrations while Eisenhower was there. During this last reprieve the California state legislature refused to substitute mandatory life imprisonment for capital punishment. Chessman then petitioned the California State Supreme Court for a stay of execution on the grounds of cruel and unusual punishment. On May 2 at 9 a.m. the State Supreme Court met in extraordinary session to render its verdict on Caryl Chessman. At 9:15 the verdict was announced. By a vote of 4 to 3, it denied Chessman's final petition. There was no more time to go further. After twelve years on San Quentin's death row, after forty-two appeals going all the way to the United States Supreme Court, after eight stays of execution reaching back to 1952, Caryl Chessman was executed within an hour after announcement of the court's decision. He was thirty-eight years old.

Chessman had made his own arrangements for disposal of the body. It was cremated the following day at Mount Tamalpais cemetery in nearby San Rafael. Caryl Chessman had no known living relatives.

On the day of Chessman's execution, protest demonstrations were held in various parts of the world and words of condemnation poured into government channels. In a state mental hospital some two hundred miles north of San Quentin, a boy who was believed by his dead mother to be Chessman's son was still learning to cope with a hostile environment. Now barely twelve years old, he knew nothing of the moment of execution, but in his disordered mind of vague shapes and sinister shadows one bit of memory nevertheless stood out clearly. He had a father whose name was Caryl Chessman. That he once had another father was long forgotten. In the boy's scarred memory of monsters and demons from hell, of dreadful pain and punishment, of women who suffered and men who made them suffer, his father's name was always on his mind. He wanted to be just like him.

In the years that followed the boy secretly collected whatever mention he could find of his father in newspapers and magazines. There was not much in the limited printed matter allowed on the ward. But whatever few things he found were treasured by the boy, and he folded them into tiny scraps and hid them in a little wallet he had once been given and which he always carried with him.

Often late at night he would take them out to read yet another time, then fold them again and tuck them away. Over the next decade and more, as the boy grew into adolescence and manhood, learning the ways of the world around him and the ploys necessary to get what he wanted, the few scraps of paper slowly yellowed with age and finally shredded into nothingness.

Outside the walls, the world had changed. Political assassination had become a weapon. The Vietnam war had toppled a government and brought about more than one revolution. Manners and morals had radically altered. A minority race had forged a new consciousness on the country. Men had been to the moon. Everywhere the tempo was faster, more hectic. Amidst all the turmoil and confusion, the name of Caryl Chessman was largely forgotten, though capital punishment had been steadily losing ground during the decade. In many ways the sixties was a time of national nightmare. It was hoped that the seventies would be better; if not better, then at least more peaceful.

On May 5, 1973, radio station KPFA, the flagship station of the Pacifica Foundation in San Francisco, broadcast a two-hour program on capital punishment. One of the participants spoke movingly of Caryl Chessman's life and death, and of his losing battle against execution. Through local affiliations the program was heard in several other areas of California.

In one of the wards of a large fenced-in hospital in the northern part of the state, the broadcast marked the actual beginning of a murderous reign of horror and destruction that would shake the sanity of the nation. The ward, radio blaring on the fateful May evening, was the home of Thomas William Bishop, *né* Owens, age twenty-five.

TWO

Thomas Bishop shut off the radio by his bedside and propped himself higher on the pillow, pounding it into shape. He looked around at the other men in the beds near his, silent figures crouched in sleep under sheets and blue blankets. His eyes closed, affording him escape from his surroundings. He stayed like that a long time.

"Chessman." He repeated the word, then a third time,

and again and again until the words slung together, exploding from his lips. One eye opened, rolled back and forth in its orbit suspiciously, and snapped shut. The mouth parted, tongue wetting dry lips, then closed tightly. His hands shot up suddenly to cover his ears. With lowered head he formed a litany of the word and while he silently chanted in rhythmic time, his mind raced down strange and devious paths.

Bishop was fair-haired, the coloring slowly turning lighter over the years. He was of medium height and weight, and handsome enough in a delicate way. His engaging smile, his friendly manner, his easy laugh—when he was disposed to turn them on—all gave him that slightly spoiled youthful male look that modern mothers seek for their daughters and advertisers for their products. That he could also be vicious, coldly calculating and menacing was less noticeable.

Constant self-evaluation had literally been forced upon him through most of his years in the institution. By trial and error he gradually discovered what attitudes and positions, what facial expressions and voice intonations would bring him what he desired. His intelligence and quick cunning served him well, and there came the time when he believed that he had learned all the rules of survival. But he practiced constantly, always on the alert for some new rule, some new twist he couldn't understand that would bring him punishment.

Late at night in the privacy of his bed, alone in the bathroom or on the grounds, wherever he had a moment to himself, he smiled and laughed and raised his eyebrows and puckered his lips and widened his eyes and made all the gestures of friendliness and innocence and sincerity as he observed them in the attendants and other patients, and on his obsession, TV. Whatever brought reward he adopted, whatever brought disapproval he discarded. In time he was thought to be improving, at least in his adaptability and social performance.

For all that he gained, however, there was an equivalent loss. He had no spontaneity, no feeling for the moment. His emotions were not tied to his body. He could smile while raging inside, he could laugh while in great pain. Sudden shifts in attitude or meaning always perplexed him and he had to be constantly on guard, ever watchful of others. He was a human robot who reacted to the emotions of others but could never act on his own feelings. In truth, he had no feelings and felt nothing. Except hatred. His hatred was monumental and encompassed virtually everything and everybody. But most of all, he hated where he was.

For the first four years of his stay at the hospital Bishop had given little indication of any awareness. A ten-year-old who acted much like an infant, he screamed and howled and cringed and noticed nothing of his surroundings, or so it seemed. By the end of the fourth year subtle changes had taken place and he began to open up, to become receptive to outside stimuli. Officials quickly congratulated themselves, without giving most of the credit to the simple passage of time. Whatever the cause, another year and he was seemingly as normal as any fifteen-year-old in matters of obeying orders and taking care of himself.

Eventually there were those who came to feel that he was curable, if not already cured of his youthful insanity. Special attention was given to him, wider areas of knowledge were opened for him. He learned swiftly, of people and places beyond the institution, of history and culture and government and law. It was an exciting time and he was a good student. But it was all useless in the end and served only to frustrate him almost past endurance. He had learned to duplicate emotion, to portray feelings he did not feel, as he had seen on TV, as well as in people around him. He had not yet learned how to conceal what was in his disordered mind. One by one those who had held hope for him reluctantly gave up.

Then the spasms began. Violent, uncontrollable rage shook his body. He was taken out of the children's wing and put in an adult ward. He was given numerous shock treatments and vast amounts of drugs. All helped, nothing cured. For two years his body raged. Then, as before, some inner resource took hold of him. The rage subsided, the spasms stopped. He was once again a "good boy" who caused no trouble. He was twenty years old.

At an age when young people look to express themselves, to tell others what is on their minds, Bishop began to study how to conceal what was on his. He found it infinitely harder than faking emotion. There were no patterns, no signs; nothing to tell him if he was doing

well or not. Lying didn't work; it was too easily discovered. Nor did he yet really know how to lie. And he
could never be sure of what people wanted to hear. A
key was needed, a key that would unlock the mystery of
what was expected of his mind. He almost despaired
before he found it.

Like most severely disturbed people who see the world
in absolutist terms, Bishop accepted extremes as the way
of life. White or black, hot or cold, yes or no, stay or go:
it was always one or the other. Opposite poles always had
ends, or extremities. To discover, suddenly and without
warning, that the center of the pole was considered
normal and acceptable and safe; to learn, not through
life's mistakes but a single instantaneous flash, that
people suspected extreme positions, were uncomfortable
with them and labeled them unbalanced, set off within
Bishop an explosion of insight that quickly fed his animal
cunning.

He had found his key. Moderation, balance, the ability
to see both sides, the willingness to compromise. All was
suddenly clear. For twelve years he had struggled in
darkness, a blind man unable to see the rules. No one
had told him, they didn't want him to know. As long as
he was kept in the dark he was not like them. As long as
he was not given the key he was in their power. But now
he had them. No longer would he be helpless before their
laughter, their mockery of him. It was all a matter of the
middle of the road.

Not that it would be easy, he told himself. They still
knew more than he did, they had infinitely more experience. But he would listen carefully and learn swiftly.
Pick a subject, any subject. Food? Sometimes it was
better than other times. Football? A rough sport but it
had its compensations. Vietnam war? People should be
helped up to a point, don't you think so? That's it. Play
the game, stay away from absolutes, don't be dogmatic.
And never, never tell what's really on one's mind.

Of course he remained convinced of the rightness of his
own beliefs. They were the crazy ones, the attendants,
the doctors, even the other patients. He was living in
madness, surrounded by it, engulfed by it. To get away he
had to become like them, he had to become mad. He had
already learned how to act like them. Now he must begin
to talk like them.

He knew the food was mostly bad, sometimes inedible. He knew football was disgusting, he disliked any bodily contact. And he knew that he liked to watch all the death and destruction in Vietnam on the TV, liked to hear the daily body count and think of all those people dying. But he was living in a madhouse and he must not stand out with the truth or they would punish him.

Within six months his key opened certain doors. He was given a battery of psychological tests which he manipulated, showing he was basically of average intelligence with no wide swings of emotion, minimum drive and expectation, and little imagination. He was given a series of aptitude tests which showed that he was just a plodding, somewhat dull person, with all tendencies and abilities within normal parameters—someone who would not fall far or rise high or take large risks.

For months afterward he would lie in bed going over every delicious detail of how he had fooled them, how he had shown his superiority by beating them at their own game. Over and over and over he thought of how stupid they would have felt had they only known it was his brilliance and imagination that allowed him to show no brilliance and imagination. The thought warmed him, and he would fall asleep thinking of being free. If they weren't careful, he would tell himself, he might just come back someday and kill them all.

In his thirteenth year at the institution Bishop was given a hearing before a group of staff doctors. He was told that the hearing was informal and carried no official sanction, but he knew that their evaluation of him and final recommendation would be required to open the last door, the one at the entrance gate. He wasn't worried. All the years of daily contact with the attendants and guards had filled him with a bitter hate, yet this paled before his consummate hatred of the doctors. They held the power of life and death, they could inflict immeasurable pain. They were demons torturing the helpless, but like all monsters they were stupid, they could be fooled.

All that was needed to fool the doctors, to make monkeys of them, was a superior intelligence. As in all things, Bishop believed himself wiser than anyone. He would outwit the doctors just as he had done on the tests. The experience they had with patients dissembling, the years of studying the intricacies of the mind, the knowledge gained over countless such interviews, all meant nothing to him. He knew how to fake emotion and he knew how to fake the mind. He had the keys.

In January 1972 the hearing was held. The three doctors listened with kindness and patience. For almost an hour Bishop talked about himself, answered questions, smiled warmly, laughed charmingly. Sitting in the brown leather chair he felt like one of them, eminent, respected, successful. When the hearing was over he thanked them politely and left the room. Going back to the ward, he did a quick two-step and clapped his hands. The attendant, amused at the nonresponsive act, thought him just another nut.

The doctors had not been amused, nor were they fooled by Bishop. They quickly saw through his deception, his carefully planned pose of impartiality and middle-of-the-road common sense. Tired, defeated in their jobs after the early idealistic years, each thinking himself a failure in his profession and neglected by his peers in private practice, they resented the patient's obvious belief that he was smarter than they. Beneath the rehearsed exterior they glimpsed the trauma that had gone largely unhealed, the threat of insane violence that lay under the surface. They recognized the faked emotions too, and regarded this as particularly ominous. A man without feeling for his fellow creatures, without a standard of moral conduct, a man raging inside with a lifetime of repressed anger, psychically scarred by years of horrendous suffering in the most formative period of life—such a man, desperate, unpredictable, was no candidate for normal society. Whether he ever would be was highly doubtful. The doctors concurred in their evaluation. Homicidal tendencies, possibly dangerous.

Bishop was so sure of his performance that he spent the next two days congratulating himself. He had done it, he had again proved his cleverness. Calmly, dispassionately, he had told of his childhood, what little he remembered of it. With huge, innocent eyes he had said there was no anger left in him. Man should live and let live. Killing was wrong, except, of course, when it wasn't wrong. When was that? Why, when the authorities said so, of course. As for his years in the hospital, he had only praise. He had learned much, he would always be grateful. What had he learned? That people should love each other. He loved everybody, though of course some were easier to love than others. He smiled, his face open, honest, sincere. Yes, he loved everybody.

When he was told that the doctors had recommended his continued incarceration, he thought a mistake had been made. Someone got the names mixed up. He checked with a staff member. No, no mistake. He couldn't believe it. Had he not performed brilliantly? Had he not proved he was one of them? The doctors, he felt certain, must surely know that he was as sane as they were. It was all just a silly mistake, it had to be. It had to.

That night he dreamed of monsters feeding on flesh, and woke up screaming. The monsters were still with him as he ran hysterically through the ward. He was quickly sedated.

When the realization came that no mistake had been made concerning him, Bishop's rage was boundless. He thought only of killing. The doctors would be first, those demons who made him suffer so. Kill them. Then the attendants and guards. Kill them. The other patients, the hospital, everything and everybody connected with it. Kill them all.

His mind dwelled on death and destruction. In his mind's eye he saw them all dying, painfully, horribly. Again and again he looked, laughing, smiling. He sat on a throne behind a big desk pressing buttons sending pain shooting through them screaming at his feet. He stepped on their heads, crushing them flat like broken eggs oozing on the floor. When he saw enough he just changed the scene but it was always the same. He had the power now, and he was doing all the killing.

Two days later he set fire to the ward. After bunching some beds together and piling the linen in the middle, he lit matches and fed the flames. The blaze was roaring by the time an attendant raced in. Bishop attacked him with his bare hands, struggling the man to the floor. When they pulled him off, he was still banging the head on the wood slats.

A half year passed before he was returned to a ward. Locked away in isolation, he made no reply when told that the attendant had suffered a fractured skull. Nothing seemed to matter to him as the spasms once again wracked his body, contorting his features and causing him to howl like an injured animal. During such times he would attack anyone near him and was kept mostly in a camisole. He was given more shock treatments, more chemotherapy. After several months the spasms subsided and gradually disappeared. He had somehow learned again to control his rage.

His new ward was on the other side of the main building and on a higher floor. A maximum-security ward, it housed those patients who had acted out their homicidal inclinations. Massive doors were always kept locked, the steel-frame windows were iron-barred. Guards with leather thongs seemed to be everywhere. For eight months Bishop lived in that prison, ate its food, cleaned its floors. He thought he was living in hell itself. For eight months he slept next to demented animals, and was surprised to find himself alive each morning. When he finally left for another ward in February 1973 he vowed never to return. He would die first.

Hospital officials, noting his good behavior since the rampage of the previous year, put him in an experimental ward in a new two-story building. Here each bed had a foot locker underneath and a night table. Six-foot plastic partitions separated the rows of beds, giving each man some bit of privacy. And here Bishop lay each night thinking about the mistake he had made, going over it again and again in in his mind. He had trusted people to act fairly, to set him free if he became one of them. He had learned to talk like them, learned all their games. But nothing worked for him because they did not want him free. They were afraid of him. He was too smart, too clever to be set free.

He knew now that he would never get out. They would keep him locked up until he died. There was no hope. And so, hopeless, he began thinking of escape.

Bishop had been lucky in at least one way. The previous year his spirit had been broken in isolation, but only temporarily. Though some attendants thought it permanent because of his new docility and willingness to cooperate, he knew better. The answer to his problem, he now saw, was not to be like them but to be subservient. Then they would not be frightened of him, not be antagonistic. It was a lesson he did not intend to forget.

After his release from isolation he became more subdued, more respectful of authority. In the maximum-security ward he promptly carried out the orders of the guards. When others caused trouble he moved away quickly. It was once again an act he was performing, but this time it worked because his new role fit their expectations of him. By the time he was transferred to the new ward it was believed that he had accepted his fate and was settling down to a peaceful existence.

In his new home Bishop rapidly became a group leader, responsible for the daily actions of several fellow patients. The job pleased him, he had a certain flair for organization. It also gave him more freedom of movement to look around the hospital grounds.

Had he been an ordinary homicidal maniac or, in the psychiatric language of the hospital staff, a severely disturbed patient with homicidal tendencies, he would have been bothersome perhaps but not particularly dangerous. There were dozens of such men in the institutions. But he was much more. His mother, Sara Bishop Owens, and his father, whoever he might have been, had created a creature with a wonderfully devious brain in a marvelously resilient body. Fate then had turned the boy into a shrewd cunning animal, trapped and badly wounded. By the time he reached his majority Bishop had become brilliantly clever at normal disguise and an expert tactician in matters of survival. He had also become an authentic monster, with no true feelings except hatred and no real goals except destruction.

In his views of the world and himself Bishop was as insane as would be expected from his tortured life. But when his mind turned to solving a specific problem, his quick animal sense and calculated contempt for normal behavior were as frighteningly precise as a surgeon's scalpel.

Propped up on his bed this early May evening, his lips silently chanting Chessman's name, the problem of escape looked insurmountable to Bishop. He touched the still-warm radio for assurance. All the programs came from outside; even Chessman was outside—he was dead. *He* would be outside too, but he wouldn't be dead. No matter how impossible it seemed at the moment, he would escape. His superior mind would do it. He would somehow find a way past the bars and the guards and the gates. He would plan carefully, pick his time and then disappear.

With eyes closed in concentration, he sorted out the problem in his mind. It divided into three parts: first was to get out of his locked building at night; second was to get through the gate, always kept locked and guarded. He felt certain he would solve each part. What was not at all certain, once free, was how he would escape detection.

The world had changed drastically during his fifteen years of institutional life; television had taught him that. Communications among law-enforcement agencies had improved to the point where the whole country was one big police network. People were more suspicious, everyone carried identification. Even bail bonds and court fines were paid by credit card.

With the outside so altered, what chance would he have? His picture would be in all the papers, on the TV. Posters would be in every police station wherever he went. People would look at him, recognize him. He wouldn't be able to get a job or a place to live. Without money or papers he wouldn't be able to travel far away or even to another country.

Perhaps he could live all alone in the woods or mountains where there were no people, but he didn't know how to hunt or cook. And he didn't know where any woods or mountains were, he didn't even know if there was a place without people anymore.

If he dyed his hair and grew a beard he might slip by for a while, but his face would still be the same, his general description still the same. The first time anybody stopped him for any reason, and he couldn't prove who he was, he would be caught. He would be hunted down like an animal.

His face set in a grimace, his eyes still closed in thought, Bishop again and again ran through the consequences of his escape as he saw them. Without money or identification, without friends or means to survive, his face and description broadcast everywhere, he would not last as he was for more than a day or two.

Satisfied in his organizational mind with the summary, he started taking it apart, running each thought over and over in his head until he began to be bothered by something he couldn't quite catch. Against his will he kept returning to it. *As he was,* he wouldn't stand a chance once he did escape. But if the police were not looking for him, Thomas Bishop, and didn't care anything about him? What if . . .

His eyes shot open in surprise. A smile slowly formed at the corners of his mouth. Suppose he was dead. He blinked in nervous anticipation. If he was dead, no one would search for him. He rubbed his hands together in the dark, thinking furiously. He had it, he had the key.

For the rest of the night into the early morning hours his mind raced, devising a plan. A hundred times he searched for flaws and found none. It was perfect, he kept telling himself. Perfect.

In the morning Bishop took his two spare uniforms to the tailor's shop in the basement of the main building to have his name sewn on all garments. When asked the reason, he said that he wanted everyone to know who he was. The tailor, nodding, told him he would have to be dead first, since the name could be sewn only on the inside. Bishop laughed, said nothing.

Afterward he spoke with the attendant who sold watches and rings to the patients. For five dollars he bought a birthstone ring, the fake stone set in heavy imitation onyx. He worked the flashy oversized ring onto his right index finger, saying that he would never take it off again. They'd have to kill me first, he announced gravely, letting the guard see the tight fit.

The next day he exchanged his radio for a small harmonica and a comb. The harmonica was wildly distinctive, silver and red, with a cross on each side panel. He took to humming on it constantly, and he soon came to be identified with it. The pocket comb, shaped like an alligator with a mouth full of teeth, was equally noticeable. He took it out often to comb his hair.

Over the following weeks Bishop keenly felt the loss of his radio, especially at night lying in his bed, but he shrugged it off. Only one more thing to find, he would tell himself. Just one more thing and he would be free. Let them laugh; his day was coming.

During that time a middle-aged man was taking a vacation he had long promised himself, and on a certain day in June he returned to California aboard the express running from Chicago to San Francisco. His face, though heavily creased, was bronzed and his body trimmer than it had been in years. Walking the streets to the bus station he decided that he had made a mistake in coming back so soon, that he should have stayed in Colorado for a month. Maybe even two months, he told himself. Or better still, forever. He smiled at the thought.

A thousand miles to the east, in a pastoral retreat midway between Boulder and Idaho Springs, he had led a momentary existence of an animal in communion with nature. He had fished—his pet passion—and he had strolled lovingly by mountain streams and through wooded hills. It was a perfect life, a life fit for a man along in years, and as he boarded the northbound bus he called himself a fool for leaving it. He hoped and prayed that, at the least, his first weeks back on the job would be easy.

Within a month Bishop had found the last link in his plan of escape. He was ecstatic, and fought to conceal his joy as he looked at his discovery. The inmate was the same height and approximate weight, had the same body structure and hair color. But his face was vastly different, dark and heavily lined, in contrast to Bishop's boyishly bland features. He had bushy eyebrows almost hiding small squinting eyes, his nose was large, his mouth set in a scowl. Lines criss-crossed most of his face, deepening the glaze of the pockmarked skin. When he smiled he provoked distaste in others rather than friendliness. He was ugly as sin, and Bishop was overjoyed. His name was Vincent Mungo and he was twenty-four years old.

Mungo was living in a ward on the second floor of Bishop's building, one of several recent transfers from other state mental institutions sent because of the experimental unit. They were all considered severe disciplinary problems, and it was hoped that they would benefit from the new unit, the first of its kind in the state, and that others could then be sent.

Bishop sought his man out immediately, offering him advice and friendship. He found Mungo aggressive, somewhat dull-witted and wholly unpleasant. He also saw him filled with despair and desperate to get out. Mungo had been in and out of mental institutions for much of his childhood and early youth. At nineteen he was finally committed by helpless relatives who could no longer control him or take care of him. Five years and three mental hospitals later he was firmly convinced that he would never leave. His despair led him to an ever-increasing hatred of authority but no further. Though readily violent if confronted, he was incapable of the sustained planning required for escape. He had never even thought of it. Until, that is, he met Thomas Bishop.

Almost from the start Bishop talked of escape to his new friend, for he too was desperate, though his desperation was far more concrete and dangerous. At first in supposed jest, then with increased insistence, he filled Mungo's head with visions of a new life. He was careful not to mention anything definite, emphasizing that no one else must know of their plan. Only the two of them were to go, only they would be free. "But how?" Mungo kept asking. "How do we do it?" And when he received no answer he would always ask, "When?" Bishop would smile. "Soon," he would say. "Very soon."

While the two men waited, one for the moment and the other for the word, the beginning of summer splashed itself up and down the California coast. In a splendid office atop a building in Los Angeles a man sat waiting for the arrival of two of his staff. He was Derek Lavery, West Coast editor and bureau chief of one of the country's biggest newsweeklies. Fortyish, silver hair crowning a large energetic body that kept itself in athletic trim, Lavery devoted his professional life to speed and facts. Each week he would assign his crew to work up stories of public interest. Though timeliness was the keynote, Lavery often developed articles of some depth on burning issues of the day that he would get out to the public before anybody else.

One such topic of the moment was capital punishment and Lavery, who was very good at his job, could feel the interest building up. He was determined to get in on the ground floor. What he needed was a kickoff story, and he believed he had found the angle.

Adam Kenton was the first to arrive for the ten o'clock meeting. He paid the cab driver and hurried into the six-story building.

"Is he in yet?" he asked the elevator man, gesturing upward with his thumb.

"Ten o'clock? Are you kidding?" The operator closed the doors. "He gets in before I do."

At the sixth floor Kenton turned left and marched down the hall, passing blowups of magazine covers hanging on the walls, each encased in glass with a small lamp above. The cumulative effect of the covers was obvious to him: nothing is as it seems. To which he often added the thought: Shoot the bastards who did it to us. At the end of the hall he opened the wood-paneled door.

"You're late," said the female voice behind the desk. But the face smiled pleasantly enough. She reached for the phone. "Adam Kenton is here," she said after a moment. Replacing the receiver, she indicated a door on her right. "He doesn't like to be kept waiting."

Inside Lavery's office he stopped. Sunlight flooded his eyes. The room was immense, almost the entire east side of the top floor. At one end was a huge living and dining area, carpeted and furnished with expensive sofas and easy chairs and tables, and a tiny kitchen set in an alcove along one side. At the other end, up several steps, was a large work area equipped with two long layout tables, design boards and rows of files stacked against the far wall. Louvered windows ran the entire length of the office and around one side of the living space. In the middle of the room stood a massive oak desk, behind which sat Derek Lavery. He motioned Kenton to a chair.

"What do you know about capital punishment?" he suddenly asked, his eyes fixed on the younger man.

Kenton crossed his legs. "Just what anyone knows," he observed smoothly. "Either it works or it doesn't work. Either it's justice or just plain revenge."

"Exactly," replied Lavery. "Nobody knows for sure so everybody has strong feelings about it. And where there's strong feeling there's plenty of steam."

"And a lot of hot air."

"That too." He gestured toward the papers on his desk. "I've been reading up on it. From what I can see this is only the beginning; it'll get a lot hotter. What we should do," he lowered his voice, "we should get in on it now."

"You got an angle?"

"Might be." His face creased but he broke it in mid-smile to scowl. "Let's wait for Ding. The son of a bitch was never on time in his life." He pushed his chair back and lit a fresh cigar from the humidor on his desk.

Kenton sat in thought. It was a good subject if handled right. After years of silent approval and thousands of executions, people were thinking seriously about capital punishment. States were stopping it, even the Supreme Court was calling it cruel and unusual. And people were separating into two warring camps.

The phone buzzed and Lavery picked it up. Another moment and the door opened to a booming voice.

"Derek, sorry I'm late."

Lascelles Dingbar crossed the room hurriedly and stuffed himself into a chair, his overweight body squealing in delight. He nodded to Kenton, at the same time pulling out an enormous handkerchief and mopping his huge brow. "The weather, you know."

"Glad you could make it," murmured Lavery in mock sarcasm. The two men were good friends, having put in almost twenty years together. Lavery knew Dingbar—Ding to everyone—to be a good legman and tenacious with facts. But he would never trust him to be on time anywhere.

Ding ignored the remark, squeezing himself further into the chair. Roughly the same age as Lavery, of average height and many pounds overweight, he had a shade of sandy hair left atop a large oval face, usually florid. His hands were soft and flabby, his legs mere pipestems, and he suffered from innumerable disorders to which he paid absolutely no attention. He could move fast if he had to, and he had the knack of putting people at ease, a valuable asset in his work. He was also a very good listener.

"We were talking about capital punishment." Derek Lavery placed his cigar carefully in the heart-shaped ashtray and looked at the two men in front of him. Neither spoke.

Swiftly and expertly he outlined the controversy on the subject in the 1950s and sixties, from the Rosenberg aftermath to Barbara Graham to the civil rights movement and the disproportionate number of black men executed. He was interrupted only by his puffings on the cigar.

"For twenty years capital punishment has been dying on its own, through disuse. But it was slow and didn't attract the headlines or the sustained passion." Puff, puff. "And without passion we have no news." He smiled briefly.

"In 1952 there were eighty-three executions in this

country; in 1965 there were seven. But for the past six years—none. Not one, nothing. Two years ago fifteen states had abolished it. Now the Supreme Court has finished the job." He clamped the cigar between his teeth. "Only they ain't."

Kenton shifted in his chair, unbuttoned his jacket.

"I said they haven't finished the job. All they really did was draw the battle lines. From now on the shit's going to be flying."

"I don't see it that way," said Ding, still mopping his brow. "When the Court ruled 5-4 against it last year, seems to me that was the end of capital punishment."

"The hell it was." Lavery shook his head. "A lot of the states will vote to restore the death penalty, some will call for a constitutional amendment. But all that doesn't interest me. What I'm talking about is the public reaction, that's where the news will come from." He put the cigar down. "Look at it this way. The do-gooders think they won and the hard-liners are watching for the first wrong move. There's maybe a thousand men in jail right now that a lot of people want dead. Meanwhile the killings on the outside go on as they always do. People are afraid to go out at night, they're afraid to leave their houses. They're buying dogs and gates and locks, and they're buying guns too. Every time somebody gets raped or killed, they scream for capital punishment." He tapped the desk. "The next time some punk knocks off a half dozen people there'll be holy hell to pay. That's where the action is, not in some court. And that's where we should be."

Kenton and Ding exchanged glances. Both were certain now that he had something specific in mind.

"If what I say is right," continued Lavery, "we should be doing stories on the issue, because it's timely and it's passionate." He blew his nose into a silk handkerchief, which he neatly tucked back in his breast pocket. "What I want for a kickoff is a lead piece on the man who was the big symbol in the sixties."

"And who might that be?" asked Ding.

"Without him," said Lavery, ignoring the question, "we might still have the death penalty. He pulled all the do-gooders together, he started the whole idea of cruel and unusual punishment. Before he came along there was just an automatic appeal and a call to the governor.

He polished the technique of appeals right to the top. He was granted more stays of execution than anybody, and he lived in the death house longer than anybody."

No one spoke for a long moment. Finally Kenton was unable to contain his curiosity. "What happened to him?" he blurted out.

"He was executed." Ding sighed, looked at Lavery. "Chessman?"

"Caryl Chessman," Lavery said softly.

The room darkened as passing clouds hid the sun. After a while Ding sighed again, a long low moan of resignation. "It was a long time ago," he whispered.

"Thirteen years," replied Lavery. "And twelve years before that on death row. But I don't want a rehash, I want a fresh look at the crime and those twelve years. The angle is capital punishment. You know what I mean," he said, glancing at Ding. " 'Was Caryl Chessman a Victim of Capital Punishment?' Something like that."

"I just remember the name. Who did he kill?" asked Kenton.

Lavery turned to him. "That's just the point. He didn't kill anybody. That's why it's a good lead story. His death got a lot of people mad and paved the way for abolishing the death penalty. That's the angle you use: he died for nothing but his death helped others to live."

"I don't understand. If he didn't kill anybody—"

"He was convicted," interrupted Ding, "of robbery, rape and kidnapping with intent to commit bodily harm. In those days, after the Lindbergh thing, that was worth execution. But his kidnapping, if I remember right," he turned back to Lavery, "was just moving the woman someplace else to rape her."

"That's right." Lavery tapped the desk with his finger. "He killed nobody. His crime wasn't worth execution. And he faced death for twelve long years."

Another silence filled the room. At length Lavery spoke. "There's another thing you should know. Right up to the end Chessman claimed he was innocent. Now, I don't give a damn if he was guilty or not, but"—he stopped to emphasize the word—"if we could cast doubt on his guilt, any doubt at all, we'd have not only the fact that the crime wasn't worth death but maybe he didn't even do it. Just remember that," he added calmly, "when you write it up."

"What's the time on it?"

"None," snapped Lavery. "I want it running in four weeks. You got one, that's all."

Kenton sucked in his breath, looked over at Ding who nodded back. They had worked together on several stories and had attended many of Lavery's briefings. When he wanted something that quickly it usually meant he was determined to go all the way with it, no matter what. They were visibly impressed.

"Actually," continued Lavery, "the idea came to me last month when I heard a radio show about capital punishment. They mentioned Chessman. Since then I've been trying to find the right lead, and yesterday it hit me. Chessman was perfect." He shoved a folder toward Kenton. "There's a transcript of the trial and a few other things the research people dug up. Like Ding says, it was a long time ago."

"That's all we got?"

"That's all we got now," said Lavery. "You get more." He leaned back in the Barcalounger, cigar in hand.

"Ding, I want you to backtrack some of the people on the crime and the trial. Talk to a few, get some direct quotes. You know the game. Adam, you handle the twelve years in the death house and the execution."

"What about our other work?"

"Finish what you can today and drop the rest back a week. I'll talk to Daniels in Assignment. Any other questions?"

Ding ponderously struggled forward in his chair. "Just one," he said softly.

Lavery, knowing the man, waited expectantly.

"This Chessman story will come down pretty hard on capital punishment. He didn't kill, he didn't kidnap as we know it today, and he spent a short lifetime dying a little every day."

"So?"

"So what do we do for the other side?"

Lavery allowed himself a big smile. "That's easy," he said quickly. "When the next real nut comes along, we'll scream bloody murder for fast execution. Society must be protected."

He stood up. "Anything else?"

At about the same time as the briefing in Los Angeles,

another meeting dealing with life and death was taking place in a California town some six hundred miles north of the movie capital. Hillside had grown rapidly after World War II, going from a sleepy hamlet of a few thousand peaceful souls to a full-fledged city of 35,000 lawful and scheming individuals. With it came industry, unemployment, delinquency and crime. Where once fertile fields at the town's southern edge gave an unobstructed view of the far horizon, now rows of claptrap housing and murky warehouses framed the area in commercial squalor. Like many such towns newly sprung from old traditions, Hillside had its tensions between early settlers and latecomers, between the north side and the south side, between well-to-do and destitute and, as anywhere, between young and old.

Over the years the city fathers had tried their best to cope with the growth pains, and while nobody accepted all the solutions, almost everybody agreed on the problems. On a sun-drenched June morning Lieutenant John Spanner of the Hillside Police Department discussed some of the more recent problems with his men.

Spanner, newly back from a fishing vacation that had given him renewed interest in life, was still a small-town cop at heart. Coming out of the army after the war, he returned to his hometown and joined the police force when it was just a five-man operation. With trepidation and some alarm he watched the town grow until now, as the number two man in the department, he rode in the cars with flashing lights and sophisticated communications, and routinely sent fingerprints to Washington and blood samples to laboratories and computer printouts to metropolitan centers.

Yet he still believed in the personal approach to police work, the individual touch, the friendly hand and the stern lecture, the slow, steady gathering of evidence from many sources until an assumption became a conclusion. At fifty-five, with too many years on the job and a lifetime of watching people, Spanner knew that they usually operated from hidden motives not easily seen, often not even by themselves. What was needed for good police work was patience and imagination and the steady buildup of seemingly inconsequential facts.

He constantly tried to get his men to see the truth, and on this particular morning he pointed out that the shooting on Redwood Road might be the result of a love triangle, since the husband was frequently away on business; that the series of amateurish house burglaries on the south side could be the work of an addict desperately seeking drug money; that the recent wave of muggings might come from a juvenile gang forming in the area. All would require patient checking, he told them, and a lot of legwork. Two of the younger cops, aware of his fine record of convictions but still addicted to the idea of guns and forced confessions, looked at each other in mock dismay. The lieutenant was at it again.

Seven miles south of Hillside but still in the town's jurisdiction, in a state hospital for the criminally insane referred to by townspeople simply as the Willows, two young men went about their normal routine. For one of them, however, there was an addition to the routine, a visit to a clump of bushes on the east lawn behind the main building. His hands hurriedly dug into the soft ground, soon unearthing a rusted tool. Two months earlier he had found it in almost the same spot, left by some forgetful gardener. Relieved, he slipped the tool inside the laundry he carried and returned to his ward, where he put it in the lockbox under his bed. Then he went back to waiting.

Three days later his wait was over. The rain began precisely at 4:55 p.m. on July 3. By evening the fluke thunderstorm had drowned the land, making a marsh of the grounds around the buildings. Water invaded everything, flooded drainpipes, ran down walls, entered hidden cracks in the foundation. Inside, wetness clung to the skin and men sat in elemental fear of nature's attack. Looking out at the terrifying night, Thomas Bishop knew that his time had come.

Earlier he had informed Vincent Mungo that they would be leaving now, this very night. At his insistence they had exchanged a set of uniforms that they were to wear in the escape. Mungo was told only that it would help confuse their captors. He was also told where he would be met at the appointed hour.

Midnight came and went, and Bishop lay on his bed preparing himself for the long journey ahead. He felt no sense of excitement. In his mind he knew what must be done, what he was destined to do. Every few minutes he glanced at his watch. At 12:15 he reached under the bed and pulled out the lockbox. Mentally he ran over the contents: a jacket, some books, his extra clothes, a pair of shoes, a few other things of no importance. He took out the jacket, it would be some protection in the rain. Then he took out the axe, rusted but still sharp. He held it in his hand a moment before sticking it in his pants under the belt. Finally he checked his pockets. He was wearing Mungo's uniform and he had everything he needed. He was ready.

At 12:30 Bishop walked away from his home for the last time, past sleeping men dreaming impossible dreams. Stealthily he opened the door to the ward, softly so the night guard in the hall office would not hear. Snaking through, he crept toward the door to the stairs. Again he passed through noiselessly.

On the stairs he quickly climbed to the second floor. Mungo was waiting. In silence they hurried up a final flight leading to the roof. Suddenly Mungo pointed to a huge metal door directly in front of them. In whispers Bishop told him that the door was unlocked from the inside, it would open. All they had to do was get past the alarm system.

From a pocket he carefully removed an aerosol spray can, holding it tightly in both hands. He pressed off the cap. Slowly, methodically, he saturated the alarm box on the door jamb with whipped cream. Thick, heavy, glutinous cream oozed everywhere. Mungo, next to him, watched in childlike fascination. The can was empty before he stopped.

A moment later, after a few healthy shoves, the metal door opened, noiselessly, silently. A quick push outward and they were on the roof. In the rain.

Bishop closed the metal door carefully, listening for the snap of the lock that sealed it from the outside. There would be no turning back. Then he walked across the flat roof to the edge and peered over. He saw what he had expected. Below was a sea of mud—dirty, slimy, but also soft enough to cushion their fall. He motioned to his partner to jump.

"I can't," Mungo shouted at him above the crashing of the rain. "It's too high. I'm afraid." Bishop glared at him. "It's too high," Mungo repeated, whimpering. Bishop nodded to himself. Now was the time, it had to be now. He reached out for Mungo, took him by the arm to the edge, reassuring him, talking calmly to him. It's only a short drop and the ground is soft, that's why we waited for rain, see? All you do is hang over the side and let yourself drop. There's nothing to it. You want to be free, don't you? This is your chance. Just hang over the edge and drop down. There's nothing to it. You want to be free, don't you?

Little by little he talked Mungo back to the edge. It was taking time and Bishop had no time to waste. Slowly, slowly he got Mungo to ease himself over the side, first one leg, that's it, then the other, good. As he did so Mungo looked down at the ground below. It still seemed awfully far. Suspended in air, hanging by his arms from a roof, soaking wet and frightened, Vincent Mungo turned his gaze upward for a last reassurance from his friend.

He froze in horror. High over his head the great axe arced downward like an avenging demon. It broke through his forehead, splitting his skull almost to the jawbone, spilling brain and blood everywhere. The eyes died a split second before the rest of him. There was no scream as the lifeless body fell to earth.

Landing nearby, Bishop set about the grim task, his axe rising and falling with insane fury. Again and again he hacked away at the head, crashing through nose and mouth and ear until only bits of indistinguishable bone were left. Blow after blow breaking bone, smashing skull, mutilating all till nothing was left that had been human.

Only then was Bishop satisfied. Breathing heavily, he rested a moment before checking the pockets. He found nothing. He put his harmonica in the right rear pocket, his comb in the shirt. Straightening up, he surveyed his work. With the face gone, the height and weight were his. The body wore his clothes, with his name sewn in each garment. It held his harmonica and comb, both distinctive. He paused. Only two things still to do.

Carefully he took out a frayed wallet, shielding it from the rain. Inside was a picture of his mother that he had carried around for fifteen years, one that all the attendants had seen many times. He stooped over the body and shoved the wallet in the left rear pocket.

Then he took his axe to the body again and calmly chopped off the right index finger at the knuckle. After letting the blood drip for a moment he placed the finger in an empty cigarette pack he had found earlier and put it in his jacket. Finally he ran off across the south lawn, shrouded in a driving rain, toward the big gray wall a hundred yards away, and escape.

The direction in which he ran was far removed from the main entrance, with its huge iron gates and sentry boxes always manned by guards. The hospital had originally been built on a hill, the landscape gently rolling down to the surrounding walls. To prevent flooding, a drain had long ago been dug under the south lawn to carry off excess water to a nearby creek. Years before, Bishop had accidentally discovered where the drain sluiced under the south wall, and he had safely lodged it in his memory.

Now at the spot, he scurried through the underbrush, frantically seeking where the ground gave way. On his hands and knees he stumbled down the embankment until he came to the wall. A wire-mesh fence had been installed across the drain under the wall. He wanted to scream. He couldn't go back and he couldn't go ahead. What to do, what to do? He looked around helplessly for a moment, a solitary figure in a watery grave. No, he would not go back. He didn't know how to swim, had never been in water in his life, but he would not go back. Making his decision, he leaped into the rushing water and sank below.

In the water he opened his eyes. They burned fiercely. Ahead, dim and murky, he saw the fence. The bottom was about a foot above the bed of the drain. Hysterical now, panic setting in, he clawed his way along the bottom of the drain and pushed his body under the fence. It would not fit. With his last strength he turned over on his back and squeezed his body through. Lungs bursting, he pushed himself upward. A second later his head bobbed to the surface on the other side of the wall. He was free.

Gasping, he fought his way to the water's edge and hurled himself onto the slope. After a long while he fumbled to his feet and continued on his way. He was finally free, and he would stay free; of that he was sure. The escape would not be discovered before morning; by then he would be far away and lost in civilization. All he needed was a quick change of clothes and some money, easy enough to get on a big holiday when people went visiting and left houses unattended. After all, it was July Fourth.

First he would hide the axe in the woods where no one would ever find it. He would bury his watch and ring. Once he got clothes he would burn the uniform. In new clothes he would be just another man, free to go where he wanted. They would be looking for a maniac named Vincent Mungo, who would probably be wearing a birthstone ring and a silver watch. He didn't wear a ring or a watch. And he looked nothing like Vincent Mungo.

Seized with a wild joy, Thomas William Bishop set out on a new life and what he believed to be his life's work.

What he had left behind in his old life was discovered at exactly 6:14 that morning. At 6:29 Dr. Henry Baylor, director of Willows State Hospital, was awakened by his wife, who talked of an urgent telephone call. Now, at 8:30 on the morning of a hospital holiday, Dr. Baylor sat in his spacious office in the administration building ruminating possible legal complications. The brutal murder appalled him, gave him a feeling of helplessness in the face of overwhelming evil. Yet as a psychiatrist he knew better than to indulge in prolonged emotional binges.

It was the escape that was more worrisome to the administrator in him. Escape always meant outside authorities, which invariably led to a certain amount of disorder. In such an institution as his, disorder could quickly become chaos. The thought made him shudder. He hated disorder.

Across the desk the chief of staff glanced nervously at his watch. Only two hours and already he felt years older. Nine years, almost ten, he had been at Willows, three of them as chief of staff. Good years, all of them, with good work done. Now this, and on July 4. He wondered why that should have meaning for him.

When the guard had called him in his bedroom in the staff wing he hadn't understood at first what was being said. Something about mother, somebody's mother. He had asked the guard to repeat the message. Even then the enormity of the matter had escaped him for some seconds.

Hurriedly dressing, he had literally run on the still wet ground to the experimental building and around the side. One look had sickened him. A doctor for twenty-five years, he had never seen anything like that. Leaving the guard holding the few possessions taken from the body, he had returned to his room and telephoned the director. Looking at Baylor now he wondered what he was thinking.

Since his arrival Dr. Baylor had found out what he could, what he needed to know for the authorities. He had questioned the guard who discovered the body, the guard at the main gate, and the available attendants in the building. The dead man was Thomas Bishop, who had committed matricide at age ten and was regarded as still having homicidal tendencies. The escapee was Vincent Mungo, a recent transfer patient who had shown violent traits. Seated now at his desk, waiting for what he already knew he would find disagreeable, Dr. Baylor sighed inwardly. With all we know of the mind, he reflected, we still can't even predict behavior. The thought depressed him further.

In the reception hall a middle-aged man in civilian clothes, still tanned, introduced himself to the nurse at the booth, who directed him to Baylor's office. A moment later he was opening an oak door. "I'm Lieutenant Spanner," he said politely to the woman behind the desk. "From Hillside? Doctor Baylor is expecting me."

The woman stopped her work and entered a door on her right, closing it behind her, while Spanner surveyed the room with a professional eye. In a moment she returned with a water pitcher, leaving the door open for him. The lieutenant smiled in thanks and entered the office. At the other end of the room Dr. Baylor rose to greet him.

"Good morning, Lieutenant."

"Doctor Baylor."

As they shook hands Spanner noted the several objects on the desk that didn't seem to belong there. He wished people would leave things alone at the scene of a homicide.

Fifteen miles away a police car was screaming down the highway toward Willows. Weaving in and out across two lanes, it passed cars and tractor trailers with equal abandon. In the jump seat sat James T. Oates of the California Sheriff's Office. Big, blond and immensely affable, Sheriff Oates was a cigar-chomping, gum-chewing, plainspoken man of political ambition whose intellect was often hidden behind his gruff manner. At this moment he was on his way to investigate an escape at the state hospital and he didn't intend to let anything get between him and his duty.

"Goddam it, Earl. Swing round that bus."

Earl turned to him. "But it's a school bus in the wrong lane, Jim."

"Well, what you gonna do," Oates wheezed in exasperation, "stop and give it a ticket? Swing round it."

The driver spat out an expletive and swung the car into the right lane. Jamming the accelerator down, he zoomed past the bus and quickly doubled back into the fast lane with only inches to spare.

Oates looked at him silently for a while.

"That's better, boy," he said finally.

Twelve minutes later they turned into the main entrance and Earl cut the siren. At the administrative building Oates jumped out and bustled up the steps. Inside he raced over to the reception booth. "Where's Baylor?" he barked, cigar clamped in mouth.

"Doctor Baylor's office is down the hall on the right," replied the nurse icily, but by the time she had finished he was already gone.

At the end of the hall he stopped, mystified, then quickly retraced his steps. Two doors back he turned a knob and walked in. "This Baylor's office?"

Unperturbed, the woman glanced up at him. "He's in conference now," she said sweetly.

"Who's in there?"

"A Lieutenant Spanner, I believe."

The sheriff let out a grunt. "John Spanner from Hillside?"

"I think so."

"I'll be right back," he said, already out the door. "Tell them I'm here."

Rushing out of the building, he took the steps two at a time. Earl was sitting at the wheel. When he saw the sheriff approach he threw his cigarette out the window.

Oates leaned into the car. "John Spanner's inside already, goddam it."

Earl frowned. "What's he doing here?"

"The murder's in his jurisdiction." The sheriff was exasperated again. "You go look at the body. Then I want you to talk to everybody you can, find out what the hell happened around here. I wanna know everything Spanner knows."

"Right now?"

"Now," he roared, already back on the steps.

In the outer room Baylor was waiting for him. He introduced himself and ushered the sheriff into his office. It had been decorated to Baylor's taste although the furniture was somewhat rearranged for the meeting. The eighteenth-century desk was small and tidy and the chair behind it, the doctor's chair, stately and tall. In front of the desk three straight-backed chairs with red brocade seats had been lined up with neat precision. A Queen Anne couch graced the side wall nearer the desk, its dainty tapered legs resting comfortably on the thick pile carpeting.

Two of the chairs were occupied, as Oates shook hands with Spanner and was introduced to Dr. Walter Lang, the hospital's chief of staff. There was no attempt at small talk. The sheriff eyed the empty chair, obviously intended for him, and wheeled instead over to the couch, mumbling something about comfort. Spanner watched Baylor's lips tighten in disapproval and he made a mental note about the man. By the time Baylor had seated himself behind the desk Oates was settled in the couch, his uniform in sharp contrast to the delicate floral pattern around him.

Disregarding the two doctors for a moment, he turned his attention to John Spanner. The man was not one one of his great favorites. He was just a small-town cop with no real motivation in him. But he was good at his job, maybe too good. He watched people all the time, just as he was watching Baylor now. He always looked for a loose thread, something that didn't fit, instead of seeing the over-all picture. In the sheriff's mind this was always a mistake in police work. A team effort, that's what good police work was all about. Use everybody's feet and muscle and brains, use every scientific trick there was to catch the bastards. Manpower and teamwork, yessir, that's what got results, that's what it was all about. Spanner was too much of a loner, he relied too much on himself and his damn intuition about people's motives. Maybe he was part Mexican, what kind of name was Spanner anyway? One thing was sure. Somebody like that was unpredictable, he always had to be watched. It took the sheriff a few seconds to realize that Spanner was now watching him. He pulled his eyes away and made a noise in his throat. Not for the first time he wished he could get John Spanner on his staff. Would serve the bastard right, he muttered savagely to himself.

"Gentlemen," Dr. Baylor began smoothly, "I take it we all know why we're here this morning." He lowered his eyes. "A most distressing incident." Lang blinked in consternation, he would not have called it just an incident. "Apparently sometime during the night," Baylor was saying, "two patients escaped from the new experimental wards by gaining access to the roof and jumping to the rain-softened earth below. The building, I should add, is only two stories. What exactly—"

"How'd they get to the roof?"

The doctor, annoyed at the interruption, looked blankly at Oates. "I beg your pardon?"

"The roof. How'd they get there?"

Spanner watched Baylor's eyes harden. "In the experimental building, doors are not kept locked—except for the main door to the outside, of course. I imagine they simply sneaked past the night attendants on each floor and walked up the stairs to the roof."

"Kind of careless, wasn't it?"

"Careless?"

"Why weren't the doors locked to the wards, to the stairs, to the roof? Wouldn't you call that careless?" asked Oates.

"Certainly not." Baylor snapped defensively. "The experimental plan was approved by the state medical society and by the department of corrections. It was—and is—merely an experiment. I would suggest if you—"

"Okay, okay," Oates said, defeated.

Mollified, Baylor began again after a moment. "As I was saying"—he looked pointedly at the sheriff—"what exactly happened when they reached the ground is only conjecture at this time. What we do know is that one of them then attacked the other in a most brutal manner."

"What was the weapon?"

Baylor looked uncomfortable and Spanner came to his rescue. "I saw the body, Jim," he said quietly. "It had to be an axe or a meat cleaver."

"That bad, eh?"

Spanner nodded, his eyes remembering the body. It was the worst hatchet job he had ever seen, and he shuddered at the maniacal fury needed to do such a thing.

Baylor continued. "After the attack on Thomas Bishop, that is—was—the dead man's name, after the attack the other patient apparently was able to leave the grounds. We don't yet know exactly how."

Oates shoved his long legs outward, leaned back against the couch. "Any chance he's still around here?"

Baylor turned to his left. "Doctor Lang?"

"No," Lang said hesitantly, caught unawares. Then, more positively, "None whatever. The buildings and grounds have been thoroughly searched. Mungo is not on the campus."

"Campus, Doctor?" Spanner asked, amused by the word.

Lang blushed. "Sorry. Just a conceit of mine, I guess. I like to think of the hospital as a kind of college campus."

Oates snorted. "I suppose the nuts in here are just a bunch of students." He turned to Baylor. "You got a file on this what's-his-name?"

"Vincent Mungo." Baylor handed him a folder from the desk. "You'll find everything we have on him. It isn't much. He was a recent transfer, you know."

"From where?" Spanner asked.

"Lakeland."

Oates looked up in surprise. "Lakeland isn't part of—"

"He was having violent episodes lately," Baylor hastily explained. "Disciplinary problems. They thought perhaps we could help him."

"They? Who's 'they'?"

Lang coughed. "I originally petitioned various state hospitals—"

"You mean nuthouses," Oates interjected.

"State hospitals," persisted Lang, "to suggest possible patients who might be helped by our new experimental program. It's the first in the state," he said proudly. Then, more quietly, "Mungo was one of those suggested."

Oates looked at him. "So this is all your doing."

Lang bristled as Baylor rushed to his defense. "Doctor Lang is highly qualified in his field and totally competent. We all have the highest respect for his abilities."

The sheriff laughed. He knew all about people sticking

together, especially those in the same racket. "No offense, Doctor," he apologized. "No offense."

He finished reading the few papers on Mungo in the folder, returning it to the desk.

"May I?" asked Spanner reaching for the folder.

"So the two of them get to the roof, just walk through doors and right past guards"—Oates was not going to let go of a thing like that—"and then they—" He stopped. "Wait a minute. Wasn't the roof door locked, for chrissake?"

Baylor regarded him for a moment. "As I'm sure you know, Sheriff," he said smoothly, "state fire laws require all such doors to be unlocked from the *inside*." He emphasized the word. "At Willows we must of course comply with all state laws." He smiled in triumph.

"Yeah, sure," Oates blustered. "What I meant was the alarm," he said, recovering. "What about the alarm? Why didn't it go off?"

Spanner glanced up from his reading. "Whipped cream," he said simply.

In spite of himself the sheriff had to laugh. "Maybe they're not so crazy after all."

"May I remind you that one of them was killed?"

"So he was just the dumb one." Oates had no feeling for crazy people, they were unpredictable.

"Horrible, horrible," said Lang suddenly, unable to forget. "His whole face, it was . . . gone."

Oates eyed Dr. Baylor. "What's he mean, gone?"

Baylor paused, licked his lips. "Bishop's face was totally destroyed," he said finally. "There were no features left, nothing at all."

"Then how do you know it's Bishop?"

"The clothes, the things in the pockets, the wallet, all Bishop's. Also from the body itself. Wouldn't you say so, Doctor? You knew the man?"

Lang nodded. "It's Bishop all right."

"What about fingerprints, just to doublecheck?"

Lang shook his head. "Bishop came here when he was ten years old. He never had his prints taken, I'm afraid."

Oates stared in disbelief. "When he was ten?"

"At that time," said Baylor, "this institution was the only one in the state with a children's ward." He smiled.

"It was experimental then. Now of course they're quite common."

"What did the kid do at ten?" whispered the sheriff.

Baylor and Lang exchanged quick glances before Lang spoke.

"He killed his mother," he stated matter-of-factly.

Oates grunted as though in pain. He had a sudden urge to be far away from all crazy people, including the nuts who took care of them. Like these two, nothing but trouble. He shook his head sadly.

Spanner, finished with the file, placed it on the desk.

"Okay," said the sheriff energetically. "What we're looking for is a nut crazy enough to kill in a rage for no reason but sane enough to escape from a prison—"

"This is a hospital," corrected Baylor.

"—prison hospital in a way we can't even figure out—"

"Yet," suggested Lang.

"Yet!" roared Oates, at the end of his patience. "Now, is that a fair summation?"

Dr. Baylor sighed, an audible sigh that carried with it, at least for Oates, a premonition of disaster. He fancied himself as having a nose that could smell trouble, and he had a lot of experience at it. Here it comes, he thought to himself, here comes the curve that's always there.

"There's one more thing, gentlemen," Baylor said slowly. He looked at each of them in turn. "This body, you see, had one of the fingers hacked off." He rubbed the bridge of his nose a moment before focusing on them again. "And I'm afraid that the finger is missing."

Nobody said a word.

The sheriff closed his eyes. He swore softly to himself. This just wasn't going to be his day. Here he was in a nuthouse looking for a maniac who had a thing against faces, and now he's told about fingers being chopped off. It all began to sound like a cult killing to him. He wondered what else was going on at Willows, and he made a mental note to do a little checking on the staff, including Dr. Baylor. He also wondered if he should take his vacation now.

John Spanner cleared his throat. "Doctor Baylor, when you say the finger is missing, could one of the guards have taken it for evidence?"

"They've all been checked," said Lang hastily. "It's just gone."

"Maybe it was valuable," Spanner said with a smile. Lang stared at him as though he were mad. "Perhaps a ring," Spanner continued. "A ring that the killer couldn't get off the finger."

The sheriff's ears perked up.

"Yes," said Lang, reflecting. "Bishop did take to wearing a ring recently, a birthstone ring, I think it was. But it couldn't have been of any value."

"Maybe the killer didn't know that. Was it on the body?"

Lang thought a moment. "No, and neither was Bishop's watch," he cried excitedly. "He always wore a wristwatch. That was gone too."

Oates was beginning to see reason again. A motive. Always look for a motive, even in a nuthouse. Good boy, John, he said silently. Aloud he asked for descriptions of the ring and watch. Lang promised to get them for him.

"So we got a motive," he said to the group. "Mungo gets this Bishop to go with him on the escape—"

"How do you know it was his idea?" interrupted Spanner. "He was only here a short while. How would he know where to get out? Bishop was here—how long?"

"Fifteen years."

"That's a long time. Maybe Bishop knew a way and was just waiting for something."

"Waiting for what?"

"I don't know." Spanner admitted. "But you don't know that it was Mungo's idea."

"So the escape came from Bishop, what's the difference? The point is they're out of the building and Mungo turns on the guy suddenly, without warning, and kills him and takes the watch. He can't get the ring so he chops the finger off and takes that too."

"Only one thing wrong with your theory," said Spanner softly.

"What's that?"

"Say it was Bishop's idea. Did you ever hear of a prisoner planning a break and telling the others beforehand where it would be?"

"They weren't prisoners," Oates shouted. "They were nuts."

"Why would Mungo kill him before he knew how to get out?"

The sheriff felt his anger rising. "Number one, you're just guessing. You don't know it was Bishop's plan. I say it makes more sense coming from Mungo. Why would a man wait if he knew how to get out? But Mungo comes in fresh, spots it right away, and it happens. That makes more sense to me."

"Could be you're right." Spanner smiled. "And what's number two, Jim?"

"Number two is I don't think it's just a theory. I think that's what happened. And when we catch Mungo you'll see it."

Spanner turned his attention to Baylor. "I don't suppose Mungo ever had his prints taken either, being he was a regular mental patient."

Baylor frowned. "No, I don't think there would have been any reason."

"I see." He pointed to several objects on the desk. "Are those the things from the body? I should take them along with me."

Oates was satisfied. "If we're finished here I want pictures and a full description on Mungo. I'll get it state-wide by tonight."

"Doctor Lang will be glad to get those for you," Baylor said pleasantly. He started to get up. "If I can be of any further service . . ." He let the sentence trail.

Spanner remained seated. "There are a couple of points that bother me a little, Doctor." He reached for something on the desk. "If you don't mind a moment more."

"Not at all." Baylor sat down again, vastly annoyed.

"This wallet, for instance. Mungo kills him and takes the watch and the ring however he can. Then he quickly searches the body. The harmonica is junk, he doesn't take it. Same with the comb. But why didn't he take the wallet?"

"There was nothing in it, Lieutenant."

"We don't know that. But the point is, he already had it out to check. Why take the time in the pouring rain to return the wallet to the body? Unless—"

"Yes?"

"Unless the killer wanted us to find the wallet." Spanner opened it. "Whose picture is this?"

"I believe that's Bishop's mother," said Lang.

"He kills his mother and then carries her picture around for fifteen years. Wouldn't you call that a little strange?"

"Most of the people here are, as you say, a little strange, Lieutenant." Baylor, smiling, looked at his watch.

"Another thing is the murder weapon. Where would he get an axe or a cleaver?"

"We're checking the entire staff of course, but I don't mind telling you that I'm equally mystified."

"And why take it with him? Why not just leave it?"

"Maybe he needed it for his work," Oates suggested sarcastically.

Spanner ignored him. "But what bothers me most is the attack itself, the insane fury it took to destroy a face like that. Why?"

Baylor smiled indulgently. "I think you answered your own question, Lieutenant. You used the word 'insane.' Some of these poor devils, when they work themselves into a rage there's no telling what they're capable of. The face is often the focal point of their rage. It's the face that lies to them, deceives them, laughs at them."

"Maybe," Spanner said, unconvinced. "Maybe so."

Oates stood up. "I have a question for you." He looked at Baylor. "What about Mungo? Will he kill again before we can get to him?"

The director frowned as he too rose from his chair. "I wish I could answer that," he said quietly. "Disturbed people are like children—they're unpredictable. I will say only that once an animal has smelled blood . . ." He spread out his hands in a gesture of helplessness.

"Any suggestions on where we might look for him?"

Dr. Baylor thought for a moment. "Not really. I should imagine by now he's trying to get as far away as he can."

"With his face plastered all over, he won't get very far."

Spanner was not so sure. "I got a feeling we might be hearing from him again."

Baylor nodded. "Homicidal maniacs, as the press likes to call them, are often very clever people. I shouldn't forget that if I were you."

He opened the door to the outer office and held it for them as they passed through. The woman stopped her typing and watched. For the first time in three hours

Baylor felt a sense of relief. "I'm told Bishop had no relatives, so we will bury the body. After the autopsy of course. Is that suitable to you, Lieutenant? Good. Then I won't keep you gentlemen any longer."

His eyes followed the two men until they were again in the hall. After reminding the woman to cancel the Fourth of July celebration on the lawn, he reentered his office and shut the door.

For the next half hour the two doctors discussed certain legal implications of the murder of Thomas Bishop and the escape of Vincent Mungo. Questions regarding policy and procedure were sure to be raised, and they knew that appropriate answers would have to be found.

"He must have gone berserk," Lang kept repeating. "Something snapped inside and he just went berserk."

"That he is a berserker is obvious," Baylor reminded him. "What is not yet obvious is our position in the matter."

"Suppose the police can't find him," insisted Lang. "Suppose he kills again. And goes on killing."

Baylor grew impatient. "See here, the police are certainly capable of finding this man. They have his description and his picture. He has nothing. Wherever he goes his face will be recognized. Kindly allow the police to do their job. Meanwhile our job is to see that no blame for this unfortunate incident attaches itself to Willows. Or to us."

Miles away two police officials were facing the problem of finding a demented murderer and an escaped mental patient. Lieutenant Spanner had responsibility for the killing in his jurisdiction, Sheriff Oates for the escape from a state institution. The only thing they knew for sure was that it was the same man. And that his name was Vincent Mungo.

THREE

During the month of July 1973 California was flooded with pictures of an escaped maniac named Vincent Mungo. His photograph appeared in daily newspapers from one end of the state to the other. His face was seen on television evening news in all metropolitan centers. Posters with his picture and description were circulated to police in most California communities. In little San Ysidro on the Mexican line, border guards were alerted lest he slip across the bridge to Tijuana. Along the entire coast, at all bridge and tunnel checkpoints, on all roads leading to neighboring states, police were searching diligently.

Actually the manhunt began on the evening of July 4. As people returned from a holiday visit with friends or a doubletime shift at the plant, they learned of the murder and escape. Killings were common enough of course, and men would always seek to flee any kind of imprisonment, but the word "maniac" has a menacing quality to it, a feeling of dread, that quickly caught the public's attention. The story appeared in the big evening papers, and the following morning's editions carried comments of hospital officials and the sheriff in charge of the investigation. Several dailies of July 5 ran front-page interviews with prominent psychiatrists on the danger to the public. In smaller communities local papers picked up the story from the wire services they used. By the end of that first week millions of California residents had heard of the demented killer, and if most of them were unable to remember the name or the face, they nevertheless tended to be more cautious among strangers, at least for the moment.

In Hillside the town's single newspaper headlined the escape and followed it with a blistering attack on the Willows hospital administration for allowing such a thing to happen. The editor reminded readers that municipal authorities had been trying for years to have the state facility moved elsewhere. Where? "We don't care!" thundered the editorial, as long as the threat was removed from the townspeople of Hillside. The next day's follow-up story tersely announced that the police lieutenant in charge of the murder investigation had placed himself unavailable for comment.

In Sacramento the governor declined to speculate on the case beyond expressing his full confidence in the police.

Everywhere the press was having a field day reporting

on the oddities that always accompany such notoriety. A skywriting pilot lettered the word "maniac" in huge smoke columns across the afternoon sky, then dropped a ton of garbage on the unsuspecting community below. Several papers wryly observed that he was just another flying nut and not the one being sought. In Eureka a woman living alone wrote a note stating that she was afraid the maniac was entering her home. She then crawled into her freezer, perhaps to hide, and pulled the door shut. She was frozen solid when they found her.

A young man with dark features was arrested on a San Francisco street for emitting bursts of obscenity to passersby and to the police who apprehended him. Seemingly unable to stop for any length of time, he was held in jail for seven hours as the maniac before it was discovered that he was an epileptic suffering from the bizarre Gilles de la Tourette syndrome, which forces its victims to shout obscenities. A food journal reported that the famous fruit-of-the-month club of Modesto was planning to start a subsidiary operation to be called Nut of the Week. And in Los Angeles a local toy manufacturer announced that his company was going to market new wind-up dolls called Mungo Monsters.

In response to increasing pressure from public officials the experimental unit at Willows was closed down and the patients were absorbed into other, more traditional wards. The new two-story building was shut temporarily until future use could be determined. Recent transfers were returned to other institutions. Dr. Walter Lang was reassigned elsewhere on the recommendation of Willows' director, Dr. Henry Baylor, who was most cooperative with state medical and correctional authorities. Everywhere the pressure was being felt, from Willows to California's famed Atascadero State Hospital. Patients were watched more closely, programs scrutinized more rigidly. Hospital personnel across the state held their collective breath, knowing that the vastly uncomfortable public spotlight would not long shine on them.

An enterprising reporter soon located Vincent Mungo's relatives in Stockton. A maternal grandmother and two spinster aunts were all he had left except, they told the reporter, for some ne'er-do-well people on the father's side who lived somewhere in the East. And who knows how many half-brothers and -sisters from that man, added one aunt spitefully. She was admonished but stuck to her belief.

Mungo's parents were dead, the mother choking to death on some mislodged food when he was fifteen and the father committing suicide a year later. Before that he had been a normal healthy boy, so the reporter learned, except for the times he had to be "helped" in hospitals. How many times? Oh, maybe six or seven before his parents died. He would act strange sometimes, shouting, and then quiet, and then all that shouting again. He did strange things too. Like what? Oh, he'd pour kerosene on neighborhood cats and set fire to them. And he'd dig big holes and cover them over so the other kids would fall in. Yes, and one time the little Smith girl, used to live across the street, she fell in one of his holes and nobody could find her. But Vincent wouldn't tell. Took them a whole day to get her out.

What about when he sawed off the planks on the seesaw in the park after they told him he was too big to ride on it? You see, it's not he was a bad boy. Just that sometimes he acted a little strange.

"Once he took some paint that must've been down in the cellar, and he painted these Nazi signs all over the Jewish cemetery on Allen Road. Oh, I tell you, I was so mortified." The grandmother harrumphed. "I don't know how many times I've told you, Abigail, that he did not do that." Abigail protested. "He did too. Everybody knows he did." She looked to her sister for support. "No," the grandmother said with finality. "He would not do that. Vincent was a good boy."

After the death of his parents Vincent Mungo seemed to fall apart. He became abusive to everyone and increasingly unruly. His actions were frenetic and disorganized; often he would mumble incoherently to himself or storm through the house and neighborhood. Yet he did nothing unlawful, nothing of a criminal nature. School tests placed him below average intelligence. Hospital mental examination indicated he was manic-depressive and paranoid.

In the three years following his father's suicide Mungo was briefly hospitalized four times. His grandmother and aunts tried their best for the boy, keeping him home with them, taking care of his needs. One aunt secretly offered herself sexually, thinking that he might be frustrated in that way since he was quite ugly and unappealing to girls.

Nothing worked, even with the best of intentions. Mungo became increasingly disoriented, his abusiveness sometimes flashing into violence. He began fighting with other youths. As his moods became more frightening, his sense of reality more fragile, his relatives saw him slipping away from them until the day came when they were no longer able to control him. Reluctantly they committed him to a state institution.

"He hated the hospital, all hospitals," his grandmother said quietly, "but there was nothing else we could do."

"When he left he cried," said the aunt, "and told us he knew he was never coming back. But we thought it was best for him. In those places they could watch him and help him get better. We thought that someday he'd come back to us all cured."

The other aunt shook her head sadly. "He never got any better." Her head kept kept moving. "He never got any better," she repeated.

The grandmother dried her eyes with a flowered handkerchief. "We hoped—" Her voice cracked. She looked around helplessly, suddenly old and very tired. "Now this," she said softly.

The reporter wanted to know if they expected Vincent Mungo to come back home. The women didn't think so. He had felt betrayed by them for committing him. In five years he hadn't written to them. Would he possibly return in order to hurt them? Certainly not. He was not violent unless provoked. All those stories in the papers calling him a maniac, some kind of horrible fiend, they were all lies. He was sick, yes, mentally ill, but not to the point of harming others—he was never like that. The brutal murder at the hospital? They were at a loss to understand it. That was not the boy they knew. Maybe something happened to him in the hospital, something terrible that made him turn bad. Maybe they made a mistake in committing him, but who can tell these things. Who knows what will happen?

"You must understand one thing," said the grandmother as the reporter was leaving. "Vincent was a good boy when he was small, and even at the end when he was here with us. He never hurt anybody, not really. If he changed later on"—she dried her eyes again—"if he changed, then it was something we don't know anything about. God knows we did our best for him."

Thomas Bishop, Mungo's "defenseless victim," as one paper called him, was not so lucky, at least in terms of relatives. He had none. No one who knew of him, anyway. The *Los Angeles Times* had one of its people check his background. His father died in a robbery attempt when he was three, he killed his mother when he was ten. The mother's parents had separated when she was a child; the father disappeared and was never heard from again, the mother was killed in an automobile accident several years later. The child, Sara, the only issue of the marriage, was adopted by her uncle, the mother's only brother; there were no sisters. The uncle was now dead, as was his wife.

On Bishop's father's side, his grandfather was dead; his grandmother, paralyzed and legally blind, lived in Lubbock, Texas. The father had three brothers; one killed in the war, one missing in action and presumed dead. The third, a hopeless victim of mongolism, had died years earlier in a Texas state institution. There had been one sister, murdered by persons unknown at age sixteen.

As the search for Bishop's killer continued, the net was widened to include neighboring states. Circulars were sent to police in Oregon, Nevada, Arizona, even to Idaho and Utah. Pictures were shown to interstate bus drivers, ticket agents, airline personnel. Citizens in rural communities were asked to note any strangers living in woods. Women were told to be wary of anyone asking for food.

In Gaines, Idaho, the local television station left a picture of Vincent Mungo on the screen when it finished its programming for the evening. In this way townspeople could see his face all through the night, not a particularly pleasant thought for some. And in Elko, Nevada, the girls in the town's five bordellos were told to watch out for any strange customers. "Stranger than what we got now?" one wanted to know.

Across the country in Washington, D.C., the National Rifle Association, coincidentally or not, sent a mailing to its members of the standard description of a person. On the card was a drawing of a man; around the drawing were the twelve things to note in describing someone: name, sex, race, age, height, weight, hair, eyes, complexion, physical marks such as scars, habits or peculiarities if any, and clothing, including hat, shirt or blouse, jacket or coat, dress or pants, shoes, and jewelry, such as rings and watches. Whatever the motivation, people were looking for Vincent Mungo.

By mid-July the police net had caught several dozen men who answered to the description of the escaped maniac. A few were close enough to be brothers, the rest bore general resemblances. All had one thing in common: they were not Mungo.

On the morning of July 7 a man was shot to death by a nervous homeowner in Bakersfield. Investigation revealed the dead man to have been a plumber's helper who was working in the cellar at the request of the homeowner's wife. She had neglected to tell her husband, who fired his pistol when the intruder didn't answer his inquiry. The dead man had been deaf.

In Ventura a woman waited behind a door for a midnight burglar. When he entered the room she stuck a knife in his back, then called police to report she had caught the killer. The man was dead when they arrived. He had been a former suitor of the woman, intent on winning her back even if he had to sneak into her house to talk to her.

On July 10, San Francisco police shot a suspect fleeing the scene of a robbery. He was of average height and weight, had brown hair above an ugly face. He wore a watch and a birthstone ring set in onyx. When questioned in the hospital he refused to say anything. Police were jubilant until it was determined that he was Robert Henry Lawson, a bank robber wanted by the FBI.

Two days later, in the most bizarre incident connected with the escape and disappearance of Vincent Mungo, a body was found on a little-used road on the outskirts of Fairfax. The head was missing and so were the arms and legs. A short-sleeved work shirt and cotton pants covered the torso, the pants crudely cut above the knees with a scissors. In the shirt pocket was a scribbled note stating "This is Vincent Mungo."

There were no identifying marks on the torso—no scars, no cysts, no tattoos. The medical examiner approximated the age as being about twenty-five and the height and weight as average, about 5 feet 9 inches and 150 pounds. He could go no further. Police noted the approximation as fitting Mungo's description, but without additional proof there was nothing more they could do. After a fingerprint check that proved negative the note was sent to James Oates of the California Sheriff's Office in Forest City.

No one ever came forward to claim the body. It was placed in a freezer locker set year-round at 39 degrees in the Marin County morgue. A padlock was put on the locker until such time as the body was identified or claimed. The file on the grisly discovery has been kept open and the details are a matter of public record.

Besides those who resembled Mungo enough to be picked up by police, and those who innocently or otherwise became ensnared in the dragnet, there were some who involved themselves for one reason or another. At least fifty men walked into police stations to give themselves up. Each was Mungo. Others, perhaps not wanting to appear in public, called and demanded to be arrested over the phone. Either through a misdirected sense of guilt or a pathological need for punishment, most of these men convinced themselves that they were the killer. Others were of course mere publicity seekers grabbing at the spotlight, even if only momentarily, and willing to pay the inevitable price.

The most tragic of the confessions occurred in Fresno during the second week of July. A woman in her mid-twenties, with brown hair and very pronounced masculine features and mannerisms, announced to police that she was Vincent Mungo. She told them a story of how she had been in and out of institutions since childhood, first posing as a boy and later as a man. She had fooled everybody into thinking she was male, so she said, and she had done this because she knew herself to be a man trapped inside a woman's body. Now she was turning herself in to be punished, she had to be punished because she had killed. The police treated her kindly and escorted her home. In the house they found a two-year-old girl dead in the bathtub. The mother had drowned her daughter in the belief that no one would care for the child when she was once again put away in the institution from which she had escaped.

On July 15 a man was wounded and captured during an armed robbery in Portland, Oregon. It was his seventh holdup of local shops in as many days. In each he announced to the proprietor that he was the deranged killer Vincent Mungo. For those who hadn't heard the name the gun in his hand worked almost as well. He would then threaten to return if they reported the robbery, going into the most graphic details of how he would kill them. After he left, the shopkeepers quickly called the police, money being an even stronger motivation than fear.

His general description matched that of Mungo. Though he wore a beard, his face resembled the picture on the flyers received by the Portland police earlier. California authorities were notified, and deputies from the Sheriff's Office flew to Portland to interrogate the prisoner. Hopes were raised in Sacramento, in Forest City and Hillside, as well as elsewhere around the state.

In the guarded hospital room the wounded man told police only that he had read of the manhunt and had used the name to terrorize his victims. Beyond that he would say nothing. Some officials believed—hoped—this to be the lie and the earlier version the truth, but continued questioning produced no further answers. He could not be persuaded to talk about himself, nor could he be trapped into giving details of the escape unknown to the general public.

When the routine fingerprint check returned from the regional center in Denver the following morning, the reason for his silence became clear. He was a wanted felon with three warrants out on him in as many states for armed robbery and assault with a deadly weapon. Hopes crushed, the deputies sadly returned home from yet another false alarm.

It soon became obvious to California authorities that their insane killer had escaped again, this time from their manhunt. At least from the initial casting of the net. Vincent Mungo was nowhere to be found. He was not in the big cities, he was not in the small towns, he was not in the woods or mountains, and he had not crossed over into another state. He had simply disappeared, or he was so well secluded that it amounted to the same thing. Apparently without money or friends, and with a face quickly recognized by peace officers anywhere, he had succeeded in eluding capture. That he had lasted the first three days was miraculous; that he had remained at large for several weeks was beyond comprehension. Yet he was somewhere within the state—he just had to be.

A stakeout had been placed round the clock on the

home of Mungo's relatives in Stockton, but he failed to show there. Another was laid at the nearby home of a man he had once threatened to kill, again without result. Police watched movie houses in the San Francisco Bay area, movies being a favorite pastime of Mungo. They checked penny arcades and amusement parks, other favorite haunts. They even looked into the hobby shops, since glue-sniffing had been his chief vice as an adolescent. No matter what was pulled into the net, their quarry slipped through.

Woodsmen and climbers in the northern edge of the state around the mountainous ranges were asked to report anything unusual. They spotted a number of campfires, but all proved to be legitimate. One climber was feared missing and police units rushed to the scene, suspecting foul play, but he showed up unharmed three days later.

In the southern part of the state police helicopters skirted much of the area between Death Valley on the Nevada border and the San Bernardino Mountains, sighting nothing out of the ordinary except the wreckage of a private plane lost a year earlier. At Barstow on the Mojave Desert an abandoned car was found containing the bleached body of a young man. Excitement mounted until it was learned that the unidentified male had been no older than eighteen and had probably been Mexican.

On July 18 the body of a woman believed to be in her early fifties was discovered in a roadside gully midway between Yuba City and Sacramento. She had been dead about ten days and the body was badly decomposed and almost totally dehydrated. Maggots had eaten away most of the brain. Yet the cause of death was readily apparent from the crushed skull and broken bones, injuries typical of a hit-and-run victim on fast roads. An autopsy revealed only that the woman had been a heavy drinker and smoker and had suffered from arthritis. Local police listed the death as a probable vehicular homicide on or about July 8, and sent a routine report to the Sheriff's Office in Sacramento. A check was made through Missing Persons to see if anyone answering the woman's description had been reported missing. None had, and because the original report stated vehicular homicide it was not until much later that the terrible significance of the date was seen.

The unthinkable, at least for the authorities, occurred

on July 19, a wet and thoroughly miserable day in much of northern California. On that afternoon an elderly woman was savagely attacked in her home and literally hacked to death. When police arrived they found blood everywhere in the room and an axe next to the body. Then their eyes widened in genuine concern. On the woman's right hand the index finger had been cut off. A quick search showed it was missing. The area was sealed off and by nightfall the house looked like a Hollywood set, with bright lights and various police cars and every law-enforcement official in the state seemingly there, including Sheriff James Oates and Lieutenant John Spanner of Hillside. The woman had lived less than thirty miles from Willows State Hospital.

Sheriff Oates grabbed Spanner in back of the house where they could be alone for a moment. "Mungo," he said through clenched teeth. "I knew it'd come to this, I knew he'd kill again." He caught Spanner's surprised look. "I mean when we didn't catch him the first few days," he said hastily. "The bastard's kill-crazy, that's what it is all right." Spanner wasn't so sure. "Let's check the axe with Willows. See if it could've come from there," he said thoughtfully. He looked perplexed, uneasy, and Oates asked him why. By now the sheriff was ready to listen to anything.

"It's the finger," Spanner told him. "I don't understand it. With the finger off, everybody knows it's Mungo, just the same as if he wrote his signature."

"All these nuts are egomaniacs, ain't they?" Oates asked plaintively. "Remember that little blond gal in Daly City that told all her friends she was the killer they were looking for? And what about all the nuts who do something dumb to get caught so they can tell everybody how many they killed?" He rubbed his nose. "They're all the same."

"I don't think Mungo's like that," said Spanner. "He seems to know exactly what he's doing. And he's been smart enough to outwit us so far." Oates frowned, not needing to be reminded of that fact. "I think he wants very much to stay anonymous, to get lost in the crowd. It's his only chance."

Oates shrugged. "So how do you explain this?"

"I can't. That's the point—it doesn't fit."

"It don't have to fit if he's a nut."

Spanner smiled wearily. "He may be a nut in the homicidal sense but they have their own logic. They plan things out like the rest of us, sometimes a lot better." He shook his head. "I'm afraid we're not going to get away with saying that because he's crazy he's bound to act irrationally. From what he's managed so far, I'd say it's about the opposite." He looked directly at Oates. "Anyway, why take the finger at all? Assuming he doesn't want the publicity."

"That's easy. To get the ring, same as last time."

"What ring?"

"The ring she must've been wearing on her—" He stopped, puzzled, as though an unexpected thought had struck him.

"Exactly," said Spanner, nodding. "Women don't wear rings on the right index finger. Some young girls might, but not an old woman like this. They wear them on the left hand, and if anything's on the right it's on the ring finger, not the index."

The sheriff swore loudly.

"When I saw the hands before," continued Spanner, "she had just a plain wedding band, where it should be. So she didn't go in much for rings."

"Then why chop the finger off?" asked the sheriff helplessly.

"I don't know," said Spanner quietly. Then with sudden urgency: "Check out the axe. And if I were you I'd talk to the neighbors and relatives. Might be more here than we know."

"What about you?"

"Me?" Spanner laughed. "I'm going home unless that axe came from Willows. This is out of my jurisdiction." He sounded relieved. "It's all yours, Jim."

The sheriff groaned and uttered an obscenity, not an easy thing to do at the same time.

In the second week of July the weather throughout the upper half of the state had become sufficiently hot to cause comment and general irritability, nowhere more than above San Francisco and extending up past the Clear Lake region. Here the air just sat still for days, hardly rustling the leaves, and people found good excuses to sit still with it. In a small rural community about forty miles from Willows State Hospital, the community where Sara Bishop had lived and died, a makeshift auction was being held on the lawn of a large two-story frame house that had recently been repainted. For many years the house belonged to an elderly spinster who had died six weeks earlier, leaving it to a favorite nephew who was now conducting the auction in lethargic fashion.

On the lawn were several dozen pieces of furniture of varying sizes and shapes. Some were eminently worthless beyond the strictly functional, others approached antiquity and were the only things that aroused any kind of spirited bidding by the small crowd on that afternoon. Along with the furniture, ranged in uneven rows on the newly cut grass, were dozens of cartons of pots and pans, ancient tools, bedspreads, curtain rods, books, old 78-rpm phonograph records, and assorted bric-a-brac. At one end were baskets of children's toys, mostly broken, and shopping bags of weather-beaten clothing. At the other end of the rows of general merchandise were numerous standing lamps with fabric shades and a huge birdcage. About the only common denominator among the items was the nephew's desire to be rid of them.

While his aunt was alive, all had graced her home. She had been raised in the town, moving to the frame house when she was still a young lady. Beaux had courted her on its front steps or in its parlor and been finally rejected; others had come once and rejected her. Dreams had been born there, and plans made. Not all came true. When her father died she took care of her mother, first as a companion, then as a nurse. She was their only child, a fact she was never allowed to forget. She was fifty-two when her mother died, and too old for children of her own. She had performed her duties with honor and virtue, and as the years passed she remained alone in the house she loved, reading her books and listening to her records and feeding her birds. She let the grass grow around the house, and collected cast-off toys, which she gave to the town's needy children.

The spinster was known by all the townspeople to have a good heart. She would visit the sick and cry at funerals and comfort the bereaved. That she loved children was obvious, that she at times also loved their mothers was something she kept to herself and safely at a distance.

When the spinster was fifty-four years old she met Sara Bishop and her shy, withdrawn boy. She felt a deep sadness for Sara and saw in the young mother much of the suffering she herself had endured for so many years. Her feeling quickly turned to love, not passionately sexual but quiet and responsive and selfless. Sara soon returned the feeling, finding a strange comfort in the other woman. Perhaps once a month they would cling together in bed, talking quietly of sorrow as desperate women do and giving strength to each other's bruised psyche. At such times Sara would often tell the spinster that theirs was the only relationship in which she had ever found any peace. The spinster would smile sadly, knowing that such peace came from their mutual loneliness.

Though she had little money to spare, the woman gave Sara sewing jobs whenever she could. She would also give the boy small gifts. She was frightened by Sara's attitude toward the boy, and for a long time she tried to shut her eyes to her friend's increasingly strange behavior. The spinster was a passive woman, taught to sit and wait. Taking action was unfamiliar to her, she had no experience at it. She was also very religious, and the idea of coming between a mother and her child was repugnant to everything she had been taught to believe.

Yet the day came when she could shut her eyes no longer, and she quietly told Sara of her fears for both mother and son. Sara, feeling betrayed once again, ordered the woman from her home and vowed never to talk to her again. Before she left that last time the spinster gave the boy a little wallet with a picture of his mother inside, taken some months earlier.

Within a year Sara Bishop was dead. When the police took the boy away, the only possession he had on him was the little wallet with the picture of his mother.

The older woman was grief-stricken at the double tragedy. With the remarkable courage she had shown all her life, she put aside her sorrow and did what she could. Aided by neighbors, she took to her home some of the dead woman's possessions, paying what she considered a fair price. The money was sent to the institution where the boy was placed, to be held for him until such time as he could make use of it.

For a long while the spinster left the boxes unopened in a darkened room, never going near them. Eventually she rummaged through the contents bit by bit, finally coming to a box of books. In one book, written by someone named Caryl Chessman, she found a sheaf of papers folded neatly in half. Putting on her glasses, she slowly began to read of the life of her friend Sara Bishop. The tears quickly came, and long before she finished the last page she was crying inconsolably.

Over the next dozen years she read the pages many times, never without tears. Each time she would place them back in the book where she had first found them. To her they seemed somehow to belong in that book and nowhere else. Someday, she often told herself, she would give them to the boy.

The spinster never visited the boy in the institution. She felt she would not be able to control her sorrow and would do him no good. She wasn't even sure if he would remember or recognize her. But she left his mother's pages in the book for him. When she died the pages were still there.

Now on this hot day, after several hours of desultory bidding, the only items left on the lawn were a worn tufted couch of uncertain origin and two cartons of kitchen utensils and books. The nephew paid a neighbor to haul away the couch in his truck. The two cartons were stored in the shed behind the house and quickly forgotten.

Far from the bucolic scene but at roughly the same time, two men in Fresno were supervising the installation of a neon sign over their new diner. They were brothers, simple men trying to make a living in the fast-food business. They knew nothing of Sara Bishop or her boy, or of the town in which she died, or even of Willows State Hospital. They had, however, heard of Harry Owens. In fact, one of them had killed him.

Don Solis was released from San Quentin in 1968 after serving sixteen years for murder and armed robbery. He considered himself lucky. He could have been sent to the Green Room like Caryl Chessman. He had been there when Chessman was executed, he was there for Barbara Graham's death and almost a hundred others. In his sixteen years he had seen men die in prison fights, go mad, commit suicide, bleed to death while others watched. He saw brutality beyond anything he experienced in the war, and it all finally sickened him. Now at age fifty-five, a little heavier and a lot smarter, he wanted only to be left in peace and to make a lot of money, this time legitimately. With his brother Lester as his partner, he was doing all right.

When Lester got out of prison in 1962 after a ten-year stretch for armed robbery and accessory, he drifted back to Fresno. Always the follower, he worked at odd jobs until Don came out. They had no money and no plans. Johnny Messick, who was in on the Overland Pacific job, had disappeared after his release in 1960. Hank Green had been killed in 1954 by a fellow inmate. Carl Hansun, who started the whole thing, had been gone since the robbery. Harry Owens was dead of course. Don still thought hard of Harry, though he wished he hadn't killed him and thereby wasted those years.

Two weeks after his return Don Solis was contacted by a local lawyer, who had a $10,000 check waiting for him. It was no joke, the check was his to do with as he pleased. No, the lawyer couldn't tell where the money came from; he was paid only to pass on the certified check that had arrived in the mail.

Shortly thereafter the Solis brothers bought a diner in Fresno with the money. They did well. Five years later they bought a bigger place and put up a bigger sign. By July 1973 Don Solis no longer thought about the original $10,000. The future looked bright.

On July 22, three days after the brutal axe murder, a second elderly woman was killed in the same savage manner, this time with a large butcher's knife. Again the index finger was missing. But from the left hand.

Her house was ten miles from the first killing, and both were within a thirty-mile radius of Willows. Panic immediately gripped the area. People stayed off the streets at night, admitted no strangers to their homes. Windows were locked, doors barred, guns kept loaded and ready. Women refused to stay home alone during the day, and many banded together with friends for protection or visited distant relatives. In other households men refused to go to work and leave their families. During that week millions of dollars were lost in unearned wages and unproduced goods and services.

By then the police were no longer in the dark, at least not entirely. The axe found at the first murder site had been checked with the Willows Hospital authorities. It definitely did not belong there. Where it did belong, and where it had been kept for many years, was in the woodshed of the murder victim. Neighbors identified it by the initials the frugal owner had scratched into the wood handle. Apparently the killer had gone to the unlocked woodshed looking for a handy weapon, perhaps he had even known of the axe.

Relatives verified that the woman, living alone in the house, had often hired handymen to help around the place. These were usually locals who were unemployable for one reason or another; most had drinking problems, some were of unsavory reputation. During the past year five or six had been seen on the property. Police set about finding and questioning each one. There was no particular urgency to their quest since they still believed the killing was the work of the maniac, who had gone to the shed looking for anything and found the axe.

After the second murder the urgency suddenly increased. Sheriff Oates called Spanner in Hillside, told him about the new killing and the missing finger. "It's from the left hand this time, for chrissake. What the hell's going on, John? Are we all nuts?"

Spanner laughed mirthlessly. "Maybe someone's trying to make it look that way."

"He's doing a damn good job of it," Oates growled over the phone.

Spanner agreed. After a moment he grew serious. "I don't think Mungo's the one you're looking for. It's not his style. Somebody's using him as a cover-up, that's why the fingers are missing. He read about it in the papers."

"But why the left hand?" Oates demanded.

"He might be just too dumb to remember. Or too careless, or drunk. The important thing is, he picks his shots and seems to know the layout. And he grabs whatever weapon's handy."

The sheriff grunted. The word suddenly stirred something in the back of his mind. "We're checking on some handymen the old lady used around the house." He paused. "You think there might be something in it?"

"Might be." Then: "Look for a connection, Jim. Somebody who knew both women and knew his way around. Chances are he's your man."

"What about a motive?" Oates objected. "Without a motive we're back to a nut like Mungo."

"Not quite." Spanner, unseen, shook his head. "These killings are too methodical, too planned for that. Whoever it is, he's not mad, just very angry. Get your connection and you'll find your motive."

By the evening of the twenty-third police learned that the second victim had also employed an occasional handyman. Neighbors remembered one some months earlier who had argued with the woman over the number of hours he worked. They didn't know his name, but the description given police matched that of one of the men known to the earlier victim. He was quickly called in for questioning, and this time the police were too short-tempered for any further evasions.

Within hours the man confessed to both murders. A forty-five-year-old uneducated laborer with a history of alcoholism and a long record of arrests for disorderly conduct, he had harbored a grudge against both women. When the escaped mental patient wasn't promptly caught he decided to kill them. Cutting off the fingers was meant to throw suspicion on Vincent Mungo but on the second job he got the hands mixed up. Both times he had been half drunk.

Why did he kill them? "They cheated me. I worked hard for them and then they didn't pay me all my money. They were too stingy to live."

Sheriff Oates was jubilant as he took full credit for the capture. He mugged for the cameras and joked with the reporters and generally made everyone feel at ease. He went over details of the two murders lovingly and lingered longest on how he had solved the case by sheer brain power. "It was all a matter of finding the right connection," he told smiling reporters. "After that the motive comes easy."

When someone finally asked about Vincent Mungo and *that* investigation, the sheriff suddenly excused himself. Urgent police business, he told them as he flew out the door.

Toward the close of the first week of July, as the manhunt for Mungo was getting under way, another manhunt of sorts was winding up. But not soon enough to suit Derek Lavery, who sat in his Barcalounger scowling at the two men on the other side of his huge oak desk.

He put the cigar down. "You had a week and even a day extra on this story. Now you say you want another week?" He looked pained.

"Less than a week," said Adam Kenton. "Just five days."

"That's a week," snapped Lavery.

Kenton took a deep breath. "I got a few more leads I want to track down."

"Like what?"

"Like a couple of ex-cons who were in the death house with Chessman."

"They out now?"

Kenton nodded.

"Where?"

"One's in Long Beach, he saw Chessman go. The other's right in town."

"And they'll talk about him?"

"They'll talk."

Lavery shrugged. "That's worth a day. What else?"

"There's a woman who worked in the prosecutor's office at the time of the trial. She remembers a lot of things that never got in the papers. But . . ." He let the word hang.

"She wants money," Lavery said.

Lavery sighed. "You know we never pay for information. It's unethical." He paused a moment as Ding coughed loudly. "How much she want?"

"A hundred."

Another sigh. "Take it from travel. Is she in town? So from now on she lives in Vegas. Anything else?"

"Just Chessman's final confession."

"His what?"

"His final confession."

Lavery looked at Ding, then back to Kenton. "What are you giving me? Chessman claimed his innocence to the end, except for the alleged confession the cops beat out of him." He put the cigar in the heart-shaped ashtray. "I never heard anything about a final confession."

"Neither did anyone else," Ding said softly.

Kenton scratched his chin. "There was a psychiatrist used to be up at San Quentin in Chessman's time. His name was Schmidt."

"So?"

"So I got a connection in San Rafael near the prison who knows a guard there. He swears the guard told him that Chessman confessed to the psychiatrist before he died. Told him he was the robber-rapist back in '48 when they caught him."

Lavery glanced over at Ding, who shook his head.

"Me neither," he muttered and put the cigar back in his mouth. "It doesn't make sense."

"The guard supposedly said that he was passing Chessman's cell," Kenton continued, "when he overheard the confession." He paused. "Personally I don't believe it, because he'd have no business being there. What I think might have happened is, he got Chessman mixed up with a man named Bud Abbott who was executed a couple years earlier."

"Who's Abbott?"

"Bud Abbott was convicted of killing a young girl in San Francisco but he never confessed, and just like Chessman, he claimed he was innocent right up to the end. But just before he died he apparently told this Schmidt in confidence that he was guilty. I have his words here—" Kenton leafed through his notes for a few seconds "—here they are. Abbott supposedly said to Schmidt, 'I can't admit it, Doc. Think of what it would do to my mother. She could not take it.'" Kenton closed his notebook, looked up. "After his execution the authorities claimed that was his confession but not everybody was happy about it." He paused for effect. "I think the guard—"

"If there is a guard at all," interrupted Ding.

"If there is a guard at all, I think he just mixed them up," said Kenton. "But it's worth checking."

"If there's no guard, you just got a lying connection," Ding said gently.

Kenton laughed. "You mean another lying connection."

"Check it out," Lavery said abruptly. "But you'll come up with nothing." He puffed on the cigar. "I'll bet you a year's salary on that."

"Yours or his?" asked Ding.

Lavery said nothing.

"Do I get the week?" Kenton asked enthusiastically.

"You get three days," Lavery growled, "and that's all you get." He turned round, looked at the giant schedule calendar tacked on the cork-lined wall. "It'll run on the thirty-first instead of the twenty-fourth." He turned back. "Anything else before we go on?"

Ding had one final thought. "At least two women identified Chessman as the attacker, and there were a bunch of others who got raped at the time. Now remember, this was long before birth-control pills and free abortion clinics so there's a good chance one or more of them became pregnant. Suppose we see if any babies were born to those women around nine months later. Might be worth a good picture spread. You know, 'Son of Rapist! Caryl Chessman Executed for Bringing This Boy into the World!' Or 'Daughter of Raped Mother and Rapist Father!' What do you think?"

Lavery and Kenton sat in stunned silence for a long moment. Sunlight streamed into the penthouse office through the louvered windows. The air conditioner hummed peacefully in the background. Lights blinked on the telephone console at the end of the desk but no rings interrupted the creative juices at work.

Finally Lavery broke the silence of the room.

"That is the most disgusting and flagrantly unethical idea I have ever come across in twenty-five years in the business," he stuck his cigar between his teeth, took it out again, "and I might add I have seen some real beauties." He slammed it back in his mouth and sat there.

"Good idea, though," said Ding.

"Goddam good idea," said Lavery.

"I can see it now," Ding said and laughed.

"Terrific," agreed Lavery. "It'd sell an extra fifty thousand copies."

"At least."

"Maybe more."

After a moment Lavery shook his head sadly and hunched forward in the lounger. "Too bad we can't use it," he said sorrowfully.

"Why can't we?" Ding asked.

"For a million reasons," answered Lavery, "but I'll give you only one. The kid would be about twenty-five now, and the son of a bitch would find you and he'd kill you or she'd kill you. Then they'd come after me." He closed his eyes. "And I have enough troubles, God knows." His eyes snapped open, ready for business. "Now what did I get for a week's salary?"

For the next fifteen minutes Adam Kenton outlined for his editor what he had learned about Caryl Chessman's twelve years on death row and his execution. From an habitual criminal and three-time loser Chessman rehabilitated himself in prison to the point where he became a recognized writer and a fair country lawyer. But the times were against him, that more than anything else killed him. It was as though a gigantic conspiracy had formed around him, crushing him slowly in its maw. There was no escape. Nine months before he was executed, the sadistic rapist-murderer Harvey Glatman died in San Quentin's gas chamber. The people of California quite properly had no mercy for such rapist fiends, and no distinction was made between a Caryl Chessman and a Harvey Glatman. Two months earlier the vicious mass murderer Charles Starkweather went to the electric chair in Nebraska. The people of America quite properly had no mercy for such criminal monsters, and no distinction was made between a Caryl Chessman and a Charles Starkweather.

The jaws began to close almost from the beginning. On his important appeals Chessman lost every time. The state of California was in no mood to order expensive retrials in a case where the accused served as his own lawyer in a capital-offense trial, or where he was not advised of his constitutional rights by arresting officers, or where he was given perhaps the harshest judgment ever handed a felon not having committed murder, or where the capital charge of kidnapping was ludicrous at least in the spirit of the law. Likewise, the country had not yet heard of the phrase "cruel and unusual punishment" or that everyone was entitled to adequate defense. Chessman petitioned himself through every state and federal court right up to the Supreme Court itself. He lost there too.

Toward the end the jaws closed faster. The California Supreme Court affirmed his conviction, the United States Supreme Court denied his appeal, the United States Court of Appeals denied a stay of execution, the California Supreme Court refused to recommend executive clemency. Then the governor granted him a sixty-day reprieve for political motives. When the reprieve was over, so were the reasons that created it. No further reprieves would be forthcoming. Chessman lost. The California Supreme Court refused to annul the death warrant. Chessman lost. The California Senate Judiciary Committee voted down a proposal for abolishing the death penalty. The death penalty won. Chessman lost. An appeal was made to an ardent foe of capital punishment, Supreme Court Justice William O. Douglas. Chessman lost. An appeal was made to another foe of capital punishment, California Governor Edmund Brown. Chessman lost.

The jaws were almost closed. A final petition for a writ of *habeas corpus* was made to the California Supreme Court. The vote was 4 to 3. Chessman lost. A last-minute call was made to the governor's office. Chessman lost. A last-ditch effort was waged before a Federal District Judge in San Francisco. He agreed to a stay of execution so that a new petition could be filed. His secretary hurriedly called the prison to stop the execution. Somebody got the phone number wrong. There was a pause. The number had to be verified, dialed again, or was it the operator who had to get the prison? It didn't matter; by then it was too late. The cyanide pellets had just been dropped that very second. Caryl Chessman had suffered his final loss. He was dead. The jaws had snapped shut.

Lavery liked what he heard. He especially liked the conspiracy idea of everything being against Chessman; that was a popular word at the moment. But it wasn't the main attraction. "Lean heavy on capital punishment as the killer," he told Kenton.

Ding had much the same to report. Chessman was a loser from the beginning. A hard childhood, reformatory at sixteen, Los Angeles County jail at eighteen. Sentenced at age nineteen to multiple five-year-to-life terms in San Quentin for robbery and assault with a deadly weapon. Escaped prison in 1943.

Transferred to Chino minimum-security that year, escaped from there. Recaptured the same year, returned to San Quentin. A three-time loser at age twenty-two. Sent to Folsom maximum-security prison in 1945, paroled 1947. Captured in a stolen car January 1948. Two women identified him as their attacker. The trial in Superior Court lasted two weeks. He acted as his own lawyer, with a court-appointed public defender as legal adviser. The jury had eleven women, one man.

"What?" yelped Lavery. "Eleven women on a jury in a rape and sex-offense trial?" He shook his head. "Chessman didn't get executed. He committed suicide."

It took only thirty hours to find him guilty of three counts of kidnapping for purpose of robbery—a capital offense—and fourteen other crimes. No recommendation of mercy. Sentenced to death in May 1948 on two kidnapping with bodily harm counts, five years to life on the third. Ding had read the trial transcript, calling it a joke as far as adequate defense was concerned. "A fool for a client," he said hopelessly. He had talked to some legal people, a few court attendants, one of the jurors. He could find none of the victims.

Of the crime spree itself, Ding considered two points of particular interest. There had been robbery-rapes in secluded areas of Los Angeles before Chessman ever came on the scene. If he didn't do them all, who did the others? And if others did some, who said Chessman did any? Two witnesses. But under that kind of emotional pressure, who can be sure? And they never really faced any expert cross-examination, with Chessman acting as his own lawyer. At the least, there was room for doubt.

"And the second point of interest?"

Ding sighed, a long luxurious hollow sound. "There's a good possibility that Chessman was impotent," he said softly. "Rumor had it that after the arrest some people wanted him to be examined but he refused. I haven't been able to check it out but it fits, in the sense that a guy like Chessman would've been too proud to reveal anything like that. It wouldn't have mattered anyway, because the big charge was the kidnapping with bodily harm."

"But if he was impotent," protested Lavery, "why go on a sex spree?"

"Maybe he didn't," said Ding. "Remember that Chessman proclaimed his innocence right up to the end. His last words to the warden, a man named Dickson, were"—he read from a small card—"'I just want to keep the record straight. I am not the Red Light Bandit. I am not the man. I won't belabor the point; just let it stand at that.' Now why would he stick to it even after all hope was gone? What would he gain?" Ding put the card away. "All I'm saying is that Chessman was a loner. He never had much to do with women. I think maybe there was a reason. Did you know that his original name was spelled Car-*ol*? His mother wanted a girl, You see what I mean?"

"No good," said Lavery. "If Chessman was impotent he would've at least tried to get out of the sex raps. Nobody's *that* proud."

Ding shook his head emphatically. "That's what I thought until I talked to somebody in legal medicine. Most impotency is temporary and no alibi against rape done at another time. Even if it's a physical defect the guy's not

clear because other things could be done that might con-
stitute sexual abuse or attempted rape, which is legally
the same as rape, at least in the gravity of the charge."
Ding took out the huge handkerchief he always carried.
"If Caryl Chessman was impotent it wouldn't have done
him any good to shout it out." He wiped his forehead.
"What he was really being tried for was taking them
somewhere and doing whatever he wanted to them." He
wiped the back of his neck. "That's every man's fantasy.
But it works only if it remains a fantasy." He crumpled
the limp handkerchief—"So Chessman had to be punished"
—and put it back in his pocket. He winked at Adam
Kenton, then turned his gaze back to Derek Lavery who
sat quietly in thought.

"All right," Lavery said eventually, pushing the lounger
back. "I think we got most of it here. The crime, the trial,
the death house, the execution. Chessman was a victim of
his times. Push the capital punishment angle, work everything around that. He was helpless from the beginning but
fought back bravely. That'll get our men readers. Maybe
he didn't do it, that'll get the women. The trial was a joke.
Play up how the years on death row straightened him
out, the redemption bit makes everybody feel good. But
he got the gas anyway. Why? Capital punishment. The
machine was oiled and needed another victim." He
grimaced. "I think we got enough to throw some doubt
on his guilt, beside the fact that he never should've been
there at all."

He wheeled to one side, his hand reaching for the telephone. "Ding, go easy on the impotency thing. I might
want to use that idea about Son of Rapist. What a spread!"
he said in awe. Then he pressed a button on the console
and left Caryl Chessman for the next story.

During the same first warm week of July, on the day
after the brutal killing of one patient and the mysterious
escape of another from Willows State Hospital, John
Spanner spent several morning hours walking around the
grounds. The rainstorm had long since given way to
streams of sunshine that swiftly dried the water-soaked
earth. Few traces remained of the storm's arrival and
none at all of the killer's departure. The body of his victim
had been removed, the alarm on the roof door cleaned
and reset. The big iron gates at the main entrance still
remained locked, the gray stone walls surrounding the

hospital still stood unassailable. Yet Vincent Mungo had walked out, Spanner reminded himself. Or flew out.

He talked to the guards at the main entrance. The gates were always kept locked, opening only for vehicles. Those leaving were always thoroughly checked out. The pedestrian arch had a small gate of its own, also locked. And nobody could climb over the gates because they locked into the massive overhead stone slab, part of the wall design. Spanner was satisfied.

At the rear of the grounds, behind the main building complex, a smaller gate was opened only for staff personnel and suppliers. A guard watched from a tiny office at the wall. Again the gate locked into the overhead design. Between the hours of 9:30 p.m. and 5:30 a.m. the gate was locked, and personnel were required to use the main entrance.

Spanner next surveyed the wall itself. He found no breaks in it and nowhere to climb over without an extension ladder. Somehow he couldn't see Vincent Mungo obtaining such a ladder.

Leaving that problem for the moment, he talked to the attendants in the experimental building. To a man they expressed no surprise at Mungo's violence, trained as they were to expect irrational behavior. He had been resentful of authority and erratic in his social performance. Spanner tactfully did not point out that those were traits common to most people. One attendant noted, however, that he would have expected that kind of violence even more from Bishop than Mungo. Why? "He was a cold fish, always watching everyone. Like he was the hunter, you know what I mean?"

In the afternoon Sheriff Oates appeared with a deputy in swimsuit and goggles. He had been told of a drain that flushed out under the wall. Always the fisherman, Spanner was immediately interested. If their man couldn't walk out or fly over, then maybe he swam under. At the ditch they found the wire-mesh fence that had been built across the drain under the wall. It extended into the water, now only about five feet deep. The deputy waded in and sank underneath. In a moment he returned. The gate was a foot short of the bottom, just about enough for a thin man to squeeze through. "Now we know how he got out," said the sheriff. He beamed at his cleverness in solving the mystery. "What I don't understand is how he knew it was here. I bet there ain't ten people in this whole damn place know that." He kicked at a stone. "He was only here a couple months, for chrissake."

Spanner walked to the edge of the drain. "Maybe he didn't know," he said matter-of-factly.

"Huh?"

"Maybe Mungo never knew about it. Maybe he's dead."

Oates followed him to the edge. He wanted to laugh, but nothing came out. He shut his eyes, opened them again. "What's on your mind, John?" he said softly.

"Maybe the body we found was Vincent Mungo. It had Bishop's uniform and all his things in the pockets. It didn't have his watch or ring so we assumed they were taken. But all that could've been staged."

"That's crazy."

"Is it?"

Oates thought furiously. The son of a bitch is trying to pull something here, but what? He can't be that nuts. Better see what he's up to. "Tell me more," he said grimly.

"The face is gone. Maybe the work of a nut, like Baylor said. But maybe so we can't tell who it was. Fingerprints are useless; neither one ever had them taken. Again we can't tell who it was."

"What about the finger?"

"That could've been staged too."

"The wallet?"

"Same thing."

He really must be nuts, the sheriff said to himself. Okay, play along, let him make a fool of himself. Serve him right, the bastard.

"Got any suggestions?" he said aloud.

"One that should work," replied Spanner.

Five minutes later they were in the records room in the main building. "Bi-g, Bi-l, Bi-m, here we are, Bi-s, Bishop, Thomas William," The clerk handed the file to Spanner. "Is this all?" he was asked. "That's it," he answered cheerfully. "Let me know when you're done." He moved away.

Spanner opened the file, Oates at his shoulder. Thomas William Bishop, born April 30, 1948. His finger quickly ran down the sheet, stopping at Physical Description. No mention of any scars, tattoos or other identifying marks. The bottom line was obviously a recent addition. Both men read it: "Small V-shaped scar on upper right shoulder below the scapula." They exchanged glances.

Soon they were talking to one of the guards in the experimental unit. Yes, he remembered how Bishop got the scar. The year before, the man had gone absolutely berserk: he set fire to the ward, then attempted to kill another guard. One of the patients tried to stop him. He stuck a scissors in Bishop's shoulder, made a few gashes. "Even that didn't stop him. Took four of us to get him off the guard."

Another twelve minutes and they were getting out of the screaming police car in front of Hillside's small hospital. "We'll know in a few seconds," Spanner said evenly. Inside they rushed to the basement, where the morgue attendant opened the drawer and wheeled out the body of Thomas Bishop. They carefully turned it over. On the upper right shoulder, just below the scapula, was a small V-shaped scar.

Outside again, the two men were a study in moods. "Can't win 'em all," said the sheriff, smiling. "You had a crazy idea, it didn't work out. Nobody's perfect." He rubbed his hands. "Can't win 'em all," he repeated.

"Guess not," said Spanner, defeated.

"We'll get him," Oates said cheerfully. "Mungo, I mean." He laughed. "By tomorrow we should have him. No problem."

"Hope you're right," said Spanner.

"Nobody's perfect. Don't forget that."

By the weekend, fishing in one of his favorite streams, John Spanner had forgotten everything. Or almost everything. He had a hunch that he had worked up to an assumption. The hunch was based on a few little signs that he thought he had detected. But it was wrong. Maybe he was getting too old. Maybe it was time he retired, God knows he'd thought about it often enough. When he felt the tug on the line he thought about nothing else.

That was July 5, the day the two police officials were at Willows. Two weeks later Vincent Mungo was still at large and Sheriff James T. Oates was no longer laughing. Not at all. On that very day the first elderly woman was hacked to death, her right index finger missing. Three days later the second body was found and although the diabolical killer was quickly apprehended, the whole episode served to publicize further the continued absence of the Willows maniac.

Yet at least one man read of the capture in the San Francisco newspapers of July 24 with uncommon interest. He read the account rapidly through, then once again, absorbing each detail. He had been certain that the elderly upstate women had been slain by the escaped madman. The killings seemed to have all the earmarks of the dedicated homicidal mind.

Naturally he was chagrined to learn that both murders had been simple pedestrian affairs committed by a lowly handyman with a grudge. And half drunk to boot! How mundane, he thought to himself. Ah, well, *à la chandelle la chèvre semble demoiselle*. He brightened at the thought and helped himself to another piece of toast. As he unconsciously chewed each morsel precisely eight times he pondered his miscalculation.

Amos Finch was an associate professor of criminology at the University of California at Berkeley. A youthful forty, still slim and athletic, he played the horses and the ladies with equal abandon. But the real passion of his life was the study of the homicidal mind, the maniacal killer, those whom society called psychopathic monsters and fiends. Finch called them his crank artists. He would tell his students in class: "You crank them up and they run out and kill, they they run down and you have to crank them up again." What cranked them up in the first place, and what kept on cranking them, was the study to which he gladly devoted his life's efforts.

Finch was marvelously gifted for such work. His steady nerves gave him a lengthy attention span, and he had a trick memory that nailed down almost everything he had ever read or seen or heard. It hardly ever failed him. He was also a speed-reader and a remarkably good writer for a scholar, able to evoke the atmosphere of a time long gone or a city far removed.

His vast knowledge of the subject had thus far produced three books, all recognized classics in the genre. *The Complete Bruno Lüdke,* published in 1963, recounted the horror story of the German mass murderer who killed eighty-six people, the modern record. Four years later *The Complete Edward Gein* appeared, which told of the Wisconsin mass murderer, necrophiliac and cannibal, in whose farmhouse police found bracelets and purses made of human skin, as well as vests, leggings, chair seats and drums. Also found were ten human heads sawed in half, another human head converted into a soup bowl, and a refrigerator full of frozen human organs.

Finch's third book, in 1971, was *The Complete Mass Murderer's Manual,* a collection of sketches of a dozen maniacal killers of history, from the infamous John Gregg family of early eighteenth-century England to the American Albert Fish in the first third of the twentieth century. Included was a graphic compilation of the hundreds of monstrous tortures inflicted on the victims and a complete glossary, the first of its kind, of terms used in the study of the homicidal mind.

Amos Finch thought of these books as his children, being unmarried, and he was as proud of them as any loving father. For his fourth book he quickly decided on a subject about whom he knew a great deal, the dread Jack the Ripper, only to learn that the excellent Donald Rumbelow of London was devoting efforts to just such a book. He then turned to a dream he had harbored all his professional life, the book he believed would be his *magnum opus:* a complete account of the vampirish Countess Elizabeth Báthory of Hungary who killed hundreds of young girls, perhaps as many as six hundred, then drained their bodies of blood and bathed in the blood to keep her skin youthful.

He soon saw the prodigious amount of work that would be required, including the learning of two languages and a stay in Europe, perhaps for several years. Reluctantly he shelved the *magnum opus* for a more suitable period of his life. Now, after a two-year layoff in which he did some preliminary work for a future book on mass murderers in the Bible, Finch was restless again. Something in the Vincent Mungo case had stirred his interest, possibly the savagery of the killing at the hospital. Unquestionably the work of the homicidal mind, he told himself. He secretly hoped that Mungo would not be caught before he had become a true mass murderer, and therefore a proper subject for a study and perhaps a book. But he never voiced the hope of course, not even to himself.

Sitting now in his study, disappointed that the two women had not been killed by Mungo, he wrote to Sacramento requesting that he be given special status in

the investigation for purposes of scholarly research. He
pointed out that as a recognized criminologist he would
be valuable to the law-enforcement officials.

During that last week of July nothing had yet been
heard of Vincent Mungo. His whereabouts remained a
mystery, though accusatory letters and phone calls were
still being received, misguided confessions still being made.
Sheriff Oates was desperate, especially since he had
assured the press that the madman would be caught "in
one or two days at most." His political ambitions were
not being helped by his continued failure in the case. On
the other hand, at least Mungo was not killing people
yet so the big pressure was not on him at the moment.
That Mungo would kill again was obvious. Oates had
been a cop too long to doubt that. He hoped that he
could get the son of a bitch in time. If not . . .

At the very end of that month, to be exact, on
July 30, a report landed on his desk that was to provide
the first legitimate clue to the killer's disappearance. The
report stated that a boy walking in the woods near his
home had found a shirt and pants mostly destroyed by
fire, both of which could have come from Willows. The
boy lived nine miles south of the hospital.

Within an hour Oates was at the site, his men fanning
out to question every household. Three hours later they
got lucky. A wife remembered that earlier in the month
her husband had complained that some of his clothes
were missing: a pair of pants and a shirt and a pair of
shoes—brown, she thought he had said. But he was always
misplacing things so she had paid no attention. Anything
else? Nothing, except— Yes? Well, she usually left a
twenty-dollar bill in one of her old purses in the closet,
just in case she ever needed quick cash. When she looked
a week ago she couldn't find it anywhere. Any signs of
forced entry at any time? She shook her head. Windows
were always open around here this time of year, it would
be easy for anyone to get in. What about animals to
guard the house? The woman laughed. They were a cat
family, had four of them running loose. One last thing:
could she remember when her husband missed the
clothes? Yes, it was when they returned from visiting
relatives over in Flint. They had spent the whole day
there and she was dead tired. What day was that? The
big holiday, the Fourth of July.

If Sheriff Oates had been desperate before, he was now in despair. Vincent Mungo had got himself a new set of clothes and some money right at the start. If he kept off the highways and got a few rides he could have made it out of the area the first day, maybe even out of the state. Or by now he could be losing himself in the anonymity of a big city. Each day he was free he became harder to find.

Oates was sure of at least two things. One was that Mungo had almost a month's jump on everybody, and that was a helluva lot of time. The other was that he was a damn sight smarter than those records and pecker-wood doctors at Willows said he was.

In his heart of hearts the sheriff hoped that if Mungo made it out of the state, he kept going clear across the country.

On the morning of July 31, 1973, a young man, well dressed and clean-shaven, handsome in a bland way, passed a newsstand in downtown Los Angeles. A banner on a newsweekly caught his eye. He stopped to read it and quickly reached into his pocket for some change.

It was not until much later that the significance of that headline would become apparent to the rest of the country.

FOUR

Thomas Bishop sat deathly still in the strange room. Against the far wall a battered television set frantically announced a sale of summer shorts. A half-eaten banana lay on a nearby dresser, its yellow peelings clashing with darkening fruit. A roach crawled across the windowsill. Outside a siren shrilled by and was soon lost in the morning haze. With great effort Bishop focused his eyes on the banner in the magazine he had just bought.

Caryl Chessman a Victim of Capital Punishment? He read it for the hundredth time, yellow block type slashed across the cover's edge. The picture below showed a bikini beauty cavorting gaily on a faraway beach. He turned to the appropriate page. At the top was a photograph, the first he had ever seen of Caryl Chessman. He stared at it a long time. Chessman had his right hand up to his face in a thinking pose, his chin resting in the arch formed between the thumb and fingers, his eyes cast down. The face was somber, the lips tight. It seemed to Bishop that the man was trying to say something but he didn't know what or to whom. After a while the face began to blur in his vision and he thought he heard his father talking to him.

Faint at first, then with brutal clarity, he listened to the sounds of demons destroying children, beating, burning, whipping small bodies in dreadful detail. All the demons were women in bathing suits, their globular breasts and butterfly bodies weaving madly in terrible temptation, trapping tiny faces, mouths open in frightful scream. Hideous noises gushed from secret recesses and in time all the demonic shapes rotted in leprous disgust, leaving only the screaming of the boy.

Much later, his eyes still fastened to the page, Bishop read of the life and death of Caryl Chessman. He read the article many times, poring over each detail of his father's crime and punishment. He learned of the rapes, as told by the accusers at the trial, of the years of caged and tormented suffering, much as he himself had suffered all those years. He saw the gas chamber with its green-splashed walls and leather-strapped chairs, heard the slow gurgling sound of death, breath by agonizing breath, until nothing remained but the body, vacant and peaceful. Eventually he came to believe that his father was not only a victim of capital punishment, about which he himself cared nothing, but of women as well.

Again and again he studied the words for hidden meanings. He felt that Chessman was somehow behind the words trying desperately to reach him. Laboriously he began to fit the true pieces together. Women were in constant and perpetual agony, suffering perhaps because of a God-given curse. They painfully brought life into the world, knowing that the only result of that life would be death. Such knowledge, visceral and inescapable, maddened them beyond endurance. In their horrifying torment they lashed out at men, those who gave them the seed of life and thereby brought them death. Using every wile at their command they enticed, enslaved and destroyed any man within their grasp, instinctively, mercilessly, in a titanic battle for survival in a totally crazed world. But they could not win, of course. They were doomed because without death there was no life, and as they sought in their monstrous grief to kill that which brought life, they accepted in their grotesque bodies the seed which brought death. And so the horrific cycle continued unbroken, leaving only victims in its bloodied wake.

Ultimately Bishop realized that the demons of his dreams were not only women monsters who had to be destroyed because they were evil, but women who suffered terribly and who desired to have their unspeakable torment ended by the final welcome release of death. That both the incarnate evil and the incalculable suffering should be lodged within the same body seemed to him as reasonable as a woman having two breasts.

After his close examination of the story was completed, he carefully tore the several pages out of the magazine and neatly folded them in half, and half again, until they could fit into a pocket. He then began to write a brief letter to the editor in a disguised hand. Unfamiliar with writing anything, he labored over the words. To an unseen observer he would have looked at those moments like a college student at his books.

In the cheap furnished room the television set was revealing the twisted emotional lives of a seemingly nice town caught in the grip of a soap opera. On the dresser the banana-half slowly turned to a soft, fragrant brown. The roach was gone from the window, and outside the noise increased as the lazy afternoon wore on toward the last night of July.

On the first night of that fateful month Bishop had sat by a window at Willows waiting for rain that did not come. His plans had been made. He knew what he had to do to get out and generally what had to be done afterward. His clothes were in order; the harmonica, the comb, the wallet, the ring, the watch, the axe, all were in readiness. He even had the can of whipped cream, bought from one of the kitchen staff at a profit of course, to silence the roof alarm, a trick he learned from a French movie on TV years earlier. Everything, including Vincent Mungo, was waiting for the one thing over which he had no control. But he hoped the rain would come soon.

His rage at being locked up was now so overwhelming that only marvelous self-control had kept him from exploding his new role of subservience. Often in past months he had been on the verge of running amok, but his animal cunning saved him each time from disaster. Vincent Mungo was part of his plan and had to be destroyed yet he wasn't one of them, he wasn't a demon. Bishop found himself wishing that Mungo were a woman.

Sitting by the window, he reviewed the plan again and again in his mind. After they jumped off the roof to the soft wet ground below he would kill Mungo with the axe and hurry to the drain, where he would slip under the wall to freedom. The axe would go with him since it was lost before Mungo arrived and might thus give the plan away if found. Without proof the gardeners would never admit to a missing tool.

Mungo's body, the face gone, would be wearing his clothes and carrying his possessions. His watch and ring would be missing. Fingerprints would be useless because Mungo's prints had never been taken since he had never been arrested. Neither had his. The plan was subtle and it was foolproof, and Bishop believed that he had once again proved his brilliance and superiority of mind.

To make absolutely sure, he built one final safeguard into his scheme, though he didn't expect it would ever be needed. When Mungo first arrived at Willows, Bishop quickly made friends with him and soon they were taking showers side by side, laughing and joking and masturbating simultaneously. Bishop surreptitiously examined his new friend's body for scars and tattoos. To his relief there were none.

He, however, had a recent scar on his upper right shoulder. He suggested that Mungo get the same so they could be buddies forever, even long after they escaped—sort of blood brothers, he said to Mungo, and winked. Mungo had at last found a friend and being somewhat dull-witted, he readily agreed. That afternoon when they were alone Bishop carefully made a small V-shaped cut on the same spot as his. Every day he dressed the wound, and it rapidly formed scar tissue. By the time of the escape they had identical scars.

On July 3 the rains came and Bishop went, over the roof and under the wall into a world he knew much about from watching television. Behind him he left his surrogate body and all the curses he could muster. He knew he was never going back.

In the pouring rain he walked for hours, heading due south, as best he could tell, trying to keep to a fairly straight line away from Willows. Somewhere along his trek he hid the axe in dense woods where it would not be found. Somewhere else he buried the ring and watch deep in the ground. The severed finger he threw to the insects.

The night was dark and fearful and afforded him good protection. No one was out, no cars moved. He felt alone in the universe and the feeling pleased him. Everything he touched filled him with delight, even the rain seemed friendly. He passed sleeping houses full of silent shadows that ignored him. Without breaking stride he crossed roads and culverts, gradually making his way unseen down the California land.

Toward morning the rain stopped. He had only a few hours left before the body was discovered. He kept moving, running at times across fields and along the edges of roads, always listening for sounds of danger. At daybreak he came to a small community bordering woods. He paused to rest, hiding in a makeshift lean-to a few hundred yards from a clump of houses. Wheezing loudly, he tried to slow his breathing down; he was desperately weary but not particularly sleepy, sheer excitement was keeping him awake. He thought of how far he had come during the night. Eight miles? Ten miles? A good enough distance for immediate safety. "But not good enough," he muttered savagely. Not good enough if he didn't change his clothes fast. What he needed was to get into a home on this Fourth of July morning or he would surely be picked up as he was.

As he was . . . The phrase made him smile, thinking of his plan and how it all had started. He suddenly wished for his wallet with the picture of his mother, that was his only regret. He had carried the little wallet all the years he was at Willows; someone had given it to him when he was very young. He loved his mother and always carried her picture with him. Now it was gone. He laughed, saddened by the loss.

An hour later he saw activity in one of the houses, people coming out. He watched as a young man and woman got into a car and drove away, his eyes following the car until it disappeared. If he could only drive . . . He left the thought unfinished. Quickly he skirted the backs of the other homes, keeping himself among the trees. The house he had been watching was at the end of the row. If he could approach it from the blind side he might have a chance. He waited another hour, then walked toward the house and up the steps, intending to ask directions if anyone was inside. He knocked on the door, waited, knocked again. No answer. He turned the doorknob. Locked. Swiftly he went around to the blind side and raised a window. In a moment he was in the dining room.

Another few seconds and he found the bedroom. From the closet he grabbed a pair of brown pants and a yellow dress shirt. He changed clothes, tightening the belt to the last notch on the loose pants. He traded his black institutional shoes, worn and mud-caked, for a pair from the closet. Almost a perfect fit. The other closet held women's clothes. He searched through several pocketbooks; in a purse was a twenty-dollar bill. Luck was still with him.

Within minutes he was walking toward the kitchen, his old clothes bundled under his arm. Something moved, ahead of him. He froze. Something else moved. He looked down. Cats. He swore softly. A bunch of cats was running around the kitchen. Under the sink he found what he needed. Kerosene. He took the can with him.

Back in the dining room he stopped at a small writing desk by the window, leafed through the papers on top. Nothing he could use. In the drawer were a handful of paycheck stubs made out to a Daniel Long. On each was a social security number. He stuck two in his shirt pocket. He also took a used envelope addressed to Daniel Long at that location.

At a clearing in the woods a half mile away he poured kerosene on the clothes and burned them. The shoes he buried farther on, then walked to the next town where he bought a small cardboard suitcase and shaving gear. After breakfast he waited with several others for the bus south. With his new dress clothes and suitcase he looked respectable, a young man on a short business trip or a brief vacation; certainly no one to be feared or even to create suspicion.

That evening in Yuba City he stopped in a bar; he had never tasted alcohol. He ordered a beer, liked it, ordered another. "That's very good," he told the bartender in his most engaging manner. The woman next to him said she drank beer now and then, mostly on hot days. "Makes you sweat, you know?" She glanced at him, smiled. "It's good when you sweat a little."

He returned the smile. When she ordered another martini he saw the roll of bills in her pocketbook. Soon they were deep in conversation. She was from Los Angeles, owned a beauty parlor there. Decided to take a month off, drive around her adopted state to really see it. "Most people don't even know what they got here," she said emphatically. "It's beautiful, really beautiful, really beautiful, you know?"

She was fifty-four years old, originally from Milwaukee. Married at twenty, her husband deserted her eight years later. No children. She worked a few jobs, then went to a trade school for four months to learn the beauty-parlor business. After six more years in Milwaukee she moved to Los Angeles. Her parents were dead, her sisters married and scattered. She worked in a dozen different salons in Los Angeles, managed a few of them over the next ten years. When she saved enough money she opened her own shop. She was good at her trade and she had a head for figures. The business prospered.

"Twenty years I'm here," she told him, "and I'm never going back." She shook her head. "Never going back." She ordered another martini. "It's too cold in Milwaukee, you know? I don't like the cold." She giggled. "I like to be kept warm." She looked at him, a warm smile painted on her face.

He looked good to her and there was no use denying that. She was essentially an honest woman and long past the coy stage, and what she regretted most about her younger years were all the boys and men she had rejected out of traditional feminine virtue. Whenever she thought of it her anger flashed, and in recent years she found herself thinking about it more and more. Such a damn loss, she would say to herself bitterly. All those lost years of good feeling and good times because she was taught to guard herself and her stupid damn virtue. What was it that her mother used to tell the girls growing up? A lady always keeps her pocketbook closed until after the marriage. Well, this lady's goddam pocketbook was going to open any goddam time she felt like it. And she felt like it right now.

She squeezed the young man's hand, rubbed against his index finger. It was long and slim, that meant he had a long slim cock. She shivered in anticipation. She could always tell the size of a man's cock by his fingers. God knows, she had seen some in her years. But not enough, not goddam near enough, she told herself bitterly.

They had another round of drinks, for which she paid. Sometime during the evening a television newsman announced the escape of a homicidal maniac from somewhere up north. His picture was shown on the screen. Nobody paid any attention. The bartender, wise and weathered, turned the volume down a bit; nut talk was bad for business. He looked his customers over; the only maniac at the moment was the dumb old blonde trying to pick up that nice-looking young guy. He shook his head sadly. They'll never learn, he said silently for the millionth time in his bartending life.

She must have had about seven drinks, she told herself on the way out. Not too much for someone who can handle it. She hiccupped. When they got to her car he helped her in. She liked that, such a gentleman. Must have had a good mother. She was not a mother herself, didn't even like kids. But if you're a mother be a good mother, that's the only way. She felt a little light-headed in the cool night air but otherwise she was fine. And she expected to feel even better very shortly.

She started the motor, touching his hand again for luck. He sat there quietly, smiling whenever she turned to him. Behind his eyes a plan was slowly forming.

A few minutes and they were at the motel. She wheeled the car round the gravel driveway to the rear, parking in front of her room. In the soft porch light he looked awfully good to her, good enough to eat, she thought lewdly. He was young, twenty-five he had said, and lately she had been seeking younger men. Not just lately, she corrected herself; for a lot of years now she had this thing for young men. The older she got the younger she tried to get them. But this was the youngest she had ever lucked into, just a boy really, and she was not going to let it get away. She would get its long slim fingers inside her if she had to kidnap and rape it. And if she had to, she would even pay for it.

In the room she turned on one small lamp. Not being romantic but realistic, she knew it would be better if the boy didn't see her in harsh light. With a giddy school-girlish squeak of delight, she sat on the love seat in front of the curtained window, pulling him down next to her. She held his hand, soon placing it on her breast. She stroked his thigh. He was shy, and she liked that. Cooing softly, she brought her face near to his until they were kissing, timidly, awkwardly. As he started to separate, she moved her hand up the back of his head and pressed forward. Their mouths joined again and she opened his with her insistent tongue, weaving in and out like a silky snake. After some moments she released him and pretended to be shocked by his wildly passionate behavior.

On the way to the bathroom she kept telling him that she had no idea he was such a real man, he just took her breath away and made her forget everything. She did not, however, forget to take her handbag with her. Several minutes later she returned in her nightgown, after he had snapped off the lamp and opened the curtains at her request. In the romantic glow of the porch light she saw his naked body, slender, boyish, and her nipples hardened as erotic sensations swept over her. She quick-ly slid under the covers, holding them open for him in smiling invitation. As he joined her in bed she loosened the bow on her nightgown and pulled the bottom up above her thighs.

Her hands soon guided his slim fingers down to her vagina. Like many women, she needed physical stimulation to become lubricated properly, and now she pressed his hand into the slow rhythmic movement necessary for her. She sensed his inexperience, and that became an added thrill. After a while she began to feel her senses melding and she knew she was drifting toward orgasm. She slipped her right hand under his waist and rolled him on top of her, expertly guiding his penis inside her moist body. With quickening motion she began her own rhythmic dance, and as she floated into sensual ectasy she murmured his name, softly, faintly, forming an end-less litany of love. Danny, Danny, Danny...

Bishop wanted to scream. He wanted to kill the woman six times. He felt sick, he felt disgusted at what she was doing, what she was making him do. She was old and she was fat and she had put her disgusting tongue inside his mouth and now his penis inside her disgusting body. She was horrible, a horrible monster that was trying to crush him, devour him. But he would fool her because he was smarter; he would learn what he needed to know and he would take what he needed to survive. Then he would kill her.

He had never been with a woman, had never seen a woman naked except in pictures somebody once had at the hospital. He wanted to find out about sex, how it felt to be with a woman. He hated bodily contact, hated to touch anyone, but he wanted to see if sex was different. He had to see if it made touching somebody else feel good. Now he saw that sex was just another trick that women used to capture men, to kill them little by little instead of all at once. Maybe if they were dead it would be good, or if they were asleep. Or maybe if they were in his power, afraid of him, willing to do anything to save themselves, maybe then it would be nice to touch their bodies.

The woman beneath him began to moan and toss her head from side to side. He thought he was hurting her and he became excited, wanting to hurt her more, but he didn't know how. Her moans became louder, her tossing more frantic. She started to shriek, quick guttural gasps. He stopped moving, looked at her. She shook his body violently up and down on top of her, getting him to move again. Seconds later she lunged up at him in a final horrible gasp, her face contorted, her lips drawn back, her eyes feverish. For a moment he was frightened, thinking the demon was attacking him. Then she collapsed back on the bed, her voice silent, her body still. Soon her labored breathing stopped and she lay there, eyes closed like a broken rag doll. He hoped she was dead.

Slowly, cautiously, he dismounted her. He put on his pants and went into the bathroom. He stayed there a long time. When he returned she was curled up on her side at the edge of the bed, her flabby face relaxed in sleep. She was snoring loudly.

The roll of bills was not in her handbag. He knew he could find it hidden somewhere in her clothes but he didn't look. He needed one more thing from her, something very important to him.

He got into bed, well pleased with himself. He had come far in one day. The authorities were searching for Mungo, and he was free and clear in his new clothes and traveling with a respectable businesswoman. Tomorrow, he told himself finally, should be even better.

In the morning he asked the woman to teach him how to drive a car, telling her that he had never bothered to learn as a kid. She was flattered of course, but more than that she saw it as a way to keep him a few days longer. She found him weirdly exciting, his inexperience and clumsiness titillated her. She wondered where he came from, wished she could find a few more like him. He satisfied her strange ways in bed, just as long as she directed him, and yet he didn't seem to expect anything sexual in return. He didn't steal her money, as others had done; he didn't ask for gifts in the morning. Just to learn to drive. Damn right she'd teach him, and get all the good feeling she could while it lasted. Boys like that didn't come along every day.

For his part Bishop was willing to put up with her vile body and awful touch while he got what he needed. He was a master of emotional disguise, and each time they were in bed he smiled and laughed and did what was expected of him. For three days they lingered on the outskirts of Yuba City. He was a good student, clever and quick, and by the third day he could drive a car as well as anybody.

The three days had been sheer ecstasy for the woman. She was sexually satisfied for the first time in years. She didn't at all mind that she had to pay for the boy's food since he had no money. She didn't even care about the hundred dollars she was going to give him when they parted. She wished only that she could keep him forever.

On their third evening together in bed the woman suddenly turned her body around and kneeled between the boy's legs. She took his penis in her mouth and slowly and deftly brought him to climax. She did not usually give oral sex to men and she intended it to be something that the boy would remember. It was more than that. Afterward he lay in bed wondering how anything could feel so good. He soon concluded that what she had done was the only real sex; it was clean and he didn't have to touch the woman and she didn't have to touch him, except for her mouth on his penis. He quickly resolved that the only sex he would ever have again would be with a woman's mouth. Not only did it feel good, he reminded himself, but it showed his complete contempt for women when he put into their mouths the very thing he used for urination.

The following day, July 8, they drove south. The woman was going to Sacramento and San Francisco on the way home. He told her he would go as far as San Francisco. The afternoon was sunny and cheerful and they drove slowly, enjoying the scenery along the way.

Several times they stopped to eat fresh fruit from roadside stands. They were a happy couple, laughing and having a good time as friends do. At dusk they stopped by a field. In such a deserted place the woman felt that they were alone in all the world and she wanted the boy to make love to her right there in the field, as was once before done to her when she was seventeen and in Wisconsin.

He smiled his warmest most engaging smile and as she got out of the car, deliciously happy and feeling for the moment like the pretty young girl she once had been, he hit her from behind with the tire iron. It was a savage two-handed blow that noisily cracked her skull. As she fell he hit her again. He then carefully ran the car over the body, the left wheels crushing the chest. Afterward he dragged the remains to a ditch off the road and covered the body with leaves and rotted wood. When he was finished he knelt down, his knees straddling the crushed head, and put his penis in the dead female mouth.

Later that evening he pulled into a motel near Sacramento. In the room he examined the woman's handbag thoroughly. The roll of bills totaled $800, plus $500 in unsigned traveler's checks; these he put in his pocket. From the wallet he extracted the woman's driver's license, thought a moment, then returned it. Too dangerous. He looked at the pictures in the plastic slots, flipping rapidly: men, women, children, bodies, faces, eyes, all staring at him in silent pose. He came to one of the woman herself, younger, slimmer, crouched on a nameless beach in a seductive manner, her brief swimsuit intentionally revealing her charms. He pulled the picture and slipped it into another pocket. The rest of the contents was the usual female junk. He put the bag in the trunk with her clothes.

The next morning he drove to San Francisco and

parked the car at the sprawling airport lot, another thing he had picked up from TV. He threw the parking stub away, knowing that the car would not be found for months. He then bused into the city, where he bought a new suit and light raincoat in a shop on Geary Street. He also bought an American Airlines flight bag into which he put his shaving stuff. His cardboard suitcase and discarded clothes were deposited in a trash barrel in the North Beach area. Not wanting to spend time in San Francisco, a focal point in the search for Vincent Mungo, he caught an early afternoon bus for Los Angeles.

He arrived at 11 P.M. and immediately checked into a nearby hotel, registering as Alan Jones of Chicago. The next morning he transferred to a rooming house on a pleasant street just a ten-minute walk from the downtown area. He used the name Daniel Long and paid for two weeks' lodging.

As soon as he was settled he visited the local Social Security Administration office and applied for a new card. He told the clerk that he had just moved his family to Los Angeles from upstate and somehow certain things had been lost, including a box of family documents. His Social Security card was among them. He showed her the payroll stubs with his name and Social Security number. The clerk nodded impatiently, she had heard it all before. What she couldn't understand was why people didn't carry the card on them at all times. In minutes she typed up a new card for him.

Next he entered a nearby bank and opened a savings account with $100. The bank officer checked the Social Security card, as he was required to do, and noted the number on the application. The address given was the rooming house. Within minutes he was issued a bankbook. A checking account also was opened, this one with $50. He was told the checks would be ready in ten days, and meanwhile he was given a book of plain bank checks.

That afternoon Bishop spent visiting a half dozen public and private institutions, from the public library to the art and natural history museums. He used his Social Security card and bankbook for references. For a minimum fee he received a membership card from each, valid for one year. All the cards had his new name.

Afterward he bought a wallet for his growing identification; it looked a little like one he had once owned.

The following morning, July 11, he called a branch of the Bank of America and complained that he was trying to get a bank credit card but seemed to be having difficulty. Could he be put in touch with their credit bureau? He was told that most large Los Angeles companies used a central credit clearing house, and was given the number. To the credit bureau he complained of a mistake in his credit rating and gave them his name and the address on the envelope he had taken from the house on the morning of his escape. He was referred to another clearing house in San Francisco which handled much of northern California.

He put in a call to San Francisco and spoke to a credit clerk about his problem. He again gave his name and the upstate address, as though he were calling from there. Within minutes he was informed that he should be having no difficulty. What specifically was the trouble? He replied that a local furniture store had turned down a time purchase of his after a credit check. His name and address were again examined, and nothing was found amiss. Have we got the right Daniel Long? he asked in exasperated fashion. Born in San Francisco on February 10, 1945? He waited for the reply, knowing it would be negative since he had just made up the place and date of birth.

The answer came swiftly. A mistake had obviously been made. Daniel Long was listed as having been born in San Jose, California, on November 12, 1943. "Good God," Bishop mumbled quickly, "that's my brother's birth date you got instead of mine." To the mystified clerk he promised to send a letter with the correct information. After supposedly jotting down the address to which the letter should be sent, and the clerk's name, he hung up.

That same hour he sent a letter to the San Jose Bureau of Records, requesting that a copy of his birth certificate—Daniel Long, born November 12, 1943—be sent to him at his Los Angeles residence. He enclosed a five-dollar bank money order to cover costs.

In the early afternoon he revisited the bank and sadly informed a different officer that his new bankbook had been lost. He had it in his jacket, and when he looked for it at home, it was gone. And the very first day too! He was told that it probably had been stolen by a pickpocket. He stammered, hardly able to believe that he could be a victim of such a thing. He was soon issued another book, giving him two for the same $100—still another trick learned from TV.

During the next week Bishop explored the city of angels. He walked along Sunset Boulevard and a dozen other famous streets, took a tour of Universal Studios. He rode the sightseeing bus and the trip to the homes of movie stars. He visited Disneyland and Magic Mountain, the Los Angeles zoo and Hollywood Park. Everything he saw amazed him; it was like being born an adult with no history and no memory. As a free man with a new identity, able to go anywhere and do anything, he enjoyed every moment.

Toward the end of the week he took a two-day trip to San Diego. He went to Balboa Park and the San Diego zoo, adding another membership card to his wallet. He bused down to the Mexican border and crossed over into Tijuana, where he walked along *Revolucion Avenida* and drank Mexican beer in dark cantinas.

When he returned home a letter was waiting. Inside was a copy of Daniel Long's birth certificate. He immediately applied for a driver's license, showing the birth certificate as proof of identity. He also furnished the several required passport-type photographs, taken at an amusement arcade. A false beard purchased in a theatrical supply store effectively hid his true features. He was quickly given a temporary permit. In a nearby driving school he paid $25 for an instructor to take him for his road test. He passed and was told that a valid California driver's license would subsequently be mailed to him.

With the temporary driver's permit as proof of identity he rented a safe-deposit box in a different bank, paying an entire year's fee. Into it he put the birth certificate and the picture of the woman in the bathing suit. Once outside, he threw away the two keys, leaving behind a mystery he believed would never be solved.

Afterward he filled out an application for a major credit card, listing his employer as the company named on the payroll stub. He made up a salary of $20,000 per year and seven years of employment. For the rest he fabricated a background, with the only facts being the place and date of birth and the upstate home address. He already knew that his credit rating was excellent. At the bottom he listed the furnished room as his summer place of residence to which the card should be sent.

On July 20 he returned to the first bank to pick up his checks. The name was correctly imprinted, and he discarded the unused plain bank checks given him earlier. While there he casually sauntered over to a waiting line at a teller's window and soon withdrew $95 of his $100 in the savings account, using the second bankbook. On the way home he destroyed the book. He now had practically all of his money back, and a validly stamped bankbook that he could take anywhere as proof of his solvency. With that and a driver's license he could never be arrested for vagrancy or even questioned beyond the moment. He had identification and he had money; he was a responsible member of society.

On the twenty-fourth of the month he paid for one more week's rent. His preparations were almost completed, and he knew that he would soon be leaving Los Angeles and the sovereign state of California.

Six days later two pieces of mail arrived for him. One was a California driver's license. The other was a credit card embossed with his new name. There was no address on the card.

The following morning he returned to his bank and cashed a check for $45 of the $50 in the checking account. Again for practically no cost he had valid bank checks that were further identification, and that could be used for cash in an emergency. On the way back to his furnished room a banner on one of the weekly magazines caught his attention.

Looking out of his window now on this final July evening, the anonymous letter mailed and the Chessman article in his pocket, Thomas Bishop brooded at length about his existence and what had been done to him in his home state. They had murdered his father and destroyed his mother, they had taken him as a child and had locked him away for most of his life, they had lied to him, ridiculed him, tortured him in a thousand monstrous ways until he himself wasn't sure at times whether he was crazy or sane. And they would have kept him a prisoner forever if he hadn't escaped. But he was smarter than all of them, otherwise he would have already been dead. They meant to kill him, just as they had killed his father.

His eyes hardened at the passing thoughts, his hand gripped the sash at the window's edge. They deserved something, the people of California, and he would see to it that they had something to remember. They wouldn't understand it, just as they never understood him, but they would remember.

At nine o'clock he put his shaving gear into the flight bag and turned off the television set. He looked around the room; everything was cheap and tawdry and smelling of goodbye. He left the keys on the dresser next to the rotten banana remains. Closing the damaged door behind him, he bade all of it farewell.

A brisk mile hike brought him to a small hotel, where he registered as Bernard Parks of Cleveland. Upstairs he lay on the bed and quickly fell asleep. At 11:50 P.M. he awakened and walked down the stairs and out of the hotel into the warm Los Angeles night in search of his prey.

On that last July morning at least one other person was equally moved by the Chessman article in the newsmagazine, though incensed would be the better word. State Senator Jonathan Stoner read the story in Sacramento on the way to his office. By the time he got there he was livid with anger. He stormed in and made several hurried calls, one of them to his press secretary who had not yet arrived. "Have him call me the minute he gets in," Stoner bellowed and banged the phone down. It was after ten o'clock, and he felt that he should be last in the office since everything revolved around him.

Jonathan Stoner was an ardent capital-punishment advocate. He believed the country was being paralyzed by a criminal element that feared nothing because there was nothing any longer to fear. Society was permissive, the courts lenient, the police disgusted, and, as usual, the middle class wound up paying for everything. The rich could afford to protect themselves, the poor had nothing to lose but their squalid lives. But the middle class, the backbone of the nation, the millions of lawful decent people of property and businesses, they were being robbed and plundered and assaulted and even murdered.

It wasn't so-called white-collar crime, the embezzler,

the forger, the tax evader, the big business deals, the political payoffs, that angered him. Stoner well understood these things, he had seen them and been around them all his political life and he was smart enough to know that grease was what made the machinery run so well. Nor did organized crime particularly disturb him; it lived off those vices men would always indulge, and it killed only its own. What filled him with rage was the violent criminal: the muggers, the rapists, the bank robbers, the petty gunmen, the thrill killers, the maniacs. They were the ones ruining the country, they were the ones turning the streets into jungles and the homes into jails.

Stoner passionately believed that all such criminals should be imprisoned forever, the key thrown away. Better yet, they should all be executed. Charles Manson should have been shot dead. Richard Speck should have been executed. Charles Schmid should have been executed. Sirhan Sirhan should have been executed. They all should have been killed, they all deserved the same death as the Harvey Glatmans and William Cooks of a few years earier. Caryl Chessman too. He got just what he deserved. Death.

Stoner looked again at the banner. He picked the magazine up, held it a moment, slammed it back on the desk. He called out to his secretary to get him some coffee. When she came in with the coffee he handed her the copy of *Newstime,* told her to get the Los Angeles bureau chief on the phone. "Find the number from information," he barked. "Tell them I want to talk to him personally. No one else," he shouted to her back. He sat down, trying to calm his anger.

The senator was a self-made man. Tall and ruggedly built, with a strong face and an iron constitution, he had clawed and fought and worked his way up the political ladder over the past eighteen years. Still only thirty-nine years young, as he liked to put it, he had political ambitions beyond the state, which he wisely kept to himself and a few intimate associates. At least, he often reminded them, until the proper time.

. He had been fourteen when Chessman was tried and convicted. He was twenty-six when Chessman was executed in 1960. While he had no recollection of the trial, he vividly remembered Chessman's death. He had almost been one of the sixty witnesses. As a young assemblyman from a working-class district he had felt a duty to witness the punishment of animals that preyed on his constituents, but he had little power as yet and was not able to attend the execution. Even then he knew that such fiends had to be destroyed if the good people were to survive.

In Chessman's case it was also personal. A cousin of his, still a teenager in the late forties and living in Los Angeles, had been raped and horribly brutalized about the time that Chessman was operating. The attack had been reported but the girl, wildly hysterical, had not been able even to describe her assailant. Afterward she was never quite the same, never marrying or even dating men. There had been no proof that the rapist was Caryl Chessman but to Stoner, who learned of the attack some years later, it all amounted to the same thing. His poor cousin had been raped at the same time that Chessman was a rapist, in the same city and in the same general area. That was enough for him.

The senator's reactionary instincts were deep-rooted and honest, as was his passionate belief in the efficacy of capital punishment. Yet he was also a clever strategist, quick to take advantage of every opportunity. In the matter of capital punishment he swiftly saw that the Supreme Court's 5-to-4 decision of the previous year was unpopular with a great mass of people. The Court's decision was now law but that didn't mean it would remain law. As a good politician he believed in the overriding will of the people, at least in emotional issues, and he was prepared to bet that within a few years most states would vote for restoration of the death penalty. After that it would be just a matter of time, perhaps only as long as it would take for several Justices to die or resign.

In his own state Stoner was absolutely convinced that the majority wanted the death penalty restored. He realized the increasing emotional impact of the issue and over the past months he had begun to think how he might be able to use that impact to his advantage. Elections were only a year away, and it might even give him recognition outside the state. He had been in just such a frame of mind that very morning when he saw the Chessman article, and now the beginnings of an idea slowly started to form in his mind.

His secretary buzzed him. A Derek Lavery was on the phone from Los Angeles. As he picked up the instrument she rushed in with *Newstime* and placed it on his desk.

For the next ten minutes the senator spoke calmly and dispassionately with the bureau chief. His voice was crisp, his tone modulated, his words precise. He well knew the power of the press. In a preelection year he had no intention of giving any editors or reporters ammunition that could be used against him.

In carefully measured sentences he outlined his objections to the Chessman piece. It was sensationalist, it pandered to the emotions, it abused the public's natural sympathy for the underdog, it distorted fact and at times bordered on fancy. Chessman was obviously guilty; he was convicted of a capital crime and he was executed for it. He was not the victim of capital punishment or anything else. He was a robber, a rapist and a kidnapper, and the only mistake made by the state was in keeping such a vicious maniac alive for twelve years at the taxpayers' expense. It was not the times that killed him but his own criminal acts. Everything else was unimportant. What? Yes, including the fact that he acted as his own lawyer. No, he did not suffer any cruel and unusual punishment but his rape victims surely did. As for other rapes at the time, he probably committed them all. In regard to Chessman's alleged rehabilitation, there is no such thing for these vicious criminals. Yes, that's right. No rehabilitation. Who said so? I said so. An animal is an animal, it cannot be rehabilitated. From animal can come only more animal. What's that? Son of animal? Is that what you said? No, I can't say that I do see the humor in it. Yes. Goodbye.

"Son of animal," mumbled the senator, shaking his head as he put down the phone.

A few minutes later the senator's press secretary came in. Young, ambitious and very sharp, he had been with Stoner for two years. Before that he had taught political journalism for a year, after graduating from Stanford. A column he wrote at the time for a local newspaper caught the senator's eye and he had been asked to join the team. The young man had plans and they did not include being a press secretary forever.

Stoner picked up the magazine and tossed it across the desk. "You see this?"

His press secretary glanced at the newsweekly. "Not my type. I go more for the sensational side of the news."

"The story on Chessman," said the senator. "Read it."

"Must I?"

"Read it, Roger," the senator said wearily.

Roger sat in the leather chair on the other side of the desk. He stretched his legs out and began reading, humming softly. After several minutes he looked up.

"What do you think?" asked the senator.

"It's a story on Caryl Chessman, who was executed thirteen years ago."

"I know that," replied the senator sarcastically. "Anything else?"

"It's well written for that kind of thing."

Stoner smiled heavily, as though he were dealing with a mental retard. "I'm not interested in the writing style," he said, annoyed. "Don't you have any opinions, for chrissake?"

"Sure I do," said Roger defensively. Then he brightened. "But I don't necessarily agree with them."

The senator looked at the young man for a long moment. His sigh, when it came, was loud and agonized. "You'll go far in politics, Roger," he said finally. "Very far indeed."

Roger smiled. The senator would go further too, he told himself, if he had a sense of humor.

"What I mean," Stoner said patiently after a pause, "is the idea of the article. It's totally anti-capital punishment."

"I see that," said the young man, serious now. "But they're beating a dead horse. Chessman's long dead and gone."

"Then they're reviving him." Stoner got up and walked to the window. "They are saying capital punishment is the real killer and Chessman just got caught in the machinery. They're making a hero out of him, how he was an innocent victim who fought a losing battle against legal murder."

"Everybody loves a loser."

The senator paid no attention. "It's the most vicious attack on the death penalty I've seen in years. They practically come right out and say we are all murderers."

"Next week they'll be on the other side," Roger assured

him. "All magazines work the same way. They don't care about sides as long as the subject is hot."

"Is Chessman hot?"

"No, but capital punishment is."

"Exactly." The senator smiled widely, walked back to his chair, sat down. "It's life-and-death, it's real, and I think it's time I get involved. In other words"—he looked at his press secretary intently—"it can be a good vote-getter if handled right."

"The public already knows your stand on the issue."

"I mean get involved personally. Make it my cause. Get all the exposure I can with it. This thing," Stoner said quietly, "is going to be around a long time, and so am I. There's no right or wrong in it beyond what the law says is right and wrong. Everything else is emotion, and that's where a good politician comes in."

"Cynical but true," sighed the young man.

"Plus the fact that I'm on the right side."

Roger laughed. "Let's just say the easy side."

"Now with this Chessman thing," the senator pressed on, "we have a ready-made handle. A convicted criminal who died for his crimes. His death made society safer, probably saved lives. But some people are making him out to be a victim." He glanced over at his aide. "It's a natural."

The press secretary considered the idea, humming softly again, as though trying to remember a forgotten tune.

"It's a hell of a way to get some national exposure," he conceded. "A lot of states are angry."

The senator nodded. "I could become a spokesman for them."

"But it won't work," continued the young man in a voice properly disappointed. "Not like that."

The senator's eyes narrowed. "Would you care to say why not? You agree it's a good emotional issue. My views are already known. All we need is a specific target to hang it on. And here we have it." He indicated the magazine. "So what is wrong with the idea?"

"Nothing's wrong with the idea," said the other slowly. "It's your handle that's no good. Chessman is dead, been dead for years. There's no drama in a dead man. People can't get worked up over what's irrevocable. You have to give them a life hanging in the balance right now. A bunch of lives would be even better. You have to give them—" He stopped, paused a moment, grimaced. Suddenly he snapped his fingers. "That's it," he exclaimed. "You have to give them lives right now."

The senator was perplexed, and his face showed it.

"You have to give them lives, Senator," the young man repeated dramatically. "Something they can identify with. Innocent victim or maniac killer, it doesn't matter as long as it's alive. Nobody identifies with the dead."

"And where do we get a live one?"

"We have one right now, right here," answered the young man, his eyes blazing. "Vincent Mungo."

He was excited now, thinking furiously. "Mungo killed once, he'll probably kill again. He shouldn't be allowed to live. If he escapes a second time he'll kill more. There's your drama, and it's real. People are either killers or victims, so everyone can identify. You keep hammering away that he should die when he's caught."

"If he's caught," suggested Stoner.

"He's a maniac, isn't he?" asked Roger rhetorically. "He'll be caught. Let's just hope he kills a few more first to make it even stronger." He laughed. "Only kidding, Senator."

The senator frowned. It was a damn good idea even though he didn't much care for it. The dead were always more comfortable to work with, easier too.

"I still think we need Chessman," he said finally. "His name is widely known, it's been a rallying cry for the bleeding hearts for years. Whoever heard of Mungo outside the state?"

"Then marry the two."

"How?"

"Easy," said the bright young man. "Picture Mungo as a reincarnation of Chessman. Symbolic, you know. A modern maniac stalking the state, ready to ravage and kill. A monster full of blood lust. Tell women he's probably after them, maniacs usually kill women anyway. Chessman died so they could live. Now this reincarnation, this diabolic offshoot of Chessman must die too. The people must be protected, and you're going to make sure they are protected." The press secretary was on his feet now. "That way you get the best of both of them," he said excitedly, "and if Mungo does slaughter any women, they'll flock to you like fish to water." He paused a moment. "Naturally I hope no women get killed."

Over the next half hour the two men decided on a press conference two days hence, on August 2. Senator Stoner would announce a campaign to return capital punishment to California. He would also begin his campaign against maniacs and rapists and killers. A lecture tour of the state would soon follow.

At the end of the meeting, as Stoner turned to other work, he couldn't help thinking of something that idiot bureau chief said earlier. It kept interrupting his thoughts. Son of animal, he had said.

Son of animal. Caryl Chessman and Vincent Mungo...

"Son of a bitch," Stoner said savagely.

On that very same night, the last of July, the son of a bitch was walking toward South Figueroa Street in downtown Los Angeles. It was after midnight and he had come many blocks seeking his prey. The area he now walked was on the razor's edge of skid row, filled with decaying buildings and sleazy industries. Drunks sprawled in doorways or argued over half-empty pints of wine. Drug addicts wandered aimlessly, sometimes jostling one another in incomprehensible stupor. Cars of youths cruised past noisily. Over everything hovered the stench of too many years of neglect. And behind it all, in darkened alleys and lonely rooms and desperate beds, came the smell of death.

Bishop gazed at the painted women, their eyes calling to him as he passed. They were old and incredibly wasted, and to him they looked like vultures waiting to devour human flesh. He shuddered and hurried along the broken street.

Several blocks farther on he saw her come out of a dingy four-story building. She sucked in the night air for a moment and then turned right, her long hair trailing over the back of her sleeveless blouse. In those few seconds he had seen that she was young and blond and had the thin legs of a pony. He crossed the street and walked faster. At the corner he caught up with her as she waited for the cars to pass by. She wore no makeup beyond a little eye shadow and her mouth was small and formed in a perpetual pout.

Bishop smiled his best smile. His eyes showed innocence, his face beamed with friendliness. His whole manner was one of charm and grace as he stood there in his expensive new suit, seeming for all the world like a handsome young man of money and power. "I believe this fifty-dollar bill could be yours," he said to her. His smile remained unbroken, his eyes no less innocent, his manner no less charming as he waited next to her holding the bill in his hand.

The girl understood his meaning. She wasn't a prostitute and she certainly wasn't a streetwalker but she understood exactly what he meant. She didn't take immediate offense to his suggestion because he looked like an interesting person. One quick glance told her that. He was sort of handsome and well dressed and charming and smooth and cool. Not like most of the men who hit on her, old lechers and hot young punks and cheap salesmen with fat hands. And he was obviously rich if he could throw fifty dollars around.

Fifty dollars was a lot of money to her. It would help pay the rent. Christ, she thought suddenly, the rent! What's today? August first, due today. Christ! She didn't have it. Again.

She turned and smiled at him. Why not? she asked herself. Any other time I'd be pleased if someone like this took me out. We'd go dancing and have a few drinks and then we'd go to bed and in the morning I'd have nothing. At least this way I'll have fifty dollars. She studied him carefully. Who knows? Maybe he's one of those rich nuts who likes to take care of girls. Maybe he's even in the movies and can help me get a break.

Her name was Kit, that was the name she gave herself since coming to Los Angeles. Not Kitty or Kitten, just Kit. She had been in town almost two years, leaving her parents' home to become a movie star. She wasn't beautiful but she was pretty enough in an offbeat way, and she had a good body though it was a bit fleshy in the thighs. She had tried to break into pictures using her body but each try led nowhere. She had lain on occasion with respectable men for money; she considered those few occasions just an exchange of gifts. Twice recently she had exchanged gifts with her landlord. She was twenty-one years old.

They walked along side by side, silent most of the way

except for comments on the weather and the condition of the neighborhood. He kept his smile on and she kept her smile on and they passed nobody and nobody saw them. Six blocks later she was home and he was with her.

She made instant coffee and had a cup. He smiled and had a glass of water. He told her he was from San Francisco, she said she liked San Francisco. She fed her cat, he smiled and watched her. After a while he put the fifty-dollar bill on the table. She let it lie there, not touching it. When she finished her second cup of coffee she went into the tiny bedroom and undressed. She called to him. He sat on the bed and looked at her fine young body; it was very different from the other body, the one that had taught him how to drive. But he was mostly interested in her mouth.

He smiled and told her what he wanted of her. She shook her head. She was old-fashioned that way, she didn't do that. No. She would open her legs for him but not that. She had tried it once and hated it. She would never do it again.

The shade was down, the room dark. She told him to get undressed and come to bed. She promised to make him feel good. He turned away for a moment and took the knife out of his inside jacket pocket. With his left hand he found her belly button. With his right hand he stuck the pointed tip of his long knife into her belly and then, still smiling, with both hands on the handle he drove the knife all the way through her body and into the mattress underneath. He continued to force the blade downward until the handle touched her skin.

In his mind's eye he saw the woman towering over the frightened boy, whipping him endlessly, the lashes biting into the boy's soft bare skin.

As a scream started to escape from the dying girl's throat he shoved the sheet into her mouth. The body was impaled and could not move but it shook horribly, uncontrollably, for what seemed like hours to the young man. Finally the last energy within its lungs was expended and it caved in and lay still.

He raised the shade for more light. The cat came in and he scratched its whiskers and put it back in the kitchen. He closed the bedroom door and removed all his clothes. Kneeling on the bed he pulled the sheet out of the dead girl's mouth and put his penis inside. The mouth was warm and very wet from escaping fluids and saliva. With his hands holding her blond head between them like a basketball, he worked the head up and down, the lips sliding and forth over his penis until he came.

When he finally got up he carefully pulled the knife out of the body. The thin blade was eight inches long, the handle four inches. The man in the hunting supply store had called it a doctor's post-mortem knife but told him it was really used for silent killing in guerrilla warfare. He had bought it that afternoon when he mailed the letter to the magazine. On returning to his room he had cut a small hole in the left inside pocket of his jacket so that the long knife could be carried concealed. It had been there all the while he was with the girl.

Looking again at the body, the young man set about his work. He cut off both breasts and carried them, one at a time, into the kitchen where he placed them gently on the table, the empty coffee cup next to one and his water glass by the other. In the bedroom again, he slit open the abdomen. Intent now, he removed and fondled the girl's organs again and again, caressing them, needing to touch them, to possess them. Nothing less would do, and he kept his eyes shut until all the dreadful visions were gone and the woman with the whip no longer hovered over the naked boy.

Satiated at last, he gazed around. The room was soaked in blood. He cleaned his knife in the kitchen sink, then scrubbed himself thoroughly and dressed. He returned the knife to the jacket and picked up the fifty-dollar bill from the table.

In the refrigerator he found some baloney and a half loaf of bread. He made himself a baloney sandwich and sat at the table eating slowly. He was in no hurry.

Sometime during his stay he took out a soft felt-tip pen he had also bought that afternoon, and carefully printed his initials in big block letters, one on each breast on the kitchen table.

Before he finally left he filled the cat's water dish to the brim and sprinkled enough dried cat food in a saucer to last for days.

The next morning, August 1, 1973, Thomas Bishop, alias Daniel Long, left his hotel of one night and caught the bus to Las Vegas. He looked good and felt even better; a young man of money and identity. He rode the big red bus out of the terminal and onto the freeway toward Nevada, following the route his mother and father had taken, unbeknown to him, almost twenty-six years earlier. From his seat midway in the comfortable coach he stared ahead, smiling all the while, and never once looked back.

FIVE

On the afternoon of August 2, State Senator Jonathan Stoner was winding up a press conference in Sacramento. His press secretary was at his side. In the strongest possible terms Senator Stoner had outlined his position on the capital-punishment issue for the dozen or so reporters gathered in the Senate conference room. He had told them of his intention to push for the restoration of the death penalty in California. He would spearhead such a campaign in every part of the state, he would lecture for the necessary funds and accept all the voluntary help he could get. He would talk to his political colleagues on and off the Senate floor.

Beyond that he intended to take his campaign to the rest of the nation, to every state if he had to, speaking to the people of the dangers they faced if capital punishment were not restored. He was confident that the majority of the American people felt as he did, and he would see to it that their collective voice was heard. He predicted that the United States Supreme Court would reverse its wholly unrealistic and unpopular decision of the previous year. It was time, he told the reporters, that the nation's highest court stopped flaunting its will in the face of the people. They must be protected and he would make sure, by God, that they were protected.

He then spoke of Caryl Chessman, referring to him as an animal who preyed on women. Chessman robbed them, he kidnapped them, he abused them sexually. He was a vicious pervert who had been a hardened criminal all his life. By the time he was nineteen he was already in prison. The state made a big mistake in giving parole to such an animal. He was soon back behind bars where he belonged. He was charged with eighteen— Stoner emphasized the number, repeated it—eighteen felony counts. Several were kidnapping with bodily harm, a capital crime. When he was arrested he admitted to some of the crimes but later, coward that he was, insisted he had been tortured. But he fooled nobody. Decent hardworking people found him guilty on all the charges. They could have recommended mercy but they didn't, and they didn't because they wanted this crazed animal destroyed for the good of society.

Then the state made another mistake. It kept the rapist fiend alive for twelve long years when he should have been killed immediately. Each imprisoned criminal costs the taxpayers $10,000 a year for his maintenance. In Chessman's case that came to $120,000. More than the senator's father had made in his whole life! And what was it used for! Was all that money used to help people, to irrigate land, to educate children, to build hospitals? It was not! It was all wasted, absolutely wasted on a deranged pervert—the senator stopped, told reporters he did not mean deranged in the sense of mentally unbalanced; most certainly not! Chessman was crazed but not crazy, in fact he was so damn smart in prison he kept the state from killing him all those years— so all that money that could have been used for good was wasted on Chessman instead.

In the end he was finally executed, which was just and proper. The various courts could have shown leniency, the high-court Justices could have recommended mercy, the governor could have granted clemency. But none of them did, none did because they knew their first job was to protect the people. At least they all knew it back in 1960. But if Chessman were alive now he'd be costing the taxpayers more than many of them made each year. And then one day he'd be paroled and back on the streets looking for new victims. In fact, thunderered the senator, the veins in his neck popping out from anger, in fact, if the death penalty had been abolished in 1960 Chessman would have been paroled by now and out on that street, right here, today, maybe stalking your wife or your daughter at this very minute, God forbid.

Yet there is still some justice in the world, and Chessman is dead and where he belongs. But now this—the senator held the newsweekly up for the reporters to see; he had to catch himself from using the words he wanted to say—this *magazine* comes along and says that Chessman was a *victim*—he shouted the word out—of the death penalty! They say that capital punishment was the real killer and that Chessman, this sex fiend and kidnapper and robber and gunman and would-be killer, was just an innocent bystander caught up in the legal machinery—here the senator's scorn was boundless—a *hero*, for God sake, who fought a valiant battle but lost simply because he lived at the wrong time.

"Well, I say he lived at the right time. This is the wrong time. When decent citizens have to lock their doors and bar their windows and keep loaded guns by the bedside. When a man can't go to work without worrying about his family's safety. When a woman can't walk the street without fear of sexual assault. When the animals can kill with virtual impunity. Five people? Ten? A hundred? It doesn't matter how many they kill. If they're caught all they'll get is a cozy stay in a YMCA with television and free room and board for a few years. Then they'll be back ready to kill again. And any time they can't make it out here, any time they get bored or lonely, all they have to do is kill again and they're back on free room and board at the country club. It's better than working for a living! It's even better than welfare! I'm amazed that more honest citizens aren't killed by these criminals just so they can get back to the free life. What's to stop them? Not society any longer. Not the courts any longer. And certainly not the fear of death. There is no more fear of death, except for their victims of course. But who speaks for them anymore? Who cares about them? They're not news."

He paused a moment to let that thought sink in to the newsmen.

"They're just the little people. Unknown all their lives and forgotten as soon as they die. If anyone talks about them, they're simply called the victim. But the killers, that's something else! They don't work or pay taxes or obey the law or live quiet lives of frustration. That's not news. Instead they kill. That makes them special. Charles Manson will be remembered and written about a hundred years from now, just as Jack the Ripper is remembered a hundred years after *his* crimes. Everybody wants a little recognition. More things are done for sheer recognition than for money or sex, as far as I can see. But the only ones who get it are the killers. Who knows all the names of Manson's victims? Or Jack the Ripper's victims? Or Charles Starkweather's victims? Or Caryl Chessman's victims? Who cares? They were just people."

The senator quickly drank from the water glass, looked at his audience.

"You want recognition? I mean *real* recognition? Your life story in all the papers, your face on television all over the country. Books written about you; what you eat, what you feel, what you think, what you don't think. Maybe even a movie about you. Why not? They made movies about all the killers and maniacs I've mentioned, including Chessman. If that's what you want, it's easy. Just go out and kill some people. They don't have to be presidents, they don't have to be big shots. Just kill enough to make a big splash in the papers. Or kill only one or two in a novel way or a crazy way, anything to get the news media interested. You too can be famous. Chessman"—Stoner again held up *Newstime* magazine —"is famous. Thirteen years after his death they're still writing about him. He was a kidnapper and sexual deviate, but he was a victim. He was fairly tried and convicted, but he was a victim. He was legally executed, but he was a victim. Meanwhile I don't ever remember reading a word about *his* victims. You know, the real victims? They're gone, forgotten. Nobody gave them a word of print. No well-known people spoke up for them. No movies were made about them. They were nothing, the little people of dull lives who never ran amok. One of them was a seventeen-year-old girl whom Chessman sexually brutalized. Two years later she was admitted to Camarillo as hopelessly insane. Perhaps she's still there. But Caryl Chessman is a hero. Who says he's a hero? The newspapers say it. The big shots say it. All those who rejoiced in the killing of capital punishment say it. All the pressure groups, the so-called peace fronts, the civil liberties organizations. To them he's a hero-victim, the perfect existential man. Christ!"— he finished the water in the glass—"next they'll be saying we're really murderers for executing him!"

The senator mopped his forehead with a tiny handkerchief; his voice became soft.

"You may say that Chessman is gone, dead and buried, and can harm us no more. But I ask you, is that true? Can he no longer harm us? His malignancy is still with us, his evil kind are still among us. They are still robbing and raping and killing. Each year the number of such crimes grows. How many more innocent victims must be slaughtered before we end this madness? How many more lives must hang in the balance?"

The senator studied the faces of the reporters in front of him. They were a hard sonofabitchin' lot to work on, reporters were; to get a flicker of interest from them was like drawing blood. But he had their interest now. And in his heart and soul Stoner knew that he would have them from now on.

"Right here in our own state there is a reincarnation of Caryl Chessman, skulking through the night, stalking his victims. A moral madman, a blood-crazed maniac capable of inflicting savage attack and ghastly death. Whom will he destroy before he is finally captured? Whom do the Chessmans seek out to ravage and kill? The helpless among us, our women. How many women will fall before this diabolic monster? Only God knows. I hope and pray none"—his face grew solemn—"but as I look around me I find it hard to believe that my hope will be realized, my prayers answered. Killers roam the streets at will, the courts turn them out, the prisons turn them loose. Who can fight such madness? How can we protect ourselves? How can our women be protected? I don't have all the answers"—a self-deprecating smile— "but I do know one thing that will go a long way toward some kind of protection, some sense of safety. We must get rid of such vicious animals once and for all. Caryl Chessman was an animal!"—Stoner's voice thundered now—"Vincent Mungo is an animal!"—the voice reverberated through the room—"He must be stopped *now* before it is too late. He must be caught and *executed*, no matter what legal steps are needed.

Killed! Just as we would kill a mad dog. If not"—the senator paused for effect, lowered his voice almost to a whisper—"then I'm afraid innocent people are going to be slaughtered. If Vincent Mungo is allowed to return to a comfortable ward where he can plan his next escape and his next murders, then there is no hope for any of us. Then we may as well all lie down with beasts and let the jungle grow over our bones."

After the press conference Senator Stoner met with Roger in his office. He was pleased, the conference had gone well. Roger agreed.

"Should make a good splash in the papers," said Stoner, rubbing his hands together. "Might even make some of the evening editions."

Roger was not so sure. "You'll be lucky to get anything in the metro papers," he said glumly. "But maybe they'll hold it back for tomorrow."

The senator stopped his rubbing. He eyed Roger suspiciously. "Why do you say that?"

"Haven't you heard?"

"Heard what, Roger?" he asked evenly.

"They found a memo that supposedly ties Nixon into I.T.T. in some antitrust settlements. The papers are full of it, all of them."

Stoner swore loudly, a long reverberating string of words not normally intended for senatorial chambers.

By the morning of August 3 several dozen letters concerning the Chessman piece had been received at the *Newstime* office in Los Angeles, all addressed to the Editor. They were duly read by the two women who handled such matters, women who were insulated from further shock by years of service in reading crank letters, anonymous notes, obscene missiles, confessions, suggestions, threats, warnings, proposals and propositions. One reader, a grandmother, had devoted seventeen years to the effort and could tell at a glance into what category a letter fell, from smut to suicide. The other had kept up a running correspondence with an anonymous letter writer for some years, not an easy thing to do. It somehow involved a mysterious third person who acted as a mail drop.

Only two of the Chessman letters had been sent upstairs for further perusal, finally landing on Adam Kenton's desk that morning. He showed them to Ding. One was from a Los Angeles librarian, who wrote that she had been attacked at the end of December 1947 in the exact area where Chessman was supposed to have operated. But her attacker had definitely not been Caryl Chessman; after twenty-five years she could still vividly remember the man's face. It was not Chessman, and she was glad that he was at last receiving partial vindication. Having read his books, she believed he had been much too sensitive to abuse women sexually or any other way.

The other letter was anonymous. It was written on cheap notepaper in an obviously disguised hand, with letters slanting both ways and much covering-up of strokes. The crossing of the *t*'s was usually well over the letter, quick violent movements that suggested extreme anger. The whole vicious forward thrust of the writing indicated the same rage. Ding read rapidly, Kenton at his side:

> Editor
> I am Caryl Chessman's son. you wrote good about my father I thank you for that but women not capital punishment is bad My father knew that I miss him and never saw him til now Write more about him.

The anonymous note was addressed: *From Hell.*

"What you think?" asked Kenton. "Crank?"

"Sounds like it." Ding rubbed his ear. "Any chance Chessman had kids?"

"Not from my end but you tell me. You did the background."

Ding shook his head. "No chance." He picked on his ear lobe. "Unless from one of those sex jobs."

"What sex jobs?" Kenton asked in feigned surprise. "He was impotent, remember?"

Ding grinned broadly. "I still think he was." He stuck his finger in his ear. "Who knows? Maybe Lavery will get that 'Son of Rapist' spread after all."

Both men laughed and soon forgot the two letters, which were routinely sent back to the files. Kenton had a story to write and Ding some people to see, and Caryl Chessman was the last thing on their minds.

As he climbed the stairs the only thing on *his* mind

was getting his rent. Twice before he had been taken for half of it, but no more. A piece of ass was fine at the right time and he liked it as well as the next man. But money was money. So why was he wearing his new suit that made him look ten years younger? He laughed to himself. Okay, so maybe if she gave him a quick jump for twenty dollars he'd do it. Sure, what's twenty dollars? But no more. He would get the other hundred dollars for the month's rent or out she went. She was a nice kid with big tits but nobody was worth more than twenty dollars. He thought of the young girl's breasts, big and firm, with bright red nipples that got rock hard when he sucked on them. Well, maybe thirty dollars, but that was tops. If she wanted more she could go whistle. It was hard enough making ends meet these days.

He climbed the third flight. Fifty-nine years old and paunchy, he owned three residential buildings in downtown Los Angeles near the skid-row area. With tax write-offs and some silent cost-cutting here and there he made a living. The hardest part was climbing all those stairs every month to collect the rents. He had a bad heart and the doctor had said to be careful. No strain no sudden shocks. Yet he couldn't trust the tenants to run mail in their monthly checks to the small office he kept; most of them were not the stable, permanent type he wished he had. After a lifetime of business dealings he knew better than to expect miracles.

At the top he turned left and walked to the end of the small hallway. The girl had always been home this time of day, she should be home now. He knocked. Waited. Knocked again. Louder. He fumbled for his large set of keys. The only rule he had in his buildings was that he have a key to every apartment. Just in case. Whenever he found a lock changed without his knowledge the tenant was out at the end of the month. He kept a close eye on his property.

He quickly found the right key, the apartment number scratched on the head with a pin. It was his system. Turning the key, he slowly opened the door in case she was sleeping. The lock was a simple snap type. He thought of telling her to get a Segal dead bolt, much safer, but decided against it. The hell with her.

The kitchen light was on. His eyes took a second to adjust from the darkened hallway. He saw the refrigerator next to the door, the stove, the sink. He looked into the room. In the center was the kitchen table, two chairs. There was something on the table. He walked toward it . . .

The man in the apartment underneath heard a loud thud. He looked up at his ceiling. It didn't sound right to him. He worked the second shift in Los Angeles County General Hospital many times. He had heard bodies fall to the floor many times. He cautiously climbed the stairs, then continued into the hallway toward the open door. Inside he saw the man on the floor. It was the landlord. He knelt down, checked the eyes, the pulse. Up again, he looked around. On the table was something his mind couldn't quite comprehend, something seemed out of place. He went over to the table. His eyes froze. Adrenaline shot through him. His brain stopped. Started. He backed away, out the door, down the stairs. In his apartment he picked up the receiver, dropped it, tried again.

The first cop to arrive was twenty-three and still lived with his parents. He hadn't seen much action yet and if he lived to be a hundred he would never again see anything like this. Though young he had been trained to note things exactly as they were. A white Caucasian male, mid-fifties, was dead on the floor, apparently of a heart attack. A woman's breasts were on the kitchen table, one next to an empty cup and the other by a water glass. On one breast was a large letter V in black ink, on the other a large M. The apartment door was open, the light on. A black-and-white cat was perched on a cabinet. Its water dish was empty, so was the food saucer. There was an unpleasant odor in the kitchen.

The bedroom door was closed. Turning the knob he kicked it back, slowly, softly, not knowing what he would find. The odor now was horrible, overpowering. It suddenly sickened him; he gagged, withdrew for a moment to the sink, then returned and went into the room. He saw what had been the girl . . .

The ambulance attendants first removed the body of the landlord. By the time they returned, top police officials had arrived. The attendants were sent away. For the moment everything, including the girl's body, would remain as found. They were taking no chances. The medical examiner had been called, the forensic section was on its way. A call was eventually made to the sheriff's office.

The murder and mutilation of the young woman quickly caused a tremor in official circles throughout the state. Not so much because of the destruction of the body, dreadful though it had been, but because it had been done by Vincent Mungo. Of that there was no doubt. He was an escaped homicidal maniac who mutilated his victims in frenzied rage. He had been at large for almost a month, probably forging a new identity and means of survival for himself. Now he apparently felt safe enough to strike again. And he would continue killing until he was caught. There was no doubt about that either.

Sheriff Oates flew in by midafternoon. He saw the body at the coroner's office. The apartment had been sealed, the cat removed, a policeman stationed at the building's entrance to ward off the curious. Fingerprints had been taken at the scene but the sheriff knew they would lead nowhere. It was Mungo's work. Anybody could have printed the initials but this was his work, Oates told himself savagely.

The body sickened him and he turned away. He thought of calling John Spanner in Hillside but changed his mind. Spanner had been right about the two old ladies and the handyman but this was different. So much for the idea about Mungo wanting to remain anonymous and losing himself in the crowd! Not any more. He had hit the big time and he would be captured by big-time police methods. What was needed now was professional teamwork. Spanner could go fish in the lake.

The sheriff decided to remain in Los Angeles for the moment. Mungo was around here somewhere and he would be here too. He wondered what kind of disguise his quarry had effected. Plastic surgery would be impossible without money or connections. That left only dyed hair or a wig and a beard and mustache. Maybe glasses. It would do for a while but not forever, Oates promised himself. Not nearly forever.

He glanced over the raw data for the uncompleted post-mortem report: breasts severed laterally—walls of abdomen laid open from breast downward to navel—several deep abdominal cavity incisions—membrane cut—renal arteries cut—liver and kidneys—

Oates stopped reading. His eyes blurred, his hands shook. For all his bluster he was basically a shy man and one not given to violation of any kind.

"The son of a bitch," he mumbled loudly. "The stinking son of a bitch."

Police photographs had been taken of the body. The killer had not touched the girl's eyes. A forensic technician took pictures of the eyes, following the theory that in violent deaths the last images were recorded on the retina of the eye. He intended to blow the pictures up; maybe the killer's image could be seen.

In the sleazy neighborhood adjoining the city's skid row, residents pranced and preened for the television cameras and newsmen who descended in droves on the area. They quickly learned of the girl's murder but killings were almost as common as empty bottles in such places and caused no undue alarm. They did not yet know the details of the butchery, or that Vincent Mungo had been among them.

Also unknown to local residents, there would not be such excitement again until the Slasher came along more than a year later and began cutting throats from ear to ear. Before he was finished nine men would fall victim to his knife. Most of them would be drunks and drifters from skid row.

Upstate the commotion over the new Mungo outrage was fierce. As Sheriff Oates flew to Los Angeles, metropolitan newsmen flew to Willows. They could interview Oates later, since he was always ready to talk at the drop of a pen to paper. Nor were they overly interested in Spanner of Hillside, he was small-town and had no name. Besides, Mungo was not local anymore. With the girl's murder he had became statewide, maybe he was even going national.

The man they wanted was right at Willows. He could tell them all they needed to know about Mungo from the mental viewpoint. And why not? He was the top man there, he was a psychiatrist, he was a nice friendly guy if you didn't interrupt him. And like any doctor, he was helpful when he had to be.

He was also waiting for them. Dr. Baylor understood what they wanted—a story for the next day's paper, an item for the evening TV news. The big shots in Sacramento and San Francisco and Los Angeles had already cleared it. There was nothing he could do. He had to be helpful.

Baylor met the reporters in the small conference room in the administration building. He smiled warmly, greeted those he knew with a nod and introduced himself to the rest. After a moment of pleasantries he launched into a brief review of Vincent Mungo's history at Willows.

Baylor then reminded his audience that up to the time of the incident—some hardened types blanched at the word, remembering the pictures of the murdered man with no face left—Vincent Mungo had behaved himself with circumspection and, though unfriendly, had given no cause for suspicion or increased surveillance. Afterward, of course, it was too late. Baylor held out his arms in a gesture of helplessness, which somehow looked unconvincing coming from him.

Someone wanted to know the specific nature of Mungo's illness and was told that the patient had been diagnosed earlier as suffering from paranoia—

How much earlier, Baylor was asked, and he brusquely mumbled something about a number of years.

—suffering from paranoia, a psychosis characterized by strong suspiciousness and eccentricity woven into a highly organized system of persecutory delusions.

"Does this mean he thinks everyone is after him?"

They all laughed.

"If he doesn't, he must really be nuts," someone else suggested.

More laughter. Dr. Baylor held his smile. He had heard all the psychiatric one-liners many times over the years.

After a moment he continued. Mungo had also been characterized—years earlier, with a smile—as a manic-depressive personality marked by severe mood swings. In recent years, his records indicated, he had become more and more depressed.

"Would this make him a maniac?" someone wanted to know.

Baylor sighed. "One must be careful in the use of such a word," he said at length. "A maniac is also a person with a mania for something, such as truth, for example."

"Yeah, except we all know what his is."

"But it primarily means a psychotic person with violent tendencies," insisted the questioner.

Baylor allowed the truth of that but stressed that Mungo had exhibited no overt violence while at Willows until the night of his escape. He granted that the man was obviously psychotic, though he hesitated to place any specific label on the illness since he had not himself examined the patient. He also granted that the violent tendencies seemed to be entering a new stage, in which the destruction urge was being acted out. Possibly, he suggested, the patient was suffering an abaissement, which is a weakening of the ego's ability to resist a powerful demand from the id. This happens occasionally to most people, the doctor pointed out, in such states as exhaustion and emotional upset. But it persists in severe schizophrenic depression.

"Does that mean he'll kill again?"

Baylor was careful in his answer. "He might, if what I indicated is in fact occurring, and if it persists."

Now the reporters were getting somewhere. What they wanted, needed, was some hot copy.

"Am I right in saying that Mungo kills because he has to?"

"Negative," came the instant reply. Baylor had spent three years in the army as a captain in the Psychological Warfare section. "That is incorrect. Nobody *has* to kill." He smiled briefly. "Along with most other psychiatrists, I don't believe in the 'irresistible impulse' concept."

"You say Mungo is a psychotic who is now acting out his homicidal tendencies. In our terms that makes him a maniac. Couldn't your people spot this beforehand?"

"It's not that simple," explained Baylor. "The patient came to us as a severe disciplinary problem, but his overt violence had been merely fighting when confronted. It's a long jump from that to killing."

"But couldn't they see it coming?"

"In a word, no. Most people at one time or another act violently. Kicking a door is violent behavior. So is throwing a glass or breaking a dish. But most people don't go from that to killing someone."

"Why does he want to kill women?"

"So far as we know, he has killed two people. One of them was a man."

"Why does he mutilate the bodies?"

"Possibly because of some monstrous rage."

"Rage at what?"

Baylor shook his head. "If we knew that we would probably know why he kills. That is, why his potentially destructive inclinations suddenly turned overt."

Another ten minutes and it was over. The doctor felt he had handled the reporters well. He had told them little, and he had certainly not given them any sensational copy that could come back later to haunt him. He allowed some pictures to be taken of him and of the hospital buildings and grounds, but that was all. Just following orders, he assured them. They left, mostly discontented.

In truth, Baylor had not kept any pertinent information from them, nor had he misled them in his answers. He really didn't know why Vincent Mungo had suddenly started killing and mutilating. There was no indication of such rage. Granted the hidden cleverness common among certain mental patients, the homicidal fury needed for such acts was not at all common. Nor was the sheer power of personality. Dr. Baylor secretly wondered if Vincent Mungo might not be having an episode of zoanthropy, believing himself, of course delusionally, to have assumed the behavior characteristic of an animal.

The late afternoon editions of August 3 carried the first news of the horrible murder in the skid row section. The headlines screamed Vincent Mungo's name. Pictures were shown of the block, the house, the apartment, even the murder room but none of the body. Certain details of the grisly deed were glossed over. All the stories contained the standard picture and description of Mungo plus a capsule mental history. Several papers incorporated the interview with Dr. Baylor into the text. Others simply attributed information to expert medical opinion. Some of the stories were subheaded with the suggestion that the madman might kill again. One paper asked if Mungo was killing because he had to kill, compelled by an irresistible impulse. All of them labeled him a homicidal maniac, consumed with rage of as yet undetermined origin.

The murder made the television evening news. Throughout the state people again heard the name Vincent Mungo. They again saw his face—ugly, brooding, sinister. One newsman called it a face from hell, straight out of a Dostoievsky novel.

That evening Senator Stoner was ecstatic, though he

properly tried to conceal the fact. Roger had been right, thank God; the big afternoon papers of August 2 had held over news of the press conference for the following day. He had thus made all the important morning and afternoon newspapers on August 3, the day of the gruesome discovery. The timing was perfect. From now on his words and actions would be news. From now on his campaign to restore the death penalty and execute Vincent Mungo would be publicized.

The senator hoped that Mungo would not be caught immediately, at least not until the campaign got up a good head of steam. That was all he needed, a little time. He didn't even consider the possibility that time was running out for some others as well.

Stoner went to bed that night and dreamed of killing Caryl Chessman with his bare hands.

SIX

The thermometer hit a hundred on Fremont Street and Bishop ducked into a small restaurant near one of the casinos. He sat at a table and ordered from the waitress. Somebody had scratched a big zero in the center of the tabletop. The circular gashes were deep and largely discolored from too many swipes of a damp cloth; tiny bits of food were lodged in the wound. He studied the ugly design for a moment, then quietly moved to another table.

A woman in the far corner was playing two slot machines at the same time. She would put a quarter in one and pull the handle, then do the same on the next machine while the windows were still whirling on the first. A determined look gripped her face. She had her system, something to do with electrically-charged energy coming from her constant motion, and she would win on both slot machines if it took every quarter she had. And every penny too!

Bishop watched the woman with undisguised interest. An obvious tourist, she was big and heavy and had rolls of loose flesh dangling from her upper arms and legs. A straw sun hat covered her head. The vast amount of exposed skin seemed to the young man to be stark white and he wondered what it would feel like to cut into all that soft flesh.

The waitress brought his order, coffee and a ham sandwich. "No baloney," she said hurriedly. "Like I told you." Then she was gone. He watched her disappearing figure. She was young and buxom and at least twenty pounds overweight. He saw her under his knife too, and his coffee got cold as he sat there thinking about it.

He had been in Las Vegas four days now, arriving in the modernized bus depot on S. Main Street in the late afternoon of August 1 after a pleasant six-hour ride from Los Angeles. An hour's stroll gave him the feel of the downtown area and brought him to a neon-encrusted but inexpensive hotel on N. 25th Street, just off the end of a shopping plaza. His intention was to stay for a few weeks and then move on to the next place, wherever that might be.

Not that he was in any great hurry to leave Las Vegas. He was fascinated by the crowds of people who nightly descended on the gaming parlors along Fremont, many of them seemingly intent on gambling away their lives. In their faces at those moments he detected a madness he had seen many times at Willows, the maniacal eye, the pressed lips, the twitching cheek of someone deep in isolation, and of course the inevitable final vacant stare of total desperation.

The vast amounts of money also intrigued him. He had never seen so much money, never dreamed so much existed in the whole world. And these people were just throwing it away, intent only on the next throw of the dice or turn of a card or spin of the wheel. To any polite inquiry they would gruffly nod in assurance that they were fine and kindly mind your own damn business.

"Get your bets down," the croupiers would plead in feigned urgency. "There's a winner coming out every time." But Bishop saw very few winners.

His daytime was spent mostly in sight-seeing. Soon after arrival he rented a car, using his driver's license and new credit card in the name of Daniel Long. The car, a Ford Pinto with unlimited mileage, was quickly his. At the hotel he had registered earlier under another name, something easy to remember, since no identification was necessary. It was a technique he had learned from a television cops-and-robbers show, and it became a pattern he was to follow in subsequent months across the country.

He spent the first morning driving around the various areas of the city, including the fabulous Strip with its two dozen opulent hotels and gambling casinos. No stops were made; this activity he reserved for the evening hours when crowds were huge and his anonymity assured. During the afternoon he visited nearby Lake Mead and Hoover Dam. The incredible view from the dam inspired him with awe; he had never seen anything like it on TV. He couldn't believe it was real. It also filled him with a certain dread feeling that he was going to fall from the great height. Upon his return to the ground he vowed never to place himself again in such danger.

The next day he drove along the Virgin River to St. George and Hurricane, arriving at Zion National Park at 2 P.M. He lunched at the Lodge, then took an afternoon tour of the park and saw famed Angel's Landing, the Temple of Sinawava and the Great White Throne. On the return trip he dined on prime ribs of beef and a bottle of Chablis, to which he had been introduced the previous evening, at a roadside restaurant. Arriving back at his hotel after ten o'clock, he slept for two hours before changing his shirt and resuming his exploration of the city's night life.

Each evening he would roam the downtown gaming section and along the Strip, fascinated by the thousands of neon lights, the great waves of people, the mounting excitement that always comes with money. He had seen documentaries of Las Vegas on television but they paled before the real thing, and as he wandered through the casinos he sometimes felt that he was back at Willows, surrounded by madmen of every stripe regardless of their clothing or uniforms. Only here he was not known and would not be sought or even missed when he was gone.

Of still greater significance was the presence of women. They were everywhere, thousands of them, maybe millions. The most beautiful women he had ever seen, especially in the big hotels on the Strip. Wherever he turned, women were looking at him, sizing him up, staring him down.

And he stared right back. He began to feel that they were his for the asking but he didn't intend to ask. Instead he would take.

Had anyone observed him closely during those nightly prowls, he would surely have seemed to be yet another tourist enjoying one of the gambling capital's best views, its women. Certainly no one would have suspected that the well-dressed and oddly handsome young man with the curious eyes was carefully choosing another victim for his murderous rage, this time one who would be able to bring him money for which she would soon have no further use.

That Bishop needed money was painfully evident to him. He had less than $900 left. Yet he knew nothing of work, neither how to apply for it nor how to seek it out. And of course there was nothing for which he was qualified since he had never worked a day in his life. With no background and no references, he was doomed to the most menial laborers' jobs. This he would not tolerate. He intended to see different places and to get as far away from California as he could, always under the cloak of complete anonymity. No one must know of him, no one must even be made aware of his existence if he was to carry out his life's real work. No! He would get the necessary money another way.

He was dimly aware that there were many illegal means of making money but he didn't know any of them. Nor did the idea appeal to him. He was interested only in survival. Beyond that a dollar bill held no value for him; it seemed like so many coupons that were traded for whatever was needed. And his needs were few. In truth, he even resented the thought that his pursuit and destruction of demons and monsters had to be tied to money, and he vowed that as soon as he had enough to survive he would no longer think in such terms. Then he would really be free to strike the demons down wherever he found them.

That there were so many of them bothered him. He began to look at their mouths, to picture their ripe red mouths on him. He saw their breasts, large masses of soft flesh that fit in the palms of his hands. And their flat bellies, smooth skin stretched over those things inside that he needed to see and to touch and to hold. Almost every woman he passed on the street, indoors, anywhere, stirred his imagination and prompted the flow of images. Faceless mouths, disembodied breasts, ripped bellies, endless organs, livers, kidneys, hearts, strings of intestines, sexual parts, mounds of muscle, bones and blood everywhere, gouged slabs of flesh, whole skins hanging in profusion bleached white in summer sun, severed arms and legs, hands and feet, all revolving in limbo in his tortured mind, all taunting his fevered soul.

He kept thinking of the millions of women in the world, millions he would never own even for a few moments. He would never get to kill them, to open them, to *possess* them. By sheer number they were beyond his reach. Even at the impossible rate of one a day for fifty years, not a dent would be made in the sheer impregnability of their numbers. The thought sickened him each time it entered his consciousness; he brooded over its implications. The demons had conspired against him, just as he was conspired against by all at Willows. But he would somehow defeat them too. One by one he would gain possession of them. Perhaps by so doing he would live forever, perhaps that was the secret of eternal youth. He didn't find it strange or even uncomfortable that such might be his destiny.

On his second night he struck up a conversation with a girl in one of the restaurants in the Dunes Hotel. Or perhaps she with him. They smiled at each other, her smile even more electric than his. They talked local gossip over their food, then of themselves. He said he was from Pittsburgh, in for a good time. She was a showgirl from Chicago, so she said, trying to break into the ranks in Vegas. It was difficult, she had no juice and things were really tight for her.

"What's juice?" he asked innocently.

She looked at him, batting her false eyelashes with equal innocence. "Juice? It's, you know, like a connection," she announced finally. "You need conections to work here."

"You call that juice?"

"Everybody calls it juice. If you don't have it, you don't work."

"How do you get this juice?"

"All depends who you are."

"Well, who do you have to be?"

"It helps if your boyfriend owns the hotel."

"Don't you know anyone like that?"

"Would I be here if I did?" She thought a moment. "I knew someone like that a while back. Really big, you know?"

"What happened?"

"He was only in town for a week."

"Can't you just go to them and say you danced in Chicago?"

"Don't mean a thing here. This is the center of the world, everywhere else is the sticks. Except maybe Broadway."

"So tell them you danced in Broadway."

"On Broadway."

"Would that do it?"

"I told you this was the center of the world. Look! The people running things here, they're the best in the business. They know all the names, they know who done what. And where and when too. And if they don't know, they just pick up the phone. Once a girl works here she can go anywhere. Anywhere! She'll get a job just like that. She's made, you know? That's why everybody wants to work here. That's why you need juice. Or else maybe the biggest tickets in the world."

"What's tickets?"

"What's tickets! Say, where you from anyway?"

"Pittsburgh," he said quickly but she didn't hear him.

"Tickets are, you know, tits. A girl needs a big set of tickets to work here."

"You don't have tickets?"

"There's nothing wrong with my tickets." She straightened her shoulders. "They'll do till something better comes along."

"But if you had big tickets you wouldn't need any juice."

"Listen! To work this town without juice you'd need a pair of tickets bigger than the Goodyear blimp."

She ordered a bottle of Chablis, for which he paid. He liked the bitter taste.

"You in for a good time?" the girl asked, wondering how much she could take him for.

"Actually I'm here visiting a sick aunt," he answered, knowing she had no money.

"I'll show you everything you need."

"She's got cancer."

"Whatever you want."

"By the time I get there she'll be dead."

"For fifty I'll take you round the world."

"What's round the world?"

"Say, you sure you're from Chicago?"

"You're from Chicago."

"That's nice."

"What is?"

Eyes locked together.

"You buying or selling?"

"You don't have big tickets."

"You don't have any juice."

The electric smiles were turned off, but in the neon night no one noticed.

The following evening he returned to the Strip, this time going to the Sands Hotel where he went into the casino. He had no intention of gambling but he wanted to watch the action for a while to see if what he was seeking might be found there. A half hour taught him it was hopeless. The women were either tourists with men in tow or locals looking for men with money. The sight of all those women with mouths agape and bodies intact pained the sensitive young man and he longed to be about his father's work. But he resolved to stick to his plan; this one time he would search out the money first.

That many of the women were prostitutes or traders of one persuasion or another didn't bother him at all. Sex was a weapon that women used against men, and so it seemed perfectly reasonable to him that some regarded it as a profession while others used it as a means of exchange. He harbored no specific ill feeling toward such women. If he sought them out it was merely because they were the most accessible to a stranger and therefore the least dangerous. Their craft required privacy. And so did his.

He left the Sands but the story was the same wherever he went. Moneyed excitement and sexual promise, he now began to see, traveled hand in hand. Men traded money and women traded sex. The winners got what they wanted, the losers got nothing. It all seemed reasonable enough. Except for the fact that women, he reminded himself bitterly, in their total demonic rage sought to destroy men by whatever means they could. They were evil and therefore had to be themselves destroyed.

As he looked around at the players he suddenly realized that the whole concept of Las Vegas—the money-sex trade-off, the idea of winners and losers—was nothing more than another bit of insanity in an already crazed world; paper people who once upon a time had sealed themselves in a cardboard castle, hoping to escape their pursuers. They were doomed of course. There was no possibility of true exchange between men and women, nor was anyone really a winner. "Only losers," said the bright young man as he threw a coin into a slot machine and walked away.

In the car again Bishop knew that he would shortly be leaving Las Vegas, just as soon as he finished what he was destined to do.

Sitting now in the small restaurant on Fremont Street in the fourth day of his stay, the child of destiny turned his attention to the newspaper. He ordered another cup of coffee as he glanced over the headlines in the *Las Vegas Sun*. On page 2 he found it, a three-column story from Los Angeles through UPI. He looked at the picture of Vincent Mungo—dark, menacing, scowling. He mentally checked his own face—light, bland, smiling. He pushed the smile wider.

The article told of the brutal murder of a twenty-one-year-old woman in her apartment in downtown Los Angeles. She had been a dancer. The body had been "savagely mutilated" but no details were given. The killer was the escaped maniac Vincent Mungo, who had left clues to his identity at the scene of the crime. Again no details were given out. The rest was all about Mungo. Physical description, background, and expert psychiatric opinion. The conclusion was inescapable. He was dangerously homicidal and would probably kill again unless quickly caught.

Bishop, his smile gone for the moment, wished people, the men at least, could understand what he was doing. But he expected no such miracle, and he instinctively realized that he would have to live out his life and deeds hopelessly alone. Just like his father.

He walked out, leaving the paper on the table. It was yesterday's news.

For the next week he rode around Vegas and the surrounding countryside, always with an eye open for his prey. One afternoon he drove out to Lathrop Wells and visited the brothel at the crossroads of US 95 and

Nevada 29. Someone had told him brothels were legal in Nevada except for Vegas and Reno, where there were so many prostitutes that no building could hold them all. It seemed a sensible idea to him.

All the action in Lathrop Wells was on the roadway: two bars, a restaurant, a few general stores and gas stations. And a flashing neon arrow set by the road, pointing to a white frame house with trees in front and a wide parking area running around the back. He pulled in along the side. Walking up to the house, he wondered if the two big red lights above the door were meant for those who had somehow missed the flashing arrow.

Inside he quickly picked, or was picked by, a young dark-haired girl dressed in ribbons of diaphanous material that floated around her as she led him into the room. Bishop had never been with a real prostitute and he looked at the girl with great interest. When she took him over to the small sink and began washing his penis with warm soapy water he noticed that she frowned. "Anything wrong?" he asked.

"You're not circumcised."

"Is that bad?"

"Just makes it harder for me is all."

"Does that way cost more?"

She shrugged. "Depends what you want."

"That's fair."

"You want a straight lay?"

"What's that?"

She glanced at him. "You know, you get inside me."

"No. I don't want that."

"What then?"

He told her.

"That's the hardest."

"Why?"

"When you're not circumcised, there's all that extra skin I gotta take in my mouth." She looked him over. "Cost you . . . ten dollars more."

"Really?"

"I wouldn't kid you, handsome." She gave his penis a squeeze, wiped it with a paper towel. "You got the money?"

"I have money."

"So get your clothes off." She steered him to the bed. "You want mine off too?"

"Will it cost me more?"

"No charge."

"I'd like to see your body."

"This your first time?"

"Yes."

"First time," she said. "Son of a bitch."

There was a pause as she undressed. "You sure you don't want nothing else?"

"Nothing else," he said.

"It's your money."

Lying back on the bed he watched the girl hunched over him, her breasts hanging down loosely. She had a soft fleshy body, the belly skin drawn tight over a layer of baby fat. Kneeling there, she looked like a snow-white vulture swooping down on his groin. He could almost feel the claws ripping into him, tearing into his flesh, the monstrous beak eating his vital organs, teeth crunching crushing bone, pulling the life from his open wounds. He wanted to kill the hideous demon. Squinting, he watched the breasts, hanging globs of fat that could be cut off so easily with his knife. He fought to keep the breasts in focus, visualizing what he would do if only he wasn't so small and helpless. Sudden stabs of pain wracked his body. Laughing now, he gave up the struggle as the life force gushed from him and his eyes closed in total surrender.

When the girl returned from the sink she began to dress. "Time's up," she said.

He didn't answer.

"You okay?"

"What's okay?"

"You sure come hard."

"Sometimes."

"Maybe you got problems. Know what I mean?"

"No."

"You kept saying 'Don't hit me. Please don't hit me.'"

"Yes?"

"Only I sure wasn't hitting you, baby."

"I'm not a baby."

"Sure, I know that."

On the way out he gave her a five-dollar tip. She asked him for it. "You take care of yourself," she said.

He wished her good luck.

The girl smiled at him. "Who needs it? What I'm selling you gonna be buying for a long time."

Upon his return to the hotel Bishop lay down and cried in frustration for a long time until he drifted into troubled sleep.

Several days of that week were spent in the desert around Las Vegas. Here, just a little way off the road, were the quiet and solitude missing from the crowded city. Here too could be seen the constant life-and-death struggle for survival as each animal, each insect, killed or was killed.

For Bishop it was reaffirmation of his life's course. All living things, from the smallest bug to man himself, destroyed life in order to preserve life. Destruction was a form of creation. Death was a form of life. To kill was to live, to not kill was to die. It was all simply a matter of who did the killing and who did the dying. He had no intention of being among the dead.

His last visit of the week was to an oasis in the Amargosa Desert, seven miles from Death Valley Junction. He arrived on August 10 and stayed overnight. Though Ash Meadows boasted a dining room and bar, swimming pool, game room, and seventeen guest rooms set motel-style along a wood porch, its prime function was a brothel, with the girls housed in a separate building away from the main lodge. Bishop's taste for seclusion had prompted him to make the hundred-mile journey. As he sat on the porch gazing into infinity, something he had heard the previous day came to mind. Ash Meadows, it had been said, was so remote that you could lose yourself and not even be missed.

Something about the immensity of the landscape, with its unbroken horizon and sun-splashed whiteness, caused an uneasiness in him. Slowly he turned his head 90 degrees and saw—absolutely nothing. He hurriedly looked backward, to the guest rooms and main lodge, for confirmation. He had a sudden feeling that out there ahead of him, stretching across thousands of square miles without a living human being, devoid of all animal and plant life, lay the meaning of death. This, then, perhaps was what death was like. Emptiness. Solitude. Nothing.

He sat like that for a long time. In his mind's eye the young man saw a boy, the frail body bruised and bleeding, being struck again and again. He watched the torturous descent of the great whip, heard the boy's desperate pleas.

"I'm sorry, mother. I'm sorry. Don't hit me."

Crack!

"I'm sorry," he screamed. "I didn't mean it."

Her eyes bulged, foam caught the corners of her mouth. Her hand raised and lowered the whip again and again across his head, his neck and shoulders. There was no escape for him.

"Please don't hit me," he shrieked. "Don't hit me. Please! Please!"

Bang!

Crouched in absolute terror, he tried to cover his face with his skinny arms. A blow seared his wrists. He lowered his hands and another slashed open his cheek. A scream of pain rushed out of the dying young man. Blood filled his mouth.

Again the dreaded whip landed.

Crack!

Slowly, slowly, the young man returned to the living. His eyelids fluttered open. Closed, opened again. He tried to focus his eyes. Everything was blurry. Faces. Faces were above him. Far away, as though through the wrong end of the telescope. They seemed to be looking at him.

He heard noises, strange sounds. Then voices.

"Easy does it now."

"Is he all right?"

"Sure. Just fainted."

He saw them now. Three men standing over him. No—one was kneeling next to him. Two fingers gently raised his right eyelid.

"He's fine. Just let him rest a minute."

A face, friendly, interested, beamed down at him.

"You must've fainted, Mr. Jones. Happens once in a while out here. The desert, you know." The face continued to smile. "Nothing to worry about."

He felt his senses returning. Eyes, ears, touch. He lifted his right hand, looked at his fingers, long slim fingers that he put to his face. They seemed cool on his skin.

He wanted to raise his head. Someone's hand carefully pushed it up from underneath. It made him woozy and he let it be placed back on the ground. He rested a bit longer.

After a while they helped him over to the porch steps. Somebody got him a glass of water. Two of the men stayed with him, telling him how the heat can sometimes affect a man's senses. They told him he should go to his room and lie down a spell. That's all it took when the heat got you. Just a little rest.

He told them he felt much better now. It was like they said, just the heat. He thanked them and they left. They would see him later in the main lodge. Meanwhile he really should lie down a spell.

The porch steps were comfortable; he finished the water, staring at the endless emptiness ahead of him. He remained like that, motionless, for two hours. Later he lunched at the lodge on cold meat and beer. After a nap he wandered aimlessly around the oasis, always with an eye on the buildings. They never left his line of sight.

In the evening he played pool in the game room with several other guests and some of the management. He knew nothing of the game, and they kindly taught him how to hit the balls into the pockets. The ivory ball was the one that did all the hitting. He told them it seemed a lot like life. "How's that?" someone asked, and Bishop said that it was always the individual, the loner in any group who does everything, who gets everything done. "Always the loner," he repeated.

"The strong-leader theory," someone suggested.

"Sure, some men are just natural-born leaders."

"Gotta be strong to get things done."

"Not strong, Phil. Smart. Smart up here." The speaker pointed to his head.

"Got nothing to do with smart. It's drive is what it is. You got to have that damn drive."

"You need a vision too," someone else said. "You gotta be able to see what ain't there and then make it happen."

"Or something that is there," said the young man, "and make it unhappen. Make it . . . disappear."

There was a long pause.

"Yeah, it's like Mr. Jones here says. You got to make a thing disappear." He slammed the nine ball into a corner pocket. The ball whirled around the cushioned corner for a moment before disappearing from view.

"Damn!"

"Nice shot, Gus."

Gus laughed. "Ain't me. It's the cue ball done all the work."

"That's right. Just what the man says, one does it all. And you notice it's always white."

"Least it ain't black or Mex."

"What color's Mex?"

"Ain't white."

"Damn right!"

"It's like my sex life," someone said.

"How's that, Harry?"

"You running round again?"

Harry took the unlit cigar out of his mouth. "One ball," he announced smugly, "does it all."

"Did he say one ball does it all?"

"That's what he said, Andy. He said that."

"Now I know why you always remind me of a pool table with half the stuff missing."

"Tell him, Lee."

Lee pointed to Harry. "What this boy needs is more balls."

Everybody laughed, including the young man.

Later in the evening he walked past the small swimming pool to the house where the girls stayed. He selected a dyed blonde with a heart-shaped mouth. But this time he didn't make the mistake of lying on the bed with her crouched over him. Instead he spread himself on the edge of the bed with the girl kneeling on a pillow on the floor.

Afterward he gave her a five-dollar tip without her asking for it. As he was leaving he said he hoped they'd meet again. Anyway, here's wishing things get better for you.

The girl laughed. Though very young, she already had the hardness that came with the life. And who the hell was he to talk about things getting better for her? What did he know about anything, the dumb son of a bitch? She looked him straight up the eye. "On this job, mister, there's nowhere to go but down."

Outside he sat again on the porch steps and looked up at the star-infested sky. It seemed to be blazing out of control. He lowered his head. Darkness was everywhere—total, absolute blackness surrounded him, was closing in on him, enveloping him, smothering him. He glanced around fearfully. Nothing. He gazed upward again. Nothing, except a hundred billion pinpoints of light shining, existing, performing just for his pleasure. He grinned nervously. Another Las Vegas in the sky. Just another fantasy land, with make-believe diamonds and flashing promise. A lot like a brothel.

He began to feel better. Darkness was not the enemy, nor was the unknown. The enemy had form and shape and breasts. The enemy had blood and bone and belly. The enemy was all around him.

After a long while he went into his room and pulled a chair over to the door, blocking it. Then he dreamed of fire, bright orange flames fiercely burning bodies. All the bodies had breasts. Slowly all the bodies blackened and charred, endless bodies bursting with boiling blood blazing down to flame-flushed bone. Whitened bones and skulls of white that looked like cue balls.

In the morning after breakfast he walked into the desert as far as he could go and still keep the oasis in sight. He wanted to see if the uneasiness of the previous evening would return. Eventually he found a spot where he could sit and rest. A canteen of water had been given him and now he drank from it, drank greedily, all the while surveying the incredible expanse of land around him. He felt like a ship's captain in the middle of a vast ocean, becalmed yet somehow beckoning the frail craft ever onward. The fearfulness returned but he fought it down.

Suddenly possessed he walked farther, on and on, until the familiar buildings had long been lost. With the sun behind him, he traveled southwest in a straight line. Somewhere to his right was the road to Death Valley Junction; he was not worried. The name intrigued him. Death Valley. The Valley of Death. He knew he would not get there, ever. He was immortal. He had his work to do and his work would last forever.

At his farthest stop he rested again. Somebody earlier had told him that if he walked far enough, several miles, he would be in California. Ever been there? He had smiled and said no. Maybe someday, who knows? Now he believed he had come far enough, he was back in his home state. A frown creased his forehead. He had no intention of returning to the people who had destroyed his parents and almost destroyed him. They were all evil, all the people in California, everybody.

He was alone in the desert, and he was back home. He suddenly wished all the people in the whole state were dead. Then he would be king of California. He liked the sound. The King of California. That's what he would call himself someday. After they all were all dead.

Dead and in Dead Valley. Right here. This is where they belong, he told himself. He jumped up. For ten minutes he shouted and screamed at the 20 million people of the state of California. In the middle of the desert, in the Valley of the Dead, in the land of his birth, he told them who he really was and all the unspeakable things they had done to him and his family. Then he told them all that he had done in return.

When he finished he told them what he intended to do in the future.

Following a light lunch back at Ash Meadows, Bishop went home to Las Vegas. Two days later he met his prey, though he didn't know it at the moment. He reached the corner of Fremont and S. Main on one of his restless walks around the casino center, hoping to find what he needed, knowing that his time was running short, when a police car pulled up at the intersection. In seconds they had stopped all traffic emptying into S. Main, allowing only those cars to pass that were turning right onto Fremont or continuing north across the intersection. Moments later a procession of limousines hove into view, heading south toward the Strip. From his vantage point a little beyond the corner Bishop watched as the funeral cortege passed the Union Pacific depot across the street and came abreast of him.

In the lead were five open flower cars, all custom Cadillacs with gleaming chrome splashbeds framing huge wreaths of roses and chrysanthemums. Behind them rolled the long sleek hearse, its black-curtained windows shrouded in sorrow. As the silent procession wheeled by, Bishop counted the cars of mourners. There were ten, each a polished limousine of impeccable breeding. All appeared to be filled with relatives and friends of the deceased.

He had never seen anything like it. Turning to his right he smiled at the woman next to him and asked if she knew who was dead. She eyed him briefly, then smiled back and spoke a name. The name meant nothing to him; he told her so. She laughed oddly. He wondered if the man had been somebody very important to get such a funeral. She laughed again and told him the man had owned a piece of Vegas, "an important piece" was the way she put it. And all those flowers and mourners? He had friends. What kind of friends? The kind that make funerals, he was told. He didn't understand. For the next few moments the woman softly explained who the deceased had really been, and as she talked Bishop remembered a movie he had once seen on TV about Al Capone, who made many funerals and who always sent a lot of flowers.

A minute later the woman was gone, after a final exchange of pleasantries. Bishop watched the departing figure, wondered if she had money. He shrugged mentally and continued on his desultory walk.

Up the block now, past the bus station on the other side of the street to which she had just crossed, the woman asked herself why she had talked so freely to a stranger. She had been absently watching the long string of black cars, letting her mind wander, when the young man spoke to her. In seconds she was telling him things about Las Vegas better left unsaid. It was his smile that had got her, really quite charming, that and his whole innocent manner. Must be getting older, she told herself with a disgusted sigh.

Margot Rule was thirty-eight years old and not attractive. Though she had soft brown hair and perfectly even teeth, she was overly tall and overly thin and had neither the face nor the figure to lure men to their doom. On this mid-August morning she hoped only to lure a man to an apartment that she wanted to rent. A real estate agent, she found her life filled with empty rooms and empty space. The work was hard, the hours long but the money was good, especially now that she had opened her own agency. She handled all the listings and rentings and a secretary took care of the phone and the details. She was always on the go, which meant she was doing all right. Best of all, the activity prevented her from sitting home alone thinking of bottles of liquor and all the things she had lost or somehow missed in her life.

Five years earlier she had thought of nothing but her family. Married and the mother of two little girls, she filled her life with washing and cooking and taking care of a house in the valley section of town. She loved every minute of it. She had been married late, at age twenty-six, to a simple man who was good to her. In his early forties at the time of their marriage, her husband was ugly and not as bright or as passionate as she but he worked hard to provide for her and the children and she loved him for it. She quickly put aside any dreams of romance and excitement and settled down to a life of security, something she had never known in her own childhood. Whenever she reflected on her life she was amazed at the good luck that had finally come to her, after an adolescence and early adulthood devoid of any real relationships with men. They were simply not interested in her. On her marriage bed, disappointing as it had been for her, she vowed to remain faithful to her husband, faithful and true until death did them part.

The call awakened her from a late afternoon nap. She struggled to understand the words but they had to be repeated. An accident, there had been an accident. Would she come to Southern Nevada Memorial Hospital? Yes. No, an accident. Just please come as quickly as she could.

In a daze, fearful beyond any hysteria, she arrived at the hospital but it was already too late. Her six-year-old and her husband had both been killed instantly. Her four-year-old daughter had died on the operating table two minutes earlier. A gasoline tractor-trailer had crashed into their car at high speed, exploding into flaming wreckage. Her husband had taken the children on an outing and now they were dead. Her whole family was dead.

For months Margot Rule's world became an endless succession of nightmares. Awake or in fitful sleep she watched the truck crashing, the awful explosion, the fierce flames. She saw the final second of fright on the faces on her children, heard their agonizing screams. At times she sensed her sanity slipping away. She started to drink to dull the pain, something she had never done before. At first the alcohol helped her to forget, helped her to concentrate more on the moment, even to sleep better. As her tolerance grew she needed more and more liquor to achieve the same effect, the same state of nothingness in which there was no past remembered. The changes were subtle but progressive. Within six months she was a raving alcoholic.

The poison had taken the place of pain. Though the ravenous beast now needed constant feeding, she didn't care as long as the hurt did not return. She went through their meager savings, then her husband's small insurance policy. And finally she sold the house, moving to a dismal apartment in a run-down neighborhood. Its many bars and general disregard for appearances suited her new life style.

Then the men came. One after another after a drink or ten drinks or whole bottles. While she remained in the house, still attached to her former life, she had maintained a certain minimal propriety, though she had already begun to sleep with strangers. In her new existence nothing mattered so everything went. Liquor, parties, men, anything that would keep her mind occupied, her senses dulled. She began to gamble and her money went even faster. For three years she roamed about in an alcoholic haze, running through almost all she had including a $20,000 settlement from the accident.

In 1971 she started going to Alcoholics Anonymous. At the outset she was brought to meetings by friends she had known earlier but had never suspected of being alcoholics. They seemed contented and secure, while she was sickly and desperate. Time had healed some of the scars of her tragedy, but the alcoholism had ravaged her mind and body. At the meetings she was introduced simply as Margot. She listened attentively as an endless series of speakers told of the horrific waste and futility of their lives as alcoholics. Each speaker stressed the importance of giving up that first drink and then handling the problem one day at a time.

Margot was impressed. She began to see that her initial grief had eventually given way to self-pity, perhaps the quickest of all roads to alcoholism. Disgusted with herself and her motives, now seen in a true light, she resolved to end the nightmare. For three weeks she stayed with friends who watched over her and supervised her drying out. When she returned to an AA meeting she had not had a drink in a month.

Her friends had been gentle with her. As alcoholics they knew of the shock to the system when the drug was suddenly withheld. Yet, though much of the shock came from the physical reaction, much was also purely psychological, and they worked on her mental attitude every day in an attempt to build up her confidence and discipline. Her nerves were raw and her temperament volatile during this time but she managed to control her outbursts for the most part. By the end of her stay she believed the road back to some kind of normal life was possible for her.

She needed satisfying work even more than money. Again through a sympathetic friend she secured a job in a large real estate agency, where she promptly set out to learn the business. At one AA gathering she met an older man, a member in his late fifties, and soon they were spending time together. It was not a passionate affair nor was it fulfilling for her, but she delighted in having a continuing relationship again.

During that summer and fall they shared many a dinner and evening on the town, all without liquor of course. They hiked along trails and drove into the desert. They fished and enjoyed water sports on Lake Mead. They visited nearby national parks including the Grand Canyon. For Christmas they flew to Hawaii.

Her gentleman friend was devoted. He was never angry or abusive. He praised her when needed and comforted her when necessary. He introduced her to some important people, whom she cultivated as business contacts. That he loved her was obvious to both of them, and one day in winter he talked of marriage. She felt much warmth for him, though it wasn't love—indeed, she had not experienced real love since her high school days and then it had been entirely one-sided—but she thought she would probably marry him eventually, for kindness was very important to her.

The marriage was not to be. In the spring of her thirty-sixth year her lover and friend died of a sudden heart attack. He was fifty-eight years old. He had exercised regularly and watched his diet. He neither smoked nor drank. Six weeks before his death he had received a yearly physical examination and had been pronounced healthy. When he died the doctor called the attack unexpected and massive.

Margot, who had once again put away her dreams of love for the reality of being loved, was numb with grief. But she vowed not to repeat her earlier mistake.

This time she would not succumb to self pity, she would not fall apart or seek to destroy herself. Most of all, she would not return to the bottle. Instead she flung herself into her work with furious energy. No task was too arduous, no assignment too challenging. She worked day and night, weekends and holidays, meeting prospective clients and tenants, befriending possible business leads. As long as she kept active she was strong, though the desire for alcohol never entirely left her. She was quite good at what she did. In September she opened her own agency.

Within six months her success was assured. The work was her passion since she had little else, and she brought to it all the energy and devotion of a mother for her children or a moonstruck young girl for her lover. She wished only that she had twice the amount of time, for she was convinced that she could do even twice as well. A suggestion that she hire other agents to work for her was rejected, at least for the moment. It was her symbolic children, her would-be lover for whom she was caring so tenderly, and she would not give up any part of it. Not yet.

In April 1973 she was given a small apartment building for rental. In May she sold several unfurnished houses. In June two men came to see her. They gave no names. Would she be interested in handling the sale of a large estate? Certainly. Could she see the principal at his convenience? Of course.

A week later she was driven to the estate. Built on two landscaped acres of prime land, the mansion was constructed in the manner of a Roman palazzo, with marble pillars around the long rectangular swimming pool and a huge terrace of Italianate tile. Inside everything was expensive and tasteful, and included all the latest electronic hardware for pleasure and security.

She was introduced to the owner, whom she recognized immediately by his name. Her reaction was to be forthright and blithely naïve, a mixture that apparently worked. The owner soon smiled upon her and dismissed his aides. She was then told what he wanted for the place, and what he would take. She was told nothing else. All details would be handled by his lawyers. On the way out she listened to a quiet suggestion that if negotiations were successful, she might be in line for a large apartment complex then being built.

On the return trip to her office, sitting in the back of a plush limousine, she wondered why she had been picked, finally deciding that it would have had to be word of mouth. Which meant she was doing well. She resolved to handle the estate sale since it was a one-time deal and assured her a large commission. But she would refuse the apartment complex if offered. Long-term involvement with those people was simply too dangerous.

Six weeks later the estate had not yet been sold, due mainly to the truly staggering asking price. One millionaire prospective buyer hadn't flinched at the cost but backed off when he learned from private sources the owner's identity. Even a respectable real estate agent and high-powered lawyers could not entirely camouflage the owner or his associates.

Now of course it was too late. The palatial home would eventually be sold, no doubt, but the funeral cortège had ended any future negotiations, at least for her. And for the owner as well. He had apparently waited around too long.

Margot Rule looked at her watch. She would be just a few minutes late at the apartment she hoped to rent. It was on Gass Avenue and was the first of three appointments she had that day. With any kind of luck she would have at least one rented by nightfall.

She thought of the long night ahead of her. There was little evening work in July and August as people left town or sought air-conditioned relaxation. Since she no longer drank or gambled the city's neon life held no attraction for her, nor did the Strip's lavish shows and restaurants beyond an occasional meal or a rare evening with clients. She would be forced to return to her well-furnished but lonely rooms. Perhaps she would sit on her green velveteen sofa and stare at her Picasso prints. Or she might turn on the TV and watch a movie or the Phil Silvers show. He was always good for laughs. Or maybe she would just lie on her bed and dream of the young man she loved in high school or all the other young men she thought she loved in her early twenties, always from a distance. Perhaps eventually she might try to give herself some physical relief, talking softly as though they were in the bedroom making love to her. "Come to me. Come to me," she would whisper. "I am wet with your love, my love, come to me." And they would always answer her. "Take me, take me. Love of my life." Their bodies would press on her, strong arms encircling her smooth breasts as they pleaded their final command. "Now," they breathed into silence, and she always cried out in joyful acceptance.

A half mile away in his hotel room Bishop no longer remembered the funeral procession or the woman to whom he had spoken. His immediate concern was as yet unresolved and he was worried. He had only $700 left.

On August 15 he attended a local meeting of AA. He had seen a television movie at Willows about three lonely men who always sought women until they found true love at an AA gathering. Except that true love for each was the same woman, a blond divorcée, which led quickly to kidnapping, murder, bondage, suicide, sadistic sex, cannibalism, necrophilia and assorted forms of violence. But that was TV and this was real life and he was running out of options in a town where the men sold money and the women sold smiles. He was ready to try anything, and what he tried most was to remember other movies he had seen for still more ideas.

The meeting was in a chapel hall right off Fremont. She recognized him immediately. He looked so much like someone she had once known from afar, the same easy smile, the same quiet manner. After the speakers she went over to him and introduced herself, laughingly reminding him of his wonderment at the passing funeral. He set his face and flashed his smile, he was all charm and friendly grace. At the meeting's end he asked if he might be allowed to walk along with her. It was a lovely night and she kindly consented.

On the way they spoke of this and that. He was in the import business and had a shop in Florida, mostly stocked with items from Central America. He had been a heavy drinker for a few years, finally deciding that was not for him. AA had saved his life. He had taken two months off to see the country but liked Las Vegas so much he didn't want to leave. For her part, she had come from Los Angeles as a child. Her husband and children were dead. She had turned to alcohol but it was two years now and not a drop. AA had also saved her life. She lived alone and had no close relatives, spending all her time at her work. She was in real estate.

At her fashionable apartment house he asked if he could see her again. He was a stranger in town and knew no one, and of course he didn't want to get too near the night life, where liquor flowed freely. At least not alone. It hadn't been that long since— He let the thought hang.

She smiled demurely, or so she hoped. To him she looked like a giant bat ready to fly, her eyelids flapping like wings. But he held his innocent expression, his hopeful air of expectancy. She looked directly at him, saw his boyish face, his clear manly eyes, his incorruptible honesty. He was *so* much the image of someone she once might have known if only she had been born pretty. Yes, she nodded shyly. Yes. Perhaps dinner tomorrow evening? he asked breathlessly. Again she told him yes.

Bishop walked home believing his problem had been solved. She lived well and was in real estate. That meant she had money. She lived alone and had no attachments. That meant she was safe. His final thought before falling asleep was that she had come from Los Angeles. In California.

The next evening they dined at the Sahara on the Strip. He was good company and she enjoyed herself, especially whenever she looked at him sitting across from her. She felt like a young girl again. They had dinner together every night after that. He never pushed and she never resisted. On the fourth night she invited him up for coffee. Afterward he kissed her on the cheek and left. On the fifth night she put on soft music before the coffee. Then she sat next to him on the sofa. They talked a bit, she held his hand. Soon he kissed her on the mouth, a long, loving kiss. She almost swooned in ecstasy. When he got up to leave she was disappointed but she did not want him to feel she was seducing him.

The following evening she showed him the view from her windows. The bedroom faced the Strip. Neon lighted the sky, holding the desert blackness at bay. He said it looked very pretty, almost as pretty as she. Standing by him, she quietly drew her arm around his waist. He turned to her, kissed her again and again. When he placed his palm over her slight breast she murmured yes, and as he gently led her toward the bed her eyes, her body, her lips were saying yes, yes. Yes.

In the morning she called her office to report she was

taking the day off. She packed a lunch for them to eat in the desert. They showered and left in her car.

Margot Rule was thirty-eight years old and had never known love, not real love, not the real love she had just experienced. Now she saw that she had been virginal all her life, now she understood what sex was meant to be, what it should always have been. She could not believe the depth of her emotions or how the young man sitting next to her had made her feel. She stole a glance at him. She loved him, more than she had ever loved her husband, God forgive her, more even than the faraway boys of her girlhood. In her woman's heart she knew this was the love she was meant to have, this was the way she was meant to feel. If there was a god in heaven she would have this love, no matter what the cost, no matter whom it would hurt. Without it she knew she would not want to live, and with it she would live forever.

Bishop sat quietly in the car knowing that he had played his part well. She was starved for love and hungry for the sex that goes with love, passionate and prolonged, the kind of sex that gave all and demanded nothing, that was receptive to her every unspoken wish, that made her feel like the most desirable woman who had ever lived. For this kind of love-making, tenderly physical yet tied to the female's emotional need for constant reassurance and eternal allegiance, a woman would do anything, go anywhere. His judgment had been correct, his timing superb. He had not gone to a prostitute or even masturbated in a week. He had given her a night of verbal and sexual love that she would remember forever. He smiled at the word. Forever was often not so very long, and he intended that for her forever would not be long at all.

During the next week they saw each other as much as her work would permit. He no longer went to her apartment, wanting, so he told her, to protect her reputation. Nor did he allow her to go to his hotel, which he changed every week so no one would recognize him, for the same reason. She thought this very loving and considerate of him. Instead they ended each evening at out-of-the-way motels where there was little chance of being seen. She would sit in the car while he registered, feeling like a wicked schoolgirl and enjoying every moment of it.

The nights were absolute heaven for her, beyond anything she had ever imagined in her masturbatory fan-

tasies. On their third such night together he asked her to
put his penis in her mouth. She had never done this
before, not for her husband, not for anybody, but she
did it gladly for him, without thought, without reservation.
He kneeled over her and gently showed her what to do.
When the sperm spurted into her mouth she took it
greedily, savoring it on her tongue, swallowing it slowly,
lovingly, as coming from him. She liked the sensation
and quickly came to believe that she was even closer to
him at such moments. Every night thereafter she would
take his penis in her mouth, working her taut lips over
the crown, waiting, wanting the sweet swallow and dec-
laration of his love, hearing his whispers in the last moments, needing to hear his whispered words, waiting with
widened eyes watching waiting for final feeling flowing
into welcome mouthful melting into loving leaving all
ahhhh . . .

By the end of that week he had learned that she
possessed $26,000, which she kept in the Nevada State
Bank. He decided he could survive on that for years.

On the last day of August Bishop told his beloved that
he wanted to marry her and to live with her for the
rest of his life. He had never loved before, not really, and
he would never love again. But he could not marry her
because he was a hunted man. Killers were after him.
He owed $22,000 to the wrong people in Florida, which
was why he was traveling and why he changed his hotel
and his name every week. His real name was David
Rogers. He was telling her only because he loved her so very
much. If she loved him, if she wanted to be with him
forever, she could save his life by lending him the money
to pay off his gambling debt. She knew what those people
were like; one day soon they would find him and he would
then be dead. They already had his store in Florida, now
they wanted his life. He asked her to go with him to
Florida. They would pay the money and get married and
honeymoon there or anywhere she desired. They would be
free to return to Las Vegas and to love and make love
forever more. If not—he shrugged in fatalistic acceptance—
he would soon be dead.

Margot did not want him dead. She loved him beyond
all reasoning, needed him inside of her, in every part of
her. Life without him would be meaningless, would not
be worth living, and suddenly she wanted very much to

live. She thought of the money. She had lost three times that much in drinking and gambling and now had nothing to show for it. At least by paying off David's debt she would have him. And she could easily make back the money now that her work was going well.

The very next day she withdrew $22,000 from her business account and $2,000 from her personal savings account for their expenses. The money, 240 one-hundred-dollar bills, was placed in a bank-deposit bag for her. Being a meticulous woman, she put a note in her safe-deposit box stating that she had taken $24,000 for expenses and was going to marry David Rogers of Florida.

The plan, at her insistence, was to marry in Las Vegas and then fly to Miami, stay there a few days, and return. She needed no long honeymoon since they would always be together. The time of departure was three days hence, September 4.

Bishop readily agreed to everything, asking only that she wait until the last day for flight reservations so no one would know. He realized it was just paranoia, he said sheepishly, but why take chances?

Margot knew David loved her. He was thirty, though he looked much younger. The eight-year age difference didn't worry her. She would always keep him as happy and contented as he was right now.

On September 3, 1973, the loving couple went into the desert they liked so much for a final outing before their marriage the following day. Again pleading paranoia, he told her the money should not be left in the house, where it could be stolen while they were gone. Blind with love, she did as he suggested and took the money with her. It was now in a small black zippered case.

In his rented car they rode up US 95 to Lathrop Wells, then turned left onto Nevada 29 toward Death Valley Junction. A few miles inside the California border he pulled the car off the road and drove on packed ground until they could not be seen.

She had never been in this part of the desert before. It was bleak and impossibly lonely. They had not passed a car or any sign of life since the cutoff about twelve miles back. She was happy to be with him but a bit frightened by the utter desolation. He reassured her and got out a blanket, which he spread on the ground some distance from the car. She brought the food over and they ate lunch and talked about their coming life together and the joys they would share. Then he got the idea.

They would take off all their clothes and make love right there under the sky. Unfettered and free, they would feel deliciously sinful. She laughed at the thought. Suppose somebody should come? But nobody was within miles of them. No, it was too ridiculous—she was a grown woman, wasn't she? Then they'd be kids again for a little while. What about the sun? Didn't he realize they would burn terribly?

He went to the car and soon returned with a tarpaulin and two wood stakes. In minutes he had constructed a lean-to, with welcome shade underneath. She chided him for having such things in his car and asked him how many other young women he had lured into the desert. Both laughed merrily at the very idea, it was so preposterous.

She was pleased with his suggestion. She had never done anything like that, and the sheer impropriety of it all made the whole thing seem delicious to her. Why not? she asked herself. She was once again a young girl and she had the love of the handsomest, kindest and most wonderful young man in the world. At that moment she felt like the fairy princess in all the fantasies of her life. She could do anything she wanted.

They undressed in front of each other, unashamed, no longer embarrassed, her eyes on his body, the body she had come to know so well in so short a time. Naked, they lay down together on the blanket. The air felt good on her skin, the shade soothing. He moved over her with the deft motion now so familiar to her. Slowly, capably, he began her on her rhythmic journey, and as her dance grew ever more frenzied she sensed this time was somehow different, different even from the other times with him. The open air, the sky, the sensation that they were alone in the universe, all heightened her awareness. She soon felt her senses rushing together, she couldn't believe what was happening as every nerve in her body fused with every other nerve, sending shock after shock shooting through her until finally she exploded into orgasmic spasms.

Even as her shudders shook the sky Margot Rule knew that she would remember these moments beyond all others for the rest of her life. No matter what else ever happened to her, this would be the supreme thrill of her existence.

After a long while she took David's penis between her lips and lovingly brought him to climax, and as his love gushed into her waiting body Bishop's hands clasped round her throat and choked her to death.

Suddenly, swiftly, without sign or signal, she who had been life, given life, held life, was now lifeless. For her, forevermore, in the spirit sphere beyond the stars, the sun would rise in the west and set in the east, and she with it.

Bishop worked quickly. He removed a watch and two rings from the body. He put the lean-to back in the car, the clothes on the front seat, to be dumped somewhere on the way home. Her lunch basket and pocketbook, stripped of all identification, would also be disposed of along the way.

From the trunk he scooped out a shovel and a five-gallon can of gasoline which he had filled that morning. He poured gasoline over the body and struck the match. Flames shot up, and he watched the fire slowly blacken the body into burning ash. Several times he poured more gasoline onto the reddish flames.

When little was left but bone and sickening slime, he dragged the remains of the blanket some fifty yards to soft sand. Here he dug a grave, small but deep, into which he shoveled the human debris. Afterward he smoothed out the sand back to the picnic spot, where he brushed away any sand and dirt on his body and hurriedly dressed.

In the car again, shovel and can once more in the trunk, he drove to the road, then walked back to the area with a branch trailing on the ground, wiping away the tire tracks.

On the return to Las Vegas he made numerous stops by the side of the road, flinging things he no longer wanted, including the shovel and empty gas can, into the desert. He also brushed out the car, removing all traces of human occupancy.

He kept the money case close to him.

In his hotel room he counted out the 240 hundred-dollar bills. He folded ten in his pocket and returned the rest to the black zippered bag, which he hid in the toilet tank after flushing the water and plugging the spout, still another trick learned from TV. He then burned the paper contents of the pocketbook in the bathroom sink. Other items such as keys and comb and mirror and makeup kit had already been discarded separately, as had the watch and rings. He kept only a picture of the woman. She was wearing a severe dress that made her look quite matronly.

That night he exchanged the big bills in his pocket for tens and twenties at a casino on the Strip, then walked out. He felt a sudden contempt for the people around him. He didn't gamble or drink or smoke. He was a moral young man in all things.

Home again, he put most of the bills with the others and placed his few possessions in the flight bag. He was ready to leave Las Vegas. He was glad.

The next morning he returned the car to the rental office, paying his bill with some of the tens and twenties. He didn't pay by credit card because he wanted no record of charges going back to California. Also he needed the card to remain valid in case of emergency. Again he wore the dark sunglasses and false beard he had bought in Los Angeles. Wearing them, it was impossible to get an accurate description of his face. He could as easily be Vincent Mungo as Thomas Bishop or Daniel Long or almost anyone else.

With the flight bag slung over his shoulder, the zippered money case tightly gripped in his right hand, Bishop boarded the noon bus bound for Phoenix. He was leaving Las Vegas on his wedding day. And leaving behind his intended bride.

She too would be missing.

SEVEN

Derek Lavery just sat there scowling. No one was in his huge penthouse office on the sixth floor of the *Newstime* building in Los Angeles. Not yet anyway. The carpeted living and dining space, the large work area at the room's other end, the enormous middle ground where

Lavery sat behind his mammoth oak desk: all were empty. But Lavery pushed the scowl wider by the minute. He didn't like it, not a bit of it. Whenever those sons of bitches called from New York there was trouble and this time was no exception. Not that he minded trouble; on the contrary, he sought it, lived with it, needed it. Without it, he often felt he would just shrivel up and disappear in a puff of smoke. But this was different. This kind of trouble he didn't need. And he didn't at all appreciate the fact that those bastards in the East had ultimate veto power just because they had financial control of the magazine. He had built up the West Coast edition almost from scratch, built it to a peak of performance. And prosperity too. Those bastards knew that! Knew they were dealing with the best man in the organization. Since all they could read intelligently was a balance sheet, they mostly left him alone to work his money miracles.

Lavery lit the second cigar of the morning. He glanced at his watch, August 15, 8:50 A.M. He pressed a button on the telephone console but no one answered. Naturally, she wasn't in yet. In his mind's eye he pictured his secretary's long slim legs, her heavy breasts as she leaned over the desk. They were always firmly encased in a bra, reminded him of the old line the salesman gave the slight young thing shopping in the bra department: Let's not make a mountain out of a molehill, dear. Christ, she was goddam Mount Everest! He was sure she wore nothing at night, just flopped around her apartment getting all the phallic symbols hot. He thought again of the breasts, must be at least ten-pounders. They reminded him of his daughter, she had big ones too. And long slim legs. But she almost never wore a bra. Half the time they were falling out of her shirts and blouses. When she took a dip in the pool all she wore was a strip covering the nipples, he could see almost everything. Twenty years old with a body like that. Jesus! She would ruin a dozen good men before she was through.

A few minutes later the buzzer sounded. He pressed the button. "Coffee," he snapped. The hell with her. Who did she think she was? He could get a hundred like her. He wondered if she was any good in bed.

Soon she brought in his coffee, a pewter cup on a

silver tray. Leaning over the desk, she placed the tray in front of him. Lavery interested her. She would have liked to look at his penis; one of the girls in promotion had sworn it was the biggest she had ever seen. That interested her too. She would hold it rigid with both hands, her long thin fingers wrapped tightly around it, slowly pulling the skin back. She liked to do that to her men. Little by little she moved her hands faster until she was masturbating them. She knelt between their legs on the bed and watched their faces until they came. That excited her more than anything, to watch their faces. They looked like animals for those few moments, total crazed-out lovely animals that belonged in zoos, or in trees a million years ago. There was a sense of danger and excitement about them at those times, something she found primitive and wild and very masculine. That turned her on more than anything else, when she was on top of a wild animal grunting and groaning underneath her. It drove her crazy with desire, and when they finally came she would watch it shoot out of them, and she would usually come herself as she put her head down and wiped the sperm all over her face, her eyes, her breasts. For those few moments she was an animal too, and when it was over she would lie down, sperm running down her face, and let them do whatever they wanted to her.

Once, only once a long time ago, did she abruptly stop as the man was about to come. She was much younger then and just fooling around; not quite ready, she wanted to wait a bit. He reared up and hit her; he went totally berserk for a few seconds and would have killed her. His hands were around her throat, strangling her, when he came to his senses. That's when she first saw the incredible power of the animal during those few moments. She had never been so turned on in her life, and as she nursed a swollen jaw and bruised throat she knew that from then on she needed the power of the animal, needed to hold that power in her hands, needed to watch the animal revert to savagery. Only then could she become part of that savage power herself.

Afterward she chose her men carefully. She would sleep with a man more than once only if his penis was big enough for both her cupped hands and he was animalistic in bed. She had no use for passive men or those who came quietly with nothing but smiles on their faces. Through trial and error she found that aggressive men were best for her, successfully aggressive men who viewed the world as a jungle and themselves as predators.

Derek Lavery was her kind of man, but he was also her kind of boss. She liked the job and the pay and she had no desire to become anyone's mistress. She was much too independent for that. Since there were always enough men to satisfy her wants, she didn't feel any particular loss in not seeing Lavery's face in bed. But if she ever quit or something happened—

Lavery glanced at his watch again; it was 9:05. They were late as usual. He could be in at eight o'clock to talk to New York but they couldn't even make it by nine. He felt the world was against him.

New York. The thought made him shudder. He had been there enough times to know he didn't like it. New York didn't have the spaciousness or the friendliness of the West. People there lived tightly packed together, they had little sense of privacy or ownership. Worse, the place was full of foreigners who took everything and gave nothing. No—whatever else New York was, it wasn't the good life. That was as clear to him as his secretary's bra.

He thought of the moneymen on the magazine; all of them lived in New York or its suburbs, right up to the publisher. He didn't like any of them. Now he liked them even less for their reaction to the Chessman piece. Not the story itself but the bad timing, what with Vincent Mungo and Senator Stoner. In the two weeks since the new Mungo killing Stoner's name was being heard across the state. His campaign to restore capital punishment was picking up steam, and everywhere he spoke he held the Chessman story up to ridicule and scorn. He linked Mungo to Chessman as a sort of symbolic son, a legatee of Chessman's alleged criminal mind and murderous mentality. The senator's tough stance and his clever linkage between the dead and the living were beginning to turn people toward the death penalty.

In a way Lavery admired Stoner, at least for his game plan. It was really brilliant. Tie the past to the present, the known to the unknown, trade on people's fears, throw in a touch of dramatics, and the result was one senator going statewide. Maybe even nationwide if he kept rolling. The issue was a good one and there was no telling how far he would be able to ride it. And Vincent Mungo was helping greatly.

An hour earlier Lavery had told New York that he was doing a story on Mungo that would scream for the death penalty. They were relieved. The New York papers had printed news of Stoner's campaign, mentioning the Chessman article in *Newstime*. Even network television had carried items about the senator's increasing impact.

What he told them was at least partially true. He intended to do a story on Vincent Mungo, one that would demand death. That's the way the game was played: on a good issue like capital punishment, hit both sides hard. Mungo was current, and Stoner's tying him to Chessman made it perfect. Even New York saw that and wished him luck.

The only problem was the angle; he didn't have one yet. Mungo had been at large for six weeks and had killed two people, maybe more. He was still free. Those were facts, not angles. There was no way to prove gross negligence by hospital officials at Willows, and no point in taking on the sheriff's office for failing to capture him.

Downstairs, Ding waddled into the building and quickly ducked in a darkened elevator. The lobby man, who knew him well, snapped on the light and shut the doors.

"What time the boss get here?"

"I came at eight. He was already in." The man glanced at Ding. "Must be important, eh?"

"His girl in yet?"

"Miss Charm? About ten minutes ago."

Ding smiled. "Why do you call her that?"

"What?"

"Miss Charm."

"She got big tits, ain't she?" He didn't wait for an answer. "That means she's trouble."

Ding studied him a moment.

"You should be a writer," he said finally as the elevator stopped.

"You think so?" said the lobby man, interested now.

"Sure thing," Ding said on the way out. "You see people for what they really are." He turned around. "And you know how to bury the truth." He toddled down the hall, shaking his head. "That's all you need," he muttered softly. "All you really need in this game."

Inside he adjusted his eyes to the sunlight flooding the penthouse office. He always thought what the place needed were a few myna birds flying around. And maybe a small beach at one end, with breaking waves and bare women. Then the other end could have some gambling tables—blackjack, baccarat, craps. Nothing pretentious. In the middle would be a bar where a bevy of big-breasted beauties sat around waiting for action. Ding had been with Lavery a long time and knew him well. What he didn't know was what the hell the bastard wanted at nine in the morning.

He looked toward the bar. It was bereft of beauties. In fact it wasn't exactly a bar at all; seemed to be more of a large desk. Behind it Lavery sat scowling, as usual. Ding blamed it all on the Barcalounger, something about it turned his boss into a scowler.

He squeezed into a normal chair, which was two sizes too small for him. He tried to scowl back but his face just didn't work that way. Whatever he did with it came out fat smiles. He sat there smiling.

Lavery took the cigar out of his mouth. "Nice to see you," he growled.

"Nice to be back."

"Where were you?"

"Sleeping."

Lavery reached for the ashtray. "Maybe you sleep too much." Missed it. "Ever think of that?"

"All the time."

"And?"

"That's what makes me fall asleep."

Lavery gave up. He knew better than to cross words with Ding; the man had that crazy kind of head that saw paranoid humor in everything. He was not aggressive, had no drive or ambition to make it big and didn't seem to care about real success. The kind he, Lavery, had carved out for himself. They had started together on a local California newspaper, both having grown up in the same area. Lavery rose right from the beginning; he had the balls and the brains and he knew how to wheel and deal. As he jumped higher and higher—night editor, city editor, managing editor, magazine offers, always moving up—he took Ding along because he was a good legman and writer. He knew what to do with words. And what he didn't know hadn't been written yet.

Lavery liked that, it was his first good thought of the day. He wanted to write it down. On the desk were two lamps, a pair of tennis shoes, plants—all dead—telephones, tape recorders, a purple elephant, a red garter, handcuffs, a tape measure and a million other items of necessity. But no pad or pen. He went back to scowling. This was not going to be his day at all. Hopefully it would soon be over, and the sooner the better. Only ten or twelve hours to go. He sat back, defeated.

"We got problems," he said turning to Ding.

Amos Finch had arisen on the previous morning at his usual time of six o'clock. With a wistful sigh of remembered pleasure he allowed the blond graduate student in his bed to continue her sleep. Standing over her he gazed at the tousled head, the shapely arched back as she slept in the fetal position, her legs jackknifed, her arms curved downward. She looked so tiny, a child's body with a woman's sexuality. He liked smaller women, found them to be the most passionate and open to sexual variety. Their small breasts and buttocks made him feel boyish again and wandering once more through the fertile fields of his Midwest youth. A half dozen times he had bedded down with midgets, enjoying each experience immensely. His secret ambition was to sleep with a dwarf.

Studying her nude form against the pink sheets, he was overcome with erotic desire and hurriedly returned to bed. He gently straightened her legs and turned her over onto her stomach. As he pressed hard against her from the rear she cooed softly, still half asleep. Her body was warm and moist and deliciously sweet-smelling to him. He slipped easily inside of her, driven on by her murmured oohs and umms. In his growing excitement he decided that his work could wait a few hours, perhaps even until delivery of the day's mail. He was expecting a letter.

Big Jim Oates had a dream. He was running for governor on a law-and-order platform. The race was close and came up a tie at the wire. Both sides waited as the last voter in California slowly walked toward them, thousands of silent people lining the approach. Oates watched intently as the figure gradually came into focus.

It was a man of average size and dark features. His steps on the carpeted floor began to boom as he drew closer. There was something familiar about him, something Oates couldn't quite catch. The man pressed forward, step by booming step, until the noise was shattering. Suddenly Oates saw him clearly. That face! He recognized it now, it was the face of the devil himself. Vincent Mungo! Oates quickly pulled his service revolver and shot Mungo six times at point-blank range. Mungo didn't even notice. He continued his slow, steady gait until he was at the head of the crowd, which closed behind him. Standing silently in front of the political opponents, he waited a moment before turning to Oates. He drew closer, their faces now only inches apart. Oates saw the insanity in Mungo's eyes. He saw something else too. He saw that he had lost. "You lose," Mungo said softly. He turned to the other man, they shook hands. As they walked away together, arm in political arm, Oates fired six shots into them, then six more, and again and again and again . . .

He awoke in a sweat, his eyes blinking. A nightmare, it was only a goddam nightmare! He glanced at the electric clock by the bed: 4:10 A.M. Groaning, he looked over at his wife asleep in the other twin bed. Only her head was visible over the flowered sheet in the air-conditioned room. His eyes rested on the head, graying now but once the color of wheat, a dark gold in the summer sky. He had loved the color of her hair, just as he had come to love her, and when they married he promised her that he would make something of himself, someone of whom she could be proud. She told him she was already proud of him beyond anything else imaginable, and from that moment on he loved her with a tenderness he knew would last unto death. Whatever he had to do in his professional life, whatever good or evil was forced upon him, whatever women he would take for sex urges, she would always be his loved one, the woman in his private heart.

Through an uncle's political connections he had become a deputy in the California Sheriff's Office. His blustery manner and affable ways served him well in the police business. Especially valuable was his ability to deal on the political level, which had moved him up the ranks until he commanded his own sections in several locales before coming to Forest City. The latest move was exceptionally good for him; it was not that far from Sacramento and the real power. Inordinately ambitious, the years had whetted his appetite for public office.

He glanced again at the clock. Still only 4:11. The hour of the wolf. The hour when more people died and more babies were born than any other. He didn't know why but he knew it was true. Every cop knew that. The hour of the wolf. Vincent Mungo was the wolf right now, and his hour would soon be over. Hopefully.

Oates quietly propped himself up on the pillow, folded his arms behind his head. If he couldn't sleep he'd just lie there in the dark with his thoughts. He often did that; a fitful sleeper, he spent many moments awake. Over the years such times frequently were the most peaceful of his day. He was equally familiar with the hour of the devil and the gun. But he was a bit unnerved that his nightmare about Vincent Mungo would come during the hour of the wolf. To a realistic man superstitious in many ways, it was not a good sign.

He had returned from Los Angeles on August 8 sadly empty-handed. Mungo had disappeared again, vanished without a trace after committing the fearful murder. Despite one of the most intensive manhunts ever conducted in the Los Angeles area, despite almost 100,000 law-enforcement officers throughout the state searching everywhere, despite the tentative entrance of the FBI into the case on the assumption that he had crossed state lines in unlawful flight to avoid prosecution, Vincent Mungo was nowhere to be found.

He was a devil, Oates reluctantly conceded, a devil in disguise. Whatever his disguise was, it had to be one of the greatest ever seen. Or not seen. In almost thirty years of police work Oates had never known anyone with so little fool so many for so long. If he had his way, Mungo would get a gold medal just before they shot the son of a bitch. Or hanged him or gassed him. That he would be killed one way or another was a certainty. It was all just a matter of time. Of that Oates was dead sure. He was also sure that if he got there first Mungo was dead. One look at the girl's savaged body had been enough. Mungo was a real-life monster and had to be destroyed.

The sheriff stared into the darkness of the bedroom, thinking thoughts of legal murder. Five days in Los Angeles had been more than enough for him. The people were different from those in the northern half of the state, more frenetic and insecure, given more to fads and surface feelings. Even though well treated, he was glad to get away. He didn't believe he would enjoy working in the southern part of the state, though he had lived there for a few years as a youngster. Sacramento would do just fine. All the political power he could ever want was right there.

He remembered an article he had read about capital punishment, and he wondered how a good magazine like *Newstime* could print that garbage. They had really made a big mistake; about the only thing they got right was Chessman's name and age.

He had been around at the time and he knew a little about the case, though he hadn't been personally involved. He knew, for example, that Chessman wasn't identified by just two women, as stated in the article, but by half dozen people as their assailant and robber. He knew that Chessman was a punk car thief and gunsel as a teenager. From friends, guards at San Quentin and Folsom, he knew that Chessman remained a punk throughout his early prison years and even after the big rap sent him to death row. But most of all he knew Chessman had been guilty of the crimes that got him gas. He was captured in a stolen car with a flashing red light similar to those used by police. The car was identified by witnesses. He was identified by witnesses. And not one or two instances but in a whole series of crimes. That was enough for Oates. Everything afterward was just legal games.

He knew one more thing not mentioned in the article. Chessman was married at age nineteen to a lovely girl with silky hair and a nice smile. Oates had once had a crush on her when he was himself a youngster and living in Glendale.

Again he eyed the clock. Ten more minutes and the hour would be over. No more wolf. He wished his problems would be over as easily. Vincent Mungo. Bang. No more Mungo.

He primed the pillow and eased his head down. In six hours he had a meeting with the police and public-safety officials in Sacramento. Was that right? He checked himself. August 10, 11 A.M. Yep! Just six hours away. The clock was set for 7:30.

As he drifted into sleep he wondered if he would ever get to see Vincent Mungo after all.

While the sheriff's plane was holding to a course due north at 22,000 feet on the bright clear morning of August 8, a sleek black Lincoln Continental pulled to a stop in front of a neon-and-chrome diner in Fresno. The chauffeur, after a few words with his passenger in the rear, slid from behind the wheel and headed for the diner. Inside he spoke to the cashier; he was polite but firm. A moment later Don Solis came forward. The chauffeur told him a man wanted to see him outside. Would he go along?

Solis looked the man over. He recognized the eyes, unyielding, disinterested, yet noting everything. He had been like that once, not quite that good. Nowhere near that good, as a matter of fact. The man was dangerous and not to be crossed. He followed him outside.

Business was light at that hour and few cars occupied the parking area. They headed for the limousine, where the chauffeur opened the rear door for him. Not knowing what to expect, Solis tensed himself. As he bent to look in, his eyes widened and his mouth sprang open in amazement . . .

George D. Little lived for his family and his business, in that order. A man of few passions, he doted on his sprightly wife and three lovely daughters and provided them with a big house in the best section of town, a ranch with fine horses to ride, cars, clothing, travel. To give them this kind of life he sold death. Specifically, funerals. He owned one of the biggest mortuaries in the state, taking over from his father before him. He knew the business well, knew all about dead bodies, and where the money was in caskets and flowers and private services. Over the years he made a good living at it, and better than good, and they got it all.

His wife often thought him a bit of a bore and much too logically sane but she loved him for his kindness and generosity, and she gave him what he needed, or at least deserved, in companionship and in the bedroom. Out of it came three daughters. He had wanted sons to carry on the business but he soon grew to love the sound of females in the house. They brightened his life considerably, and by the time they were young ladies he adored them. They could do no wrong.

Two of them did everything right, at least in their father's eyes. They accepted their parents' life style and position in local society, they enjoyed the abundance of money, and generally behaved themselves as well-to-do girls with nothing in their heads beyond the moment.

The oldest daughter was the problem. She did not quite fit, was not quite content. At thirteen she wanted to be a rodeo rider, at sixteen she was going to be the first woman astronaut. When she was turning eighteen her goal in life became clear to her. She would be a movie star. She was pretty and she was clever and she would make it big in the movies. When her sisters laughed at her she just gritted her teeth still one more time and walked away. When her parents refused to listen she just grew silent. They would be sorry someday, she kept telling herself. They would see, but it would be too late.

Mary Wells Little hated where she lived and hated horses and especially hated her father's business. Funerals! Ugh! What she wanted, needed, was some glamour—bright lights, good times. Show business, that was for her. She'd go to Hollywood and become a movie star. Then she would get on the Johnny Carson show and she'd sit down next to his desk and talk about all kinds of interesting things. Mostly about herself of course. Then afterward they'd go out to dinner and dancing. He'd hold her in his arms and they would whirl around the floor for hours and hours, and at daybreak he would take her home to his beach house by the ocean and they would make mad passionate love. She was barely eighteen and still a virgin and she wanted Johnny Carson to be her first lover. Please God, make it all happen for me! Please! Please!

The next year Mary Wells was nineteen and no longer a virgin, but she still wanted to be a movie star and be on the Johnny Carson show. She would lie on her bed at night watching him on television from faraway California. After a while her long pony legs would open and she would feel him inside of her, on top of her, all over her. He was the symbol for everything she needed, he was the end of the rainbow. She would get him if only she could get away from home. She would somehow do it.

She had to. "Johnny," she would whisper as she watched him, felt him inside her, "help me, please help me. Please, Johnny! Please!"

The following summer she bade her parents goodbye. She had finished one year of college and that was enough. Almost twenty, she was going to Hollywood. They stormed and pleaded and cried, and still she left their home. They couldn't stop her. At the door her father, overwrought, screamed names at her and told her never to come back. He didn't mean it but she did. She silently vowed never to return to the house or the town.

A week later she found a small apartment in Los Angeles. She changed her name to Kit and began making the rounds. Youthful and full of energy, she was out to conquer the world.

Within a year her world had crumbled. She had done her very best but luck did not smile on her. Slowly she changed from wide-eyed innocence to hardened indifference. She began exchanging sex for job offers or even promises of offers. Eventually she exchanged sex for gifts. She worked many part-time jobs, mostly at night so her days were free to seek movie parts. After a while her searchings became more infrequent until finally, toward the end, there were none.

She got a job in a dance hall because she needed money. It was hard work, and she hated it, and one night after work she stood outside a few moments to breathe in the sultry air. A young man saw her from across the street, hurried over. At the corner he caught up with her . . .

The body was released to the father by the coroner's office on August 5. They had tried to patch it up, to bring some kind of order back to the body, but the father was an expert in such matters and would not be fooled. Because he was himself a forensic man who spent his life with dead bodies, he was finally allowed to read the coroner's report. Unlike the average layman, he understood precisely what was written in the report, and as he read he saw exactly what had been done to his daughter. Tears welled in his eyes, he found it hard to swallow. The one who had done these things was a devil; no man could have committed such destruction without losing his sanity. Either that or he was already a raving lunatic, furiously homicidal. Vincent Mungo was all that and more.

George D. Little took his oldest daughter home to Kansas to be buried. He did not tell his wife or his other two daughters what had been done to Mary Wells. The following day he buried her in a sealed coffin in the family plot, near a grove of trees in the carefully landscaped cemetery. Only the immediate family was in attendance.

On August 7 the bereaved father returned to Los Angeles. He did not expect the police to catch the killer of his little girl. Half devil, Vincent Mungo was beyond the power of the law. He had been free for a month, against all odds. He would remain free unless other forces were used.

In Los Angeles the father made discreet inquiries based on information given him by certain businessmen back home. On the evening of his return he sat in a sleazy topless lounge off Sunset Boulevard waiting for a man who would perhaps be able to have Vincent Mungo found. Found and killed. Not only killed but destroyed.

George Little was not a violent man, nor was he much given to flashes of anger. Yet he knew he wouldn't be able to keep his sanity if he didn't do everything in his power to correct the great wrong done him and his family. He had to do everything he could, and he intended to do the ultimate. Only then could he again find peace with his family and his work and his life.

In the lounge he waited impatiently, surrounded by young girls with bare breasts bouncing to the music.

Senator Jonathan Stoner was dozing when the phone interrupted his catnap. He had slept little in the three days since the discovery of Vincent Mungo's latest victim. Interviews had been given to reporters from one end of the state to the other. He had already been on television and radio, with a half dozen further appearances scheduled for succeeding days. Lecture offers were pouring in from local communities and schools. Suddenly everybody wanted him. His castigation of Mungo fed the public's craving for a personification of evil. He was the hero, Mungo the devil. Everything was simple after all.

The phone blared again in his ear. He shook his head awake. If he didn't get some real sleep soon he would keel over. His hand reached out.

"Stoner."

Roger's voice was a beat late, as though far away.

"Good news," he said loudly. "Five colleges lined up already, with TV spots in Denver and Houston so far. Others sure to come. They think you may be onto something."

"Where you now?"

"Houston."

Stoner chewed his lip in thought.

"Listen carefully. I got a call this morning from Danzinger in Kansas City. His people are very interested in what's going on here. They'd like to know more. You run up there and set the deal. At their convenience." Pause. "This is a big one, Roger. If we get them with us it means access to the whole Midwest. You know? So get there right away and work it out. Next week would be a good time for me but the sooner the better."

"Okay. What about the other schools on the list? There's still a good dozen that should come through."

"You'll just have to take care of them by phone when you get back. If they want me—"

"That's not the problem, for chrissake. The thing is lining up the TV spots in the big towns. It's a bitch at the beginning, at least until you get the steamroller effect going for you."

"If we get it."

"Look. I'll go up to Kansas City now, then take care of as many as I could on the way back. Okay?"

Stoner thought quickly.

"Okay," he sighed. "But get here soon's you can. I'm up to my ass in mail and every other goddam thing."

He called his wife to say that he would be working late again. Yes, on the go, as always. Then he called his mistress and told her he would be right over. What he needed was some good rest and relaxation.

John Spanner hadn't believed it when he first heard the news on the radio. After a month of freedom Mungo was virtually safe from detection; he apparently had found a perfect disguise and a way to survive. Why blow it all in a moment of rage? No, it didn't make sense and everything Mungo had done thus far had been eminently sensible. So much so that Spanner was filled with increasing doubt about the validity of determining anyone's sanity. Or insanity.

His first thought had been that someone was again imitating Mungo, as the handyman had done two weeks earlier. It was a good way to shift the blame for a murder. A known killer was always easier to digest in the public mind than was the fear of the unknown. Too often in the police mind as well. With a killer on the loose, responsibility could be dribbled away; in a murder investigation that sought a killer's identity the responsibility was clearly defined. Which was why police generally accepted the theory of multiple murders, and potential killers often duplicated the method of operation of those who were highly publicized. As with Vincent Mungo.

But as more details became known of the Los Angeles murder, especially the fearful destruction of the body, Spanner began to realize that his time was not mere imitation. Mungo had returned to the world with a vengeance. If anything, this latest attack was apparently more savage even than his killing of the other mental patient on the night of his escape.

To Spanner this was an ominous sign. Much experienced in such matters, and by nature and temperament attuned to the nuances in aberrant behavior, he saw or thought he saw a pattern emerging that could precipitate a reign of terror in the state. Assuming that Mungo could be held within the state at all. His disguise seemingly allowed him freedom of movement so he could as easily move away, move anywhere he chose. Free to stop or go like anyone else, he would be a plague descending on people. Or a wolf among sheep. Spanner preferred not to think of the consequences.

He couldn't shake the conviction that the insane mutilation of the bodies was the key to Mungo's sudden passion for murder after a young lifetime of noncriminal behavior. People suddenly killed for an infinite variety of reasons or for no reason at all. But the butchery afterward had to come from something in the man's dreadful past, something that wouldn't let go of him. Which was why he chanced blowing his cover, his whole new identity, whatever that might be. He did it because he had to do it. That meant he would do it again. And again. Until he was captured or killed.

The prospect made Spanner flinch. If he was right

about the present pattern coming out of the past, it would be virtually impossible to predict where or when Mungo would next strike without knowing about that particular past locked into the man's crazed head. He, Spanner, had read all the records on Mungo going back to the beginning; there was nothing in them that gave a clue to his present rage beyond the fact that he was paranoid. Nor was there anything in the newspaper accounts of his background or relatives.

With nothing to go on for motive or opportunity, without an idea of the new disguise or identity, the police would be powerless to take any action. Except to wait until he made a mistake or got caught in the act. Each time he wasn't caught meant still another innocent victim would be killed horribly.

Spanner had a feeling that Mungo would become a mass murderer before he made a mistake.

Beyond that, the lieutenant knew that he, everybody, was up against the most dangerous, most elusive killer in all the world: the man who kills at random for no discernible reason. Such a man was impossible to stop. Without even a description, he was invisible. Just the thought of a monster like that loose in a city or state or even a country made Spanner shudder and filled him, as it would any policeman, with a cold dread.

On August 5 he finally called some four hundred miles downstate to Dr. Walter Lang's new post. It was a Sunday and two days after they had found Mary Wells Little. Lang was familiar with Mungo's record. More important, he had examined Mungo, talked with him. Maybe Spanner could get a few questions answered.

The hospital reported the doctor out but due back at 6:30 P.M., when he would return the lieutenant's call.

Willows was exceptionally quiet on the morning of August 4, or so it seemed to Henry Baylor after the news conference of the previous afternoon and the endless phone calls and meetings. He usually took Saturdays off, enjoying his quiet weekends at home with his wife. But this weekend was different. The head of an institution like Willows should be at his post, he kept telling himself, in times of trouble. He wondered just how much trouble this time would bring.

He couldn't understand why the police didn't apprehend

Mungo. They had his picture and description, his habits and vices, where he liked to go, what he liked to do. He had nothing, not even much intellect. Yet after a month he was still free and the police had no idea where he was. Except that he might be in Los Angeles, because he had just murdered someone there. But he might as easily be elsewhere already, murdering still another somebody, for all they knew.

Baylor was becoming increasingly bitter toward the police. He had always enjoyed the best of relations with them, being himself a policeman of sorts as director of a state hospital for mentally ill criminals as well as others. But now he was being caused embarrassment and perhaps even trouble. After Mungo's escape he was able to jettison the experimental program and get Dr. Lang reassigned, thus keeping himself afloat. This pacified state officials for the moment. But a new killing had again turned attention to Willows and himself. There was little point in sacrificing anyone else on staff; the next head would probably be his. He grimaced painfully at the though that Mungo might kill yet again.

He answered the phone on the third ring, remembering his secretary was out. It was Adolph Myers of the California State Department of Corrections, calling from Sacramento. A meeting was being held in the capital within the hour. Yes, right up to the very top. That's right. About the latest killing of course. Something would have to be done, some . . . readjustments might have to be made. Certain people were unhappy about the whole thing. Very unhappy indeed. No, predictions were impossible. Much too early to tell anyway. If only the police would get him. Well, there was still a chance. Yes, in a few hours. What? Of course.

Dr. Baylor cradled the receiver, knowing he would be going through the motion many times that day. He wished he were in Sacramento instead of having to wait for their call. He didn't like disorder and he didn't like to be interrupted. But most of all he didn't like to be kept waiting when he was waiting for something.

Frank Chills couldn't get the image out of his head. There they were on the table like two scoops of ice cream. Or a giant boiled potato, peeled and cut in half. He had seen severed arms and fingers and legs but never anything like that. Two years in the Medical Corps and nine years an attendant in a general hospital and he'd never seen that before.

He belted down another drink. And he didn't even get a chance to look in the other room! Son of a bitch, he said to himself, he'd like to get his hands on the guy. He would cut him into little pieces.

Frank liked his liquor and thought he'd better have another. It was only nine o'clock and he still wasn't totally drunk on this Friday night. Or even drunk enough to get rid of the terrible memory of that morning. Earlier he had called County General Hospital to report in sick for his four-to-midnight shift. Now all he wanted was to forget the sight of the girl's breasts. He ordered another drink.

The night owl editions were already on the newsstands, their headlines screaming murder. Buried on a back page was a brief item dated Friday, August 3, about a local woman reported missing for several weeks. She had been taking a motoring vacation around the state. Her name was Velma Adams and she owned a prosperous beauty salon in west Los Angeles.

By midnight Frank Chills was so drunk he had to be helped to the door. He had told everyone in the bar about finding the murdered girl. Nobody wanted to hear it, all they wanted was a good time at the beginning of a weekend in a hot city.

As he slowly struggled homeward Frank wished, just wished that the killer would start something with him. He'd rip'm apart. Kill'm, s'help me! He threw up on a car fender.

By the time he finally made it home and to bed, Friday night had turned into Saturday morning.

The call from Sacramento came through at 3:40 Saturday afternoon. Dr. Baylor answered the phone. He was distressingly angry because of the long wait but he controlled his emotion and his voice. The meeting, he was informed, had gone better than expected. The police rather than the Department of Corrections was receiving most of the heat. However, they were not out of the woods by any means. Certain reform measures would have to be taken at all state facilities. Particulars would be discussed at a future date. Also, there might be some necessary changes in personnel. No, nothing was said about any of the directors. Not yet anyway.

The call ended with the admonition that if the killings continued—well, anything could happen. Baylor, a conservative psychiatrist and efficent administrator, clearly understood.

He left his office after four o'clock and spent Saturday evening attending a dull party where the host insisted on playing obscenely loud music. Baylor and his wife departed early and on the way home he wondered, as he often did, why some people never seem to grow up. It was as though they were caught in a time warp of childhood, forever trapped in impossible dreams or irreconcilable nightmares.

On Sunday evening at 7:30 Dr. Lang returned John Spanner's call. He apologized for being out earlier but Sunday and all that. Spanner in turn voiced his regret for bothering the doctor. He just had a few thoughts he wanted to check out for a moment if Lang would be so kind.

Did the doctor think that Vincent Mungo was capable of the violence done to the Los Angeles girl?

"Yes. Definitely."

Where did such anger come from?

"Demonic rage, I would call it. Probably surfacing after years of being buried in the unconscious. Most such rage is slowly worked out by the person but sometimes it's just capped. Then one day it blows and he goes berserk."

Could Mungo control the rage?

"Not if it became strong enough."

Even if it meant discovery and capture? Or death?

"Even then." The doctor paused. "But usually this kind of rage is accompanied by feelings of invincibility, so that the person doesn't ordinarily think in terms of capture. He's simply so superior that detection is quite impossible. It never really enters his mind. Not seriously anyway."

Would this kind of rage follow any pattern?

"It might. Everything is cyclic in a sense, and Mungo undoubtedly has his inner clock ticking to his rhythm.

But without sufficient examples there'd be no way to predict the pattern."

"You mean without more killings."

There was a silence.

"I'm afraid so," Lang finally said.

"Why the mutilation?"

"Well, it's obviously sexual. But exactly what signficance it has for Mungo can't be known until we study it further."

"You think what he's doing now is connected to his past in any way?"

"Everything's connected to the past, Lieutenant. At least as long as there's memory. Even after, we have automatic reflexes and cell-conditioning."

"You examined him, Doctor. What did you think of him?"

"I found him marginally aggressive, maybe a bit slow in thought. And filled with suppressed violence."

"Then what he's doing doesn't surprise you?"

"Not really. Though I didn't think he had the spark needed to blow. I guess we can never tell for sure."

"But you're sure that's Vincent Mungo out there."

A long pause.

"Doctor Lang?"

"That's an odd thing you said."

"I just wondered if it fit your mental pattern of Mungo."

"In lieu of anyone else, I would have to say yes."

"Just one more thing, Doctor. Would you say Mungo was a sadist?"

"Yes, I'd say he had strong sadistic instincts. That type very often does."

"Could these . . . instincts be outgrown?"

"Not usually."

Afterward Spanner sat on the porch steps for a long time smoking his pipe and thinking strange thoughts. By the time he went to bed it had become August 6.

"What I don't need is another day like this," Senator Stoner said that night in the arms of his mistress.

Lying lazily across the ruffled sheet, she pulled him closer to her as she slowly opened her thighs.

"I'll help you relax," she purred. "Then later you can tell me all about it."

* * *

The man was heavy, hard. His dark suit closed around him tightly.

"George Little?"

Kit's father looked up from the table, pressed his lips together in acknowledgment.

"Let's walk."

They passed through the rear of the topless lounge and out a back exit. In the alleyway a large black sedan idled. The man opened a door. "Inside," he commanded.

As George Little climbed in, a man glanced at him from the opposite seat.

"You wanted to see me about a contract on Vincent Mungo . . ."

That was the evening of August 7. Twelve hours later another man climbed into a different car some two hundred and fifty miles away in Fresno. He stared in disbelief at the solitary figure in the back seat.

"Carl?"

The man smiled. "Good to see you, Don." He waved a finger at the chauffeur, shifted his attention back to Solis. "Been a long time."

"I thought you were—"

"Dead." Kept the smile. "Everyone did. That's why I'm still alive."

"Jeez, I can't believe it." He shook his head. "Where the hell you been?"

The big limousine moved effortlessly out of the parking area, its engine humming softly. In the plush interior not even the hum could be heard.

"We're going for a little drive," Carl Hansun announced casually. "Can the place do without you for a half hour?"

"Sure, sure. No problem." Solis still couldn't believe it. He kept thinking maybe it was some dumb cop trick. But he recognized the tall, bony figure even after all that time. "How long's it been?" he asked.

"Twenty-one years," replied Hansun. "And five months."

"That long?" It once had been a lifetime to Solis, rotting in prison. But now, sitting next to a friend he once had, it all seemed like just the day before yesterday. "Christ, we must be getting old."

Hansun looked pained. "I'm two years older than you. Don't rub it in."

"When I never heard from you I figured—well, you know."

"I read about it in the papers. Tough break."

"Could've been worse," Solis said quietly. "They had me on death row for a couple years."

"So I heard."

"But I got out okay. Did my time and took my walk."

"Good man," said Hansun smoothly. "And now you're a responsible businessman. Successful too, from what I saw back there."

Solis shrugged. "It does all right for me and Les. Hey you ain't seen my brother yet. Boy! We'll have some party tonight. Just like the old days."

"Some other time," Hansun said quickly. "I'm a little pressed now." He settled back. "How is he anyway?"

"Les? Oh, he's fine. You know Les. Never says much." He wondered why Carl didn't want a get-together. Maybe he was sick. "You okay? I mean, your head and all?"

Hansun tapped his skull. "Never felt better. Got a new steel plate, this one guaranteed for life." He lit a Camel, inhaled. "Still got only one good lung," he said between coughs. "Not allowed to smoke but I sneak one here and there—you know how it is."

Solis studied him a moment. "You look good, Carl. Like somebody important, a big shot or something. It's like you're rich, that's how you look." He grinned. "Are you rich, Carl?"

"I got enough."

"Yeah, but who says what's enough?"

Hansun sighed. "That's always the problem."

"You in the rackets?"

A smile. "Not really. I got a lot of construction up north, went there after L.A. Sunk every nickel in the business and built it big." His voice grew soft. "Now I own it all. Some other things too."

"Must be nice, all that money."

"I got no complaints. Me and the wife, we live pretty good."

"Still the married man."

"Still the same woman. Almost thirty years now." He grunted. "It must be love."

"Must be."

They rode in silence a few minutes. Don Solis wondered what Carl could suddenly want with him after twenty-one years of nothing. The only thing he knew for sure was that it wasn't a social call. And no need to ask how he was found. Carl looked like he could buy anybody or anything, including information.

"You read the papers much?" Hansun asked finally.

"Here and there."

More silence.

"This capital-punishment thing is getting serious."

"It's all talk."

Hansun glanced his way. "I'm talking business now. I'm not talkin' talk."

Solis listened.

"The right politics helps business make money. But it costs a bunch of money to get the right kind and it all comes out of the business. It's like they say, one hand washes the other." Pause. "We got some people in Idaho—the right kind of people—and a couple here in California we want to get elected. They know how business should work. So we help them now and then they help us, and everybody makes money. It's simple."

"Who's we?"

"Business associates. You know."

"And you got some things here too?"

"Upstate mostly."

"What's the angle on capital punishment?"

Hansun grimaced. "All of a sudden it's a big issue in this part of the country. I don't know why but it is. Gonna buy a lot of votes."

"Lose a lot too."

"That's where you can help us, at least in this state."

Solis saw the pitch coming.

"You knew a guy named Caryl Chessman."

"Chessman? Sure, in the joint. But that was a long time ago, twenty years." He rubbed his nose. "Besides, he's dead."

"He's got a big name around here, people remember him. Mostly for the capital-punishment thing."

"So?"

"Some people are using Chessman," Hansun explained patiently, "as the handle to a hot issue. The right people, you see what I mean?"

"Which side they on?"

"The backlash is strong and getting stronger. We think

it'll be a big factor in politics for years. State politics anyway."

"So they want to kill Chessman all over again."

"Better than let him go free."

"He's dead, for chrissake."

"But we ain't."

Another long silence.

"Where do I come in?" Solis asked eventually.

"You knew Chessman, talked to him a couple years."

"So did everybody."

"But he only told you."

"Told me what?"

"He was guilty, what else?"

Solis hooded his eyes. "He never told me nothing like that."

Hansun smiled. "You forgot about it over the years. Never thought of it. But now he's in the papers again and you remember. He told you he did those robberies and rapes and if he ever got out he'd do more."

"I don't get it."

"There's a state senator pushing the death penalty; soon a few congressmen will start. We want to help them all we can." He wet his lips. "They use Chessman to show how capital punishment protects people from dangerous criminals. But some don't believe Chessman was guilty or don't think he should've died. So you come along and say he was guilty and deserved death. You knew Chessman in prison, where men got nothing to do but talk about the past. A lot of people will listen to you."

"The politicians know about this?"

Hansun shook his head. "To them you're legitimate. They won't know until we tell them at the right time."

"It won't work. The newspapers'd check me out right away."

"That's what we're counting on. You were really in with him. Now you're an ex-con small businessman trying to make an honest living. You got nothing to win and everything to lose, but you had to do the right thing anyway. You're perfect for this. You got the credentials and nobody could prove it didn't happen."

"Any guy in the joint at the time could do the job for you."

"Except you got a few things they don't. You're respectable now, and you know how to keep your

mouth shut." Hansun glanced quickly at his friend.
"One more thing, Don."

"What's that?"

"You owe me a big move," he whispered, "and now
I'm calling it in."

"Like that, eh?"

"The business you own came from a check for ten
grand."

"You?"

Hansun nodded.

Solis didn't like it. He just wanted to make a buck
and stay out of trouble. Now he was back in. Even if
they couldn't disprove his story he'd still be in danger
from the bad publicity, from the anti-death fanatics
and Chessman freaks. He'd probably lose the business,
and if they ever found out he was lying he'd lose the
rest of his life too. They'd crucify him right back into
prison.

But he couldn't say no. He owed a debt and it was
being called. Carl and his crowd were playing for big
stakes and a refusal now would mean only one thing.
Someday he'd hear a knock on the door. Or maybe he
wouldn't hear it at all.

"What's in it for me?" he said quietly, defeat in his
voice.

The meeting in Sacramento broke up at 1:30, and
Sheriff Oates felt he had been under a steamroller.
The day was hot and the people angry. Especially the
big shots from the gonernor's office. How could Mungo
escape a dragnet of a hundred thousand police and peace
officers? It was now August 10. How could one man
whose face was known remain free for almost forty days?
Not only remain free but go out and kill again? How in
hell could such a thing happen?

There were no answers. A lot of theories from the
dozen men gathered in a state conference room, but nothing definite. Mungo might be disguised as a woman. He
could've somehow had plastic surgery done secretly. Perhaps he was living with someone who kept him hidden;
that way he needn't go out except to kill. Or maybe he
already had a place well stocked for him before he
escaped; his relatives could've been in on it. The most
bizarre suggestion was that Mungo was dead and his

role taken over by someone else equally insane. Oates rejected this because it seemed obvious that the man who savaged the girl was the same fiend who mutilated the other inmate at Willows, and that man was Mungo.

With no answers, new plans were made. Extra men would scour the Los Angeles neighborhood, knock on every door if necessary. New impetus would be given to publicizing Mungo's description; television stations would be asked to cooperate. A dozen state investigators would be assigned full-time to the case, setting up a central command in Sacramento. Finally, a reward of $50,000 would be offered for information leading to the arrest of Vincent Mungo. Conviction was guaranteed.

On the way back to Forest City the sheriff, now relieved of sole responsibility for the capture, had the uneasy feeling that new plans alone would not be enough. There was something strange about Mungo's ability to disappear and reappear at will. And something positively demonic about his hatred of human bodies. Oates found himself beginning to believe once again in the devils of his youth.

Four days later Amos Finch arose for the second time that morning. Unlike his previous resurrection this one was successful. The strawberry blonde slept on as he showered and dressed. At his mailbox he sorted through the day's bills and brochures until he came to the letter he had been expecting.

In the kitchen of his house near the Berkeley campus of the University of California, he prepared his usual breakfast of orange juice, freshly squeezed, lightly buttered toast and black coffee. As he ate leisurely he glanced over the letter. Sacramento's reply to his inquiry was a polite rejection. They did not think it would be feasible at this time to assign civilians, no matter how experienced, to the Mungo investigation. What they really meant, he well understood, was that they didn't want any nosy professors snooping around. Here it was August 14; they had taken three full weeks to say no. He was disappointed.

He was amused at the authorities' lack of imagination in not realizing they needed help. Without being privy to inside information, he could've already told them a few things. He could tell them, for example, that Vincent Mungo did not kill the young woman in Los Angeles.

In the Willows killing only the face was destroyed,

supposedly by Mungo. In Los Angeles the body apparently was greatly damaged but the face was untouched. If there was no logical motive behind either mutilation, if each was a simple act of rage, or seemed certain, then the conclusion was inescapable. Each had been killed by a different person. Homicidal maniacs operated in set patterns, just like anyone else, and it was incredibly harder for them to break out of their patterns.

Amos Finch was aware of the horror of his conclusion. Somewhere in California was a second maniacal killer, infinitely more dangerous than Vincent Mungo. Faceless, nameless, unknown and even unsuspected, he was driven by a rage so great he destroyed whole bodies. Under the guise of Vincent Mungo he could do anything, go anywhere. Anywhere . . .

EIGHT

On the morning of his wedding day in Las Vegas, Bishop bought a ticket for Phoenix. Toward evening he emerged from the bus station on E. Jefferson. He was not impressed by what he saw or felt. Phoenix was oppressively hot. The late afternoon sun shone on everything within reach, baking man and metal alike. Shade was rare and offered little solace from the stark sunlight. Bishop removed his jacket and rolled up his shirt sleeves; the raincoat bought in San Francisco had been discarded in Vegas, much to his relief now. He was not used to such heat, it stuck to him like a straitjacket. Within minutes his shirt was soaked as sweat ran down his ribs and back. His eyes blurred, his hair suddenly felt matted. Flight bag and zippered money case in hand, jacket under the arm, he trudged down the street, already weary.

His first look at the city reminded him of a miniature Los Angeles, all plastic and glass and steel. Everything that wasn't straight up seemed absolutely flat, flat and squat; endless rows of squat tract houses and little lawns on perfectly even land, all manicured and symmetrical and incredibly, irrevocably flat. Yet the streets were wider, the spaces larger. There was less crowding, less impatience. The tempo seemed a bit slower to him. Slower, too, was his own pace in the blistering summer heat.

In a half hour he had seen enough, or at least as much as he could stand. He ducked into an air-conditioned restaurant on E. Washington and ordered a steak and coffee. When the steak came he ate ravenously. At Willows he had eaten mostly casseroles over the years, and he found himself developing a positive passion for real meat.

The man around the bend in the counter watched him eating. As he pulled his possessions even closer to him, Bishop smiled in his direction. "Kind of hot out there," he said in friendly fashion.

"Ain't the heat," snapped the old man. "It's the damn humidity."

"Is it always like this?" Bishop asked.

"Only in the damn summer." The old man sugared his coffee. "The winters is just hot."

Bishop continued working on his steak. He had eaten nothing since the previous evening in Las Vegas after his return from Death Valley alone. In the morning he had been too busy.

"It's the damn canals."

He looked up to find the old man staring at him.

"It's the damn canals," the man repeated.

"What canals?"

"The damn canals they got all over this town. Right in the streets." He shoveled in more sugar. "The damn sun pulls the water right out and makes everything too humid." He stirred the coffee. "I read that somewhere." Put the cup to his parched lips.

"They got canals in the streets?" Bishop asked in surprise.

"Damn right."

"What's in the canals?"

"The damn water, what else?" He eyed Bishop suspiciously. "Don't you know 'bout the canals?"

Bishop slowly shook his head. "Never saw them."

"They there all the same." He reached for the salt shaker. "Everybody knows 'bout them."

"That's the salt."

"What's that?"

Bishop pointed. "You got the salt there."

"Damn right." He poured salt in the cup. "Too much sugar's no good for you."

Bishop went back to his steak. As he ate he kept thinking about canals filled with water in the streets. It seemed like a good idea to him, certainly better than the dusty streets of Los Angeles. Suddenly he saw himself fall in the canal. He couldn't swim.

"How deep is the water?" he abruptly asked.

The old man looked at him with blank eyes. "What water?"

"The water in the canals in the streets."

His eyes came alive again. "Damn deep," he said vehemently. "So deep nobody knows for sure."

"Why don't they send divers down?"

"They do. Only they never come back. Soon's they go down nobody ever sees them again."

Bishop didn't believe him.

"It's the damn truth, s'help me," said the old man. "Not only that but lots of people drown in them canals, and their bodies never come up either."

"Why don't they drain the canals?"

"Can't." He ordered more coffee.

"Why not?"

The old man took out a cigarette. "The damn water is used for irrigation. This whole town lives on irrigation." He broke off the filter and stuck the tobacco end in his mouth. "If they ever let the water go, this damn town'd die overnight." He lit the broken end. "You ever see a town die overnight?"

Bishop shook his head.

"I seen it once. In New Mexico when I was no older'n a pup. A little place called Los Rios." He took a deep drag on the cigarette. "One night a dust storm hit. Rained dust all night, not just grit but big rocks of dust. Sounded like bombs going off. By morning everything was buried, must've been a hundred foot deep. Killed every living thing in town." Took another drag. "For years they tried to find that damn town." Sugared his coffee again. "Couldn't find it. The whole damn place was dead and buried in one night." Put in the salt. "Never found it again neither. Not so's I know 'bout." Dunked his cigarette in the coffee. "Same thing'd happen here if they ever drained off the damn canals." Stuck it in his mouth. "The banks over on Central Avenue need the water to wash all the dirty money they get. The squatters need the water to flush their damn toilets. And the rest of us need the water to get the electricity to run the damn air-conditioners 'cause the water makes everything so damn humid." He picked up the cup. "Without it we'd all turn to dust by tomorrow. The whole town." He swallowed the coffee, ran his hand across his mouth. "Dust to dust," he said softly. "Dead and gone." He looked into the drained cup.

Bishop shoved his empty plate across the counter. He slowly drank his coffee. After a while he placed the cup on the plate; they seemed to belong together.

"How'd you get out?" he asked finally.

"Get out?"

"From the dust town. You said everybody died and was buried."

The old man gave him a toothless grin. "A giant bird come down and pulled me out just as I was sinking. Carried me far away."

"A giant bird?"

"Big as a house." He chuckled. "Bigger."

Bishop got up. "You better hope he don't come around again."

"Why's that?" asked the old man at his back.

"He might drop you in the canals this time," said Bishop over his shoulder.

Later that evening he checked into a quiet hotel on Van Buren and slept soundly. The next morning he rented a car, again using his Daniel Long identification and disguise. He told the clerk he expected to be in town only a few days on business. In truth, he found little in Phoenix to hold him and he intended to remain just long enough to give them something to remember him by.

Three weeks earlier, on the morning of August 15, certain people were trying desperately to remember him, though they had never met him and knew of him only by one of his many aliases. Derek Lavery officially began the meeting at 9:25, when Adam Kenton finally arrived.

A story on Vincent Mungo was needed, and quickly. One that would demand the death penalty. The snag was that a legitimate angle was also needed. They didn't have one. Not yet anyway. The Chessman piece had been easy;

he was dead, executed. The angle was that he hadn't deserved death. Mungo was a lot harder. What they needed
was not so obvious.

"Then we got it," said Ding suddenly.

"Got what?"

"The angle."

"What is it?" pursued Lavery.

"I don't know."

"You just said—"

"We need what's not obvious. Right?"

Lavery nodded, suspicious now.

"Since it's not obvious to us, that must mean we already
got it." His face beamed angelically, his eyes shone. "Otherwise it would be obvious that we didn't have it."

"That's right," said Kenton. "We have got it, but we
can't use it—"

"Because we don't know what it is," finished Ding.

"If we knew it, we wouldn't need it."

"Obviously."

Both men glanced at Lavery, sputtering incoherently.

Twenty minutes later the most obvious thing in the room
was the grin on the editor's face. He had found his angle.
Something in what Adam Kenton had said at one point:
Everybody assumed Mungo was crazy. But suppose he was
crazy like a fox . . .

Crazy like a fox.

That was their angle. Maybe Vincent Mungo was not
really crazy at all. Maybe he knew exactly what he was
doing. And therefore deserved the death penalty.

He killed the other inmate to get whatever the man had
on him. The girl's murder could have been a sexual thing.
Both bodies were then mutilated to make it seem he was
nuts.

Who was Vincent Mungo anyway? Just another young
man in a hostile world. Angry, resentful. His mother
choked to death, his father committed suicide. He was
brought up by women, he was considered strange. He had
problems, he had fits. So did a lot of people. They didn't
all kill and destroy.

"That's it," said Lavery. "That's the angle we go with.
Assuming it's legit and he's not really nuts. Let's find out."

Kenton was to dig into Mungo's record in the upstate
hospital.

"Willows."

"He was there a few months. I want everything he did up there. Who he talked to, what he ate, where he slept, who his friends were, his enemies, what the guards thought of him, everything you can get."

"What about the other hospitals? His years at home? His people?"

"No." Lavery held out a pointed finger to emphasize his words. "Whatever happened to him happened at Willows. Before that he was just another guy walking around. If he hatched any kind of plan, it was at Willows." He turned to Ding. "I want you to check into other killers who used the insanity laws to get away with murder. See what happened to them, if they got out and what they did afterward. Especially if they killed again. Make them recent if you can. Then we'll pull everything together and match Mungo to it." Back to Kenton. "You look into Mungo."

Kenton nodded. "I just hope he doesn't look into me."

"If he does," said Lavery quickly, "look out." He glanced at the calendar on his desk. "I want it for the September 4 issue. That gives you five days."

"Not much time," Kenton told him.

"We need it running soon as possible. Mungo's been out a month already."

"Six weeks now," said Ding, who always liked to have the last word.

"That's just a long month," said Lavery, who never liked to give it.

Don Solis had taken a week to get his story together. He had spent almost two years on San Quentin's death row. In 1952 he had been whisked up in the elevator to the fifth floor, strip-searched and deposited in a ten-foot by five-foot cell. He had paced that cell a thousand times; three steps one way, six steps the other way. He had been fed twice a day, let out for exercise in front of his cubicle each morning. He had listened to music and the outside world on earphones. Between the pacing and eating, the exercise and music, he had watched men walk to their death. Some walked bravely, others had to be supported or even carried. Almost all wanted to live longer. Just a little bit longer, please. A month, a week, even a day, anything. Anything at all.

He had talked with many of them; there was little else

to do on death row. He had known the good and the bad, the famous and the infamous, the killers and the cripples. He had known Caryl Chessman.

They had talked often, he and Chessman. Talked of the things they did or would like to do, their dreams and fantasies, their hopes and fears. They respected each other and got along well, at least well enough for two men facing death.

Sometimes Chessman talked of his youth and how everything seemed to go wrong. His mother, whom he had loved dearly, was paralyzed in a tragic automobile accident. His father, a weak but kind and gentle man, tried to hold the family together financially. It was impossibly difficult. Chessman began to steal in his earliest teens to help with family expenses. He was soon caught. After that his juvenile record grew until finally he was sent to reform school. As a child he had been considered a musical prodigy but a bout with encephalitis ended the promise of a career in music. Acutely intelligent, embittered by the truly incredible misfortune constantly stalking his parents and himself, the youth isolated himself from society's acceptance and turned to a life of crime.

By age seventeen Chessman was committing armed robberies and shooting from stolen cars at pursuing police. He carried guns, he formed gangs, he sneered and bragged and bullied his way around. He knew it all. But misfortune still dogged him. He was eminently untalented as a criminal. Before he was twenty years old he was imprisoned in San Quentin. The die had been cast. His entire adult life, with minor exception, was spent behind bars. Eventually his young wife, whom he had married in Las Vegas, divorced him. Several years later his mother died of cancer in agonizing pain. Her death was a severe blow to him. She had been abandoned as an infant in St. Joseph, Michigan. Once he had spent thousands of stolen dollars in an attempt to learn, through private detectives, who his mother's real parents had been. He learned nothing. That seemed an apt appraisal of Chessman's life, at least to Don Solis at the time.

On rare occasions the two men would get in a competitive spirit when recalling past deeds. Chessman usually won since he had done many things and was much more vocal. But Solis could always point to the men he had killed in wartime. Chessman had killed nobody. But he had come close a lot of times, he kept insisting.

Solis remembered one time they were talking about women and he told Chessman about the Italian peasant girl he had raped during the war. A bunch of American soldiers had caught her in a barn during a lull in the fighting around Salerno. They kept her in that barn all night taking turns at her. Did everything to her too.

Chessman said that was nothing. He had raped at least a half dozen women in Los Angeles, forcing most of them to give him oral sex which he particularly liked. He was the famous Red Light Bandit who had robbed couples in lonely spots, sometimes taking the women to his car for sex. He never thought any of them would identify him because of shame. When two women did, he decided to bluff his way through. He was smarter than any dumb cop, and he wouldn't give them the satisfaction of knowing they got the right man. Also, his mother was alive at the time and he'd never do anything to bring her grief. Now they could all go to hell. He'd beat the rap yet! He would somehow get out through legal means, and then watch out! He'd pay them all back for the years they'd kept him locked up. When the time came he would rob and rape his way clear across the country. He'd show them, he'd show them all!

That was the story he, Solis, would tell Senator Stoner. Caryl Chessman had admitted he was the Red Light Bandit and had stated that once he got out he would continue his activities. Proof? For one thing, the attacks stopped completely as soon as Chessman was arrested. For another, he was captured in a car that had merchandise from one of the robberies still in the back seat. Then, too, in the police station he confessed to almost all of the robberies and attacks, though he later repudiated the confession. Oh, just one last thing. On that prison day when he admitted his guilt, Chessman bragged that one of the women he had raped told him she liked it but she was cheating on her husband with a mutual friend and he was going to get her in a lot of trouble. Chessman also bragged that a young girl he attacked had a large mole on the small of her back that looked like a flower.

Why was he coming forward after all these years to tell what he knew? Because he was a legitimate businessman now. He lived by the law and recognized his responsibility to tell the truth. He hadn't thought of Chessman for many years and believed that what he knew just didn't matter any longer. Now he saw that he had been wrong, and he wanted to tell the truth to others so that he could go back to his quiet, peaceful life.'

Satisfied with his story, Don Solis, against his better judgment, picked up the receiver in his office and called Stoner in Sacramento. He gave his name and said he would like to speak to the senator about Caryl Chessman. He was told that Stoner was out of town but would return on August 17. Could he call back then? Solis left his number and agreed to call again in two days.

When he cradled the phone his palms were covered with sweat.

Two thousand miles away Jonathan Stoner was having the time of his life. For two days he had been wined and dined by the political bigwigs in Kansas City. He had met and talked with the top men, the bottom men and a half dozen groups in between. He knew they were sizing him up and so he was on his very best behavior. From all the attention accorded him, Stoner could only conclude that they were thinking of backing him nationally. To see how he went over, of course. He already had firm commitments for exposure throughout the Midwest. And he was doing a creditable job of exposure on his own in the western states, though more attention would have to be given to Washington and Idaho. He felt certain that the Southwest would fall in line, especially if he got the backing he now expected.

Stoner was well pleased with himself. He was still youngish, still in good shape. He intended to pay even more attention to his physical appearance and style. He would affect a mod look, but a bit sterner and somewhat westernized of course. If he went national, there was no telling how high he could go. Governor, United States senator. And then?

He smiled at the thought. A boy from the California valley, from the lower middle class. The goddam working class, for chrissake. Harry Golden was right. It could only happen in America.

After a while he stopped daydreaming. There were a lot of problems to solve before dreams came true. In two days he would be home, with much to do and important people to see. A dozen TV shows were waiting for him, innumerable speaking engagements. A lecture tour had been arranged for later in the month. Roger was doing a good job, a terrific job. Now he had to do his job. He had to convince these old bastards that he was a hotshot, a sure winner if they gave him the chance. All it took were the right keys to open the right doors; that's all he needed. Give him the exposure, push him across the country. He'd do the rest. Goddam right he would! He'd smile and shake and kiss and take. Yeah, and if he had to diddle a few, he'd do that too. He had the guts, he had the drive, he had the ambition, the brains, the body, the style, the look. He had it all.

And he had the issue too. Capital punishment was national, a nationwide concern. It was moving across all economic levels but most especially with the moneyed whites. The phony liberalism of the sixties was dying. Too many people were being hurt in the pocketbook, where it counted. Too many were being killed. Things were getting out of control. Maybe the death penalty wasn't the whole answer but it was a damn good start. It was big and getting bigger, and it would take him along with it. By then he'd find other issues of national concern. A man grew as his responsibility grew. Stoner firmly believed that. Look at all the dumb sons of bitches who became near-great presidents. The office made the man. Especially if he was straight to begin with. Stoner was straight.

He suddenly thought of Vincent Mungo. God bless him! Wherever he was, Stoner hoped that he could hold out a while longer.

Meanwhile he had work to do. He called his mistress to tell her he would be back in two days. He called his wife and told her he'd be back in two, maybe three days. Then he put on his best face and went into another meeting.

While the senator was having the time of his life in Kansas City, a woman with saddened eyes was identifying a body in the Sacramento morgue. Cause of death was massive injuries suffered when struck by an automobile; since no one had reported the death to police it was listed as a probable vehicular homicide. The identification was positive. The body was that of Velma Adams, who lived in Los Angeles and owned a beauty parlor there.

She was fifty-four years old and had been traveling alone around the state on vacation.

The woman viewing the body was the manager of the salon. A native Californian, she had known the deceased for seven years. She had reported her employer missing on August 2, already a week overdue. Twelve days later she was notified that a woman answering the description had been the victim of a hit-and-run between Sacramento and Yuba City. A close-cropped photo of the face, taken in the morgue, was shown to her. Would she be willing to go to Sacramento for formal identification?

Afterward she talked to the sheriff's deputies. The dead woman's car was missing, along with her money and clothing. In light of the missing possessions the file on Velma Adams was changed from vehicular homicide to possible murder. A description of the car, a tan Buick hardtop with a "Save the Whales" bumper sticker, and the license plate immediately went out. Since almost six hundred cars were stolen each day in the state, the search might take some time. The manager understood. She would be informed of any developments.

On the way home she thought of the dead woman. They had been good friends but she knew her good friend had not left a will. Which meant she would get nothing and would probably lose her job under new owners. However, she knew a man in Los Angeles who was very good at handwriting. Especially other people's. She would call him as soon as she got back.

That evening a man in San Francisco watching television was suddenly struck by an odd thought. Why hadn't that fellow sent in his proper birth information so his credit file could be corrected? What was his name? Long—Daniel Long, that was it. It's been about a month now. Well, business procedure is sixty days. We'll wait another month, thought the credit clerk, who was really very conscientious about his job. He stuck it in his memory file and promptly forgot it as the movie came on.

The next morning Don Solis again called Stoner's office. The senator was expected back later in the day, if the caller cared to leave a message. Solis replied that he had valuable information concerning Caryl Chessman. No.

He would talk only to Stoner. He was told that the senator planned on being in the office the next day even though it was Saturday. Solis promised to call back then.

George Little was concerned. It had been ten days since he gave a Los Angeles man $25,000 to kill Vincent Mungo. To kill him and cut the body into sections. Little intended to see the sections before handing over the other $25,000. To gloat over them and thereby dispel his grief. He especially wanted to look at the face, to make certain it was Mungo. And to stare into the eyes of the devil himself.

Sitting in his Kansas home, his wife by his side, his other two daughters out on the town, he wondered if he should call the number given him in Los Angeles.

Around midnight Jonathan Stoner was relaxed enough to tell his mistress about his triumph in Kansas City. Much as he liked to brag to her, he left out one interesting detail. During his sojourn he had been introduced to some political favorites, women of beauty and quality who were apparently turned on only by men of enormous political power. They were a new breed to Stoner and they excited him. He already foresaw the day when his mistress would no longer be worthy of his attentions. He was moving up in every way.

For her part, his mistress hoped only that he wouldn't discover the tape-recording equipment she had installed months earlier. She was wise to the ways of men and the world and had no intention of being suddenly dumped by her lover-boy senator, at least not without remuneration. She was twenty-five years old and had to look out for herself.

Her bed was wired to a tape recorder grinding away in a closet. The mechanism was voice-actuated, working only when sounds were made on the bed. It was simple and efficient and very expensive. The equipment and installation had cost over a thousand dollars. She expected to get it back someday with a great deal of interest. Until then she listened with wide-eyed fascination to anything her lover said.

Henry Baylor did not believe in premonitions of course. He was a doctor, a scientist of the mind. Precognition and inner voices were components of the occult, and the occult quite properly had no place in the discipline of science.

Still, as Baylor puttered around his home on Saturday morning, he had a strong feeling that he was not yet out of the woods, so to speak, in the matter of Vincent Mungo's escape from his institution.

What particularly bothered him about his feeling was that he paid any attention to it at all.

The following day was Sunday and Senator Stoner had planned to spend it at home with his wife. But something had come up, something important. He knew she would understand, and he'd certainly be back by evening. His wife, a plain woman and long-suffering, understood even more than he knew.

On the way to his office he thought of the phone call about Chessman. Could the man be legitimate? He would find out, and fast. But if it were true, if Chessman really had admitted his guilt, it would find out, and fast. But if it were true, if Chessman really had admitted his guilt, it would be helpful to the campaign to restore capital punishment. And to his own personal campaign as well. He just hoped the man was telling the story straight.

Starting in Fresno that morning, Don Solis arrived in Sacramento just in time for his meeting with Stoner. He had called back the previous day and told the senator the bare outline. Now he would have to give him the whole chapter. He was ready. He just hoped the senator was in a receptive mood.

On Tuesday morning Amos Finch called John Spanner in Hillside. It was now August 21, and he had thought about it since receiving the rejection note from Sacramento a week earlier. Spanner was the man to see; he had been on the Mungo case from the very beginning, as Finch remembered from the papers of early July. He probably knew more about Mungo than all those idiots in the state capital. At the least, he would be a good start.

Finch still had that feeling about Mungo, that he could become a true mass murderer. But the major interest at the moment was with the elusive shadow behind Mungo, the other killer no one knew about. No one but

Finch. He was sure his theory was right. That there should be two maniacal crank artists running loose at the same time stretched even his imagination. Yet, not having that instinctive police mistrust of all coincidences, he simply attributed it to bad luck. Or good.

The only way he could visualize the other man was as the specter of death. The Grim Reaper, shrouded in mystery, scythe in hand, collecting its victims. Hiding behind one of its own creations lest anyone catch a glimpse of its reality. As long as Mungo remained free the other was safe. Perhaps Mungo was being hidden by the other or protected in some way. Perhaps they even shared the same body in the sense of a wonderfully devious schizoid personality.

Finch was thrilled by the thought but was quickly forced to reject it. The idea of two distinct identities simultaneously being homicidal, both with ungovernable destructive urges toward the body, each with its own area of specification, was beyond even the imagination, let alone logic. There was nothing like it in all the literature of murder. Finch the expert could vouch for that. Such a find, were it ever discovered, would be the coup of the century. Beyond anything known. Beyond even Jekyll and Hyde, which was merely a personality battle between good and evil. But this! A battle for supremacy on the most elemental level in man's makeup: murder. The thought was staggering, and Finch reluctantly dismissed it from consideration or even hope.

As he waited for Spanner on the phone Amos Finch sought a name for his monster. He intended to include him in his next course at Berkeley and to write about him as well. But he had to learn much more about the Grim Reaper. The name came easily, in seconds. Where he was, what he did: the California Creeper.

Finch wondered what John Spanner would say about his monster.

On August 22 a call was made from Kansas to Los Angeles. The man who answered said that Vincent Mungo had not yet been found. He indicated that the target might have left town.

That same afternoon someone in Los Angeles called New York. Derek Lavery reported that the Mungo story was ready to go. New York was pleased. He told them the story came out strong for legal execution. They were delighted. It would help to offset the unfavorable image Senator Stoner was giving them with the Chessman issue.

Afterward he read the rough draft again. Ding had done well on finding killers who had escaped death through an insanity defense, some of whom had been eventually released only to kill again. Included was the horror tale of Jed Smith of Oregon who killed half his family in a murderous rage and vowed in court to kill the other half. After five years he was released from a state mental hospital. Three days later he killed the rest of his family.

Ding ended his section with the calm observation that Charles Manson would be eligible for parole in five years. In 1978.

For the main body of the story Adam Kenton had combed through Vincent Mungo's brief record at Willows. There wasn't much.

Mungo had apparently become increasingly violent, more resentful, more afraid. No one seemed surprised that he had finally killed. A staff doctor believed that the mutilation of the face meant he hated his father. The man had deserted the boy of sixteen, committing suicide, which was the ultimate weakness. The boy had to become strong, had to have power over others, the ultimate power of life and death. In killing his only friend Thomas Bishop he was killing his father symbolically. Hence the facial destruction.

What about the murdered woman in Los Angeles?

He probably hated his mother too. She deserted him, died, when he was even younger.

But the face was left untouched.

Men who kill women in maniacal rage seldom harm the face. They destroy the body. It's eminently sexual of course. An aberration.

Thomas Bishop was Mungo's only friend at Willows; he stuck to Bishop like glue. No doubt planned all along to kill him at the right time. The poor sap. Probably looked like Mungo's father.

Only two things in the article surprised Lavery. Vincent Mungo had told a doctor at Willows that he and the devil were blood brothers and would be together forever. This was just days before his escape and was, at the least, an odd choice of words. He then asked the doctor if he knew how to play chess.

The other surprise was Mungo's place of birth; it was not Stockton, where he had lived all his life, but Los Angeles. And his parents got married a year after he was born in October 1948.

Lavery made a few deletions and indicated areas for clarification and sent the manuscript back to the fourth floor. He was satisfied. New York was waiting, eager to run the story in the next issue.

Senator Stoner was getting used to television. He had made a half dozen appearances in the past three weeks. Now he was on again, this time in San Francisco: a half-hour news special about capital punishment. He wore the prescribed blue shirt and light suit and slim tie. He stood still for the makeup and loop cord. Then he spoke forcefully and with genuine emotion about the problem of crime control and restoration of the death penalty. He denounced Caryl Chessman and Vincent Mungo as terrorists, no different from the self-styled revolutionaries who terrorize whole cities. They had to be stopped, he insisted, before society was thrown into chaos.

"Crime is too important to be left to the police," he declared passionately. Beyond a certain point it became a job for the politicians, who must revise laws in accordance with the will of the people. And it was their will that monsters like Mungo must die. Politicians ignored that will at their own peril. He did not intend to ignore it, and he hoped that the people would continue to support him. He would do his job no matter what. He was herewith serving notice on the criminals.

"If survival comes down to them or us, by God," he thundered, "it's going to be us."

At the end of his portion of the program Stoner quietly announced that he had incontestable proof of Caryl Chessman's guilt for those who still regarded him as a victim or hero. He didn't mention *Newstime*, not wanting to give it any further publicity.

After the show he told reporters of Chessman's admission of guilt to Don Solis. He knew the story would make all the media. It would confuse the enemy camp and demoralize the Chessman old guard. Best of all, it would keep the issue alive and Stoner's name in print.

The next morning all the major newspapers carried items about the senator's startling revelation concerning Caryl Chessman. Newsmen talked to Solis at a 10:30 conference in Stoner's Sacramento office. Solis filled in the details. He seemed hesitant and unsure of himself in the glare of publicity but generally told his story as planned. As he spoke he began to visualize the talks he had with Chessman all those years ago. He remembered one time Chessman had said he was the Red Light Bandit and he talked about some of the women and how he was going to beat the rap and what he'd do when he got out. As Solis remembered these things he came to see them happening in his mind's eye, and he himself began to believe as he heard Chessman once again tell him about the girl he got in the back seat of the car and how he forced her to lie down on the seat on her stomach . . .

It was obvious to the senator and his press secretary that the story would be good for days, perhaps as much as a week with any luck. Now, if only Mungo could keep the ball rolling!

Carl Hansun was pleased. On August 29 he read in the Idaho papers about Stoner's newest headline-grabber in his capital-punishment and personal publicity campaign. That evening he watched excerpts from the interview with Don Solis on the TV news. Between the two he made and received a number of phone calls.

The idea had been a good one and was worth the added $10,000 Solis would cost. The senator was their kind of man, a businessman. So were the others. Anything spent to help them get reelected the following year would be returned with considerable interest.

Hansun just hoped his friend didn't get too cute with his story. If anything went wrong Solis would have to take all the blame himself. He'd know better than to trace it back to Idaho.

On the last day of August a tan Buick hardtop with a "Save the Whales" bumper sticker was spotted in the sprawling parking lot at San Francisco International airport. The license plates matched those of the car belonging to Velma Adams of Los Angeles, slain six weeks earlier. In the trunk police found the woman's pocketbook and clothing. Examination revealed no bloodstains in the car's interior. A fingerprint check failed to turn up any suspects. The Buick was towed away and a report filed with the Los Angeles police.

September 1 was a Saturday, and Amos Finch drove north out of San Francisco toward Hillside and John Spanner. The weather was warm, the air clear. Traffic was heavy at times on this Labor Day weekend, and Finch finally arrived in Hillside at 1 P.M. He was an hour late, much to his annoyance.

He found Spanner waiting for him at home. The lieutenant seemed unruffled and immensely affable. Finch liked him immediately, even more so after learning that he had read *The Complete Mass Murderer's Manual*. The two men soon discovered they shared a passion for finely prepared fish as well as aberrant criminal behavior, and they spent a mutually delightful several hours discussing both.

Spanner had never married, much to his regret at times. When confronted by male friends he would simply say he never found the right one. But it was more than that of course. He had a solitary quality about him that made women uneasy, at least those who might have had designs on him. He enjoyed being by himself and didn't seem to need the constant companionship of others. His fishing and his work occupied most of his waking hours, and whenever he felt the need of a woman he afterward soon again felt a desire for solitude. It was a pattern that had held through most of his adult life. As he grew older he found the need for women lessening. But he was still sometimes dismayed that no one cared especially for him. At these times he believed himself too selfish, and the thought bothered him even more than the loneliness.

Now, however, he had no such thoughts as he listened to Amos Finch describe his theory of a second homicidal maniac. He was impressed by Finch's knowledge of the psychopathic mind, a knowledge certainly deeper than his, though sadly lacking in practical experience. For example, Finch seemed blissfully unaware of the statistical rarity of the coincidence he was suggesting.

Two killers were just too much. Then, too, he accepted without proof the idea that both mutilations were committed with no reasonable motive.

This Spanner refused to grant without further evidence. The mutilation of the face might have been done to prevent identification, the destruction of the girl's body to suggest insanity instead of deliberate murder by someone known to her, perhaps a relative or lover. There were other possibilities. Maybe only one of the killings was an act of rage. Spanner still held a suspicion that something strange had occurred at Willows in the early morning hours of July 4, still had a feeling that Vincent Mungo might have been the victim of a diabolical plot. But he didn't know what or how or even by whom. The body had been Bishop's right down to the scar. He felt he had exhausted all possibilities of investigation.

When Finch had said over the phone that Mungo did not kill the Los Angeles girl, Spanner's ears had opened. They were still open but his eyes were seeing something different.

He told Finch about Mungo's sadism. As a youngster he had poured kerosene on cats and set them afire. In a house a few miles from Willows, Mungo had found fresh clothes on the night of his escape. He probably also had taken the kerosene with which he later burned his hospital uniform. In that house were four cats. With kerosene in hand he let them alone. Perhaps he was just in a hurry. But in Los Angeles the killer was in no hurry; he could easily have butchered the cat as well as the girl. Instead he apparently fed the cat.

Another oddity was Thomas Bishop's missing jacket. Assuming he took it with him that night because of the heavy rain, where was it? Why would he have given it to Mungo before he was killed? If it had been taken from him afterward, it would've been soaked with blood. The first blow must have been struck suddenly, without warning, so Mungo couldn't have demanded it from Bishop under threat. They were friends until the axe fell.

Finch recognized the problem of inconsistencies, especially in aberrant behavior. Loose ends, things left unanswered, riddles unsolved. But he regarded these as minor compared to his theory of two killers. It covered, in his opinion, all the known facts.

At the end the conclusions were several. There were

two killers of similar purpose, or Mungo had killed Bishop and destroyed the face for unknown reasons. Or someone, Spanner suggested mysteriously, had devised an incredibly complex and brilliant scheme.

After an excellent fish dinner the two men promised to keep in touch and work together should new thoughts arise. Both reluctantly agreed that the next move was up to the killer, or killers.

By Labor Day the September 4 issue of *Newstime* had been on the stands for several days. Sales were good, well above average. The cover was a real shocker, with the composite picture of Mungo and the murdered girl's disemboweled body. The photo of the body had been bought from someone in the medical examiner's office and handed personally to Derek Lavery for a goodly sum of money. It was worth the cost.

Sheriff Oates read the story over the weekend. It confirmed his growing suspicion that Vincent Mungo was somehow much smarter than all the doctors who had examined him, otherwise he could never have lasted this long.

Senator Stoner also saw a copy over the weekend. He immediately began fuming. He wanted a target to flail against, as long as he held the upper hand. Now *Newstime* had stolen some of his steam by demanding death for Vincent Mungo. But to come down hard on them he would have to appear soft on Mungo. That was out of the question.

He decided to do nothing for the moment, hoping the source of the idea would be obvious to all. Having no confidence in the public's intelligence, he doubted it.

Sometime late on the evening of September 6 Bishop found what he had been seeking in Phoenix, Arizona. His two days in town had seemed like two years. The city was still an oven. He had bought a map and driven to all the local points of interest, filling a day. At night he cruised the E. McDowell area of topless bars and prostitutes but nothing appealed to him and he soon returned to the hotel room. It was air-conditioned.

His second day was spent driving in the surrounding desert. The land had barren beauty that intrigued him, it was somehow different from the deserts of Nevada and

California. He stopped often along the deserted roads to take a mental stretch. After a lifetime at Willows, unlimited space made him feel a bit claustrophobic. Darkness engulfed everything by the time he got back to Phoenix. He ate a quiet dinner before continuing his search.

It was late and she was temporarily inactive but he looked like such an easy mark. She was sure she could get him in and out fast.

In her apartment, to which they had come unseen, he told her what he wanted. Right there in the living room, with all his clothes on.

She had guessed it. A real fast mark! "Sure, honey," she said in her sexiest drawl, "I'm always ready to put my love where my mouth is." She smiled sweetly, her eyelids fluttering. "Just as soon as you put your money where yours is."

He took out two twenties.

"But not in here," she said, taking them out of his hand. She indicated a closed door. "I got somebody sleeping over." He looked startled. "Don't worry," she whispered, "it's just my kid. He's with me for a couple weeks' vacation." She pulled his hand. "He's only five," she added as an afterthought.

Bishop's eyes shrank to pinpoints as he was led into another room. He was furious. A woman who left her boy alone while she went out looking for men! Who kept the boy with her while she took strange men into her bed! He could hardly believe that anyone would be so vicious, so inhuman. He thought of his own mother. She had been a saint. And so good to him. He had loved his mother dearly.

His eyes followed the woman as she got a pillow from the bed. She was evil, he told himself. She was an evil demon and he was glad he had met her for he knew how to handle evil demons. Yes, he most certainly did.

She placed the pillow on the floor and knelt in front of him. As she opened his zipper he pulled out his long knife from the jacket pocket. He whispered to her and she raised her head, her mouth open. With one swift stroke he cut her throat, almost severing the head from the trunk. He jumped back to escape the squirting blood as she sank to the floor, her eyes already dulled.

Inserting the long blade in her vagina, he slit upward to

the navel. Cutting the flesh back, he lunged savagely with the knife at the sexual parts again and again. Finally exhausted, he deftly cut out the belly button with the razor-sharp edge and wrapped it in a handkerchief from his pocket.

Before leaving the room, his shoes and knife wiped clean of blood on the bedspread, Bishop cut a letter C with the point of the blade in each breast. This one was for his father, he reminded himself with grim satisfaction.

He wanted people to know of his father, to read of him again. But he realized he had to go about it in a mysterious manner lest they get too close to his true identity. A letter would be sent before he left Phoenix. He would slowly lead them to his father, always making sure he was far enough ahead of them in time and space.

Back at his hotel Bishop slept for a few hours. In the early morning he returned the car and bought a bus ticket to El Paso. The girl's body would surely be found that day; by then he would be far away.

In the station he glanced over the newsstand and saw Vincent Mungo staring back at him from one of the magazines. Bishop paid his money and sat in a corner, his face buried in the story. It made no sense. Why didn't they write the truth? It was the women who destroyed in murderous detail, seeking revenge and release. Women were a different species from another planet, a devil universe, and he was a warrior in an endless space war between good and evil. Why couldn't they see that?

For a long time he sat quietly, the black money case on his lap, the flight bag by his side. Behind his eyes he saw his friend Vincent Mungo lying dead in the rain. Sometimes the innocent were slaughtered along with the guilty. He hoped he wouldn't have to slaughter too many of the innocent. But he must vanquish the enemy regardless of consequences. He was the demon hunter, and he was very good at what he did.

On the bus he turned again to the copy of *Newstime*. Leafing through it, he came to a brief article naming Caryl Chessman and his eyes rounded with interest. It was about California politics and capital punishment as well as Chessman.

As the big bus raced for the Texas border on the morning of September 7, 1973, Thomas Bishop settled back and slowly read how his father had allegedly admitted attacking women to a convict named Solis who was being used by a senator named Stoner to advance capital punishment and himself.

The mutilated body of Janice Hill was discovered by her five-year-old son, who awakened that morning at 8:30 and went into his mother's bedroom. Phoenix police found the woman's breasts placed neatly between her feet. On each breast was a letter C, obvious knife cuts. Her sexual parts had been hacked to pieces. The belly button was missing.

A call was quickly made to Los Angeles police, who in turn notified Sacramento. Vincent Mungo had apparently struck again, this time in Arizona. The trail was widening. And so would the net.

The official reaction to the latest outrage was swift. By that afternoon Arizona police were searching everywhere, photos of Mungo in hand. The FBI jumped in, promising to provide more than laboratory assistance and out-of-state checks. Sacramento offered full cooperation from its investigative team, and sent Sheriff James Oates to Phoenix to fill them in on what was known of Mungo. Unofficially the reaction in California was one of relief; Mungo was no longer just their problem.

No one understood the terrible significance of the carvings on the breasts. None could even guess at the meaning, except for the obvious obscenities. But there was virtually no doubt as to whose devilish work it had been.

The evening news gave the details of the new atrocity to all of California. At Willows, Henry Baylor was dismayed, dreading what it could mean to his position. He roundly cursed the incompetent police, the inefficient Dr. Lang, and his own incredible bad luck. It was a display of emotion he seldom allowed himself.

In Sacramento, Jonathan Stoner was overjoyed. Mungo was going big. With him he carried the imprint of the senator from California.

In Berkeley, Amos Finch again called John Spanner. They readily agreed that the madman was after women and that the Willows killing was either a fluke or something much more sinister. Finch intended to give

Spanner's ideas more thought, though he said nothing over the phone.

In Los Angeles, Derek Lavery congratulated himself for a coup of perfect timing. Mungo was the day's rage and his picture was on the cover of *Newstime*.

In San Diego, a Los Angeles man in town for a few days called Phoenix and asked if the mob there could reach out for Vincent Mungo. There was a contract on him.

And in Kansas, George Little felt sorrow for the dead woman's parents. He knew what they were going through.

By the following morning Sheriff Oates had given the Phoenix authorities all the information he had on Vincent Mungo. The city was combed from end to end. Nothing turned up: no killer, no clues. Someone said that if Mungo was still in town he'd have to be invisible. Oates blanched—it was happening all over again. He almost told them they were looking for the devil himself.

Over a twenty-four-hour period Arizona was searched by thousands of men, all to no avail. Mungo was nowhere. He had slipped through once again. Or flown over or swum under. There was one other possibility. Maybe he just vanished in a puff of smoke.

NINE

The letter to the Editor arrived in Los Angeles on the morning of September 10. It had been mailed the previous Friday in Phoenix. The woman who opened the letter in the *Newstime* building had other things on her mind as she turned to her co-worker. "So then I told my son he was wrong and he should . . ."

She stopped, the color draining from her face. Her mouth sprang wide, her hands began to shake. After a moment she called to her friend who was starting to turn toward her. She called out again, very softly. The cheery grandmother left her own desk and came over to the woman's side.

"Really, Thelma, I wish you wouldn't do that. You always stop in the middle of a story just when it's getting good."

Thelma did not hear a word she said. Her eyes were on the object removed from the envelope. It was a human navel. She had spread the tissue open and there it was. With a slip of paper underneath.

She gingerly fingered the paper free of the tissue and unfolded it. Both women stared at the two words: Another one.

At the bottom was a third word.

A signature.

Manson.

Ten minutes later the envelope and its grisly contents rested on Derek Lavery's huge oak desk.

"Interesting," said Ding finally, breaking the room's unearthly silence.

Lavery stared at him, not knowing whether to laugh or shout.

"I got a goddam belly button on my desk just lying there, unattached to anything, and all you can say is *interesting!*"

He sounded personally offended.

"Not the navel, that obviously belongs to the Phoenix woman." Ding sighed. "The note. That's what interesting."

"Tell me about the note," said Lavery.

"What's to tell? It either means he's killed before and this was another one or this was his first and another one is coming up. If he's killed before, it could be Mungo. The M.O. sounds the same."

"But is it Mungo?"

"The note says Manson."

Lavery looked pained. "Charles Manson is behind bars where he belongs."

"A follower, then. He had them, you know. Crazies with nothing to lose. Outcasts with paranoid fantasies. They could easily do something like this."

"But did they?"

"I don't know," Ding said weakly. "They could have."

Lavery gave a disgusted snort. "That's all you can say, for chrissake? A journalist—"

"Reporter."

"—like you, and all you can say is you don't know? You remember Manson, you wrote enough about him. What's that you called him? A nobody who wanted everybody to know what he was. I liked that one. And what was the other? A cunt cultist with delusions of adequacy. That was good too. You had the punk down cold." His voice turned to stone. "But now you can't answer a simple question about the little bastard." Paused for effort. "C'mon, try. Does this feel like his kind of thing?"

Ding hated to think when he was being pressured.

"Does it?"

"No, I don't think this was a cult killing," he said finally. "It seems spontaneous and random, but—"

"Manson's were spontaneous and random."

"That's the point. They really went in just to kill. But here the kill seems almost incidental to wrecking the body. That makes it different."

"What about Manson's name on the note?"

Ding frowned. "It means something but I don't know what."

"So we're back to Mungo."

"Not necessarily. Could be somebody else taking up the sport."

Lavery blinked in surprise. "You mean a second maniac?"

"It's happened before."

The editor thought of the possibilities for circulation. Wow!

Ding pointed to the desk top. "First you better call the cops," he said softly. "That thing's been there long enough already."

The evening news reported the existence of a note indicating that the murder of a Phoenix woman had been the work of followers of Charles Manson. A Los Angeles police spokesman called the note genuine. The morning headlines loudly announced that Manson was once again in the news, and the papers printed the contents of the note. Dozens of people throughout the state renewed their secret vows to kill the son of a bitch should he ever set foot outside a prison.

* * *

Amos Finch didn't believe it for a minute. He had accepted the existence of two killers when each seemingly presented a different psychological *modus operandi*. He had himself postulated the theory. *Naturellement!* But to suggest that two or more crank artists were operating separately with the *same* hideous passion for destruction of the body was utter nonsense. The police were fools. Consummate asses! As always, they saw only the obvious, the straight line, the simple point. They had absolutely no sensitivity for the nuances of human conduct, the immense subtleties of any interaction. Give them another hound to chase after, and they would miss the fox every time.

He could think of a half dozen interpretations of the signatory word, including the obvious one of misleading the authorities. Why the killer should want such misdirection could only be guessed at for the moment. Then, too, it could be a misspelling of "mansion," the main house, which might have significance for the killer. Or a corruption of the Old French *masson,* a master builder who works with stone; in this case, headstones, as in a cemetery. Or "manson" could simply mean son of man, with all that implies. There were many possibilities.

The only impossibility was the idiotic belief that one or more youthful thrill seekers committed these incomparably artistic murders. Finch knew better. There was a thread of majestic insanity running through them, weaving them into a mosaic of absolute logic and invincible order. True mass murderers were always loners, always working out of their own mathematical rectitude. Whether this one was the California Creeper or the Willows maniac, or whether the two were really one remained to be seen. But that only one of them was now operating was a certainty. *Sans doute.*

Amos Finch waited with undisguised anticipation for the next murder. That there would be more was also, in his mind, without doubt.

John Spanner, for other reasons, arrived at much the same conclusion. A lifetime of police work had taught him to mistrust all coincidence. The maniacal slaughter had started at Willows and had continued in Los Angeles and now in Phoenix. And God knows how many others not yet discovered! In all the known killings the M.O. was basically the same, and the method of operation was the one thing Spanner had learned to trust. People usually didn't change their ways of doing things; each person operated out of a particular view of the world, and his actions came out of that view.

Why Mungo, if it was Mungo doing the killing, should suddenly start writing cryptic notes was unclear. But why not? Maybe he wrote one for Los Angeles but it was lost or went unrecognized. Maybe that was part of his pattern. If so, there would be a note the next time too.

John Spanner also was sure that there would be a next time.

Sheriff Oates called Spanner on Tuesday from Forest City but he was out for the day. Oates wanted to ask him if he had figured out what kind of disguise Mungo used that enabled him to escape detection. Oates didn't really believe the man was a devil. But he also didn't believe Mungo was himself any longer. Who the hell was he now?

Senator Stoner was angry. He took time out from his lecture tour to publicly ridicule the police theory that Charles Manson's followers were behind the horrible murders. It was Vincent Mungo and no one else, as any fool could see. Stoner was no fool. He saw that he had cast his lot with Mungo the maniac, and he wasn't about to cast off in another direction now.

On Thursday Sheriff Oates called on Lieutenant Spanner for a friendly chat. They talked mostly about their problem. Spanner reminded the sheriff that in his case it was purely academic since he no longer had any responsibility in the matter. Oates nodded glumly; he was still officially involved.

"But if he keeps moving on," said the sheriff, brightening, "my troubles'll be over."

"Still think it's our friend?"

"What do you think, John?"

The lieutenant was annoyed for a moment but shrugged it off and smiled. "It's the Willows killer you're looking for. He did them all."

"Mungo!"

The word was spat out, like a curse.

Spanner said nothing. He had once mentioned his idea

of what happened at Willows on that rainy July night. He didn't intend to be laughed at again.

"Why he'd cut them like that is beyond me. What's he get out of it?"

"He hates women."

"The sap at Willows was a man." Oates grumped in his throat. "Maybe when he kills men he destroys the face and with women it's the body." Grumped again. "Can't trust these nuts to do anything logical."

Spanner sat there stunned. He had never thought of that. Of course! The male face and the female body. The power that could hurt him and the temptation that could defeat him.

After Oates left, Spanner sat quietly in his office and thought back to his first meeting with Dr. Baylor the morning of the murder and escape. What was it Baylor had said? For many patients the face was the focal point of all their rage. It was the face that lied to them and laughed at them. And at a place like Willows all the faces were—male.

Jesus, Spanner kept repeating to himself. Maybe he really was getting too old for the job.

On the day after Sheriff Oates' visit to Hillside, Bishop was winding up a week in El Paso. He liked the town, liked its warmth and color, its open spaces, its two cultures. He promised to return, knowing he would never be able to keep the promise. A wanderer, he had no home and no roots. All he had was his work, and for that he had to be always on the move.

In quiet moments he found himself asking why he was chosen for such an impossibly lonely life. But he knew the answer. He was his father's son, the only son of his father, Caryl Chessman, who commanded him, and so he had to go about his father's business. In secret and in silence. The enemy was everywhere and he was so small and helpless.

Perhaps if his mother were alive. But she deserted him, left him alone. His father too. They both left him alone. He needed them and they had left him all alone.

He loved his mother dearly. She was dead.

Sometimes he would look at the picture of his mother that he carried in his new wallet. She was a very tall, thin woman with brown hair and perfectly even teeth.

She wore a severe dress that made her seem matronly. Occasionally he showed the picture to others, a girl perhaps or someone in a bar. He was very proud of her, she looked just like a mother should look.

He was proud of his father too, and wanted everyone to know about him. And about his son. But he had to be careful.

Before leaving Willows he had removed the two pictures of himself from his file in the administration building. He was friends with the clerk and often brought him pieces of fruit. One day the clerk went to the men's room; it took him only a minute to find the folder. Afterward he destroyed the two photographs, burned them.

He was not only unknown and unsuspected but unphotographed, at least as he really looked. The man with no face.

And no fingerprints.

He was the perfect killing machine.

Now on his last day in El Paso, Bishop wrote another letter, this one to Senator Stoner, whom he had read about and seen on television. Stoner was an authority figure. He was stern and strong, and he had great power. He could make people do things. He could command and people would obey.

The letter began: "My Master . . ."

On that same day another note arrived at the *Newstime* building, postmarked Lordsburg, New Mexico. This time the message was a bit more explicit. Derek Lavery read it over again: More to come.

He stared at the signature.

Son of Man.

At his side Adam Kenton frowned. Something was shadowed in the back of his mind, something having to do with the signature, but he couldn't pull it out. Not at the moment anyway.

Obviously Manson and Son of Man meant the same thing.

But what?

By early afternoon the airwaves crackled with the news of another letter that seemed to indicate Manson followers were involved in the sensational murders of young women. Everyone remembered Manson and now here was the Son of Man, whoever he was, carrying on the slaughter even more fearfully than his predecessor or leader.

It hit him suddenly, without warning, later in the day.

"My God!" he yelled at the top of his voice.

Of course. That was it!

Manson. Son of Man.

Chessman.

Son of Chess-man.

Now he knew who the killer was and why he was sending the letters to the magazine.

He even knew why the women were being slaughtered.

Kenton speared the phone to ring upstairs.

With the sudden flurry of interest in Charles Manson and his followers since receipt of the first note at the beginning of the week, news of Vincent Mungo was temporarily shunted aside as the media capitalized on the notoriety of the Manson name.

It was only momentary of course, for Mungo was soon back in the headlines as the true significance of the notes became horrifyingly evident.

"Let me get this straight. You say he sent the notes here because of the *Chessman* story?"

"Of course," said Kenton. "Caryl Chessman's the key to the whole thing."

"Why Chessman, for chrissake? What's he got to do with it?"

"Don't you get it? Mungo believes Chessman is his father. Think of the signatures. Man-son. Son of Man. Son of *Chess*-man." Kenton gulped air. "When Mungo read the Chessman story he sent us a letter saying he was Chessman's son. We thought it was just another crank." He looked at Ding ruefully. "What else could we think?" Back to Lavery. "But now look at the letter. It says women are bad, not capital punishment. Women! And it says Chessman knew that."

Lavery studied the sheet of paper in his hand. He wished he had seen it earlier. Maybe he would've caught the link right away.

"You think it's Mungo?"

"He killed up at Willows when he escaped. Then the real

killing started." Kenton shook his head. "It's Mungo all right. You can bet on it."

"So what've we got?"

"We got one helluva story is what we got. Mungo is Chessman's son somehow. Or at least he thinks he is. He kills women because they're bad, or at least he thinks they are."

Lavery glanced again at the letter. "Why'd he address it *From Hell*, on the top like that? What's it mean?"

"Maybe his life *was* hell being Chessman's kid," Ding blurted out.

"He *ain't* Chessman's kid."

"He *thinks* he is. That's the same thing."

Nobody spoke for a long moment.

Then: "Maybe he *is* Caryl Chessman's son." It was Kenton.

Lavery eyed him as though he were nuts.

"What do we really know about Mungo? Mother dead, father dead. In and out of hospitals a dozen times. A grandmother and some aunts in Stockton—all women. But when we did the story we found out he was born right here in L.A. And his parents didn't marry until a year later. Why?"

"You might have something." Ding's instincts were working now. "Nobody ever checked that angle. Who knows what happened twenty-five years ago? Maybe—"

He stopped.

Kenton's mouth was open, as if he were seeing a ghost.

"What is it?"

"You said twenty-five years ago."

"What about it?"

The voice was a whisper, as though coming from the grave. "Twenty-five years ago in L.A. Caryl Chessman was—"

"Jesus Christ!"

The three men looked at one another in silence. If they lived to be a hundred, none of them would forget the electricity of this moment.

"Jesus Christ," Lavery repeated, wetting his lips.

Bishop awoke in darkness. Oftentimes late at night he would wake up in a cold sweat, his eyes closed, seeing the woman standing over the frightened boy. In her hand the great whip rose and fell endlessly, cutting deeper into the boy's frail body. Now it told him that his time was at hand. He had spent a pleasant week scouting the city, seeing what he had to see. Now the time had come to do what he had to do.

He dressed in the dark, slowly. Only the bathroom light was clicked on, to check the money's hiding place once more. His jacket went on last, hiding the long knife. Outside, his shadow loomed large across the desolate land under the late night sky.

When he finally returned, two more women had been added to his growing list of victims. One of them was a Mexican national from nearby Juarez. She was well known to border guards. The other was a young El Paso woman he had found someplace along Alameda. She was alone and he was alone and there was talk of an exchange. Now she would be alone forever.

The next day, a Saturday, he left for San Antonio on the early bus, money and flight bag in hand.

It was September 15, 1973.

He left behind two female bodies that were literally shredded. Only the faces and feet were untouched. In each mouth was stuffed a page of the magazine story on Caryl Chessman.

The bodies were discovered late Saturday night. Local police had never seen anything like it. They first suspected the carnage was the work of some wild beast. When it was finally tied to the Mungo killings, they felt that a monster had been in their midst.

In subsequent years the crime became known in Texas police annals as the El Paso Massacre, and local people still talk in whispered words of that fearful mid-September eve.

On that same Saturday that saw Bishop speed to San Antonio, police were again at the home of Vincent Mungo's maternal grandmother in Stockton, California. The previous evening, after hearing new evidence presented by the Los Angeles bureau chief of *Newstime*, sheriff's deputies once more interviewed the relatives. They were told that Mungo had been born in Los Angeles because his mother lived there at the time. For how long? About two years.

During that time she met and eventually married the boy's father. They hadn't married right away because he, the father, insisted on first saving enough money. Even though the woman was pregnant? Yes. They finally married about a year after the birth. When she first arrived there? Yes. So they knew each other for two years before they married, is that right? Yes. And a year before Mungo was born? Yes.

"Let's see, that would make it mid-1947."

"Vincent was born in October 1948, so that would be about right."

"She knew the father since 1947 but didn't marry him until 1949."

"Yes."

"Why?"

"I told you, he wanted to save enough money."

"For what?"

"For them to get married."

Between Friday night and Saturday noon police checked with the father's close relatives in the East. Apparently he hadn't gone to California until April of 1949; before that he had never been west of Chicago. Soon after his arrival in Los Angeles he met and married Mungo's mother, in August of that year. She told him she was widowed, her husband killed in the war.

Now police were back in the house, and leading them was Sheriff James T. Oates. He had once again been put in charge of the investigation. Since Vincent Mungo had left the state and therefore the jurisdiction of California, the special task force had been disbanded by the governor's office, except for liaison work with the other states.

Oates was in no mood for gray-haired old ladies. Or for lies. He told the women point-blank that they had been lying, and he demanded the truth. Mungo's mother had met her husband in 1949 and married him some months later, when the boy was already almost a year old. Since he couldn't have been the father, who was?

The grandmother began to cry.

"Who was the father?"

Her cries became louder.

Oates was exasperated.

"Who was the father?" he shouted over her sobs.

One of the aunts shifted her eyes away. "We never knew," she said softly.

The grandmother looked at her helplessly.

"Vincent's mother was attacked about six months after she went to live in Los Angeles. In January 1948. She became pregnant. The baby was born in October."

"Did they catch the man?"

"No."

"Ever find out who he was?"

"No."

Oates thought fast. The dates matched. Chessman was free for most of January 1948 and doing his rapes and robberies. He wasn't caught until the last week.

"Was Mungo ever told about it?"

The aunt looked at him as though he were crazy. "Of course not."

"Could he have found out, maybe from a nosy neighbor?"

"Nobody knew but the three of us. Naturally we never told anyone."

"How about the mother?"

"She'd be the last to ever say anything."

"She told no one?"

"No one."

"Not even her husband?"

The aunt turned ashen, she found it hard to speak.

Oates pounced. "She told him."

The grandmother shrieked in sorrow.

Her daughter nodded. "Years later," she whispered. "She became angry at him one night and told him she'd never been married."

"Why didn't she tell him the truth right away?"

"She was ashamed." The aunt smiled grimly. "You know how men look at a thing like that. They always think a raped woman asked for it."

Oates let that pass. He believed it himself, at least most of the time.

He had only one more question.

"Would the husband have mentioned it to the boy at any time? Was he like that?"

The other spinster sister snorted her disapproval of the dead man.

The grandmother stared with vacant eyes.

"He could have," said the aunt finally. "Yes, he could have. He—changed later on."

Oates thanked them. At the front door he turned, smiled warmly. "By the way," he said disarmingly, "did the mother ever think the man could've been Caryl Chessman?"

Not that any of them knew about. The aunts remembered reading of Chessman years before, but his name never came up in connection with their sister.

Outside, Oates grinned in satisfaction. The pieces were all coming together at last. Mungo's stepfather, probably bitter at the mother, had told him he was the offspring of a rape. He had no real father. Somewhere along the way Mungo had found out about Chessman. The dates were the same, the location the same. It had to be. Caryl Chessman was his father. He determined to avenge his father's death. He hated women, was always surrounded by them at home. But girls his own age didn't like him. Why didn't he kill the women in the house? That type of nut doesn't kill relatives, only strangers. Then the women had him put away for good. One day he escaped, killing the other nut who got in his way. Or maybe he was the one who told Mungo about Chessman. If he did, then he had to die. Sure, it all fit. It was Mungo all along and he was crazy and he was a devil or a magician. Either way he was out to kill a lot of women unless somebody got awfully lucky and killed him first.

By late Saturday afternoon the news media had the story. All the metropolitan Sunday editions carried lead articles on the Mungo-Chessman link. Twenty-five years after his trial and conviction, thirteen years after his execution, Caryl Chessman was again front-page news.

In Sacramento, home from an astoundingly successful lecture tour, Jonathan Stoner was happy to read about Mungo being Chessman's son. He had been saying that for months. Merely symbolically, perhaps, but it amounted to the same thing. People would remember he had tied them together.

He was hot now. Everything he touched turned to gold. He could do no wrong.

By Sunday morning people in the western states knew that the maniac had struck again. Not just once but twice. And in the same city. Texas authorities were frantically circulating thousands of posters of Mungo, secured from California. Police were keeping a sharp eye on all strangers in the smaller Texas towns. In

Austin a $20,000 reward was announced for the killer, dead or alive. Posted reward money for Vincent Mungo now totaled over $100,000.

Sheriff Oates was not surprised by the new killings, nor was John Spanner. Both men expected, dreaded, just such an occurrence. Spanner even more than Oates felt that Mungo was beginning to lose control. The intervals between murders were shortening, the horrific brutality increasing, if that were possible. The lieutenant thought that Mungo might even go all out in one gigantic suicidal bloodbath if he could get his hands on something like a machine gun. What a madman could do with such a weapon in a crowded place terrified the normally placid policeman, who now accepted that it was indeed Vincent Mungo being sought. Weary, discouraged, Spanner had discarded his instincts and settled for the obvious.

Not so Amos Finch. With each killing he saw the shadowy character of a monumental mass murderer emerging more clearly. He still clung to the two-killer theory, with Mungo simply retired after his escape and the unknown California Creeper the real homicidal genius. But he brooded over Spanner's original idea. If it was the Willows maniac, which one? Spanner swore the body was that of Mungo's partner. But without the face, who really knew for sure?

On Sunday evening Derek Lavery got a call at home. New York wanted a quick story on the Mungo-Chessman connection for the next issue. With the El Paso killings Vincent Mungo had hit the big time. Newspapers would headline anything about him, television would schedule special reports. From now on, every bit of sensationalism would be squeezed out of Mungo to meet the insatiable public demand.

At nine o'clock Monday morning Lavery told Adam Kenton to get busy on the assignment. Keep it short and simple. Run through the murders, the letter addressed *From Hell*, Mungo's birth, his discovery that he was probably a rape case, the two notes, his picking Caryl Chessman as his father, the possibility of it being true.

As always, there wasn't much time. New York wanted it fast. Meanwhile Ding would be working on another segment of the same story.

Capital punishment was a sure thing. The people

seemed to want it, if for no other reason than that it made them feel safer. The politicians would soon be jumping on the bandwagon. Within three or five years California would restore the death penalty, Lavery was certain of that. All of which meant the issue was a good one for the forseeable future, just as he had predicted.

But it was time to move on to the next level. The insanity plea. He would again steal the thunder from Stoner and the rest by publishing a series of articles blasting the whole concept of an insanity defense.

Legal insanity still followed the old McNaughton rule, which required proof that a defendant did not know the nature and quality of the act and did not know that the act was wrong. Basically it was a matter of determining if the defendant could distinguish between right and wrong. If he could not, then he was declared innocent by reason of insanity. Furthermore, if a judge found that the accused was mentally incompetent, meaning he was not able to participate in his own defense, he would not even be brought to trial, no matter what crimes he might have committed.

Lavery believed that both parts of this concept of criminal insanity—the idea of mental incompetency and the McNaughton rule as used in criminal trials—were foolish and dangerous. Or at least he believed that he was very good at spotting trends in mass thought.

He saw it coming as the next important step in the capital-punishment issue, and he intended once again to be there in the beginning.

The opening position would be that the whole concept of legal insanity should be abandoned. Discarded, wiped off the books. There would be no such thing as a legal-insanity defense. Every person accused of a crime, no matter how mentally ill, no matter how obvious the illness, would stand trial for the act itself. Afterward, if the defendant was found guilty, the judge would take appropriate action in sentencing the convicted person to a mental institution rather than prison.

Criminal law would thus be protected from the present hysteria and confusion surrounding an insanity defense. More importantly, as Lavery saw for his own purposes, it would correct the growing alienation of the public over the great injustice in the criminal-court procedure. People were becoming enraged as confessed murderers were declared not guilty and given a few years in a rest home.

Derek Lavery intended to pick up these people as readers, as many of them as possible. He believed they numbered in the millions, and their numbers were growing each year.

The Mungo-Chessman piece would kick off the campaign. Mungo's psychopathology would show. But the story would also list the murders in gory detail and catch the reader emotionally.

Then, the angle: A boxed article showing how an insanity defense could be used to thwart justice. Mungo would be found not guilty by reason of insanity and returned to Willows or the like, as though nothing had happened, as though at least five people, and God only knew how many more to come, had not been butchered, were still alive. Meanwhile Vincent Mungo would be planning his next escape and his next series of human slaughter . . .

Stoner was not amused. He had gone through various stages of disbelief before the truth dawned on him. The letter was genuine. It had really been written by Vincent Mungo and sent from El Paso. The son of a bitch had taken time out from his killing to write a stinking letter, for God's sake! The senator had been given an account of what was done to the bodies of the El Paso women. He still found it hard to believe. And the same went for the letter in his hand.

He read it again: "My Master—We do your bidding. The streets will run with blood from my knife but it is your voice that commands. The demons are everywhere around me but I will win and the people will rise up at your destruction and laugh and scream. You are the devil. My knife is sharp and ready for work so you will hear from me. They cannot catch me when you can. I will live forever."

Stoner glanced at the signature, "V. M." But the initials were crossed out.

Underneath was scrawled one word: "Chessman."

The man was crazy. Stark raving mad. A homicidal lunatic was stalking the cities killing at will. No one was safe. No one.

He wondered if Mungo could hold out for one more

month, all he needed was another month and he'd be on his way. Then Mungo could go to hell where he came from, and where he belonged.

The senator told his secretary to get Roger in Chicago. He intended to use the letter to whatever advantage he could before turning it over to the police.

Two days later, on September 20, Margot Rule was officially reported missing to Las Vegas police by worried friends. It was soon learned that she had withdrawn $24,000 from her bank on September 1. Her car was found in the garage. None of her clothes seemed to be missing from her apartment.

Nobody knew of her brief affair with David Rogers of Florida. Nor of her planned marriage to him. She had told no one.

The following day in Los Angeles the will of the late Velma Adams was filed for probate. It was found in a desk drawer in her aparment and named her good friend and manager of her beauty parlor as sole heir.

On September 25 Dr. Henry Baylor was removed as director of Willows State Hospital and reassigned to another post. Officials termed the move routine and denied it had anything to do with the celebrated Mungo case. The reassignment was duly noted by the Hillside *Daily Observer* and picked up by several metropolitan newspapers.

Dr. Baylor was reported on vacation and unavailable for comment.

That Friday, September 28, a credit clerk in San Francisco called the home of Daniel Long in northern California near the Willows hospital. Long knew nothing about any trouble with his credit rating and had indeed been born on November 12, 1943. No, he never made a call regarding his credit and had not spoken previously to the clerk. There must be some mistake. The clerk thanked him and afterward reported the incident to his supervisor, who told him to note it in Daniel Long's file.

Long discussed the strange call with his wife. They agreed it might have something to do with the time a thief broke into their home and police had suspected the notorious Vincent Mungo.

After five days of not wanting to become involved with the police and maniacal killers, Daniel Long finally phoned the sheriff's office in nearby Forest City. He decided it was the right thing to do.

In Fresno on the evening of October 1, Lester Solis was shot to death as he stepped into his car. His brother knew the bullets were meant for him. The next morning he found out why. Police arrested a thirty-six-year-old religious freak from Los Angeles who believed that Caryl Chessman was the son of God. A member of a fanatical desert sect that believed all prisoners were latter-day saints, he hated Solis for bearing false witness against Chessman, the son of God, who came down to earth to release all prisoners but was betrayed by his own people. All men were brothers, the religious freak believed, who must rise up and kill those who do evil. Unfortunately he had killed the wrong brother.

By October 2 the issue of *Newstime* with the Mungo-Chessman story was already sold out. People were fearful, and they were angry. They wanted fiends like Mungo punished and they didn't understand about mental illness or insanity when a person could walk around in society and feed himself and pay rent and function day after day. That was all *they* were doing. So what made him so special that he was crazy and able to get away with murder? They didn't want to hear it. They wanted him dead.

On October 3 a court order was secured to open Margot Rule's safe-deposit box in Las Vegas. Inside was found a note saying she had withdrawn money and planned to marry David Rogers of Florida. Police in that state were notified.

During the last two weeks of September and the first days of October 1973, David Rogers, alias Daniel Long, alias Thomas Bishop, was extremely busy. His unholy activity caused a reign of terror unequaled before or since in a half dozen states. In San Antonio he left behind a female body almost totally eviscerated. In Houston, two more.

In New Orleans he struck down three women. The police pathologist reported them to be the worst violations he had seen in thirty years. A quiet man given to understatement, he suggested that whoever had done the mutilations had lost all human feeling.

Police well knew the identity of the satanic killer. A *V* or *C* had been carved somewhere on each victim. In addition, the M.M.—method of mutilation—was the same in all cases. There was no doubt in anyone's mind that the fiend was Vincent Mungo. His work became so well known that the new term M.M. joined the standard M.O. in the police lexicon. As did the word "mungo-maniac."

From New Orleans Bishop turned suddenly north. Straight up to Memphis and then St. Louis. Afterward three more victims were found.

In those horrific weeks calls were made from Los Angeles to all the cities he had passed through, but the mob was having no better luck than the police. Railroad and bus stations were watched but Mungo's face was not seen anywhere. Besides the contract that had to be honored, the mob had received unofficial requests for help from various law-enforcement authorities. A nut like that? They were happy to oblige, if only he could be found.

Those same weeks also saw Senator Stoner going national along with Vincent Mungo. He had made it. His name was becoming a household word in the West, he had conquered the Midwest and the central states, and he would soon do the same in the East. He was being asked to talk in New York and two TV appearances had already been scheduled. The media smelled a winner. If things kept going right he was a cinch to run for the United States Senate. Or was it governor?

Capital punishment had really caught fire. The timing was perfect, everything clicked. Mungo had helped of course, but he was no longer needed. Stoner hoped they got the son of a bitch fast. He should not be allowed to run around killing women and violating their sacred bodies. Maybe the police were inadequate, maybe they needed prodding. Perhaps he should look into that angle. It might be good politics.

* * *

On October 4 Bishop arrived in Chicago. He found a
cheap hotel on Dearborn and then set out to find the
city. He didn't rent a car; unlike the West and Southwest, public transportation was adequate. Nor did he
want to use Daniel Long's identity any further except in
an emergency. By now they could have discovered what
he had done. He needed a new identity and he intended
to get one as soon as possible.

Meanwhile he rode the local buses and trains, walked
the downtown area, ate in small restaurants on side
streets. Chicago was incomprehensible to him. Big,
sprawling, unknowable. Everything was congested and
jammed together, there were people everywhere. It was
all a bit frightening, yet he found the movement of the
city, and its anonymity, exciting as well. He felt as though
he could remain lost for a hundred years, a thousand, and
he wondered if New York would be like that.

On that same day in California, Sheriff Oates returned
Daniel Long's call to Forest City. He listened quietly
as Long told him of the credit clerk and the mysterious
stranger. Could it mean something? In five minutes
Oates was speaking to the clerk. What day was it?
Where did the call come from? What exactly was said?

He called Long again and got his birthplace and date.
Then a call to San Jose. Did a Daniel Long request
a birth certificate within the past three months? Yes?
Where was it sent?

Oates could hardly believe it. The first concrete clue
to Vincent Mungo's new identity. Maybe. He felt like
Columbus discovering America. Then he remembered
that Columbus was seeking the Orient.

He picked up the phone to call Los Angeles.

TEN

The ten days that shook Chicago were among the happiest in the young life of Thomas William Bishop. He was twenty-five and a half years old and had not known freedom until exactly three months before when he walked away from a locked building behind a big wall on a dark and dangerous night. After years of waiting and months of watching he had seized the moment— rather, had made his own kind of moment, from which there would be no turning back. With the first fall of the axe his new life had begun, and he gratefully accepted the deadly mission for which he believed he was destined. More than that, he embraced it and the sense of freedom that came with his new existence. No longer would he have to sleep and wake, eat and fast, live and die by someone else's clock, always in the shadow of the big gray wall. No more would he say yes sir and no sir and lower his eyes and hold his tongue and agree with everything said by anyone who said it. Now he would do the talking, he would make the rules regarding himself and he would do whatever struck his fancy. From now on they were the ones who had to be careful, all of them. He was the master of reality, and he held life and death in his hands.

The sense of power was absolute and he enjoyed it absolutely. In three months he had made his way across two-thirds of the country, alone and in complete control, learning as he went, striking as he left. His wake was strewn with the butchered bodies of the enemy and as in any war of diabolic purpose, no mercy was expected and none given. From the initial murder at Willows, through the slaughter in Los Angeles and Phoenix, the war machine rolled relentlessly eastward, moving inexorably across the face of the land, un- mindful of state boundaries or local jurisdiction. As the death toll mounted, as the fearful destruction increased, authorities on all governmental levels sounded the alarm. A Texas mayor deputized all males in his city. A state's attorney general alerted the militia. The governor of Louisiana was asked to call out the National Guard. In Memphis police went on double duty, and surrounding towns imposed temporary curfews. In St. Louis all leaves of law-enforcement personnel were canceled. In a hundred cities and a thousand towns from the West Coast to the Mississippi River men were regarded suspiciously, stopped for questioning, detained for hours; in some cases, beaten and arrested. It was no time for strangers who looked anything like Vincent Mungo or accosted women or couldn't prove their identity or ran away or acted belligerent or talked funny or even walked around.

As the bloody trail lengthened so did the coverage by the news media, most especially television. Their appetites whetted by the prodigious publicity given the Charles Manson murders of the previous year, TV newsmen scurried about in a frantic effort to report every bizarre detail of this fresh sensation. In news circles it was an even bet at the moment that the mungomaniac would go bigger than Manson. The story had all the ingredients: it was occurring in more than one city or state, it was affecting in one way or another a large share of the audience, and it had the forbidding elements of mental illness and violent sexuality. In short, it had everything to draw national attention and as network coverage increased, along with column space in newspapers and magazines, the nation eventually came to realize, or was led to believe, that it was locked into a secret guerrilla war with an unseen enemy who sought total destruction of at least half its population. That the enemy was one man, if indeed it was only one man, which many seemed to doubt, made the struggle no less fearful. Like the plague, the enemy was moving at will, covering more and more area, striking wherever and whenever it pleased. The outer fringes of the populace were ready to believe anything. Some science-fiction aficionados saw it as the beginning of an invasion of alien beings from another galaxy, a vastly different life form that had no use for female earthlings. Others, mostly men, saw it as just retribution for the sins of mankind.

Law-enforcement officials nevertheless regarded it as strictly a police matter. The FBI was involved, on direct orders of the United States Attorney General; the investigation bureaus of a dozen central and western states were coordinated in a joint effort, as were police departments in all the struck cities. Thus far nothing new had surfaced beyond the fact that Vincent Mungo, rightly or wrongly, thought Caryl Chessman his father and had now taken over his father's role in avenging himself against women. The letter to California State Senator Stoner proved that. The initials "V. M." had been crossed out and the name Chessman written underneath. FBI lab reports concluded that the handwriting was the same as in the letters sent to *Newstime*. All were regarded as genuine. As to present appearance, plastic surgery had been ruled out so police and special agents at airports and train and bus depots in the larger cities concentrated on young men with heavy beards. These were politely asked to show proof of identity; if none was forthcoming they were held until identified by others. Only the clean-shaven who did not resemble Mungo were allowed to pass unchecked.

The Daniel Long thread, discovered by Sheriff Oates, was just beginning to be unraveled by California authorities. In a matter of days Los Angeles police, working back from the address to which a copy of Long's birth certificate was sent from San Jose, would open a bank safe-deposit box containing the certificate, dated November 12, 1943, and a picture of a middle-aged woman. Identification of the woman as Velma Adams, a beauty salon owner who was found murdered on a road between Yuba City and Sacramento in mid-July, would add still another victim to Vincent Mungo's growing list.

Police would also find a savings and checking account in the name of Daniel Long in a different bank. A further search would produce a record of a driver's license issued to Daniel Long in Los Angeles at the end of July. The picture on the license application would show a young man with a full beard. A car-rental clerk in Phoenix would describe Daniel Long as a bearded man wearing dark wraparound sunglasses. The conclusion would be inescapable. Vincent Mungo was traveling as Daniel Long, with a complete set of identification including a driver's license and credit card and checkbook. His identity, sent to the proper authorities, would

not be given to newsmen for a few days so that Mungo
might be caught somewhere posing as Long. If not, the
story would then be circulated in the hope that Mungo,
forced to discard the Long name, would have no other
sets of identification. Without papers, a bearded young
man, he would soon be caught. Maybe.

For the moment, however, all that was known about
the California maniac was that he had been in and out
of mental hospitals for much of his young life and was
now free again and killing women without apparent
design or pity.

Free again! Lucky me, thought Bishop standing on a
Chicago street corner on his first day in the city. Free
again after a lifetime of madness and pain! His eyes
took in the buildings overhead, the sidewalks crowded
with people, the endless streams of cars. He had never
felt so alive, so exhilarated. His sense of freedom was
total in the midst of such huge crowds, and he suddenly
realized that he was more invisible in a big city than
he could ever be on a deserted mountainside or forest
range or even in a small country town. Chicago was
unlike anything he had ever seen. Los Angeles was
nothing like it, nor any other city he had passed through.
All of them had space and the space always swallowed
up the people. But here the hordes of people dwarfed
everything; even the buildings seemed to bend toward
them. He stood still for a long moment allowing the
world to pass around him. Soon he saw that it was as
nameless and faceless as he, and he began to feel that
at last he had found the kind of place in which he
could survive. A big city. Surrounded by millions of
people virtually living together yet unknown to one another, with at least half of them the enemy.

For several days Bishop explored the Loop area and
rode on the elevated trains. He walked through Grant
Park and gazed at the hundreds of boats in Chicago Harbor. He visited the Shedd Aquarium and the Field
Museum of Natural History and the Adler Planetarium.
He watched the planes take off from Meigs Field. He
rode the sight-seeing boats on Lake Michigan and viewed
the Chicago skyline. He walked the length of the Gold
Coast along Michigan Avenue and then onto Lake Shore
Drive with its endless luxury apartment houses and its
small beaches. On the fourth day he found the Oak Street

beach. The air was cool and there were few strollers as he came up from the underpass. She was sitting alone on a bench near the curve in the walk. He sat nearby and soon struck up a conversation. He was new to Chicago, coming in from San Francisco for a visit. It seemed like a nice town but kind of cold to people alone. She smiled. She was alone too. In from Milwaukee on a two-day business trip. He said he had never been to Milwaukee. She told him he wasn't missing much.

"You staying around here, are you?"

She nodded, indicating the Drake Hotel across the street. She had a meeting in the afternoon and then would be free until the following morning, when business again reared its ugly head before an early evening flight back home.

Bishop said he had some free time too.

She had told him of her schedule because he looked good to her at the moment. He was young and clean in appearance and he had the nicest smile. She was afraid of only two things: dirt and poverty. Dirt brought disease and poor people brought misery, and she had seen enough of both in her life. As she glanced at the young man now seated next to her she saw no dirt and smelled no poverty. Beyond her twin fears Lilian Brothers was an emancipated woman of twenty-nine who took her pleasure as it came. She was fond of good food and expensive clothes and capable young men. Unfortunately she couldn't always tell a man's capabilities by his looks but she was almost always willing to give it a try. Unmarried, she supported her parents, who lived with her, though she often stayed elsewhere overnight. In Chicago, to which she came occasionally in her career as a successful buyer, she knew some people but lately they had begun to bore her with their sameness. She longed for a fresh experience.

After further pleasant talk they agreed to meet that evening for dinner and drinks.

During the afternoon Bishop took care of some business of his own. He first changed a half dozen hundred-dollar bills into tens and twenties at different banks in order not to draw attention to himself. There was no real danger because the bills were old and had no consecutive serial numbers.

Afterward he went to a large post office that had

tables set up for the use of customers. In the adjoining trash barrels he found three envelopes addressed to a Jay Cooper of Chicago. In one of the envelopes was a statement of earnings and contributions from a workers' pension plan. On the offical-looking form were Cooper's name and post office box address, his birth date and Social Security number. Bishop stuffed some folded advertisements from the barrel into the other two envelopes and slipped all three letters in his pocket.

His next stop was a branch of the First National Bank of Chicago, where he opened a savings account with fifty dollars in the name of Jay Cooper. He showed the letters as proof of identity and the pension-plan form for proof of his Social Security number. He then went to the local administration office with the form and received a new card, since his old one had been stolen along with everything else in his wallet. Imagine! Mugged in early evening on a Southside Chicago street! He just didn't know what the town was coming to anymore. Neither did the clerk, who sympathized with his sentiments and just casually glanced at the bankbook as proof of identity.

Back on Michigan Avenue he stopped in the Playboy Club lobby where he bought a membership for fifteen dollars. In the Playboy Hotel next door he rented a single room for the night, paying in cash and receiving a copy of the bill. He now had valid proof of a Chicago residence for Jay Cooper.

In Grant Park he became a member of several cultural institutions, with a card from each in his new name. He bought a twenty-dollar gift certificate in a Marshall Field store, filling in his name as though the certificate had been given to him by friends. He had the name written on a phony college degree that was sold in a novelty store for a joke. Finally, he had small white cards printed in dry type with the name and a false address.

In the taxi on the way to the motor vehicle bureau he studied the pension-plan form. Jay Cooper was thirty-two years old, according to his birth date of 1941. Not too old to be inpersonated! He, Bishop, would simply be a youngish thirty-two. At the bureau he told the clerk he had been mugged three nights earlier over on the Southside and had lost his wallet with all his identification and money and had spent the night in a hospital. The theft had been reported of course. Now, after several days spent at home feeling woozy, he was trying to get things in order again. He showed the clerk his bankbook and other cards, including his Playboy membership. He had lost not only his driver's license but his union card, two credit cards and a bunch of other things. He was just beginning to replace them but of course his license was the most important. No, he didn't remember the number on the license. Next time he'd be sure to copy it down at home. But who would ever dream he'd be mugged?

The clerk was properly sympathetic. His niece had been attacked in the same general area the year before. He didn't understand why the police couldn't do anything about those people. In minutes the computer found the right Jay Cooper, working from birth date supplied by Bishop on the application form. The clerk noted the license number on the form and then filled out a temporary driver's permit in Cooper's name. A new license would be mailed to him, which he could bring in to have validated. About how long would it take? Three or four days, usually not more. Bishop thanked him and walked away whistling to himself. He now had a new set of identification, perhaps not as complete as that for Daniel Long but good enough temporarily. As for guessing that the real Jay Cooper had a driver's license, it was hardly a guess since the vast majority of males between twenty and sixty-five have such licenses. He was just playing the odds, and they were all in his favor.

In the hotel room he took the Daniel Long papers out of his wallet and burned them in a large glass ashtray, then refilled the wallet with the new set. The bankbook went into his jacket pocket, along with the pension-plan letter and the Playboy Hotel key. Afterward he put most of the remaining bills into the black zippered bag in the toilet tank. a quick shower and shave and he was ready for the evening. On the way out he made certain his long-bladed knife was in its proper place.

Later, Lilian Brothers had to admit she was having a delightful time. They had dined high in the Chicago sky, almost a hundred stories up, in a most fashionable restaurant. Oysters Rockefeller, giant mushrooms filled with crabmeat, escargots Bourguignonnes, mousse au chocolat. And endless champagne. Then a perfectly scandalous show in a club on Rush Street, followed by more drinks at still another place and a quiet cab ride home. She really didn't want the night to end. He had been attentive and charming and actually quite different from her other friends, though she couldn't say exactly how. And he did have the very nicest smile. Finally back at the hotel, she held onto him tightly as they got into the empty elevator.

In bed she showed him how she liked her sex. She crouched on all fours and he was to approach her from the rear. Dogstyle, she called it. Bishop found it disgusting. When she was finally satisfied she slumped down and rolled over in a sleep position. He tried to put his penis in her mouth but she mumbled something about being too tired and maybe in the morning. He tried again and she pushed him away.

Bishop was suddenly furious. With a guttural gasp he lunged at her face, his hands clenched tightly into fists. She was happily drunk and sleepy and utterly defenseless. A blow caught her cheek, another an eye, then her nose, her mouth. In seconds she lay still, beaten unconscious by the savage assault. The blood excited him. With fingers he smeared it on his chest and shoulders and arms. He felt animalistic. Grunting, he forced the woman's mouth open as ribbons of discolored mucus gushed out. Giggling now, his body streaked with red, his maddened eyes mere dots of flamed desire, Bishop plunged his penis into the pool of blood. The sensation was electric, and his mind instantly forged a pleasure connection between the blood on her face and his hardened lust. His thoughts raced ahead to future connections as his hand moved her head in a rhythmic motion. The blood flowed freely from her wounded mouth, and what remained eventually came to mingle with his spent passion.

The next day, the fifth of Bishop's stay, Chicago read of the insane murder and a shudder ran through the city. Those in power knew they were up against an authentic monster; one look at photographs of the carnage convinced the most skeptical. Some regarded it as an elemental force of nature, much like the Chicago wind or fire. But consensus affixed the slaughter to

Vincent Mungo, last reported to be in St. Louis which was not that far away. Yet nothing was definite. Unlike Mungo's other bestial attacks, there were no carvings on the body or any removed parts. Several newsmen speculated on a Mungo imitator, a home-grown maniac with his own diabolic design, his own diseased desires. One reporter reminded his readers of the infamous Edward Gein of nearby Wisconsin, and what he had done to his victims. The editor would not, however, allow any mention of the particulars, in defense of public morality if not its sanity. But the point had been made. Imitators were a distinct possibility and part of a horrific tradition stretching back to Jack the Ripper and far into the dim past.

Working on the assumption that Mungo himself was in their midst, Chicago police immediately formed special units tied into the investigation and communications grid that linked the struck cities and states all the way back to California. They quickly learned that Mungo was traveling under the name of Daniel Long and had grown a beard. He had rented cars with a credit card made out to Long. In his possession was a checkbook imprinted with Long's name. Police began canvassing the city's hotels, searching for recent arrivals who looked like Mungo or who wore beards. Pictures of the killer had literally been run off overnight. In the Pasadena on Dearborn and Ohio streets, the clerk had no one who resembled Mungo but one young man sported a flowing beard. Yet he couldn't be their man. Why not? He was Oriental.

Other units checked out the car-rental agencies and the airlines and trains for anything in Long's name. Also visited were the department stores and expensive clothiers and jewelry shops. All banks were notified to watch for the California checks. Mungo's clean-shaven picture appeared in the newspapers next to the California driver's license photo with a beard. Radio and television also carried a description. And all terminals were watched round the clock.

Police tried to reconstruct Lilian Brothers' last day and evening. She had apparently left her hotel before 11:30 A.M., since the maid cleaned the room at that time. Only one person had slept in the bed; the maid was positive. At 10:30 A.M. a friend had called and she answered, so her departure from the room was set at about eleven o'clock. At noon she had lunch with two women friends and then had gone directly to a fashion showing. Afterward she attended the usual cocktail party and was driven back to her hotel by a male business acquaintance. The time was 5:30 P.M. She had a headache and said she would see him the following morning at a company conference. At 7:15 P.M. she asked the desk clerk to change a twenty-dollar bill; she was apparently on her way out. That was the last time she was seen alive, or at least was remembered. Police needed to know what she had done after that hour. They also wondered what happened that morning between eleven o'clock and noon.

On the sixth day a cab driver reported that he might have taken the dead woman home. His fare had looked like her but he couldn't be sure. At any rate it was not the Drake but about a block away, on the other side of Lake Shore Drive, across from that Oak Street beach. That's where they got out.

They?

Yeah, her and this young guy. He looked young anyway but it's hard to tell. They kept in the dark, if you know what I mean.

Description?

Tall, good build. Wore a light jacket. Had a lot of hair all over his face, you know how some guys get. I don't go for it myself. Too messy, you know?

The driver, who was only five feet two inches, was shown the photograph of a bearded Vincent Mungo. It could've been the man in his car that night, but who can be sure behind all that hair?

In the first days of investigation dozens of leads were checked out, including restaurants and theaters and just about the whole run of city night life. Nothing worked, though one waiter insisted he had served the woman that same evening. She had been with a man who wore sunglasses. Not the wraparound kind, no. They looked like prescription. No, no beard. About thirty, medium height, thin frame. Nothing really noticeable about him. But the waiter remembered the woman because she reminded him of his former wife—she had the same dishonest eyes.

Who paid the check?

He did.

Credit card?

Cash.

No one else could confirm the presence of the woman at the restaurant that evening.

If police went with the waiter and cab driver, Lilian Brothers had dinner with someone who was afraid to come forward, perhaps a married man, and then somehow met and took off with Mungo posing as Daniel Long of California. Since the descriptions were so different, two men were obviously involved. But who was the clean-shaven man and where did he go? And why did the bearded man and the woman get out on the far side of Lake Shore Drive when the hotel was across what amounts almost to two highways? Police were inclined to be skeptical of both stories since there was no corroboration for either one.

Which meant they had absolutely no knowledge of Lilian Brothers' movements on the night of her death.

Or for that missing morning hour.

In his hotel room Bishop followed the news of the sensational murder. He had guessed right about the Daniel Long discovery and had secured identity just in time. They would never penetrate the new disguise because it had been done clean, as he had learned to do from years of watching television. For all his megalomania Bishop realized how much he owed to the television writers, who always seemed to come up with better ways to outwit the law on the crime shows. Yet it was his superior intelligence, so he believed, that enabled him to refine those ideas to fit his purpose.

He had met the woman by the Oak Street beach and they had walked down Michigan Avenue to dinner, he wearing expensive sunglasses and his hair combed differently. Afterward they walked to Rush Street and a crowded club, where no one would remember them, then to a nearby saloon, equally crowded. The cab finally took them to Lake Shore Drive by Division Street. They used the underpass to cross over to the beach, where they sat a while on the grassy knoll across from the Drake and exchanged meaningful glances. Eventually they went in the side entrance and slipped unnoticed into the elevator.

Before entering the cab Bishop had put on his beard, which he carried in his jacket. The outfit had been costly—an actor's professional-type equipment—and looked very real. The woman was just tipsy enough to think it all quite funny and him a comic genius. Especially when he told her he was Jack the Ripper and didn't want anybody to recognize him. She screamed with laughter. If someone in the hotel had remembered him, it would have been as a heavily bearded man. At dinner and afterward he would have been seen as just a bland young man hard to remember, much less describe, beyond the sunglasses and odd hair style. He thought it all out carefully. People, he was quickly learning, were amazingly unobservant and nonresponsive in public. They could look right at you and not see you at all! And what they usually remembered were vague impressions having a minimum of reality. Which suited him just fine.

In the woman's hotel room he removed his disguise. She was quickly passionate and he followed her desires, all the while thinking of his own. Disgust was etched on his face, but she did not see it for he was behind her.

Much later he returned the knife to its place in the jacket and lay down next to what was left of the woman. He mentally set himself to awaken at 8:30 A.M.

In the morning he took a shower, washing himself clean of all the blood and bits of flesh. He decided against leaving any reminders of his identity. By now they would know of his work. Better still, they would be made to guess, and a certain mystery might be useful to him. Might even sidetrack them a while.

On the seventh day Bishop rested, wandering out only for food. When he moved freely again it was to Old Town, along N. Wells Street. Here he found a whole colony of young people and hundreds of small shops catering to youth. He also found the singles bars, where people came to meet others. On his second visit to such a bar he told someone he was in town for a few weeks, a casino dealer in Las Vegas on vacation. She was originally from Harrisburg, Pennsylvania. Hated it, nothing but dirty politics and dirty politicians with fat hands. Ugh! She had moved to New York but found it too frightening and eventually made it to Chicago. She liked it here, the people were friendly and there were millions of them around but it didn't have the paranoid feeling of New York. At least she didn't feel it. This was her third year in the city. She was twenty-three years old.

He asked her what she did for money.

"I'm an artist's model." She laughed. "Only there's not too much work around right now."

"What can you make when there is?"

She shrugged her blond head. "Depends who it's for. Anywhere from ten an hour." Her eyes searched his. "Why do you ask?"

He smiled warmly, a boyish grin of good feeling and good intentions. "I don't know anybody here. It'd be worth it to me." He paused. "Would you model for me?" he added softly.

"What kind of art you into?"

"None," he answered matter-of-factly. "I don't know anything about it."

She laughed. She couldn't help it, caught by surprise like that.

"You're crazy, you know that?" Her giggles sounded musical.

He nodded his head in agreement. "I can afford to be," he roared in delight. "I got plenty of money."

In a local shop they bought two thick steaks, the best filet cut, and twenty dollars worth of other foodstuffs. She promised to cook for him. Her two-room apartment was small and incredibly messy but she laughed it off. She was in good spirits. And why not? Her money was just about gone and here was food for a week plus who knows how much money in the hand. Fifty dollars? Maybe even a hundred. She would let him stay all night, her mind was made up to that. She would fix him a great meal and then take off her clothes and model for him. The thought made her smile. He knew nothing about art, so her modeling would be simply standing there in different poses while the bulge in his pants got bigger. In a way that was a waste because she really had a good model's body, even though her thighs were a bit heavy and her belly was inching up. She swore once again that she would do something about that starting tomorrow.

Meanwhile she would pose for him and he would get all hot, and then they would go to bed and maybe she'd get hot too and they'd have a good time, and in the morning she would have some money to live a little longer.

She wondered if he would want to see her other times while he was in town. That would be good for her. Thinking about it, she resolved to treat him extra nice. Really something special.

The meal was very good; he told her it was the best he'd eaten in a long while. They ate slowly and drank red wine out of cardboard coffee cups but he just sipped his. She rolled two joints of marijuana and gave him one. He refused it, told her he took no drugs. He didn't tell her he was a moral man who was horrified by all the evil around him. He sat there grimly watching her get high, a pleasant smile on his face.

Afterward she sat him on an artist's stool and slowly undressed for him. He watched her carefully, noting every part. He had seen enough females by now to appreciate her firm, youthful body. Suddenly he felt an excitement within himself and he hated her for it. As she stood nude before him he saw that she was a natural blonde, and an idea slowly worked its way into his disordered mind.

On the eighth day of Bishop's stay in Chicago the headlines screamed murder for the second time. A brutal, fiendish killing of a young woman in the Old Town section. The papers again wrote of the California killer, though again no initials were carved on the corpse. What the reporters didn't write, what they couldn't print, was the condition of the body. Even the medical examiner could not credit what his eyes were seeing.

Within hours a rumor was spreading throughout official Chicago that the madman would be shot on sight. Shot at least a dozen times to make sure, and perhaps even made to disappear. No Chicago police officer was heard saying it, no one spoke of it, but it was tacitly understood that Vincent Mungo would not be left alive to be judged insane and sent to an institution from which he could one day again escape and continue his dreadful carnage. If caught—*when* caught—he would never even reach the police station. That much was certain. Chicago would take care of its own.

On the ninth day Bishop returned to the large post office and asked for the contents of his mail box. He told the busy clerk he had left the key at home. For identification he showed the driver's permit. In a moment he walked out with four pieces of mail, one of them Jay

Cooper's new license. Another was a note from a friend visiting in Europe, and two were advertisements which he discarded. At the license bureau he paid the fee and had the card stamped. It was taking a chance asking for Cooper's mail but worth it. Had the clerk known Cooper, he would have said he was a friend who had been asked to pick up the mail while the other was out of town for a few days. The key was really left at home but he hadn't wanted to go all the way back or to be hassled over who he was so he just said he was Cooper. No harm done. And he would have walked away, promising to return with the key. In reality he knew that people with post office boxes seldom knew the clerks. They wanted to be inconspicuous, their movements unobserved, their mail unnoticed. Which was usually why they paid for boxes instead of getting free delivery at home.

Now the real Jay Cooper would never know about a duplicate driver's license, nor would he miss a few advertising brochures. And mail from Europe was always being lost. It had been a clean job and the fake Jay Cooper, the fake Vincent Mungo, the fake Thomas Bishop felt so elated he started to cry. In his hotel room the real Thomas Chessman lay down to rest and wondered why he hadn't been given his true name at birth. He had no way of knowing that on the birth certificate he was really listed as Thomas Owens.

That evening he went to the Playboy Club to celebrate his conquest of Chicago. He walked past the square bar into a large dining room, where he was seated in an alcove facing a buffet table. A bunny in purple served him. Her name was Sunny and she smiled warmly. He kept looking at her mouth and she kept wetting her lips. When she brought him a second beer he gave her a twenty-dollar tip and she became even warmer. He told her he was tired and she got him a plate of food from the buffet. He thought that was very nice. When he left he tipped her again. She smiled and asked where he was from and he smiled and told her New York. Her tongue darted out again and he told her she had nice lips.

On the way home he stopped in another place and had a few more beers. Next to him a black girl was drinking a martini. She wore a white blouse and gray pants and looked bored. He sat staring into his beer and thinking of Sunny. People were dancing to rock music on a small stage set at one end of the room. Strobe lights played over them.

"Do you dance?"

He turned to her. She smiled at him but her smile wasn't as warm as Sunny's. She wore glasses.

He shook his head. "No, I don't," he said politely. "But I like to watch."

"This place is creepy," grumbled the girl. "They don't like single women sitting at the bar. And you can't dance unless you're a couple at a table."

"I never learned how," he said after a moment. "I'm from New York," he added by way of explanation.

"You in on business?"

"Just looking around." He went back to his beer. "This is a tough town."

"Same as anywhere, I guess."

"A little more here."

She glanced his way. "Depends what you want."

"In New York if you spread the money around, the girls come to you. Know what I mean?"

"Same thing here once you learn the game."

"I don't play games. Got no time for that. I like to show a little money and buy what I want."

"That's a good way all right."

A pause.

"Where you staying?"

He turned back to her, studied her lips. They never moved. "I'm at the Playboy," he said finally.

She frowned. "They keep a close watch over there."

"If a girl's dressed, she just goes in the elevator. Who's gonna stop her?"

"They do sometimes. From what I hear."

"So then they call up and the guy says he's expecting company. He paid for the room so it's nobody's business what he does. See what I mean?"

"That's right."

He finished his beer and picked up his change, leaving a dollar tip. "I'll be in room 830 later on. If you're in town for the night, stop over."

"Maybe I'll do that."

He stood up to leave and she touched his arm. Her smile was hidden now.

"I'm not cheap," she announced in a business voice.

He looked at her but couldn't see her eyes through the thick glasses.

"Neither am I," he answered and walked away.

Outside he breathed in the cool night air. The moon was silvery and riding high in the sky. Thinking about the girl, he laughed to himself all the way home. She'd be at the Playboy and up to room 830 if she had to fight her way through tigers. He had given her a smell of money and made it seem like he was an easy mark.

He wouldn't be there, but somebody else probably would be when she knocked on the door long after midnight. He hoped it'd be a woman. Would serve her right. Serve 'em both right.

The hell with them all. He giggled. That girl would never know how lucky she was that he wouldn't be there to greet her. Lucky for her he was too tired to be at his work. He corrected himself. His father's work. Well, by now it was the work of both of them. Yes, very definitely it was now the firm of Chessman and Son.

He was still snickering when he got to his room.

On the tenth day Bishop left Chicago. There were those who would later say that he left the city in ruins. He had killed two women, but the miasma of fear that surrounded each incalculable destruction lingered long after his departure. While it was never reported officially, details of what had been done to the two women soon became common knowledge, and eventually the two became ten and the ten stretched endlessly. For years afterward mothers would use the Chicago fiend as an example of warning to wayward daughters, and men would swear they were nearby or next door or even in the same room when the madman stalked his victims.

On that last day Bishop arose early.

After breakfast he walked along the beach front on Lake Shore Drive for the last time. He was sorry to be leaving and he hoped someday to return. Chicago was his kind of town. But it was time to go.

At noon he checked out of his hotel and walked south on State Street, past Heald Square and the Chicago River, all the way down to Jackson Boulevard, then turned west to Union Station. He had decided to take the train to New York since all the bus terminals were being closely watched. Though he was in no danger, carelessness could always be harmful. He didn't intend to be careless. The previous day he had bought a coach seat for New York leaving Chicago at 2:30 P.M. Now it was almost time.

Union Station looked like a giant bank vault to him, all hollow and cavernous and full of empty space. In one corner by a flight of imitation-marble stairs was a church directory listing eleven different services. Christian Science was first. He thought that added a nice homey touch to the cold room. Past the rows of empty benches he continued to the shopping area in front of the track gates. He bought a paper and some magazines. Across the aisle he ordered a frozen chocolate shake at a candy-colored stand. He asked for water but they didn't seem to know what it was or where to get it. They told him to try Coca-Cola.

When the gates opened he filed past the quiet man who carefully eyed the crowd. The coaches were in the rear of the train and first class toward the front, with the dining car and bar car in between. He wished he could have had a first-class roomette where he'd be by himself, but that was too conspicuous. Porters always remembered the people in first class. Nobody looked at those in coach.

He found his seat and put the flight bag on the floor. The zippered money case he kept close by his side. His seat companion was a college student from Maine who liked to talk. In due time Bishop made up a whole history for himself as they talked along.

During the first few hours he went through the magazines and newspaper. The weekend section of the paper had a long article on the Mungo case. There were many factual errors and, even worse, the author had made Vincent Mungo into a raving lunatic. Bishop didn't think he raved and he obviously was not a lunatic. Nor was Vincent Mungo really Caryl Chessman's son, not *really*. He had just made it seem that way so no suspicion would fall on him since he was legally dead. He didn't know where they got the idea that Mungo really was Chessman's son. *He* was.

He thought about writing a letter to the newspaper in which he would correct all the errors. Except for his real identity of course. But he soon saw how dangerous that would be. He was a star now, and stars had to put up with anything people wrote about them. That was part of the price of being a star, even an unknown one. You had to suffer in silence. He was very good at that, at silent suffering. He had been doing it all his life. He forgot about writing and went back to reading.

Eventually he walked through a few of the cars. Almost all the seats were filled. The trip would take about twenty-one hours along the scenic Lake Shore route through upper New York state to Albany, and then down to New York City. Dinner would be served until nine o'clock, the bar open till midnight. After that it would be bedtime for those who could sleep in a chair. Bishop again wished he had a bedroom of his own.

At eight o'clock he entered the dining car and was seated with an elderly couple who liked to drink even more than they liked to eat. They didn't talk much except to complain about the food and the service. The liquor apparently was passable. After dinner they headed for the bar car. A few minutes later a young woman was seated across from him. She was thin and fair-skinned and had mousy brown hair and looked very timid. He smiled at her and made some introductory comments and soon they were talking as people do at a dinner table. She was a librarian in Omaha, Nebraska, doing some traveling on a three-week vacation. She had never been to New York. From there she was going to Florida and would then fly home.

He hadn't seen her when he walked through the coaches. She said she had a bedroom because she couldn't sleep sitting up. He nodded understandingly; he had trouble sleeping that way himself. Toward the end of the meal he asked if she'd like to have a drink in the bar car. Perhaps later, she said, if she didn't fall asleep first. He told her he'd be there about eleven if she cared to join him.

He didn't mention the meeting to his seat companion, who was getting off at Buffalo in the early morning hours and intended to sleep until then.

At 11:30 he was on his second can of beer when she walked into the car. She looked around timidly, saw him and rushed over, as shy people usually do. He made a place for her and they had several quiet drinks together. He bought her a nightcap at midnight, Scotch and water, and another beer for himself, and suggested that perhaps they could finish the drinks in her compartment since the bar car was now closing. She hesitated, but he laughed off her alarm by saying that was the least one weary traveler could do for another who couldn't sleep in a chair. If he had a private room he would certainly offer its use to her. She blinked a few times in thought and finally agreed, more out of exasperation with herself than anything else.

He had to get something from his seat and would see her in about five minutes. She told him her compartment letter, two cars forward, and he said he'd be there right away. Walking back to the coach Bishop thought rapidly. He had left because he didn't want to go forward with her. If anyone had noticed them, they were seen leaving in opposite directions. Now all he had to do was get to her room unseen, at least as himself.

He stopped in the bathroom at the end of the first coach. All the lights were out, people were sleeping. He quickly transformed himself into a bearded man. He waited a few minutes before walking back through the almost empty bar car and the darkened dining car. Tucked under his jacket was the zippered case he always carried with him. The flight bag was left under his seat, out of the way and unnoticed.

In the next car he crept silently down the carpeted aisle. Her room was the last one forward, compartment A. At her door he whisked off the beard and returned it to the pocket and set his face in a mask of boyish innocence.

He knocked softly and the door slowly was opened for him. . . .

The editor-in-chief leaned back in his chair and stared at the paintings hanging on the walls of his spacious office. There were four of them, large canvases that depicted famous New York scenes. They were arranged so a viewer could start with the South Ferry panorama and move on to the square at Fifth Avenue and 23rd Street, the canyons of upper Sixth Avenue, and finally the Hotel Plaza and the beginnings of Central Park.

Each of the paintings seemed to suggest movement and the ceaseless activity of the great city in its headlong rush to unearth the next bit of business. But underneath the sweep of motion could be felt the geometrics of the city, the pattern of unchanged daily life, much like the river that forever flowed yet remained the same. Martin Dunlop envied the artist his comprehensive view of man's creations, the quick confidence of his judgment. If only life were really so simple!

Outside, the jumble of traffic along Sixth Avenue, the Avenue of the Americas, was its usual Monday-morning mess. Horns blared insanely, oaths were muttered and curses delivered, nerves cracked amid scraped fenders. And hordes of people gave rise to an incessant chatter that was dulled only by the intermittent rumble of the subways underneath the street. Around the corner in Rockefeller Center things were quieter as chauffeurs conversed in conspiratorial tones, their gleaming Cadillacs and Lincolns stretched lazily along the brief boulevard. The editor-in-chief found himself once again wishing that his office was on that side of the building, even though it was high enough for him not to hear anything through the sealed glass windows.

A noise jarred his thoughts and he shifted his eyes from the paintings to a leather couch set against the wall to his right. The white-haired man cleared his throat again and pushed himself off the couch. Dunlop placed the folder he had been holding back on the desk and sat there motionless, his thick body resting while his mind raced the implications of the subject.

"Do they have anything?" he presently asked.

Managing editor John Perrone, functional head of the newsweekly, was one of the most respected editors in American journalism, as well as one of the most feared. Both the respect and fear came from his often ruthless but totally professional handling of a worldwide network of writers and researchers who strove each week to bring the news to millions of readers. His power was immense, his responsibilities heavy. Generally regarded as being without equal in his dramatic flair for the big story, for tomorrow's fresh sensation, he was just as often accused of manipulating the news for the benefit of the publishing empire he served so well. Which was why he held his job and kept his power.

"I think so," he said after a moment. "That's why I brought it to you." His tone was subdued, his eyes steady. But he was already feeling the emotional pitch of the story possibilities. "There's nothing definite about a psychological profile, as we know. But this one seems to match Mungo pretty well so far. If it has any validity as a projection, we might be in for a bloodbath that could make Charles Manson and Richard Speck look like a pair of country preachers. The Institute doctors feel Mungo's worked himself into a state of megalomania. He thinks he's invincible, and he's out to get vengeance for his father on women, any women."

"It's not definite that Caryl Chessman was his father at all."

"That doesn't matter anymore. Mungo's made his decision and he's gone too far to stop now. Blood feeds on blood and if the doctors are right, he's beyond recall. Wherever he is, all he sees are dead mutilated bodies. What we have to decide is, should we go after him ourselves? We've got contacts and connections around the country that even the police don't have. If we could get him or get to him first"—the fervor grew in his voice—"we'd pull off the story of the year."

"There was a time," Dunlop said with a smile, "when we just reported the news."

"Times change," growled Perrone. "Besides, I'm not saying we interfere in police business. Just that we run our own parallel investigation. Newsmen are supposed to uncover facts. All we'd need in this case is a concerted effort—a special company task force that would report only to us and work out of the New York office. They'd have no other duties until he was caught, one way or another."

John Perrone stopped. He had made his plea as strongly as he could. For years he had chafed whenever Dunlop referred to the role of the newsman as a simple reporter of the news. Yet he was never really certain where the man stood on the issue. For himself, he well knew that the media often made the news. Indeed, it was almost impossible for the reporter not to become part of the report. He was painfully aware of the Hawthorne Effect: that is, people under observation perform differently by the very fact that they are being observed. And he believed the same held for anyone questioned after an event. Furthermore, all news was private until made public, and the very gathering of it was already a form of manipulation. That seemed obvious.

Martin Dunlop pressed his lips together in concentration and turned his eyes again to the paintings. There was a feeling to them that suggested the New York of a hundred years earlier, though the technique was modern and the architecture contemporary. Gazing at them, he sometimes wished he were living in the nineteenth century; he had an idea that things were much simpler for an editor then. Not easier; God knows an editor's life had never been easy since Adam and Eve were penciled out of the Paradise story by the Directing Editor Himself. But things were less complex a century before, if only because there was less of everything. This was the news and that was it. Simple. Direct. The editor-in-chief liked the simple and direct. And one thing he didn't like was having to make instant decisions involving something that could get out of control. He wished Perrone would go away. The man was the best in the business, but right now he wished his managing editor would just disappear.

Martin Dunlop turned his thoughts to Perrone's idea. The company perhaps had the resources to ferret this Mungo out. It could mean possibly interfering in police matters and withholding information. It might even prove dangerous, and could certainly lead to charges of manipulation. But it would be a fantastic editorial coup if successful. Dunlop had no illusions about the fierce competition among the news magazines in the tight-money year of 1973.

"All right," he sighed, still looking at the wall paintings. "I'll take it upstairs."

John Perrone said nothing. His boss was a good editor and a brilliant communications businessman. He had expected no less from him.

Dunlop wheeled round. "I'll get back to you before lunch." He smiled to indicate the meeting was over. "It is a most interesting idea. I hope we can work something out."

After Perrone had left, to return to his own office and a dozen pressing problems of the new week's issue, the editor-in-chief again read the doctors' report. He closed his eyes at the finish. There was no doubt that Vincent Mungo would kill again, and keep on killing. He would not stop suddenly, like Jack the Ripper. It didn't take a doctor to see that.

Still frowning, he buzzed his secretary to call upstairs.

That same morning in Berkeley, California, Amos Finch solved a problem that had been bothering him for many weeks. He finally figured out how to tell if the body of the man found murdered at Willows State Hospital on the morning of July 4 was really that of Thomas Bishop, even though the face had been bludgeoned beyond recognition and the body itself already buried.

At 10:40 A.M. the editor-in-chief of *Newstime* magazine rode the elevator to the twenty-fifth floor to see the chairman of the board of Newstime Inc. He expected the meeting to be brief.

As the elevator doors opened on the twenty-fifth floor Dunlop stepped into a thickly carpeted foyer with original lithographs on the wood-paneled walls. He turned left and walked into the reception area, smiled briefly at the woman seated behind the silvered desk, and continued along the blue-carpeted hall. Eventually he came to the end, where he rounded a corner into a huge board room.

At the far wall the woman looked up briskly from her desk as he crossed the room.

"Mr. Dunlop. How nice to see you."

"Mrs. Marsh." The editor-in-chief glanced toward the closed door to his right. "I'm a minute or two early."

"He's expecting you." She flicked up a switch and announced his presence, waited a moment, then smiled briefly, and Martin Dunlop walked past her desk into James Mackenzie's private office.

The room appeared just as he had left it the last time, some weeks earlier, and all the times before that. Cluttered, informal, passionately untidy and yet somehow eminently livable. It went with the flowers and a Greek fisherman's cap and blue tennis shoes and a clay pipe. And all of them, including an urbane charm and grace, went with the rangy man who turned to greet him.

"Martin, good of you to drop in."

Mackenzie indicated a chair and Dunlop quickly sat down. He was asked about the magazine and the new issue in preparation, and he soon found himself mentioning some ideas he had wanted to keep under wraps a while longer. But a few points scored were a few points gained, and as they talked business he almost forgot his reason for being there.

"Now what's all this about Vincent Mungo?"

Martin Dunlop instantly switched his thoughts. In minutes he explained that *Newstime* had funded a Rockefeller Institute study of the killer. Based on the Institute profile, and most especially the projection of increased bloodshed, his managing editor believed—and he quite agreed—that the company should set up a large investigative unit aimed at tracking down the madman. If successful it would mean millions of dollars worth of free publicity that couldn't help but benefit all areas of company operations. And *Newstime* would of course print the whole story, which should bring in much added revenue. He ended his brief explanation by placing the profile on the desk.

Mackenzie reached for the green folder without a word. As he read, his lips pressed together time and again in a show of distaste. When he had finished he pushed the folder back across the desk and sighed loudly.

"What are the negatives for the organization?"

Dunlop recited them quickly. Several times he used the phrases "interfering in police business" and "withholding of information." He watched Mackenzie's frown deepen. When he got to the part about "manipulating the news" the frown burst open.

"That is politically indefensible at the moment, as I'm sure you know, Martin. The Nixon administration is just waiting for something they could sink their fangs into. They haven't forgotten"—the contempt in his voice was unmistakable—"Mr. Agnew's direction."

A few more minutes and there was nothing left to say. A big task force was out. A major company effort was out. Any publicity, even any mention of such a project, was out. There must be no interference with police or withholding of information, though in the matter of individual reporters this was often difficult to prove. Finally, there must not even be a suspicion that anything was being done to manipulate the news. God forbid!

Back in his own office, the editor-in-chief summoned his administrative aide. Patrick Henderson, a youngish man of impeccable background and discretion, was often used as a sounding board by his employer. Henderson regarded loyalty as an art to be constantly practiced, and he could be particularly hard on those who strayed or made too many mistakes. Some thought him Dunlop's hatchet man, and he was admired and hated in about equal proportions. If any of this ever bothered him he managed to hide it quite well, and all that seemed to concern him at the moment was the refusal of James Mackenzie to authorize the plan.

"It's a mistake. A big mistake. The prestige for the magazine would be enormous, something they'd talk about for years. Just the thought of bringing such a person down in ruins— It's staggering. Surely Mackenzie must see that."

The editor-in-chief shook his head in sad reply. "Mac knows what he wants and doesn't want. And what he doesn't want most right now is anything that could be used against us in Washington. Which means he doesn't want a big group in on this thing, or any kind of company-wide effort." He spun his chair around to look out the window. The sky to the west was very blue. "And he doesn't want any publicity. In fact, if anyone even mentions such a project he'll probably get fired." He repeated the chairman's final words. " 'There must be no chance of incident between us and the administration at this time. Or even the police—at least nothing we can admit to. There must be no formal project and no plans.' " Dunlop paused a moment, then added on his own: "No public plans anyway."

"But nothing can be done," protested the aide, "without using all the resources of the company. What's needed is a major campaign under a central command that can have spotters everywhere and be fed continuous information—"

"And become public knowledge a half hour later." He swung the chair back to face Henderson. "The orders were clear and absolute. No publicity."

"Then there's nothing we can do."

"Nothing that would attract attention," corrected Dunlop. "Which isn't exactly the same as doing nothing."

Bishop had remained with the corpse all night. He did not sleep but sat silent by the window watching the passing landscape, the girl's still body beside him on the bed. He felt a power within him as he gazed out at the dark and deserted countryside. Sleep was death, and all the silent towns were filled with the dead. Only he was alive to witness the utter desolation. Only he had the power.

In the morning he put the corpse in the tiny bathroom. She had been strangled so that no blood would get on the sheets. When the porter buzzed the compartment to ask if he could make the bed, Bishop ducked into the bathroom and locked the door. In an excellent girlish voice he shouted out a yes through two closed doors. He turned on the water tap as the porter entered, to let him know the occupant was using the bathroom. When the porter left Bishop thanked him, again in the girlish voice. Afterward he locked the compartment door and stretched the girl's body across the red flower-patterned seat. He placed the white hand towels underneath the body and pulled down the shade. Then he took out his knife.

John Perrone and senior editor Fred Grimes, the *Newstime* crime specialist, met with Dunlop at noon. A big company task force was out because of the need for complete secrecy. Private detectives were out because of the possibility of being compromised. What they needed was someone in the company with the instincts of a detective and the abilities of a reporter. A man who knew the company operation and could use it to investigate and track down Vincent Mungo.

One man.

Martin Dunlop rubbed the bridge of his nose, looked over at his wall paintings. From Central Park down the breadth of Manhattan to the Battery all seemed peaceful. In the dim background the Statue of Liberty promised hope.

He turned to his managing editor.

"Who," he asked softly, "is the best investigative reporter on the magazine?"

John Perrone glanced at Fred Grimes. They seemed to agree without a word being spoken.

"The best investigative reporter in the whole damn company," Perrone announced grandly, "is one of my own senior writers, Adam Kenton."

"And he already owns the story," said Grimes.

"Where is he now?"

"In the L.A. bureau."

"Get him," said editor-in-chief Dunlop. "I want him in my office tomorrow morning."

The Train ground into Grand Central at 1:30 P.M., an hour late. Bishop threw the bloody towels in the toilet bowl and stuffed the body on the seat. In blood he wrote "C.C." on the mirror. Opening the compartment door a crack, he listened for a moment. There was no one in the aisle. He quickly slipped out.

All was confusion as people left the train.

When he got to his seat he picked up the flight bag and slung it onto his left shoulder. From under his jacket he removed the zippered money case and held it in his right hand as he walked through the car and off the train.

On the long walk down the platform to the track gate Bishop smiled happily. He had given New York a present to announce his arrival. The King of California was in the Empire State.

He had a feeling it was where he belonged.

At the end of the platform he passed through a marble maze and suddenly he was in the hub of Grand Central terminal. To him it looked like a science-fiction city, with millions of people running back and forth. He was struck with awe. It was more beautiful than anything he had ever imagined.

He pushed his legs forward and slowly entered the maelstrom. Far ahead was the biggest clock he had ever seen. He walked toward it and was soon lost in the crowd.

The date was October 15, 1973.

Remember it.

In the official lexicon of the New York City Police Department, it eventually came to be known as Bloody Monday.

BOOK TWO

Adam Kenton

ELEVEN

He was a loner who liked a woman when he needed one and never really thought about them the rest of the time. Whatever tender feelings he may once have had for women in general were lost in the backwash of a disastrous early marriage, but Adam Kenton didn't notice anything missing. He lived out of suitcases and knew bellhops and bartenders by their first names in a hundred tank towns across the country. His work often kept him on the move and for him one city was the same as another, all of them corrupt and full of men with murderous intent. He was fascinated by power, and since men held all of it these were the people he frequented. Suspicious of everybody, trusting no one, he saw monsters everywhere, ready to pounce on the unwary. Politicians, bankers, businessmen, revolutionaries, public servants of every stripe, merchants of every persuasion, all were greedily stealing whatever they could. Government or private industry made no difference, they all had their fingers in the pie. His job was to find them out. In darkened corridors or crowded rooms, on empty street corners or busy boulevards, through mountains of paper and miles of records he searched, sought, questioned, demanded, threatened, cajoled and wheedled his way to facts and figures that could help in the pursuit of his prey. An air of quiet desperation often accompanied such movements, and over the years this kind of furtive solitary activity had made its mark on the patterns of Kenton's mind. He had no real friends. In his disordered view the stale smell of corruption seeped through everything and everybody, and though his puny efforts had met with some small success he soon came to realize that the quest for incorruptibility was futile and perhaps even dangerously corrupt in itself. Yet he persevered though his personal life was empty, his human existence meaningless, and his twice-a-week sweat socks all had holes in them.

Of average height, wiry in body and loosely coordinated, Kenton yet gave the appearance of grim purpose and determination. It was mostly his eyes, which could instantly open wide in mock belief or close to narrow slits to indicate suspicion and distrust, as well as accommodate all shades of disbelief in between. His face, heavily lined, also told of his singleness of mind, at least to those able to read it properly. The lips were thin, the nose sculptured, the cheeks hollowed and high. With his face closed and eyes narrowed he presented a formidable force indeed to those from whom he sought something. Very often it was enough to get him what he wanted.

Most recently working out of the Los Angeles bureau, he was now suddenly being recalled to New York. The Telex message had given no reason, not a word beyond the imperatives of the move. Nor had the call from the executive editor been any more helpful except for the assurance that all would be explained upon his arrival. Eminently suspicious, his immediate thought was that he had been getting too close to the power structure in his articles on the irrigation scandal. Or was it the searching look he was giving California State Senator Stoner? Or maybe even his investigation of illegal Mexican immigrants. Whatever the story, he was close to something and somebody was beginning to hurt. So he was being reassigned. He trusted his own company no more than any other and often had fantasies of digging into *Newstime* operations at the highest levels. But what troubled him most at the moment was the name of Martin Dunlop on the Telex message. He had never met the august editor-in-chief. Only his boss, John Perrone, spoke to Dunlop. And Dunlop spoke only to God, who in this case was called James Mackenzie. Yet here he was, recalled on Dunlop's direct orders. He frowned at the thought of what it could mean.

Past groups of sleepy travelers and impatient personnel he picked his way out of the TWA terminal and into a yellow cab. He was going on a special assignment, that much was certain. Feeling a rush of anticipation, he lay back and closed his eyes to the late night gloom that surrounded the fleeing cab on its headlong flight into the midst of Manhattan.

On the front seat next to the driver an early-bird edition of the *Daily News* screamed murder in Grand Central Station. A young woman's body, gutted like an animal's, had been found on an in-bound train at 4:40 Monday afternoon. The train, the Lake Shore Limited, had arrived at 1:30 from Chicago. The savage murder was believed to be the work of the California madman Vincent Mungo.

Kenton had written several pieces about Mungo of course, including the recent story that had been such a success. What he didn't yet know, as New York slipped into Tuesday morning, was that Mungo had struck again. Or that he would be asked, *ordered*, to go after the story of the year. Long afterward he would be heard to say more than once that had he known what lay ahead of him at that moment . . .

By eleven o'clock Tuesday morning Adam Kenton knew why he had been summoned to New York and what was expected of him. He had been given the Rockefeller Institute profile to read and had then listened to Martin Dunlop and John Perrone discuss the project at length. As they briefed him, his eyes grew smaller until only pinpoints of light remained. He was to track down Vincent Mungo for the glory, and benefit, of the magazine and the company. He would conduct what amounted essentially to a one-man operation, headquartered in an unmarked office on the seventh floor, away from prying eyes. Everything he needed would be given him. He would have virtually all the resources of the company at his command. His authority would be unquestioned, the funds unlimited. Only time was in short supply; if he didn't get to Mungo before the police did, the entire effort would be wasted and the project labeled a failure. Naturally nobody wanted that.

There was, unfortunately, one small catch.

The entire operation had to be conducted in total secrecy. No one outside the company would know of the search. That was on direct order of James Llewellyn Mackenzie himself. Even within the Newstime organization only a few top people would know of the existence of such a project. There would be no reports written or files kept. Nothing would be on paper. All communication from the field would be shredded each evening. Inquirers would be told only that Kenton was gathering material for another cover story on Vincent Mungo.

That was it.

Just a simple clandestine operation involving dozens, perhaps hundreds, of people in the field who could be told nothing. Searching for a man who had eluded the combined efforts of federal authorities and the police of a dozen states and cities across the entire length of the country. And working without benefit of any time schedule, since the whole thing could blow up at any time with Mungo's capture by police.

Added to which were no clues to Mungo's latest identity. And no witnesses to his present appearance. At least none alive.

As each of these desperate facts sifted into his consciousness, Kenton wondered if the three men in the room realized what an impossible assignment they had handed him. Surely they must see that there was no chance of success, barring a miracle.

Of the few things in which he still believed, miracles was not one.

Several times during the briefing he wanted to ask what idiot had dreamed up the idea of a magazine searching secretly for a mass murderer. Besides being insane, it sounded damned illegal! But his reporter's instincts warned him that the answer was already right there in the room.

Something suddenly stuck in his suspicious mind. California Senator Jonathan Stoner was now riding his own crest to national prominence. He didn't need Vincent Mungo any longer; at best Mungo was an embarrassment, at worst a political liability. The sooner Mungo was killed off the better it would be for Stoner. The one thing the senator didn't need at this point was adverse publicity.

Kenton silently vowed to learn what he could of Stoner's activities, past and present, just in case that was part of the reason he was now in New York. He did not intend to be sidetracked from a story by anyone, and most certainly not by his own people.

". . . and you'll start immediately. Set things up as quickly as you can. You'll have whatever you need."

Dunlop was speaking and Kenton found himself nodding in agreement, much against his will.

"Everything will be routed through Grimes here. He'll be your liaison in the company." The editor-in-chief turned to the leather couch. "Fred, you know the ropes in this kind of operation. See that things run smoothly." He looked around. "Anything else?"

"Just one thing," said John Perrone. "If we want this kept secret, I suggest we adopt a code name. Something only we know about."

"Good idea."

Fred Grimes' brow wrinkled in thought. "It all started with the Rockefeller Institute profile on Mungo."

"Mungo shouldn't be mentioned."

"But the report can. Adam's supposed to be doing a story on Mungo."

"Fred's right," said Perrone. "It's the perfect cover."

"What is?"

"The Rockefeller Institute Profile: R.I.P."

"R.I.P. Ripper," cried Grimes. "The Ripper—"

"The Ripper Reference," said Perrone quietly.

Dunlop pursed his lips, then nodded. "It'll do." He turned to Kenton. "Use it on all communiques to the field. That's it then."

He reached for some papers on his desk. The meeting was over.

As the trio reached the door Martin Dunlop called out.

"Mr. Kenton, allow me now to offer my personal congratulations on the swift success of your mission. I know I speak for Mr. Mackenzie when I say the company is deeply indebted to you."

John Perrone and Fred Grimes exchanged quick glances on the way out.

The sly son of a bitch, Kenton muttered savagely to himself. He's fixed it so I can't fail or I'm through. And if I do somehow pull off the impossible, he'll wind up with all the credit, sure as shit. Either way I lose. The sly son of a bitch.

Still muttering, Kenton's sly mind had already begun to search for effective countermeasures. He was damned if he'd let some superslick country editor get the best of him.

Adam Kenton knew he was a good investigative reporter. Better than most and as good as the best of them. He researched his subjects carefully, dug thoroughly for facts, and always applied the human equation to his findings. How did this or that benefit the subject? If the answer was not clear he dug further. In his constant, sometimes frantic search for information he never allowed himself to forget the truth that men invariably acted out of self-serving motives. Whatever was done, whether by individuals or groups or even whole governments, ultimately was done for self-interest. His job was to discover that interest. The conclusions were then usually inescapable.

His only present regret was that he was not working for a paper like the *Washington Post.* For an investigative reporter Washington was the in place at the moment, the place where the news was literally being made by reporters digging into a corrupt government.

Short of that he was satisfied with *Newstime*. It was relatively honest for a mass magazine that served an incredible array of vested interests. The chief sin was not in what it printed, which was for the most part straight-forward, but in what it neglected to print. Some Machiavellian mind at the top, perhaps Mackenzie himself, had discovered that it was less troublesome to omit something altogether than to slant it. Once locked in print an article was open to censure, but an omission could always be called simply an oversight. It was a much more subtle and sophisticated way of managing the news, though no less reprehensible. Yet in his six years with the magazine Kenton had seen nothing of his pulled or even materially distorted. It was, even by his cynical standards, a pretty good record.

He was regarded by his peers on the magazine, and by the press corps in general, as a gifted, occasionally brilliant reporter who usually got his story whatever the odds. His investigative instincts were superb, and he had more than once refused offers from private industry. He liked writing about real people and he liked reporting the news, but most of all he liked to dig underneath the news to write about what was really happening. That gave him a sense of power, and power to a newsman, as he well understood, was what it was all about.

He had quickly come to the attention of the assistant managing editors, who soon began using him for the more difficult stories. Within a year he had become a staff writer, in three years a senior writer. He worked in a dozen cities and was always somewhere in the field, always on the move. Several times he was offered a supervisory position in one of the bureaus; each time the offer was refused. He was a maverick journalist who intended to continue doing the one thing that turned him on, and sitting behind a desk was definitely not it.

In 1972 he was sent to California, where he worked on the bizarre Juan Corona case. A Mexican-American, Juan Corona had been accused of killing at least twenty-five migrant workers over a two-year period. He was finally sentenced in the California courts to twenty-five consecutive life terms.

Later that year Kenton moved on to New Mexico, where he investigated a fantastic land-grant scheme that would have netted millions of dollars to a few unscrupulous real estate operators. The entire story appeared first in an issue of *Newstime*.

After several special assignments he returned to California in April of 1973, assigned to the Los Angeles bureau. The whole political climate of that state was in turmoil and could be, so some responsible people in New York felt, a harbinger of what was to come in national politics.

Kenton kept his investigative pores open and was soon deep into a number of stories. The articles on Caryl Chessman and Vincent Mungo, and one on the rise of Senator Stoner had been just a few of them.

Now here he was suddenly back in New York, where he didn't particularly want to be, and saddled with an impossible task that promised only trouble. He had nothing to go on, nothing to work with except his own skills. And those were hardly up to finding one man out of more than one hundred million in the fourth-largest country in the world.

Yet he had to admit that if he could somehow work the miracle, if he could get to Vincent Mungo first, his name would become a legend of investigative reporting. Assuming he could prevent Dunlop, the big corporate cheese, from stealing the glory. Or John Perrone from downgrading his role.

Assuming all that, including the possibility of miracles,

he would not only be plugged into the power but he would be part of the power itself, if only temporarily.

It was worth a shot, or so he thought at the moment. Which meant he knew he had no choice.

Back in Perrone's office he was asked what he needed for a start. A getaway car, he had replied grimly. Nobody laughed. He settled for a WATS line covering the whole country and a complete listing of *Newstime* reporters and stringers in all cities. He also wanted everything written about Vincent Mungo, from the smallest country rag to *The New York Times,* as well as copies of all important documents, starting with Mungo's birth certificate. Perrone had promised to put two researchers on the job immediately; both would be his for the duration of the project.

Anything else?

For the moment, no. Except—Kenton had smiled—he would require the full list of all *Newstime* confidential sources of information, Perrone's famed information spies. Without the list, he forcefully observed, he would be severely restricted in his ability to reach out quickly for a vital fact or a needed name or even a covert operation.

The managing editor had cautioned that the list was available only to three or four top men on the magazine. How could it remain confidential if allowed to circulate? Kenton had replied that only he would see the list, that in any event he would be solely responsible for its confidentiality and eventual return. A hurried call had prompted Perrone to consent.

If asked, both Perrone and Fred Grimes would have had to express a certain sympathy for their supersleuth at that moment. They recognized the difficulties he faced, the impossible odds he bucked. Yet they passionately believed it was worth a try. They wished Kenton good luck.

Now on the seventh floor he sat in his new temporary office looking out the window and thinking of California. Just twenty-four hours earlier he had been in sunshine and warmth, and here he was in a barren room on a dark and dreary New York day. It didn't seem fair somehow, and had he believed in the gods he would have cursed them roundly. As it was, he blamed John Perrone and Martin Dunlop and everybody at *Newstime.* But most of all he blamed Vincent Mungo.

He turned to watch the wizened man march into the

office. Military bearing, iron-gray hair clipped short, dark ferret eyes. He had heard the name before. Otto Klemp, the company security boss. Klemp introduced himself formally, allowing the ghost of a smile to disturb his rigid features. He allowed nothing else.

His message was brief and precise.

"While you are on this assignment you will live at the St. Moritz in rooms kept by the company. You will tell no one of your work beyond the cover story. *No one*, in or out of the organization. If your cover is blown for any reason, if the secrecy is compromised in any way, your assignment is automatically canceled." Again the ghost of a smile. "We will be watching your progress closely, very closely. Your quarry, as you know, apparently arrived in New York yesterday. The same day, I believe, as did you. Interesting, *nein?*" His hand was on the door. "In Austria they tell of the fox who dressed like a hound. When the chase began he ran with the pack. Everything went fine—until the wind shifted."

Klemp seemed to click his heels as he turned and slipped through the narrow opening. Kenton watched the door slowly close behind him.

Of all the traits that combined in Adam Kenton to make him the best investigative reporter on the biggest newsmagazine staff in the country, traits that had in a brief decade brought him a certain measure of renown and respect, and that would ultimately lead to a Pulitzer for his investigation of the sinister forces behind the movement for repeal of the Second Amendment to the Constitution of the United States, perhaps the most important was his ability to adapt himself to the roles of those from whom he sought information. In mannerisms and speech he seemed to blend into their public identities. His sympathetic understanding and acceptance almost invariably prompted a flow of confidences not normally given to reporters. Whether it was businessmen or politicians or bureaucrats or the police, he understood their problems. He was really one of them.

This metaphoric quality was coupled with an intense concentration that often enabled him to think like his adversaries. He constantly asked himself the question: What would they do next? Or: Why did they do that? His guess was usually correct. Only it wasn't ever just a guess but more of an instinctive leap into their minds.

This mental bit of magic, grounded in voluminous information and a brilliant imagination, probably more than anything else had led to the nickname of Superman given him by his peers, not without a strong touch of envy.

Average in everything including his clothes, appearing ordinary except for his eyes, he was able to become whatever was needed.

Beyond that, he had put in ten years at a job that required an ability to fight dirty and a stubborn refusal to quit. For whatever success he may have achieved he had paid a price in his increasing paranoia, his detachment from women, his negativistic outlook. The years had made him shrewd and tough; they had also brought out his hunger for power and the strong streak of sadism underneath. In his growing isolation, his fantasies of perfection and incorruptibility were becoming more fragmented. Yet the shrewdness and toughness were the dominant strengths of Kenton's professional life, and were ignored by others only at considerable peril to their freedom of operation or even liberty.

At age thirty-five, with a desperately poor childhood behind him, with a college degree paid by four years of menial jobs, with a disastrous marriage and two years in Vietnam, plus ten years on the firing line, four of them at newspapers in the boondocks and the last six in the big leagues at *Newstime*, Adam Kenton was just about immune to everything but good luck. And he certainly wasn't going to be fazed by veiled threats from within the company.

His only reaction to what Otto Klemp had said was to narrow his eyes to slits and think furiously.

A half hour's reflection convinced him of two things. There were some people in the company who really believed that he could scoop Vincent Mungo out of thin air and deliver him to the Corporate Powers, ready to give them the story of the year.

And there were some who wanted him to fail.

As his thoughts finally shifted toward the problem of an invisible madman who seemed to be worth a lot of money to a lot of people, John Perrone came into the room and sat down. He looked worried.

"So Klemp's been here already, eh? I wondered how long it'd take him. I saw him upstairs and he told me to make sure you had anything you needed. He stressed 'anything.' I think the man likes you." He hesitated. "Or else he's afraid of you. Does he know something I don't?"

Kenton glanced over at his boss. "Maybe he's really Vincent Mungo and he knows I'll find out." He grinned at the idea.

"It's no joke," said Perrone.

"Neither is this damn assignment."

"Don't underestimate him. Klemp is as tough as they come, and he's totally dedicated."

"To what?"

"To the job."

"Whose job?"

Perrone frowned. He never felt comfortable talking about Klemp.

"Mackenzie's," he said finally, "if it got down to that. And of course his own. But his actual job is to keep everything locked and everybody in line. Real gung-ho on security, you know the type."

"I've met a few."

"His passion is to keep secret things secret."

"And dead things dead?"

Perrone looked around the empty office.

"That too," he answered quietly.

Somewhere a clock struck the hour. Twelve noon. Only 9 A.M. in California. Kenton pursed his lips in thought. He would still be in bed, hoping for a few more minutes. Instead he was in a sealed glass cage surrounded by enemies and saddled with a lunatic who was his sole means of escape. If he didn't get Mungo he would lose his reputation, if not his job. Sure, he'd get other offers but he liked his work and he liked *Newstime*. It had style and class and it suited him just fine. He sighed. There was no way out; he was trapped and he would be forced to do what they wanted, at least this time. But in doing so he would, by God, keep his eyes open to the Senator Stoner angle, and to Otto Klemp and everyone else in the company. And if he found anything wrong pounce like the Baskerville hound itself.

He shook his head. It was settled, and as his mind turned to the chase he slowly began to see himself as the fox. What would he do?

"You've got to come up with something, Adam. And fast. My ass is all the way out on this one. Spend whatever it takes. I'll see that you get everything you want from this end."

It was the managing editor. He was still here, still talking.

Kenton pulled his thoughts away from the chase. His eyes widened, his face softened, the sly look disappeared. He turned to the other man.

"It's not a matter of money. This so-called madman's had whole states after him, with all their resources." He snorted in derision. "No, I'm afraid not. If it was that simple he'd be long dead."

"Then what?"

"Information. We need information. Lots of it. We must know everything about him, from wherever we can get it. And then—"

"And then?"

Kenton smiled. "Then maybe we can outfox him."

Each man sat with his thoughts for a moment. Perrone was the first to speak.

"I've already assigned two researchers to work with you. They're to know nothing of course."

"That will be difficult."

"Try your best."

"What about Grimes? Where does he fit in?"

"Fred will give you all the help he can. He's our crime expert and knows everybody on both sides of the fence. Technically he's your superior but on this job he'll do whatever you say. He's already been told. Does that bother you?"

"No, as long as he plays it straight."

"Fred's a good man. He can be a lot of help."

"What's the chain of command?"

"You report to me directly. No one else."

"Is that an order?"

Perrone looked at him sharply. "If it has to be."

"What about Dunlop?"

"I'll handle him."

"And Klemp?"

Perrone thought for a moment.

"Him too," he said finally.

"How many know about me?"

"Six from the magazine know we're going after Mungo. Dunlop and his aide Patrick Henderson; my executive editor, Christian Porter; Mel Brown, who heads up Research; and Fred and me. From the corporate side, Mackenzie of course, and Otto Klemp. And the group vicepresidents for magazines and newspapers—they had to be told. That's about it for the moment."

"Ten little Indians," said Kenton thoughtfully.

"Some of them are big."

"Ten little big Indians." He grimaced. "I want a list of everyone with their titles. If I'm playing I want to know who's sitting at the table."

"You'll have it this afternoon."

"And keep them off my back. I'll have enough to do without them hanging around."

Perrone nodded.

"One more thing," he said softly. "Martin explained why we want this project to be top secret. Besides the usual competitive reasons, we can't afford to get involved politically right now in anything that even smells like press manipulation. What he didn't explain was where that left you. If you're picked up for interfering in police business or withholding information or any kind of covert operation, we can't help you."

"I figured that," said Kenton.

"As far as the company is concerned," continued Perrone, "you're doing a story on Mungo and that's all. In practice, of course, the magazine will call for your release and have its legal staff in court. But as to any provable criminal charges—"

"I know," said Kenton mechanically. "If I'm caught I'm on my own."

"In this particular case I'm afraid that's about it. Naturally there would be some financial arrangement made if that happened. And of course a job when you returned. But I just wanted you to know what you're up against."

"I think I already know what I'm up against," murmured Kenton.

Perrone stood up, obviously relieved. He walked to the door. "Do your best on this, Adam. If you get to Mungo before the cops do, he's worth his weight in gold to all of us." He turned the knob.

"By the way," called the gold digger from his desk. "Just for the record, who picked me for this impossible assignment?"

"I did," said the managing editor on the way out. "Me

and Fred Grimes. We figured it was a job for a superman."

The closing door brought with it a quietness that swept through the room. In due time Kenton shook himself out of his deep reverie and left the office. Through the lunch-hour streets he fought his way over to P.J. Clarke's where he had a fillet of sole and a bottle of beer. He saw no one he knew. Although surrounded by people in the crowded restaurant, many of whom were no doubt in the communications industry, he felt himself more alone than he had ever been in his life and he wondered at that moment if Vincent Mungo, wherever he might be in Gotham City, felt that way too.

Had he really been Superman, his X-ray vision could have told him that Vincent Mungo was indeed in the city and no more than a mile from him, his phenomenal hearing might have picked up Mungo's soft humming as he attended to business, his blinding speed could have propelled him swiftly to the site, his incredible strength would perhaps have prevented still another murder and mutilation.

Because he was not Superman he did none of these superhuman things and would not learn of Mungo's latest outrage until the evening news. Meanwhile he ate his lunch in silence and took a cab back to the office. On the desk he found a stack of clippings about the California killer, the beginnings of what he had requested earlier, and he began going through them methodically. After a long while the phone rang.

Chief of research Melvin Baker Brown had given him the two best researchers on the staff. They were already at work getting things he wanted. And if there was anything special he needed, or if he ran into informational difficulties, he should just give a call. What's that? Yes, that shouldn't be too hard to work up. A little strange perhaps but hell, everything on this one is strange. Sure, he'd have it in the morning. Hopefully. When? No, that's impossible. The whole thing has to run through the computer. That's right. Okay. Will do. And good luck, hear?

He replaced the phone and returned to his reading. Every so often he made a note on a sheet of paper; eventually the page was filled. Before starting another he lit a cigarette and smoked quietly. As he finished, the door opened. It was Fred Grimes.

"Been delegating a little authority upstairs," Grimes began jovially, "just in case I get stuck down here in the pits. Always wanted to do that." He sat down in front of the desk. "How goes it?"

"Feeling my way."

"Uh-huh. Bet you don't feel so good right about now."

"I've felt better."

"Amen." Grimes grew serious. "I know they think it can be done, especially John and Martin Dunlop, and they got you all wired to do it. But what do you think?"

"I was just going to ask you the same thing."

Grimes stared at him a moment. "You want it for real?"

Kenton nodded.

"I don't think you have a chance in hell."

"Why not?"

"The guy doesn't kill for any of the normal reasons of personal profit or revenge or even love. He picks on strangers. That means he can strike anywhere. So you got no motive. Without motive you can't look for opportunity. So you got nothing. If he doesn't make a mistake he can go on forever. Or retire like Jack the Ripper. If he slips up, the cops grab him. So what chance have you got?"

"That's about the way I see it," said Kenton. He sounded discouraged.

"You can always quit."

"No good. They'd just say I was Vincent Mungo in disguise."

Both men laughed.

"Now that you mention it there are no prints, and with a face change you could almost pass for him. A little old maybe."

"Killing ages a man, haven't you heard?"

"Well, you must've had your share, all right."

"Thanks, pal."

"Seriously, I'm glad you're going to give it a try."

"Even though there's no chance?"

"Even so," Grimes crossed his legs. "You're the best they got here, and somebody should be doing this kind of investigative reporting. It's what the business is really all about. Or should be anyway." He smiled, embarrassed. "So where do we start?"

"At the beginning." Kenton pointed to the papers on his desk. "I've learned a great deal already this afternoon. The Rockefeller profile, for instance, suggests—not concludes, just suggests—that Mungo might be killing only women out of hatred for his mother rather than love of his father. Unconsciously of course. His notes indicate he's emulating Chessman and that's obviously what he thinks. But when it comes to violence, hate is usually a much stronger motive than love. Now I think, you see, that the doctors might just be right. It's something I never even thought of when I was doing the L.A. stories on Mungo. Maybe it's the thing everybody's missed in searching for him."

"Sounds good for a start."

"There's more. I checked the ages of the victims. All were between seventeen or eighteen and about forty— roughly the child-bearing age. No little girls, no older ladies. Just women who could have children."

"So he hates women and children."

"That's not all. From my earlier work on Mungo I know about the mutilations, stuff that never got in the papers in any graphic detail. It was mostly the sex organs and the breasts, the things for reproduction. Hacked to pieces. Just butchered beyond belief." He paused. "You begin to see what I'm getting at?"

Grimes thought rapidly.

"Mungo murders and mutilates women who could bear children because he unconsciously hates his own mother. He hates her because of something she must have done to him when he himself was a child." He glanced over at Kenton behind the desk. "How'd I do?"

"Good so far."

"There's more?"

"He's killing now," Kenton said slowly, "because he's reliving the horror of whatever it was the mother did to him when he was a child. Or I should say he's still living in that horror. He still sees himself as the child, defenseless against attack, unable to protect himself."

Grimes saw it. "But now he's a man and able to protect himself. He's killing women who could be mothers like his own mother."

"No!" Kenton smiled. "He's not a man, not in his

own mind. He's still the child living the horror and doing whatever the terrified beast in his nature can do to survive." He smiled again. "When pushed for survival we all revert to animality, you know."

"But you can't have him literally living as a kid," objected Grimes, "and killing as a man. You can't have it both ways. He's either trapped in that phase of his childhood and living it over and over just as it happened, or he's not. If he's in it, then he's living it exactly as it was. So he couldn't very well go around killing women unless he——"

His mouth sprang open in shock.

Their eyes met.

"Exactly," said Kenton softly.

Grimes sat very still for a long moment.

"You're not serious," he said at length.

"Very serious." Kenton lit a cigarette. "He killed his mother somehow as a child and now he's killing her over and over again. He can't help it. He's locked into that period of his life. For him his childhood is right now, right here in the present. He's caught in it and he'll go on feeling the terror and doing the killing until he's stopped. Only now it's much more complicated because of sex. He feels the sex instincts of the man and that gives him some of his drive."

He took a deep drag of the cigarette.

"Also it's much more dangerous now. Whatever his mind thinks in that insane part of it, he is physically a man with a man's strength and cleverness. The murders prove that. Wherever he's been since childhood, however many years that might be, he's developed a cunning that borders on sheer genius. He was obviously born with a high intelligence; his letters indicate that. They're expertly disguised, for one thing. Put that together with an absolute animal cunning for survival and you've got somebody brilliant enough to kill his way cross-country while laughing at the police. Think of it. He leaves clues, he writes letters, he announces his intentions. And still he's not caught."

He paused, lowered his voice.

"What he's done, I think, is to let the rest of the world in on his desperate struggle for survival. That's the Chessman angle, as I see it. He might sincerely believe that Caryl Chessman was his father; I don't dispute that. But he's unconsciously adopted that as his cover story. He's correctly gauged Chessman, at least from what I know of the man. His flashy arrogance, his hunger for publicity, his drive to be recognized. And he's trying to be like Chessman, to do what Chessman would do if he were here. Or what he *thinks* Chessman would do. That means of course that he believes Chessman was guilty twenty-five years ago.

"Now the two things are feeding each other. He survives by killing women who are his mother, and he kills women in celebration of his father. In the process he's turned into a monster that may be unique in crime, at least for America." He ground the cigarette in the ashtray as smoke flared from his nostrils. "What we're up against, don't you see, is an incredibly brilliant psychopath with the emotions of a terrified child and the animal instinct to live, caught in an eternal moment in the mind but where the deed is endlessly repeated in the real world." He shook his head in wonder at the thought. "The ultimate human killer. Seemingly normal, entirely functional, and totally, irrevocably programmed for mass destruction." He looked at Grimes across the desk. "A hundred like him, you know, could destroy a whole country."

The late afternoon rain had already started, as promised by the morning weather forecast. Drops the size of quarters splashed against the windows and ran down the glass to form small puddles on the casement ledges. In the wet streets below, solitary travelers sloshed homeward or toward the nearest safe refuge. Across the New York sky darkness gathered early in the face of the storm.

Fred Grimes rubbed his hands together in nervous reaction. When he spoke his voice crackled, as though he hadn't used it in a long time.

"Vincent Mungo's mother died when he was fifteen. She choked to death on some food. Whoever you're talking about, it's not Vincent Mungo."

"No," said Kenton in a tone of absolute conviction, "it's not Vincent Mungo."

In the distance thunder could be heard, but Grimes was oblivious to everything except his own breathing in the closed room.

"Who then?" he asked eventually.

"I don't know." Kenton shrugged helplessly. "It could be anybody.

"That's how he's been able to get around so easily. No one even knows what he looks like." It was not a question.

Kenton nodded.

"He could be somebody Mungo went to after his escape, somebody who took over the identity. Mungo could be hiding now, living a quiet life somewhere. Or most probably he's dead, killed by the impostor."

Grimes eyed the papers on the desk. "You got all that just from reading about him?"

"I've been thinking about him for weeks, asking myself where such maniacal hatred came from. Now I see it's right there in the profile. His mother. Something she did to him, but it had to be while he was very young. That's when any of us is most vulnerable; by the time we grow up we have other resources we can use to fight back. That insane kind of hatred had to come in childhood. If what he's doing now is a reenactment of that time, as I think it is, then it means he killed his mother originally. Or tried to kill her. Only he can't admit that to himself, no one could. I'm sure he's blocked out the memory, and right now he believes he's always loved his mother." He sat quietly for a few moments. "God only knows what he thinks happened to her. Or what he's using for a substitute."

"You can't prove any of this."

"No, I can't," said Kenton heavily, "but just the same it's what I'm going after. I need an edge, something to start me thinking like him. If my guess is right, maybe there's a slim chance I can get to him."

"What's your next step?"

"Mel Brown called before. I asked him to run a computer check of all known cases of matricide in California in the past twenty-five years. That might get us something."

"Why California?"

"It's a start." He pulled at his earlobe. "Since the killings began there, I'm hoping our mad genius is a native or at least lived there as a child. With such a list we can see how many are dead or in mental institutions and maybe narrow it down."

"Anything I can do?"

"Plenty. You can get that WATS line in here fast. Starting tomorrow, I want to be on the phone. And another desk for the researchers or yourself when you're down here. You can work up a list of the top brass in the police department for me. Also the mayor's office, with phone numbers for everybody. I'll need a dictaphone machine and a telephone recorder. Tell them to hook up the recorder to the junction box with the adapter set so it works when I pick up the receiver. I also need a small safe in here, one with a double combination lock. And I'm still waiting for several lists from John Perrone."

Grimes jotted some things down on the back of an envelope.

"I'll do what I can," he said cheerfully.

Outside, the rain blanketed the windows as the storm took hold of the beleaguered city. Somewhere north of New York lightning downed three heavy-duty transmission lines, and a man in Con Edison's energy-control center quickly blacked out a dozen Westchester communities and cut voltage in the city by 8 percent. In the office the light dulled a bit but neither man noticed it as each busily pursued his own thoughts. After a while Grimes inhaled deeply and stood up.

"There's one fatal flaw in your theory."

His voice jarred Kenton from deep concentration. "Only one?" he asked with a smile.

"One that's important, anyway."

"Go ahead."

"He killed his mother when he was a kid. Now he's a man and he's killing again. But what happened to him all those years in between? How come he wasn't killing all along, if he's locked into his childhood as you claim?" He shook his head. "Something's wrong there. Where was he for those years and what was he doing?"

Adam Kenton walked over to the window. "I don't know," he said softly, watching the ribbons of rainwater rolling down the smooth glass surface. "Not yet anyway."

He stared at his reflection, clearly visible against the black background.

"What you said about the child and the man. It reminded me of the time they found Jesus preaching in the temple after three days away from home. I think he was twelve at the time. When they questioned him the boy said, 'I must be about my father's business.' Or words to that effect."

He turned around, his face solemn.

"That funny thing is, you don't hear about him again either until he's a man."

TWELVE

Amos Finch felt guilty and he didn't like the feeling one bit. Not at all. Guilt was a middle-class aberration that had no business being in his psychological system. It was cheap sentimentality wrapped in emotional tinsel. It was pedestrian and bourgeois and counterproductive. Even worse, it was irritating. There simply was no excuse for allowing common standards of morality to cloud his fine perceptions. None whatsoever. He was not middle class, he didn't subscribe to its beliefs or accept its judgments. Nor did he intend to be governed by an obsolete set of values that proscribed selfish conduct. Selfishness kept the race going, and he was one of the superior breed that rose above mere moral considerations. No, he had nothing to do with guilt that came from looking out for one's own interests regardless of the suffering of others. He had no neurotic excesses. He was coldly analytical and detached.

But in truth Amos Finch was feeling guilty.

For three days he had known how to tell if Vincent Mungo was alive or dead. Or at least, if Mungo had really escaped from Willows State Hospital some three and a half months earlier. And for three days he had said nothing to anyone. A hundred times he had found himself at the phone about to call John Spanner in Hillside, and each time he had stopped.

When he analyzed his motives it all seemed eminently reasonable. He was watching a genius at work, an artist in action. Whoever the California Creeper really was just didn't seem to matter anymore. Identity and past life were meaningless now. Only the present meant anything. And what it meant was that he, Amos Finch, was witness to the emergence of a truly monumental mass murderer. A killer of incalculable guile, one perhaps destined to rank with Jack the Ripper and Bruno Lüdke. And perhaps even to surpass Lüdke's record of eighty-six women victims, if only left alone.

That was the rub.

For the sake of society, such a monster had to be captured or destroyed. Species survival demanded it. A defective organ must be removed for the good of the body. A defective individual must be removed for the good of the group. Vincent Mungo was defective. He was killing his own kind. He was cancerous.

He was also a genius and an artist and the most exciting thing to come along in Finch's lifetime of studying mass murders. He could be, should be, *must be* the crowning achievement of that life! He would be the subject of a definitive study, itself a work of genius and art. Written of course by the world's leading scholar on multiple murders. The book's title? *The Complete*...

That's when the guilt feelings began.

Finch wasn't going to give up his killer so easily. By now he had a vested interest in him, a proprietary interest that had become almost a mania. Each morning he listened to the news to hear if another victim had been added. Each evening he worked on his preliminary notes of the case, intending to include it in his courses at Berkeley the following semester. In between he collected everything he found printed about Vincent Mungo. He had his students looking too. No mention was too slight, no publication too obscure. He ran classified ads in several Bay area newspapers as well as in the *Los Angeles Times*, offering to pay for any item having to do with the celebrated killer, no matter how indirectly. He was undoubtedly the first to see Mungo as a collectible. While the primary purpose was scholarship, the monetary value was a definite consideration. He knew, for example, that personal items of, say, Jack the Ripper would be worth a fortune to interested collectors. He intended to become the foremost collector of the new Jack Ripper. Scholarship would be served and a fortune made. He wanted it all, anything and everything. And when he had everything, he wanted more.

The longer his collectible remained free the more celebrated he would become. And the more valuable, both in terms of the artifacts of his existence and the need for a definitive study of that life. Assuming he would continue his kills, of course. Finch had no doubt about that. His man seemed to be programmed for killing, as though it were a reflex action, involuntary, unable to control or prevent.

Sooner or later the end would come; Finch knew that and accepted it. He did not expect the man to stop suddenly, to go into retirement or die providentially. Yet the scholar in him, the scientific mind, wanted that end to be stretched out as far as possible. He saw it much as an experiment in the laboratory, where the knowledge gained was cumulative. In that sense there was no cutoff point, no time when the learning process was enough, the knowledge sufficient.

Only this wasn't the laboratory, nor were the madman's actions a controlled experiment. Decency demanded an end to such monstrous activity. Instinct demanded it too. And so did society.

Amos Finch was caught in a classic dilemma of science. One going back to Dr. Frankenstein and beyond.

Some weeks earlier he had settled in his mind that Vincent Mungo was not the killer being sought. With the growing notoriety, more and more had come to be written about Mungo until most of the facts of his life were known. When these were compared to the deeds of Jack Ripper, it was obvious to Finch that they were two different men. As far as he could tell, Mungo had virtually none of the qualifications needed to perform such deeds. Not the drive or the skill, much less the level of intelligence and imagination. He was a simple clod who existed, like most people, on the lowest rungs of function and achievement. To consider him equal to the genius at large was an artistic sacrilege.

Which left only two possibilities. Jack Ripper was either Vincent Mungo's partner on the night of the escape from Willows or he was someone totally unknown who started his murderous career after the escape and took Mungo's name as a cover. If it was indeed Mungo's companion who was found at Willows, then Jack Ripper was unknown. And Vincent Mungo among the missing. But if it was Mungo's body on that sodden earth, its face bludgeoned beyond recognition, then the maniacal killer was almost certainly the other man. Thomas Bishop.

Finch knew how to tell which one it was.

Maybe.

It all depended on a single anatomical feature.

If he could prove that the madman was not Vincent Mungo but very probably Thomas Bishop, the police would immediately circulate Bishop's picture and description nationwide. After that it would be only a matter of time before he was caught or killed. The only reason authorities had been unsuccessful so far was that they were looking for the wrong man.

The scholar in Finch didn't want that.

His instincts as a man fought his drive as a student of aberrant human behavior. At that moment he was too closely involved to notice his own aberrant behavior in not notifying officials immediately.

On Monday morning he had figured out a possible solution to the problem first raised by John Spanner. It had come, as he knew it would, after weeks of being worked out in those layers of mind beneath consciousness, where riddles are unraveled without direct thought. But he hadn't gone to the phone; he needed time to think. Then Monday evening brought him the news of the young woman found murdered on a train in New York.

Which was about the time he first noticed that irritating feeling.

Tuesday was mostly spent vacillating between the phone and his work. In the evening he learned of the second woman killed in New York, again apparently by his star subject. The irritation increased, and by Wednesday he found himself defending his position aloud. Which might have seemed perfectly reasonable except for the fact that he was alone in his study.

Amos Finch did not normally talk to himself aloud. Any manifestation of indecision was repugnant to him. If anything, his view of life leaned toward the overly simplistic: things came up, decisions were made, life went on. Indecision and vacillation were products of a lesser mind, as seen mostly in women and other domestic pets. That he should now be subjected to them irritated him still further.

That evening he went out to dinner with a young female friend. Deciding that talking to a woman was preferable to talking to oneself, he explained his problem to her, in hypothetical terms of course. She was flattered to be taken into his confidence; she had never before heard him talk about anything but sex and horse racing. And she understood perfectly. When he had finished his lengthy monologue about a superior man torn between conflicting desires, she smiled sweetly at him and told him that the solution was really very simple. He just had to do his thing.

She was twenty years old.

He stared at her and said nothing.

Later in bed, after he had done his thing, Finch finally came to a conclusion. No matter what the problem, he would never again try to talk intelligently to a woman. Not about important things anyway, or even the unimportant, beyond facts. It just wasn't worth the effort.

On Thursday morning he met his ten o'clock class and had difficulty concentrating on his lecture. In his afternoon class someone mentioned the latest crank artist in a deprecating way and he became annoyed. And highly indignant. Vincent Mungo was the latest and greatest! Yes, that was correct.

Except for two things.

He wasn't the greatest, not yet anyway.

And he wasn't Vincent Mungo.

At home again, he worked on a cipher puzzle for relaxation but he knew what he had to do. The decision had been made.

Bon Dieu! . . .

What he hated most about guilt feelings was that they made one feel so damn—*guilty.*

He called the Hillside police department and caught John Spanner as he was leaving. Spanner listened with growing excitement as Finch explained what should be done to determine the identity of the Willows body. Although out of the chase, the lieutenant had retained a keen interest in the Mungo affair and silently regarded it as his one supreme failure. Yet in the back of his mind a suspicion continued to lurk that he had been somehow close to the truth.

Now he would hopefully have a chance to prove it one way or the other. With luck. With a great deal of good luck.

He promised Amos Finch that he would look into it immediately and that he would call back when he had anything definite to report.

In minutes he was out of police headquarters and on his way.

Derek Lavery heard about it Monday afternoon. John Perrone had personally called to tell him that Vincent Mungo was apparently in New York. A woman's butchered body had been found on a train coming in from Chicago. It was Mungo's work.

Lavery was impressed by the news. Mungo had made it clear across the country. With his face known everywhere, leaving a bloody wake, he had still somehow managed three thousand miles. And he was supposed to be a mental case!

The Los Angeles bureau chief was also impressed by something else. John Perrone didn't usually phone him with a bit of interesting news; normally it was Christian Porter or even one of the several assistant managing editors. Lavery suspected it had something to do with the recall of Adam Kenton. That made two of them in New York—Adam Kenton and Vincent Mungo. And both on the same day. Which was quite a coincidence.

A cover story, thought Lavery. They wanted Kenton for a cover story. But a major one this time, the full treatment. Mungo was big news now and swiftly getting bigger. With the right hype he could become a national sensation. And he, Derek Lavery, had started it all with his story on Caryl Chessman and then the two on Mungo. Kenton had done most of the investigative work on all three, with strong help from Ding, so he was the logical choice for New York. Besides being the best they had on the magazine, except for himself and Ding of course. But he and Ding were a team, indivisible, and geared for stories with a wider scope. Adam Kenton was a loner and perfect for an in-depth look at Vincent Mungo. They were basically the same type anyway.

In truth he had been relieved when Mungo left California and the western states. He liked things done in a professional way, that is, everything kept at a distance. Never anything personal. Yet Mungo had made it personal by sending the letters, especially that one with the female . . . part.

That was unforgivable in Lavery's view. While it made for a good story, it necessarily involved him in the grubby details of direct police contact and it demoralized his mail room. Worst of all, it put him in a position of having to react to others instead of acting out of his own autocratic view and unquestioned authority. He had suddenly felt impotent.

He enjoyed being the captain of the ship and directing his vast energies outward from his Barcalounger. His enormous penthouse office was his captain's quarters, and he didn't like being drawn down into the boiler room. It unnerved him. He was a mover, a shaker, a leader of men. When he gave an order it was obeyed. But if he had to involve himself with petty details and people's emotions, then all his power was gone.

Without power, who was he?

By Thursday, Derek Lavery had almost forgotten about a homicidal maniac named Vincent Mungo. He had been given another reporter from the Chicago bureau to replace Kenton, and he was nursing along a number of stories, including a second one on the insanity-defense issue, which Ding was putting together. As far as Lavery was concerned, Mungo was John Perrone's New York headache now. His and Adam Kenton's.

And right where they all belonged.

He told his secretary to make a dinner reservation at the Yacht Club. Over the weekend he intended to go sailing.

At about the time that Derek Lavery's secretary called the Yacht Club, John Spanner was slamming the brakes to a screeching stop in front of the Hillside hospital. A minute later he was in the morgue records room checking the file on Thomas Bishop, DOA from Willows State on July 4, 1973. His fingers shook as he pulled the pictures of the body from the folder. There it was, impossible to miss. The body supposedly of Thomas Bishop. Whoever he had been, he was circumcised.

From the tiny morgue office next to the lockers,

Spanner called Sheriff Oates in Forest City and asked him to get to Vincent Mungo's family in Stockton and find out if Mungo had been circumcised. Yes, that's right. Circumcised. No, no joke. Try to get the information as soon as possible. At police headquarters. Or later at home. Right. That's the idea.

He did not tell the sheriff why he wanted to know such a thing, and Oates did not ask.

Next he called Willows and spoke with the new director, a Dr. Mason. He identified himself as the police official originally in charge of the murder investigation several months earlier. If the doctor would be kind enough to have someone check Thomas Bishop's file for a physical description. Specifically, if Bishop had been circumcised. Developments in the case necessitated that information. He realized that such things might not normally be in a file, but Thomas Bishop had been there for most of his young life and a complete description could be part of his record.

Dr. Mason promised to attend to it immediately and return the call. Hillside police headquarters? Yes, of course. Just as soon as it was received.

Spanner drove back to his office filled with dread.

Something would go wrong.

But nothing could go wrong.

If Bishop's file at Willows didn't have the answer, then he'd get it from the hospital record at birth. And if that didn't work out he'd find another way. Maybe some of the attendants or inmates had noticed Bishop in the shower, maybe he had a homosexual relationship with one or more of them. Or perhaps some relative somewhere remembered. Damn it, there had to be a way.

Twenty minutes later Dr. Mason was on the phone to report no mention of a circumcision in Thomas Bishop's physical-description data. But the doctor warned that it should not be taken to mean he was not circumcised, only that there was no mention one way or the other.

Spanner understood.

"One strange thing in Bishop's file, though."

"Oh?"

"Or rather not in the file, which is the strange part."

"What was that?"

"Every inmate folder has two photos, one taken on admission and one usually taken within the previous two years. In Bishop's case this would mean a picture of him as a young boy and another as he looked now."

A pause.

"The strange thing is—"

"Yes?"

"Well, both pictures are missing."

Spanner's heart quickened.

"There apparently are no pictures of Thomas Bishop anywhere."

That was it!

No pictures of him in his file. He had gone there as a boy. So no pictures of him as a man anywhere. It was too much of a coincidence. The policeman in Spanner rebelled at the thought.

He got out his own file on Vincent Mungo, put together at the time of the Willows killing. The information on Bishop was in it. Born April 30, 1948, in Los Angeles County General Hospital. Mother: Sara Bishop Owens, deceased. Father: Harry Owens, deceased. The mother was killed by the boy at age ten. But how did the father die?

Spanner intended to find out.

He asked Communications to request immediate help from the Los Angeles police. What he wanted was the full record of Thomas Bishop at the hospital in which he was born. Also, he needed all information regarding the death of the father, Harry Owens.

Hopefully, morning would bring some answers. After a half hour's attempt to work on other things he gave up and went home.

At eight o'clock he was awakened by the phone while dozing in front of the TV. It was Oates. He had talked to Vincent Mungo's people in Stockton. The boy had been circumcised at the hospital where he was born. Perhaps someone had thought that Mungo sounded Jewish. Or maybe it was just done routinely, in view of the fact that no father seemed to be around. Though the mother's family was Protestant, no one objected to the circumcision. It didn't seem important.

No chance of a mistake?

None. Why?

He told Oates that the Willows body had also been circumcised.

With the body gone, how did he know?

The pictures that were taken in the morgue showed the circumcised penis. It was the one thing they had never thought of.

Until now.

No, it was a civilian.

Spanner told him about Amos Finch and his ideas on the killer. Or killers. And how Finch had solved the riddle of how to identify the dead man.

Except he hadn't really solved it yet, Oates pointed out. All they knew now was that it could've been Mungo. But if Thomas Bishop also had been circumcised, they were back where they started.

Los Angeles was checking on him now.

It would just be a matter of time.

All they could do was wait.

When he finally drifted into troubled sleep, John Spanner dreamed that he stood helpless, unable to move, as a figure slowly approached from a great distance. When it drew closer he saw it was of average height and weight and dressed in man's clothes. Still nearer came the figure until he was able to see the face. It had no features. Nothing. Just a small hole where a mouth should have been, out of which came a sound of maniacal laughter.

As the figure drew abreast, a hand mechanically opened to reveal a long thin knife of incredible sharpness. Spanner watched in mounting horror while the hand with the knife rose higher and higher and higher until it blotted out all light in front of him and he stood in the dark screaming against the insane laugh as the knife plunged downward through his eyes to softened tissue turning the sockets to rivers of blood. . . .

THIRTEEN

Bishop rose early Tuesday morning filled with enthusiasm. He intended to do many things on his first day in New York. In his narcissistic mind the city lay before him like an extension of his own body, open, waiting to be touched, to be caressed in the warm glow of self-gratification. He would walk its streets to feel the blood coursing through its veins and arteries, he would stand on crowded corners and listen to its heartbeat. In the nameless faces and faceless bodies of its inhabitants he would find the ultimate onanistic thrill of knowing that the Power was now among them. He was the Power and he alone knew that he held absolute life and death over all around him. At any moment, in the while of a whim, he could strike down any one of them, any number of them, without design or effort, as they scurried about their meaningless duties, their empty lives. The thought was delicious. He would look at them, the women of New York, and in their eyes he would see that for which they longed so desperately and worked so diligently. They would find through him the release from their pain and madness. He would give them their due, which was death. And for his benevolence they would honor him by taking into their vile bodies for the last time the seed of life which they both craved and feared. It was justice. In the final moment of suffering they would become part of him and he them, and even as he was reborn in the agony of orgasm they would be released in the ecstasy of death.

He alone would choose upon whom to bestow this final ultimate blessing. Nor would he, could he, be stopped. They were waiting for him by the millions, not knowing who he was or when he would strike, but waiting in frantic hope nonetheless. He would not disappoint them. Though the quest was endless and victory seemingly impossible, he would continue with his mission for in truth he could do no less. His was the Power that prevailed and he survived only by its exercise. Now in New York, where he believed he belonged from the very beginning, and in which he intended to remain at least for a while, Bishop had no doubts that he would continue to be safely anonymous as he prowled the largest city in the world. That it might not literally be the very largest city in the world didn't bother him; it was eminently big enough. Nor did he doubt that he would find enough work to keep him occupied. He had already noticed in his few Monday hours that women were everywhere. Dozens of them, hundreds, thousands, millions of them. They were absolutely everywhere, just waiting for him. Everywhere.

Meanwhile the city lay open before him. He would search out a place to live, a crowded area of young people with little money where he could go unnoticed. He would secure still another identity, this one virtually undetectable. He would funnel the hundred-dollar bills he had in the black case into legal channels, so that he could draw from the amount or add to it. He would fabricate a whole history in order to give the appearance of roots, should anyone become inquisitive about a newcomer to town. Finally, he would create some slight business venture in order to have a seemingly legitimate source of income, one at the barest survival level, to be sure, yet enough to allay any suspicions about how he managed to survive.

Since he wasn't going to travel, at least for a while, and would not be in bus stations or train depots where police were watching, he decided to grow a beard. It was a common practice among young men now and would enable him to blend in more easily. In the unlikely event that his true identity were discovered, he would be safer with a beard. The authorities had no photographs of him any longer but they would be able to come up with a good drawing of his face. Putting a beard on the drawing would render it almost useless, and he could always change the shape of his own. It was the best he could do short of plastic surgery, which he ruled out as being too risky even though he now had the money. A surgeon would surely become suspicious and notify the police. While he believed himself perhaps immortal, Bishop somehow knew he was not bulletproof.

All this and more would he do in the days to come. Winter clothes had to be bought, maybe even some light furniture and bedding. Books about New York had to be read, the city divided into areas and studied. With living quarters and an established identity, with a new face and the proper money, he would be truly invisible. And with invisibility would come invincibility. A face in the crowd, one of the masses, a workingman, able to slip in and out, appear and disappear, undistinguished, unrecognized, unseen.

Untouchable.

Not as the leper, slow and cumulative.

But as the plague, swift and deadly.

In the tickings of his heart, in the twistings of his mind, Bishop knew this all would come to pass. But first—

First he would offer up a sacrifice in celebration.

He would perform his ritual in thanksgiving for his safe arrival upon these shores. In the beginning he had intended to move ever onward because to remain fixed was far too dangerous. As he crossed the mountains and plains, the cities and towns of America, eventually he came to realize that New York was his true destination, his star in the East. The wisest of men by his own definition, he did not try to fight that which compelled him to follow the star. Unlike others, he was aware of his destiny and accepted it without bitterness.

Now he had arrived safely at his destination, at least for the present, and his star shone overhead. It was time to celebrate.

By 8:30 that Tuesday morning he was already out of the dingy hotel of one night's lodging. He turned into Broadway in the eighties and headed downtown. The air was cool and crisp, the start of one of those bright October days for which New York is famous. Bishop shivered against the cold; his jacket seemed suddenly inadequate in such weather, and he decided it would be prudent to buy something warmer as soon as possible. And perhaps a heavier shirt and a cap of some kind. He noticed the men in suits, apparently on the way to office work; most of them wore topcoats. The younger people he saw were dressed in the fashion of youth everywhere; in denim and corduroy and outer jackets of every description and indeterminate origin. Boots of leather or plastic, usually well scuffed and worn under bell-bottom pants, were the standard footwear for both sexes. He gazed down at his own shoes, now worn beyond redemption, and made a mental note. They would have to go too.

On Broadway and 73rd Street the chill drove him into a small restaurant, where he ordered ham and eggs and black coffee. His lifetime in an institution had equipped him for an early breakfast and early dinner, and though he had changed his eating habits to conform to his new-found freedom the idea of breakfast seemed reasonable to him. His table was by the window, a square slab of wood on a center stand and topped with red Formica. The four chairs were the straightback kind, one had a hole punched into its oval seat. He bypassed it for the window slot.

Sipping his hot coffee he watched the hordes of people, all of them intent on their separate journeys. With closed faces and rigid bodies, they rushed past or waited for buses or dove between cars against the light. They behaved *en masse* as though they needed desperately to go somewhere and had precious little time to get there, and after a while Bishop became uneasy watching them. He finally turned away as his mind flashed on an image of rats scurrying in a maze that he had once seen on television. They had nothing to do and nowhere to go but they kept up their frantic activity. He wondered what all the people had to do and where they needed to go. In five minutes he had seen more people than he had in five months at Willows. It was still a bit scary and he was glad he hadn't come upon them his first day out.

His ham and eggs were brought over and he ate hungrily, staring into the plate. He saved the toast for last, to go with a second cup of coffee.

As he lifted his eyes from the empty dish he saw the girl at the next table. She was sitting alone with a cup in front of her, its handle chipped. Her hair was disheveled, her eyes vacant. She sat motionless save for a slight swaying of the head. Though she stared in his direction she gave no indication of having seen him. For a moment he thought she might be ill but then he remembered all the

TV shows he had seen about drug addicts. They looked just like the girl at the table. That same kind of vacant stare, that same nodding of the head. He kept watching her, fascinated.

A man eventually came from behind the counter and told her it was time to go. She didn't hear him. He said it again. Still no notice. He gently took her arm and raised her to a standing position, then slowly escorted her to the door. He pushed it open and led her out to the sidewalk and a metal pole by the curb. She appeared not to care.

Back in the restaurant the man rubbed his hands briskly as he returned behind the counter. He was a New Yorker, wise to the ways of many life styles and much experienced in the neighborhood. He knew better than to startle a junkie, to come upon one suddenly. Junkies might do anything. The best way was to touch them gently and lead them firmly. They were sick people who needed help they didn't get. He felt sorry for them even though most of them were pigs. Like the girl he had just got out. He would never trust a junkie, not even for a cup of coffee. Without money they were the poorest of the poor, and that was the worst thing of all to be in New York. Or the South Pole too.

Bishop had noted the episode carefully. The man was very gentle with her, very considerate. Which meant he loved her and was sorry she was a drug addict. It was sad and Bishop giggled softly. He was already learning about New York.

He went back to his coffee and toast. People were still scurrying in all directions. Traffic was backing up, horns were blowing. Someone dashed madly across the street, causing brakes to squeal in the far lane. Others seemingly dared cars to hit them.

A female drug addict. He considered the possibilities. Here, on Broadway in New York City, a woman with dead eyes was killing herself with evil drugs. Trying to end the horror of what she was. Probably many others were doing the same. Women who couldn't stand the awful suffering any longer and in their madness turned to drugs of death. Women too old or too ill or too crazed to destroy any more men; women ready to die, wanting to die, crying out to die.

Maybe he could help some of them.

He was still thinking about helping women when the young man came over to the table. He took the broken chair, slumped down on it. His hands reached up for his sunglasses. "You holding?"

Bishop turned to him. "Holding what?"

"Your dick," shot back the other in exasperation. "What you think I mean? Scag. You buying or selling?"

"What's scag?" Bishop asked. He had the feeling that the youth in pink jeans and flannel shirt had mistaken him for someone else. Someone who spoke another language.

"You a narc or something?"

"Not really."

"You from the mob?"

"Not really."

"Which is it?"

"Really not."

"You just come in for a cup of coffee, is that it?"

Bishop didn't understand what was so strange about that. It was a restaurant, wasn't it? Why did people go into restaurants except to eat? But maybe New York was different. Maybe it had restaurants where no one went in just for coffee, maybe even where no one went in to eat anything. But then why did they go at all? He would try to learn what he could.

"I also had ham and eggs," he said helpfully. He thought that might make him seem all right.

"No shit," said the youth in disgust.

"No shit," said Bishop, trying to follow the leader in order to understand what was expected of him.

The pink-jeans-and-flannel-shirt looked at the speaker for the first time. He didn't see a cop or a hood. So what was it?

"You from here?" he asked suspiciously.

"No."

"From where?"

"There."

The youth nodded in sympathetic understanding. "Rough."

"Rough enough." Bishop began to believe the man was totally insane.

"So you holding?"

"Holding what?"

That did it for the jeans-and-shirt. He could see only

a pure, dumb hick who probably didn't know one drug from another. And he had some sugar pills on him.

"I got some dynamite shit," he whispered hoarsely. "You want a dime?"

"I have enough money. Thanks anyway."

The youth mumbled under his breath. "I mean heroin. Top stuff. I got it in pills. Two for ten bucks."

Bishop looked at him reproachfully. "I don't take drugs," he announced with an air of injured dignity.

"So get 'em for a friend."

Dignity turned to the window. The girl was still by the curb, leaning up against the post. An idea came into his head. "All right," he said, turning back. "I'll buy two of your drug pills. But only for five dollars." He remembered a TV show in which a narcotics officer told how drug dealers would sell to strangers for double the price. He was too smart for anything like that.

"Five dollars," he repeated, "or nothing."

The youth didn't even hesitate. Reaching into his shirt pocket, he took out two transparent capsules filled with a white powder and shoved them into the waiting hand.

From his jacket Bishop pulled several bills, careful not to reveal the black money case concealed underneath. He unfolded them; the smallest was a ten. The young man said they wouldn't change it in the restaurant, but he offered to go across the street to the cigar store and get change while his amigo finished his coffee. It would only take a minute.

Bishop thought that was very nice of him. He watched as the dealer crossed Broadway, dodging cars and buses. Somewhere on the other side of the crowded avenue he lost sight of his ten dollars.

Twenty minutes later, his second cup of coffee long gone, Bishop sadly got up and paid for his meal and left the restaurant. He reminded himself to be more careful in New York. The city might contain some thieves.

Outside he walked over to the girl. Her head was slowly bobbing up and down. Passersby would stare at her for a second and then hurry onward, never breaking their stride. She seemed oblivious to them.

"Where do you live? Can I take you home?" He put his hand on her arm in a gentle manner.

Her only response was to shake herself free.

Several minutes of talk got him nothing but moans from the girl and hostile stares from others. Even mention of the drug didn't excite her. He decided it was too dangerous for him to be standing there. His intention had been to get her home, assuming she lived alone, and to feed her the drug and then end her misery in celebration of his arrival. Now he saw that would be impractical for him to do.

Regretfully he shoved the two caps in a pocket of the girl's threadbare coat. She would probably take them as soon as they were found. He knew that heroin sometimes killed people. Overdose, it was called. He hoped they would kill her.

Without a backward glance he walked away, wishing he had bought even more of the pills.

Over the next several hours he walked around Lincoln Center, which reminded him of Willows, and then the beginnings of Central Park at Columbus Circle. He sat on a bench and ate a bag of hot chestnuts. He rambled through the southwestern corner of the park as far as the bridle path. There were few people about at this time of day, and he felt an odd excitement in being virtually alone in the heart of the big city. The terrain was vastly different from Chicago's Grant Park, where it was all landscaped and flat and open. Here it rose into hills and deepened to valleys; variety was everywhere, and the rough hand of nature was allowed a certain sway. Bishop liked what he saw of Central Park and he promised himself more at another time. Perhaps with a woman whom he could take into the deep woods . . .

By noontime he was again on Broadway. At 54th Street he passed an automobile showroom, where he stopped to look in the window at the foreign cars. He saw her reflection in the glass as she came up next to him.

"Need some loving, handsome?"

He turned to her, unsure of himself. "You talking to me?"

She smiled cruelly. "Don't see nobody else here, do you?"

"You can't be talking to me because I'm invisible," he told the girl. He didn't like her smile.

"And I'm a twelve-year-old virgin," she said. "You want a quick fuck?"

"I don't think so."

"Blow job?"

"I don't think so."

"Three-hole combination?"

"I don't think so."

She looked exasperated. "You know anything for sure?"

"I know you're not a twelve-year-old virgin."

Her eyes folded over. "You not only invisible," she whispered in an ugly tone, "you not even here."

He watched her walk away, her long brown legs working like giant pistons. When she got to the corner she turned back. "Faggot," she yelled.

In his mind's eye he cut her into four pieces and then sliced each piece into more pieces. He would have liked to work on her in Central Park; nothing would've been left but bleached bone.

He finally found what he was looking for on Eighth Avenue between 46th and 47th Street. She was young and soft and nicely plump. She was also alone and waiting for business. He told her he meant business only if she could take him to where she lived. He wanted no hotels; instead he would give her the hotel cost plus her fee. Take it or leave it.

She needed money and he needed privacy. To her he looked respectable enough in his suit, just another crazy businessman who wanted to get his rocks off during the lunch hour. She took it.

In her nearby one-and-a-half-room apartment he quickly strangled the girl and put her body in the bathtub, where he cut the throat and drained the blood. Now he could literally feel the animal cunning seep through the pores into his senses. When he had finished he refilled the tub with lukewarm water and rinsed himself thoroughly.

He was the wolf who had washed in the blood of the lamb.

He was the traveler who had made his thanksgiving for a safe journey.

He was the demon hunter who had done the work for which he was destined.

On a vanity mirror the wolf left its paw mark in blood. Underneath, the demon hunter scrawled one bloody word.

By six o'clock that evening the traveler had found a haven. He had spent the afternoon downtown, having earlier determined that the Lower East Side and the

Soho district best fulfilled his requirements of a crowded area of young people with little money. He liked the variety of the Lower East Side, its splash and color and vitality, its small shops and packed humanity. But much of it sounded foreign, which would not suit his primary requirement of anonymity. He needed to blend into sheer invisibility and could do so only among his own kind. After looking at several places between Houston and Canal streets he finally settled on a large loft in Soho.

The three-story building on Greene Street was an old converted warehouse. A loading platform on street level was used during the day for storage by several local outlets renting space by the square foot. The second and third floors had a separate entrance. He would occupy the second floor. The third was unfinished and partially boarded up at the bottom of the narrow staircase. He would thus have the only key to the front door. In effect he had almost total privacy, since he would be alone in the building for much of each day and all night and weekends. Yet he was surrounded by thousands of young people living in similar quarters.

The loft was ideal for his purposes and Bishop quickly grabbed it, though he hadn't intended to spend quite so much. The monthly rental was $195 and he had to give an extra month's rent as security to the owner of the building. His intention was to live on the money he now had for a long time to come, and he didn't relish spending any more than was absolutely necessary.

Officially, the loft was only his working studio because under city zoning laws the area was not set up for living accommodations. Nor was his building licensed for living space. In practice, of course, all the thousands of tenants actually resided in their working studios, though legally they simply didn't exist. Which bothered no one in the neighborhood, least of all Bishop, who rather liked the idea of being surrounded by people who didn't exist. Half of whom he longed to make literally true.

His working studio/living loft had a gas-fired heater and a double sink and small toilet with a bathtub. The owner offered him the use of a refrigerator and stove, both already installed, for a one-time payment of $75. He accepted the offer, realizing a refusal would mean losing the place. A folding cot was thrown in free, as were the few pieces of furniture left by the previous tenant, who had to leave suddenly for a job elsewhere.

On Canal Street he bought some bedding and towels, a lamp and light bulbs and two extension cords. He also picked up a coffee pot and saucepan and a transistor radio. He examined the gleaming sets of knives in the various sidewalk displays but decided that his knife was yet sharp enough. There was still a lot of life in it, and death too.

That night Bishop went to sleep in his new home, safely tucked into a warm blanket over clean sheets, his portable radio softly playing on an end table next to the folding cot. He was elated over his progress so far and excited at the prospects for the future. He would remain in New York as long as he was accomplishing his purpose. Certainly for the winter, barring unforeseen events. And perhaps longer. Perhaps a lot longer, and maybe even forever. It was surely big enough to accommodate his very special needs. He liked everything about the city, as he instinctively knew he would.

Mostly he liked the way people just accepted anyone at face value. With the right money, you were whoever you said you were! He suspected that with enough money in New York you could be anybody you wanted to be in the whole world. It was all an insane game with everyone playing and nobody blowing the whistle. To the building's owner he was from Ohio, having left his parents' home to live on his own. He wanted to paint and so he came on to New York. He had a little saved up and he would work at something for more while he followed his dream. His name was Jay Cooper and he was twenty-three years old.

No questions asked. He had the money.

Bishop found the whole idea absolutely incredible. He had enough money now to be anybody. But the only one he wanted to be was Caryl Chessman's son and the famous slayer of women. And he already was that! So he didn't need the money. Except he needed it to pretend to be someone he didn't want to be in order to hide who he really wanted to be. And was!

He fell asleep giggling with delight.

On Wednesday morning he read about himself over coffee in a local shop. She was twenty years old, a prostitute. Her body had been found drained of blood and grossly mutilated. No one had been seen entering or leaving the slum tenement in which she had lived on West 49th Street. There was no appearance of robbery, nor could any reason be given beyond total insanity. Which brought up the name of Vincent Mungo.

The paper made much of the word written in blood on the mirror. "Chess." Quite obviously standing for "Chessman" and meaning the so-called son of Caryl Chessman, Vincent Mungo, who just as obviously had done the slaughter. It was pointed out that during his lifetime Caryl Chessman had answered to the name Chess. Everyone called him by that name and it was the only one he used.

A clever editor headlined the story "Chess Man Strikes Again."

The name was to stick.

On that morning Bishop read the story and thought the name in the headline interesting. It tied him even closer to his father, and it was certainly accurate on just about every level. He worried, though, that they might be getting too close to the truth, even if only inadvertently. He hoped his beard would grow swiftly. Until it was fairly full he would continue to wear the fake beard when outside, just as he had done when renting the loft from the owner.

After breakfast he visited a bank in the downtown area, opening a savings account as Jay Cooper with an initial deposit of $2,000. Nothing to attract anyone's attention. A further $6,000 would be slowly and quietly placed in the account over the next many weeks. The mailing address given the bank was a store on Lafayette Street that acted as a mail drop for a monthly fee, payable in advance—another thing picked up from TV. He had paid for three months before going to the bank. The address given the proprietor of the mail drop, as required by law, was the Chicago address on Jay Cooper's driver's license. All perfectly legal.

According to his plan, a further $8,000 would be carefully placed in another bank when he had secured a new identity and papers. These two bank accounts in two different banks would be immediately available should the occasion demand it. Even if one cover was blown, the other would be there waiting for him. Under the circumstances, since he couldn't go into credit cards or anything beyond such local paper as bankbooks, at least for the moment, it would have to do.

The rest of the money would be hidden at home, to be used for living expenses and kept ready for an instant emergency. The savings book would be proof of his solvency, and the home business he intended to set up as a front was to be proof of his legitimacy.

After the bank he walked down lower Broadway to City Hall, where he stopped in Modell's and bought some winter clothing. A heavy flannel shirt, wool socks, thermal underwear, heavyweight denim pants and a hunter's cap with ear flaps. And most important, a three-quarter suede leather jacket with a fiberfill lining. In the basement he got a pair of brown boots with rubber soles and heels. Also a flashlight and extra batteries, a metal can opener, a toothbrush in a plastic case, and a few tools.

In the afternoon he bought a used portable television set in a sidestreet repair shop near his new home. He paid $40, for which he got a thirty-day guarantee. After that the man would charge only for parts for the next year. Bishop thought it reasonable. To the same man he paid $150 for a Nikon 35mm camera and tripod and a quantity of photographic equipment, all of it third-hand but usable. He regarded that as a bit steep but necessary for his purpose.

A search in a neighborhood junk shop got him a dozen old photography and fashion magazines full of female models. From a wholesale supplier on Canal Street he purchased two huge rolls of white filler paper, each three feet wide. Down the block he picked up a staple gun and a roll of one-inch masking tape. His final stop of the day was to a local market, where he bought all his favorite foods: chocolate ice cream, a steak which he intended to eat raw, baloney and bread, and a can of sliced pineapple. That evening he gorged himself into a stupor and fell asleep watching a TV show that featured a double rape by a gang of toughs, a murder in which pools of blood were shown close up, a child thrown out of a fifth-floor window by a parent, and a shoot-out between police and a gunman holding hostages. All of which occurred in the first fifteen minutes. The program was called the "Eleven O'Clock Evening News."

Thursday morning Bishop awoke early as usual. He wanted eventually to stay up most of every night and sleep very late in the mornings, the way civilized people do, but he knew it would take a while to adjust to that kind of schedule. He had spent too many years in institutional life with its clockwork mentality of early to bed and early to rise. Changes would require time and he had plenty of that, so he believed. All he wanted, everything he needed, would come to him in due time. Of that he was sure. Meanwhile he would use the mornings to best advantage and do what had to be done.

He went to a lumber yard on the Bowery and ordered a dozen eight-foot strips of wood. These he carried home, together with· a pound of finishing nails.

The small business venture Bishop had decided upon was photography, which offered him the opportunity of seemingly working at home with no supervision or schedule while maintaining a supposedly legitimate source of income. If needed, proof of self-employment would be the professional camera he had bought. In addition, he would purchase a few checks each month in different banks and make them out to himself, using fabricated names as payers. He would thus appear to be in business and making an income, though one on the most meager survival level.

With the eight-foot strips of wood measured three feet apart along one wall of the loft, the bag of finishing nails and a plastic-handled hammer in his hands, and the two rolls of white filler paper set on the floor next to him, Bishop went to work. Slowly, carefully, he nailed each strip to the brick wall, hammering the two-inch nails into the mortar between the bricks. Hour after hour he kept at it until all dozen strips were firmly embedded along thirty-six feet of wall space.

The strips themselves gave the appearance of a huge structural framework on the wall, unfinished and sadly neglected. But not for long. The three-foot-wide rolls of paper were stapled onto the wood, top to bottom, in eight-foot sections. Each edge overlapped the one previously stapled, until the entire framework was covered with eleven vertical curtains of white.

A thirty-six-foot-long section of paper was then stapled horizontally across the bottom of all the wood strips, over the earlier layer of white. A second piece was fastened above that. And finally a third, extending a foot over the eight-foot-high framework.

By the time he had finished it was late afternoon, his stomach was growling, and his legs hurt from stepping on and off a chair to reach the upper part of the construction. But the difficult job was over. At least half of the loft wall was now a suitable backdrop for photography, as well as a canvas for pictures and film.

After a baloney sandwich he went back to work, searching through the old magazines for photos of female models. He pulled out several dozen he liked. Using the roll of one-inch masking tape, he studiously fastened them on top and bottom along the canvas in an artistic arrangement. The effect was quite startling. The wall seemed suddenly to come alive, transformed from a sea of white to something bright and cheerful, and very professional.

In front of the new backdrop he placed the tripod mounted with the Nikon. On a low chest of drawers, battered but serviceable, he arranged the rest of the photographic equipment, including several lenses and a light meter. Everything was finally in readiness. Now all he needed was the model for a shooting session, even though he had never snapped a picture in his young life and knew nothing about the camera.

He intended, however, to know the model intimately. All of them.

That night he dined on more baloney sandwiches and a quart of milk while watching a news special on Vincent Mungo. The program began with stills of the Willows hospital, then quickly ran through the cities struck, lingering longest on Chicago. New York was last of course, and the newsman asked rhetorically what new horror Vincent Mungo had in store for the city.

In his peaceful photographer's studio Thomas Bishop just smiled and sat silently, baloney sandwich in hand.

On Friday morning he threw out the folding cot. It was lumpy and didn't give the necessary support. To replace it he bought a six-foot by four-foot piece of foam rubber, two inches thick, and a flowery mattress cover. That would be his bed. He would put it on the floor, which was the proper place for the body to lie. Like anyone, to do his best night's work he needed a good day's rest.

The next afternoon he went to Barnes and Noble and picked out five books on New York. One was called *The Insider's Guide to New York*, and holding the book made him feel like an insider. Which made him feel good, since he was tired of being the outsider. He wanted to be part of his adopted city. Temporarily at least.

Another was *New York at Your Fingertips* and from it he learned that Grand Central Station, which he believed must surely be the most beautiful room in the whole world, was ten stories high. One room rising ten stories to the vaulted ceiling! He remembered his first sight of it less than a week earlier; he had not been prepared for such magnificence, could not imagine such size and splendor. He had since dreamed about it. In his dreams he was alone in the huge room, without clothes, racing around the marble floor. It was all his—the great lights danced only for him, the hidden voice spoke only to him. Suddenly the track gates opened and women, naked, defenseless, their flowered heads lowered in submission, long hair flowing over sinewy shoulders, silently swarmed into his room. Thousands of them. Their faces fevered with anticipation, their eyes blazing out of control, they softly melted into one giant luminous iris as the silver knife flashed again and again in his hot hand . . .

In still another of the books he discovered that New York had several chess clubs, where players could meet over a friendly game at minimal cost. For the solitary player, games could be arranged.

At the checkout counter the girl asked him if he was new to the city.

"Been here all my life."

"Five books on New York?"

"Born right up the street."

"You like to read about it."

"Now I live in the Empire State Building."

"Nobody lives there."

"On the top floor."

She smiled in disbelief.

"I can look in your bedroom window."

"You don't know where I live."

"At night I watch you take all your clothes off."

Her smile disappeared.

"I can see everything you do in bed and how much you like to—"

"That's ten sixty-five. Out of twenty."

She put his change on the counter and started ringing up the next purchase, not looking his way again.

He picked up the money and the shopping bag with his books.

"I'll see you later," he whispered on the way out.

When Bishop got home he heated a can of soup and wolfed down a sandwich, then spread the books on his new pallet and began reading about the big city. He was asleep before he finished the first one.

Sunday dawned bright and beautiful, a perfect October day, and he spent the morning in a long, solitary stroll about the deserted streets. All the way to Battery Park at the southern end of Manhattan. In the Wall Street area he did not see one other person. He felt like the last human on earth, and he wondered if he was being watched by alien eyes behind closed windows. But there were no aliens besides himself, and all the windows were blank.

Soho, like most of downtown New York on a Sunday, was mostly empty and as he walked the blocks in the afternoon the emptiness hung heavily in the air. He was reminded of Willows, not the buildings with the men but the wild places, which were lonely beyond endurance. He had once liked to be alone but that was long ago. Now he wanted to be surrounded by herds of people. They were sheep, he saw them as his sheep, and he was the wolf in sheep's clothing. While he was among them he was safe.

Eventually he went into a neighborhood bar on Broome Street and West Broadway, where plants hung in the windows and the menu was written on a blackboard in colored chalk. He sat at a table for two. About thirty young people cavorted around him, at the other tables and at the bar itself, and he wondered what the attraction could be. For him a bar was somewhere to go for a specific purpose, and as he looked around he saw very little purpose in the actions of others. The women especially interested him and he watched them with big sheep eyes. Several of them noted his interest, unaware of the sinister possibilities, and instinctively increased their coquetry. All reflex action of course, programmed by nature in the language of love. Which was also survival of the species.

In that sense Bishop too could be seen as part of nature's design; weeding out the weak, snaring the strays. Much as the chameleon at the approach of an enemy, he blended into his surroundings to the point of invisibility. And like the beautiful Venus's-flytrap, he was made by nature in the form most desirable to his prey.

He smiled at the waitress and ordered a hamburger and a beer. When she brought him the beer he told her he was a newcomer to the area. Moved over to Greene Street after six months uptown. Didn't like it there. No neighborhood feeling, if she knew what he meant. She nodded, noncommittal to strangers. A smile and a nod, that was all. It was her protection.

With the hamburger he told her he was a photographer who did his work in his new studio loft. Did she ever do any modeling? She had classic bone structure. And a lovely face, very sensitive.

She smiled and nodded. No, no modeling. Not interested. But she gave him an extra smile in payment for the compliment. Value given for value received. Seconds later, busy at another table, she forgot him. Just one more hard-on wanting to get laid or sucked. Who needed it? She was in a quiet period, coming down from a love affair. It would be a while before she opened up again.

When he paid the bill he asked her where she was from. She said Boston and he said Missouri. He was from Missouri, and he hoped to see her again. He left a dollar on the table.

Later at home he checked his beard in the mirror. Not bad for one week. Really heavier than he had expected. Already he looked different, more worldly, yet more sensitive as well. And certainly more interesting. Another week and it would be full enough. He had now stopped wearing the fake beard, didn't need it anymore. Just one more week and he'd be safe. A different person, to go with all the other different people he already was or had been or would be.

Staring at himself in the bathroom mirror Bishop was not aware, nor would he ever know, that almost all the truly great mass murderers of modern times wore beards, or beards and mustaches, or just mustaches alone at some point. Lüdke, Vacher, Karl Denke, Albert Fish, Ludwig Tessnow, Peter Kürten, Adolph Seefeld, Béla Kiss, among others. A strange parenthesis to history, whatever its meaning.

Jack the Ripper?

Though he was never caught, a few people might have seen him just before or after some of his ghastly murders in London's Whitechapel during 1888. Descriptions of men seen with several of the slain women differ but most speak of some facial hair. Perhaps the most important such description, given by a man named George Hutchinson in the absolutely dreadful murder and mutilation of Mary Kelly, mentions a mustache that was curled up at each end. And of course the major candidates for the identity of Jack the Ripper—Dr. Neill Cream, the Duke of Clarence, Montague Druitt, George Chapman—all sported mustaches or whiskers.

When Thomas Bishop finally went to bed on Sunday evening, neither knowing nor caring about Jack the Ripper or anyone else, he had a feeling that it was going to be a good week for him. He was settled in his winter quarters and he could now map out his campaign. Like a general in battle, he would marshal his forces for attack.

He would awaken in the morning and it would be Monday, and Monday would be the start of a new week. And a new life.

FOURTEEN

By Wednesday morning Adam Kenton had his WATS line, his dictaphone machine and his telephone recorder. The safe with the double combination lock and the second desk would come later in the day. He looked around his temporary office with grim satisfaction. There was something cheerless and deadening about such places, sterile was the proper word for them. All smoothness and glass and angles. All eminently functional but nothing more. No curves or softness or subtlety. Nothing to please the eye, only the orderly mind. He hated the modern office buildings with their glass skins and angular momentum, and he always felt trapped inside them. The same with the high-rise apartment buildings. He would never live in them, not if he had a choice.

Right now he had none and, trapped or not, the work awaited him. He sighed and settled in behind the desk. At least he could call people, that was some consolation.

And he could dictate thoughts and ideas on the Ripper Reference for later playback, a habit picked up in earlier days when he ran fast and worked on so many stories that he would lose the thread of some of them. Information was his currency, and anything lost or forgotten was money down the drain. Talking into a machine that could later talk back to him kept his mind clear for new facts. It also served as a continuing progress report.

He picked up the receiver to check the telephone recorder. The tape began to turn. He tried it several times. Each time the tape would stop when he replaced the receiver. A cable ran from the telephone junction box to the monitor outlet on the specially adapted recorder, causing it to function only when the phone was in use. Both sides of conversations could now be taped for future reference.

His first calls were inside the plant. He reminded John Perrone that he needed the list of all *Newstime* reporters and stringers in the country, as well as the confidential list of informational sources. Both were promised within the hour.

He called Mel Brown about the computer check on matricide cases in California during the past twenty-five years. Not ready yet.

"What's holding it up?"

"Incomplete listings mostly. California lumps matricide with patricide. In the case of mental institutions, they also separate insanity convictions, so to speak, from incompetency commitments. The ones who go right to the funny farm without any trial have their records sealed as far as any mental-health information is concerned."

Kenton groaned.

"It's not as bad as it sounds. The record is sealed only to prevent outside exploitation or some well-meaning soul from torturing the poor son of a bitch with what he did. It's really done as part of the psychiatric therapy. But the killing itself is a matter of public record of course, with the police and the courts and even the newspapers. So it's just a question of getting it from other sources and then matching it up with the lists of those in the mental hospitals around the state."

"Sounds like it could take forever."

"Not really," said Brown. "We don't have to go through all the institutions, remember. Even that wouldn't be much for the computer. But all we need are the places where they put the nuts that kill. There aren't that many. I should have it all wrapped up for you tomorrow."

"Is that a promise?"

"During the Ming Dynasty of ancient China somebody scrawled on a wall 'Never promise, never disappoint.' That's still good advice. I'll do the best I can for you."

Kenton snapped on the dictaphone machine, and for the next fifty minutes he talked about what he knew of Vincent Mungo and what he had learned in the past twenty-four hours. He referred often to a sheet of paper filled with notes from his reading of the previous day. Basically it appeared that Vincent Mungo had escaped from Willows State Hospital after killing another patient. Someone then took the name to disguise his own identity. But how did he know Mungo wouldn't be quickly caught? Or give himself up? Or write a letter denouncing the impostor? Only one way. The impostor had to know Mungo was already dead. How? He had already killed him. Which meant he knew Mungo. From where? The home? One of the institutions?

Next point. Why would the killer want to disguise his own identity? The logical conclusion: he was someone known to authorities. Someone they already were looking for or would be looking for at the slightest suspicion. Someone with a record of some kind in the hands of authorities of some kind. Perhaps someone who had already killed women. Perhaps already killed—his own mother?

Next point. Why assume Mungo's identity? Police were searching everywhere for him. Conclusion: it had to be Mungo because of some direct connection between the two men. If Mungo were sought the killer would go free. But what were the specific circumstances of that connection? It had to be something they were in together at some time. A partnership? A homosexual relationship? Look for somebody Mungo was close to, a male. When? Primarily in recent years because the killer had to be somehow connected to Mungo and known to authorities, and Mungo was only twenty-four years old.

Next point. In the killer's letter to the Los Angeles bureau—the letter addressed *From Hell*—he had written a strange sentence: "I miss him and never saw him till now." *Never saw him till now.* Why? Chessman's picture was in plenty of newspapers and magazines at the time. He was a famous man. People all over the world knew about him. Anyone could have seen his picture. Unless, that is, it was somehow impossible because someone was locked up or shut away. Prison? An institution?

Next point. The horrific mutilations are perhaps attempts at destroying the womb, indicating the killer's fearful hatred of his mother. They are so indicative of derangement that he could be acting out what he had experienced earlier as a child. Conclusion: he killed his mother. But what of the time between the matricide and now? Why wasn't he killing all along? Strong possibility: he could not. If he killed his mother he would've been placed in a mental home.

Final point. Why pick on Caryl Chessman? The killer seemed really to believe that Chessman was his father. There must be a connection between them, something that links them together. What was the Chessman connection?

Analysis. Vincent Mungo was dead, killed by someone who knew him well in the fairly recent past. Someone from either his home life or the institutional years. Someone sought by police or open to immediate suspicion if Mungo was not the killer. Someone with a record, police or mental. Perhaps for killing women. Someone who could not see a picture of Caryl Chessman, probably because of being confined. Someone who had a link to Chessman at some point. Someone who perhaps killed his mother at an early age. Someone from a mental ward, who would not have access to Chessman's picture. And would be known to police and quickly suspected. And would thus have to come from Vincent Mungo's institutional life.

Action: Look for someone who was recently released —within the past few years—or who escaped from a mental hospital that also housed Vincent Mungo. Look for someone to whom Mungo was noticeably close while inside. Look for someone who killed his mother at a young age, or who was so obsessed with the thought of having killed her that he was institutionalized and now acted out the obsession. Look for someone who had a connection to Caryl Chessman.

That final thought intrigued Kenton the most. He had a feeling that Chessman was somehow the key. Everything else seemed roughly in order, though there were a million loopholes and inconsistencies in the theory he had developed. An insane mental patient who kept killing his mother and who knew Vincent Mungo. That paralleled the known facts quite well. And all his further deductions and conclusions were based on that premise. So it was sound, although full of the paradoxes that made life interesting.

But the Chessman part came out of nowhere. Beyond the publicity angle to show the world his dreadful fight for survival, what need did Chessman serve the killer? The recent discovery that Mungo might be Chessman's bastard son was irrelevant since Mungo was not the killer. Whatever the answer, it had to come from the killer himself. That much was certain. Wasn't it?

Kenton knew from sad experience that all the pieces of a theory had to fit or it would prove worthless. But Caryl Chessman was the stumbling block, the piece that didn't fit, the riddle. He would solve it or he would have to start over again. His gut instinct told him his interpretation of the facts was correct, his educated guesses accurate. So the link he sought to Chessman was there. He had only to find it.

With his thoughts spelled out verbally, Kenton placed the sheet of notepaper in the electric shredder that had conveniently appeared behind his desk during the night. He turned to the two lists that had finally come down from Perrone's office, sealed and marked confidential. Inside also were the names of those who knew of the assignment that had brought him to New York. He glanced over the names and titles and was quickly impressed. Apparently a lot of money really was riding on his tail. He wondered what they would say if they knew it wasn't Mungo they wanted at all.

And what they would do if he didn't come up with the right name.

In a half hour he had checked off dozens of people he intended to call. He also made his own list of those who might prove helpful, the majority of them in California. He silently thanked the gods that he was already deep into the story, and that much of it had taken place where he knew a great many important people.

His research assistant came in with more clippings on Vincent Mungo. He told her to dig up everything she could find on Caryl Chessman. Remember Chessman? She shook her head. Too young at the time. But she had heard of him. Executed in California for murder, wasn't it?

He corrected her. Not murder. Chessman didn't kill anybody. Some sex crime, then. She blushed. No, not that either, he told her. Actually, Chessman was killed because of a crazy law that specified death for robbery with bodily harm. The most brutal rape, with the girl beaten and left for dead, was not punishable by death. But slap someone while stealing a penny! That was a capital crime.

Her feminism flared up. How horrible!

That's California for you!

He mentioned that he had a special assignment that might require some things beyond the scope of a cover story. Could she do whatever was needed and keep her mouth shut? He coughed delicately. What he meant was, without a lot of questions. He had no time for questions right now.

She smiled at his male insecurity. What exactly did he have in mind for her?

Research of course. He looked at her closely for the first time. She was young and pretty. And very desirable. Perhaps sometimes when he—

"If it's research, sure. I know my job and when to talk and not talk."

He also wanted all the mental institutions Vincent Mungo had been in during his life. With the dates and names of staff doctors who saw him. That was urgent. Also a list of all patients released from those places over the past five years. And those who escaped too. Mel Brown could probably help work that up.

And which should keep her busy for a bit, he thought approvingly.

Fred Grimes called. He would be down later to give Kenton the names of New York's top cops and the mayor's administrative aides.

Anything else he could do at the moment?

Yes, he could use his contacts to find out if anybody

new in town had been looking for identification documents in the past two days. Or more probably, over the rest of the week. Their man might need new papers and try to get them through one of the independent retailers who buy whole blocks of such documents from organized crime.

If he's not Mungo why would he need them? Why not just go under his own name since he's unknown?

"Except he is known, though the police might not know it yet. He's a mental patient—"

"You're telling me."

"No, a real one who either escaped or was released. Someone got close to Mungo while they were in together."

In California he posed as Daniel Long. When that was discovered he somehow got another set of identity papers. Now he might be looking for a new name, just in case. If so, he might try to get it from a local supply.

"Who would they look for?"

"He'd be fairly young, say between twenty and forty. White, probably Christian—"

"How do you know that?"

"Mungo had a collection of Nazi stuff in his room at home. And he once painted swastikas in a Jewish cemetery. He wouldn't get too close to anyone not white or Christian."

"Anything else?"

"For the moment, no. Except that he'd be new to the city and would probably stay in a low hotel and use a mail drop somewhere."

"Not much to go on," said Grimes after a pause.

He was right but it was all Kenton had. A young white Christian man. Unless it turned out to be an old man. Or an Oriental. Or a woman. Or the man from Mars.

Grimes said he would see about getting some heat on the people who push the identification racket in the city. But he didn't expect much. There were just too many retailers around, it was like sifting sand.

Kenton thanked him anyway. Sometimes sand had a way of sticking.

When he returned from lunch the second desk was installed against the wall in back of the door. And behind his desk, squarely between the window's edge and the other wall, stood a small safe. The double-lock combination was typed on a card left on top of the safe. He wondered what Otto Klemp would say about such a breach of security. Which reminded him.

He called a number on Long Island and read off the ten names of those who knew about his assignment. He wanted a look at their income-tax returns. The last two years should do it.

The next call in the city. This time he gave the names of the top dozen officers of the whole Newstime empire, starting with Mackenzie himself. What he wanted was a complete financial statement for each man—everything. Assets, holdings, trusts, shelters, offshore, the works. And dates for each. On the usual cash basis naturally. Payable on delivery, as soon as possible.

When he got through to John Perrone he told him that he needed $9,000 for expenses. Perrone didn't want to hear it, didn't want to know about it. All that kind of thing should be routed through Fred Grimes.

Kenton apologized.

"How's it going?"

"It's going."

"Keep it up. We're counting on you."

Grimes was more interested but didn't want to discuss it over the phone. Kenton assured him the recorder was off. He didn't use it inside the company, that would be counterproductive. Grimes said it was his own phone that worried him. Anyway, he'd be down in a while.

Five minutes later the second research assistant came by, an older man who smoked Chesterfields and had an amused glint in his eye. He had been gathering documents on Vincent Mungo's life, starting with a copy of the birth certificate from Los Angeles County General Hospital. Kenton liked him right away and told him to use the other desk whenever he was in the office. He also gave him roughly the same talk given the young woman earlier. He was on a special assignment that could be a cover story on Mungo or might broaden out to include even more. He didn't specify what "more" could mean, and the older man didn't ask. He had sized Kenton up immediately as a professional, and in his own way he was a professional too. Very knowledgeable about a great many things, he was at the point in life where he no longer tried to change the world, but rather was content to watch it with a certain amount of detachment and even amusement. He was good at what he did and he carried his wisdom lightly. At least until he was asked a direct question.

"What do you think of Senator Stoner?"

"He's an opportunist," said the older man, "like most of them."

"You don't like him."

The man shrugged. "No better or worse than others, I suppose. At least he talks up for what he believes."

"Or says he believes."

"In politics that's the same thing. You believe whatever you talk up today. Tomorrow takes care of tomorrow."

Kenton was developing a positive affection for the older man. Even cynics needed other believers.

"In the immortal words," he began, "of Adolf Hitler—"

"*Der vogel ist gefallen,*" said the man who spoke five languages. "*Lange leben die vogel.*"

Both men laughed. Kenton knew very little German but he got the idea.

He told the researcher what he wanted. Everything on Stoner, good and bad. His background, his family, his friends, his business interests. Most especially his business interests. Ditto for a man named Don Solis, who gave Stoner's campaign a big push with his revelation about Caryl Chessman's guilt a while back.

"Find out who this Solis really is, and what he got out of it, if you can. He owns a diner in Fresno. You'll come across him in the recent stuff on Stoner. Let me know what you dig up."

The next hour was spent talking to *Newstime* reporters and stringers in California. To each he patiently explained what he was seeking. Any stories they might have heard about a boy who killed his mother. Going back as much as twenty-five years. Maybe it didn't make the big papers, maybe it was just local gossip. But he wanted to know about it, and fast.

His reasoning was obvious, though he didn't mention it. Within hours of Mungo's escape from Willows the state borders had been closed, so to speak. That meant he couldn't have got too far. Whoever he met had to be in California or Nevada, or Oregon at the farthest. But most probably right in California. Maybe even where he lived or grew up. Somebody somewhere must know or have heard of a boy like that.

He didn't really trust Mel Brown's computer.

At four o'clock Fred Grimes came down, apologizing for not wanting to talk on the phone but with Klemp around anything was possible. He gave Kenton the names of the top police and mayor's aides, all with unlisted numbers. The sheet was put in the safe.

"About the nine thousand dollars. Care to say why you need it?"

Kenton frowned. "I'd rather not," he said softly.

"Cash?"

"Mixed bills. No consecutive serial numbers. You know the routine."

"It'll be laundered, don't worry. Tomorrow okay?"

"Fine."

"If you need more just let me know. I can get it for you overnight."

"Operating expenses?"

Grimes nodded. "Comes out of a nonprofit slush fund. The Committee to Save Freedom of the Press."

"Sounds good anyway."

"Every big combine has its own laundry service for wet cash, doesn't matter what it's called. Just that it works. Too many things going on now that can't be recorded."

"Including me."

"This is nothing. Think of the oil companies or the drug manufacturers, what they must be spending under the table. Everybody knows what's going on. It's an open secret."

Kenton lit a cigarette. "Ever get the feeling you're working for the mob," he asked absently, "instead of big business?"

"All the time," said Grimes with a quick laugh. "They're just the opposite side of the coin. The only real difference is we retire our people while they kill theirs."

Thursday morning at 9:30 Otto Klemp was waiting for him with a few words of advice. "Don't exceed your authority." He wouldn't say any more. Both men knew that for the moment Kenton had a blank check on the company, and short of firing everyone or burning down the building, he held unlimited power. But that power was just an illusion of course, and would instantly disappear if he reached too high.

"Whenever you step out of your class," said Klemp, not unkindly, "you step down."

Kenton wondered how much he knew.

The first ring broke into his thoughts and he grabbed for it. Mel Brown had the computer information for California. A total of ninety-seven known matricides in the past twenty-five years, excluding whole families killed and those individuals who killed themselves immediately afterward.

"Of the ninety-seven, sixty-eight are presently in prisons or mental hospitals, sixteen are known dead. Which leaves thirteen unaccounted for, but three of those are over fifty years old and two others are women. Of the eight remaining, two couldn't possibly be your man."

"Why not?"

"One was blinded by his mother but he managed to get his hands round her rotten throat, I am happy to say. Acid of some kind. The other was released after losing both legs to diabetes."

"So you got six left."

"What next?"

"Find them. Where they are, what they're doing. As quick as you can."

"Will do."

"Much obliged. And Mel—"

"Yeah?"

"I got Doris working on Caryl Chessman and a few other things. But more important right now, I need that list of everyone released or escaped from California mental hospitals of any kind in the past five years. See what you can do on that, would you?"

"Sure thing."

For the rest of the day the phone hardly left his ear as he talked to the West, to contacts of his own and to names from the confidential sources. He needed information, anything they might know about Vincent Mungo or Caryl Chessman or a boy who had killed his mother. But he was still fishing in the dark. He didn't know the right questions to ask yet or even the right people to call. It was all preliminary work, to get out as many lines as possible. But it was also frustrating. And if his theory was wrong it would all be useless.

He was morally certain that his quarry was not Mungo. But he could've missed the rest of it. His man needn't have started with matricide; he could be killing now because he *hadn't* killed his mother. Maybe she died giving birth, maybe she ran away when he was very young. He might have been in an institution with Mungo for other reasons, and just decided to kill women when Mungo escaped and he saw he could take over the identity. Maybe he's plain crazy. Maybe he's afraid of men and so he picks on women. There were a hundred ways to look at his insanity.

Thinking like that depressed him further and he tried to stop it. When he had a strong feeling about something it was usually right. Why should this be an exception? All the odds were with him.

Toward the end of the day he called Mel Brown to check an idea. Of the six men still open, was there any way to find out when they had killed their mothers? At what age?

Yes, it was possible. Assuming they were at least sixteen at the time. Younger than that the courts sealed the record though it was known to the doctors wherever they were placed. That way, if the boy ever got out there was no stigma attached for something done while still a child. The newspapers couldn't mention it later on, for example. Or he couldn't be denied his civil rights because of it. Did Kenton still want that information?

He did, though he believed the boy killed his mother when he was younger than sixteen. If he killed her at all, that is.

Friday morning he was in the office before nine o'clock. He got the phone on the second ring. It was Mel Brown.

"Don't you people ever sleep up there?"

"Sleep? Say, how you think the mailman makes it through the rain and snow to keep his appointed rounds? We tell him what route to take to get there."

Kenton had to laugh in spite of himself. "What have you got?" he asked after a moment.

Two of the six matricides were out of the picture. One had killed his mother when he was forty-three, the other at thirty-five. Of the four left, three were under thirty at the time and one under sixteen. The names were Morgan, Dufino, Terranova and Rivera. Rivera was the one under sixteen.

Also ready were the names of those released or escaped

from California mental institutions in the past five years. There were a lot of them.

"Good. Match your four against them."

"Already done."

"And?"

"Two of the four were released over ten years ago. Rivera was one of them. Naturally their names don't appear on the list. Does that let them out of your consideration?"

"They're out."

"The third was released four years ago. His name is on the list. But he's now serving a prison sentence in Washington."

"Is that confirmed?"

"It is."

"So he's out too."

"The fourth escaped last year. Not heard from since. Disappeared completely."

"What's his name?"

"You're not going to believe it."

"Try me."

"Louis Terranova."

The name meant nothing. "So?"

"I forgot you writers don't read," said Brown with a touch of exasperation in his voice. "Terranova was the name of the man Caryl Chessman claimed was the real Red Light Bandit twenty-five years ago."

"Good God!"

"That's what I said. Could be just a coincidence, though. Lots of people with the name. Anyway, he's forty-seven now. Which would've made him twenty-two in Chessman's time. Killed his mother in 1950 when he was twenty-four. Been in the mental wards the last twenty-two years till his escape a year ago."

"Where'd he crash out?"

"Lakeland. It's down around—"

"I know it."

"You want me to get a background on him?"

"Everything you can."

"What about the figures on the matricides? You need them?"

Kenton sighed in disappointment. "No. Between the ones still in and those who've died or are too old or sick, there's nothing left."

"Except maybe Terranova."

"You sure you got all of them for those years?"

"All the recorded ones, which may not be the same thing. Those who stood trial and were convicted and sent to prison, those who were found innocent by reason of insanity and sent to hospitals, those who were declared incompetent to stand trial and were put away. For these last, the information came from court sources rather than the state mental health agencies. Naturally, as with any unofficial count, something could slip through."

"What about the kids under sixteen?"

"That's a different story. There the court records themselves are sealed tight, so all information had to come originally from newspaper accounts at the time it happened. The papers wouldn't print the kids' names but they usually give the sex and age, and that can then be compared against the names of surviving children. Believe it or not, there are people who make a living doing such things for people like you."

"Any chance of a killing like that missing the papers?"

Mel Brown shrugged in reflex on his end of the phone. "Anything's possible. Especially in California."

At 10:30 Doris brought the list of mental institutions in which Vincent Mungo had been placed during his life. There were five. Atascadero, Willows, Lakeland, Valley River and Tremont. Plus the psychiatric divisions of the Stockton and San Francisco General hospitals. All with dates of commitment and names of the doctors who attended him. Kenton saw that one of them was Lakeland, from which Louis Terranova had escaped the year before. He looked at the dates of Mungo's stay at Lakeland. It included all of 1972.

Maybe he was getting lucky.

For the next half hour he talked into the dictaphone machine, bringing himself up to date. He took calls from Long Island and Manhattan. Long Island would be delivering at 12:30 P.M. The usual arrangement. Kenton had to think a moment—it was more than a year since he had used the service. Manhattan wanted to know where to deliver a package. He named the St. Moritz at nine o'clock that evening, Suite 1410.

Fred Grimes came in with $9,000 cash which Kenton put in the safe. He had met John Perrone in the hall upstairs. Maybe Kenton should give him a ring. Also, he had talked to some people about identity papers the fake Vincent Mungo might seek. Without a picture it was virtually impossible to watch for him. There were just too many men in New York buying phony sets of identification every day. The city was the center of the trade for the whole country plus everybody coming in from Europe. With nothing to go on, nothing could be done. Sorry.

Kenton took it in stride. There were other lines to throw out. One was the mailing address. Assuming Mungo wanted a new identity, he would need somewhere to which things could be sent. He wouldn't use wherever he was staying, most likely a cheap hotel or rooming house since none of the women he killed had much money. It would make him too conspicuous and might lead to suspicions. And he couldn't rent a post office box because he'd have to give a home address, which had to be verified by the local mailman. His best bet would be a mail drop, of which there were many around the city. Mostly small stores and shops that took in mail for clients, who usually paid by the month. They would come in to pick up their mail inconspicuously, and then quickly disappear until their next visit. Mail drops were not normally places of social gathering, nor were the clients generally very friendly. It was the type of operation that might appeal to his prey, and Kenton carefully explained the idea to Grimes.

"What we need is just the names of those who signed up this week, that's all, and the addresses they gave. Then we hire a dozen private detectives to check them out quickly. A look at them would be enough. We eliminate all but the young white males. Those we go after one by one. Can't be that many in a given week."

"Suppose he doesn't sign up till next week? Or next month? Maybe he wants to rest a while."

"No, his pattern is to do everything necessary as soon as possible. He's imaginative and thorough and very practical. That's what has kept him safe all this time and he knows it. There'd be no reason for him to change the pattern." He glanced over the material on his desk. "I've been reading and writing about our man for weeks now and I'm beginning to get a glimmer of how he operates. If he decided to get a mail drop he'd do it right away. He always takes care of business first."

"But how do we go about getting the names? They won't give them to us."

"Not to us, no. But to a city official." Kenton flashed a smile. "That's where you come in. Get somebody at City Hall to authorize a pickup of the names. Tell them we're doing a story on mail drops. If they balk, refer them to Perrone. That should do it. But naturally I'd rather he didn't get too involved."

Grimes was dubious. "You think it'll work?"

"It might get us to him first. If I can only find out who he really is."

He spent the next few minutes reporting his progress to John Perrone. Then a half hour with George Homer, his other researcher, who gave him a quick report on Jonathan Stoner. Much of it he knew from his own investigation of Stoner but a few things were of interest, especially the senator's mistress. He hadn't known about her, since that kind of thing didn't come into his earlier look. He told Homer to keep digging.

At noontime he took $2,000 out of the safe and put it in a separate envelope. After a fast sandwich down the block he walked to the public library at 42nd Street. In the massive reference room he sat at one end of a long table in the very last row on the left. A man sat across from him, intent on a book he held in both hands. In front of him, toward the middle of the table, was a manila folder. Kenton took out his envelope and placed it next to the folder, then opened the reference book he had selected on his way to the seat. A moment later the man softly closed his book, picked up the envelope and left the room. When Kenton had finished reading several pages of his book he opened the folder and studied the contents.

By 1 P.M. he was back in his office, the folder in the safe. It was 10 A.M. in California and time for work. For the rest of the afternoon he was on the phone talking with staff doctors who had attended Vincent Mungo in the various institutions, their names taken from the list prepared by Doris earlier. Several were out or unavailable but called him back later in the day. He wrote down the names of those patients who were closest to Mungo in each place, according to the records and the best recollections of the doctors. Two in Atascadero, two in Lakeland, and one in Willows, as he remembered from his research for the earlier story on Mungo. These were the only ones he seemed to have had anything to do with in the last five years. He had not been in Valley River or

Tremont since adolescence, and though Kenton called both he did not bother with names.

He most carefully questioned the doctor at Lakeland but could not get him to say that Mungo had been friendly with Louis Terranova. Yes, he remembered Terranova, who had been there for a number of years. He believed the two men never knew each other and certainly were not friends. But he was close to two other patients, didn't you say? As close as that sort could get to anybody. Which isn't very much, you know. Was either of these two patients guilty of matricide? Perhaps as an adolescent? The doctor wouldn't answer that. Such information could come only through official channels, and never over the telephone. No, absolutely not. Well, what were they in for? Not that either.

At Atascadero it was much the same story. The names of two friends were given and no more. Neither doctor was surprised, however, by Mungo's insane violence. Not at all. When that brooding type blows, there's no limit to the madness.

At Willows he talked again to a Dr. Poole, who had attended Mungo for the months he was there. Poole reminded Kenton that Mungo's only friend in the institution had been a patient named Thomas Bishop, whom Mungo killed on the night of his escape.

Kenton wrote down the name without interest.

Could Mungo have had another friend, perhaps one he saw only at certain times? Definitely not. No homosexual relationships? Not the type. Never said anything about somebody at another hospital whom he knew or admired? Never talked about anyone.

At the Stockton and San Francisco psychiatric divisions Kenton talked to two staff doctors who had seen Mungo. No, no friends. Their facilities were short-term. People were in and out all the time, and there was little chance for close relationships among the patients. Vincent Mungo was not particularly memorable to either one of them. He had been a patient several times in earlier years, according to the records. His homicidal proclivities were not apparent then, though he obviously had a violent nature and sadistic tendencies. Too bad.

Kenton thought a moment about what he now had. Five men close to Mungo when he was inside, where it counted. He looked at the names. James Turnbull. Peter

Lambert. Carl Pandel. Jason Decker. Thomas Bishop. He crossed out the last name. No use chasing a dead man.

He sent the names up to Mel Brown to match against those who had escaped or had been released in the past five years. He already saw they didn't match those of the mother killers, including Louis Terranova.

Another good idea down the drain.

Mel Brown eventually called back to say that the only name on the list was Carl Pandel, released from Lakeland in May 1972. The other four were either still inside or dead and thus out of the running. At least their names were not on the list of those released or escaped. Kenton reminded him that the final man, Thomas Bishop, had been killed by Mungo while escaping from Willows. Which was why he had crossed out the name. Brown thought it familiar, now remembered reading it at the time.

What about Pandel?

Would he check on the man first thing Monday? Maybe he killed his mother as a boy and the record was sealed. Maybe he lived in a small country town that had no newspaper. Maybe he's young and white and Christian and crazy and in New York killing women.

It was almost eight o'clock before Kenton left the office for the weekend. The last thing he did was to put $6,000 from the safe into an envelope and stick it in his pocket. He also took home the folder from Long Island and all the unread material from his desk.

At nine o'clock a man delivered a small package to his rooms at the St. Moritz. He gave the envelope of money to the man, who counted it in front of him. Afterward he had dinner at the Italian Pavilion, dining alone in the garden. A half hour with a prostitute in a Lexington Avenue hotel relieved him of the week's tension, and he returned home to sleep soundly.

On Saturday and Sunday he stayed close to his quarters reading the complete financial reports on the dozen men who headed the *Newstime* empire. It was well worth the considerable expense, especially since it was their money. From the reports he learned many useful things, some of which could be most helpful should they try to thwart his efforts or reduce his authority or steal his glory. And he now knew something else about one of them, at least one of them, that surprised and shocked him, and he was not a man easily shocked.

When he drifted into sleep Sunday night Adam Kenton felt good about the week coming up. He had all the balls bouncing in air, all under control and in perfect rhythm. He was at his investigative best. No matter how many things he worked on, he would handle them. It was all a question of timing and balance, and genius.

As his eyelids fluttered heavily, he didn't notice one of the balls slip beneath the corners of his mind.

FIFTEEN

John Spanner was crushed, deflated. Finally defeated. He had been so sure, not in the sense of hard fact or even circumstancial evidence but in a primary gut feeling. An instinct that had gradually developed over twenty-five years of police work and had never totally let him down. Until now. For more than three months, since the very morning of the Willows murder, he had in turn fought the feeling and indulged it. No matter how he tried he could not shake loose the suspicion that something had gone amiss in the investigation of that murder, something planned and executed by an insanely devious mind, something that had resulted in the ultimate appearance of the fiendish killer known as Vincent Mungo. The suspicion gnawed at him and grew in his mind until he began to see the outlines of a diabolical plot. And the shadowy figure of the devil lurking behind it. Thomas Bishop.

Now he saw that the devil was within himself and the plot was a creation of his own restless imagination. Even more, of his willful desire. He had wanted to beat Sheriff James Oates, to show the man how brilliant he was. And to demonstrate once again to his own department the absolute necessity of finely imaginative police work. Most of all, he had needed to prove to himself that he was still valuable, his skills and knowledge still important to a rapidly changing world.

Pride, that monstrous measure of self-worth, had goaded him on and now had vanquished him. Nor was he the first to fall under its weight; a thought that did not comfort him in the slightest.

And it was all for nothing.

He held the report in his hand on this grim Friday morning, but he did not have to read it again. Thomas William Owens, a.k.a. Thomas William Bishop, had been routinely circumcised at the hospital in which he was born on April 30, 1948. The mother was listed as Sara Bishop Owens, age twenty-one; the father as Harold Owens, age twenty-three. Their religion was Protestant. The baby weighed seven pounds, nine ounces at birth. There were no complications and the child was duly take home by his parents. End of report.

Within minutes of receiving the information from the downstate police he called Los Angeles and talked with a hospital administrator. Was there any chance of a mistake, the slighest possibility? Usually none, he was told, at least insofar as the records were concerned. Human fallibility was something else of course. The administrator double-checked while he waited. The wait would be longer than expected since the file was twenty-five years old and therefore in an annex storage area. His call would be returned as soon as the information was available.

Spanner sat quietly in his office for twenty minutes, dejected, knowing what the answer would be. When it came he was prepared. The report was accurate: Thomas Owens had indeed been circumcised by Dr. Timothy Engles, whose signature attested to the fact. Would the lieutenant wish to talk with Dr. Engles? The administrator would try to get the number for him if the doctor was still practicing or living in the area.

It wasn't necessary and Spanner thanked him. There was nothing else to do as the invincibility of sheer fact impressed itself anew upon his orderly mind. He had been wrong from the beginning on this one fact, which could instantly destroy the most beautifully wrought police theory.

That was Thomas Bishop's circumcised body they had found at Willows on the holiday morning of July 4. And it was Vincent Mungo who had escaped and was presumably killing women.

The pictures missing from Bishop's file had just been misplaced. Perhaps prints had been made for newspapers when he was killed and the originals stuck in another folder, perhaps simply never returned.

Spanner gave his disappointment a long last sigh and reached for the phone.

In an ornate home in Kansas a man sat at his desk and gazed around his study for the hundredth time that Friday morning. The room was dark, the curtains closed; only one small lamp burned in the far corner. On the desk lay heaps of correspondence of every shape and size, all scattered and disordered as though a north wind had blown over them. The bookshelves lining the walls were in disarray, the sofa by the louvered windows groaned under the weight of newspapers from all over the country. More newspapers flooded the carpeted floor, while still others overflowed the three caned chairs in the middle of the room, the most recent being those from New York.

The man closed his eyes in weariness and brought his right hand up to press against them. He had been awake for much of the night and up since five. Lately he hadn't been sleeping well at all, or eating or working well either. The strain of his daughter's death, the unbearable grief he was feeling, were beginning to affect his health and had already impaired his work habits and social life.

Beyond even the sense of loss was the feeling of terrible injustice done him. His baby was dead, butchered by a lunatic whom he had paid to have destroyed. Yet Vincent Mungo was still living. After three months he was still hopelessly alive and killing women, with no end in sight. No one seemed able to stop him, even to get near him. The police couldn't find him, the underworld couldn't find him.

How was that possible? The underworld was supposed to be able to find anybody. Especially those hiding from the police or society in general. That's what he had been told, what he had been led to believe all his life. Everyone knew that. The underworld was always "they." If "they" were after you, you were as good as dead.

Then why wasn't Vincent Mungo dead?

Were they in league with him? Was it some kind of plot to get money from decent citizens? Were the police in on it too? All those millions and billions spent for police protection and in reality no one was protected but the police themselves. They were never mugged because they carried guns; thieves never burgled their homes because they would be shot, and if a policeman ever was killed a whole city would be turned upside down. But the police had never done anything for his daughter. They hadn't protected her and they couldn't find her killer. So what good were they to anybody? He would never again see them as other than scavengers who prey on people, parasites who take all they can and give nothing in return.

At least the underworld didn't pretend to protect families.

Maybe the money he offered them wasn't enough. Fifty thousand for Mungo. Maybe they expected more. But how much more? How much could one life be worth? Or one death?

For some weeks now he had been thinking about the money, that perhaps he should offer them even more. He had some savings, some land he could sell. What he needed was peace of mind, that above all else. It would be worth any price.

At 9:30 A.M. Kansas time he dialed Los Angeles, getting the number from a scrap of paper he kept in a locked drawer of the dest.

"Any news about Vincent Mungo?" he asked the gruff voice that answered.

"Who wants to know?"

He gave his name for what seemed the hundredth time in the past few months.

"Nothing yet," said the voice with disinterest.

"Why can't they find him?" shouted the man in Kansas in a sudden fit of anger and despair. His voice cracked at the end.

"I just take messages," came the bored reply.

"All right," said the Kansan, regaining composure. "I have a message. Tell them George Little will pay double for quick delivery. Do you understand that? Double!"

"Got it," said the voice. "Double for delivery."

"Double for *quick* delivery."

"Sure, sure, double for quick delivery. Got it."

George Little hung up and buried his face in his hands. In a moment his shoulders shook with grief as his iron reserve crumbled. He could no longer control his sorrow and it eventually ran its course Afterward he stared into the darkened room for a long time.

In Sacramento, Jonathan Stoner arose at 10:30 relaxed and refreshed after a late-night political party. He showered and shaved, perfumed and dressed himself in a leisurely manner. There was no need to hurry on this Friday, no need at all. In fact he had the entire weekend free. And even more if needed, since he wouldn't be leaving for the East until the following Wednesday. That was five days away, five whole days he had to himself. Well, almost. He would have to spend Sunday with his wife; she had seen very little of him in recent months because of his travels and campaigning but not once did she complain. He loved her for her patience and understanding and would never dream of hurting her in any way. Then on Monday he would have to be in the Senate at least for the morning on an important roll-call vote concerning capital punishment. And of course the usual last-minute preparations for the tour would take up part of Tuesday no doubt. But in comparison to most other weeks, especially of late, he was as free as a bird.

Except, that was, for the matter of his mistress.

The state senator frowned in thought. There had been some good times with her, some very good moments they had shared and things they had done together. He had used her not only for relief in bed, at which she was extremely capable, but oftentimes as a sounding board for ideas or just somebody to whom he could pour out his frustrations. He had confided much to her during the three years of their relationship, much information as well as his hopes and ambitions and fears and hatreds.

Her bed was a most comfortable place to give verbal vent to his feelings, and it soon became for him a sort of psychiatric couch, with his unwitting bed partner in the role of silent psychiatrist. He sometimes wondered at her easy compliance and submission but each time concluded it was love for him that fueled both her passion and her patience. He suspected a great many women secretly loved him, or could love him, or would love him, and he regarded all this as perfectly natural.

Now she would have to go, and he would miss her heavy breathing and labored sighs. He would miss too her soft, quiet eyes that gazed at him lovingly as he talked after their bouts of passion. But he would be firm. His mind was made up, his decision final.

"We are through." That's what he would say and that's all he would say.

Stoner flirted with the idea of sending her a telegram instead but rejected it as possibly being incriminating. Perhaps a telephone call would do. He dreaded any excess of emotion and women were always getting emotional, especially when men were leaving them. Which was exactly what he intended to do.

For the past several months his star had risen in the East and had not yet set. Indeed, across America his name was beginning to be heard as a protector of fundamental Republican virtues and an ardent foe of what he termed centralism. The capital-punishment issue was itself only part of a still larger split in American political thought between ever-increasing centralization of government, with its attendant self-inflating bureaucracies, and a return to the more traditional, local approach to governing bodies. The senator believed he saw what was happening and therefore what was coming, and he regarded himself as the spokesman for all those who were beginning to demand more control over their own lives. He expected to ride his star to the summit, and there was no room for a local mistress.

Still, the idea was to be covered in all things at all times. The mistress would have to go, another take her place. That was only natural. One from the power-struck breed of woman he was now meeting. But what did he do in the meanwhile? He would have no female body for relief, nothing steady anyway. No one to confide in, or talk to, or gloat over. His wife of course. She was an angel, very ethereal and much too pure for him. He could do little with her.

Perhaps he should wait a bit before telling his mistress they were through. How long? Another day? Week? Until he found her replacement?

With a rush of pleasure Stoner recalled their last time together in bed. He had lain naked on his back while she knelt above him. Slowly she lowered herself onto his penis, deeper and deeper, until her skin touched his. For a long moment she remained motionless, as though impaled on him. Then she began to move ever so slowly, rhythmically, her Venus lips expanding and contracting in controlled muscular spasms as his body writhed in sensual delight. What was it that he had shouted through clenched teeth, unable to contain himself any longer? "Take me, you bitch." As he exploded inside her the bitch quickly lifted a hand-held massager out of the ice bucket and ran its icy fingers over his abdomen and chest, sending him into ecstatic shock.

Thinking it over, Stoner wondered if he wasn't being too hasty. She really was very good at that sort of thing. He shook his head. All the same, she would have to go.

There was only one thing to do. He would tell her, and quickly. That very weekend. Better still, on Monday or Tuesday, just before he left for the East and New York. That way he could get her in bed a few more times.

She would be crushed, naturally. What woman wouldn't? But he'd give her a few hundred dollars for old times and just say goodbye.

He was moving up in every way.

It was eleven o'clock before Sheriff Oates returned to his office in Forest City. He found the memo from Hillside and immediately called John Spanner.

"Good or bad?" he asked when he finally got through to the lieutenant, who had been interrogating a prisoner in another section of the building.

Spanner couldn't hide his disappointment. He had expected to be able to tell Oates that the Willows killer was known at last. Instead he was being forced to confess failure once again, and to a man who had never subscribed to his theories or methods. He wouldn't blame the sheriff for laughing at him.

"It's all bad," he replied with sadness in his voice. "Circumcised?"

"Right down to the bone."

Oates was not surprised. It would've been too much to expect after all this time that they'd come up with the answer so easily. Besides, he didn't think it was Bishop, though he wasn't sure about anything anymore. Neither did he think it was Mungo. The best brain in the world couldn't have survived this long and, from his record, Mungo was no brain. Nor was anyone that lucky. Men disappear all the time but this one was right out there killing women whenever he felt the urge. Only one answer was possible. He hadn't been caught because he hadn't been sought. But who was he? And where was Mungo?

"Got any suggestions?" asked Spanner after a moment. "I'm open to anything from now on."

He was grateful to the sheriff for not laughing. It might indicate a change of mind or perhaps just professional courtesy. Either way he was immensely relieved.

"It could still be Bishop," said Oates kindly. "Both of them were circumcised and so was the body. We're no worse off than before."

"Except we have no proof," protested Spanner, "and that was the last chance to get any."

"Maybe the record's wrong. Hospitals make mistakes, you know."

"I already checked. No mistake. It's right in his file, which hadn't been touched in twenty-five years. Doctor's name and everything." His sigh of defeat was long and clearly audible over the phone. "I've given up on Bishop. I guess it has to be Mungo."

"I don't think so," said Oates slowly. "Not anymore."

"Who, then?"

"Damned if I know. But not Mungo. He would've been picked up by now."

"A friend?"

"Or someone he met after he busted out."

"But what happened to him?"

Oates coughed. "Maybe he got himself killed or went into hiding, I don't know."

A pause. Then, Spanner: "You sound like Finch now."

"Who?"

Spanner reminded him of the Berkeley professor who had figured out the circumcision angle.

"He's said almost from the beginning it wasn't Mungo."

"Who's he got in mind?"

"Nobody particular, just a mad genius."

"Doesn't help us. If it's not Mungo or Bishop we need a suspect, a name. *Something*, for chrissake."

"Jim, do you think there's a chance this—this nobody may have nothing at all to do with the Willows killing?"

"Either that," said Oates heavily, "or Mungo's out there laughing like hell at us. Personally, I hope the son of a bitch is dead and gone. One thing sure. If he ain't dead and I get to him first, he won't be around to go back to a nut house."

Carl Hansun finally got out of bed at noon after an all-night poker session. His head ached, his throat hurt and his hands shook; all of which meant he had enjoyed himself in his night out with the boys. At age fifty-seven he was in reasonably good health for a man with a bad lung and a steel plate in his head. Except for his constant coughing from the cigarettes and occasional stomach pains whenever he boozed it up too much. Tall and still comparatively thin for his years, he ate sparingly and exercised regularly. A millionaire now, Hansun planned to live a long time enjoying his money.

While he shaved and dressed he had the cook prepare his usual breakfast of grapefruit juice, a cheese omelet, and coffee, after which he lit his first Camel of the day. At the moment he found himself alone in the huge Idaho house, save for the servants of course. His wife of many years was visiting her ailing mother in Washington, his younger son had returned to college. The older boy, Carl, Jr., now lived in New York, a move his father hoped was only temporary. After five months in a state hospital getting over the depression caused by an unstable wife's suicide in their California home, the young man had spent a year with his parents before moving on to New York where he had some college friends. He wrote regularly and seemed to be doing fine. Still the father worried, as good fathers often do.

By one o'clock Hansun was being driven to the first of several meetings he had scheduled for this Friday afternoon. His business interests were varied and he gave personal attention to each of them. A meticulous man, no less now than twenty years earlier, he saw to every detail of his affairs. Much of his later success was attributable to this methodical nature, as well as to a certain ruthlessness in business matters.

To anyone who might have known him for the several decades, he would appear to have changed very little.

His fortune of course. A dozen added pounds, a bit less hair, a few more lines in his face. And the name change. After leaving California he had changed it to Pandel, since Carl Hansun was wanted for an armored car robbery. In Idaho, Pandel lived quietly on his share of the money, soon surrounding himself with new associates. In the fifties and early sixties there was big money to be made in the West and Carl's fortune grew rapidly. So did his power and influence.

Now he had four cars, and as he stepped out of the limousine the door was held open by the chauffeur-bodyguard who quickly followed him into the office building.

Assistant Director Henry Baylor arrived at his new home at 2 P.M., his devoted wife by his side. Both of them were exhausted from their travels and glad to be back.

The house was an A-frame, with a small front lawn and a garden on one side. The living room and den were downstairs, a kitchen in the rear. The cathedral ceiling ended at the stairwell, which led to two upstairs bedrooms. Baylor intended to use one of them as his study. A third room would be set aside for overnight guests, what few there might be. The doctor's new position did not afford him quite the authority or prestige he had enjoyed at Willows.

The Baylors had been away for one month, the first vacation in more years than they cared to remember. Three weeks spent in Hawaii, exploring craters and native life styles, with the final week given over to a leisurely drive up the northern California coast from San Francisco to the doctor's new assignment, a state facility near the Oregon border. Smaller than Willows, it did not house those judged criminally insane. Nor did it normally accept behavioral problems from other institutions.

After some political and administrative maneuvering Baylor was assigned to the number-two spot at the facility. He resented the move of course. In his view the police were entirely at fault for not quickly capturing Vincent Mungo. Within Willows the blame lay with Dr. Lang, who had brought Mungo there.

Yet politics necessitated some sacrificial offering and, as head man, he was the logical target. Baylor understood this; most of his professional career had been spent in administrative capacities. What he could not accept was their callous disregard of his stature in demoting him to assistant director. For more than a decade he had been a full director of state institutions. This latest move was a severe embarrassment to him, and the fact that it was merely temporary didn't make it any more palatable. He was not accustomed to waiting around for someone to retire.

He sat now in his new furnished home, provided by his employer, and wondered if he should wait the year—no, actually fifteen months—until he became the director. Perhaps he should himself retire. He was fifty-eight years old and had put in twenty-five years with the state. A quarter of a century was a long time, and there were other things he might want to do.

The bus from San Diego and Los Angeles pulled into Fresno just after three o'clock. Don Solis was the last to leave, his gym bag in his hand. He walked the few blocks from the station to his hotel, where he undressed and lay naked on the bed for a half hour, resting his weary body and weaving fantasies of incredibly gifted women. Though Fresno was his home, he had never felt a sense of permanency anywhere and so he lived his life out of dresser drawers in hostile hotels, always paying by the week and leaving behind nothing of value. It suited his style and at the moment his frame of mind as well.

Solis was jumpy. Ever since his brother's death he felt trapped, as though his whole life was beginning to close in on him. Actually the feeling began even earlier, when he first agreed to do what Carl Hansun wanted. He had played his part well and Senator Stoner got a lot of publicity, for which Solis was responsible. Then his brother got killed and he was responsible for that too.

Now he saw it was all coming apart for him; all the wrong things he had done in his life would catch up with him. His brother's death was just the start. There were many others. The killing of Harry Owens, twenty-one years earlier, was not one of them, at least in his eyes. But it had changed his life, lost him much time and led indirectly to his involvement with Caryl Chessman and Senator Stoner. That made it important and he thought about it a lot lately.

He took a fast shower, a habit acquired in prison

where everything was done quickly in order to have even more time in which to do nothing. After an equally rapid shave he dressed and left the room, double-locking the door behind him. On the stairs he mumbled a greeting to a young couple he had seen previously. The girl looked about sixteen but already had the ripe lushness of womanhood, her long legs shapely, her breasts heavy. She wore a blouse with three buttons open and a brief skirt that revealed the promise of muscular thighs. Solis snapped her into his mind for a future fantasy. The boy couldn't have been more than twenty, and he guessed that they were runaways from home having a sexual orgy before reality caught up with them. He wondered if the boy knew what to do with it. Of the girl he had no doubts; he had known too many like her in his own youth. And a few since then too.

At the corner he paid for his ticket and pulled the Dodge out of the parking lot. It felt good to be behind the wheel again after those long hours on the bus. But it had been worth the time and effort. He had needed to see Messick again, to spend a few days away from home, to get his head straight and his perspective back. He thought of Johnny Messick, fifty now and doing all right in San Diego. They had been friends for many years, even though they hadn't seen each other for most of those years. The two of them, and his brother Lester of course, had been tight long before Carl Hansun and Hank Green showed up in Los Angeles. Long before Harry Owens too. They should never have met Hansun or the others; they would've been better off. All those years wasted in prison, for all of them. All wasted.

He had told Messick about Hansun's visit to the diner, about the anonymous gift of ten thousand dollars he used to start up the business, about the story he was asked to tell Senator Stoner regarding Caryl Chessman, for which he had received another ten thousand. The story that got his brother killed. And now apparently was causing more trouble. He had been approached by a national newspaper wanting to do a feature on his prison relationship with Chessman. Naturally he had refused. He had also received several calls warning him to keep his mouth shut.

Messick had listened carefully, his thin lips pressed in worry. He was not in the organized rackets himself but he was friendly with some of the mob and knew the score. He told Solis to be cautious. Caryl Chessman's friends could be after him, Carl Hansun's people might be afraid he would talk, someone in the business might resent his squealing just on general principles. Remember Albert Anastasia and Arnold Schuster? Or he could be the target of some real nut, like the one who hit his brother.

Solis agreed; anything was possible. But Hansun really worried him. He was sorry he had started the whole thing. Now it was too late.

No it wasn't, Messick had pointed out. Not if he went to Stoner and laid it all out for him.

But Solis couldn't do that. The senator had gained from his story, he would not want to hear anything different. Those politicians were as bad as the mob when it came to protecting themselves. Besides, it was over now and Stoner was riding his own crest. He didn't need anything local anymore.

What about the newspapers? Once they had it, no one would get to him about keeping quiet.

Then they would for *not* keeping quiet. And anyway, he didn't want to talk to anyone. He wasn't a canary. All he wanted was to be left alone.

Before he left San Diego he had given Messick an envelope containing the full account of his dealings with Carl Hansun, beginning with the armored-car robbery in 1952 and going up to what he had recently been asked— told—to do. It included Hansun's Idaho construction company address, got through a contact who checked the limousine registration from the license plate noted by Solis on the day of the visit.

If anything happened to him, Messick was to give the envelope to the police. That way, at least he would be avenged. Johnny Messick had promised he would take care of it.

Now on the way to his diner Solis tried to relax. Business was still good and he was making money. The cops were not looking for him so he wasn't going back to prison. Maybe he would get out of this okay. All he had to do was tell Carl about the envelope, but not who had it; that was his life insurance. He would make Hansun see that he was no threat as long as he was left alone.

In the parking area Solis cut the engine, his mind made up. On Monday he would call Idaho and get to Hansun through the construction company. A half hour in a business library had even given him the new name. The president of the company was listed as Carl Pandel.

Mr. Pandel would see that he meant business too.

Now, if he could only get rid of the feeling that everything was about to blow up in his face.

Friday was a late day for Amos Finch, and he didn't arrive home until almost four o'clock, his last class ending at three twenty-five. No sooner was he in the door than the phone's insistent ring brought him on the run. It was John Spanner calling from Hillside. He had tried the house several times during the day; he hadn't wanted to bother the professor on campus.

The news was not good. Both Mungo and Bishop had been circumcised as infants. Bishop's records named a Dr. Timothy Engles. The records were double-checked by the hospital administration in Los Angeles.

Finch expressed his surprise and disappointment. He had played the law of averages, expecting one of the two to be circumcised. That would have told them which was which. But with both the same, the idea lost its value. He was very sorry.

The lieutenant sighed over the phone. No more sorry than he. Were there any other suggestions Finch might have? Anything at all?

Not at the moment, no. There was of course a difference in motive between circumcising for cosmetic purposes and because the foreskin was too tight but the operation itself was basically the same. It would be too much to expect the same doctor to have done both and to remember them after twenty-five years. Besides, pictures wouldn't reveal anything since the difference might have been in the reason but not the result.

The ears could possibly have told something. There were experts who claimed they were as distinctive as fingerprints. But of course they had been hacked to pieces with the rest of the face and head. And the same for the teeth. Too bad the killer's maniacal fury had been so thorough.

Almost like he planned it that way, said Spanner, who couldn't seem to let go of his obsession.

What about footprints on the hospital certificate? That was often done immediately after birth to prevent any mix-up of infants.

Spanner told him that had been checked long ago. Los Angeles had started such a procedure only in the early fifties. Too late for their needs.

Both men agreed it was another piece of bad luck.

Afterward Finch reviewed his feelings about this latest development. Had he proved Thomas Bishop was alive, since only Bishop and Mungo were missing from Willows, he would have gained some recognition, especially if Bishop had proved to be the maniac and was quickly apprehended. Instead, the identity was still a mystery and the man still apparently safe from capture.

Amos Finch didn't know whether to be happy or not.

For his own part, John Spanner was definitely on the unhappy side. Both Finch and Sheriff Oates believed the madman was not Bishop but someone who had come along after Mungo escaped. Now he, Spanner, was thinking the same thing. Bishop was dead, Mungo was dead or missing, and the nameless killer was in New York. So be it.

On his desk was the report from the Los Angeles police concerning the death of Harry Owens, shot twice by an accomplice named Don Solis during the robbery of an armored car in Highland Park on February 22, 1952. Solis and three others were soon caught, one man escaped. Owens left a wife and three-year-old son.

Spanner felt sorry for the boy. Lost his father at three, killed his mother at ten. Spent the rest of his young life in a mental home, and then was horribly murdered. Not much of a life at all. He wondered what had happened to the boy in those seven years he was with his mother before he—

The lieutenant stopped, went back over his thought. He killed his mother. A woman. And now the unknown maniac was killing—women.

No, it couldn't be!

It was just another crazy coincidence. Life was full of them and he really must stop looking for connections all the time. Lots of men kill women. Always been like that, probably always will be. Almost like a sport at times. That was the way men looked at women, wasn't it? As sport? To be plundered one way or another. And then dumped.

Sure, just a coincidence. Bishop killed a woman at age ten and was put away for fifteen years where there were no women, at least none available. As soon as he was out, women were again killed. But they were being killed all the years he was inside too. And besides, he was dead.

Just a coincidence.

Against his will, a doubt began to creep back into the lieutenant's mind.

Several hundred miles to the south Johnny Messick finally tooled his car into the driveway at six o'clock. It had been a tough day and this Friday evening promised no relief. For most of it he would be in the downtown San Diego bar he owned with a partner. But at least he had a few hours to rest first, and that would be enough to get his juices flowing again. He wasn't a youngster any longer.

Inside the house he turned on some lights. Dory wasn't home yet, so he had a little time. With a penknife he slit open the envelope Don Solis had given him that morning and took out the sheets of paper. After fixing himself a drink he sat down and began reading.

Messick was comfortable in San Diego and had his hand in a half dozen things, most of them outside the law. He did some fencing of stolen goods, some gambling and prostitution, a little smuggling. Nothing big, nothing flashy. Just when an opportunity arose. He was too small to be bothered by the mob and too well known to be harassed by police. Neither greedy nor stupid, he paid off whatever was needed and spread the money around locally to civic and charity groups. All he wanted was a living.

He owned a car and a boat and a small house on a nice street. For six months he had been living with one of his dancers at the bar. Before her there had been others. He had a little money in the bank and a piece of land in Mexico, small and remote, that no one knew about. It was an easy existence, though some days were harder than others, and Messick had no intention of losing any of it.

He folded the sheets and stuffed them back in the envelope, many things now clear to him. When he was released from prison in 1960 he went home to San Diego. Three weeks later a lawyer handed him a certified check for ten thousand dollars, a gift from an anonymous donor. He had used it for operating money to get himself started. For thirteen years he hadn't known who sent him the money. Carl Hansun. The man who got away. The one who had made it big, and in Idaho of all places. What the hell was in Idaho?

Hansun had sent him the ten grand, and Don too. Then forgot about them. But not really. When he needed something he reminded Solis of the debt. Which meant that he, Messick, was into him the same way and one day would have to pay off. Years meant nothing to those people. A favor was payable on demand. Or else.

The letter was still in his hand. He could give it to Carl and cancel the debt. But that would mean a bullet in the head for Don Solis, and probably the same for him. They were the only two who knew the connection between Idaho and the California robbery. He had a feeling that his best protection was in keeping quiet.

Only one thing bothered him. Hansun knew where he was and could get to him any time. Still, the man hadn't made a move in all those years. So he was safe as long as he played dumb.

Messick went over to the steel desk and put the letter in the small built-in strongbox, then walked slowly into the bedroom to rest up for the long night ahead.

At exactly 7:15 P.M. Roger Tompkins left Senator Stoner's offices in the state capital, a slim briefcase under his arm. Inside were copies of some papers, and in two cases the originals, that might prove interesting to certain well-placed enemies. Roger was taking no chances; he intended to secrete the papers should they ever be needed. Of late the senator had been acting a bit aloof, as though he would not have much further use for some people around him. With his new-found prominence his eyes were growing bigger by the week, as was his self-image. Roger had no intentions of being left behind. He was very good at what he did and he expected to remind Stoner of that, as forcefully as necessary. The papers were simple insurance.

In truth it was he who had started the senator on his road to fame. Vincent Mungo had been his idea; tying Mungo to Caryl Chessman was his idea too. Even working out the logistics of the campaign came under his direction. Stoner would still be an obscure state politician were it not for him, and Roger would not let him forget that.

At twenty-six, he had vaulting ambition of his own,

and he expected to ride Stoner as long as needed. Meanwhile he was getting his name known in the East and in Washington, D.C., where it counted. When it was time to leave, he would be the one to do the leaving.

The senator was not the only one moving up.

By Sunday evening when he returned home from his favorite fishing spot, John Spanner had resolved his doubts about the Willows maniac. The fact that Thomas Bishop as a boy had killed his mother really had nothing to do with someone who went around destroying women. The whole psychology was different.

Besides, Vincent Mungo was a much better suspect in just about every way. He had been virtually raised by women, with no men around for balance except a weak father at times. His mother deserted him by dying. His grandmother and aunts betrayed him by committing him, probably for life. Girls found him ugly and never had anything to do with him. He apparently believed, probably was told, that he was the son of Caryl Chessman, a product of rape. His moods of violence had been rapidly escalating, according to records. His sadism was well known, as were his admiration of strength and disgust at any weakness.

On Bishop's side was only the fact of his mother's death when he was ten years old. Someone obviously different from the youth of twenty-five who had been quite friendly and helpful in his recent institutional life except for several outbursts. He had no connection to Chessman. His father had been a drifter, killed in a robbery attempt in 1952. His mother had been a housewife. He was not known to have been a sadist or even cruel-minded.

Maybe Oates was right on this one. Don't look for the loose threads. Go for the preponderance of evidence, for the obvious. Then why didn't the sheriff or Amos Finch think it was Mungo anymore? Because he just wasn't smart enough to last this long.

But was Bishop? According to his records he was just another plodding under-achiever showing little imagination or drive. Pretty much the opposite of any brilliance, and hardly someone to outwit the authorities of a whole country.

On paper, especially with the Chessman connection, it would have to be Mungo all the way.

And if not Mungo, then, as the others believed, somebody completely unknown. God help them all!

Spanner had already decided that over the Christmas holidays he would go back to Colorado for a week or so and look into buying some land. It might be time he retired.

SIXTEEN

By Monday, October 22, Chess Man, variously known as the Willows maniac, the California Creeper, Jack Ripper and the subject of the Ripper Reference, had been in New York for a whole week but no one was celebrating, except perhaps the rest of the country. Nor was he yet the object of the biggest manhunt in New York City's history. That would come shortly.

Bishop spent part of that Monday in the main public library reading out-of-town newspapers from neighboring communities in northern New Jersey and Long Island. Quickly he weeded out those that contained no obituaries. Further elimination, based on the average weekly number of death notices and the information given in each, narrowed his choices to three. Of these, two were in Long Island and the third right across the Hudson River. On the basis of accessibility he chose the nearest. The *Jersey Journal* covered the various communities of Hudson County, one of which was Jersey City where the newspaper was headquartered.

In the general reference section he looked up Jersey City in *Webster's New Geographical Dictionary*. It was a port town and the county seat. Population was over a quarter million. A railroad center, it also was noted for the manufacture of chemicals, paper products, locomotives, clothing and toys.

Bishop read the entry several times, skipping over the early history going back to 1630 and the Indians. The place seemed perfect for his needs. A quarter of a million people! Too big for everyone to be known. A county seat with all the records readily available. And a transportation center with people moving around causing confusion. He'd be just someone else trying to survive. It was perfect.

He got the paper's address from the Jersey City phone directory.

At a nearby newsstand he bought a copy of the *Jersey Journal* which he read over coffee in a donut shop. From a bus dispatcher he learned the fastest way to Jersey City was by underground train from 33rd Street and Sixth Avenue. He walked down to find the station beneath a giant department store. The man in the change booth told him the trip took twenty minutes, through several stops and a tunnel under the river. To Bishop it sounded simple enough as his devious mind planned the next move.

On the street again he went to a telephone-answering service he had found listed in a show-business weekly. It was in the midtown area and its rates were advertised as the very cheapest around. He paid for three months in advance and was given a handful of cards with the service number and name, as well as another number for his own use. In return he gave the name Jay Cooper and the mail-drop address on Lafayette Street.

Bishop wanted no telephone where he lived, nothing official to link him to the place. Especially nothing originating in the past week or two. Authorities might go through all recent utility orders when he didn't turn up in their search of city hotels and rooming houses. For the moment at least he was fully insulated from prying eyes, and thus safe.

His electricity and gas were part of one set of meters for the entire commercial building, so there was no record of him. The bill was paid each month by the owner. Since the building and area were not zoned for residential purposes, he was not listed as living there. Again no record. The Soho apartment had been a lucky break and he was quick to see its advantages.

Yet he needed a phone number for his photographic pursuits, just as he needed a mail drop for identification purposes. He had to be able to get in touch with prospective models, and they with him. Which was why he had bought a copy of the show-business newspaper. He found no photography models listed but he did find the telephone-answering service.

His last stops of the day were the offices of two local

papers read by many young New Yorkers who followed
free-lance careers. In each he ran a brief classified adver-
tisement for photography models to pose for distress-type
pictures for detective magazines. Only those females eighteen and over would be considered. At the bottom was
the number of his service.

The idea had come from a television documentary about
a California rapist and murderer who lured his victims
with talk of payment for modeling assignments. Before his
capture a half dozen women had died in his studio. Bishop
planned to do even better.

Home again, he spent the evening reading about Jersey
City in a newspaper and New York in books. After a
while he couldn't tell them apart.

At 10:30 A.M. that same Monday Adam Kenton was in
Martin Dunlop's office explaining his need for the list of
those who knew why he had been brought to New York.

It was really very simple. His curiosity had been aroused
as to why he had been chosen for such an assignment.
The job was extraordinary, to say the least, and required
a high degree of tact as well as investigative skill. Since
they evidently agreed on him, it indicated a certain confidence. He merely wanted to know who had such confidence in him. It would tell how he stood with the company.

Dunlop was satisfied for the most part. He told Kenton
it was John Perrone who had singled him out as the best
man for the job. He, Dunlop, had agreed. The others went
along with the selection, which indicated nothing but simple acquiescence for the moment. Of course his success
in the search would dispel any doubts some may have
held as to the choice. Naturally he would also find his
position in the company appreciably improved.

Kenton thanked him for his vote of trust and promised
to do his best. He already had some leads that looked good.
Dunlop reminded him that time was always short on a
thing like this.

Afterward Dunlop called in his aide. He wanted
Kenton watched by someone outside the organization. A
private agency would do. Also everything in the man's
past that could be used against him if necessary. And a
tap on his office phones.

Where was he staying in town?

Henderson said the company rooms at the St. Moritz.
He was told to see what could be done about a tap there
too.

Back in his own office, Kenton returned a half dozen
calls from California. Nothing yet about a boy who
killed his mother but didn't make the newspapers. Or even
anyone who tried and was put away. On Vincent Mungo
the only new information was an unsubstantiated report
that his father had committed suicide because of homosexual urges that had become uncontrollable. That, and a
rumor about a Berkeley criminologist who didn't think
Mungo was the killer. Kenton wanted to know more, including the man's name if he existed.

Before noon Mel Brown called about Louis Terranova.
He was out of the picture. Escaped from Lakeland
exactly one year earlier, in October 1972, after six years
there. First was in Atascadero for sixteen years. Before the
matricide lived in Bakersfield with his mother. Was a little
funny even as a kid but no police trouble. Didn't know
Caryl Chessman, was not in Los Angeles in 1947–48.
Didn't know Vincent Mungo, was never in Stockton. No
record of knowing Mungo in Lakeland. It was a very
big place.

So the Chessman angle was out, but not Mungo. Not
entirely. They could have known each other, been close
friends, without the doctors or anyone being aware. As
he said, it was a big place.

Oh, didn't he mention it? Terranova was black.

Black?

Schwarze. And his mother was Jewish.

A black Jew? No, he hadn't mentioned it before.

Part of the researcher's strange sense of humor.

In the afternoon Kenton read through the material Doris
had collected on Chessman, much of it familiar. There
was a lot, and more to come. Including copies of his
four books. He had received a vast amount of publicity
in the last decade of his life. Did Kenton really want all
of it? Might as well have everything, but most especially
the years 1947 and before. Someplace there had to be a
connection to the maniac. It couldn't have come from the
final dozen years in prison, so it had to be while Chessman
was still free.

At one point in his reading Kenton had a sudden thought.
He looked up Chessman's birth. St. Joseph, Michigan,

1921. In 1947 he would've been only twenty-six. Young enough for anything. But someone around Mungo's age wouldn't even have been born yet. So how could the connection be between Chessman and the man he sought? Answer: It couldn't.

It would have to be someone older. Like the killer's parents.

Damn! It was always coming back to Vincent Mungo.

His mother supposedly was raped by Caryl Chessman. His father supposedly told him he was Chessman's bastard son.

But he would not accept Vincent Mungo. No, it was not Mungo. Therefore the connection was from Chessman to someone else's parents. When he found it he would know the killer's identity.

Unless—

He called Los Angeles, a contact in the courts, and asked for the names of those women who had accused Chessman of sexual assault. At the trial or before, perhaps in a police station. Or even any women who had said to anybody that it might have been Chessman.

If Mungo was a possibility because his mother had allegedly been raped by Chessman, then other victims might have borne children from such an attack. He thought of Ding's idea about Son of Rapist. Maybe not so crazy after all!

Within an hour he had the names he needed and was talking to a California information agency. He wanted to know if any of the women listed had given birth in 1948, and if so, the sex of the infant.

At 3:40 Fred Grimes reported that he had received the okay to collect recent names from the city's mail drops. Two special peace officers would visit all such places in Manhattan over the next several days. He assumed only Manhattan was wanted.

Kenton said the Bronx, Brooklyn, and Queens too. But Manhattan first. Staten Island wasn't needed, because at checkpoints like the ferry terminal everyone could be stopped. But the other four boroughs were impossible to police thoroughly, with subways and buses constantly on the move.

Grimes wondered about New Jersey. Maybe the maniac was staying over there, right across the river. Or Westchester or even Connecticut. Had Kenton thought about that?

He had, but the objection to Staten Island held for those as well. Without a car it was simply too dangerous. And he wouldn't have a car.

Why not?

He rented cars in Phoenix and probably in other places. He came to New York on the train from Chicago. He couldn't have much money and he wouldn't want to get involved in the red tape of owning a car in New York, with registration and parking tickets and the danger of being towed away. He'd be showing proof of his identity all the time. That didn't fit his pattern of complete anonymity, not at all.

By 4:20 Kenton was hurrying into police headquarters on Centre Street, late for a meeting with a deputy chief. If the cops got to Chess Man before he did, he wanted first crack at the story. That way, his assignment wouldn't seem a total failure to the big shots at *Newstime*. It was worth ten thousand to him. What the cops did with the money was their business.

Upstairs he outlined his plan to the official. He just wanted to help out somehow so he could be credited with assisting the police. He was doing a cover story and it would lend a certain authenticity. Which would in turn give the story strong reader appeal. For this he was ready to pay ten thousand cash. Perhaps for the retirement fund . . .

The deputy chief said he would think about it. There were ways an investigative reporter could help the police, especially if he had vital information. It would be his duty to report whatever he knew to the authorities, who might want him around at the capture.

Just what he had been thinking, said Kenton with a smile.

On the way home he reviewed the meeting. He had struck the right balance of public service and professional interest. He wanted nothing illegal, merely a little preferential treatment for which someone's retirement fund would come to benefit.

Naturally he said nothing about the Ripper Reference. Or his ideas on the identity of the Chess Man. It was all just insurance anyway. He still hoped to beat everyone to the killer. At least he had one big advantage. He knew who it wasn't.

Six hours earlier in the same building, though on a different floor, top police brass had met to discuss Vincent Mungo. A special homicide task force was set up, with thirty detectives assigned to the search under a deputy inspector. The command post was to be the 13th Precinct on East 21st Street. Special patrols and stakeouts would be conducted and all leads pursued. Men had already been visiting the city's lesser hotels and rooming houses, showing pictures of Mungo with and without a full beard. Other men distributed photographs to restaurants and supermarkets. Mungo had to sleep and eat. He would be caught. He also apparently had to kill. Surveillance would be increased in areas where prostitutes walked the streets. He might be captured in the act, preferably beforehand but streetwalkers were always expendable. The main thing was to get the maniac.

The police brass was confident. They had his face and description and M.O. He was a stranger to New York, with little money and no friends. Where could he go? How could he hide? And he was a madman besides—a nut, irrational. How could he stack up against 27,000 of New York's finest? Someone suggested that if he stuck to preying on local prostitutes he wouldn't last long at all. They were the toughest in the world.

The meeting ended on a note of assurance. It was just a matter of time and he'd be in their hands. Probably only days, maybe even hours.

Bishop's train pulled into Jersey City's Journal Square shortly before ten on Tuesday morning. He walked up some steps to the street and found the building that housed the local newspaper. Inside, he pretended to be a journalism major in college who wanted to do a class report on the *Jersey Journal* in the period after the Second World War. Would he be able to look at some back issues? Say between 1945 and 1950?

The clerk was most helpful. All back issues were now on microfilm, one year to a roll. At that time the paper was called the *Jersey Observer*. Any serious reader could certainly review whatever rolls were needed, and even have blowups made of desired pages. Yes, indeed.

Where would he find them?

The public library. The entire microfilm collection could be seen at the main library on Jersey Avenue. The paper kept actual copies around only for the past few years.

Didn't it have its own set of microfilm?

Yes, but that was just for internal use.

Bishop put on his most innocent expression, his friendliest face. His eyes shone, his smile sparkled. He was all charm and manners.

Could he possibly look at the paper's film for just an hour? One hour, no more. He was from New York and didn't know his way around the city. He'd be very quiet and no one would even realize he was there. It would be such a great help to him.

The clerk, a kindly man, knew he should say no. Company policy forbade any reader use of the set. But the boy seemed so helpless, so bewildered. Reminded him of his own youth. He too had often been flustered.

He led the helpless youth to a room in the rear of the building. The microfilm was on a shelf, boxed and dated. He pulled out the years 1945 to 1950 and showed the young man how to operate the viewer, cautioning him to roll each film back to the beginning after he had finished.

"One hour, mind you, and no more," he said on the way out. The door clicked softly and Bishop turned to 1945.

An hour and forty minutes later he found it. Thomas Wayne Brewster, three, died at the Medical Center on September 1, 1949. The only child of Mary Brewster and the late Andrew T. Brewster, killed two years earlier in an auto accident. Interment in Holy Name Cemetery, Jersey City, on September 4.

It was perfect. Three years old. Only child. Father dead. Mother probably remarried, maybe moved away. No one to remember him. Three years old meant he had almost certainly been born in the city. Now only the birth date was needed.

Another half hour and he stepped from a bus on West Side Avenue. A brisk walk brought him into the Catholic cemetery. Once inside the gates he quickly saw the futility of searching among the headstones. There were thousands of graves, endless rows of plot and stone seemingly stretching to the horizon. He went into the groundkeeper's office.

Could he be directed to the grave of Thomas Wayne Brewster, buried on September 4, 1949? He had known the family years earlier but had never before visited the cemetery. Now he was in the area and would like to pay his respects to the deceased.

The records book was opened for that time, the name and date checked. Brewster. 1949. September 4.

Within ten minutes he was standing over the grave. The headstone had two wreaths carved on it and in the center a figure of the Blessed Virgin Mary. Underneath, two names had been chiseled into the smooth surface. The father, Andrew T. Brewster, born 1918, died 1947. The son, Thomas W. Brewster, born 1946, died 1949.

His trip had been for nothing. There was no birth date.

On the return to Journal Square he thought of several ways to learn the child's correct date of birth but rejected each as too dangerous. He couldn't afford to draw attention to himself or even be asked for identification. Certainly not at the moment.

An idea finally came that might work with no risk to him. Infants usually were born in hospitals, and hospitals kept records. It was just a question of finding the right one and pressing the right button for the information that he wanted.

The telephone book listed eight hospitals for the city but only one was all maternity and it was part of the city system. Assuming his parents didn't have much money, the boy could have been born there. Poor people had their babies in city hospitals. He had been born in one, or so he had read in a newspaper months back. Vincent Mungo too.

He called Margaret Hague Maternity from a closed booth. He was Father Foley of St. John's on the Boulevard, asking about the birth of one of his parishioners years ago. He had been sent a mass card from relatives now living in another state. The mass was due to be said that very week. But he needed the birth date of the deceased. Yes, that's right. It would be most helpful, thank you.

He gave the name and year and waited patiently. Several minutes later he got his answer. No one with the name of Brewster was listed for 1946. Was he sure it was Margaret Hague? Not positive, no. What about the baptismal certificate, wouldn't that have the date?

Yes, but with the church expansion program everything was misplaced or in transit. He just thought this might be faster. Thanks anyway for the help.

Bishop closed his eyes for a moment. He had to think quickly on that one.

The answer was the same at the Jersey City Medical Center. On the third call he got lucky. Christ Hospital on Palisade Avenue had a 1946 record of Thomas Wayne Brewster. Mother was Mary, father Andrew. Religion was Roman Catholic. The baby weighed eight pounds, eleven ounces.

Date of birth: May 3.

Father Foley thanked the woman and hung up.

At Christ Hospital the middle-aged clerk returned the file to its proper drawer. She was a bit surprised that the parents were Catholic. Now, of course, everything was opening up but that was almost thirty years ago. She didn't think there were too many Negro Catholic families at that time.

At a nearby post office Thomas Wayne Brewster purchased a five-dollar money order and sent in his request for a birth certificate to the Registrar of Vital Statistics in Jersey City. He had been born on May 3, 1946. The certificate should be sent to him at 654 Bergen Avenue. The address was that of the local YMCA where he had just rented a room, paying for one month in advance.

Back in New York Bishop bought a pair of eyeglasses with heavy brown frames. The lenses were almost clear glass but wearing them gave him a different look. He also bought some hair coloring. He intended to lighten his hair that night. His beard was nearly full. With eyeglasses, sandy hair and a beard he would not really look like Thomas Bishop anymore, just in case they somehow discovered he was not Vincent Mungo. Which, of course, they would never do. He was too clever for them, for any of them.

Don Solis called Boise, Idaho, about the time Bishop was returning to New York. It was still morning in California. He had tried the day before but Hansun was out. Now he again asked for Carl Pandel. This time he gave his name instead of saying "a friend."

Soon a very surprised Carl Hansun was on the line.

He listened carefully as Solis gave him the number of a pay phone in Fresno. He was to call there in exactly ten minutes from a safe phone of his own.

Ten minutes later Solis picked up the receiver in a Fresno pay booth. He did most of the talking. There was a letter that would be given to authorities if anything happened to him. In the letter was all the information on Hansun, going back to 1952, including the new name and location. This was not blackmail. He wanted only to be left alone. He had done the job and had been paid off. Nothing further was owed either way. If he wasn't bothered, the letter would never be seen. His brother was dead and all he wanted now was a quiet life. He would not talk to anybody about the Chessman thing with Stoner. Or anything else. As long as he was left alone.

He hung up after telling Hansun to call off his bloodhounds.

Senator Stoner had a million things to do on Tuesday evening before he left for the East. And of course he wanted to be home with his family on his final night. Which was why he had a last matinee with his mistress in the afternoon. It was delicious as always. Afterward he told her they were through. He had other plans which did not include her. He was sorry.

He put three bills on the table by the bed. One hundred dollars for each year.

She was expecting it, knowing the senator. He was always predictable. Lately he had been going through all the motions of a male in flight. His new fame was giving him a big head and even bigger ideas. She wouldn't, couldn't, stand in his way of course. But it would cost him something to be rid of her.

She asked him to listen to some tapes. Then she told him what she wanted.

Fifty thousand dollars.

She had quite a few tapes.

He could buy all of them, and he would get his money's worth. She would hold none back. There were no duplicates. Once she got the money, he would never see her again or hear from her. She was not dumb enough to squeeze him, not with the people the senator knew.

Just fifty thousand and he'd be rid of her forever.

If not, she'd give the tapes to his political enemies and to the newspapers. The *San Francisco Chronicle* would love to hear them, not to mention *The New York Times* or the *Washington Post*. Some of the things he had done along the way, the deals, the people, would make interesting reading to authorities as well as the public. Then there were his many comments on the politicians and plain folks, the growers, the laborers, the small businessmen who put him in office. He really did like to talk.

It was either the money or his career, if not his freedom.

She wanted the money before he left on his trip.

In Los Angeles a Republican district leader sent a mailgram to Washington, D.C., before he left his office that afternoon. It went to the congressman from his district. A friend of his in the state penal system had been called by a *Newstime* reporter in New York, who said he was writing a cover story on Vincent Mungo for the magazine. But the odd thing was that the reporter seemed interested only in Caryl Chessman, who had been executed in a Republican national administration. The district leader wondered if there was anything in it. Especially in view of the total animosity displayed by *Newstime*, normally a Republican-oriented magazine, toward the Nixon administration.

Wednesday promised to be a busy day for Kenton and he got to the office a bit early. By nine o'clock he was hearing from Mel Brown. Apparently Carl Pandel was white, Christian and twenty-six years old. His wife had committed suicide two years earlier, which put him in the rest home for five months. Then a year with his parents in Idaho. His father was big in construction among other things.

Young, white, Christian and crazy. Good so far. "Did he kill his mother too?"

"His mother is very much alive. Sorry about that."

So he didn't kill her. But he wanted to all those years. Then he drove his wife nuts to where she killed herself. Or maybe he killed her and made it look like suicide.

"Where's he now?" Kenton asked.

"Right here."

"What?"

Brown chuckled. "He's in New York. But—" He paused for effect. "He's been here for months."

Down but not out. "When did he get here?"

"July."

"When in July?"

Brown didn't know.

"Find out the day he arrived. And how. Also where he lives and what he does for money. If the old man's that rich, maybe the kid doesn't work."

"What's your idea?"

"He could've come here, then gone back on a bus or coach train where there's no record. And slowly made his way east again."

"Too complicated for a nut."

"Who says he's nuts?"

"Even half."

"Let's find out."

He got Fred Grimes on the fourth ring. They might have a lead. He wanted the best detective outfit in New York, and their best man checking on Carl Pandel. Mel Brown would have an address in a little while. Another dozen should be ready for the mail-drop names when they came in. How was that going?

"Only started yesterday," said Grimes, "and there's a lot of drops. Even just Manhattan."

"When do you think?"

Grimes thought a moment. "Probably Friday. That should do it."

"Let me know."

For the rest of the morning, between bouts with the telephone, Kenton listened to George Homer talk of Senator Stoner and Don Solis. Stoner held stock in a half dozen blue chips, perhaps fifty thousand dollars total. He owned two homes, in Sacramento and Beaumont, Washington. Some land in northern California and Idaho worth possibly another forty thousand. All on the surface. Underneath, no one knew for sure. There was talk of deals but that was standard for most politicians. He was a rank opportunist obviously, and probably much more. The trouble was proving it.

His mistress was more interesting, at least for the moment. A model, twenty-five, two years' college. Had a brain to go with the body. Been with Stoner three years but not exclusively, though he might not know that. Apparently he paid for her apartment. Not known what other arrangement they had.

What was interesting about her?

A while ago she spent over a thousand dollars for recording equipment. Voice-actuated equipment. She had the heavy stuff placed in a closet, hidden out of sight.

Where was the other end?

The bed.

Which meant she probably had tapes of Stoner talking crooked or dirty or both. Tapes she'd want to sell, either to him or someone else.

Kenton had to admit that raised some possibilities. Now what about Don Solis?

Solis killed an accomplice in a payroll robbery in Los Angeles in 1952, a man named Harry Owens. In San Quentin, Solis knew Chessman since they both were on death row. That was the basis for the story he gave the papers about Chessman confessing his guilt.

After a few years Solis switched from death row to life and finally parole. When he got back to Fresno he opened a diner with his brother, who had been in on the robbery. Where the money came from was a mystery; Solis had none. The robbery money had all been recovered except for the one who got away. About a hundred thousand. Now Solis owned a bigger diner and was doing all right. He was not in the rackets that anyone knew about.

Was the money a payoff for something Solis did? Or was the Chessman story a payoff for the money? That would let Stoner out. The money was five years before the story.

Kenton told Homer to check out a rumor about Mungo's father being a latent homosexual. Also he was to call all the criminologists at the University of California in Berkeley until he found one who didn't think Mungo was the killer. He should also look further into Stoner's business affairs, especially the land he owned. When did he get it? From whom? And he should read all the material on Chessman, in case Kenton had missed anything.

At 12:30 P.M. New York time the information agency in California called about possible rape victims who had borne children in 1948. Only one woman who reportedly said Caryl Chessman might have been her attacker gave birth during that year. The infant was a girl.

Dead end.

The killer was a boy.

Carl Hansun was worried. He lit a Camel and took a deep drag into his one good lung, which set him into a paroxysm of coughing. It was all the fault of that dumb son of a bitch Solis. Talking to him like that. And how did he know the new name? Only one way. He got the license number from the car that day and traced it back to the company registration. Who owned the company? Carl Pandel. Same first name. Not so dumb at all.

He didn't like taking the car so deep into California, but even after all these years he still wouldn't travel to the state by any public transportation. Too dangerous. They might remember his face or discover his real name. It was all in his head of course. He was a new person with a new identity, and nobody cared after twenty years. But he couldn't help it.

Now Solis knew who he was and had it in a letter, and the old stuff too. Maybe enough to even put him away for a while. He was fifty-seven years old, a rich man, and he couldn't take chances any more. Solis was the only one who knew about him. No—Johnny Messick too. The last of the old gang. But Johnny was all right; he wouldn't talk. Besides, he didn't know anything about Idaho or the new identity.

Solis was the one. He would have to be watched; where he went, who he saw. The letter would turn up somewhere.

Hansun crushed the cigarette. He would get his associates to talk to the mob in Los Angeles.

Stoner was leaving for Kansas City on a two o'clock flight. At 10 A.M. he took fifty thousand dollars from the wall safe in his home and put it in a manila envelope. Twenty minutes later he gave the envelope to his mistress. In return she gave him fourteen reels of tape in a shoe box. At home again he listened to the tapes in the privacy of his study, just a bit from each to make sure he got the right ones. Then he took them to a nearby woods and burned everything in a roaring fire. He watched fifty thousand dollars go up in smoke, and he was glad he wouldn't ever see his former mistress again. He was so angry he could easily kill her.

When he left for the airport he kissed his wife and told her that in two weeks he would return the conquering hero.

Bishop went out for a walk that evening. In a Greenwich Village bar he talked to a young woman drinking white wine. It had been a hard day's work and what she needed more than anything was some civilized talk and nice manners. He had a good face and a fabulous smile. His voice was soft and he seemed very civilized. She accepted a drink from him. Two hours later she accepted his offer to escort her home.

By the time Kenton finally left the office he felt he was leaving his voice behind. For almost two hours in the afternoon he had talked into his machine, reviewing his moves. Then to John Perrone, a progress report, and to Christian Porter, who apologized for not calling sooner and wanted to have lunch the next day, and to Mark Hanley, an assistant managing editor, from whom he got the names of the Rockefeller Institute doctors who had prepared the profile on the killer. Several times to Mel Brown, to Fred Grimes, to Otto Klemp, who reminded Kenton that any breach of security would mean the end of the assignment, and to assorted others in and out of the company and around the country. Weary and discouraged, all he sought at the moment was quietness.

He ordered a steak and mushrooms at the Bull and Bear, dining in an alcove well away from the noisy bar. On nearby Park Avenue he hired a working girl to service him, telling her he wanted no talk, no words. He paid her double to lie silently by his side for an extra amount of time. Later at the St. Moritz he sat soundless in an overstuffed chair, the room dark, his eyelids closed.

Was it just his imagination or was there someone following him?

For two days Deputy Chief Gunther Charles had thought about the proposition. It all seemed reasonable enough. The man was writing an important story for a big magazine. He wanted to make it as authentic as possible and to get all the publicity he could. Helping the police would insure its being accepted as genuine and would certainly guarantee publicity. Especially if he was credited with assisting the police in capturing Vincent Mungo. That should easily be worth ten thousand.

On the other hand, where would he get that kind of money? Reporters didn't have ten grand to give away. So the magazine would pay. But why? Why all that money for a story? They wouldn't even get an exclusive out of it. Everybody in town would be writing about Mungo.

Somehow it didn't sound right.

On Tuesday he had a man look into Adam Kenton even though Fred Grimes had set up the meeting. Everything checked out. Still, it was unusual for a magazine to try to buy police help. Though the proposal was seemingly not unlawful as presented, police acceptance could cause some unwarranted assumptions. Particularly since a lot of money was involved.

On balance, he was for it. Such an arrangement could lead to a whole new source of revenue for the PBA fund to go to families of those officers killed in the line of duty. But it could also become a secret source of graft. He decided to pass it on with his reservations.

Now on this Thursday morning, he picked up the phone and called his counterpart in the detective division.

"Lloyd? Gunther here. You busy for the next five minutes? . . . Good, I got something for you. . . . Could you? Yes, I'll come over."

Outside his office he told the man on duty where he'd be in case the PC called on that kidnapping.

"Anybody else I'll be back in fifteen minutes."

"Right, Chief."

"And tell Anderson I want to see him before the demonstration at City Hall."

"It's on at noon."

"Before, not after."

The sergeant busied himself as his boss walked away. He didn't envy the man his job.

Charles talked with Lloyd Geary for almost a half hour about the *Newstime* offer, noting that he was sympathetic in principle though he wasn't sure how it could be controlled or even if it was legal. Since the offer was concerned with the Mungo search, he thought Geary should know about it.

Deputy Chief Geary had headquarters command over the special task force set up to apprehend Vincent Mungo. He regarded his detectives as the best in the business, and it was mostly due to his influence that his men were under divisional supervision rather than direct control of individual precinct commanders. This gave them greater autonomy and supposedly make for more efficiency, though some in the department felt the reverse was true. Gunther Charles was known to be one of these and Geary, now alone again, carefully reviewed what had been said.

To him it sounded downright illegal. Not in giving preferential treatment to a particular reporter—that was done all the time—but in taking money for it. Even money given for a nonprofit fund. He knew nothing about corporate tax law but he was sure it couldn't be deducted as a business expense. Which meant there was something wrong with it.

He didn't intend to be caught in any squeeze play. When he got the 13th Precinct on the phone he told Deputy Inspector Dimitri he wanted to see him at four o'clock. Yes, at headquarters.

Deputy Inspector Alex Dimitri didn't like the offer at all. He had listened to his superior's views on the matter and had agreed with him that it would be foolish to involve the department in any money deals with newspapers or magazines. On the other hand investigative reporters sometimes got information denied the police and could thus prove useful. Geary believed an agreement should be made with the reporter for an exchange of ideas. Nothing more, and no discussion of money. Just an exchange of ideas and information. It wouldn't hurt and could help.

Dimitri was in charge of the task force. He was an experienced detective and homicide expert, rising rapidly from the ranks in a brilliant career. He made few mistakes. Industrious and imaginative, he allowed nothing to interfere with his various pursuits. Which was why he had been given this latest assignment. That, and because he had enemies in high places. Or so he was firmly convinced.

Back in his command post at the 13th Precinct, he called the number given him for Adam Kenton. He would tell the man that the department was willing to cooperate to the extent of sharing whatever was known. Maybe Kenton had something he could use. After three days he already saw that Vincent Mungo was going to a bitch to find.

At home that night Alex Dimitri wrote a letter to a friend in Washington, a high police official like himself. They had met years earlier at an FBI course for metropolitan police and had kept in touch, writing regularly and seeing each other every few years.

Toward the end of his brief letter Dimitri mentioned his new assignment to capture the notorious Vincent Mungo. He also told of the *Newstime* offer and his suspicion that the magazine was trying to get Mungo for the publicity value and just wanted to see how much the police knew. He never did trust investigative reporters. What kind of a job was that for a grown man?

The California congressman was having a good time at the party, the first he had attended in at least two weeks. Though parties went on continuously on the Washington political scene, several every day of every year, the congressman had just got himself a new mistress, a pretty little thing from the Senate office staff, and she was keeping him busy.

At one point in the evening he talked to someone on the Committee to Re-elect the President and remarked in passing about the supposed *Newstime* story on Vincent Mungo that focused entirely on Caryl Chessman. He had received a mailgram about it from one of his people back home. "Probably nothing," he said to his acquaintance, drink in hand. "Who cares what happened to Chessman? It was all a long time ago anyway."

The committeeman, who drank only club soda with a squeeze of lime, cared quite a bit. Eisenhower had been president when Chessman was killed. The execution was put off a couple of months so Ike could visit South America without running into mass demonstrations, always a sore point with the enemy even after all these years.

And who had been Vice-President under Dwight David Eisenhower?

The committeeman left the party a bit early. He had a memo to write. Most especially in view of the fact that *Newstime* was presently considered to be strongly in the enemy camp.

It wasn't so much that she worried about her friend, but New York could sometimes be a scary place for a girl alone. Which was one reason they talked on the phone almost every day and even had the keys to each other's place. Just in case.

She had things to tell her friend, girl talk about the new job and the boy she had gone out with who had the most incredibly big . . . she just couldn't get used to the word cock, and always blushed when she said it. She wished there was a better word for it.

She had called several times the night before and a half dozen times earlier in the evening. No answer. Her friend would normally have been home from work long ago. Probably staying over with some guy, she thought as she climbed the two flights. Still, she was here now. Might as well knock on the door, in case the phone was off the hook or not working.

When she got no answer she decided to use the two keys. It was silly, but why not? Maybe her friend was sick or had passed out from those damn pills she was always taking. First the Segal, then the Fox lock. That was the right order.

The kitchen light was on. She looked at the huge calendar with the male nude over the tiny breakfast table. He was not as big as the boy she had the other night. She shivered with remembered delight. It really did make a difference if they were extra big.

She instinctively reached up to tear off the daily sheet. It was no longer Wednesday. In fact Thursday was almost over, and soon it would be Friday, October 26. Only a month to Thanksgiving and two until Christmas. She liked Christmas, but another one so fast! At twenty-three she was getting too old too fast.

The lights in the living room were on too. There was a half-empty glass of wine on the end table by the couch. She walked past it toward the bedroom. The door was partially open, the light off.

She ran her hand along the wall and found the switch as she turned her face into the room.

SEVENTEEN

"Jesus!"

The first homicide detective to arrive from the special task force closed the bedroom door softly, as though he were in a funeral parlor, and walked noiselessly over to the couch. The wine glass was still on the end table. What he had just seen filled him with a certain dread. Thirteen years on the force, eight of them a detective involved in murder, and he had never seen anything like it. Earlier in the week he had wondered about the fuss made over one crackpot killer. Why all the heavy attention? Now he knew.

At that moment he would have killed the man with his bare hands, easily and without thought. Stripped the skin right from his body, as was done to the girl in the bedroom. And worse.

He shook his head, trying to focus on the others in the living room. Two beat cops from the 6th Precinct, one a sergeant, and the building's superintendent. Did they feel what he was feeling? Did they sense the evil still lurking in the room? It was real, and he knew if he reached out he could touch it. He hoped he wasn't going to throw up.

His mouth was dry and his hands shook slightly. He was not the man to believe in devils. In his experience the devil always turned out to be somebody with a motive and a sadistic nature. Now he wasn't so sure. The thing responsible for what was left in the bedroom could as easily be beast as man, but a beast with human capabilities. And maybe superhuman powers for evil. If that wasn't a devil, what in hell was?

He suddenly thought of the girl who had discovered the remains. She apparently had run screaming into the hall. Ten minutes later she was still screaming as she was gently led away. He expected the screams to be with her for a long time.

Upon his arrival the detective had put in a call for the deputy inspector. One look told him it was their man. Now Dimitri entered the apartment, his manner quiet, his voice subdued. It was nearly midnight and he had been home sleeping when the word came. He made good time over the Queensboro Bridge, the siren whining all the way downtown to Greenwich Village where the woman had lived. In the interim several other members of the task force had arrived, men still on duty, and they congregated now in the kitchen, their eyes studiously avoiding the nude male on the calendar as they discussed the murder in hushed tones. Hardened veterans all, they were nonetheless shocked to a man.

Dimitri got himself a glass of water from the sink and drank it slowly, staring into the transparent liquid. His headache was worse, and this latest massacre was not going to help it any. He couldn't quite grasp the bestiality of the attack. He had seen classified photographs of some of the victims across the country, including the one in Grand Central and the prostitute on West 49th Street. But seeing it up close for the first time was—awesome; he could think of no other word for it. Something like this, if seen by the public and perhaps repeated two or three times, could easily lead to mass hysteria.

No pictures. That was the first clear thought as his police mind began to function again. Only the forensic boys. No reporters allowed in the apartment—nothing! After the lab was through the remains would be taken to the morgue, whatever was left. The press could shoot the place in the morning. Meanwhile he would make a statement.

Next order of business. A meeting of the task force heads at ten o'clock in the morning. Everybody. The killer must be caught, and quickly. There were other things that could be checked besides hotels and rooming houses. Maybe he got a cheap apartment or a car. They would look at recent electricity turn-on requests, new residence phone orders. Visit used-car lots and search through parking tickets and moving violations for any California identification. There were dozens of places that could be checked for new faces—where he ate or got his mail or banked or got a beer or a haircut—if only they had enough manpower. Dimitri had a feeling they would soon get all the manpower they needed.

After a while he sat on the couch and called his second in command at home on Long Island's North Shore. One of the privileges of rank, Dimitri reminded himself, was to be inconsiderate to subordinates. Unlike Captain Olson, his assistant on the task force, he did not have a great need for country privacy. His home in Queens was separated from the houses on either side by narrow driveways.

"After one," Dimitri said when Olson finally came on the phone. He didn't ask if the man had been sleeping, nor did he apologize for waking him up.

"Where?" asked a tired voice trying to rouse itself.

"Greenwich Village."

"He's moving around."

"Worse than that," said Dimitri slowly. "I got the boys checking but from the looks of it, she was not a prostitute."

Both men knew what that meant. Killing prostitutes was one thing, easily overlooked by society up to a point. But the killing of a decent woman was entirely different matter in police circles, which always followed public morality.

"That could be trouble," suggested Olson. "Anyone see him?"

"Not yet but they'll search more in the morning. The lab's coming now."

"Want me in?"

"Nothing you can do here," growled Dimitri, "unless you want to see a real horror show." He wished he hadn't been reminded of what was in the next room.

"No thanks. I'm a family man."

Dimitri stiffened. He was a family man himself, with four children to Olson's two. That made him twice as good, and he resented the captain's implication that he was a bloodthirsty voyeur. But he quickly swallowed his resentment. Olson hadn't meant anything disrespectful.

"Get in a bit early if you can. We'll have to fight off the media, not to mention headquarters."

"The PC know about it yet?"

"I expect he'll hear it from Lloyd Geary. Soon as I call him."

He rang off and dialed the deputy chief's home in

Bronxville. Geary, watching a late movie, answered on the third ring. Dimitri swiftly explained what had happened. Would Geary notify the Police Commissioner? He would. And he would be in touch with Dimitri in the morning. . . . "What meeting? . . . Oh, yes, good idea. Fire them up. This thing had better be stopped now before it gets out of hand."

Dimitri, visualizing the destruction in the bedroom, believed it was already out of hand. But he kept the thought to himself.

The local precinct cops had gone, some of the others were just leaving. Dimitri had no desire to be with the lab people, not while they were working inside. He had seen enough.

"Inspector?"

It was Murphy, the first to arrive from the task force. His eyes were red with fatigue, his mouth grim. He sat down heavily, slowly ran a hand over his jaw.

"What he done in there. Suppose the guy turns out to be—not human. I mean, suppose he's something we don't know anything about. Nobody knows. Maybe some strange kind of horrible animal."

"You mean like the Abominable Snowman or Bigfoot?"

"Something like that. Only worse. Maybe it has the power to become human or even to hypnotize people to see it as human. Then it could never be caught or killed or—"

The look on the inspector's face stopped him. Dimitri had much the same thought when he viewed the body—animal cunning and primeval savagery—but he realized it was not good thinking for a police officer. Animals didn't make good suspects. Or good arrests.

"He's human all right," Dimitri said, "just barely. And we'll get him too. One way or another."

Their eyes met in understanding.

"One thing sure," Murphy said, rising from the couch. "Whatever it is, it'll never stand trial."

At 9:20 A.M. in Washington, D.C., in an office less than a half mile from the White House, a youngish man in a dark suit sat at his desk and read the memo for the third time. *Newstime* was preparing a cover story on Caryl Chessman, using Vincent Mungo as a front. Reporters from the magazine were digging up everything they could in California. In view of the fact that the President was

Vice-President under Eisenhower at the time Chessman was executed, it could mean a major attack on the administration. The fanatical hostility of *Newstime* toward the Nixon people made it a strong possibility.

The man placed the single sheet on his excessively neat desk and smoothed it out carefully. The memo was from one of his staff on the Committee to Re-elect the President. Even though it seemed a bit far-fetched, this was no time to take chances. The press was becoming increasingly vehement in its denunciation of the President. *Newstime* was a good example. A long-time Republican supporter going back to the days of Herbert Hoover, it was now a leading critic not only of Nixon but of his entire administration. In the past six months it had published four highly critical articles.

Still, how damaging could a story on Caryl Chessman be to his chief? He should probably forget about the memo. There was nothing definite about the report; it could as easily be a straight news story. But suppose it wasn't? Suppose *Newstime* had found something explosive to use against the government, something that would feed the rumormongers at the *Washington Post,* for example? Once they got their rabid teeth into it, once they smelled blood, there would be no stopping them. Not that they could find anything, mind you, or print anything but lies and distortions. But why give them even that opportunity? Why give them anything but the cold contempt they deserved?

The still youngish man was inordinately proud of the Nixon administration, and most especially of the Committee to Re-elect the President. Using specific techniques, some of which he had himself created or perfected, the Committee had seen the President through reelection. It had been a difficult time and they had done their job well, so well in fact that it was a virtual landslide. Only seventeen electoral votes for McGovern. Seventeen—in the whole country! And a plurality of eighteen million! Unbelievable.

Now they were faced with an even bigger task, one of enormous implications. Instead of disbanding after the '72 elections, as they were expected to do since the President could serve only two terms, they were entrusted, at least partially, with an awesome responsibility. Nothing less than to seek ways to implement a movement for a third term. Such a movement would require the most precise kind of manipulation since it would have to come directly from grassroots support, from the American people themselves. Or at least be made to appear that way. Only a prolonged groundswell of emotion that eventually erupted into thunderous assents across the entire country could produce sufficient leverage to have the Twenty-second Amendment repealed. The Committee to Re-elect the President might finally have to change its name or even go underground, but its creative capabilities were equal to the task before it, and it would, God willing, succeed in its holy mission.

The Committee executive liked the political life very much and intended to remain in the center of all the immense power. Nothing must interfere with that destiny. Sitting now at his desk, he came to a decision. Best to play it safe. In the matter of his subordinate's memo concerning the *Newstime* story, he would kick it upstairs. Meaning the White House.

At about the same time that Friday in New York City, *Newstime* investigative reporter Adam Kenton arrived at his office, morning paper in hand. He opened it on the cluttered desk and stared again at the headline: "Chess Man Claims Second Victim in City." On page 3 he read the gruesome details for the tenth time. What he read confirmed his belief that his prey had a fix on Caryl Chessman—the word "Chess" had been printed in blood on a wall of the victim's apartment—and that he was acting out the killing of his mother, either real or imagined. Kenton stubbornly clung to the conviction that it was real. The story also told him something he had never fully realized until that moment. The man was totally committed to his insane course and would not be stopped except by death, final and irrevocable. Except by death . . .

The phone interrupted his thoughts. Fred Grimes had news of Carl Pandel from the detective agency. Pandel had arrived in New York on July 10 by train; was afraid to fly, according to California information. He worked part-time for the Museum of Modern Art, two days a week, in the membership-services section on the main floor. Mostly to be around people, it seemed, since the money wasn't much. Started there August 1. Hung out with a few college friends, had a small place on the upper West Side near Columbia University. Father sent him

$800 every month through an Idaho bank to his account here. Spent most of his time at home or the movies when not with his friends, was a movie freak. No known female attachments in New York at the present time.

Detectives had been on him since Wednesday, tailing him from when he left the apartment to his eventual return. No unusual movements observed thus far. On both evenings he got home around eight o'clock, at which time surveillance was discontinued for the night.

So there was no way of knowing if he had gone out again, perhaps down to Greenwich Village to kill. Asking other tenants if he had left the building later in the evening, assuming anyone saw him, would prove nothing and might tip Pandel to the fact that he was being watched.

It was a bad break, and Kenton blamed himself. He told Grimes he wanted a twenty-four-hour surveillance until something happened. Starting immediately, if not sooner.

Then he added it all up. July 10 in New York, and Vincent Mungo had crashed out July 4. Two days of work a week, leaving five days free. And giving him a sort of alibi. If his fear of flying was just a cover, it could've been done. He could have slipped back and forth across the country by plane during August and September, paying in cash under a phony name each time. At least he was still a good possibility.

That over with, Kenton called the 13th Precinct. Deputy Inspector Dimitri had assured him that the Department was interested in an exchange of information but no mention was made of money. He took this to mean the police had no leads and were afraid to accept money from a magazine. Which meant they would be of no help to him. With no insurance left, he would have to get to Chess Man first.

Dimitri had nothing for him beyond what was in the papers. He did not bother to mention that the police were widening their investigation to include local used-car dealers and apartment-rental agencies. And Kenton didn't reveal in return his investigation of Carl Pandel or the mail-drop names that private detectives were already running down.

Each promised to continue the free flow of information.

At the Rockefeller Institute he spoke with the two doctors who had drawn the profile of the maniacal slayer and Ripper Reference subject.

Was there any chance that the person they profiled was clinically sane?

None whatsoever. Not in their opinion.

What about legally sane?

They couldn't say for sure. Legally he might be considered sane if he knew the difference between right and wrong. But in this case his actions were so bizarre that probably no judge would declare him competent to stand trial.

So he would be sent to an institution for the criminally insane.

That is right.

An institution like Willows in California, from which Vincent Mungo had escaped.

Yes.

Would he ever be set free?

Probably not.

But was there any chance that he might someday be free again?

In such matters there was always that chance.

Free to destroy again . . .

Kenton thanked the doctors for their time and wheeled round to face Otto Klemp, who had entered the office without a sound. His thick glasses effectively hid his probing eyes.

The two men stared at each other for a long moment.

"Why am I being followed?" Kenton finally asked when Klemp had seated himself.

"Are you being followed?"

"For the past few days, maybe longer. Aren't they your people?"

The security chief permitted himself a smile. "You called me down here to tell me I'm having you followed?"

"I called you here to tell you to stop it." Kenton reached for a pack of cigarettes, took one out, lit it. "I don't think Mr. Mackenzie knows about this or would allow it. I'll tell him if I have to."

"You mean I'll tell him if you have to." Klemp stood up. "Is that all?"

"Just a word of advice. See that it stops. I have enough problems looking for Mungo without having to watch you over my shoulder every minute."

Klemp carefully removed his glasses and began to polish them with a small cloth. "Now I'll return the advice, Mr.

Kenton, equally free. Anybody can find out anything about anyone else, all it takes is money. And we all have something to hide. Presidents, kings, businessmen, the FBI. Everybody. You too. For example, you call yourself Kenton but you are not really of that family. You were left on a doorstep as an infant. The Kentons took you in and kept you as their own since they had no children. You knew that of course. But did you also know of your mother? Most likely she was a high school girl named Jenson who was extraordinarily generous with her—favors? So generous in fact that no one could say with any degree of certainty who your father was. A short time later her family moved away. Interesting, no?" Klemp slowly put his glasses back on. "The advice I spoke of is this: *Always* watch over your shoulder because something might be gaining on you." He adjusted the glasses on the bridge of his nose, his eyes never leaving the other man's face. "As I had occasion to tell you once before, Mr. Kenton, whenever you step out of your class you step down." With a polite nod of the head he turned away and marched to the door.

Kenton, whose foster parents were dead, had not known about the Jenson girl and had never really wanted to hear anything about his actual mother or father. Nor was he much impressed by the news though he knew he would someday have to try to find her, now that he had a name.

But that was for the future. His main concern at the moment had the door opened.

"Give my regards to the Western Holding Company," he blurted out. He hadn't meant to say it, didn't want to tip his hand just yet. But his mind was filled with disgust for the shabby thing Klemp had just said.

The effect was startling. Klemp stopped in mid-step, his hand still on the door. He did not turn around but his shoulders hunched ever so slightly, enough to show he had been stunned.

Kenton smiled in smug satisfaction.

"Like you say, anybody can find out anything," he shouted as the door closed softly.

When he ran the scene over in his mind one thing became clear. He would have to get some spectacular results on his assignment since Klemp made a powerful enemy in the company, one with access to Mackenzie himself.

He was still weighing it all when George Homer came

in full of information. As far as he was able to determine, the rumor about Vincent Mungo's father having been a homosexual was just that. A rumor, with no basis in reality. The man had apparently been very gentle, except when drunk, and certainly weak in action, if not character. Not too effective in anything. One of the probable causes of his suicide was his wife's death. He didn't seem able to do much without her.

With regard to Senator Stoner, his home in Sacramento had been bought legitimately on a twenty-year mortgage, paid off in nine years. Not an unusual thing for politicians. The house in Beaumont, Washington, a flamboyant affair, was given to Stoner and his wife by her parents, who had a bunch of money. They lived in Washington. Stoner's land in northern California and Idaho was another story. Both properties were bought separately over the past six years from the same realty outfit, the Rincan Development Corporation. For twenty thousand—evidently in cash—and now worth about forty. But the interesting thing was that both were in narrow areas of valuable mineral deposits. When the states allowed further development, the value would zoom. Which should be fairly soon.

A fortuitous purchase for the senator.

Fortuitous or otherwise.

Homer had also discovered the Berkeley criminologist who had been saying in his classes that Vincent Mungo was not the killer. His name was Amos Finch. He was a recognized expert on mass murderers and his books on the subject were considered classics. He lived quietly in a rented house near the university campus. His only vices seemed to be women and horses.

Kenton smiled to himself, thinking that only Homer could get away with such an observation.

Finally, he was in the process of going through the Chessman material. There was plenty, more than he had expected. What he had read thus far seemed either grossly maudlin or inflammatory. Chessman apparently induced very little middle ground. Should he continue?

Yes, and he should also look into the Rincan Development Corporation. Whatever he could get. That was important. Also how close California and Idaho were to allowing mineral development on those lands. And would he get the name and phone number of Stoner's mistress in Sacramento? Maybe they could make a deal with her.

"Use Doris for whatever you need. I gave her back to Mel Brown part-time."

Homer laughed and said he was a bit old for that sort of thing. She was much nearer Kenton's age.

Remembering her full-bodied blouse, Kenton quickly agreed and said he would have to look into it.

At the phone's first insistent ring he spun around, and was back in the chase.

Otto Klemp had just finished a chase of a different kind, one that had taken him only a few hours, and he now stood in the office of Martin Dunlop. He was not happy.

"You investigate someone in the company and neglect to tell me? You have him followed without my consent?" His voice sounded incredulous. "That was not smart, Martin. I am responsible for all internal security. Or did you forget?"

Dunlop frowned. "I just didn't want to bother you with this."

"But now I am bothered even more." His lips formed a cheerless smile. "Your thoughtfulness is appreciated but, as you can see, it has helped nobody. Kenton is no fool, he knows he is being followed. Did you think less, hiring a pack of amateurs?"

"They were highly recommended," he said coldly.

"They are bungling *idiots*," shouted Klemp, who quickly lowered his voice to a whisper. "Now it will be more difficult to do properly. And more expensive." He gazed stonily at Dunlop. "What else did you purchase?"

"What do you mean?"

"Any telephone taps?"

The editor-in-chief looked uncomfortable. "Just the office phone. They said they couldn't do the St. Moritz."

"Amateurs," Klemp repeated scornfully. "Anything else?"

Dunlop shook his head.

"So from now on I will handle all security matters and you will manage your magazine." He smiled. "Maybe we do better that way."

"Just make sure you find out what he's up to."

"I already know what our young man is up to. I was aware of it almost from the beginning."

"And when will we get the benefit of your knowledge?" asked the editor-in-chief sarcastically.

Klemp shrugged. "It is quite simple. He is a maverick, a rebel who must always tilt at windmills. He sees a chance to investigate the company and perhaps slay a few dragons, and he cannot resist. He is an idealist, incorruptible and full of moral rectitude. He cannot bend, and so one day a windmill will break his fool neck. Until then he is the most dangerous animal on earth."

"But can he find this Vincent Mungo?"

"Possibly. He is really very good at what he does."

"Then he had better do it on his assignments instead of snooping around the company."

Klemp went to the door. "He'll probably do both. By the way," the security head said on the way out, "he asked about the Western Holding Company."

He didn't turn around to witness Dunlop's startled reaction.

Across the river, in an office of the Board of Health and Vital Statistics, an official copy of Thomas Wayne Brewster's birth certificate, complete with the raised seal of Jersey City, was being mailed to him at his residence, 654 Bergen Avenue.

Both buildings were in the same mailing zone and the envelope would normally arrive the following day.

Jonathan Stoner had put in three tough days in as many places starting with Kansas City, and he was now in D.C. still working hard. He had a lot of people to meet, big people, and a lot of talking to do. He hoped to hear some big talk in return. That was very important at this stage. He had come a long way, and there were people from the West and Midwest power centers who believed he was going far and were ready to back him. Now the eastern power bloc would look him over but Stoner wasn't worried. He was riding high and his time was at hand.

He had expected to call on the Vice-President for publicity purposes. To be greeted officially by the Vice-President was a symbol of one's coming of age in the Washington political arena. But Agnew had resigned earlier in the month, and Gerald Ford of Michigan had not yet been confirmed by Congress. There was no one to greet him.

Roger Tompkins, who was handling the advance work for the tour, did the next best thing and got him invitations to all the good parties during the three days he would be in town. Which suited Stoner just fine since they promised to be the only bright spots in an otherwise endless round of meeting and talks. Even better, a California congressman had promised to fix him up with one of the young girls on the Senate office staff. He was told they all did it like rabbits. A small-game hunter himself, Stoner could hardly wait.

After Washington he would be heading for New York on Tuesday, where he was to appear on a TV news program Wednesday evening and then on *Meet the Press* the following Sunday. It was national exposure of the most vital kind and he fully expected to be a smash. Of course he would say all the right things and conduct himself in a very virile masculine manner. Smart and sexy. How could he fail?

The possibility never seriously entered his mind.

On Sunday night Adam Kenton dreamed that he and Chess Man finally came face-to-face. They were on the Golden Gate Bridge, on the same streetcar coming into San Francisco from Marin County. Only the streetcar somehow ran without rails and had enormous windows, all of them painted black. People constantly walked back and forth in the dingy, crowded aisles. At some point Kenton and Chess Man came together. They immediately recognized each other.

"You!"

"You!"

Accusation was in both voices. Kenton saw Chess Man reach for a weapon and quickly pounced on him. The two men struggled as the streetcar swung wildly out of control and smashed through guard rails until it plummeted from the bridge, falling finally in an endless arc through time and space and black bottomless ether . . .

When Kenton awakened from his disturbed sleep the strongest impression was of Chess Man's face, his identity. Kenton had known him right away. It was Otto Klemp.

* * *

Captain Barney Holliman was a good cop and a staunch Republican. When he got the letter from his friend Alex Dimitri in New York he noted with particular interest the part about the *Newstime* reporter who was trying to corner Vincent Mungo before the police. That sounded like interference with police business, or so it seemed to Holliman. Such interference was illegal and could lead to embarrassing consequences for the magazine.

The captain didn't know the politics of *Newstime* since he wasn't a reader, but he regarded most of the media as liberal and therefore highly suspect. On that basis he thought he might pass along his item to a friend on the President's internal security staff.

In his college days in the Midwest Franklin Bush had been an editor of the undergraduate newspaper, and there were those who could still recall the sting of his biting criticism. Anything liberal or flamboyant was sure to draw his ire. After graduation he had turned to politics, working as a legislative aide to several Republican leaders before joining the White House staff in the spring of 1972. Though he didn't turn out editorials any longer, his writing now confined to reports and recommendations for proposed legislation, he read actively a wide spectrum of the press and was as easily at home with the *Christian Science Monitor* as the *National Review.*

One of his coeditors on the college paper was a young man who became a professional reporter and was now on the staff of the *Washington Post.* Bush saw him once in a while for a few beers and a sandwich even though Pete Allen's paper almost daily vilified the President. Allen was on the metro desk handling mostly nonpolitical news, and so Bush did not hold him personally responsible for what the Ben Bradlees and Carl Bernsteins and Bob Woodwards were doing to the Nixon government.

At his invitation the two of them met at a bar near the *Post* on Tuesday afternoon. Bush bought the drinks and steered his companion to a dark booth in the back corner. He was so secretive about it that the bartender wondered if the wrong clientele was beginning to frequent his place.

"I need some information," Bush said when they were settled. "Thought maybe you could help."

"What's it all about?" asked Allen.

Bush told him of the report from the Committee to Re-elect the President and the possiblity that *Newstime* was working up a hatchet job on the President via Caryl Chessman.

"Chessman?" Allen was startled. "That's a long time ago."

"Our second year of college when they executed him. I remember you wrote an editorial blasting the state of California for its action. You called it murder and blamed everyone from the governor on up and down. You were really incensed about it."

"I remember," said Allen.

"That's why I came to you. I need to know if there was any connection between Chessman and Nixon other than the fact that he was Vice-President at the time. You know all about Chessman. Can you think of any tie-up that could be used now against the President? Anything at all?"

"Is this for publication?"

"Christ, no, strictly off the record. I'm asking you for a favor, that's all. I just don't want to send this kind of thing upstairs unless there's something to it. He's got enough troubles."

"Chessman and Nixon," Allen said slowly. "Interesting."

"Must be, for *Newstime* to pull this Adam Kenton out of California to work on it. I hear he's the best they got."

Allen gave no sign of having heard the remark and Bush attributed it to professional jealousy.

"What do you think?" he asked quietly. "Any connections?"

"Might be," said the other nodding his head. "They're both from the same general area around L.A."

"So are Mickey Mouse and Charles Manson."

"Chessman's full name," said Allen deep in thought, "was Caryl Whittier Chessman. Named after John Greenleaf Whittier, the poet. Chessman's father was a direct descendant of Whittier. There's a town near L.A. that was also named after the poet. And in the town is a college, again with the same name."

"Whittier College in California," whispered Bush. "Nixon went there. He was undergraduate president."

"Exactly." Allen smiled. "Just a coincidence of course. Now if I remember correctly, the town was once a Quaker settlement and the college a Quaker school. Caryl Chessman's family was Quaker, going all the way back to Whittier and even before. And Richard Nixon's people—"

"—were Quakers too." It was almost a shout.

No one spoke for a long moment.

"Just another coincidence," Bush finally said, shaking his head.

"Of course. What else could it be?"

"Lots of people went to that college. And there are millions of Quakers."

"But not all of them get to be Vice-President," said Allen, staring into his glass. "You remember how long Chessman was on death row?"

"Nine or ten years, wasn't it?"

"Twelve. He went through seven stays of execution during those years. Each time his lawyers hoped to get the original verdict set aside. They had plenty of good cause too—everything from outright fraud regarding the trial transcript to denial of due process. While all that was going on year after year Chessman saw dozens of confessed killers get commuted to life or even go free. But his turn never came. The state wanted his life, wanted it badly because he had decided to go out fighting. Finally it seemed he had used up all his chances. The execution was set for February 1960.

"That same month the President of the United States, Eisenhower, was due to go to South America on a goodwill and defense-treaty tour. With preparations already made, reports were sent to Washington from a number of South American countries citing the certainty of anti-American demonstrations if Chessman were killed. The word from Uruguay was especially disturbing. Why there instead of Peru or Colombia is another story, but it was serious enough to frighten the striped pants off the State Department. They didn't know what to do, especially in view of the bad mauling given the Vice-President a few years earlier. You might remember the famous picture of Nixon's car being shaken by an angry mob, with him still in it. Anyway, communications were suddenly opened between Washington and Sacramento. The next thing anyone knew, Pat Brown had granted Chessman a sixty-day reprieve, his eighth stay of execution but the first time California had done something for him. Eisenhower went to South America and there were no demonstrations. Everybody was happy. Except Chessman. When the sixty days were up Eisenhower was back and Chessman was out. He got the gas and everyone got the message. It had been a political trade-off, sixty days' grace—allowing the President safe travel—for a promise of noninterference in states' rights, at least in the matter of one Caryl Chessman. When it was over they pulled the plug. But the thing I most remember was this rumor at the time that the one behind the whole stinking deal was the Vice-President himself, Richard Milhous Nixon."

Silence seemed to flood the bar as the two men became aware of their own breathing. Each sat stone-still with his thoughts of the political dealing that had gone on during Chessman's final days. Toward the front the bartender was mixing martinis for a couple of recent arrivals, while several regulars stared moodily into the silvered mirror between the two cash registers.

"Did you ever see any confirmation of this rumor?"

"No, but that doesn't mean it wasn't true. I was just a college kid. What did I know?"

"The *Post* might have something on it. Could you check the files for me, on the quiet? Shouldn't take you long."

"I suppose so," said Allen. "But what would it mean now? At the most, it would be embarrassing to Nixon. It's not like anything illegal was done. That kind of double-dealing goes on all the time in politics, and somebody always gets hurt. You know that."

Bush shrugged. "I just want to make sure before I send the report upstairs. Do it for me, okay?"

"I'll let you know what I come up with."

"Call me at home on this, will you? Not the White House. Too many phones there—have problems."

Allen looked at him sharply. "You mean the whole White House is bugged?"

"I didn't say that." Bush was flustered. "Just call me at home. Okay?"

"Sure, sure. No problem," said Allen, suddenly thoughtful.

"Much appreciated." Bush got up from the booth. "I'll do the same for you sometime."

"You bet you will," the *Washington Post* reporter murmured to himself as he followed the White House staff member out the door.

While Bishop was busily dissecting his fourth New York victim, the third not yet having been discovered, Adam Kenton conducted a long phone conversation with Amos Finch in Berkeley. Wednesday was an early class day for Finch, and Kenton caught him already back home by 1:30 P.M. California time. The *Newstime* investigator introduced himself and mentioned that he was doing a cover story on Vincent Mungo. Reliable sources had told him that Dr. Finch, an eminent criminologist, did not believe Mungo was the maniacal killer. Neither did he.

Would Finch comment on his belief?

Finch would and did, at great length. It was obvious to him that a clod like Vincent Mungo could not commit such a brilliant series of crimes. What was being seen was nothing less than the work of a classic mass murderer, in the very best tradition of Jack the Ripper and Bruno Lüdke. Certainly the outstanding example in recent American history and perhaps eventually of the twentieth century. One who apparently began his public life about the time of Mungo's escape. Perhaps he killed Mungo or the man simply disappeared of his own volition or even died accidentally.

Finch mentioned John Spanner's theory, now discarded, that Mungo's partner on the night of the escape was the one they sought. His name was Thomas Bishop.

Bishop? Wasn't he dead?

Killed by Mungo during the escape. Spanner had once believed it was the other way around. Finch explained the circumcision angle and how it had failed to support the theory. Which left them with no clue to the maniac's identity.

Kenton had no interest in the dead. What he needed was flesh and blood. Did Finch have any specific suggestions about what kind of man the maniac might be?

Indeed he did! As a matter of fact, he was in the process of collecting material and writing preliminary notes for a book about the Chess Man. All the great mass murderers had style. Chess Man had style too, and he was rapidly getting the numbers as well.

As the criminologist ran through the litany of qualities such a monster needed—the sum total of which was a superior mentality and a genuine alienation—Kenton kept thinking that he was no longer alone in his convictions about his man. He wasn't exactly warmed by the thought. It was always more fun to be the only one who knew something. At least until he wrote about it.

Being a good newspaperman, Kenton did not reveal his own beliefs on the matter or any of his sources for those beliefs. He could, for example, have mentioned his idea that Chess Man had killed his own mother and was now reliving that experience. Or that there was some connection between his parents and Caryl Chessman. Instead he pumped all the information he could from Finch, some of which he found most useful in his laborious and painful reconstruction of the killer's psychic identity.

The two men promised to stay in touch. Both shared, for the present, a consummate passion in mass murder.

Afterward Kenton spent a half hour at his dictaphone machine. Then he called Senator Stoner's former mistress in Sacramento. She denied knowing Stoner and professed to have no knowledge of any tapes. Kenton repeated his name and phone at the magazine, should she change her mind. He was of course prepared to pay handsomely for such merchandise.

She hung up on him, but not before noting the name and number.

At 8:30 that evening Pete Allen dialed Franklin Bush's home in Georgetown. Allen was still in his office at the newspaper.

"I just finished checking our files for 1960, the first five months right through Chessman's execution. It was just the way I said. Rumors, but nothing definite. The original communique to Governor Brown came from the State Department, over the signature of an assistant secretary of state. There were purported phone conversations between Washington and Sacramento, one of which was reported to have been initiated by Vice-President Nixon. But again no substantiation."

"Maybe not at the time," said Bush softly, "and maybe not from the Washington end. But there could be something in California that ties the President to the Chessman thing."

"Could be," admitted Allen, "but I still say, so what. Nixon has always been known as a hard-nose. And there's nothing wrong with a Vice-President interfering in State Department matters. Maybe Eisenhower asked him to see what he could do. Or maybe *Newstime* is interested in Chessman for another reason, having nothing to do with Nixon. You ever think of that?"

Bush thanked Allen for his help and promised to return the favor. He put the phone down, his mind made up. In the morning he would send the report to Bob Gardner himself. Which meant it would probably get to the President. Let them figure it out. He had enough to do holding things together on his level.

At the *Washington Post* Pete Allen typed up a brief summary of his meeting with the White House aide. Included was the observation that the White House might be tapping most of its own phones, beyond even what the Watergate hearings had disclosed. On the way out he dropped the memo on the desk of his section chief. Better safe than sorry, said the conscientious young man to himself as he turned up his mackinaw collar on a wind-swept and deserted 15th Street NW.

By the time he got home and to bed, October had slipped quietly into November.

EIGHTEEN

Bishop slept soundly that night, a long luxurious sleep devoid of the nightmarish monsters and hideous demons that forever filled his nocturnal hours. When he finally rose, fully rested, it was already after nine o'clock Thursday morning. He boiled the water for his breakfast coffee while he dutifully brushed his teeth and did his daily exercises. With infinite care he then made up his bed, folding the sheet and blanket precisely, as he had learned to do all those years in the institution. That over, he sat silently at the breakfast table, coffee cup in hand, and stared at the dismembered body of the young woman spread out on the cold cement floor in front of him.

It had been one week since the killing in Greenwich Village and for most of that time Bishop had gone quietly about his life, doing whatever was necessary to insure his safety and continued comfort. On the previous Thursday he had deposited an additional $2,000 in the bank under the name of Jay Cooper, bring the total to $4,000 in the savings account. According to the plan he had devised, a second $4,000 was soon to follow. Another $8,000 waited to be deposited in a different bank as soon as the new identity was secured. The remaining $6,000 of Margot Rule's money would be kept hidden at home for living expenses and emergencies. He had found several loose bricks at the back end of the long wall and had chiseled out enough of a space behind them to hide the bills. It was a good job for a man who had never worked with his hands. Only a close examination would reveal that the mortar was not intact.

That afternoon he had gone again to Modell's on lower Broadway across from City Hall, where he purchased more wool socks as well as a six foot muffler and an insulated vest to wear under his suede leather jacket. Not used to the New York chill, he had no intention of freezing to death. Wrapped in wool, wearing his hunter's fur-lined cap, his sheepskin-collared jacket and heavy brown boots with rubber soles and heels, Bishop believed he might be able to survive.

On Friday morning the headlines had screamed the latest Chess Man outrage and he read about it over coffee in a local donut shop. He had come to like reading of his exploits in the newspapers, and began to see himself as a heroic figure. Much like the Batman on television. No one knew who Batman was but he fought the forces of evil and he always won. Which was exactly what he, Bishop, was doing. He too was fighting the evil demons who would destroy him, destroy everyone, every man they could. And he too would always win.

Reading about himself that day in the coffee shop,

Bishop came to a decision. In his next encounter with the powers of darkness he would leave word that the Batman had struck again.

The final Saturday and Sunday of October were spent mostly in meditation. With the TV blaring loudly, he would sit in front of the set hour after hour, his eyes glued to the screen, his mind empty of all thought. Slowly, ever so slowly, his focus would turn inward as his vision blurred to pinpoints of light, to shimmering suns of pure white and to final fiery incandescence. Transported, in his mind he would see strange and wondrous things, shapes and colors and textures beyond comprehension, beyond anything even his disordered imagination could fantasize. In such state he was oblivious to everything external, seeing all, feeling all, knowing all from within.

As the intensity eventually lessened, he would begin to form shadowy figures that slowly hardened into the hated enemy. Demonic beings lashed out at him, diabolic bodies sought to ensnare him. Opening like the petals of a giant flower, feminine forms slithered round his arms, his legs, pulling him irrevocably toward their center where they would close over him, squeezing out the juices of his life, crushing his bones to pulp. But he fought them valiantly, going from flower to flower until all were leveled and he stood solitary and fierce against the next terrible onslaught, and the next and the next.

During the weekend Bishop also visited a chess parlor on 42nd Street, above a clothing store. Here he watched dozens of players, all of them passionately involved in the game. He talked to a few—one was a truck driver who had learned chess while in prison. "There was nothing else to do," he told Bishop, "nothing at all." So he was forced to take up chess. Eventually he came to love it.

For his own part, Bishop didn't reveal that he too had learned chess in an institution. Nor did he mention that he was considered a very good player. Not wishing to cause undue comment, he allowed the truck driver to win. Everybody seemed pleasant enough in the parlor and he felt comparatively safe, especially with his horn-rimmed glasses, lightened hair and full beard. People, mostly men, were constantly entering and leaving the place, and when Bishop finally left he promised he would return.

On the way home he had picked up the latest issues of a half dozen detective magazines. In each he found photographs of female models in distress-type poses, some bound to chairs, others sprawled on floors at the feet of sadistic males, all of them seemingly moments away from death. In the apartment he put them with his photographic equipment where they could be easily seen.

Monday morning saw Bishop once more in Jersey City at the YMCA on Bergen Avenue, where he had rented a room the previous Friday. The Y was in an area of heavy traffic, and his appearance occasioned no special interest. To the clerk who gave him his letter, he was just another faceless young man in a world full of travelers. Nor did the name Thomas Wayne Brewster have any significance. Both man and name were immediately forgotten.

To Bishop it had seemed a perfect choice. He needed a Jersey City address and wanted not merely a mail drop but an actual residence. The Y was cheap and it was anonymous. He didn't intend to live there of course, but it would be a convenient backstop in case of emergency. From a lifetime of television he had learned all about evasive action. Meanwhile he would pay each month in advance and collect his mail whenever any was expected.

After examining the birth certificate and mussing up the bed to show occupancy, Bishop had gone to the Social Security Administration office on Kennedy Boulevard, where he filled out an application for a Social Security number on form SS-5. He printed his full name as Thomas Wayne Brewster, his place of birth as Jersey City. For his mother's maiden name he put Mary Smith, his father, Andrew Brewster. His mailing address was 654 Bergen Avenue, date of birth May 3, 1946, his present age twenty-seven, sex male, color white. He checked the appropriate box for having never before applied for a United States Social Security, railroad, or tax account number. At the bottom he signed his new name.

When his turn in line came he handed over the application form and his newly acquired birth certificate as proof of his identity. After being examined the certificate was returned to him.

The woman with the big glasses behind the desk told him he would receive the new Social Security card at his mailing address within four weeks. He told her he was starting a job the very next day. Could he somehow get a card immediately, or at least a temporary number? She said that was impossible. All new cards were sent out from Baltimore. But she could give him a form saying he had applied for a Social Security number which would be given him shortly. Bishop smiled his warmest. That would be fine.

He watched the woman as she gathered the papers neatly. In his mind's eye he saw her face break apart like a jigsaw puzzle and the blood flow out of her mouth and neck and chest as his long knife skewered her to the chair. The vision remained with him even after he had left the office.

A half hour later he deposited $2,000 in a commercial bank near Journal Square, showing the bank officer his temporary card. He had been living in Canada since childhood and was just now returning to his native state. He would give his new Social Security number the moment he received it. Meanwhile he had all this money he didn't want lying around . . .

The bank officer nodded understandingly and had him fill out the application card for a savings account, leaving the space for the Social Security number temporarily blank. Within minutes Bishop walked out with a blue bankbook in the name of Thomas Wayne Brewster.

His next stop was a local Motor Vehicle registration and license agency where he paid five dollars for a driver's permit, good for three months. With the permit he was given a driver manual containing a summary of New Jersey's traffic laws. The written examination for the license would be based on the contents of the manual, and he was told to study it carefully.

That evening Bishop spent hours at home memorizing facts from the booklet. Many of them seemed frivolous and not relevant to driver safety but he kept at it. When he finally felt confident of his knowledge he went out to prowl the city, this time finding what he needed on Third Avenue and 10th Street.

She was standing under a clock that said 12:30 and

she was open for business. When the John mumbled that he'd like some action at her place, her first impulse was to shoo him away. Her trade was mostly cars, passing cars that could whisk her to a darkened street where she would give the driver a quick blow job right on the front seat. Then straight back to her corner to wait for the next car. Fast and easy! She liked blow jobs the best because she didn't have to take off her clothes or even open her legs. There was no strain or struggle, just a little simple mouth action and the money spilled in. She had once figured she swallowed at least a gallon of the stuff a week. All that pure protein was probably what kept her so healthy the year round. Yessir, she was strictly carriage trade. Lincolns, Cadillacs, Buicks, even Fords and Chevies. Almost anything but Volkswagens; she had once sprained her neck in a Volkswagen. The forced vacation had cost her at least a thousand dollars.

But it had been a slow night so far and she was chilly. The end of October was never her best time; too late for hot pants and too soon for the big boots. When the John told her what he wanted and said he'd pay double to go to her place, she popped her gum and nodded glumly.

She lived on 13th Street between Second and Third Avenue. A room in the rear, with a bed and a dresser and a hotplate on a small table. The two chairs made the room seem crowded. She hung her cotton coat over one of the chairs and flung off her boots. The impact raised dust in the cracks of the wood floor. She got in bed with her clothes still on and he got in bed with his clothes still on, and as she put his penis in her mouth and closed her eyes she didn't think to ask him why he was still wearing his boots.

Much later, just before his departure, Bishop stuck his finger in a pool of thickening blood and printed his latest public name on the dresser mirror. Then he disappeared into the gloom of Gotham like a bat out of hell.

On Tuesday morning he had returned to Jersey City, going right to the Driver Qualification Center at Roosevelt Stadium. He presented his birth certificate and driver's permit, and quickly passed the written examination and eye test. With his permit stamped for practice driving, he made an appointment to take the road test the following week.

In Journal Square he stopped at an auto school and paid thirty-five dollars to have a licensed instructor accompany him in a registered New Jersey vehicle when he took the road test. He was told to be at the school 7:30 on the morning of his appointment.

Back in New York by early afternoon, Bishop walked from the underground train terminal to 630 Fifth Avenue at 50th Street, across from St. Patrick's Cathedral. He rode the escalator to the government passport office on the mezzanine, where he filled out a passport application and paid his money. The lines were long, including one for pictures in the building's basement. He didn't like the idea of having his picture taken but there was nothing to be done. At least, he kept reminding himself, with the glasses and beard he didn't look much like Thomas Bishop.

By the time he had finished everything it was after four but he considered the afternoon well spent. Barring acts of God or war, his passport would be ready for him within a week.

That night at home Bishop was jubilant. He already had the birth certificate and would soon possess a driver's license and Social Security card and passport. With them he would be safe anywhere.

But more than that, they would form the basis of the first new identity that was truly his own. All the others had either belonged to people still living, like Daniel Long and Jay Cooper, or were complete fabrications, like Alan Jones and David Rogers. Each carried with it a certain danger, a clear and present reminder that he was merely imitating someone who might discover the impersonation, or else be asked to present proof of the existence of someone who never existed at all.

But Thomas Wayne Brewster did exist, was once alive, and lived no longer. The records were there for all to see. *His* records now.

Long live Thomas Wayne Brewster!

TWB.

Bishop suddenly stopped, startled by the thought.

TWB.

Thomas William Bishop.

No!

That life was over too. Finished. Dead and buried the

night he escaped from Willows. The night he became Vincent Mungo. And a dozen other men in the past four months, including the infamous Chess Man.

Chess Man frowned in delight. He had been glad to get rid of Thomas William Bishop. Even that name had not been really his. It was still another creation for someone who didn't live, who had never lived at all.

No one had been Thomas Bishop, least of all he.

He was Thomas Chessman.

That was his true identity. He was Caryl Chessman's son, and the world knew it because he had told them. And he would go on telling them.

He was also Thomas Brewster.

But no one would ever know that.

In his ecstasy over his new existence Chess Man promised himself a party, a real celebration at home with just the two of them. Himself and the very first photographer's model who came to his house to pose for detective magazines.

By Wednesday the neighborhood newspapers with his classified ad were on the stands, and he called his answering service. Someone had already left her number. He phoned immediately. Could she come that afternoon? An assignment was overdue and required about three hours' work. Prevailing rates of course. Paid at the end of the session.

She needed the money, had modeled only once before for a clothing catalogue, and didn't know how the game was played. The furthest thing from her mind was treachery and death. At twenty she was immortal. She agreed to meet him at a local restaurant, from whence they would go to his downtown studio. He would be carrying a copy of *True Detective* so she would know him.

At three o'clock he arrived back home, the model by his side. For an hour he took pictures of her bound to a chair, gagged and trussed on the floor, roped in a kneeling position and generally appearing distressed. Bishop had bought the ropes earlier that day in a discount store on Canal Street. Much to his surprise, he liked the feel of rope in his hands and the pleasure it gave him when he tied knots. And most especially when he was tying them around a female body.

The film in the camera came from a nearby photography supply shop. Bishop had decided to use real film since he wanted pictures of his model victims bound and gagged. While he couldn't have the films developed commercially, he thought someday he might learn how to set up his own darkroom facilities. Meanwhile he had the clerk show him how to load the film and operate the camera. He also bought a book on photography as a hobby.

When he had shot several rolls of legitimate pictures and they had taken a break he again tied the model to the chair, this time tightly, and gagged her. She suspected nothing of course, since these were the kind of photos wanted and it was all part of the session. She was trying to be very professional. As he hovered over her she thought he was merely gauging distance and light. He arranged her hair differently, he opened her blouse a bit to show more cleavage. She blinked. Suddenly he ripped the blouse down the front and yanked it off her. She wore no bra. He then feverishly slit apart her brief skirt with a single-edged razor blade and struggled it from her body. As the now terrified girl strained against the ropes he photographed her from various angles, acting the complete artist, shouting at her to do this or that in mock imitation, smiling all the while.

Finally tiring of the camera and his own frantic efforts, he surreptitiously got out his knife and approached the still struggling girl from behind and calmly cut her throat, left to right, with one swift stroke. He quickly loosened the ropes as the lifeless body slumped to the concrete floor gushing blood fiercely. With a short sob of triumph he removed the girl's panties and then disrobed himself. Kneeling over the corpse he wallowed in the blood, scooping some in his hands and forcing it into the dead mouth, now no longer gagged. After a while he placed his streaked penis in the reddened mouth and moved rhythmically until he climaxed.

For a long time he lay with the body, joined to it by blood. When he again moved it was with knife in hand, preening over his prey.

Eventually he showered and slept, a long, luxurious sleep free of the demons that normally prowled his dreams. A twelve-hour sleep of the innocent—or was it the damned? Bishop knew only that he felt rested and at peace.

Now on this Thursday morning of the first day of November, he sat with his coffee and gazed at the girl's remains. The blood had long since dried on the cement floor but water would wash it away. The body would be taken upstairs and dumped there. The place was empty; even the stairway was mostly boarded up. A perfect grave. He would put all of them upstairs. Drain the bodies of fluids so there'd be no foul smell and bury them up there.

Just like *Arsenic and Old Lace,* which he had seen so many times on television. Except upstairs was much better than down in the basement. Safer too. Sometimes people dug up basements for one reason or another but nobody ever dug up a top floor. Teddy Roosevelt was crazy in the movie so he didn't know any better. But this wasn't like the movies and he wasn't at all crazy. Unless maybe like a fox.

Bishop's only regret was that the world wouldn't know of his deeds at home, since the bodies would never be discovered. At most it would simply be a matter of a growing number of women missing. Eventually certain suspicions might be entertained by the authorities but they'd never give him the credit without proof. They were all secretly jealous of him. He was doing what they couldn't do, what they longed to do if only they weren't so cowardly. He was fulfilling all their deepest desires, their unconscious cravings. And why not? They were men and had the same chance he had. Only he took his chances. He showed them all up, and so they were angry with him. He would have to be very careful.

After breakfast he carried the remains of the corpse upstairs, where he threw it in a storeroom filled with old cartons and assorted junk. He heard scratchings in the room and caught a glimpse of a large rat diving under a pile of rubble in one corner. Rats didn't scare him, he had seen too many of them over the years. Huge institutional rats, the biggest kind there were. Backing out, he found a metal swivel chair which he carried downstairs.

In his apartment again he washed the blood off the floor and put the rope in the closet, coiled and ready for the next photographic session. The gag, a piece of towel, went on the shelf. He took the film out of the camera and placed the several used rolls in a smooth cardboard box he had brought home from some store. The lid was snapped on. Inside was room enough for at least a dozen more rolls of film. He left the box on the floor by the tripod.

When he rang his answering service he was given two more names but he decided to wait a day before calling. There was no hurry. He would get around to them, to all of them sooner or later. He was the demon hunter and he would never die as long as even one woman lived. Like the vampire, he was the undead. He could not be killed. And if, strangely, he were killed, he would still somehow return to his work. Of that he now was certain.

On the way home he bought a *Daily News*. They had finally found the Third Avenue and 12:30 girl.

Robert Arthur Gardner sat motionless behind the specially designed desk, his arms tightly folded, and stared out of steel-gray eyes across the broad expanse of his White House office toward the great central hallway and the President's quarters beyond. In the hushed corridors men moved softly on thick carpet, their manner subdued, their voices low. Only an occasional self-conscious cough betrayed the excitement some still felt at being on such hallowed ground.

Now on this Friday morning, Dean Gardner reached for the two-page report on his desk as the buzzer from the outer room sounded.

"Yes?"

"Franklin Bush is here."

"Have him come in."

Gardner glanced over the report quickly as the door was opened to allow entrance to the spacious office. When he had finished his perusal he returned the document and looked up as though caught unawares, an automatic smile creasing his bland features.

"Good of you to drop in, Frank. Sit down." He indicated the grained-leather chair nearest him. "Cigar?"

Bush shook his head. "Gave 'em up years ago. Thanks anyway."

Dean Gardner picked one out of the burnished humidor. "Good idea," he said as he unscrewed the aluminum cap and pulled the cigar out of its silver container. "Going to have to try it myself sometime." But there was no conviction in his voice.

The younger man watched the veteran aide light up, sending swirls of bluish smoke toward the ceiling. He noted his report on the desk. There was another sheet next to it.

"What do you make of this Chessman business?" asked Gardner when he had the cigar lit to his satisfaction. "I mean, do you really believe an executed convict could in any way damage the President of the United States?"

Bush thought that an odd question. Why else would he have submitted the damn thing? Or be called here now?

"What interests me most about your report is not so much the possibility of such an occurrence but that you saw fit to involve a reporter in something that was, and is, essentially an administration matter. A *private* matter, if I may say so. And not just a reporter but one from the *Washington Post,* of all papers! Don't you think that a bit strange under the circumstances?"

Bush suddenly understood why he had been summoned upstairs. To his superior it must have appeared that he had consorted with the hated enemy and given it privileged information. An unpardonable sin.

"It wasn't that way at all, Bob. I didn't tell Pete Allen anything he couldn't have found out for himself."

"Didn't you, now? Then what exactly did you tell him?"

"Only what everybody in California and New York already knows. *Newstime* is preparing some kind of story on Chessman that will most probably end up attacking the President."

"It seems we already know about that, thanks to you." Dean Gardner had often found sarcasm effective in dealing with recalcitrants. "What we don't know is why you find it necessary to sit down with the *Washington Post* and discuss our affairs. Do you have dinner with them often?"

"It was just a couple of beers."

"Then the price has gone down."

Bush felt his anger rise. He had done nothing wrong, nothing to warrant a charge of betrayal. If he had used bad judgment in talking to a reporter, then that was the worst of it. Gardner should have known how dedicated he was to the administration, how motivated he had become in the past year.

"I did what I thought best," he said sharply. "Pete Allen's helped me before and I've helped him. We're friends."

Dean Gardner puffed furiously on his cigar. He did not intend to engage in a shouting match with a subordinate. Certainly not in his own office, where he had most meetings taped.

"There is no such thing as friendship with the news media," he said between clenched teeth. "You know what the *Post* is doing to us. The lies it prints day after day."

"I'm aware that most of the press seeks to destroy this administration but I hardly think one man is such a threat to us. He doesn't even handle political news."

The senior staff member sought to restrain himself as his anger mounted. One man indeed! What would this newcomer know about the dangers of the press and how much one man could do? History was full of just such examples, single men bringing down whole governments. Look at Émile Zola and the wretched Dreyfus affair! He shuddered in indignation.

"In the future, Bush, in the future do you think you could restrain yourself from such close contact with the enemy?" His voice rose dangerously. "Just so we in the White House could feel comfortable around you? After all, a man is known by the company he keeps. You and this—this *reporter*," he shouted, "are making us feel very *un*comfortable. Do you understand?"

Franklin Bush blew.

"Are you asking me to end a fifteen-year friendship with Pete Allen?" he screamed.

"That's *exactly* what I'm asking," Gardner screamed back. "The relationship is *unhealthy*. End it!"

The two men stared each other down, the eyes fierce.

Neither spoke for a long moment. Outside, the sprinklers revolved on the lawn, guards patrolled, tourists gaped. In other parts of the White House men sought to make their work winnings larger or their losses less as each went about justifying his job should a superior summon him to task.

Then, finally, Bush, his eyes glossing over: "I don't think Pete is as bad as most of the reporters I've met," he said softly, "but I can see what you mean about the enemy and how it looks. From now on"—he sighed—

"from now on I won't ask him for help or give him any or talk about business with him at all."

"Or even be seen publicly with him."

"Or be seen publicly with him," he repeated in defeat.

"Then we have nothing more to discuss," said Dean Gardner picking up some papers from his desk. "I will handle this matter of the Chessman story. You need not concern yourself further."

Bush nodded glumly and hurried out of the office. Being himself a veteran of the political wars, though certainly not as battle-hardened as the older officer whose quite magnificent quarters he had just left with his tail between his legs, he had no illusions that his little error in judgment would soon be forgotten. He knew of too many instances in which political mistakes had returned to haunt their owners. Still, he had extricated himself as best he could and with the least possible damage. It could've been much worse—his stupid anger flaring up like that. He lived well and had some power and prestige. And he had almost thrown it all away over a dumb friendship. Christ! Maybe he was getting senile at thirty-three. Some bright young man he was! Who cared about reporters? They were all sons of bitches anyway.

For his own part, Dean Gardner had no intention of forgetting the incident. It was to be lodged in his memory like a stone, ready to be hurled should the need arise. And, of course, a memo from the office tape for the files. Meanwhile there was more pressing business. The Agnew resignation aftermath, the GOP fund-raising scandal, the mess over the White House tapes. A dozen things like that, all coming at once.

He frowned at the papers in his hand. Caryl Chessman wasn't going to hurt the President. The lower-echelon staff people just didn't have the whole picture. *Newstime* was digging Chessman up as a part of a story on Vincent Mungo, which was itself probably a cover for what they were really after. He reached for the other report on his desk. It came from a member of the internal security staff, who in turn had received the information from a Washington police captain. Apparently *Newstime* was trying to capture Vincent Mungo by themselves, trying to pull off the story of the year. Which could lead to charges of interference in police business and, even more important, manipulating the news. Now *that* was something the administration could use. It was just what Nixon and Agnew had been saying all along. The media manipulated the news to suit themselves. If they did it in a simple thing like the search for a maniac, God knows how far they went in political news where it really mattered. Something had to be done to stop them, or at least to curtail their power.

It might also serve to take the spotlight off the White House.

But could it be proved? What if the magazine was just digging up a little more dirt on Nixon? Or really doing a story on Mungo? True or not, maybe he could manipulate it somehow to do the most damage where it counted. He would check it out with the President just to make sure. Might be a good opportunity.

"Maybe we can get their tapes," he mumbled as he pressed the button for his secretary.

"But we already *know* they tapped the White House phones," said the section chief to one of the editors at the *Washington Post*. "What else do you think Pete can come up with?"

"We know they taped *some* of the phones and office meetings, like Nixon's. But suppose it's even more extensive than we realize? Get Allen to see what he can find out from this guy."

At a few minutes past noon the President returned to the White House from a meeting with his foreign policy economic advisers. Dean Gardner was waiting for him.

Gardner was one of the three or four men who could get in to see the Chief Executive almost at will. He exercised the privilege as often as he deemed necessary, usually when there was trouble. In recent months he had been exercising it more and more.

On this occasion he had several worrisome areas to bring up, some suggestions to make, and a few items of possible cheer to relate. One of these was the *Newstime* interest in Vincent Mungo. Perhaps something could be made of it.

At 12:20 the phone in the outer office rang. He waited for the buzzer, then picked up the receiver.

"Mr. Ramsey for you."

"Put him on." Pause. "Jack? . . . Yes, I'm coming over now. Be right there."

He left his office, on the way telling the male secretary that he would be with the President. When he returned he wanted to talk to Gould in the Justice Department and then to the Attorney General. In that order if possible.

In the hallway he made a left and hurried to the stairs. As always, the corridors were empty, those on business preferring not to linger between their destinations. From the walls portrait faces gazed in fixed expression. Lights shone everywhere, illuminating each square inch of surface.

He climbed the wide staircase quickly and took a right turn at the top. In the moment he was being ushered into a room by a security man who held open the door. Jack Ramsey, the appointments secretary, looked up from his desk.

"Try not to be more than ten minutes, Bob. He's got a one o'clock meeting of the Budget Council." He smiled professionally. "We're running a bit late."

"Like always," said the visitor pleasantly.

"Always," Ramsey agreed. "Go right in. He's expecting you."

Dean Gardner strode briskly across the room to a pair of huge ornate doors. He knocked twice before entering the Oval Office.

"Mr. President."

At precisely that time in Fresno, California, Don Solis placed a call to San Diego. He was in his room in the ancient hotel, and the number had to be routed through the hotel switchboard. After making the connection the desk clerk wrote down the number because it meant money to him. He was being paid to note all phone calls to or from the occupant in 412.

In Sacramento a young woman tried to call New York City but all the circuits were busy. She decided to do some quick shopping and try again in an hour.

And in Kansas a funeral director with long thin fingers dialed Los Angeles for the hundredth time in recent weeks. He knew the number from memory.

It was almost twenty minutes before Dean Gardner finally

got to the small matter of the *Newstime* article. He briefly explained the report from the Committee to Re-elect the President which had come to him through Franklin Bush, and the memo from the Washington police captain to a member of the internal security team. If his guess was correct, the magazine might be guilty of withholding information from the police in a murder investigation. Maybe even of aiding a criminal in flight to avoid prosecution, which was itself a Federal crime.

"But the best part is that they might be open to a charge of manipulating the news," said the senior presidential aide.

The President stopped drumming on his desk. *Newstime* had turned against him, spewing out garbage every week about his administration. They had become part of the superslick liberal press. Traitors all around him! He turned to his left.

"Bob."

"Mr. President?"

"Find a way we can get the bastards right now. *Right now!*"

In the *Newstime* building in New York, Adam Kenton was just leaving for a lunch date. It had been a most productive morning and as he got into a cab at 47th and Sixth Avenue, he wished they could all be like that.

In the space of three hours he had learned more than he cared to know about the Rincan Development Corporation, as well as something about one of Vincent Mungo's few institutional friends which seemed strange indeed. He intended to look into it further. In addition, he had been given the first twenty-two eligible mail-drop names, all young white men, all possibilities. A dozen detectives were still checking out the original list of recent Manhattan clients, compiled the previous Friday. There were hundreds.

He had immediately sent the names up to Mel Brown to see if one of them matched any of his lists.

Then just before noon a call from Inspector Dimitri. The police had widened their net but found nothing so far. Did Kenton have anything yet?

Since it didn't matter any longer, he told Dimitri about Carl Pandel. Private detectives had been watching him round the clock for more than a week on a hunch that he might be the maniac. The suspicion was grounded in certain facts that had come to Kenton's attention while following his magazine story, but was not strong enough to warrant police involvement. When the Third Avenue whore's body was found late Wednesday night, that let Pandel off the hook. He had been watched continuously and hadn't been downtown the entire week. No possibility of mistake. He was clear.

What were the facts that had led Kenton to suspect Pandel?

He would rather not say. It was all academic now anyway, and he told it only as a gesture of good faith so Dimitri would reciprocate should the occasion arise.

Dimitri promised he would and Kenton believed him. The police needed all the help they could get. So that too had been a positive part of the morning, even though the Pandel angle hadn't worked out.

In the taxi he reviewed George Homer's findings on the Rincan Development Corporation. It was a multimillion-dollar real estate investment company with large land holdings in Washington, Idaho and northern California. Capitalization was adequate and the directors were seemingly above reproach. The firm mainly concentrated on land with valuable mineral rights and lumber holdings. By some complex legal machinery it also was involved with leasing for exploration and buy-back arrangements. Senator Stoner had apparently acquired his land on such terms, which made it doubly desirable should exploration proceed satisfactorily and all options be exercised. Evidently both California and Idaho were close to allowing development.

Through a series of interlocking companies, the real estate outfit had access to related interests from construction to lumber mills, with all of them operating under an umbrella organization based in Boise, Idaho.

Two facts surprised Kenton and bothered him too. The parent combine that had spawned the half dozen separate firms was called the Western Holding Company. And the man who headed it up was named Carl Pandel.

He had told Homer not to go any further with that line of investigation. It was too close to home; no use getting him in trouble with the magazine. Kenton would look into it himself.

After lunch he made a call from a public phone. If he was being followed, then his office phones were surely tapped as well. Which didn't really bother him that much since he was doing nothing beyond the company's scope. Except for a few calls here and there, such as the one he was now making. He wanted full information on a Carl Pandel of Boise, Idaho, who headed the Western Holding Company. The usual double price on anyone outside the New York area would be all right. Yes. Delivered to the St. Moritz over the weekend. No office calls accepted. Repeat: no office calls. He hung up.

Two messages awaited him. John Perrone and a Miss Kind from Sacramento. He rang Perrone first.

"John?"

"Everything okay?"

"Far as I know. Why?"

"I'm getting pressure from upstairs. Dunlop and Otto Klemp both. Anything I should know?"

"Just that I'm being followed and my phones are tapped."

"Who?"

"Inside."

Perrone hit the ceiling. He'd get back to Kenton.

After a quick cigarette Kenton went into the empty office next to his and called Stoner's former mistress in Sacramento. She just happened to find one tape of the senator talking—informally. She had made it merely for a keepsake of him. There were no others, of course. On it he did say some rather interesting things, but she would be willing to part with her only keepsake if it could be of value to somebody.

"How much value?"

"Twenty thousand dollars."

He told her nothing was that valuable. The most he could do was five.

She couldn't let it go for less than fifteen.

He might be able to dig up ten if it was mostly political and money talk; he wasn't interested in sex. And of course he'd have to hear it first.

She let him listen to a few minutes of the tape over the phone, enough to satisfy him. If he wanted it all—one hour's worth—it would cost him ten thousand in cash. Delivered in her hand.

Kenton knew the tape would enable him to do the right kind of story on Stoner. Just as the *Washington Post* was uncovering the Nixon illegalities, he would uncover those of the California senator.

Something else he could tell from his listening. It was a compilation from a lot of tapes. What she obviously had done was to take the most damaging sections from different tapes and run them on one reel. That meant she had a buyer for all the tapes, undoubtedly the senator himself. It also meant she had only the one reel left, as she said. But a very valuable one. Smart girl.

He took down her address. If he flew there the next day he could hop down to Los Angeles to see Ding and the others and be back at work on Monday, with no one in New York the wiser.

She had herself a deal. He would see her the following day, Saturday, in Sacramento. With the money.

He immediately rang Fred Grimes, told him that ten thousand was needed by nightfall. All hundreds. Laundered twice if possible. Grimes said he'd try his best.

At four o'clock Kenton gave George Homer his dictaphone tapes to study over the weekend. Maybe Homer could spot something he had missed.

Mel Brown reported none of the mail-drop names matched anything on his lists. Which meant each of them would have to be investigated separately. Kenton agreed. He hadn't really expected Chess Man to use his own name in New York since he seemed to like other identities, such as the Daniel Long one. Still, it had been worth a try.

John Perrone came down personally to apologize. He had talked to Martin Dunlop and then to James Mackenzie himself. He didn't intend that his writers be hounded by their own magazine. Though it wasn't mentioned, Kenton visualized the battle that must have taken place. Perrone was a fighter when it came to his staff, and he usually won. This time was no exception. The telephone tap would be removed immediately, and so would the tail.

Kenton thanked him.

"You must be up to something for Klemp to go after you like that," said a curious Perrone.

"Just my job."

"Getting close?"

"Closer, I think. Might have a story on a politician along the way. You interested?"

"Is he news?"

Kenton glanced at his editor. "He's big news now, and he'll be even more news afterward."

Perrone grimaced. "You got any big news on Mungo yet?"

"Everything except where he is and who he is," Kenton replied. "By the way, you ever hear of the Western Holding Company?"

Perrone shook his head. Never heard of it.

At 4:50 Fred Grimes called back. No good on the money until morning. About ten o'clock.

Could he bring it to the St. Moritz? It was important.

He would.

Before leaving the office Kenton opened the safe and took out the $2,700 from Grimes' most recent deposit. He put the money in his pocket, not even glancing at the mound of papers inside. Most of them were about Vincent Mungo. Or Caryl Chessman or Senator Stoner or the *Newstime* big shots or the New York cops.

One piece of paper, near the bottom, was about a man named Thomas Bishop. It came from the *Los Angeles Times* and gave the background of the mental patient killed by Vincent Mungo in his July 4 escape from Willows State Hospital. The brief notice included the facts of Bishop's father's death in a robbery attempt when the boy was three, and the mother's resumption of her maiden name of Bishop, which she used for the boy as well. It did not, however, mention that the boy had killed his mother when he was ten. That information was sealed by court order because he was a minor at the time. The mother was listed simply as dead. For his own part, Kenton hadn't really read the tear sheet, since it concerned a man whom he also had listed as dead.

On the way home he again rang a local number. The merchandise he ordered was to be delivered to the St. Moritz on Monday morning. Not over the weekend. On Monday morning at nine.

Saturday at 10:30 A.M. he put ten thousand dollars in his jacket pocket and took a cab to Kennedy, where he boarded a noon flight to San Francisco. He left no word of his plans at the hotel. A little past four that afternoon, California time, he knocked on Gloria Kind's apartment door in Sacramento. For the next hour he listened to a tape of Jonathan Stoner. It was worth the ten thousand, at least for his purposes.

Later he flew down to Los Angeles and made some calls and saw a few people. He stayed at Ding's house overnight. The next day he took an early flight back to New York, sleeping most of the way.

In New York again, Kenton bought a Sunday *Times* and read it in the cab going home. He didn't notice the date. It was November 4.

Thomas William Bishop had been free exactly four months.

To police officials across the nation it was more like four years.

To a score of women it was forever.

And the score kept going up.

NINETEEN

In his studio apartment Bishop bound the girl tightly to the swivel chair. She was a blonde, very pretty, and she had a lovely mouth that photographed well. He had been at it for an hour on this Sunday evening and was just finishing up his second roll of film. The one on Saturday was not nearly as good or as pretty, and a single roll had been enough for her. Except for the pictures he had shot afterward, of course, while she was struggling. He knew those were the best even though he couldn't see them. After this he planned on using actual film only for that kind. And maybe a few pictures once he had done his real work.

He focused now on her face as he told her to look fearful. Yes, indeed, she had a fine mouth, and he would be feeling its warmth soon. Very soon.

Three females in four days, all of them young and able to bear children. He had finally found the fountain of youth. It was in the field of photography. And it would keep him young forever.

* * *

In another part of town Senator Stoner was also focusing on the beautiful face of a young woman. Sitting across from her at a tiny table in the Palm Court of the Plaza, he studied her features much as a connoisseur of wine would savor the bouquet. Before too long he expected to have her in bed where he could kiss that sensual mouth and bite the hardened nipples and spread the firm thighs for frantic acceptance of his gift to her. Which was only fitting and proper, as the senator saw it. He had done his work well and deserved a bit of sport. Almost a week in Washington, relieved only by a helpful young thing from the Senate office staff. Then New York and interviews and news shows and finally *Meet the Press* that very morning. He was a smash of course. Direct and sincere and honest as the day was long. Except the days were getting shorter as he reached November.

At some point his companion looked at him and smiled warmly. While it wasn't exactly the look of love, it surely seemed to Stoner to suggest the sigh of sex. He quickly searched for the waitress. In the morning he would certainly have to thank the political hack who had set it up for him.

As they waited on the steps for a cab to his hotel, the senator hoped that she would be as good as his mistress. He really missed her loving ways. And ways of loving.

At just about the time the Senator Stoner was giving a lesson in political thrust, his former mistress was packing her three-piece matched luggage set for an extended vacation in the Islands. For years she had wanted to visit Hawaii, perhaps live there a while. Now she had the opportunity. She would put the most expensive furniture in storage in San Francisco, the rest would be left in the apartment. The rent for November hadn't been paid yet so she could save that three hundred dollars. Her mink coat would be stored, the recording equipment and the car sold. All in San Francisco. With sixty thousand dollars she could buy anything she needed.

It seemed to her like a good time to leave Sacramento. Especially before the senator got back. She had about four days, which was more than enough.

As the rains came down in the wet New York night, Adam Kenton finished his late-hour meal in the hotel dining area and went upstairs to his rooms. It had been a long and tiring weekend, and Monday morning would come around all too soon.

He had much to think about. In his mind he listed them by name: Chess Man, Senator Stoner, Otto Klemp, Carl Pandel, the Western Holding Company, John Perrone, Martin Dunlop. That was just for starters. He was sure there were others, there were always others, including some he didn't even know about yet. Life always did that to him. To everybody, he supposed.

In the back of his mind was a nagging suspicion that all the names were somehow linked together. It was crazy of course. They were not connected in any way; Senator Stoner, for example, surely had nothing to do with Chess Man. How could he?

Yet Kenton, for all his newsman cynicism, had a strong mystical side to his nature and believed, at least viscerally, in a centralist universe where most things that happened on the human scale were interrelated. A kind of great chain of being. The trick was finding the connecting strands. Usually they were buried too deep to be found or linked too tenuously to be seen. Which made life the jumbled mess it was ordinarily, at least on the surface. But they were there, and it was up to him to find them. And to follow them until all the pieces were connected and the picture was complete.

In his bedroom he sat on a Danish loveseat and smoked a cigarette, his mind turning back to Friday morning and something Mel Brown had told him about Vincent Mungo's final institutional friend. Thomas Bishop was dead but, still, it was a bizarre coincidence. Or else a Byzantine connection. His job was to discover which, and to fit it into the scheme of things.

Apparently Thomas Bishop's father had been killed in a robbery attempt when the boy was three, killed by another member of the gang named Don Solis. The very same Don Solis who was with Caryl Chessman on San Quentin's death row and who helped Senator Stoner so much by revealing Chessman's alleged confession. The same Don Solis who received a mysterious bankroll when released from prison, and a recent money offer from a tabloid for a feature on his prison relationship with Chessman. But Solis had refused, according to Mel Brown's information. The reason was unknown.

Brown himself had missed the Bishop-Solis connection the first time around, since the father was named Harry Owens. Bishop was the mother's maiden name, which she evidently used for the boy as well as herself. All of which meant something or nothing but Kenton had to know either way. For his part, he hadn't paid much attention to anything concerning Thomas Bishop in the material he had read because the man was dead. He was seeking a live villain, not a dead victim.

On Friday he had been too busy with important things to call Amos Finch, who mentioned Bishop in their phone conversation. He had called that morning from Los Angeles but Finch was out or not answering. He would try again in the morning from his own office. Because of the name change, it was possible that Harry Owens had not been the father. Then who? Caryl Chessman? Was the mother raped by Chessman? Her name wasn't on the list of women who claimed Chessman as their attacker. But maybe she hadn't reported it. Many women suffer in silence.

What did it matter anyway? The man was dead.

Most probably the widowed mother was so angry with Owens for the shame he had caused her that she resumed her maiden name after he was killed. Women do that all the time. Then she found it easier to use that name for the boy too. Very common.

But he had to know for sure. He would just check out where and when Thomas Bishop was born, and the name on the birth certificate. Might even ask Finch for the phone number of the California cop who had once believed Bishop to be the maniac. That should do it.

At the moment he was mostly interested in why Don Solis had refused money to talk about Caryl Chessman, especially after he had talked publicly about him, presumably for nothing. Was that just a coincidence, now that Chessman and the deadly Vincent Mungo seemed tied together?

He also wondered whether Solis knew that the madman's first victim was the son of the man he had killed. Was that just a coincidence too? And where had the original bankroll come from? Kenton suspected that he might have to talk to Mr. Don Solis sooner or later.

He finished his cigarette and changed into his pajamas. It was after eleven already and the morning was coming up fast. The bed felt good and he stretched luxuriously before turning on his side. The last thing he remembered thinking about was Thomas Bishop, who had been approximately the same age as Vincent Mungo. And Mungo's one friend in the institution just before the escape. Before Mungo killed him. But why was he there at all? What did he do to be put away like that . . .

Carl Hansun crushed the empty pack and flung it angrily away. Here it was just after nine o'clock and he had already finished his smokes for the day. And he still had a couple of hours before bed. It wasn't fair. There was a time he could have smoked all he wanted but he didn't have the price of a pack. Now he could afford a million cartons of Camels, enough to light up a city, and he wasn't supposed to smoke at all. But he did it anyway, against his doctor's orders. A pack a day. More than that and the doctor wouldn't be responsible.

And now the whole pack was gone and the day wasn't over yet. Some big shot he was!

He sank heavily into the oversized easy chair, collecting his thoughts. It wasn't really the smoking that had him upset, that was just a minor irritation. What it was—he felt his stomach muscles tighten, the anger rising in him again, and he fought to bring it under control—it was his longtime good friend and former associate Don Solis who had his insides in knots, his blood boiling. The miserable bastard had prepared an account of their association going all the way back to the robbery twenty-one years earlier. Including the Stoner episode, and even his new name and location and everything. The miserable bastard! He never should've bankrolled Solis when the ungrateful prick came out of prison.

And what did Solis do with the account when he finished? He gave it to that other longtime good friend and former associate Johnny Messick. Another ungrateful prick!

He tried to calm down. Anger would do nothing. Only a cool, logical mind could be trusted to figure out the next step. All he knew at the moment was that something had to be done and the next move was up to him.

The San Diego number that Solis had called through his hotel switchboard was traced to a house on Valley Road. The house was owned by John Messick, who lived there with his latest tramp. That meant Messick had the envelope. Who else would Solis trust more than Johnny? Hansun shrugged. Sure, they were tight in L.A. long before he came on the scene. Messick would hold it gladly, figuring he wouldn't even know they were in touch. And he didn't, not until the phone call.

Now it all was clear.

The way Solis had it planned, his insurance was the letter in the hands of somebody unknown to Hansun. As for Messick, he figured he was safe as long as Hansun didn't know he was wise to the Idaho identity and location. An obvious act of hostility by both men against someone who had bankrolled them when they were down and out.

Carl Hansun got so mad at the thought he reached into a table drawer and pulled out a pack of Camels and broke it open. In a moment smoke was pouring out of him. He sat stonily still and fumed for a long time. He had helped both of them and all he had asked in return from Solis was a small favor having to do with Senator Stoner. From Messick he hadn't even asked anything in thirteen years. He had proved himself a friend and expected the same from them.

Instead they had consorted to betray him. To put his position and even his freedom in jeopardy. Don had returned the favor, all the while planning to stick a knife in his back. And Johnny had twisted it. They were equally guilty.

He had to get the letter and destroy it. It wasn't just the old robbery rap; he might even beat that since it was so long ago. But Stoner was a big man now, and getting bigger, and he had a piece of Stoner. It wouldn't do to have the senator investigated like they were doing to Nixon. He might be the next governor or United States senator. After that, who could say? And he owned a *piece* of the man!

Nor could he allow his past to interfere with his complex business activities. He was Carl Pandel and he controlled a half dozen companies. He was one of the state's leading citizens, admired and respected by some very powerful men. He was a man of power himself. Whatever else might happen, that position was not to be disturbed.

He would have to get the letter.

Which still left Don Solis and Johnny Messick.

He would do something about that too.

Which would leave only him.

He checked his watch. His loving wife would soon be

home from her Sunday-night hospital committee meeting. He missed her whenever she was away, no matter how brief a time it was. When she came home they would play a little cards or watch TV or just talk. After all these years they still liked to talk to each other, still had much to say.

He ground out the cigarette and put the pack back in the drawer. He wouldn't smoke anymore before bed. No use staying angry. Business matters always came up that had to be taken care of, no more and no less. He would take care of them, as he always did.

He walked into the kitchen and got himself a glass of grapefruit juice. Then he sat on the porch and waited for his wife.

The object of Carl Hansun's anger also intended to go to bed shortly, and not alone either. For sixteen years Don Solis had lived without women, and after five years of freedom he was still trying to make up for lost time. They were there to be used, like tissues or plastic bags, and he intended to use as many as possible. The more the merrier and the younger the better. Young teenage girls were the best of all, to his way of thinking. They were still full of the juice of life.

At the moment one of them was in his hotel room, sharing a pint of bourbon. She was sixteen, a runaway from a small town near Fresno, and she lived down the hall with a young man who had picked her up on the road. He was away on a job and she was bored.

Solis had seen the two of them in the hall a number of times and little by little had caught her eye. He seemed to have the right rhythm for very young girls of a certain type, who found him slightly menacing and therefore a challenge. The first time he saw her alone in the hall he started a conversation. It wasn't overly subtle but it was effective. She giggled and sighed and rolled her eyes and was thrown off balance. He had sized her up correctly. After that it was easy.

Now he watched her as she took a long pull on the bourbon, her huge breasts thrust forward in obscene fashion. When she finished smacking her lips he kissed her, placing his hand firmly on a breast. She moaned in acknowledgment and drew tighter. By the time he had inched her to the bed her hand was on his penis. He opened her blouse and she did the rest as his eyes widened in anticipation. She had a roller-coaster body and he had his ticket right in his pants. He would ride her as long as the park was open.

Consciously carnal, the teenager shivered with thrills as she felt his thing explore her. It felt very professional. She hoped he had a lot of staying power because she surely needed it. Needed something, for certain.

To Solis, smothered in sensuality, life was looking up again. He had the business with Carl Hansun straightened out, and his letter was safe with Johnny Messick. He was making money in the diner and he would make even more. He had plans.

Throughout the night, between bouts of sleep, the two combatants fitfully coupled and uncoupled as the flesh moved them.

Kenton awakened at 8 A.M. right on schedule, rested and alert. By 8:30 he had showered and shaved and was ready to sit down to breakfast, which he ordered sent up. When the awaited merchandise was delivered at nine o'clock he was in the middle of two eggs fried pancake style and a muffin burned black. He gave the man one thousand dollars in cash and watched it being counted. Twice.

For the next twenty minutes he read about Carl Pandel, Senior. Besides heading up Western Holding, Pandel controlled or was a principal in all the satellite companies, including Rincan Development, of which he was chief executive officer, and the Pacifica Construction firm, which he owned outright and served as president. He was big money and had big political clout. He was also fifty-seven, his wife fifty-six. Two sons, Carl, Junior, now in New York, and Charles, in his second year at Stanford. Owned property in Idaho, Washington, Oregon and northern California. Lived in Idaho at least twenty years. Served in a number of administrative capacities in Boise and on several state commissions. A Republican, Pandel was known for his generous political contributions. Investment portfolio included a dozen major stocks, mostly in energy-related fields, and a wide assortment of state and municipal tax-free bonds. A heavy trader in lumber, mineral and precious metals commodities on both the West Coast and Chicago commodity exchanges. Also the Calgary Exchange in Canada. Believed to hold major equity in several Canadian mining ventures. Believed to have a Swiss bank account. Traditionally made unusually low income-tax payments for such a high gross income. Had individual trust funds set up for wife and sons . . .

The financial report went on and on and as Kenton read it through, he noted two obvious conclusions. Carl Pandel was apparently interested only in his own land and mineral ventures in the West and held no directorships or corporate seats on the boards of other businesses or in other geographical areas, such as New York. Pandel also was seemingly not himself involved in the business underworld, though he might have associates who were so involved. Such men often did.

Kenton noticed there was nothing in the report about the man's background and early years, and he wondered about it. But since his interest was focused entirely on the present, on what was happening at the moment, he soon let the thought slip from his mind.

He had found nothing unusual about Pandel or his business activities, nothing that would shed any light on either Chess Man or Senator Stoner. Evidently it was just a coincidence that the man who was behind Western Holding had a son who was a suspect in the search for the maniac. Coincidences happened all the time, even stranger than that. Like the fact that Senator Stoner got valuable land for next to nothing from a satellite of Western Holding. Or like the fact that the top corporate people at Newstime —Mackenzie, Dunlop, most of the other big shots—all had a piece of Western Holding, which was very big in lumber which made paper for things like magazines. Even though the antitrust laws frowned on publishing corporations owning forests. But Newstime didn't own any forests. Western Holding did. Newstime people just owned a piece of Western Holding. It probably was a smart buy and they all saw it and simply bought at the same time. Just another coincidence.

Adam Kenton didn't believe in coincidences. He was willing to admit that the Pandel boy coming briefly into the picture was an oddity. But the Stoner deal was strictly malodorous. So was his company's fancy footwork, though everything was no doubt legal. He knew what to do about Stoner but he wasn't sure about Newstime. He'd probably just tell them to sell their holdings. The stink from the Stoner publicity would do the rest.

Assuming they printed the story when he wrote it.

God help them if they didn't! He would be forced to go after all of them like an avenging demon.

The power of the press. And didn't he love it!

When he had finished his reading and his breakfast Kenton took the report to his office and put it in the safe. The time was 9:50 into the morning of November 5.

Inspector Dimitri's meeting was just breaking up at the 13th Precinct on East 21st Street. The mood this time was not quite so confident as that of the initial assembly two weeks earlier. By now the homicide detectives were beginning to realize they were up against somebody a little more resourceful than a slobbering madman or a wild-eyed berserker. Their enemy was shrewd and dispassionate. He went about his hideous business with a professional instinct, his every step calculated. Much like a chess player plotting his next move. He was obviously a master of disguise or else possessed the legendary cloak of invisibility. Thousands of hotel people in the city had his picture— dark, menacing. Other thousands of posters were in supermarkets, post offices, car-rental agencies and sales lots, bus and airline terminals, gas stations, banks, anywhere he might be recognized. Sooner or later their efforts would pay off; at least they were still sure of that. Most of them anyway.

The latest victim had been found the previous Wednesday evening. This was Monday morning. Four days and no further killings. None discovered, at any rate. A few of them, the inveterate optimists, thought the worst might be over.

Dimitri knew better. His man had found a hole somewhere. Or had made one for himself, which was really all he needed. With a base of operations, he could sneak out whenever he wanted, and then slip back. Wherever too. He was already branching out. Not only prostitutes but girls living alone. Next time it could be any female anywhere.

But why the change to bat man? Why write a new name? What was its significance? There were some in the Department who believed the latest killing was the work of an imitator. Yet the M.O. was identical to the others. It had to be the work of the same madman. The imitators would come later, after the original was dead and gone.

Dimitri frowned in thought. He hoped he was around

to see it. Couldn't tell for sure, though. They never did catch Jack the Ripper.

Meanwhile he had ten more men and could use a hundred. But the net was widening every day. Something was bound to fall in.

For no reason he suddenly had a vision of vampire bats. They lived on blood. Maybe that was what Chess Man meant. He was a vampire bat. He could not be killed and he would not be captured.

Dimitri had a helpless feeling that things were going to get worse before they got better.

By eleven o'clock Kenton had listened to the entire Stoner tape for the second time. On it was talk of the land purchased from the real estate outfit, as well as mention of several other questionable and highly suspicious business deals. One section concerned the Solis incident. It sounded as though someone had set up the whole confession story to benefit Stoner but no names were mentioned. There were other things too, sleazy political deals and scatological opinions of prominent politicians and much obscene sexual material. All of it added up to enough for a withering investigative report on Senator Stoner.

Kenton put the tape in the safe. He would work on the article concurrently with his other investigation, mostly at night. It shouldn't take him more than a week.

John Perrone called to assure him that all phone taps had been removed. In turn he was told that the story on the politician would be in his hands by the following Monday, hopefully. He wanted to know who it was. Kenton told him.

Perrone asked for a preliminary discussion first and a look at what they had in the way of information. That seemed fair under the circumstances and Kenton agreed. Ordinarily his stuff would go through a senior editor and then to one or more of the assistant managing editors before reaching Perrone's exalted desk. But he was on special assignment and responsible to Perrone personally. He wasn't sure that was altogether a good thing in this instance.

At 11:30 he called Amos Finch in Berkeley but got no answer. From Mel Brown he learned that Thomas Bishop had been born in Los Angeles in 1948. He didn't have the exact date or the hospital, if any. Kenton quickly sorted through the stack of papers on Vincent Mungo from the safe. What he sought was near the bottom. All about Bishop's father's death and the mother resuming her maiden name. Which meant that Bishop was Owens at birth and his mother had nothing to do with Caryl Chessman. No! It meant only that Bishop wasn't Bishop at birth. Best to make certain. He skipped down the notice until he found what he needed. Born in Los Angeles County General Hospital on April 30, 1948. Just about the time Chessman went to prison for good.

He called Los Angeles. The administration office wasn't open yet. Frustrated, he stared out the window at a gray New York morning.

Eventually he called Fred Grimes. When would the private detectives be finished checking out the Manhattan mail-drop list?

By that evening. Why?

Forget the other boroughs. They should immediately get on the twenty-two young white males. Plus whatever other eligibles they came up with. A total screening job.

What would they look for?

Anything out of the ordinary. Anything recent. Maybe someone just moved in but didn't say from where. Maybe he acted funny. Maybe he liked knives. Maybe anything strange.

Chess Man lived in Manhattan, Kenton was sure of that now. He had studied his prey for a month, thought of him, dreamed of him, lived with him in his head until he was almost beginning to feel what Chess Man was feeling. Like any animal, he wouldn't stray too far from the kill.

At 12:15 Kenton again called Amos Finch. Still no answer. He tried Los Angeles County General. The administration office was open and he was put through to one of the hospital administrators, a Mr. Hallock. He identified himself and briefly explained what he wanted.

Thomas Bishop? Yes, of course. He seems to be suddenly very popular. Umm. Yes. Born right here, April 30, 1948. How do I know? Had the same question couple weeks back. A policeman. Had the file right here on my desk. Only his legal name was Owens. Father was Harold Owens, mother Sara Bishop Owens. Guess that's where he got the Bishop from. Not legal though, unless he had it changed. What? Yes, I'm positive. Thomas Owens. One of forty babies born that day. I checked them all just to make

sure I got the right one because the policeman kept saying
Bishop and it's really Owens, you see. But I knew who he
meant of course. With all the publicity when the poor
man was killed, I certainly knew who Thomas Bishop was.
He was Thomas Owens.

What's that? The policeman? Yes, I think his name was
Spanner. That's right. Lieutenant Spanner. . . . Upstate
somewhere. A town called Hillside, I believe he said. Had
to call him there when I found the information. . . . No,
afraid I didn't keep the number. Quite all right. Glad to
be of help.

Spanner! That was the name Amos Finch had mentioned. The cop who had once thought that Thomas
Bishop—

Kenton grabbed for the earliest Mungo papers. He had
seen that name before. He had seen it—there! Lieutenant
John Spanner of Hillside, who had jurisdiction over the
killing at Willow State Hospital. The killing of Thomas
Bishop.

He quickly read through the account. Thomas Bishop's
face had been obliterated. Totally. Nothing was left. His
identity was established largely by the clothes and personal
possessions. It was a brutal, fiendish slaying. The work,
it was said, of an absolute madman. Vincent Mungo.

Kenton lowered the paper.

Or an absolute Chess Man.

Chess Man.

Chess.

A master chessman. Every move carefully planned and
brilliantly executed. He had made no mistakes. He had
crossed a continent and shocked a nation. He had killed
whenever he wanted and eluded capture wherever he went.

Mad he might be, but he was far from crazy.

He was also far from caught.

And he certainly wasn't Vincent Mungo.

In later years Adam Kenton was to recall that moment
many times as his mind made an intuitive leap, his imagination sparked a cerebral current that instantly fused all
obstacles and impossibilities of an insanely devious and
sinister scheme.

The idea grew even as his hand reached for the phone.

Pete Allen had tried a half dozen times to get through to
Franklin Bush. Each time he was told the same thing. Mr.

Bush was in conference and couldn't be disturbed. But he would be given the message that Mr. Allen had called just as soon as he was free again.

On the last call Allen hung up abruptly. He didn't think Bush would be free again for a long time. Being a good newspaperman, he didn't take it personally. But he wondered how his friend's superiors had found out so quickly about their meeting. Was the White House staff being spied on? Were they all followed wherever they went?

Or was he the one?

The *Washington Post* reporter went in to see his section chief.

In the White House, Bob Gardner leaned back in the leather lounge chair that rested on a double thickness of plastic sheeting. Being somewhat shorter than the average male, Gardner had his chair fully raised and his specially-designed desk lowered several inches to give himself the maximum height advantage. The needed modifications helped to increase his feeling of security, which was one of the presumptives of power.

It had not been a particularly good Monday morning, all things considered, and Dean Gardner was not at his affable best. Demands for the President's resignation were growing, following statements calling for such action by Democratic Senators Tunney of California and Inouye of Hawaii. Sunday's *New York Times* had suggested resignation in an editorial, as had the *Detroit News* and the *Denver Post*. So had Joseph Alsop, long a Nixon supporter, and some TV newsmen, such as Howard K. Smith. The bandwagon was beginning to roll and Gardner definitely didn't like the feel of it.

To make matters even worse the President was acting aloof, having abruptly left for Key Biscayne on Thursday and remaining in seclusion all weekend. And Wednesday evening he was due to make a televised speech to the nation on the energy crisis.

Dean Gardner sighed. He was going to suggest that the President end his speech on a personal note by saying he would never resign. Maybe that would stop some of the foolishness.

He buzzed his secretary. He wanted to speak to Ned Robbins of the White House legal counsel. On his desk was the Bush report suggesting that *Newstime* might be guilty of federal crimes as well as manipulation of news. Rumor had it that the weekly magazine was preparing an editorial strongly advising the President to resign. But pressure, as Bob Gardner well knew, could be made to work both ways.

In a few minutes he had Ned Robbins, who was very smooth and knew all the right people. He picked up the report.

"Ned? The President has asked me . . ."

In New York Adam Kenton bit into the sandwich sent up for lunch. Corned beef on a roll, with Russian dressing dripping all over. Next to it the piece of pie looked anemic. He rested his feet on the desk and took a few minutes out to eat. His eyes fell on the dictaphone machine. George Homer had returned the tapes earlier, thanking Kenton for taking him into confidence. He had found the analysis of the problem compelling. He had also found no major flaws in the idea that Chess Man was not Vincent Mungo. But that was only half of the equation. What of the other half? Did Kenton also have a good idea who Chess Man was?

Kenton said he was still working on it.

Homer had brought down the remainder of the Caryl Chessman material as well, including the four books Chessman had written. He let it be known that he felt himself to be a qualified expert on the subject, having read everything. With Chessman, Senator Stoner, the maniacal killer, and sundry other areas of interest in and out of the company, it seemed to Homer that they were working on quite a few different stories at the same time.

Suppose they were all connected, Kenton had said.

What if they were all one story?

He finished the corned beef roll and wolfed down the pie with swallows of coffee. John Spanner had been out to his earlier call but was expected back at 1 P.M. California time. He glanced at his watch. It was after two o'clock in New York. Two hours to go. Meanwhile he had already spoken to Dr. Poole at Willows. Vincent Mungo did not know how to play chess; the man was not at all interested in such things. How about Thomas Bishop? Yes, Bishop had played chess. In fact he was a very good player. Really excellent.

Kenton had expected no less.

As his idea grew, so did his excitement.

For the next hour he reviewed the various parts of his puzzle, speaking into the machine, going over the pieces again and again. His original analysis still held up. He was seeking someone close to Mungo in the recent past. Thomas Bishop was his only friend at Willows. He was seeking someone who would be immediately suspected if not for Mungo. Thomas Bishop would be known as the killer if Mungo's body had been found. But it was supposedly Bishop's body that was found, so he had the greatest alibi in the world. He was dead.

The only major piece missing was the connection to Caryl Chessman. And that, he hoped, would be found hidden somewhere. Eventually. But only if his idea was right. If it wasn't, nothing lost. Except maybe everything.

At three o'clock Kenton at last got Amos Finch at home. Did Finch know that Thomas Bishop and Vincent Mungo were both born in the same Los Angeles hospital, only five months apart? He did not. Did Finch know that Bishop's mother lived in Los Angeles at the time of Caryl Chessman's attacks, the same as Vincent Mungo's mother? He did not. Did Finch know that Bishop's father was killed by a man who was in prison with Caryl Chessman for years, who knew him on death row and talked to him many times? He did not. Finally, did Finch know that Thomas Bishop was an expert chess player? No, he did not.

Chess, as Kenton saw it, was the key to the puzzle. A superb series of chess moves brilliantly planned and executed. He reminded Finch that Vincent Mungo, who didn't know the game, asked the doctor at Willows if he played chess. Why? Because he had been hearing his one friend explain their daring escape plan in terms of the game. Mungo was much impressed even though the game meant nothing to him.

And ever since then everyone had been assuming the comment applied to Caryl Chessman! Assuming that Mungo was identifying himself with Chessman publicly for the first time, although still symbolically. How ironic that such a simple statement should work so strongly in Bishop's behalf.

Finch was excited and delighted. Even he in his pure scholar's heart knew that his California Creeper, the now acknowledged equal of Jack the Ripper and the other master artists of mass murder, must finally be brought to rest for the good of all.

And, of course, should it indeed turn out to be Thomas Bishop, he, Amos Finch, expert criminologist and recognized authority on mass murderers, would receive a certain amount of credit and would himself become a footnote in the pages of history. How splendid!

Any proof yet?

Kenton was working on it. He would be in touch soon.

Something in what he had said to Finch suddenly bothered Kenton, something elusive that kept slipping away from him. A word? A fact? What was it? He was missing a connection somewhere. Or was it just his heightened imagination? Was everything his imagination? All of it?

He would soon see.

At five minutes past four New York time, he called John Spanner in Hillside, California. Spanner was back in his office in police headquarters. Kenton introduced himself, mentioning Amos Finch and Mr. Hallock in the Los Angeles hospital, and quickly explained his mission. He was doing a *Newstime* cover story on the escaped Willows madman, who was now in New York. Amos Finch had mentioned the lieutenant as having once held a belief that Thomas Bishop might be the madman rather than Vincent Mungo. He was interested in that belief because of some information that had come to him, even though Finch had also said the current consensus was that it was neither Mungo nor Bishop.

Spanner wanted to know if Finch had explained how the circumcision angle didn't work out.

He had.

And that there were other expert police authorities, like James Oates of the California Sheriff's Office, who believed it was someone unknown?

Yes.

What information had come to Kenton?

Just some oddities that by themselves meant little but might contribute to a general impression.

Such as?

Things like both men born in the same hospital at almost the same time, and Bishop's father killed by a man who knew Caryl Chessman in San Quentin.

The police had known about those two, of course.

As he said, just oddities. The main thing actually was a feeling much like in a chess game, a series of moves that gave evidence of a certain cool precision and brilliance.

When he learned that Vincent Mungo did not play chess, he quite naturally turned to other areas. At the moment he was particularly interested in the body found at Willows. Would the lieutenant remember if there had been any recent scars on the body? Knife scars, perhaps, or from some other sharp object, most especially on the arms or shoulders?

There was a small V-shaped scar on the upper right shoulder that had looked to be fairly recent. How did Kenton know that?

Only a guess. Mungo told a Willows doctor that he had become blood brothers with the devil. He probably meant it symbolically, but it could also mean the ritual arm cutting and mingling of blood between two men.

Spanner remembered the scar vividly since he had specifically looked for it when he first tried to prove the body was that of Vincent Mungo. Now he wondered if he had been too hasty. Could it be possible—? No, that was a long time ago. Four months, a lifetime. He wasn't going to start that business all over again. Absolutely not. It was all settled in his mind. The Willows maniac was not Vincent Mungo or Thomas Bishop but someone unknown to any of them. That was obvious and the New York reporter would soon learn it for himself.

"Lieutenant Spanner?"

He pulled his attention back to the phone. "Yes, I'm here, Mr. Kenton."

"I asked if you knew where Bishop came from originally. Before Willows, I mean."

Spanner shook his head to clear it. Bishop? Bishop had always been at Willows. There was no before. No, that wasn't right. He had lived with his mother when he was a boy. But Spanner couldn't remember where and he said so.

Had he always lived in Los Angeles, perhaps?

No, that wasn't right either. It was coming back to Spanner now. Bishop had been born in Los Angeles, but after the father's death the mother had moved to San Francisco, and then eventually to— Damn! What was the name of that town?

Spanner told Kenton he couldn't think of the town but it was about forty miles from Hillside. Just a small country place. As a boy Bishop had lived there with his mother— Justin! That was it. Justin, California. About forty miles west of Hillside and two hundred miles above San Francisco.

He repeated that to Kenton.

And after Justin?

After Justin came Willows.

Kenton didn't understand. As a boy Bishop had moved with his mother from Los Angeles to Justin—

To San Francisco.

To San Francisco and then to Justin.

That's right.

And after Justin he was put in Willows for good?

Yes.

No other mental hospitals?

Just Willows.

Kenton tried to figure it out but it didn't make sense. How old could the boy have been?

Spanner told him.

"Ten!" It was more a scream than anything else. "Thomas Bishop was placed in a mental institution when he was *ten?*"

He couldn't believe it. What did the boy do?

"He killed his mother," said the lieutenant softly. "Didn't you know that?"

In his own tiny office on the twelfth floor of a New York skyscraper, research assistant George Homer was suddenly struck by an odd thought that came out of something he had heard on the dictaphone tapes over the weekend. Kenton had mentioned that Vincent Mungo once talked about chess at Willows, and that it obviously referred to Caryl Chessman.

But did it?

Homer loved the game of chess. He had been at it for over forty years, and he found it incomparable for sharpening one's wits. At the moment he wondered if perhaps he wasn't being just half-witted instead. Still—

For many minutes after his California conversation, Kenton, face immobile and body rigid, stared at the silent phone in front of him. His mind reeled and he fought to bring it back under control. Thomas Bishop had killed his mother at age ten. Bishop! It had been right there under his nose almost from the beginning and he hadn't seen it. All the conditions were being fulfilled. Everything he had

said weeks earlier, everything needed to discover Chess
Man's identity. But he had been so sure of himself that he
had lost sight of the most important condition of all. Chess
Man was someone who as a boy had killed his mother and
was now reliving the experience over and over. The only
thing missing was the connection to Caryl Chessman, which
had to come through the mother or father. It was there
somewhere, it had to be. And he would find it.

When he moved again it was mechanical. A call to Mel
Brown.

Thomas Bishop killed his mother in California and went
to a mental institution. Why wasn't he on the matricide list
of ninety-seven names?

How old was he when it happened?

Ten.

That was why. Under sixteen the court records were
sealed shut.

But the list supposedly included those under sixteen
whose matricide made the newspapers at the time.

Which meant that Bishop's didn't make the papers. In
the cities they usually print the fact of the crime but not
the name of the youth of course. But in small towns they
often just list the death as something else. He probably
came from one of those.

Why wasn't Bishop's matricide mentioned in all the Vincent Mungo stories that told how he killed a fellow patient
at Willows?

Because newspapers were not allowed afterward to print
the fact of matricide if the killer was under sixteen at the
time it happened. Sealed records meant exactly that.

At least his name should have been on the list of released or escaped mental patients in the past five years.

How could it be? Thomas Bishop was not released from
Willows and he did not escape. He was officially listed as
dead.

Dead.

Kenton walked the halls for a few minutes to clear his
head. Something still was twitching in the back of his mind
but he couldn't bring it up. Try! Try! When did it start?
All right. It started— It started when he was talking to
Amos Finch about Bishop's being born in the same hospital
as Mungo. That's right. And his mother living in Los
Angeles at the time, and his father getting killed by someone who later came to know Caryl Chessman—

Kenton froze, his hand suspended at the nape of his neck.

Bishop's father killed by someone who knew Chessman. Christ!

The connection!

That too had been there all the time. He didn't yet know exactly how it worked but it had to be that. From Chessman to Bishop. Through Don Solis.

All the pieces were coming together.

If nothing came along to blow them apart.

When he got back to his office George Homer was waiting for him, seated at the second desk reading a copy of Batman comics.

Batman! Kenton felt a sudden chill in the room. That was the latest signature of his prey. "Bat Man," he had signed himself on the victim's mirror. Did he think he was fighting the forces of darkness? Or was he a vampire bat that fed on blood?

Homer looked up and smiled. "Just trying to see why he would choose such a name." He closed the magazine on the desk. "Not my usual fare, you know."

"Got any ideas?"

"Not about that, no." He swiveled round as Kenton moved to his own desk nearer the window. "Something else though."

"Always willing to listen."

"Might mean nothing."

"Try me."

Homer paused a moment, pursuing his lips into a thoughtful frown.

"Do you play chess?"

"Not really. Do you?"

"Yes, I do as a matter of fact. Still haven't mastered the damn board. But you know something about the game, right?"

"Sure. Doesn't everyone?"

"That's just what I was thinking before. Most people know about the game even if they don't play it themselves."

"I just don't have the patience for it. But it's funny you should bring that up. Chess has been on my mind more in the last few days than almost anything else."

"On the tapes you say somewhere that Vincent Mungo mentioned chess to a doctor before he escaped with his only friend, the one he was supposed to have killed. And that it was probably a reference to Caryl Chessman."

"What about it?"

"Well, chess is a funny game, you see. It's got all those strange-looking pieces. Now, I'm sure this is just a coincidence and has nothing to do with what you're working on. But the pieces are separated by their shapes into different kinds. There's the King and the Queen, the Rook and the Knight and the Pawn. And there's also this other piece, you see, called the Bishop—"

"Jesus H. Christ!" said Kenton and leaped out of the chair. He didn't know if he kissed Homer or just shook his hand.

At the moment he was sure of only one thing. Chess Man's real identity.

For almost a month he had known who it wasn't.

Now suddenly he knew who it was.

"Bishop!"

The roar was both an accusation and a shout of triumph. *"Bishop!"*

Nobody shouted back.

He still had to be found.

TWENTY

In the eight-day period between November 7 and the 15th, four young New York women—free-lance models, students, one a mother, all having a need for extra money or men—disappeared from their homes and regular routines, never to be seen alive again. Their dreadfully mutilated bodies would not be found until the morning of November 16, along with three other fearful remains. The ghastly discovery was to trigger a manhunt unparalleled in the city's history, a manhunt involving law-enforcement officials and local politicians in bitter acrimony as civil liberties were widely and indiscriminately violated in the first flush of frantic activity, a manhunt embracing thousands of searches and hundreds of seizures by elements ranging from the police to groups of private citizens to the mob. Its like would not be seen again until the Son of Sam killings four years later.

On that same morning, November 16, in Fresno, California, the owner of a local diner stepped into his Dodge hardtop and turned on the tape deck to Sinatra. As the music flooded the car he began feeling better already.

At about the same time in San Diego a sedan quietly pulled up to a small one-story house on Valley Road, near the end of the block. Two men slowly got out and walked up to the front door. They seemed in no particular hurry.

Earlier that Friday morning in New York City, four men rendezvoused in lower Manhattan at a restaurant near the Criminal Courts Building on Centre Street below Canal. From there they proceeded by car to a further destination. Three of the men carried guns. The fourth, quite ordinary in appearance except for his eyes, sat next to the driver and led the silent group. Hands clasped on his lap, he kept wetting his lips in nervous anticipation.

As Kenton celebrated on the evening of November 5 his certain knowledge that Chess Man was in reality Thomas Bishop, young madman-about-town, the subject of his celebration prepared for bed. He had to be up and away at 6 A.M. and he needed eight hours of sleep. The necessity itself had always vexed Bishop and, while he enjoyed the moments before sleep when he would lie in bed and plot and plan, he resented the idea of having to spend one-third of his life in dreamy pursuit. Especially since all his dreams were nightmares in which he was usually pursued by the most frightful monsters from the deepest recesses of the subconscious mind, wherein lurked all the hideous ogres of his origin. Oftentimes in the dead of night he would scream himself awake, only to find the demons out of reach until he again lay down and die. Over the years they had never relented, nor had he, and in due time he came to regard the battle as one unto death itself.

Sliding under the covers on this blustery night, Bishop checked the alarm on the clock by the bed and turned onto his stomach, with his arms curved over his head. He fidgeted for a long while in that position before surrendering to sleep. To a spider near the ceiling the dark shadowy object thrashing below might perhaps have seemed to be some immense beast with rounded body and giant claws, an incalculable enemy, different and fearsome and not to be fought, but by then Bishop was already locked in mortal combat with his own kind.

At midnight Adam Kenton had a final drink and went upstairs to bed. He too had a full day planned and though he could operate with five hours' sleep, a Scotch hangover was not the ideal companion for a workday. With a great deal of persistence and a bit of stumbling he finally maneuvered out of his clothes and into bed. He tried to concentrate on a riddle someone in the bar had posed—Who shaves the town barber if he shaves only those who do not shave themselves?—but he was asleep before he could even repeat it.

Kenton had told no one of his new knowledge. All evening he had thought about it, weighing its import, wary lest he do the wrong thing. After weeks of frustration and disappointment, false leads and blind alleys and poor assumptions, the impossible had happened. He had succeeded where thousands had failed. With a lot of hard work, some imaginative investigating and a sprinkle of luck, he had discovered the identity of the notorious Chess Man. He was sure of it. Thomas Bishop was his man, his madman, his maniac, his batman, his superman, his manson, his son of man. His Chessman!! He had all the pieces of the puzzle but one, and they all fit. The last piece would fit too.

Now he awaited the miracle. No! That was not right. He *hoped* for a miracle. He would work hard for it, give it all he had, his very best. With work and some more luck, maybe a miracle would happen. If the impossible could happen, why not a miracle? Against all odds he had found out who Chess Man was. Now he needed to know *where* Chess Man was. And he would know. By God or the devil himself, he would!

Meanwhile he would tell no one. Bishop was to be his secret. To tell the police at this point was useless. Without proof it was merely suspicion, and in truth he had no proof. What he knew to be a certainty was all in his head, and none of it was demonstrable. The pieces of the puzzle were all shaped by his desire, his passion. They fit because he willed them to fit, because he chose to see them that way. Without him they were shapeless and nonexistent. His certitude was nontransferable.

A name in the hands of the police would do nothing, except perhaps scare away the fox. The authorities in California had a name, the correct name. At least a few of them did. They suspected Bishop, maybe even knew in their hearts he was the one. Yet nothing was done because they couldn't get any proof. And he wouldn't stand any better chance now, especially since there were no pictures of Bishop. Those from his file at the state hospital were gone, according to Spanner. Which meant Bishop had taken them before he left, another audacious move. And which further meant the newspapers didn't have any to print at the time of the escape, at least none he had seen in the material on Vincent Mungo. A tight drawing could be made for the newspapers and posters but by itself it would mean little. With all the possibilities of beards and hair dyes and even cosmetic facial surgery, positive identification was virtually ruled out.

No! The fox would have to be caught on its own ground, not scared away. And for that it would have to be made to see the viewpoint of the hound too.

Kenton hoped he wasn't just rationalizing his wishes. He wouldn't want to be responsible for even more women being killed, but he believed he had the best chance of catching his prey. After all, he had been thinking like the fox for a long time now.

Unfortunately, in his zeal he forgot something Otto Klemp had once told him about the fox who dressed like a hound and ran with the pack. Everything went fine. Until the wind shifted.

Bishop was up with the alarm at 6 A.M. He washed and dressed, ate a bit of breakfast and was out of the house at 6:30. By 7:15 he sat in a Jersey City auto school waiting for an instructor who would take him for his driving test. At 8 A.M. they were already on line at Roosevelt Stadium. When his turn came he presented his driver's permit to the state inspector, who had him go around a small section of local road, make a U-turn, back up and park. He passed the test and was given a temporary sixty-day license at the Driver Qualification Center, a large room on the second floor of the stadium building. He was also given the permanent-license application form. Back in Journal Square, he completed the form at a post office and mailed it along with an eleven-dollar money order to Trenton. Within thirty days he would receive his permanent New Jersey driver's license, valid for three years, at his Jersey City residence address.

Bishop now had two of the four basic pieces of identification: a birth certificate and a driver's license. The passport would be his in a few days, and the Social Security card within a month. He was on his way.

Before returning to New York he deposited another $2,000 in his new bank account as Thomas Wayne Brewster, then spent a half hour in his room at the YMCA rocking in a chair as he inspected his new license. On the way out he mussed up the bed again.

Back in New York he killed the afternoon in the chess parlor on 42nd Street, where he won three games in a row. On his final game a number of people were watching and he deliberately lost.

Kenton spent most of the morning in meetings. At 9:30 he played the Stoner tape for his managing editor, then told him what he knew of Stoner's activities. Perrone agreed there was enough for a story pulling the California senator off his high-flying pedestal. But he wanted to talk it over with the editor-in-chief, probably the next day. Could he have the tape and Kenton's notes? They would be returned of course.

Kenton graciously consented. Why not? Trusting no one, remembering the Nixon tapes, he had made a duplicate at Ding's house in Los Angeles on the previous Sunday. The duplicate tape was in the St. Moritz safe. And should a sudden earthquake swallow up his notes, he could rewrite them from memory.

He did not tell Perrone about the duplicate. He did, however, suggest that only the two of them should know of the existence of the Stoner tape for the moment. And Dunlop of course. Which made four, including Patrick Henderson.

"Can he be trusted?" asked Kenton.

"About as much," said John Perrone, "as a cobra around your neck."

Throughout Manhattan a dozen private detectives were beginning a complete screening of young white males who had rented space in local mail drops during the initial week of Chess Man's arrival in the city. There were twenty-seven names, five more than the original twenty-one. For each of them records would be checked, neighbors questioned. Whatever it took, however it was done, the needed information would be secured.

During the afternoon Kenton was mostly on the phone to California. To contacts in Red Bluff, sending them to the nearby country town of Justin, where they would seek people who had known Thomas Bishop and his mother. To Justin itself, talking with the editor of the local weekly newspaper, from whom he wanted copies of any mention of the mother's death in 1958. To Dr. Poole at Willows State Hospital, asking him to help assemble a drawing of Thomas Bishop from memory. And to an expert sketch artist in San Francisco, who would go to Willows to put together the drawing.

The contacts from Red Bluff, two stringers who knew their way around, were told to find out exactly how the mother died, where she was buried, what happened to her son, who got the family possessions. Anything and everything they could. They were to talk to a hundred people if they had to. If there were a hundred people in the town.

The newspaper editor was most cordial. He had heard of Adam Kenton, and of course he was thrilled to be able to help out *Newstime* magazine. Unfortunately he had not been around in 1958. That was old Mr. Pryor, the original editor, long gone now. He had taken over the paper in 1963. But he would do his best to find the death notice. Did Kenton have a date?

He did not. All he knew was that the boy was ten at the time and he had been born on April 30. So the editor should look from May 1 right through to the end of the year. The name was Bishop. Mother's name Sara, the boy Thomas.

Kenton also would have wanted any mention of the Bishops during their years in Justin but he knew better than to ask for such a thing. The paper's past was not on microfilm, nor did it have an index. It was not, after all, *The New York Times.*

At Willows, Dr. Poole was agreeable to the idea of a composite sketch of Thomas Bishop and felt certain that he could come close to reality, provided the artist followed his directions. But permission would first have to be secured from the administration. Kenton talked to Dr.

Mason, Willows' director, who immediately gave his approval. In doing so he did, however, make a mental note to call the police lieutenant from Hillside.

In San Francisco the sketch artist would leave for Willows in the morning and would hopefully have the drawing on the way to New York by nightfall.

By 4 P.M. Kenton felt he had done all he could with California. He called Fred Grimes. The private detectives were to get a picture of each of the twenty-one men they were investigating, a recent picture. Nothing more than six months old, even if they had to take the photographs themselves.

Grimes said it was up to twenty-seven now.

Then twenty-seven. But he wanted a clear photo of each man. That was vital.

He counted the money left in the safe, about a thousand dollars. He looked through the Mungo papers for anything he might've missed on Bishop. He put all the secret financial reports and income-tax returns together in a separate envelope. He did the same for John Perrone's confidential list of information spies.

Kenton wondered about the information spies, especially such high-placed people as cabinet officials and judges and senators. What made them do it? They signed a pact with the enemy, they violated the trust placed in them. In the search for truth, itself just another form of power, the battle was always between those who made it and those who made it public. Between the players and the observers. The population, the audience, was both the hostages and the spoils of war. A newsman's job was to get the facts out, to be the observer who transmitted reality, truth, to the public. There was no morality, only objectivity. The players could not be objective because they were involved, they had vested interests. Only the observers, those on the periphery of power, could objectively report what was happening. And thus become themselves part of the power.

This essentially was what the news game was all about. It had nothing to do with the public's so-called right to know. Nobody had an empirical right to know anything. Whatever was told to someone was a gift or a curse, but either way had nothing to do with any inalienable right to know. That the public knew anything at all was merely a by-product of the eternal struggle between the players and the observers, the protons and electrons, mutually attracting and repelling. There was only one real arena of action and it was the center ring. Faces might change but the sides were constant. And spies with interchangeable masks merely muddied up the clear-cut struggle. They were tolerated but not particularly liked by either side. When they were discovered, their usefulness to their acknowledged side was at an end. They were powerless.

Kenton felt no sorrow when such spies were found out, most especially when it was a newsman who had gone over to the enemy. It was the same as if he had let Senator Stoner go for money, or given up on Chess Man out of pity.

No, he would never do that. He would never lose his power.

Toward the end of the workday James Mackenzie received a call from Washington, D.C. An acquaintance, though not a friend, and a man of some influence. They talked for ten minutes.

Afterward Martin Dunlop was asked up to the chairman's twenty-fifth-floor office.

John Perrone spent a bad night. Not only did he have the problem of the Stoner article but now the whole Ripper Reference project was being shut down. Martin Dunlop had said only that the wrong people in Washington had found out about it. What he meant, as Perrone well knew, was that pressure had been exerted to return the magazine to its traditional political sympathies. Mackenzie had of course refused. Which left him no alternative to scrapping the private search for Vincent Mungo.

Perrone understood the reasoning and even the necessity for such a move, though he didn't agree with the decision. What worried him was Adam Kenton's reaction. Kenton was not only the best investigative reporter on the magazine, he was also a fanatic about anything he went after. Perrone himself had thought the Mungo idea great and had wanted Kenton for the job because he was the best. He also wanted him out of California and Senator Stoner's hair.

Stoner was Perrone's image of a good politician in theory if not in practice. Though overly ambitious, he stood for the old-line traditional American virtues that had made the country strong. Self-reliance and rugged individualism and a religious cohesiveness within the family. These were the virtues the magazine had always extolled. Along with Stoner, Perrone believed that an increasingly strong centralist government was bringing the country to economic and social ruin. He looked for men like Stoner to support, men who preached the rock-ribbed Republican canon of limited government and free-market capitalism. In an age of dreary socialist rhetoric, where last year's liberal became this year's conservative, and where leftist labels stretched to infinity, such men were increasingly hard to find.

There was also a personal interest of sorts in Perrone's view of Stoner. In his own earlier days the managing editor had been greatly influenced and even materially aided by the Rintelcanes of Washington, a powerful western family of money and Republican sentiment. One of their daughters was married to Senator Stoner, a plain woman he himself had once thought about seriously.

Now Perrone supposed he would have to give the okay for the Stoner piece. His reporter had enough to call for an investigation, and if *Newstime* didn't publish it he'd go elsewhere. Stoner was just too greedy and too dumb. An investigation would probably nail his career; certainly it would take him out of any national consideration. Perrone felt sorry for the in-laws and most especially for the wife. At least he would do his best to keep out the sexual stuff. She deserved better than that.

But what about the Ripper Reference? How would Kenton take that?

The call from the managing editor's office came at 9:30 while Kenton was dictating some thoughts he had put together overnight on Thomas Bishop's psychology. With an annoyed air he turned off the machine and went upstairs. His boss was waiting for him, alone and in a somber mood. Something was wrong, and Kenton quickly guessed that it concerned a certain California senator whose wife's parents were good friends of the man seated behind the desk.

"You changed your mind on Stoner," said the reporter gruffly. "You're not going to print it."

John Perrone sighed, wishing life were so simple. He suspected Kenton knew of his relationship with Stoner's in-laws and wondered if he should act offended by the remark.

"Don't be presumptuous," he finally said. "I already told you there's enough for a good story. Providing Martin goes for it."

"But will you recommend it?"

"I always recommend whatever I believe in," snapped Perrone, stung by the implication.

Kenton smiled. "Nothing personal, John. I know you're the best in the business, always were." He sat down, crossed his legs as he stretched them. "So what's up?"

Perrone told him.

Kenton just sat there, his legs still crossed, the smile still on his face. A paranoid personality, suspicious of everyone and everything, he expected constant treachery and deceit. Often satisfied, he was seldom surprised. He thus tried to prepare as best he could for the power plays of others.

Perrone watched him for some moments, the smile, the posture, the eyes. Finally he could contain himself no longer.

"Well?"

The voice in answer was flat, lifeless.

"It's a mistake."

Perrone had somehow expected more.

"A mistake?" He frowned. "Is that all you can say?"

"It's a mistake that will have to be corrected."

"How?"

"It will be done," said the flat voice.

"But how? Mackenzie himself gave the order."

"Then he will himself change it."

"I doubt that," said the managing editor. "For what it's worth, I think it was the wrong decision, but I told you what he's up against."

There was no longer a smile on Kenton's face. His eyes blazed and he sat very erect and tensed.

"I know who Chess Man is," he suddenly blurted out, "and he's not Vincent Mungo." He stood up. "I also know how to get to him."

A speechless Perrone heard him ask for a meeting in the afternoon with James Mackenzie and Martin Dunlop. Preferably in Mackenzie's office.

On his way out Kenton decided it was time he used some of that unlimited power he was supposed to have in the company.

* * *

After lunch Bishop went uptown to pick up his passport. It was waiting for him. A slim green booklet, very official-looking, with his name and birthplace and picture. Even the seal of the United States. He was Thomas Wayne Brewster. It said so right in the book, an official document of the United States government. And good anywhere in the world. Except Cuba, North Korea and North Vietnam. Bishop had no intention of going to those three countries. At least until he had taken care of the women in the rest of the world.

Home again, he prepared himself for a six o'clock photography session. As always, he would be meeting the model in some local restaurant, a copy of *True Detective* in hand.

The meeting in Mackenzie's office was set for three. Before that hour Kenton saw Otto Klemp privately. His message was brief and very much to the point. If Klemp didn't agree to continue the Ripper Reference, Mackenzie would be told that he was a clandestine contributor to, and a long-time backer of, the American Nazi Party. If Mackenzie wasn't interested, the newspapers would be. And that, said Kenton, was known as blackmail.

He also mentioned the Western Holding Company to Martin Dunlop, again privately.

At the three o'clock session he told the group that he knew the madman's name and history, and would soon have a picture of him or at least a drawing. He was also close to locating his prey.

Mackenzie wanted to know how close and was told perhaps a week, maybe only a matter of days.

No one else was aware of his knowledge, Kenton asserted, so there could be no charge of interfering with police business or withholding information. Not yet anyway. They still had a good chance at the story of the year.

Mackenzie wasn't convinced. The pressure would get worse. If the police got wind of anything they would be around like flies. So would the mayor's office. Yet the newspaperman in him cried out to get the story.

What did the others think?

John Perrone felt right from the start that it could be done and should be done.

Martin Dunlop thought they should continue. A story like that was worth a limited risk.

Otto Klemp sat silent a long moment, gazing thoughtfully at Kenton, who stared back at him with eyes unwavering.

Finally Klemp shrugged, ever so slightly, and turned his attention to the chairman. If Kenton was that close to victory, he said softly, why retire in defeat?

Mackenzie frowned, looked at Kenton and made an executive decision. The search would continue for one week if necessary, after which their position would be reviewed. He told Perrone to hold the editorial calling for the President to resign. Scheduled for the next issue, it would also be continued for a week. The matter was settled.

Back in his office, a jubilant Kenton called California. The Justin newspaper editor read the brief death notice over the phone. There was no mention of any matricide. Apparently Sara Bishop had been found dead in her home on December 28, 1958. Her sole survivor was her son, Thomas Bishop, age ten, who was placed in the care of the state. They had been residents of Justin for five years, had most recently lived in the old Woods' house, three miles out of town.

That was it.

Kenton hoped Mel Brown was right about small-town papers usually not reporting things like matricides.

The editor was proud he had found the mention at all; stayed up half the night looking for it in the files. He had finally come across it in the last issue of the year, dated December 31.

Kenton thanked him profusely and promised to stop in when he was up that way again. Meanwhile could the editor send a copy of the notice on to New York? It would be most helpful.

He rang off.

Damn small towns anyway. If the papers didn't print what really happened, what good were they? Now he had to rely on the two stringers who were combing the town, prodding people's memories. Suppose nobody recalled the mother and boy? Thirteen years was a long time. Almost as long as having to wait a whole day for important news.

Kenton went home early. There was nothing else to do.

United Airlines Flight 35 left San Francisco International

Airport for Hawaii at 1 P.M. Pacific Standard time with a full passenger list. Included aboard was Gloria Kind, who intended to live in Hawaii for a while. Her furniture had been stored, her mink coat placed in a furrier's vault, her car sold.

She had not, however, sold the recording equipment. It was packed in a separate section of the warehouse, ready to be sent to her on one day's notice.

Some twenty hours later Senator Stoner flew out of St. Louis on a silver jet bound for San Francisco and home. He was a bit weary and would be glad to get back. His trip had been an immense success by all standards of publicity and political promise. Even Roger, the perennial pessimist, had to agree he was a smash.

Stoner wondered if now was the time to get rid of Roger. Lately he was spending most of his hours ingratiating himself with the right people instead of working on them in the senator's behalf. Besides, the operation now needed a chief of staff who had some national stature. Like Tom Donaldson of Chicago.

He would have to give that serious thought.

Kenton was impatient. The drawing of Thomas Bishop wouldn't arrive until the following day, Friday. But at least he could get something from the stringers in Red Bluff. They had spent an entire afternoon and evening in Justin talking to the locals. What had they learned? Sara Bishop was well remembered by many people. A strange woman, not too balanced, maybe a bit sick in the head. Very aloof, frightened of everyone, even hostile. Especially to the men. Kept the boy tied to her. Beat him often, probably whipped him. Burned him too. Everybody knew that. Sometimes the boy would be home from school for a week because of the beatings or burns.

One day the boy killed his mother. Got her unconscious somehow and put her in the wood stove. Fried her till there was nothing left but bones. When the police came the boy was sitting in front of the stove, full of cuts and dried blood. In his hand was a piece of charred flesh he had been eating—

What?

A piece of charred flesh he was eating. Near as they could figure it, he'd been there about three days. Just sitting in front of that dead stove, the fire long gone. The local authorities said only that the mother had died, but everyone in town knew what happened. And apparently no one was surprised either.

What about the boy?

Naturally they figured him for crazy so they sent him to Willows, which was the closest state mental hospital. Also, it had a separate section for killer kids.

What happened to the house and the mother's possessions?

The house was closed up, nobody wanted to live in it. Eventually it was sold to newcomers. Some of the stuff was taken by a woman in town who had been the mother's only friend. She kept it all in boxes, and when she died some of it was auctioned off by a nephew who'd inherited the woman's home. He still lived there. Far as he knew, about the only things left from that time were a couple cartons of books and junk that he kept in a back shed.

Kenton wanted them to go through the cartons. Looking for any pictures or letters or diaries or papers of any kind. Anything personal about the Bishop woman and the boy. If the nephew had a list of the people who bought any of her things at the auction, they should be questioned too.

Red Bluff would reluctantly return to Justin on Sunday. Meanwhile Kenton would receive their typed report.

He rang Fred Grimes. By Monday he needed pictures of all the twenty-seven suspects being investigated. Pictures by Monday, not later. They should get on that right away, even sooner.

John Perrone called to give him the go-ahead on the Stoner article. Dunlop agreed they had enough. The tape and notes were on the way back to him.

With Bishop in the works, Kenton turned to Stoner. He could see nothing but trouble ahead, and he wondered if Martin Dunlop really expected to cut all references to Western Holding in the story. It was either that or sell all investments in the Idaho combine.

Kenton knew which one he would strongly advise.

In Hillside, John Spanner mulled over the information he had just been given. The *Newstime* reporter had commissioned a special drawing of Thomas Bishop, a memory composite of eyewitness descriptions, to be done by a former police artist in San Francisco. Which meant that somebody else thought Bishop might be the Willows maniac.

If asked, Spanner would help all he could. He suddenly felt more alive than he had in months.

The line at the parcel post window was longer than usual for a Friday morning, and the clerks could be heard grumbling in raspy voices. The young bearded man held his package tightly with both hands and moved forward slowly with the line. On the bulletin board against the nearby wall were printed notices of one kind or another, many of them in English and Spanish. He read some of them to while away the time. Most were concerned with various official post office regulations, and he found all of them incomprehensible. Soon he was second in line, and then first.

He walked up to the windowed ledge and pushed his package forward.

"Nothing breakable," he told the clerk. "Just some soft toys."

The composite came in the morning mail, heavily encased in cardboard and tape. Kenton slashed open the protective covering with a scissors edge and pulled out the drawing. On the desk next to it he placed the standard police photo of Vincent Mungo.

They were like night and day.

Not a shred of similarity in face or eyes or even skin. Mungo was dark, almost swarthy, and slightly menacing. His eyes seemed to be dull reflectors pulled over empty sockets. The lips were full, the nose oversized. Bishop was fair, with finely chiseled features and smooth skin and crystal-clear eyes. The lips were thin, the nose sculptured in the classic Anglo-Saxon mold. He looked as innocent as an uncrushed egg.

One could never be mistaken for the other, even by someone stone blind. Kenton immediately saw how Bishop was able to travel so freely across the country. He was automatically passed over a thousand times by watchful eyes seeking anyone who remotely resembled Vincent Mungo. With Bishop there wouldn't be a shimmer of suspicion.

Kenton saw something else too, though not immediately. How much Vincent Mungo looked like—Caryl Chessman.

He put the two faces in the safe to await Monday's arrival of the local pictures.

In the mail he also found the death notice of Sara Bishop from the Justin weekly paper. It was brief and contained no surprises. He placed it in the new folder marked *Bishop*.

Time was running out and yet nothing more could be done until Monday. He was banking everything on coming up with Bishop's new face and identity in the search of mail-drop clients. If that didn't work out, he was through. He had lost. There would be nothing else to do and no time to do it. But he was a winner, not a loser. Bishop's face would be there, staring up at him. Complete with a name and address. He had come too far to be fooled now. He alone knew his man was Bishop, not suspected it, like Spanner and others. He *knew* it. Knew how it was planned and how it was done. Knew how Bishop thought and what he felt. All the twists of mind and turns of fate that brought him three thousand miles to New York. Brought both of them all the way to New York. And destiny.

Kenton had run with the fox. And with the tiger too. Over the weekend he would work on the Stoner piece. He was hungry for blood.

At 6:30 that evening a bearded young man bought the latest issue of *True Detective* at a downtown newsstand. The cover promised assorted murders and mayhem and the photograph showed the usual beautiful female in distress. Minutes later, the magazine under his arm, Bishop walked into a restaurant on Spring Street. It was a busy time and no one paid him special attention. He sat at a small table toward the rear. The magazine was placed conspicuously at the table's edge, its cover showing.

As he drank his coffee a young woman entered the restaurant, her manner uncertain, her eyes seeming to search. Soon she was at his table.

"Are you the photographer I'm supposed to meet here?"

Bishop looked up, nodded. His smile was electric.

"I'm Helena. We talked on the phone before."

He rose slightly and offered her the chair opposite him.

"Helena. How nice to meet you. I'm Jay Cooper and I have this rush job . . ."

* * *

Sunday night was Dory's turn to work the bar, and by the time she finished her shift she was tired. Her feet hurt, her legs hurt, even her crotch hurt. From overwork, she thought meanly, blaming all her ills on the man she was living with. Damn that Johnny Messick anyway. Didn't he ever get tired of it? She pictured herself going home and falling into bed. He'd be on her before she could turn over. Nothing would stop him either. If she said she had a headache, he told her to shut her eyes. If she was too tired to move, he used her body stone-still. And he never let up on the sex. Sometimes she really believed he was a little sick in the head somewhere. But at least she had a nice place to stay and a car and she didn't have to work her ass off more than twice a week instead of the usual five or six days straight. It paid to let the boss stick it in. If somebody had to, get the boss and the bread. Only, Christ! he overdid it all by himself. A year of him and she'd have nothing left to give the next boss.

At the car she fumbled for the keys and didn't notice the two men until they were on her. The one with the gun shoved her in the front seat, they climbed in around her. She was not to scream, not to say anything. They just wanted her to listen for a minute. She lived with John Messick. He had a letter they wanted. The letter was signed "Don Solis." Maybe the name was on the envelope. Maybe the envelope was sealed. Maybe there was no envelope. What she had to remember was the name. Don Solis. Papers with the name written somewhere. If she could get that letter they would pay her ten thousand dollars.

Ten thousand! Just to give them a letter or help them get it. Messick probably kept it somewhere in the house. He wouldn't put it in a safe-deposit box, in case anything suddenly happened to him. And he wouldn't hand it to someone else since it wasn't really his. But they had to be sure.

Did he have a safe at home? Maybe in a wall or inside a desk. Or maybe in his office in the bar. She should keep her eyes open. Even if she couldn't get the letter herself, if she found out where it was, she would still get the money. Provided they could get to it. But it had to be done fast. She worked again on Tuesday night. They would see her then. If she crossed them, if she told Messick or anyone, they would hurt her. But she had nothing to worry about if she did what they said. And she'd have ten grand for herself.

Dory was scared. As she drove home her hands shook and her teeth ached. She was also thinking furiously. Ten thousand dollars. She had never had that kind of money. At age twenty-one she had never even seen that much. With ten thousand she could do anything, go anywhere. Go far away.

It was ten o'clock Monday morning before Fred Grimes got the pictures from the detective agency, twenty-three in all. Four others were still being processed and would be delivered later. It had been a costly operation, said the agency manager, very costly, but . . .

Grimes nodded. At this point cost was not a consideration. Kenton was on unlimited company funds, and Grimes just paid the bills. In cash.

By 10:30 Kenton was comparing each photograph with the drawing. Most were tight close-ups taken with a telephoto lens, as had been requested. One by one they were studied, examined, scrutinized. One by one they were rejected. At the end, only three remained possibilities. All wore beards.

He turned to the reports on the three. One of them lived with his parents and ran a mail-order business from a home workshop. The mail drop was the business address, a changeover from an earlier drop, which had closed when the elderly owner died. Another was a young married man who apparently carried on correspondence affairs with males in other cities. He had received about a dozen such letters since opening the rental box, as well as several magazines that listed names of similar-minded people, who were initially reached through letters sent to the magazine and forwarded. For a fee of course.

Neither man was Thomas Bishop.

The third was of more interest. Age twenty-five, lived alone in a downtown tenement. Claimed to be an artist of sorts, no visible means of support. In town about a month. Previous address: Venice, Florida. Name: Curtis Manning.

Kenton told Grimes to have the agency check Manning out with Florida right away. The particulars of his leaving there, and a picture. He wanted it by the morning.

When would the last four photos be ready?

Early afternoon.

One possibility out of twenty-three. And only four more to go. Kenton decided not to panic yet.

In the *Daily News* building on East 42nd Street the package arrived in the mail room and was routinely sent upstairs to the seventh-floor editorial offices, since it was addressed to the Editor. There an editorial assistant opened it because no individual name was specified. Under the wrapping was a white cake box. A rubber band held the cover down. The editorial assistant removed the rubber band and lifted the cover. Her split-second impression was that they were some strange little cakes or—

As her hand automatically reached into the box, the scream had already begun somewhere deep in her throat . . .

Johnny Messick slowly awakened to the most wonderful feeling all over his body. For a moment he thought he might be in heaven and he wondered how he had made it. He slowly opened his eyes, not daring to move. As focus returned he saw Dory's head bobbing up and down in front of him. She was kneeling between his legs, facing him. Her silky hair brushed against his belly. Goddam! She was giving him a blow job, and just the way he liked it too. Waking up to it. She hadn't done that since the first few weeks they got together. He closed his eyes and relaxed, trying not to think of anything.

Dory had made herself wake up before him. She had given him sweet sex the night before, tired as she was, without complaints, with much forced passion. Lulled him to sleep with the soft syrupy slurping of body on body. And now this. She slid her tongue along the shaft of his penis to the head, then pursed her lips over the crown, tightening them as she accepted him fully into her mouth. Slowly she ran her taut lips up and down the stem, holding the skin back with her thumb and index finger. As she worked her movements into a rhythm she could already begin feeling the tightening of the scrotum, which would soon send the milky white substance shooting into her waiting mouth.

At least he came quicker than some others she had known in her young life. Which was a blessing, Dory thought wearily, as his breathing grew heavier. But fast or slow, she would make him so mellow he would tell her anything she wanted to know. And what she wanted to know was worth ten thousand dollars.

The thought excited her so much she forgot to close her throat muscles as his sperm slammed into her tonsils and sluiced down past pink tissue and all recall.

It was 12:30 when the news came through from Red Bluff. They sounded excited, both literally talking at the same time. Most of Sunday had been spent in Justin. The nephew had been very cooperative, allowing them to browse through the cartons in the shed at their leisure.

First they found the usual household junk, all of which could have belonged to anybody. Kitchen utensils, old clothes and linen, a few rusted tools, a Strongboy leather strap, well worn. Stuff like that. A lot of books too, mostly all yellowed with age and falling apart. After a while they looked among the books and found some handwritten notes on sewing, a child's school notebook, a few drawings. And plenty of papers with figures added up, like somebody going over what money was left.

Finally they came to a book called *The Face of Justice* by Caryl Chessman—

Kenton's heart quickened.

—and inside the book were about a dozen pages folded in half, all of them filled with writing about a young girl growing up and all the things that went wrong in her life—

Had she been raped?

More than once, it seemed.

Did she name Caryl Chessman?

She talked a lot about him.

Was there someone called Harry Owens?

He was the guy she married.

Kenton knew the author, though he had never met her. It was Sara Owens, mother of Thomas Bishop.

He had found the Chessman connection. The last link, the final piece of the puzzle. It was just as he knew it would be. Through the parents. Except he had thought it was the father, by way of Don Solis. But it had been the mother all along. Sara Bishop Owens.

He told Red Bluff to send him the pages immediately. Also the other writings. One of them was to go back to Justin and buy the cartons from the nephew and send them on to New York too. And they were not to mention their assignment to anybody. That meant nobody.

The fox looked around the empty office. Slowly he changed back into the hound.

Inspector Alex Dimitri stared at the female parts in the box. From at least two women, as near as he could tell, maybe more. How the devil could anybody tell? He rubbed his eyes, trying to pull himself together. He had three daughters of his own.

There was no note, just a name scrawled on the box.

Chess Man.

Two questions concerned him at the moment. Did they come from women already found? Parts had been taken from the bodies, so it was possible. But somehow he doubted that. Then where were the new victims? In their homes, not yet discovered? Or—

He suddenly was chilled to the bone. If Chess Man had a secret place where he not only lived undisturbed but to which he could bring victims unnoticed, he was practically invisible. A rat in a hole. A bat in a cave. He could go on forever storing bodies away. Cutting them up for packages or maybe Christmas gifts—

Dimitri felt his own sanity slipping away. The boys were right. There was no way the maniac would ever reach a courtroom. He was too dangerous. And not just because of what he was doing. But he touched the insanity in everyone, he fed it. Fed the monster that was in each person from the very beginning, that had been pushed down over millions of years but was always and forever waiting to be released.

The inspector closed the cover on the cake box. He hoped the forensic people would come soon.

Kenton heard the news of Chess Man's latest mailing at 1:20, a call from a *Daily News* friend. At 1:50 he was given the last four photographs from the mail-drop investigation. Four young white men, one of them bearded, all of them clean-cut and strong-eyed. Typical American youth.

Unfortunately none of them looked anything like Thomas Bishop.

Kenton groped for his chair, stunned. Something had gone wrong. How could he be so mistaken, so off base?

Bishop needed a mailing address. Too dangerous wherever he was living. So he would get a mail drop. And his psychology would prompt him to get it right away.

It made sense.

Except Bishop wasn't there.

And he probably wasn't Curtis Manning of Florida.

That left nobody.

For much of the afternoon Kenton stared at the blank wall nearest him. After a while he didn't see it any more as he returned in time to his own painful childhood. His foster parents had been older people who had no children of their own. They were bitterly poor and knew little about raising a boy. It was not their fault. They were not cruel and he loved them while they lived, but he had suffered terribly in ways he would never get over.

As he became the lost boy again his eyes slowly filled with tears and his mind eventually turned to another boy who had once suffered desperately, inconsolably, and who had finally found a certain peace in madness.

Nor were the two boys so very far apart, except in degree.

At home now on this dark and fearful night, with a torrential rain hammering at every exposed nerve, Bishop put on the TV, prepared to be entertained until he fell asleep. Instead he received the shock of his young life. The show was a police detective series from San Francisco in which a youthful killer was finally captured through his telephone-answering service. To Bishop the similiarities were startling.

He leaped off his pallet bed, badly frightened. He had made a major mistake, a serious error that could destroy him. It was already too late. They knew all about him and were outside his door even now, waiting to pounce. He looked toward the door, imagining them on the other side. Dreadful demonic shapes out of hell itself. *Them!*

His fright quickly turned to rage, the involuntary frenzied rage of the caged beast. His features contorted, his body shook in spasms. Soon he was howling like a wounded animal maddened by pain. He rolled on the floor, unmindful of his head banging on the cement. He tore at his own limbs. He punched himself and beat himself without direction, all the while shieking in total derangement. Were he not alone in the house he could easily have been heard from above. Were the wind and rain not thunderous he would surely have been heard from the street.

After a long time the rage was spent and he lay on the floor in peaceful stupor, his clothes shredded, his body lacerated and bloodied. No longer did the animal howl as the glazed eyes closed in merciful sleep.

Kenton dreamed of a time of coldness and hunger; of his boyhood, helpless, isolated, unable to act or even understand. Of the white rabbit of his youth, and the black cat. As he lay in bed now, safe against the ravages of night but not those of the past, he was not at all sure whether it was a time of waking or sleeping. Or if the boy was real. Or even the man.

Bishop slept into the morning on the cold cement floor and awoke ravenous. He washed his animal body and soothed it with ointment and then ate breakfast. Fearful no longer, he set his mind to work on his problem.

He had made a fatal error in getting the answering service. Several in fact. The photography idea itself was valid but not his execution. To have the women leave their names with his service meant someone had a list of them. Sooner or later the service would become suspicious, and that list would be matched against the list of missing women. All had called Jay Cooper just before they disappeared. How odd. But the police would find it more than odd.

Also sooner or later a model would leave his name as her destination in a note to a friend or relative, or become suspicious beforehand and report him to the police. Granted no one knew where he lived, which was why he always met them in public places and took them home only when he was certain they had come alone. And granted they were all amateur models, half-crazed artistic types and semiprostitutes and desperate women needing money or kicks or both, none of whom would know enough to first check prospective clients and always leave full information on appointments. Still, something would eventually go wrong. Maybe already had for all he knew. They could be after him right now, knowing his name and the mail-drop address.

That was his third mistake. The answering service had the mail drop on Lafayette Street as his address, to be given to the police. He could not go there again. At least there he had given the Chicago address, so that wouldn't help them. But they could get to his home through the owner of the building. He had rented to Jay Cooper. When he saw the name in the paper he would call the police. So the apartment was no good anymore either.

Bishop frowned in disgust. He blew it all on a bad move. All his work, his plans, his New York identity. All gone. He had no doubt they would expose him in another week. Maybe only a matter of days if any more women disappeared. And he had an appointment for that very evening!

He added up the score. The apartment, the mail drop, the telephone, the photography. He had lost it all. New York held nothing more for him.

But what if he hadn't watched that show? Thank God for television!

He went to work quickly and efficiently, destroying his Jay Cooper identity, refilling the wallet with Thomas Wayne Brewster's driver's license and birth certificate. In the pocket with the wallet also went his new passport. At the local bank he closed out his savings account, pointedly saying he was returning to Chicago. Home again, he removed the money hidden behind the bricks. An hour later he had over $21,000 in the New Jersey bank. It was only temporary, he assured himself on the way back. Half would be returned to New York when he found another place to live in his new identity. Until then at least the money was safe. No one knew of Thomas Wayne Brewster, and he would make no more mistakes.

Fred Grimes had the bad news when Kenton finally got to the office. Curtis Manning was straight out of Florida. Family still lived there. He was sensitive, artistic, different from other local young men, and he had decided New York would be more responsive to his needs, whatever they might be. The pictures matched. It was Manning all right.

Kenton already knew it. Not factually, not the specific details, but in his gut instinct where he lived. Manning would have been too perfect. Madman, Chess Man, Bat Man, Manning. Everything was Man. Bishop had a problem identifying as a man. It would have been an incredible piece of irony for him to take over the identity of someone named Manning. Maybe in novels or in the movies they could get away with things like that, where everything was planned in perfect circles and things always seemed to fit exactly. But not in real life. Nothing ever worked out perfectly in real life because there was no director or central casting or even stage manager. It was all hit or miss.

And this time he had missed. That was it and that was all. Somehow he blew it. He had spent half the night trying to figure what had gone wrong, and he still didn't know. It was a valid idea—that much was certain. He couldn't compete with the cops in checking hotels and public places. Nor could he put thousands of men on the streets.

Instead he had studied his prey until he felt things, knew things about the man. Bishop lived in New York, in Manhattan. He would want to stay near his kills. He found Manhattan exciting, all those millions of women at his fingers, all around him. A madman's dream. He would find a place to live. But he wouldn't want to call attention to himself so he'd get his mail elsewhere. What mail? Pieces of identification mostly. Part of his pattern was a constant search for new and safer identities. Apparently he would not, could not stop.

So he, Kenton, had picked something Bishop would do. Something the police wouldn't think of, not knowing the man. The city's mail drops. And he picked the first week, which was also in Bishop's pattern of immediate action.

When he pulled up the net, Bishop should have been inside.

Only he wasn't.

And Kenton didn't know why.

He asked Grimes again if the city officials had gone to all the drops in Manhattan. If they got all the recent names from each other. If the detectives checked all those names for eligibles. If they investigated all twenty-seven finalists.

As far as Grimes knew, the answer was yes to all.

Kenton went back to staring at the wall.

In the early afternoon Kenton took a long lunch and then worked for an hour on the Stoner article, his mind far away. Toward the close of the day a thought popped into his head and he called Mel Brown. The secretary reported him away for the afternoon on business and Kenton said he'd call again in the morning.

Bishop left the lights on in the studio. He didn't expect to be away very long. When he returned with the model it would be his last opportunity to play photographer, a role he rather liked, and the thought saddened him. He would at least try to make it an outstanding performance, one the model would remember for the rest of her life.

Outside the air was brisk, and Bishop shuddered a bit as he turned left into early evening shadow.

She was late as usual, and as she ran out the door she dashed off a note to her roommate that she was going to model for a magazine with a photographer named Jay Cooper. Somewhere downtown, she didn't know exactly where.

Back in a few hours.

Dory made herself walk over to the car. This time she wasn't frightened by the two men, not terribly anyway. Her mind was on money and they had it. And she had what they wanted, at least the information. She told them the letter was kept in a steel desk at home. Messick had this room that he used for business and making calls, it was really a second bedroom. Earlier in the day when he was out, she had looked at the desk. On the right side was a little door, like a safe. It opened with a key but it didn't look all that strong.

Was she sure about the letter?

She shook her head. Don Solis. Right. She was sure.

They believed her.

When would she get the money?

When they got the letter.

She couldn't open the safe by herself.

They would take care of it. All she had to do was open the front door for them. Friday morning. They'd get the letter and she'd get the money.

What about Messick?

He wouldn't know anything about her part.

And what should she do meanwhile?

Nothing. She'd done enough already.

Kenton thought Mel Brown might see something he missed. The detectives checked everybody for those who could fit the description. Came to twenty-seven. Then they got pictures and reports on those twenty-seven.

One thing Brown couldn't understand. How did they check everybody initially?

By taking a quick look at each one.

That was what he couldn't understand. Were they all available to be looked at? Nobody traveling for a few weeks or away on a job? Nobody giving a wrong address? And did every single name have a local address that could be checked out?

Eyes narrowed, Kenton called Fred Grimes. Would he ask the detective agency if they had any names they could not reach, names with no local addresses? Right now?

He got his answer in minutes. There were eight names with no local addresses given. They all were out of state. Many individuals and firms from other areas of the country kept convenience addresses in New York from which the mail was routinely forwarded. The agency considered the eight to be of that type and didn't list them because it was presumably looking for an individual who actually lived in the city.

What about Manning in Florida? He was out-of-state.

True. But he had given a local address as well.

Kenton wanted the eight investigated immediately. That very minute. Each had to be verified by the renter. And he wanted the information by 5 P.M. if at all possible.

In Sacramento, Roger Tompkins told Senator Stoner of the several original letters and copies he had in his possession which might prove embarrassing to the senator. They would, however, remain in his possession since he had no intention of resigning from the senator's staff. Not at the moment anyway.

Stoner said nothing. As a politician he knew all about power.

At 11 A.M. Kenton informed James Mackenzie that he was close to Chess Man but he needed more time. Mackenzie said they were running out of time. It had been a week now and he had hoped—

Maybe just a few days, Kenton pleaded.

The others in the room were in favor of continuing.

Mackenzie told John Perrone to go ahead with the editorial calling for the President's resignation. They would take their chances.

But—he could not guarantee more than a few days. Another week at the very most, when the new issue would be out. That was it.

By 4:30 Kenton had answers on five of the out-of-state rentals. Three were small industrial firms in Ohio, West Virginia and Wisconsin. The fourth was a man from a hollow in Kentucky who was a mail addict and liked the prestige of a New York address. The fifth was from New Mexico, a woman who used the drop in her mail-order occult business. All had been verified.

The three left, all individuals, were from Denver, Los Angeles and Chicago. The search was on. They would know in the morning.

Los Angeles. Kenton thought of Bishop's stay in Los Angeles after the escape. Of his mother being raped there, his father killed there. Of Caryl Chessman's life there. Of his own Los Angeles article on Chessman, which must have been a beacon to Bishop and a godsend to Stoner. Everything came out of Los Angeles.

Now Bishop was in a box.

Kenton had a feeling it was Los Angeles.

The roommate was worried. Pam had not been home all night or all day. Now another night and she still wasn't home. It wasn't like her. She had no steady boyfriend. An art student, she stayed home mostly and worked.

The roommate looked again at the note. Model for a magazine. Jay Cooper. Somewhere downtown.

Well, she'd give her until morning.

Bishop had a change of heart. He had intended to leave that morning, after disposing of the final model. Now it was after nine at night and he was still at home. He had already decided to take nothing extra with him, not the camera or any of the books or his radio or even his extra clothes. He would start all over again as Thomas Wayne Brewster. Everything different. But he wanted one more final night as Jay Cooper in the only real home that had ever been his. The danger was there and it was real. Yet he was giving them too much credit. He was far too clever for them. He was the Chess Man, the Bat Man. They could never kill him or even capture him. He would outlast and outlive them all. What did they know about him? Nothing. And they never would.

He was going to go out to a bar and pick up a woman and take her to his first home on his last night and hold a final celebration. She would be part of his celebration, a very big part.

In the morning he would leave alone, as he always was and always would be. World without end.

At 8:20 A.M. Pam Boyer's roommate called the police to report her friend missing. She gave the particulars and read the note, including the name Jay Cooper. The information was routinely dispatched to Missing Persons Bureau. Because of the current publicity concerning several such women, the report was also marked for special attention Task Force.

At 9:10 Jay Cooper left his home for the last time. Wearing his wool socks under brown boots, wrapped in his muffler and suede leather jacket, and carrying only his portable TV set, he walked to a subway that would take him to a new life.

He was alone.

At 9:25 Adam Kenton was told that it was not Los Angeles that hid Chess Man behind its New York mailing address. The rental was paid by an irate client who apparently used it for purposes not entirely legal. But he was confirmed as its lessee and he was not Thomas Bishop. Nor was it Denver, where the customer was a self-employed businessman who was in New York one week a month.

It was Chicago.

Jay Cooper was a Chicago resident who knew nothing about a mail address in New York City. It wasn't his. How could it be? He didn't even like New York. Hadn't been there for years.

It was Bishop.

Somehow he'd been able to latch onto Jay Cooper's identity. The rest was easy. No, not easy. Just a lot of thought and careful planning. That was never easy.

Kenton had the face and he had the name. All he needed was the address.

Now was when he should go to the cops. From here on in he could be accused of anything and they'd be right. He was withholding, interfering and probably a lot more.

But he hadn't come this far to hand it over to someone else. He wasn't built that way. Never would be.

Mackenzie had given him a few more days.

He would take them. And the consequences too.

By ten o'clock he was talking to the manager of the midtown detective agency, explaining what he wanted. An all-out effort to locate one man. His mailing address was downtown, so he probably lived downtown. East Village, Bowery, Soho. Copies of the drawing of his face would be ready by mid-afternoon for the detectives. They should show it everywhere in the area, especially in stores and restaurants. Other operators were to go after the name. Jay Cooper. Somebody must've heard it. He paid rent under the name. Maybe worked or had a phone or rented a car or applied for something. Cost was no object. Whatever it took. The manager was to throw everybody he had into it. If that wasn't enough he should get more.

Kenton was to be kept informed. Right through the night at the St. Moritz. They should work round the clock. He needed results and he had no time left.

Elsewhere in midtown a telephone operator for an answering service thought she probably was being silly, but it seemed like all those girls who disappeared had called one of her clients. She remembered hearing their names on the phone. Johnson. Daley. Ubis. Boyer.

She stared at the names in the paper. Lots of people have the same name. Sure, that was it. She was just being silly.

November 15 was a day Adam Kenton afterward swore he would long remember. He sat in his office hour after hour, unable to work or even concentrate. Each time the phone rang he jumped for it, then had to tell people to get off the line. Several times he checked with the agency. Each time the answer was the same. Almost fifty people were in the field. Other shifts would take over in the evening. They would work all night if that was what he wanted.

At 6 P.M. he finally went home. He ate a quick meal and spent the evening watching television with the sound off. He didn't think he would sleep at all but eventually he did, the phone by his ear.

* * *

The telephone operator decided that maybe she should mention her suspicions to her boss. Even if it was silly, so what? They were supposed to be alert and conscientious, weren't they?

So that was what she would do in the morning.

The call came at 7:43 A.M.

Kenton leaped up so suddenly he knocked over the ashtray, and crushed cigarettes spilled onto the floor as he speared the receiver.

They had found Jay Cooper. Where he lived. A three-story building on Greene Street in the Soho district. Had a loft there. No one else living in the building at the present time.

They had found him through a petition filed by the building's owner to have the property's tax assessment reduced. He was listed as a business, Jay Cooper Novelties, since the area was not zoned for residential use.

A man was already stationed near the house, watching it.

Kenton said he would meet them in forty-five minutes. Where?

In Ray's, a restaurant on Centre Street near the Criminal Courts Building that opened at 7:30.

All the way downtown in the cab Kenton kept thinking that something would go wrong. When he got there the restaurant would be gone or the phone call was a wrong number. Something crazy.

But they were waiting for him, three bulky private detectives with guns. And now as they rode in silence, Kenton in the front seat, his hands clasped on his lap, he hoped his luck would hold out just a little longer.

In Fresno, California, Don Solis listened for a few seconds to Sinatra singing "It Was a Very Good Year." He hummed a few bars. He was feeling good on this bright Friday morning and his future looked even brighter.

He didn't have a worry in the world.

With soft music filling the car, he reached out and turned on the ignition and his whole future blew up in his face.

Farther south, in San Diego, two men walked up to a

home on a quiet street. They were soon let in by a young woman.

Once inside the house they shot the woman with silencer-equipped pistols, then went into the bedroom and killed John Messick in his sleep.

In the second bedroom one of them got a short crowbar from under his jacket and in seconds had the desk strong-box opened. They took the envelope marked "Don Solis."

Within three minutes they were out of the house and in their car again.

The sedan stopped down the block and four men got out and walked to the loft building. One of them used some small tools on the front door. Soon it opened and they entered cautiously.

They quickly were at the second-floor landing, guns drawn. Ahead of them the door was open. They peered into a large room with a white-papered wall and a camera mounted on a tripod.

Nobody was home.

Two of them squeezed through the boards to the top-floor landing and slowly started up the stairs. . . .

Inspector Dimitri had compared the name given him by the telephone operator with that in the previous day's report of a missing young woman. They were the same.

Jay Cooper.

Something sick began crawling around in his stomach.

A downtown photographer who used young models.

He had just sent men scurrying everywhere in search of a Jay Cooper when he was called to the phone.

"Adam Kenton, from *Newstime*."

Dimitri shook his head. He was busy.

"He says it's urgent. About Jay Cooper."

Thus began the biggest manhunt in New York's history, a brief and bloody moment in the beat of the nation's largest city. Before it was over, dozens of lives would be irrevocably changed, others ended. Careers would be ruined, some started. Two men, both hunters, yet each knowing the fear of the fox, would finally meet face to face. And an incredible mystery, forever unsolvable, would come to haunt Chess Man collectors and the general public alike.

To this day the various police files on Thomas William

Bishop have never been officially closed. Nor has the actual FBI report of the investigation ever been released.

Over the years newsmen and writers of true crime would point out curiously that Jack the Ripper was never caught, and that similar or even identical murders and mutilations of females have taken place in different countries at roughly seventy-five-year intervals, about the life span of the average woman.

And there are those who still believe that on some dark and dreadful night, the demon will again flash his knife and plunge it pitilessly into private parts. They wait, just as a fearful city and anxious nation waited during those last awful weeks of November 1973.

And waited . . . and waited . . .

BOOK THREE

Thomas Bishop
and
Adam Kenton

TWENTY-ONE

For most of those two final weeks New York was turned upside down in the frantic search for Jay Cooper. Reports came in by the thousands and each one was noted and investigated. He was seen in the observation tower atop the Empire State Building, on subway platforms deep underground, in buses and cabs, theaters and restaurants and supermarkets, at Coney Island and the Cloisters, on bridges and boats and trains, even in church. At least a half dozen of them, ranging from Methodist to Buddhist. None proved accurate. He evidently wasn't sightseeing or traveling locally or viewing shows or eating or praying, as far as anyone knew. Nor was he walking around or sitting in parks or standing on street corners. He apparently wasn't even sleeping.

Every hotel in the city was checked for a Jay Cooper. Young men fitting the description were asked to show identification when they registered. From the Plaza and St. Regis to the welfare traps on the Upper West Side and the bottle cribs on the Bowery, from Washington Heights to Bronxville, the center of Queens to the heart of Brooklyn, all hotels were investigated. Even the rooming houses in each precinct were visited, along with religious and social shelters of every kind. Anything that housed men on a daily or weekly basis was inspected, right down to deserted warehouses along the riverfront and empty buildings in slum areas where homeless men stretched out. Neighborhood clubs were looked into, as were the back rooms of Chinese laundries. Known hoodlum hideouts were rousted, whorehouses raided. Even a carnival tent show near Kennedy Airport that used local talent for geeks and goons was searched. Jay Cooper wasn't to be found.

Within twenty-four hours thousands of prints of Kenton's drawing were made and quickly distributed to bars and restaurants, barbershops and banks, private massage parlors and public baths, anywhere and everywhere a man might go for food and drink or a hundred other needs. The circulars showed a pleasant-faced young man with light hair and a steady eye, a far cry from the menacing pictures of Vincent Mungo. This young man seemed most friendly and charming and obviously incapable of harming anyone. His name was Thomas Bishop, though he was known publicly as Chess Man.

In the following days many hundreds of men were stopped by police on the streets, on public transportation, in parks and sports arenas. All were asked for identification. Those who had none or who acted suspiciously were immediately seized. Their crime was that they resembled Thomas Bishop, or at least were white and not overly ugly. Most were soon released without apology, some were held for further questioning on other matters. Police were in no mood at the moment to hear about civil liberties. Or to act subtly. At the slightest suspicion that he had been spotted, at the merest rumor that he was nearby, they blanketed the area, raided premises, searched homes, accosted strangers, leveled guns at suspects. Word went out to get the job done; excuses and apologies would have to be made afterward, if at all.

Police were visible at the city's major checkpoints: the bus terminals, especially those at Times Square and the George Washington Bridge, the ferry slip for Staten Island, Penn Station and Grand Central Station, the airports, the bridges and tunnels. Roadblocks were set up on all major arteries leading to Long Island and Westchester County. The harbor patrol searched all pleasure craft, the Coast Guard took care of merchant vessels. An international incident was narrowly averted when the captain of a Rumanian cargo ship berthed in the Hudson River threatened to shoot any American who came aboard. Diplomatic fingers quickly reached halfway around the world to Bucharest but the Rumanian government was adamant in its refusal to allow a foreign inspection of its vessel. Finally a Rumanian police official was dispatched to New York, at American expense, and he conducted the examination, print in hand. The result was negative. Bishop was not aboard the *Moldavia*.

All known sex criminals in the city were visited, their homes or rooms checked, on the theory that the madman might be an acquaintance of one or more of them. High police officials recognized that these were not basically sex crimes but they were determined not to overlook any possibility, no matter how remote. Two of the sex offenders were finally held on other serious charges.

Youthful detectives frequented the city's chess parlors, its more popular singles bars, student hangouts and frat houses, lonely-hearts gatherings, partner parties and sexual-encounter sessions—anywhere young men and women might meet. Others checked out the homosexual areas, the private clubs and baths, the gay bars, the truck stops, the pet pits and fist fairs. There was always the chance, according to some police psychiatrists, that Chess Man's derangement stemmed from a strong homosexual identification. Local units warned prostitutes and harassed them off the streets, at least temporarily.

Female detectives were sent to model agencies, to YWCAs and other such hostels, to nurses' quarters and convents, to wherever women congregated without men. A recurring nightmare was that Chess Man, deprived of other outlets for selecting his victims, might go berserk and enter some kind of female facility, where he would turn mass murder into wholesale slaughter.

The police department was taking no chances. Officially the position was to smother any criticism with activity. It was better, the lieutenants told the sergeants who told the rank and file, to overly react than to leave an opening. If they didn't get the madman, and quickly, residents would begin wondering why they had a billion-dollar police force in which men received high pay for semi-skilled work that others in private industry were doing for one-third the cost, and from which those same men retired after twenty years on pensions that were bigger than many New Yorkers' working salaries. Naturally nobody wanted people thinking about such things. Which meant they had to produce, had to get Chess Man fast. It was a political thing, a power play, and the police were caught in the squeeze.

The mob had an even worse problem of credibility. They had contracted to do a job, for which they had received the initial payment. More than three months later they hadn't yet completed the deal. Chess Man was making fools of all of them. Being true businessmen, mob leaders knew that would eventually hurt them where it counted. In the money. Something had to be done.

With the start of the massive manhunt, the mob went to work. In places the police could never go, to people the police would never know, the word was passed. The killer of women was wanted. There must be no refuge for him, no food, no rest. He had to be hounded out of hiding. In the hard underbelly of New York life, in the home of the hustle, in gambling and drugs and loan-sharking, in every racket from the garment district to the union hall, the cry was heard in every part of the jungle. Get him! He had to be found. Alive or dead, the king of the jungle wanted his head.

There was another consideration. The elderly and venerable and generally acclaimed man of most respect had been personally contacted by one of the top men in the police department. His help was needed. In this one, everybody's neck was on the block. For certain concessions grudgingly given pursuant to a successful outcome, Mr. G. had agreed to commit his forces to battle.

No public mention was ever made of the secret meeting of course; no memos were written, no notes kept, no reporters tipped off. Since that day police spokesmen have repeatedly denied any involvement whenever the rumors are revived. But such denial is itself part of an old tradition, almost as old as the temporary mutual-aid pact worked out by two men of power on a bench in a tiny concrete park on Sullivan Street one brisk November morning. More than fifty thousand men from both sides of the coin, police and mob alike, were joined in the search.

Which left some eight million private citizens. In the days following the release of Chess Man's new name and likeness, while police were hauling in hundreds of unlikely suspects and the mob was rousting out dozens of underworld denizens, groups of people chased hapless individuals who were said to be Bishop or were thought to look like him or act like him or talk like him or maybe just walk like him. All that was needed to start vigilante action was a rumor, a scream, a shout. Or sometimes just a word, and someone would be forced to flee for his life. In certain areas hysteria ran high. Several suspects were badly mauled by crowds before being rescued by police. One was dead on arrival at a Queens hospital. His head had been literally crushed with a baseball bat. Youthful, somewhat backward, a stranger to the neighborhood, he was not Chess Man. Nor was the young man in the Bronx, shot as he ran from a screaming woman he had just molested. In all, eight men required hospital treatment due to crowd action during those hectic weeks. None of them was Jay Cooper.

After seven dismembered bodies had been removed from the top floor of a commercial building on Greene Street on the cold crisp morning of November 16, Alex Dimitri stood in a corner of the second-floor loft while his men went through the routine of searching and cataloging everything. There was evidence all over the place, enough to satisfy a dozen TV cop shows. Evidence of the photography hobby, including rolls of film; evidence of the mail drop, including letters addressed to it; evidence of the answering service, of being a recent arrival in New York, of coming from a warmer climate, of being young and average in height and weight, of having light hair, of a beard, of money in the bank, of an institutional past, of a fondness for baloney sandwiches and a liking for chess. And, of course, a passion for mutilation.

What Inspector Dimitri didn't know at that moment was that Bishop had removed all evidence of New Jersey or his new identity. He had vowed to make no more mistakes. In his wallet when he left were documents attesting to the fact that he was Thomas Wayne Brewster. The only thing old in the wallet was a picture of a rather plain woman in a severe dress, a woman whom he believed to be his mother but who looked very much like Margot Rule of Las Vegas.

"You should've called me yesterday," Dimitri growled, trying to control his anger. "You had the name twenty-four hours. Maybe we could've got to him sooner, maybe while he was still here."

Adam Kenton didn't agree and told him so. It was obvious Chess Man had left at least a day earlier and probably more. The bed was cold, there were no fresh food scraps, nothing to eat in the refrigerator. The garbage was several days old. The most recent newspaper was dated Tuesday.

"Today's Friday. If he left Tuesday or Wednesday he had plenty of time before we got onto him. Even yesterday morning would've given him enough time." Kenton shook his head, perplexed. "Something tipped him off, started him running again. But what?"

"Who knew about him from your end?"

"Nobody." Which wasn't quite true as Kenton thought about it. George Homer had known, and probably Mel Brown and Fred Grimes. And some people in California. And he had told Mackenzie and Klemp and Dunlop and John Perrone that he knew who it was, though he hadn't given them the name. Any one of them could have warned Bishop if— Stop it! he told himself. Nobody was in league with the maniac. That was too much even for his paranoia. "Nobody," he repeated softly after a moment. But he resolved to watch Otto Klemp even more closely. And the rest of them too.

"You made a mistake," Dimitri said gruffly, his finger in Kenton's chest. "Don't make any more." He walked away still angry but his mind made up. Nailing the reporter on charges of withholding information would bring only more trouble at a time when he needed good relations with the press. God only knew where the madman would lead him, and a sympathetic press was important. But if it wasn't for that, Dimitri barked to himself on the way to the kitchen, if it wasn't for the goddam power politics all the time he'd nail that bastard's ass to the cross. To the goddam cross! Goddam right he would. Jesus! They almost had him.

The *Post*, New York's afternoon newspaper, was first on the street with the story. Radio and television were already broadcasting the news. Chess Man had been identified as Thomas Bishop and not Vincent Mungo, who presumably had been murdered four months earlier. Bishop had come to New York from Chicago as Jay Cooper. He had left California by way of Los Angeles as Daniel Long. Other aliases in between, if any, were unknown at the moment. Through exhaustive investigation local police, aided by an alert telephone operator, had been able to penetrate the latest disguise and trace Cooper to a house on Greene Street in the Soho area of lower Manhattan. He had apparently vacated it some days earlier. Left behind were the bodies of seven young women, all horribly mutilated. Six of them had been reported missing in the past several weeks. In the apartment were found sections of anatomy removed from the corpses. There was reported evidence of necrophilia and cannibalism.

The papers, though not the earliest broadcasts, mentioned the fact that an investigative reporter for *Newstime* magazine, working independently of the police but with their knowledge and approval, had discovered Chess Man's latest identity and location at about the same time.

By early evening, details of the sensational find had been rounded out and TV news shows ran special reports that showed the house and apartment and third-floor storeroom where the grisly discovery was made. Also shown was the drawing of Thomas Bishop secured from California by *Newstime* journalist Adam Kenton before the actual location of the murder site. The public was asked to note the face and to be on the lookout for such a man. A special police phone number would be operating round the clock.

The news ended with a brief on-the-spot interview with Deputy Inspector Alex Dimitri, who headed up the special task force assigned the job of catching the killer. In reply to a question Dimitri said Chess Man's capture was imminent, now that his identity was known, and implied that the police already were following leads.

In the early-bird edition of the *Daily News*, on the streets by 8 P.M. that Friday evening, the drawing of Bishop's face was on the front page. Next to it was the same face with a full beard, a composite sketched by a police artist and based on the remembered observations of the Greene Street building's owner, an official of a downtown bank and a local shopkeeper. The eyes still gleamed in open friendliness but the face somehow seemed a bit less boyish, a trifle less innocent. The story, on page 3, recounted the finding of the bodies in what the paper chose to call a "house of horror" and went on to tell of the police investigation that had culminated in the near-apprehension of the "Greene Street ghoul."

Adam Kenton's parallel investigation was also mentioned in the body of the story, though few details were given. It was noted, however, that the *Newstime* reporter had actually located Chess Man's residence while police were still searching, and had then called them. Either the private detectives had been talking or the magazine's publicity machinery was grinding into action. Or both.

The New York Times had the most comprehensive coverage of course, including an interview with Kenton in which he told of his assignment to do a cover story on Chess Man. During his inquiry he had come to the conclusion that the homicidal madman was not Vincent Mungo at all but rather Thomas Bishop, whom Mungo was supposed to have killed on the night of his escape from a California institution for the criminally insane. The opposite actually had occurred, and Thomas Bishop had then begun his cross-country reign of terror, arriving in New York on October 15.

Toward the end of the interview Kenton was quoted as saying he would have to conclude that Chess Man was an absolutely brilliant strategist, a consummate chess player who seldom made a mistake. He was also incurably, hopelessly homicidal.

Unlike the police, the journalist did not seem quickly confident that capture was imminent, or even inevitable.

It was two o'clock that afternoon when Kenton, who had finally left Greene Street to Dimitri's men in baggy suits and blue serge, was called upstairs to James Mackenzie's office. News of the discovery was already public knowledge and he was greeted warmly by Mrs. Marsh. Another moment and he was shaking hands with the chairman of Newstime Inc.

Mackenzie looked pleased. The strain of the past weeks seemed to have been lifted from his shoulders, and a certain spirit was again evident in his voice. He indicated a nearby chair as he took his own seat behind the cluttered desk. Plants framed the windows at his back and hung suspended by invisible wire from the ceiling.

"We did it," he said expansively, the exuberance gushing out of him. "We flushed the fox out of his lair. He's on the run now, and the police can take over from here. Meanwhile we get the credit—part of it anyway—and the publicity. And we don't have to worry about Washington accusing us of manipulating the news."

He reached for a gold-fluted box on the desk, opened it and offered a cigar to Kenton, who declined with a shake of the head.

"Of course, we didn't get everything we went after. We don't have Chess Man and the story of the year. We don't even have an exclusive on what happened this morning, except for your account, naturally. On the other hand," said Mackenzie, leaning back in his green brocade chair, "we don't have the threat of political or even criminal charges." He smiled. "In a trade-off, I'd say we came out a good bit ahead. What about you?"

"It's not that simple," said Kenton after a pause. "Everything we wanted is still out there."

The chairman suddenly looked pained. "I don't think I understand."

"Chess Man, Thomas Bishop, is a homicidal killer to the ultimate degree. He won't stop until he is himself killed. He's a robot, an engine of destruction that cannot stop on its own. He's also a genius in some ways, easily the most clever criminal mind America has produced. With our resources, with what I know of him, we still stand the best chance of finding him. He is unique in our time, and I think it's worth any risk. Any risk at all.

"Think of what it would mean if we could pull it off. *Newstime* captures the American Jack the Ripper. *Newstime* captures the most sensational murderer in modern American history. We would be in all the reference books, we'd be talked about a hundred years from now. More important, our circulation would go up like a rocket. We'd sell more copies of those issues with the story than anybody's ever sold before." He took a breath. "All we have to do is find him."

"And the police?" asked Mackenzie.

"I don't think they'll get him. He's too smart, too resourceful. He plans ahead, he doesn't panic. And he doesn't make mistakes. Or hardly any. I got to him because I started thinking like him. The police got there this morning only because he made a mistake with his answering service. But he won't do that again. So all they'll have to work on is luck, which is just a fancy word for coincidence. And I don't believe in coincidence, not that much anyway.

"But I can think like him. He's a television manqué. He's been locked up since he was ten and most of what he knows comes from the tube. It's all flat emotion and extreme behavior and evasive action, but for some strange reason I can think like that myself. A month ago I came to New York, the same as Chess Man. Like him, I had to start from scratch. Learn the terrain. Set the rules. When I determined he wasn't Mungo, when I discovered he was Bishop, it all began to fall into place. I became Bishop. In my mind I moved through the city as he did. I figured out what he would do and how he would do it, where he would go and whom he would see. Finally it led me to where he lived. I didn't miss him by much and I still don't know how he learned there was danger. But I did it once and I can do it again."

Mackenzie turned to the window, his eyes seeming to stare for a long moment at the surrounding plants. He longed to be at his weekend home in Sterling Forest, where he could walk the fields far away from the city's endless decisions. He glanced at his watch. In a few hours he would be in the limousine on his way.

"As you say," he began finally, "it would be worth a great deal to the magazine, to the whole company. I think you're quite right about him. He's unique and will be remembered when the other homicidal minds of our century are long forgotten. Much as Jack the Ripper is remembered today beyond all others.

"But I must concern myself at the moment with the practicality of such a venture. Granted you could find him—and you will admit, Kenton, you will admit that is granting a lot—what about the police reaction? Won't they be watching you closely from now on? We were lucky this time, with that inspector taking a broad view of things. What about the next time? We may not be so lucky. And what about the whole Washington aspect? They'll be back on us, especially after the Nixon editorial."

Kenton leaned forward in his seat, his hand spread on the desk. His voice was one of appeal.

"The police won't bother us because I'll let them know everything I do, now that I got the ear of the top men. If I get to him first they'll give me a crack at his story. I won't hold him, he's much too dangerous even as a prisoner. So we'll have no trouble with them."

"And Washington?" insisted the chairman. "They would love to point to an operation like ours to show they were right all along. What would stop them?"

"They won't know anything about it. If the police don't charge us with anything, Washington can't very well accuse us of manipulating the news. All we're doing is running a parallel investigation, which is legitimate. Only we'll try to come in a little ahead of the cops. If it ends in a tie we'll still get all the glory. We can't really lose."

Mackenzie was not so sure. He had hoped to end the matter while they were still ahead. Yet to walk away now was to leave the challenge unanswered, and he had always been a fighter. Then, too, there was damn little opportunity nowadays to take chances. Real chances, not just paper-money gambles. And his newsman instinct told him Kenton was a man worth gambling on.

The chairman of Newstime fixed his steel-gray eyes on his reporter. "Do it," he said with finality. "But make it good."

John Spanner heard about it that afternoon. He sat in his office a few minutes, dazed. He hadn't expected it, not really, though God knows he had certainly hoped for it long enough. Now here it was at last. His feel for the subtleties of human behavior was as good as ever. And as needed as ever too.

He suddenly felt important again. It didn't matter that the New York reporter hadn't given him any credit; that would come in the magazine story. Those fellows were basically honest and he would be given his due, he was sure of it. From now on he would be a local hero. More important, he would have the respect and attention of his men when he talked to them about the value of the imagination in police work and the gradual piecing together of clues to form a deduction.

Thinking about it, Spanner decided he might not retire after all.

In Forest City, Sheriff James Oates swore softly, though not particularly in bad humor. Earl had just brought him the news that the Willows maniac had been identified in New York as Thomas Bishop and not Vincent Mungo. Which meant John Spanner had been right all along. Damn him and his feelings and his crazy ways! There had to be some Mexican blood in him somewhere, there just had to be.

Oates put down a file he had been reading. At least that explained why Mungo had never been caught. He was dead. And no one was looking for Bishop, so he passed right through. Simple. It answered all the questions. Except nine or ten. Like how could a mental nut whose records said average intelligence and no imagination pull off the slickest crimes of the year, of any year? And then just go on killing, with nobody getting near him? He had fooled everybody, the son of a bitch had fooled *everybody!*

Except John Spanner.

The sheriff picked up the phone and called Hillside.

* * *

Amos Finch took the long way home from his final class, spending an hour in bed with a young lady who was far from ill. At his own door again, he was greeted by the ringing of the phone in his study. It was Lieutenant Spanner with the good news.

Had Finch heard?

He had not.

Afterward they spent some moments congratulating each other. Then, in a more serious vein, they agreed to offer whatever help they could to Adam Kenton in New York if he continued his search for Bishop.

As he replaced the instrument Amos Finch resolved to begin the preliminary work on his *magnum opus,* his life's work. *The Complete Thomas Bishop.* It had a certain ring to it, and decidedly better than *The Complete Vincent Mungo.* Finch could not know at that moment, of course, that the title would have to undergo further changes.

He would start immediately. And none too soon, for he suddenly had the strongest belief that his California Creeper, the only absolutely authentic contemporary genius in his line of work, would not last much longer.

At 6:30 that evening Kenton was interviewed on TV. He told of his search for Chess Man and of his discoveries, or at least as much of the truth as he could tell, as he had done earlier to *The New York Times.*

He was careful to point out that his discovery of Chess Man's real identity had come out of the normal research done on such assignments. When it was suggested that he had done in one month what the police of the country couldn't seem to do in four months, Kenton smiled modestly and praised the vast Newstime resources.

After a suitable pause he went on to note that the New York police had been seriously involved only that one month, and they had cracked the Jay Cooper disguise about the same time he had. Which wasn't at all the same as unmasking the madman as Thomas Bishop, of course, but Kenton didn't mention that.

In his Idaho home Carl Hansun had changed channels till he got his favorite news show, then sat down to watch. He wasn't particularly interested in the sensational revelations about the California homicidal maniac, nor did he pay much attention as Adam Kenton's image flashed on the screen. Senator Stoner was well on his way to power, so the whole Vincent Mungo thing no longer bothered the Boise businessman. He was waiting to hear of more local news, or at least local western news.

He grimaced in remembrance. Twenty years ago they were good men, Don and Johnny. Dependable and ready to do the job right. Straight shooters all the way. He shook his head sadly. Funny what the years could do to a man, how they could change him into somebody else. Someone even friends wouldn't recognize anymore.

That was what happened to Solis and Messick. They had changed, turned into greedy scavengers who knew no loyalty. Animals, no good to anybody.

Carl Hansun shrugged wearily. He wouldn't miss them, not at all. Those years were gone forever.

Henry Baylor heard about Thomas Bishop in his rather cramped institutional office near the Oregon border. Thomas Bishop had killed Vincent Mungo and taken his place. In doing so he had destroyed reputations as well as lives. There would be many more questions now, more probes and scandal. Everything would be reopened, gone over again, this time more thoroughly. It was not a pleasant prospect, not at all.

In his favorite easy chair at home, Henry Baylor sat and thought about things for a long time. Bad enough he had to take the humiliation of being removed and demoted. But he was about to be cast in the spotlight again as the man who let the fiend escape, this time a fiend who had been in his custody for years and who had fooled him completely.

It was, he finally decided, the last straw.

The father of Mary Wells Little had seen the face on television the previous evening, on the news, It belonged to someone named Thomas Bishop. He and not Vincent Mungo had killed all those women, one of whom was Mary Wells Little.

Her father continued to stare into his private vision of hell at this early morning hour. He would not be cheated out of his revenge. No! He still wanted his daughter's killer. Only the name had been changed, and the face he was paying to destroy.

But he would not be cheated.

* * *

The meeting started at 8:30 Saturday morning in police headquarters. In command was Deputy Chief Lloyd Geary, at his side was Alex Dimitri. They faced almost a hundred police officers from captain to sergeant. Most were detectives of various grades. Less than half were from Homicide. The rest came from Robbery and Rape and Vice and Narcotics. Even Juvenile and Administration. The Department was throwing everything it could into the search.

Geary began with a brief background of Thomas Bishop running through the killing of his mother and his years at Willows State Hospital in California. There he grew up on television and learned a lot about the world outside, much of it the wrong kind of thing. He was immensely clever and resourceful. As a boy he had apparently been mistreated by his mother to the point where his mind eventually snapped. Now he was either killing women out of revenge or he was locked into his childhood and killing his mother over and over. Either way it seemed he would not, could not stop by himself. He must be stopped by others. The police. Them.

The pictures were ready. A drawing of Bishop, clean-shaven, and the bearded photo from Daniel Long's California driver's license application. More would be run off during the day. By nightfall all precincts in the city would have enough pictures for local distribution.

Geary closed his remarks with the observation that the Police Commissioner expected a quick end to the reign of terror. Everybody was feeling the heat and nobody liked it. That very morning his own wife had told him to be sure and get the son of a bitch. In thirty-one years of married life, Geary hastily explained, he had never heard his wife use that language.

Alex Dimitri took over and rapidly went through procedures and assignments. Afterward he noted that Bishop had withdrawn $8,000 from the bank, enough money to move around. At least that much, maybe more. Which was a piece of bad luck. On the other hand, it might make him leave the city or even the state. He might already be gone. He had told the bank official he was returning to Chicago. But unless such a move was definitely established, the search would continue.

If Bishop remained in the city without identification he

would soon be caught. The inspector was certain of that. But if he already had another identity he was now using—

Dimitri let the thought hang.

The meeting finally ended at 9:40, after specific assignments had been given out.

The hunt was on.

In his lair across the river the fox lay on the bed, his eyes vacant, his mind blank. Opposite him, a flower print broke the bareness of the white wall. On an end table next to the bed a plastic-covered shade dulled the glare of the lamp. Two wood-backed chairs rested in the far corner, and near the window the polished dresser mirror cleverly gave the small room added dimension.

Bishop noted none of this. His eyes opened and shut automatically but nothing registered. Nor did anything disturb his dormant brain. In truth Bishop was in a trance of his own making, a self-induced semihypnotic state that served to bring all his functional parts back to normal. It was a survival trick he had learned slowly and painfully many years earlier at Willows. Oftentimes when he was confused or frightened or helplessly angry, he would put himself in a kind of stupor where outside stimuli were blocked along with all mental processes. Time briefly stopped for him as his body and mind sought a new equilibrium. Eventually balance would be restored and everything returned to normalcy. In his institutional life it had saved him many times from rash acts that would have brought quick and painful punishment.

This latest trance was triggered by the news of the past twenty-four hours. When he had first heard about it on Friday afternoon he refused to believe such a thing. They simply couldn't have discovered his real identity. Impossible! He was too smart for any of them. Yet there it was, on the TV, in the newspaper. His own name. With a drawing that certainly resembled him. Then by nightfall the license photo from California.

Because of his error he had expected them to get to Jay Cooper and then to the house. Which meant they would also secure a description of him from the landlord. But he assumed they would think him Vincent Mungo. They would show a picture of Mungo to the landlord, and because of the full beard worn by his new tenant and the certainty of the police he would say yes.

Just to be on the safe side, on Thursday evening in his YMCA room Bishop had dyed his hair dark and cut it short, then shaved off much of his beard until only a trim goatee remained. With the heavy horn-rimmed glasses, he looked different enough to cause no suspicion. Now, with a general likeness of his own face everywhere, it was doubly important that he appear as different from it as possible.

What had confused him, what frightened and angered him was their discovery that he was not Vincent Mungo. That was not supposed to happen. He had planned everything so carefully. Vincent Mungo was free, Thomas Bishop was dead. Yet they had found him out. He was no longer invisible. He was Thomas Bishop, son of Caryl Chessman. Everyone knew about him. The only safety he now had was his new identity as Thomas Brewster.

On the Friday late news he learned how he had been discovered. Too shaken to go out for a late paper, already having read the brief story in the afternoon *Post* a dozen times, he relied on the television, his lifelong mentor, to give him whatever knowledge he needed. Huddled in bed, he watched a magazine reporter named Kenton tell of the month-long search for the elusive killer and the series of events that had finally led to Greene Street. He had earlier heard a police inspector say that capture was imminent and they were already following up leads.

Now, as Bishop slowly came out of his hypnotic state on this sunny Saturday morning, his body and mind restored from the stormy emotions that had swept over them, his nerves soothed, he began to evaluate his position and to plan his moves, not as a fox in jeopardy but as the hunter in control again.

He was relatively safe in his new quarters for the moment. The day clerk had paid little attention to him and he had no dealings with anyone else. His money was equally safe, temporarily. But he would soon have to change his residence of course. New York police were checking all hotels, probably even recent apartment rentals. When nothing turned up, somebody might get the idea of asking surrounding towns for help. Even so, they would be looking for those who had registered this past week so he was presumably safe again.

Still, he couldn't afford another mistake. The best plan would be to remain in the Y for about a week and then move to a New York hotel, after the police had finished checking them all. Some of his money would be used up that way but at least it would get him back into the city, where he could continue his work. Nothing could be done in his present town since they would immediately go after the hotels.

There was one other alternative. He could move on, now, this very day. Leave the New York area completely. Go to another city with his money and his knife. He was supposed to keep moving anyway, that was the plan. To be here and then gone, like the wind itself. Unseen, known only by its effects, by what it left behind.

Except there was nowhere left to go. He had come three thousand miles across a hostile continent to New York, to Mecca, where there were more people, more females, than anywhere else. A cramped, spaceless city where anonymity was virtually assured. He could've been safe forever if he hadn't made a dumb error. Bars with women on every block, and around every corner another town. New York was heaven for him, a city of ghouls and demons, and he longed to send them all straight to hell.

Where else would he be in such demand for his specialized skill?

Bishop thought of the places he had been, the things he had seen. None of them compared to New York for what he needed. And the other big towns on the East Coast were obviously just cut-down versions of New York. Only Miami sounded interesting, perhaps because he had once been David Rogers of Florida. He thought he might like to go there someday to see about the women.

The TV was on as always, and when a special news report interrupted the regular programming Bishop turned his eyes and ears to it while his mind held onto a thought.

The Police Commissioner looked out over the cameras. He didn't particularly like a live broadcast at eleven o'clock on a Saturday morning. In point of fact, he didn't particularly like the idea of a news conference at all, especially in such a sensitive matter. But the mayor and city officials had felt it would help allay public fears concerning Chess Man.

A family man himself, the commissioner well understood the emotion and how debilitating it could become. He wished he could somehow dissipate the fear and ease the pain. But only Chess Man's death or capture would do that, and he was unfortunately not in a position to announce either one.

What he could do, however, was bluff a good game and tell New Yorkers that his police had strong leads. Which was not entirely false. They knew, for example, that Thomas Bishop had at least $8,000 on him. If he had no new identification and couldn't put the money in another bank, maybe he would be dumb enough to show it around, and somebody would spot it for the police. Or he could be mugged for it. Maybe even killed. They also knew he might be on his way back to Chicago and out of their immediate responsibility. And of course they finally had his prints as a sure means of identification. In fact, they knew everything about him except where he was.

The Police Commissioner smiled warmly and began the press conference in his most confident manner. . . .

As he listened on the TV to the head of the New York police say there was no place he could hide, Bishop decided on his next move. He would go to Miami for a week and then return to New York where he would live in a hotel. Miami would be better than staying in his room, since the day clerk might become suspicious if he passed by too many times. They had his new name and he had to protect that identity at any cost. Once gone, there would be no need to think of him or even remember him. He would just leave the Y quietly, unnoticed, throwing the room key down a sewer.

An hour later Bishop was on his way to Newark Airport. He was wearing his one set of clothes, his only worldly possessions again. The television set had been left behind. In his pocket were a thousand dollars he had kept out of the bank. He felt a sudden sense of excitement in once again being on the move, and he wondered if his original mistake had been in settling down at all. As much as he had liked the loft, as much as he wanted a place of his own in which to live safe and secure, perhaps he was destined, doomed, to travel endlessly on his eternal quest. Maybe after all the years he was now fit only for that kind of existence. The thought depressed him almost beyond endurance.

At the airport he bought a one-way ticket to Miami

under a fake name. Sometime during the afternoon he was lifted into a shimmering sky by a silver bird that flew southward. Bishop soon found himself relaxed and smiling on his maiden voyage. His only worry was that the silver bird might fly too near the sun.

By Saturday evening Adam Kenton was already well into into the story he was writing on the unveiling of Thomas Bishop. He had just three days to deadline. Mackenzie wanted it in the next issue of course, as did everyone. With John Perrone's blessing he had shelved his article on Senator Stoner, but only for a bit. He intended to have that ready for the following week. To Kenton it represented a one-two punch that would be the high point of his career thus far. The downfall of two invidious men of power. It would rank second only to the Watergate investigative series by Woodward and Bernstein.

Power, as Kenton knew so well, came through fear as much as from publicity. Bishop, or Chess Man, held the power of life and death. In killing indiscriminately he had demonstrated a willingness to use that power to its fullest. Hence the fear, which only increased his hold over others. This was the same principle used in political power, with its built-in system of rewards and punishment. What Kenton railed against was not the existence of that power but its misuse. For him that was Chess Man's ultimate crime. And Stoner's. And that of any leader who flouted the law, or ordered the destruction of a city or the extermination of a people.

Misuse of power. Kenton was always fearful that he would himself be guilty of that if given the chance. And so he ran from any real personal power, and perhaps all responsibility as well. Alone and powerless, he fought the demons in himself by constantly exposing the demons in others, for in truth he saw only a difference in degree between himself and a Stoner or a Nixon. Or even a Chess Man.

Concerning Chess Man, he was pleased about solving the mystery of identification. Certainly John Spanner had helped, and also Amos Finch. But even so, that was only half the problem. Where was the man now? When would he strike again? Kenton believed he had made a bad mistake by not finding his prey in time. Now he had no leads, nothing to go on except his knowledge of the man, his feelings and instinct. He would have to start all over again.

Something within warned him that he was running out of time.

TWENTY-TWO

"Adam?"

The glare from the silent television screen reached out to Doris sitting up in bed, her legs jackknifed under her chin, her eyes looking down at the long darkened form lying next to her.

She kicked her legs out and lay down beside him. "You're going to find Bishop, aren't you?"

"If I can," he whispered. "I practically had him and I let him go. If I had followed my original thought I would've got to him in time. I *should've* got to him in time. It was my fault."

"Why's he killing like that? I mean, what he does to them."

"He's crazy."

"But only to women." She shivered. "How could anyone hate that much?"

"Maybe he thinks he's God."

"God doesn't hate."

Kenton deftly rolled his body onto hers, his arm circling her waist. "How could he?" A low growl. "He made you, didn't he?"

Much later he told Doris he would probably kill Bishop if he could. If he ever got anywhere near him again.

"Is there a chance?" she asked hopefully, her hand on his chest.

"There's always a chance," he answered unconvincingly, his hand resting on the flat of her stomach. He couldn't help thinking what Bishop would do to her body, those breasts, that abdomen. He shuddered. But was Bishop really so very different? He himself had often thought of killing women, especially in his more youthful years. Of torturing them and making them suffer. But that was just fantasy. Just typical male fantasizing.

Wasn't it?

That was Monday night and Kenton had just finished the article on his search for the notorious mass murderer. He had begun in California four months earlier with a story on capital punishment and Caryl Chessman, just about the time that Thomas Bishop had escaped from a state mental institution housing the criminally insane. The journey then took both of them across the country over the next months, finally ending in a run-down building on Greene Street in New York City. Only it wasn't really the end at all. Bishop, Chess Man, had escaped again.

The article would be the lead feature in the next issue, though not the cover story. Chess Man had already been given a cover in the person of Vincent Mungo and reader reaction had been critical, many accusing the magazine of sensationalizing the affair and thereby indirectly condoning his crimes. This criticism of giving undue publicity to a murderer was also repeatedly leveled at network television of course, as had been done the previous year in the coverage of the Charles Manson killings; but once again all such remonstrance seemed to fall on unconcerned ears. The public, as one disgusted critic put it, apparently had the right to know—and know—and know.

None of which bothered Adam Kenton. He had done his job, or at least part of it. Thomas Bishop was the chessman, the madman, the fox. Finally falling asleep that night, Kenton felt he was halfway home.

The next morning he awoke to the news that the celebrated killer of two dozen women had confessed. In the early Tuesday hours of November 20 he had walked into the 24th Precinct on Manhattan's Upper West Side and calmly confessed to the murders. He had killed them all. Los Angeles, Phoenix, El Paso, San Antonio, Houston, New Orleans, Memphis, St. Louis, Chicago, New York. And other places he couldn't remember. Many of them, so many he had lost track. He was a killer. He killed women. A lot of women. He couldn't help it. He was twenty-six years old and he couldn't stop himself. His name was Carl Pandel, Jr.

By 8:30 Kenton was talking to Inspector Dimitri. Pandel was not their man. The poor bastard's wife had committed suicide and he spent half a year in a nuthouse. He had even met and become friendly with Vincent Mungo while there. And he had left his own home in July to come to New York, at just about the time Bishop was escaping from Willows with New York as his destination too. But Carl Pandel was not their man. He didn't kill anyone, certainly not the women.

Kenton quickly again ran through the investigation he had conducted on Pandel, which had cleared him of at least one of the New York murders. And if he didn't kill them all, he didn't kill any. Dimitri reluctantly agreed. The young man had been in an excited state when he confessed. He claimed he needed to be punished—which usually meant psychiatric help was needed rather than punishment. Yet he knew enough about Chess Man's movements to be taken seriously, at first anyway. Nor could any confession be disregarded at the moment, no matter how improbable.

Dimitri sighed wearily. Pandel's confession was only the first; more were expected. It went with the job. But for a while there, his had looked especially promising to the inspector's men.

And Pandel now?

"In Bellevue for observation. They should have word on him by the end of the day. Maybe he just went over the edge a bit, happens a lot to that type."

What type was that?

"A nice young guy. Very quiet, very polite. Maybe too polite, you know? That's always a bad sign."

Kenton laughed. The police mind saw suspicion everywhere. Next to them, real paranoids didn't stand a chance.

He told Dimitri to treat Pandel with care. His father was a very big shot out West and he might not be so polite.

The murder of Don Solis made all the California papers because of his recent publicity in the capital punishment controversy. On Monday Ding had called Kenton in New York to tell him that Solis was dead. He hadn't heard.

"How'd it happen?"

"Dynamite. They wired his car."

"Sounds like mob."

Ding agreed.

"So we'll never know for sure about Caryl Chessman."

"Not from Solis anyway."

Kenton didn't bother to mention how he had originally tied Solis to Bishop. It was too late now anyway. Nor did he bring up the Son of Rapist idea that had seemingly spawned so much truth.

Ding meanwhile congratulated him on finding the madman. At least his true identity, which was more than anyone else had been able to do. Kenton was becoming a hero in California. Even Derek Lavery went around calling him one of the best. And taking credit for the whole thing of course.

Afterward Kenton wondered if the Solis killing had anything to do with Senator Stoner's capital punishment campaign. It wasn't a Chessman freak who got him or even a death-penalty hater. Dynamite usually meant the mob. But how could they be connected to Stoner through Solis? If anything, he had helped Stoner. Kenton soon decided there was no connection between the two, nothing he could use in his story on the senator.

In San Diego the murders of John Messick and Dory Schuman made only the local papers. It was a professional job obviously, an execution. Messick had been involved in any number of small-time illegal operations. Maybe he got in somebody's way. Or got a little too greedy and had to be taken out. Police weren't overly concerned and had no reason to look beyond their own areas. Homicide by persons unknown was the finding, and the case kept open in police files. Several years later a Sunday-supplement feature on the double slaying would trace the car that might have been used by the killers to a Los Angeles man, Peter "Pistol Pete" Mello. The car's license number had been found in the slain woman's handbag, scribbled on a scrap of paper. Mello, an ex-con with mob links, disappeared at the time and was never heard of again.

At the office on Tuesday morning Adam Kenton accepted delivery of several cartons of books and household items sent by the stringers from Red Bluff. They had bought everything left from the last home of Sara Bishop and her boy in Justin. Sara's papers and writings had been sent earlier of course. Now here were the final belongings of the mother and son in two corrugated boxes bound with baling cord.

Kenton cut the cord and slowly removed the contents piece by piece. He examined each item, leafed through each book. It was all junk, worthless. Yet soon all of it would be valuable because of a woman's tragic life and a boy's hopeless descent into madness. The hard-bitten investigative reporter was suddenly overcome with anguish that such a thing could happen. His crusted heart filled with despair as his hands grasped a worn leather strap, the hide frayed from use, the stamped name faded almost beyond recognition: Strongboy.

When he had finished his examination, he carefully placed the cartons on the floor against a wall. They would be given eventually to Amos Finch in Berkeley, most of the stuff anyway. Finch was collecting Chess Man material and would no doubt write a book on him. In which he, Kenton, would hopefully occupy a prominent place.

Kenton was not himself a collector, except of papers perhaps, and he fully intended to keep Sara Bishop's pages about her life. Unless her son wanted them. They belonged to him.

And after him?

After Bishop there was only a blind and paralyzed paternal grandmother in Texas who had never seen the boy. He had already checked.

There was no one else. Thomas Bishop had no known brothers or sisters. And of course no children of his own.

He was the last of a line.

A line of warrior kings, thought Kenton in his own paranoiac fantasy. A noble and savage breed. And very rare.

Thank God, said his logical mind.

Amen, said the rest of him.

On that same morning John Perrone phoned near Spokane, Washington, after having taken several days to decide that he owed the call to his close friend and mentor. In a few moments he was speaking to Samuel Rintelcane himself. Though almost a generation apart in age, the two men shared an ideological viewpoint that encompassed not only political and economic outlooks but social morality as well. It was Sam Rintelcane who had given the young Perrone his first boost up the ladder. And it was the same man who had once hoped that John Perrone would marry his daughter. It was not to be.

Now Perrone had to tell his good friend the bad news. Senator Stoner, his son-in-law, was about to be the subject of an investigative piece in *Newstime* that would probably crush any hopes for national prominence, if not do worse. He was apparently involved in some illegal business deals, among other things. There was a tape of him talking about himself and others, evidently made by a mistress. It was easily enough to warrant a further investigation of the senator by state governmental agencies.

Perrone said he would, naturally, try to keep the sexual aspects out of the story, in regard for Helena and the family, but as for the rest—

Rintelcane understood. His son-in-law had been stupid and had been caught. If *Newstime* didn't publish the facts, someone else would. He was grateful that Perrone had told him in advance. Did he have permission to prepare his daughter for the shock?

Of course. And Helena should use her judgment about letting the senator know ahead of publication. Whatever she decided was all right.

It was a sad moment and both men wondered how the revelations would affect the senator's wife. She had always been passive and unassuming, content to live in her husband's shadow. She was not a strong woman, or so they believed.

Neither one knew how much Helena Stoner had already withstood in her sixteen years of marriage to a profligate and inordinately ambitious man. Or just how strong she really was behind her quiet demeanor.

By evening a preliminary report was in on Carl Pandel, Jr. He evidently wasn't dangerous or even crazy, at least by New York standards. Doctors at Bellevue suggested he was still blaming himself for his wife's suicide two years earlier. They expected him to snap out of it sooner or later. Until then, his was a relatively harmless delusion except for the trouble it caused others. He was, they found, incapable of hurting anyone. He loved animals and children and, though shy, enjoyed normal relationships with his male friends.

They intended to hold him for another week or so, just to make certain of their findings. But his confession that he was the much-sought mass murderer of women was obviously based on total fantasy.

The Bellevue doctors further suggested that he be gently admonished and dismissed should his harmless delusion cause him again to confess to such killings. It was, they stressed, not an unusual occurrence for a person suffering irreconcilable guilt over the death of a loved one. In time those feelings would disappear and with them would go the delusion and other manifestations.

Kenton looked over the report given him by the inspector. It sounded reasonable to him, and just about what he had expected.

"I hope this hasn't taken you from the real pursuit," he said laconically.

Dimitri grunted in response. It had been five days since their fearsome discovery on Greene Street, and still no trace of Chess Man. Not a word, a whisper, a warning. Nothing. He had disappeared again. The inspector said as much.

"Not disappeared," corrected Kenton, "covered himself, like the chameleon."

"Covered himself with what?"

"With another identity."

Dimitri wheezed. How many identities could one man have? And how did he get them all? By the time police found one he was into another. It was uncanny, unnatural.

"Got any suggestions?" he asked Kenton, exasperated.

No suggestions. No ideas. At least not for anyone's ears at the moment. He had written the Chess Man piece and was now working on Stoner. That was crucial. In between he tried to see things the way Bishop would. He had a new name, that much was certain. Probably a New York name. How did he get it? From local outlets. Didn't Fred Grimes say this was the center for the fake-identity racket? Or he could've stolen somebody's wallet at the beach. In November? So a steam bath, or a gym, or a sex orgy. Maybe he was a homosexual. Easy enough to get a wallet that way. Or he could've gone to a cemetery and just picked out a name. Or the death notices in local papers. Or gossip in a bar. Or half a hundred ways a clever man could figure out. And whatever else he was, Thomas Bishop was a clever man. So clever he seemed to be able to get whatever he needed.

But how did he get physical possession if it wasn't bought or stolen? He would need an address but not a mail drop again. Too risky. Had to be where he lived, except there was no place for him to live in the city. Not with any degree of safety. So where would he go? What would he do? Kenton didn't know. He didn't have the answers, not yet anyway.

"No suggestions," he said quietly to Dimitri.

Dean Gardner returned to Washington on Wednesday from a Republican policy committee meeting in California. Many matters awaited his attention, among them the *Newstime* editorial calling for the President to resign. The magazine was not the first to do so, nor would it be the last; of that Gardner was certain. Yet it was a particularly severe blow to the administration because of *Newstime*'s prestige and its traditional Republican identification. The President was angry and, thought Gardner, for good reason. It was a vicious stab in the back and indicative of the moral decay sweeping the country. When people of similar interests didn't stick together, something was radically wrong.

Especially galling to Dean Gardner was the fact that his little power play via Ned Robbins hadn't worked. He wasn't accustomed to failure. The Washington political scene did not pay off for failure, only success. He would quickly line up a dozen newspaper and magazine endorsements of the administration, to repair some of the damage. And he would get back at *Newstime* for its treachery. By God, he would! He'd investigate every one of the bastards who ran it, right down to the color of their underwear. Everyone working on the maniac story too; that had started the whole thing. There must be plenty they were doing wrong. Everybody did wrong!

He would call Treasury. The IRS had a big field force in New York. So did the FBI, and a few other agencies he could think of for that kind of work. All would be pleased to accommodate the President of the United States. Pleased or else.

Carl Hansun listened as his contact in New York told him of his son. The boy was in Bellevue Hospital's psychiatric ward but was due to be released in a day or two on the signature of a private psychiatrist, whom he was to visit. That was already in the works. He wanted to continue living in New York and had no intentions of returning to Idaho at the present time. In fact, he was distressed that his family knew of his confession. Apparently it was an aberration caused by lingering guilt over his wife's death. Such things, the contact had been told, often happen to people but disappear in time.

Wasn't there any way to get him home?

Evidently not at the moment.

Anything he needed?

Nothing beyond the usual. There would be the added doctor and lawyer fees of course. But the boy seemed in good spirits. He had his apartment and his friends and he looked forward to being with them again.

Carl Hansun was worried about his son. He didn't understand how anyone could confess to killing women. Who would want to kill them? Without women, where was the joy of life? He had been in the army and he had seen what life without them did to men. It brutalized them, took away the civilized part of their nature, turned them into animals. Without women to give softness and beauty to life, what good was it all?

Now his own son confessed to killing them. That meant he had thought about it. Didn't it?

Or maybe he still just felt guilty about his wife, like the doctors said. But nobody blamed him. The girl was moody, high-strung. She was so insecure she needed constant reassurance and attention, more than any man could give. She always felt betrayed since no man could live entirely for her. Hansun had warned his son. The girl was trouble. Her life was torment and she would make his life the same. But the boy loved her, wanted her, needed her. He wouldn't listen. They got married and two years later she was dead and he was locked up in California, where his father couldn't even visit him. But he finally got the boy home again, and eventually his mind had cleared.

Now this.

Hansun couldn't understand it. Where did guilt feelings come from? He never felt guilty even when he was wrong. Maybe the boy was just too sensitive and would grow out of it. He thought of his younger son. Nothing sensitive about him, he'd fight tigers. Just like his father. Had a good head for business too.

Meanwhile his people in New York were taking care of things. He was a power in the Northwest but New York was different; somebody might get curious about him. He hoped it wouldn't be necessary to go there. The boy should come home anyway. What the hell could he do in New York he couldn't do in Idaho?

Sometime late that afternoon a man in Miami returned to his beach locker to find his wallet missing. Nothing else had been taken—not his expensive ring or his electronic watch. There was little money in the wallet; he knew better of course. Still, it had all his identification. He cursed loudly as he banged the locker door shut.

By Friday, Adam Kenton was well into his exposé of State Senator Jonathan Stoner of California. He expected to be finished by Monday's deadline. Once the story became public, he was sure the newspapers would pick it up and continue the investigation. He had no personal animosity toward Stoner—they had never met—but he regarded the senator as unfit for public office because he had abused his power and privileges. A miniature White House, Kenton had written somewhere in the article; and he intended to hound all such men out of office. He didn't regard that as an abuse of *his* power.

Two days earlier the top executive of the Newstime communications combine had met briefly in the twenty-fifth floor boardroom and voted to divest themselves of all interests in the Western Holding Company. A forthcoming magazine piece on a California state senator would name one of Western's operations as buying political favors and would call for an investigation. The staff writer of the article knew of the corporate investments and had recommended immediate and total divestiture.

To protect their vital concern in a huge future source of wood pulp, an equal amount of equity would be purchased in Western Holding through Crane-Morris, a Colorado-based mining group controlled by Globe Packaging, Midwest packer of foodstuffs. Globe was itself a joint venture of Great Lakes Shipping and the Trinity Foundation. Three of the five-member Trinity board of directors were Newstime executives, including James Mackenzie. And Great Lakes Shipping, a Delaware corporation, was owned outright by James Mackenzie's wife's family.

The meeting lasted only fifteen minutes, after which several members repaired to the executive dining room. Martin Dunlop was not among them. He was chairing a discussion at the Columbia University School of Journalism on the opportunities for investigative reporting.

Before he went fishing on Saturday, John Spanner read of his nemesis in the latest issue of *Newstime*. He found himself mentioned a number of times in the early part of the article. Kenton had given him full credit for his deductions and surmises; he had seen through some of Bishop's incredible plot. But not all of it, nowhere near all of it. As Kenton fitted the pieces together, as the various parts of the puzzle took shape, the complexity slowly became evident. The sheer brilliance of the mind behind the scheme was staggering. Even at that early stage all the moves had already been planned.

As Spanner read on he began to see Thomas Bishop, the maddened child who had killed his mother, growing to young manhood, still in pain, still insane. Only by then he had learned to conceal his homicidal urges, to control his emotions. He had fooled everybody, all the doctors. And after his escape, the police too. Even him. Lieutenant John Spanner, fooled by a twenty-five-year-old mental patient who had spent almost his entire life behind walls. And who just incidentally was the most imaginative and resourceful mass murderer of modern times, as Kenton stated in the article.

Spanner closed the magazine. He didn't feel bad at all. Not really. He had been up against the best.

What it had needed finally was someone not so set in police ways, someone with equal imagination, to work it out. Adam Kenton had done it, he had crashed through and almost got the killer of women.

Almost.

The one word that stood between success and failure.

In truth, Spanner didn't give the New York police much of a chance. They were casting for trout in a stream that held a shark. And he had strong doubts about Kenton doing any better. Bishop had made mistakes he wouldn't be likely to make again. Not unless—

There was one flaw in Bishop's planning, as Spanner saw it. His ego, the same monstrous ego of all such maniacal minds. Spanner had come across it before in his own police work and had occasionally been able to use it against his prey. Perhaps Kenton could do the same. Or by now Bishop might be so sure of himself he would try anything, risk anything.

The lieutenant refused to dwell on the implications of such a thought.

Over the weekend the Chess Man piece in *Newstime* was read as well by others who were involved in the search, or had been once. In his Berkeley home Amos Finch was delighted with Kenton's progress thus far. The man had made some imaginative moves to get at the truth, moves Finch himself could have made, to be sure, with the proper information and resources. But he was not an envious man. Having finally decided that his latest and greatest crank artist must be caught, Finch waited anxiously. He wished only that Bishop could be captured alive. It would be like finding a living dinosaur or a creature from another galaxy. The knowledge gained from such an encounter, should Bishop talk, would be of great benefit to all, and not least to Amos Finch, who would be writing the definitive study of the man's life and deeds. But he knew better than to expect the impossible.

In Los Angeles, Ding thought the reporting superb, which was only natural since he had started the whole thing with Kenton back in July when they worked on the Caryl Chessman story. He sometimes found himself wishing he had been chosen for the assignment—it was a reporter's dream. But he was strictly the California type, wouldn't know how to operate in New York and wasn't about to try.

Near the Oregon border Dr. Baylor read of Thomas Bishop without emotion. Having tendered his resignation to the proper authorities, he was no longer involved. In six short weeks he and his wife would be free to leave the second-rate institution, the wretched town, the uncomfortable house. They would travel and enjoy life again, meet new people. The world was a big place, and Henry Baylor had his fill of mental defectives and criminal minds. In the future he would deal only with normal people who had minor neuroses. That would be the extent of his private practice.

Meanwhile he naturally wished success to the police and all those concerned with the apprehension of Bishop. Personally, he didn't think the madman would ever be caught.

If anything, he expected Bishop finally to kill himself, or allow himself to be killed—which amounted to the same thing—in one last grandiose public display of alienation and contempt. What the authorities didn't seem to understand was that his present course of action was self-destructive as well. Degeneration was taking place and he would wind down. It was only a question of time. No one was totally alienated from his own species, no matter how bizarre the conduct. That unconscious thread of species survival that ran through all humans was Bishop's Achilles' heel and would finally be his undoing, even if nothing else intervened.

Dr. Baylor was certain of that. It was what eventually stopped all true mass murderers, from a Hitler to a Bishop. Drove them to destruction or irrational madness leading to the same thing. The degenerative process, which was cumulative and could not be controlled. A species could not kill its own kind indefinitely and indiscriminately. That was abhorrent to nature. Which was why national leaders in wartime had to tell citizens that the enemy was not human. They were fiends, devils, demons, gooks, savages. Anything but human. But even then the reaction set in sooner or later.

In the matter of individual mass murderers Baylor found the evidence overwhelming. He knew, for example, who Jack the Ripper was and why he suddenly stopped his horrific slaughter of women. The murders stopped because the degenerative process finally overcame him after an incredibly satanic slaying, and he committed suicide. Weighted his pockets with stones and jumped in the Thames River, where his decomposed body was found on December 31, 1888, some seven weeks after the last murder.

The name of Jack the Ripper was Montague John Druitt.

Baylor even knew why he had killed women. His father left a large estate to three daughters instead of to him, forcing him to teach school, which he hated. And his mother went insane and he believed he was following in her footsteps. Inheriting nothing from his father and only insanity from his mother, blaming all his misfortune on women but not being able to touch his mother or sisters, he turned to other, more accessible women, women of the streets. Each murder became more horrible, each mutilation more gruesome, until he lost control entirely with the body of Mary Kelly. Self-destruction followed.

Dr. Baylor recognized that different cycles were required for degeneration to take over. For Jack the Ripper it had been perhaps half a dozen women, for Thomas Bishop many more than that. But the end was the same for all. None could escape. Nor would Bishop. His time, as Baylor knew, was running out.

Unfortunately it was coming too late to restore the doctor's career.

In Miami a young man with dark hair and a goatee read of himself in a national magazine. It was not a pleasant experience for it brought back terrible memories of the kind that filled his nightmares. Afterward he sat a long time in thought, protected from the burning sun by a hat and beach umbrella.

He wondered about the reporter. The man was no fool, not like the others. He was clever, a good hunter. But was he also a good fox? A hunter should know how it felt to be on the other side. He knew. He was hunted and was himself the hunter. That made him the best. The other could be only second best. Still, that was more than anyone else. Thinking about that, he slowly began to develop a feeling of kinship with the reporter. Maybe, he told himself, they had something in common.

He wondered if Adam Kenton played chess.

Sheriff James Oates thought he should've been mentioned in the article. Didn't he start on the murder investigation the very first day same as John Spanner? And didn't he listen to Spanner's crazy ideas when no one else would? He spent months following Mungo—*Bishop*—all over California. He knew as much about the man as anyone did. It wasn't fair that Spanner got all the credit. He was just a local lawman with no ambition. He didn't want to be a state senator. Or the governor. So the credit meant nothing to him. Why waste it?

Oates was jealous. Publicity on a national scale could've helped his political chances. There were some people who thought he might do well running for office. This could have given him a push. And he really was in charge of the search for the maniac for most of those early months. It was really all his responsibility.

His responsibility.

Oates had a sudden thought. At least they didn't say anything bad about him in the article. And that was something good.

On Sunday evening Helena Rintelcane Stoner told her husband that he was going to be the subject of a damaging story in *Newstime* the following week. She had learned of it from her father. Apparently an investigative reporter had uncovered illegal business dealings. The story could seriously hurt his career.

Stoner was wild with anger. It was all lies, invented by his political enemies. Lies and distortions and false accusations without a shred of evidence. He had done nothing wrong, certainly no more than any other politician in looking out for the people's interests. His general honesty was above reproach. It was big business that was after him. Big business and the power brokers in the East. They couldn't buy him so they would try to break him. His enemies at home too. They were all in it, all of them. They wanted to destroy him.

After he had calmed down, the senator tried to figure the angles. Obviously someone was out to get him. But who? He was certainly friendly to business and all the major vested interests; he supported all the right causes, he didn't interfere with underworld concerns, he was liked by the Midwest power sources and now by the East, both of whom regarded him as a winner. He had not stepped on any big toes and was not involved in any big scandals.

It made no sense. Here he was shooting for the sky and somebody was trying to shoot him down. His only real enemies were archliberals and all the other crazies and one-worlders and welfare-staters. But their power was spread out, they didn't usually concentrate it on a single subject. The whole thing was crazy. Who would feed information about him to a reporter? And *Newstime,* for chrissake? Somebody was kidding. *Newstime* was as much a part of big business as he was.

Before she retired for the night the senator's wife, an honorable woman, told her husband that she would of course stand by him. She did not bother to mention that she came from a family of quality and good breeding. Or that she had known of the senator's various women for years, knew all about his sordid little affairs, his brief trips and overnight business meetings, his reputation as a sexual athlete. Not a woman of excess energy, she intended to keep her marriage vows because loyalty and patience were virtues of the well bred.

For his part Stoner saw his wife as an absolute angel, a woman filled with all the kindness and generosity of spirit that a man needed in life, and certainly much too good for him.

Whenever he was mad at her he called her a dumb Jew bitch.

He didn't know how he had missed it earlier. Probably in his anxiety over the story he hadn't looked any further after the ending. But there it was, in a separate section by itself, on light-green paper with a black border.

Seated now at the wobbly table in his small cheerless room, Bishop began reading the pages of a woman's tearful review of her life, written by his mother sixteen years before, scribbled on sheets of paper and put away between the pages of a book written by his father that same year, the year he was nine and still living with his mother, whom he loved dearly.

As he read of her youthful dreams and the things she later endured, he saw his mother bending over the silent boy, caressing him, her soft hands smoothing his troubled features, her face smiling at him, her eyes alive with love, her mouth calming him with words of reassurance. She had loved him so very much and had always taken such good care of him. He was the luckiest boy in the whole world to have a mother like her.

He read the pages many times that night. After a while he took out his little wallet and looked at the picture of his mother in her severe dress, tall and stately and firm. He kept the picture next to the pages as he read on and on.

Alex Dimitri was in no mood to be crossed on this late November afternoon. It had been ten days since Greene Street. Ten days of the most intensive manhunt the city had ever seen, and still no sign of Chess Man. Despite countless searchings and raids and swoops, despite a thorough shaking up of neighborhoods, Thomas Bishop was still free. Which didn't look good for Alex Dimitri. He had just been chewed out by Lloyd Geary, who had himself been put on the carpet by the Police Commissioner, who naturally had heard from the mayor's office just that very morning.

The *Newstime* story hadn't helped any.

Personally, Dimitri liked it. He was mentioned favorably and his task force singled out as a possible solution. But overall the Department seemed no better than any other police group in the country, and perhaps worse. None of them had been able to get Chess Man. But now his face was known, his real face. And his real name. He had no one helping him or hiding him. What was holding things up? Why wasn't he caught? People were beginning to wonder.

On the other hand, he hadn't killed any more women in the ten days. That meant they were at least keeping him bottled up.

Maybe.

Dimitri wet his lips nervously. Suppose they found another apartment with seven more bodies hacked to pieces. God forbid! New York would panic. There'd be vigilantes on every corner. People would die. Not to mention a big shake-up at headquarters. He'd probably be forced to retire, or maybe given a post at the other end of Staten Island. All things considered, it wasn't a very bright future.

Now, to round things out on this Monday afternoon, it seemed that the damn magazine reporter was working on another story somewhere and couldn't be disturbed at the present time. *Couldn't be disturbed!* Dimitri would've liked to wring his fool neck. All he really wanted was to ask Kenton if he thought Bishop might have skipped town. A man answering his description had left a note on a plane to Miami saying he was Chess Man and he was starting a new life, leaving behind New York and all the killing.

By Tuesday the issue with the inside story of Thomas Bishop had sold out. With no cover picture, with just the banner across the top screaming "Chess Man," the magazine had sold more copies than any issue in several years. Which meant Chess Man had captured the imagination of the public. Or was it the media hype that had captured the public? John Perrone didn't care. Either way, he had been right about going after the madman. Now, if Kenton could only come up with the same miracle again, this time nailing the killer for good, they might all be in line for some awards.

That morning Kenton had turned in the Stoner piece. Perrone found it factual and convincing. It examined Stoner's land acquisition, naming names and dates. It went into other business dealings, again with facts and figures. Finally, it discussed some of Stoner's personal views as they might affect his public performance and hinted that a tape existed of the senator airing many of his own thoughts. Perrone edited out a few sexual references, and the piece was soon on its way to publication in the next issue. Because of Stoner's national look the story was certain to create a sensation of sorts, following in the wake of the Chess Man bell ringer. Adam Kenton was becoming a power in investigative journalism.

On the seventh floor, meanwhile, Kenton was already back on Bishop. His one fear during the past week had been that his prey would be somehow cornered and killed by police. He didn't really believe it could happen but he knew the gods sometimes played strange tricks. Now they were giving him another chance, his last one.

Where to begin?

With Bishop's pattern; that was the only constant. His pattern was to seek new identities and to get each one on his own. All he needed to start accumulating papers was a birth certificate, and all he needed for that was a name and date and place of birth. Alive or dead? Dead would be easier and much safer. Somebody born and died in New York. A male around his age. He could get the name and place of birth from an obituary column. How about the date of birth? Vital statistics records were closed to the general public. And he couldn't very well go to the relatives of the deceased. Too risky.

What about a live person like Jay Cooper of Chicago? No good. That could mean anywhere in the country for the place of birth; but he needed it fast, so it had to be local.

Suppose he had come to New York with other identities besides that of Jay Cooper? Suppose he had identities from every city he passed through?

Kenton squirmed in his chair, annoyed at the thought. In that case, he had to admit, they didn't stand a chance in hell. Not until Bishop made another big mistake.

Would he?

No, said Kenton firmly, knowing the man he had never met.

On that same day in Miami a young man removed a wallet from a cabana at a private beach by posing as a waiter. The wallet belonged to an equally young man. No one saw the thief or remembered the waiter.

It came to Kenton that night at a most embarrassing moment. He jumped up from the bed, suddenly excited in a different way. Doris became so angry she was almost dressed before he could talk her out of leaving the hotel right then. All she knew was that he kept repeating something about the hospital.

By Wednesday Senator Stoner had called everybody he knew and pulled every string he could. He even talked to John Perrone himself. Nothing worked. The article was on the presses; in a few days it would be on the newsstands.

Stoner was furious. He would of course deny everything, at least everything illegal. For the rest, people were broadminded these days. They would forgive some indiscretions on the part of their elected leaders. Sure, look at John Kennedy and his women. And Mendel Rivers and his drinking. There were hundreds of examples. Maybe he could blunt some of the attack by being open and honest, maybe even turn it to his advantage. Naturally he'd be open and honest only about those things they would find out anyway.

It was really very simple. All they had to do was call the hospitals in the city to find out if anyone had been asking about birth dates of males born there. Not city agencies or any kind of organizations, only individuals. Only strangers. Asking hospital record rooms about dates of birth. Just of males born between twenty and thirty years ago.

Mel Brown would work on it, using some of his people. Shouldn't take too long.

Just New York City?

Maybe Long Island and Westchester and northern New Jersey, to make sure.

That would take a bit longer.

* * *

Kenton assured Inspector Dimitri that it didn't matter if Chess Man had left the city. He would be back. Where else could he find anything like New York, with all its women and its places to hide? He'd never find that anywhere else, not in this country anyway. For what he was hunting, New York was the biggest national game preserve there was.

But did Kenton think he was gone?

No.

That meant he could be turning another apartment into a slaughterhouse while they were talking.

Kenton hesitated, thinking of Greene Street.

Well?

Yes, he could be. Were any women missing?

No more than usual, said Dimitri.

Both men thought of it at the same time.

Suppose he was killing the usual?

"Some ideas work out and some don't."

Mel Brown's research team had called every public and private hospital in six metropolitan counties. They had come up with nothing. No record of unauthorized requests for birth-date information, no recollection of strangers wanting any such information.

Wednesday was Mrs. Majurski's day off. Wednesdays and Sundays. She liked a split week, made the work seem less tiring somehow. Her married daughter kept telling her it still amounted to five days every week in that hospital, but she didn't mind. At least she was around people. Her husband was dead, her two sons lived away, the daughter had children of her own. Mrs. Majurski lived alone with a giant tiger tabby cat and a heating pad that was always on when she was home. Which was most nights and all day Wednesdays and Sundays.

On Thursday morning her co-worker in the hospital records office told her of the call from New York. The woman was thrilled. Imagine! *Newstime* magazine calling them.

Mrs. Majurski immediately remembered Father Foley. But they didn't mean a priest, did they? He wanted the date of a boy born in 1946, which was between twenty and thirty years ago. But a priest? She decided to ring Father Foley and tell him about the magazine, maybe he could see what they wanted. Now what did he say? St.

John's on the Boulevard. She dialed the rectory, asked to speak to Father Foley.

There was no Father Foley at St. John's. Mrs. Majurski prided herself on her memory, hardly ever made a mistake. He had said St. John's. She was sure of it. How strange.

The clerk at Margaret Hague Maternity Hospital had answered truthfully the previous day when asked about unauthorized requests for information. She hadn't even thought of the priest who had called weeks earlier. A strong Catholic in a strong Catholic town, she regarded all priests as authorized. They were like police and firemen. She wouldn't dream of giving out information to strangers.

The call to Mel Brown as head of research came in the early afternoon, a Mrs. Majurski from Christ Hospital in Jersey City. He listened a moment and then hurriedly patched the call through to Adam Kenton, asking the woman to begin again.

She had given information on a hospital birth to a local priest over the phone, but now she discovered there was no such priest. She called St. John's parish earlier that day, thinking Father Foley might want to get in touch with their magazine. But he didn't exist—

When did she talk to this Foley?

About a month ago.

And the baby's name he was interested in?

Brewster. Thomas Wayne Brewster. She had just looked it up again.

Date of birth?

May 3, 1946.

Kenton sucked in his breath. Bishop was born in 1948. Just two years apart. Close enough.

He thanked the woman, told her it was a criminal-investigation story they were working on. He'd keep her informed.

Just one more thing, she said quickly.

Yes?

She thought she should mention that Thomas Wayne Brewster was a Negro.

Kenton's eyes closed in despair.

A Negro?

She had noticed it at the time because there weren't that many Negro Catholic families in the forties.

Afterward Mel Brown tried to console him.

"It was a good try."

"Not good enough."

"He'll slip up again. Then you'll get him."

"Then the police will get him."

"So stay on their good side."

"It's hard," said Kenton, "and getting harder."

Brown agreed. "You think this Foley was our man?"

"It fits. Except the kid was black."

"Maybe he didn't know."

Kenton's ears opened.

"Maybe he didn't know before he called the hospital or he wouldn't have bothered."

"So the woman told him."

"Did she say that?"

A minute later Kenton was again talking to Mrs. Majurski. He was sorry to bother her, but did she tell Father Foley that the baby was Negro? It was very important.

She did not.

Was she sure?

Positive. He didn't ask and besides, she didn't even notice it until afterward.

Kenton then called a well-placed political contact in Newark. He needed two questions asked of Vital Statistics in Jersey City. Fast.

In twenty minutes he got his two answers. Thomas Wayne Brewster died on September 1, 1949, at age three. Curiously, a birth certificate was issued to Thomas Wayne Brewster on October 26, 1973.

The certificate was mailed to that name at the address given, 654 Bergen Avenue in Jersey City.

Mel Brown quickly determined that the address was the Bergen Avenue YMCA, near Journal Square. With a shaking hand Kenton dialed the Y and asked for Thomas Wayne Brewster's room. Seconds later he was told that Mr. Brewster was not registered.

But he had been registered there?

Oh yes.

When was his last day?

He had paid to the twenty-fifth.

This was the twenty-ninth.

When had the desk clerk last seen him?

Who was asking?

Kenton hung up.

It was Bishop, he was sure of that. He had found his man again. And missed him again, this time by four days. But it might as well have been four years. Slowly he smoked a cigarette. The phone rang twice; he didn't answer. For the first time he began to smell defeat. He was going to lose Bishop, he knew that now. There would be no more chances.

When he finished the cigarette he dialed downtown.

"Inspector Dimitri."

By six o'clock that evening Thomas Brewster's former room at the Jersey City YMCA had been searched and the desk clerk questioned. He had no recollection of the man and was certain he hadn't seen him in weeks or he would remember. Brewster had paid a month's rent in advance. He had not returned the room key when the month was up. The cleaning personnel said the bed hadn't been slept in during that time, except for several nights a few weeks back.

Upon reflection the desk clerk did remember a letter Brewster had received at the very beginning of his stay. He hadn't noticed the sender's name or the return address. Since that day he had not seen the man. He had a vague impression of a beard but that was all. He could not positively identify the license photo of Daniel Long as being Thomas Brewster.

The letter had to be the birth certificate. Brewster received no other mail at the Y. Fingerprints in the room matched those known to belong to the maniacal woman slayer.

Chess Man's latest identity had been discovered.

To no avail. Whether he was Bishop or Brewster or the devil himself, the trail was cold. Even worse, it told police that he had secured a back-up position long before needed. He was obviously taking no chances. Which meant he had any number of them. And probably a different identity to go with each.

Police naturally wanted the discovery kept secret in the hope that Chess Man would use the Brewster name elsewhere, but they were already too late. Someone in the local Vital Statistics office had told the *Jersey Journal* about a corpse getting a birth certificate. And Adam Kenton had called his contact at the *Daily News* right after he talked to Dimitri. He didn't intend that his efforts be lost in the subsequent police investigation. Especially since he didn't think he would ever get close to Chess Man again—if indeed he had ever been close at all.

By late evening the news was being broadcast across the nation. Stories in both New York morning papers included mention of Adam Kenton as having once again unmasked the homicidal madman. Primarily because of the continuing and increasingly dramatic Washington findings, investigative journalism was the year's rage, and Kenton was rapidly becoming a favorite of the New York media.

Inspector Dimitri was furious of course. Possessing the police mentality, he believed that as much as possible should be kept secret from as many as possible for as long as possible. In the matter of Chess Man, that meant everything. If he had his way the public would know nothing at all about such affairs. Which would leave the authorities free to do their job without interference. Since he didn't have his way he tried his best to be friendly with the press, never knowing when he might need their support. But he didn't really trust them, any of them. Here he was doing all the worrying about Chess Man, having all the responsibility, and a lousy goddam reporter was getting all the credit. Just because he got there first.

But he had to admit Kenton was good. A reporter with the skills of a detective. Unfortunately, what he needed at the moment were a few detectives with the skills of a detective.

Friday newspapers around the country were again featuring the infamous Chess Man. He was considered hot copy and good for extra sales. Sometime after three o'clock that afternoon Bishop bought a paper in Miami. As always, he delighted in reading about himself but this time his delight was tempered with concern. He had worked hard to become Thomas Brewster and now it was useless, wiped out. They were getting close to him, or so it seemed.

He sat at the small counter in the downtown bus station, a young man in cotton slacks and a sport shirt opened at the throat. His winter clothes were in his hotel room and his casual dress in the Miami sunshine occasioned no special interest. He smiled as the woman behind the counter drew near.

"More coffee, please," he said politely.

To an observer the pleasant-faced youth would not have

seemed out of place in a city of easy charm and informal manner. He drank his coffee and read his newspaper and calmly hid his insanity.

Only his eyes showed his force of concentration.

The Brewster discovery was a blow; he hadn't been prepared for it. At once he had lost all his money and the identity he had fashioned with such great care. Nothing was left except the two new wallets he had secured for future use. At least they gave him an identity.

Nevertheless there was danger. He had no history to go with the new names; they belonged to other men. He would not be able to withstand investigation. And with no money he would not be able to move around.

Bishop liked Miami, had stayed two weeks instead of just the one. Now he was doubly glad he had. In New York he might already have been caught as Thomas Brewster.

He thought of remaining in Miami but quickly decided it was impractical. The city was too open, even though women were plentiful. There was no anonymity as in New York.

Though distressed at his misfortune, Bishop felt rested and relaxed and ready to be about his father's business again. He would return to New York with his new names and get a cheap place somewhere with the money he had left while he sought more.

He paid for his coffee, showering the woman with another smile. He would leave for home that very day. But first he would have to say goodbye to Miami, just in case he never came back.

If he wasn't loved, at least he was needed.

Much later on the bus, his eyes drooping, his body relaxed, a hand draped over the armrest, Bishop fell asleep and dreamed of things beyond his control. He fought bravely, as always.

Somewhere in Georgia, a train blew midnight and November turned to December.

TWENTY-THREE

Adam Kenton was dreaming. It was Saturday morning and in his dream he rose from his bed to answer the phone.

"George Homer here. Sorry to bother you like this but I've just had an idea about our boy. Got a minute?"

The dream was real.

"Sure," Kenton grumped, forcing his eyes open. "Go ahead."

"By now I think I've read mostly everything there is on Caryl Chessman. His psychology is fairly obvious, as you probably know; the swaggering and braggadocio typical of someone insecure around other people. In his case, particularly women. And I had this thought, you see, that it might have come from some sexual inadequacy. You even hinted at that in a Chessman article some time back."

Kenton remembered Ding's idea about Chessman being impotent. "Go on," he said quietly.

"Suppose we leak a story to the press that Caryl Chessman couldn't possibly have been Thomas Bishop's father. That he was physically incapable of achieving parenthood."

"What'll it get us?"

"It just might get us Bishop. He glows in the fact that he is Chessman's son. Suppose we take that fact away from him."

Kenton saw what Homer meant. Bishop obviously adored Chessman, and being his son gave him the psychological crutch he needed. If that were suddenly taken away from him, he might cave in.

"If Chessman wasn't his father, who was?"

"Harry Owens, a nobody. Killed in a robbery by one of his own gang. That should bring Bishop's spirits down a bit. It's Chessman that keeps him hyped up, that makes his whole insane view of the world work for him. He's avenging his father. But if his father was just a small-time thief who did nothing, it makes him out to be nothing too."

It might just work. At the least it would fill him with self-doubt. As the son of Sara and Harry Owens, he was a nobody again. Even worse, all his killing would have been in vain.

"One thing sure," said Kenton. "When he reads it he'll blow skyhigh."

Homer agreed.

"He'll get in touch with you somehow. He will be forced to, no matter what the danger. Like all mass murderers, he has a compulsion to keep the record straight. That way, when he's caught he can justify his behavior."

"You think he wants to be caught?"

"They all do. They kill because they're alienated; the murders are an extreme expression of their extreme alienation. But they don't really want to be alienated; no one does. So unconsciously they hope to get caught, which is the only way to end their unbearable isolation."

Homer paused a moment.

"He'll get to you," he repeated ominously, "one way or another."

That was the plan, then. If Kenton couldn't get to Bishop, he'd make Bishop come to him. And in the process, when Bishop learned he was not Caryl Chessman's son, maybe he'd come apart.

"What do you think?" asked Homer.

Kenton thought he was right.

The news from Florida reached New York at six o'clock that evening. Less than an hour earlier a twenty-eight-year-old Miami woman had been found murdered in her apartment in the city's northwest section. Murdered and mutilated. The body—what was left of it—had been discovered by a neighbor and the building's superintendent after repeated calls during the day had proved futile. Miami police suspected the gruesome find might be the work of the celebrated New York woman killer because of the condition of the body. That, and the two words smeared in blood on the refrigerator door. "Chess Man."

"I just heard," said Kenton when he finally got through to Dimitri at the 13th Precinct. "You think it's him?"

The inspector blew into a large handkerchief. He was

coming down with something he hoped might be triple pneumonia.

"How could it be?" he answered sarcastically after a moment. "You assured me he didn't leave town."

"Nobody's perfect."

"You telling me."

"So what's your idea?"

"I don't have any."

Kenton wondered if he should mention the plan to lure Chess Man into the open; a little help would be a good thing. But he quickly decided against it. Dimitri might try to stop him.

"It could just be a diversion," he said softly, and the man on the other end grunted.

"Some diversion."

"This is where he belongs and he knows it," continued Kenton, almost adding: It's where he wants to be caught. But Dimitri would just laugh at him and he wasn't in the mood for that right now. Too many things to think about. Like how much danger he was walking into, assuming Bishop went for the bait. The more he worried, the stronger became his conviction. It would work.

The *Newstime* investigator sat quietly in his hotel room, racing his mind through all the ways Chess Man could get in touch with him. The phone, a letter, a third person, maybe even a secret meeting. Would he go? Yes, with a gun in his pocket. Maybe even two guns. But he'd go, damn right he would. It was too late to stop now and he had come too far.

The phone rang at 6:30 and Kenton had a flash of Thomas Bishop calling him. He stared at the instrument for a few seconds. Then he slowly reached out for it.

"Who?"

Not his prey, not yet.

He talked to his contact at the *Daily News,* giving him the story about Bishop not being Caryl Chessman's son. Yes, it was legitimate in the sense that there was some indication that Chessman might have been impotent. But he needed it handled as an interview, that was important. He had to be listed as the source. And his residence was to be included too, the St. Moritz.

Fifteen minutes later the story was settled. It would make the late finals, meaning the Sunday-morning editions. "Chess Man Not Son of Chessman." Who said so? *News-*

time expert Adam Kenton, who had been tracking the killer for months and knew more about him than anyone else. Which wasn't hard since no one really knew anything about him, though some people once thought they did.

Now only he knew it all. Except where the man was and what he would do next.

The big land cruiser rolled into the Port Authority bus terminal at 9:30, right on schedule. In the rear of the bus Bishop stared out the window until most of the passengers were gone. Good to be back? He wasn't sure. In a way New York had everything he needed but now there was danger as well. Adam Kenton had bulled his way through Vincent Mungo and through Jay Cooper and through Thomas Brewster. The man was an absolute bloodhound.

Bishop finally sauntered out of the silent bus and across the lobby crowded with weekend travelers.

There was only one way to beat a bloodhound and every fox knew it. He was doing it right now.

Doubling back.

The call from Fred Grimes came at 10:45. He had just heard from one of his mob sources that a man bearing a resemblance to Bishop's description had been seen in the Port Authority terminal earlier in the evening. The spotter just noted the general likeness and thought nothing more about it since the man's hair was dark rather than light and he wore a goatee. And of course a great many men fit the category of medium height and build.

On a whim the spotter checked the bus the young man had been seen leaving moments before.

"Guess where it came from," Grimes whispered.

"Only one place it could be," answered Kenton. "Miami."

By the time the man had raced after the suspect he was swallowed up in the crowd.

Bishop had decided that the safest place for him would be the Upper West Side, where he had stayed on his first night in New York. There were seemingly hundreds of small hotels in the area, many of them run-down and accustomed to renting rooms by the hour with no attention paid to the occupants. He rode the subway uptown and got off at 96th and Broadway. The streets were a Saturday night fever of Latin music and great masses of people, all apparently bent on having a good time.

In a drugstore he bought a bottle of the lightest blond hair dye and a cream rinse, a razor and shaving soap, some small cotton balls and a pair of rose-tinted sunglasses with delicate frames. He also picked up a ten-dollar vinyl travel bag into which he put his purchases. At a nearby discount outlet he paid for a tiny portable radio and some extra batteries. These went into the black bag too. Soon afterward he got a room for the night in a grubby little hotel off Broadway in the nineties. The place was murky and cheap and he signed some fictitious name. No one cared.

Upstairs he listened to music as he set about altering his appearance once again. He assumed that by now the police would conclude he had dyed his hair. The natural choice would be black. Or he might be remembered from the Miami bus station as a young man with dark hair who had bought a ticket to New York City on the night of that killing. Or even by the driver or other passengers. A man with dark hair and a goatee. That would have to go too. Along with the thick glasses. All of it, everything.

First he washed his hair in the small sink behind the door. A cracked mirror hung above the sink and he kept looking at his progress in the dim light of the one ceiling bulb. It took several washings to rinse out the dark coloring, even with the chemical preparation. While his hair dried he shaved off his goatee. Eventually he applied the bleaching mixture, following directions carefully so it would be as light a blond as possible.

He again was wearing his New York clothes, chiefly the suede leather jacket and the heavy workboots with the rubber soles and heels. He now had only a pair of corduroy pants, which he found adequate for the weather, and a wool shirt. Everything else, including the Florida clothes he had bought, had been left in his room in Miami. But not his hunter's cap. That had come with him and was resting on the hook that held his jacket.

Sometime near midnight he wrapped a towel around his head and went to sleep. He couldn't go out and he had no television. He didn't know what else to do.

At about that time Inspector Dimitri was in his command post at the precinct, surrounded by members of the special task force. He had been personally told of the man spotted in the bus terminal, a voice on the phone giving him the information. He knew of course about the mob helping in the search, though he wasn't aware of any of the arrangements. He also knew there was a contract on Chess Man. Obviously the mob had missed him this time, and to show good faith they were letting the police in on their discovery.

No matter. Only the information counted. Was it reliable? Dimitri thought it fit the facts pretty well. And Kenton had said Chess Man would return to New York, didn't he? Which was right before he said Chess Man hadn't left at all. Still, if that was really their man in Miami, and if he had really killed the woman there, it made good sense to get out right away. Miami was no New York—far from it. There weren't a million holes for him to drop into, or crawl out of, whenever he felt in a killing mood.

Alex Dimitri believed Chess Man was back in New York and had been seen.

"It looks like he's back in town," he told his men. "This time we won't miss him, I don't care how many names he's using. According to our information"—he didn't say from where—"he now has dark hair and a goatee. Which should help us, since he doesn't know he was seen. Forget light hair, forget beards. Tell all your contacts what we're looking for. That's it."

He turned to Captain Olson, his second-in-command. "We'll keep his new look quiet as long as we can. Even a few days might be enough to flush him out."

At 10:30 Sunday morning Bishop went out for a breakfast of a cheese omelette, toast and coffee. It was a sunny day of little wind, and the young man in the warm jacket walked several extra blocks just for the exercise. He felt alive again in the deadening anonymity of New York.

His hair was now a whitish blond that seemed a good match for his fair skin and smooth face. Two weeks in the Florida sunshine had produced no appreciable tan since he had kept himself covered most of the time. When he checked in the mirror before leaving he was well pleased with the different appearance he had created. Wearing his new delicately framed sunglasses, he bore little resemblance to the dark man with the goatee.

He could think of only one further refinement to complete his changeover. On the way home he bought an eye pencil with which to give himself a noticeable scar running down a cheek along the mouth lines to the jawbone. His description, as he well knew, contained no mention of facial scars.

He also picked up a copy of the *Sunday News.*

John Perrone liked to play tennis on Sunday mornings at his home in Rye, unless he was nursing a hangover from a Saturday night party. This was one of those Sundays, and so he stayed in bed reading the papers instead. First the *Times,* as befitted the managing editor of a top newsweekly. By 11:30 he was starting on the *News.* He never got past page 3.

There it was staring him in the face. A headline saying he was not Caryl Chessman's son. He never was and never could be Chessman's son because Caryl Chessman had been impotent.

Impotent!

Bishop was beyond anger. They were trying to take away his very reason for living. Make a mockery of his father, a liar of his mother. Trying to make people believe his real father was a common thief, a *nobody.* A man who did nothing with his life. A man no one cared about, no one missed. They were saying *he* was nothing because his father was nothing.

They?

Who were they?

Adam Kenton.

Bishop read the interview again. Caryl Chessman had been impotent and therefore couldn't have raped Sara Bishop. She had made up the story for reasons of her own. Perhaps she was going mad herself, there were indications of that. She had the boy by Harry Owens, and after he was killed in Los Angeles she moved north. Eventually the boy went mad as well. But Chessman had nothing to do with any of it, not with the mother or the boy. He never even knew they existed. Nor did they know of him until Sara Bishop got it into her head that she had been raped by Chessman, which she apparently told the boy at some point. But he was really the son of Harry Owens and all his killing was in vain. What was more, he knew it.

Lies! Lies!

Bishop threw the paper aside. He was shocked by the accusations regarding his mother. She had loved him dearly and would never lie to him. He was Caryl Chessman's son and always would be.

Even worse was the statement that he was acting falsely. Bishop felt hurt and insulted. Over the past weeks he had developed a certain respect for the *Newstime* investigative reporter. Now he saw how foolish he had been to think that any newsman could treat him fairly. They were jealous of him, all of them, envious because he was doing the impossible. Adam Kenton was as bad as the rest of them. Worse! He knew more so he should know better.

Bishop lay on the bed like a stone, unmoving, his eyes closed, his mind locked in confused thought. He'd show Kenton. He'd show them all. What did they know? He was his father's son. He was the demon hunter.

He would give them a sign by which they might know him. Something they would remember forever.

John Perrone finally got Adam Kenton at 1:15 at the hotel. He had been calling for hours, where had Kenton gone? For a walk in Central Park. On Sunday morning? It's the best time, the park is empty, the air is clear. Besides, it's afternoon. Perrone should try it sometime, get out there and commune with nature. Anyway, what was on his mind?

Plenty. And it all had to do with the interview in the *News.*

"What was the idea?"

"What idea?"

"Saying Chessman was impotent. You were the one who first reported that the lunatic was his son, for chrissake."

"I reported that the lunatic *thought* he was Chessman's son. There's a big difference, you know."

"Not that much once the police found out it could be true."

"I don't believe any of it myself."

"Why not?"

"Take Vincent Mungo. His mother said she was raped, told her family. And it supposedly happened in the time and place that Chessman was operating. So now the police say he did it. But there's no real proof she was raped. No police report at the time, no doctor's examination. Just her word. It could as easily have been a lover who left when she got pregnant."

"And Thomas Bishop?"

"All we have is Sara Bishop's writing years later. No dates, no specifics. Maybe she imagined the whole thing, or made it up for some reason. If you read her words carefully, it begins to sound like a romantic fantasy in an otherwise dreary existence."

John Perrone was perplexed. "How could you have written about Chessman's son if the man was impotent? That doesn't make sense."

"I don't think he was impotent."

"Then why say it?"

"Because I need something to get Bishop so angry he'll have to show himself, something that will make him take chances." Kenton lowered his voice to a whisper. "I've run out of miracles, don't you see?"

The managing editor saw. "If Bishop does start coming apart," he said, his voice equally low, "you know who he'll be coming after."

"Of course," said Kenton. "That's exactly what I'm counting on."

The impromptu meeting in the inspector's office began at four o'clock. He wasn't in the best of moods as he stared at the *Newstime* reporter and Fred Grimes, who Kenton had insisted be present.

"Do you have any idea of the danger," asked Dimitri gravely, "any idea at all?" His eyes rested on Grimes for a moment. "And you, Fred, I'm surprised you let him do this. You know what could happen."

"Fred knew nothing about it," said Kenton matter-of-factly. "I told him after you called me."

"Then what's he doing here?"

"Let's say he's representing the *Newstime* management. I wanted all of us to be clear on what I'm trying to do so there'd be no misunderstanding. It's obvious we can't get to Bishop again through his identities, like we did with Jay Cooper and Thomas Brewster. I'm sure he's not using mail drops or getting mail wherever he's living. It's too dangerous now, and he doesn't need it anymore. I think he has enough new names for a while, probably from the cities he was in before New York. Or maybe from Miami."

"We're still not sure he was there."

"I'm sure. But it's not worth asking Miami police to check all missing wallets for weeks back. There'd be hundreds of them. The same goes for all the big towns he's been in."

"If he had other papers when he came here, why'd he get the Brewster ID right away?"

"Because all the others were out-of-state, far away. He needed something local that wouldn't cause suspicion, that would make him a member of the community, so to speak. Remember, you were looking for somebody from California. The only way he could've got a local ID was from someone he met in another state who lived here. But apparently he wasn't that lucky, so he had to get one fast."

Dimitri grunted. It made sense.

"When we got to Brewster, Bishop ran out of time. He couldn't get another local since the mail was too dangerous, so he had to fall back on the ones from other cities. Or maybe he had none and that's why he went to Miami."

"Or maybe," said Grimes in reflection, "he was getting papers on other local names the same time as Brewster."

"That too," conceded Kenton.

"So he's got other names now," growled Dimitri. "What's that have to do with the interview you gave about Chessman not being his father?"

"Everything. With his new identities there's no way we can get to him, so I'm trying to make him come to us. To me. He's too smart to be caught in a police trap but I have no connection with the police. To him I'm probably just a nosy reporter who's been writing about him for a long time. He read that first piece about Chessman back in July and probably everything since. When he reads what I say now he'll find a way to me. His anger will make him do it."

"That's what worries me," said Dimitri gruffly. "He might try to kill you."

"I don't think so. He'll want to explain, to have me set the record straight. I'm no personal threat to him."

"Neither were the women."

"Evidently he thought so."

"Still does," Grimes pointed out.

Dimitri studied his nails for a moment. There was really nothing he could do about it; the paper was already out. He would try to protect the damn fool of course, but anything that happened was his own fault. His own stupid fault. Who did he think he was? Superman?

"You'll have a bodyguard," said the inspector. "Round the clock."

Kenton shook his head vigorously. "No bodyguard, that's out. I don't want him scared off."

"A tail, then."

"Just so I don't see them."

"Is there anything else you would like?" Dimitri asked with exaggerated politeness. "Anything we might've missed?"

Kenton glanced over at Fred Grimes, then returned his gaze to Alex Dimitri. He smiled pleasantly but his manner was determined. "If I do flush him out, I want your word that your men will not immediately kill him."

"What makes you think they would?"

The reporter shrugged. "In every city the police have vowed to kill him on sight. New York is no different. I understand the feeling. A wounded animal like that is too dangerous to live."

"Then why do you want him kept alive?" asked the inspector suspiciously.

"Right now he's the biggest story around. I've worked hard to get near him and I want everything he has to say. That's my job."

After another examination of his nails Dimitri agreed. "If it's at all possible," he added swiftly.

There were no further demands.

"You think it'll be soon?"

"Tuesday's the fourth," said Kenton by way of an answer.

"What's December fourth?"

"Five months since Bishop's escape. He might want to celebrate."

They didn't understand.

"Five months," said Kenton softly, "completes the pentagram. In mystical lore once the holy pentagram is sealed after a series of sacrificial killings, any further discovery is impossible. After Tuesday, don't you see, Thomas Bishop will be free forever."

There was a strained silence.

Finally somebody cleared his throat. Dimitri: "You're not serious."

"Why not?" said Kenton with a defensive shrug. "In

matters of great madness anything's possible. You seem to forget that in many ancient cultures madness was synonymous with magic. Even today in some South American groups, demented people are considered the true magicians of the tribe. They are thought to possess a 'special understanding' of things hidden to others."

"But Bishop?" The voice was incredulous.

"Don't you think he has magic? His hideous desires, his sexual sadism, his sheer invisibility. All are far beyond the normal range. What is magic but a supernatural power over natural forces? Bishop's absolute madness gives him this kind of absolute power. And if that isn't real magic, what is?"

Nobody answered him.

"God forgive us," intoned Kenton slowly, "but the Thomas Bishops have become the true magicians of *our* tribe."

At 7:30 that evening, washing down a hamburger with lemon soda at a Broadway stand, his blond hair framing a face marred by an ugly scar, Kenton's magician came to a sudden realization concerning what he must do. Of course, that was it! He continued to stare at the three women in the corner booth, obviously good friends. They had given him the answer. A superstitious man, he regarded that as a sign.

An hour later the early-bird editions were on the streets. Both morning papers mentioned Adam Kenton's latest startling revelation about Chess Man. In the *News* an editorial demanded a review of the whole insanity-defense issue. *The New York Times* was content to report the possibility that Thomas Bishop might not be the son of Caryl Chessman, as had been generally believed. With copies of both papers under his arm Bishop checked into another seedy hotel, this time in the high eighties off Broadway. Again he received no undue notice as he paid for one night, careful to show only a few dollars.

In his room he intended to read of himself and then make the final preparations for his plan. The section he needed from the Manhattan Yellow Pages was already in his bag, filched from a phone booth. He also had a few pads and some pencils. The rest he would get in the morning.

Meanwhile he simply had to control his mounting excitement. He would soon show Adam Kenton and all of New York that he was indeed who he claimed to be, the son of his almighty father, come down from the heavens to rout his enemies.

Horrific images of destruction flashed across his disordered mind and he calmly accepted them all as reasonable and natural.

It was 9:30 before Inspector Alex Dimitri finally got home to Queens. He didn't like Sunday work, and lately it seemed he had been doing a lot of it. His wife didn't much care for it either. Traditional people, they believed Sunday was supposed to be spent with one's family in relaxation. As it happened, the eldest daughter worked in Manhattan and lived in a hotel for women, another was engaged and the third away at college, so Dimitri hardly ever got to see them anymore. But much of the blame was his, for they were often around on weekends. There was one son, also in college.

As he settled down in his favorite chair with the evening newspaper, the father again wished his children hadn't grown up so fast. He missed the years when there was always youthful noise in the house, and he and his wife Evelyn would often talk of those days. For the hundredth time he silently vowed to stop all the Sunday and late-night work and stay home more with his own.

Just as soon as he cleaned up the Chess Man thing. Just that, and he'd have plenty of time.

At ten o'clock Adam Kenton stormed out of Doris Quinn's fashionable apartment on East 77th Street. They had quarreled over his affection for her, or rather the lack of it. She had wanted more than he was prepared to give—an old story to Kenton. Over the years he had been with many women, most of whom sooner or later presented him with escalating demands. When he suggested that everything for him was temporary and held no meaning beyond the moment, women invariably became hurt, angry, resentful. He couldn't understand it. Having no sense of permanency, he distrusted all declarations of undying love or eternal allegiance. They seemed foolish and insincere to him. But most of all he disliked anyone who couldn't enjoy the pleasures of the moment, who always sought assurances for the next hour or the next day or the rest of life itself. He had no such guarantees to give.

In truth, he didn't himself know what the next moment would bring to his existence. That he had no emotional life was obvious even to him but he didn't know how to change the condition, since he felt nothing for people. Nor did he particularly want to change. His satisfaction came from power, from being around it, involved with it. Women, largely powerless, didn't normally enter that consideration. They gave him no satisfaction beyond their company when needed. For him they were essentially harmless creatures of little consequence in the scheme of things.

He couldn't understand how Chess Man could go around wanting to kill them, wasting all his energy and purpose in seeking their destruction. His view of women, thought Kenton, was hopelessly distorted.

In Rye the streets were generally deserted by 11 P.M. For most of its residents, hardworking and affluent, Sunday night was a time to gather strength for the workweek ahead. For John Perrone on this late-night evening it was also a time of deep foreboding. Try as he would he couldn't shake the conviction that irreconcilable tragedy was imminent. It had to do with Adam Kenton's plan to snare the demented killer, or at least establish some communication with him. But it would lead instead to acts of madness. Madness!

The managing editor had good reason to trust his present sense of doom. Many times such intuitive feelings had been proved correct. Though not overly superstitious or even religious, he had been reluctantly forced by fact to accept the phenomenon of precognition—if not in specific detail, then at least in outline. A practical man, willing to use every tool, Perrone wasn't about to deny his own experience. Oftentimes such feelings worked and that was all he needed to know.

At the moment he also needed something to take his mind off the foreboding, something violent and visceral and gory that would ultimately lull him to sleep. In *TV Guide* he found two possibilities, *The Texas Chain-Saw Massacre* and the Eleven O'Clock Evening News. He chose the news.

* * *

By 11:30 Kenton had downed six or seven Scotch-and-waters and felt reasonably relaxed. He weaved out of the English pub near Doris Quinn's house and piled into a cab. Some twenty minutes later he was in his rooms at the St. Moritz. Another few minutes and he was ready for bed, his mind dulled by drink.

Further uptown a young man in a cheap hotel left his room to use the pay phone in the hall for the tenth time.

Kenton was struggling with the covers when he heard the first ring. He grumbled and decided not to answer. At the fourth insistent ring he let out a curse and grabbed for the instrument.

"Who's that?" he yelled into the mouthpiece. And immediately burped.

No one answered him.

Annoyed, he repeated the question. Even louder this time.

A voice politely asked if he was Adam Kenton.

"Yes!"

"Mr. Kenton? I've been trying to reach you all evening. My name is Thomas Bishop. I have been reading the things you've written about me and my father . . ."

Though trained as a reporter, with ten years on the firing line of instant emergencies and a young lifetime of quick decisions and fast movement, all Kenton could remember of the brief one-sided conversation was that he would be hearing from Chess Man again very soon. And so would the rest of the world.

Six minutes later a lonely lion in the nearby Central Park Zoo roared a midnight challenge and it was December 3.

TWENTY-FOUR

Bishop left his hotel room before eight o'clock in the morning. He had much to do in the next few hours and an early start was vital. After a quick breakfast he boarded a crosstown bus on 86th Street, which took him through Central Park to the East Side. He transferred at Lexington Avenue to one going downtown and got off at 64th Street. On the next corner was his first stop, the Barbizon Hotel for Women. Fixing his face in a wide smile of good fellowship, he entered the lobby and turned left to the front desk.

His cousin was coming in from California for a few months and he wanted her to stay at a safe place like the Barbizon, what with all the terrible things happening in the city nowadays. She insisted on an upper floor, for a view. How high—

The desk clerk was most helpful, pointing out that the building rose twenty stories, though residence rooms were available only on the first eighteen floors. Yes, there was a swimming pool of course. Also a health club and sun terraces. And for maximum security, all elevators were attended at all hours. His cousin would find it quite safe and most convenient.

Another half dozen quick questions told Bishop everything he needed to know. He thanked the man and walked back through the busy lobby to the street where he rejoined the working throng.

In his room the previous evening he had found three midtown hotels listed in the Yellow Pages as being exclusively for women. There were undoubtedly others in the city, he had told himself at the time, but he wanted something centrally located, something that would receive wide public attention. That was important. He intended to create a sensation and he expected everyone to be made aware of it. He would show them a vision of hell itself so that all might know his true identity. Like his father, he was a god among men. His divine mission would never end. Nor would he.

A few minutes' walk down Lexington Avenue brought him to the Ashley at 61st near Park Avenue. Fourteen floors of women. He smiled and asked questions of the kindly clerk.

Four blocks farther down was the last such stop, the Allerton House at 57th and Lexington. Seventeen stories, a small lobby brightly lit and easily crowded. Bishop didn't stay long.

Afterward he picked up some telegram forms at a Western Union office.

By 10 A.M. he was back on the West Side. In a discount clothing chain he bought a cloth coat and print dress, a button-down sweater, two brightly colored scarves, and a pair each of women's gloves, shoes and stockings. They were for his sister, too sick to go out. The cashier, knowing the area, chewed her gum and took his money. Next door he selected some makeup—lipstick, eye shadow and liner, rouge and powder. Also a hair brush and a pair of cheap gold earrings. The clerk looked at the scar on his cheek and turned away.

The last thing he bought on the way home was a full blond wig.

In his room again, Bishop carefully made himself into a woman. He shaved his legs and put on the stockings, then walked around in the wide-heeled shoes to get used to them. He slipped into the dress, finally managing to zip up the back. The sweater went over the dress. Trying on the cloth coat, he was satisfied that it covered the dress length. The scarves would lend a bit of color to his intentionally subdued outfit.

Next he sat at the sink with the cracked mirror and applied the eye makeup, after washing his face of the scar and giving himself an extra-close shave. Then some coloring on his cheeks with the rouge, a fine layer of powder to smooth over any facial roughness, and a generous smear of lipstick, which he expertly drew on his full lips. Lastly came the blond wig, fitting tightly over his own hair brushed smooth and swept straight back. Earrings completed the startling transformation.

Afterward Bishop examined himself scrupulously in the mirror. He was pleased with his new appearance. In a quick walk across a cavernous lobby to an elevator, he would fool unconcerned eyes. Especially if the lobby were dimly lit. Which it was.

He had already made his choice of hotels.

Another ten minutes of admiring himself brought no further improvement and he turned to his final packing. Into the shoulder bag went his portable radio and extra batteries, the hair brush and second scarf, the telegram forms and pads and pencils, and all the makeup and shaving stuff. Finally his post-mortem knife. There was no more room and nothing else to take. All his own clothes would be left behind except for the hunter's cap. He

stuffed that in the bag too, just in case. That was it, all
done. The new sunglasses and gloves would be worn.

He was ready for instant immortality.

A few minutes before noon Bishop left his squalid
room without a goodbye glance. To him it was just another
stopover in a lifetime of one-night stands. As always and
forever, he would not be coming back.

In the murky hallway he passed another resident, who
soon stared after the blonde with cunning eyes. Downstairs the wino behind the desk wondered where she had
come from. She looked a helluva lot better than the usual
run of hookers who paraded around the area. Either that
or he was into the sauce a little heavy this morning.

Outside, Bishop quickly got a cab on Broadway, the
driver braking smoothly for the trim blonde. She gave her
destination in a timorous schoolgirlish voice and he turned
left on 86th Street. As he gunned his cab through the park
he stole smoldering glances at his passenger in the rear-
view mirror.

At a distance Bishop looked striking. Even from a few
feet away the lithe figure appeared desirable. Average in
height, the body was slim, the legs shapely. But the best
part was the face; soft, feminine, even sexually alluring
with its shadowed eyes, high cheekbones and pouting lips.

In truth Bishop found his latest disguise exciting. More
than that, he found the thought delicious. He would vanquish his enemies by turning their own weapons against
them. Like a fox in the guise of a hound, he would become
one of them in order to gain access to their castle. Once
inside he would reveal his true nature and wreak his vengeance on all within. He would lay waste to the castle and
leave it in ruins.

His plan was to start at the top floor, room by room,
woman by woman, working his way downward, floor by
floor. He would announce himself at each door in his
girlish voice, a member of the hotel staff with a telegram.
Brought to their rooms through the courtesy of the management, a nice gesture. Unsuspecting, they would open
their doors.

Working quietly, taking his time, he would go from one
to another. Not all would be home, or answer his knock,
or be alone—in which case he'd announce his mistake,
the supposed telegram in his hand. It was really for some-

one else, the right room number but the floor below. Sorry for the inconvenience.

But many would answer and be alone, would open their doors and smile at him, reach out or even let him in. A great many of them. And why not? They were in a hotel for women. Safe, secure, protected. That was what they were paying for. Danger was elsewhere, someplace else in another part of town.

But coming closer.

He got out of the cab at 62nd Street and Lexington Avenue, giving the driver a large tip and receiving a last lascivious look in return. He would walk the rest of the way, just around the next corner actually. Then no one would see him entering the hotel, or at least pay any attention to him.

Coming closer.

With his powdered face and blond wig, his slim figure and soft clothes, his stylish shoes and gloves, the travel case slung over his left shoulder, Bishop walked down Lexington Avenue to 61st and made a right turn into the peaceful block.

Closer.

Past moneyed stores and expensive houses he walked, passing shoppers and chauffeurs, office workers on their lunch hour and women of independent means.

Close.

The red fabric canopy was just ahead of him. He steeled his eyes, fired up his warmest smile and added an exuberant bounce to his bearing. He was the picture of young womanhood, poised, assured, self-confident. The kind that was always noticed but never suspected.

Now with a final rhythmic clicking of heels against pavement, she entered through the glass doors and continued onward into the lobby of the internationally famous Ashley Hotel for women.

It had been a bad night all around for Adam Kenton. He was sure he didn't sleep more than two or three hours. Because of his drinking he had missed some of what Thomas Bishop had said to him, missed it or instantly forgot it. Not that Bishop had revealed anything specific about his plans; of that Kenton was positive. But still he wanted every word said, every pause and inflection. That was his livelihood and this was the biggest story of his life.

He immediately called Dimitri but couldn't get him. Even inspectors had to sleep sometime, to be with their families. The message would be given to him. When? When he was available.

Kenton woke up Fred Grimes to tell him of the call. Was it really Bishop? Yes, it was Bishop. No mistake about that. How did he know? He had never talked to the man, never heard his voice or even his breathing.

Didn't matter. He knew who it was right away. Something about the timing of the call, how it was handled. He couldn't explain it but he was certain he had talked to the madman himself.

Well, not really talked to him. More like listened.

What was said?

That something special would be happening very soon. Something so special that all the world would be talking about it for years to come. It would be a sign that Bishop had been sent on a divine mission, that he was truly Caryl Chessman's son and doing the work of his father.

But what was he going to do?

Kenton didn't know.

Afterward he thought of phoning George Homer or even John Perrone. But they could do nothing at midnight, nobody could. He sat up and smoked cigarettes and drank water, trying to clear his head. At 12:30 A.M. Dimitri called. He didn't seem particularly disturbed over Kenton's inability to recount Bishop's exact words, asking only that Kenton try to keep him on the phone as long as possible if he called again.

For the rest of the night the hound slept fitfully, pacing and growling, angry at himself, his prey, everybody. In the morning he felt anything but rested. A shower and shave helped a bit and breakfast a bit more. By ten he was in his office. Or rather John Perrone's office, telling of his midnight caller. His idea had worked; Homer's idea actually. Their man had taken the bait and established contact.

But for what purpose? asked Perrone. And what would the sign be? And when? Those were important questions.

Kenton had no answers. Not at the moment. But if Bishop called once, it meant he would do it again.

Perrone was not so sure. He had awakened with the same dread feeling of imminent disaster that had filled his Sunday-night hours. Something was going wrong, horribly wrong. Chess Man was demented and homicidal. He was also vastly unpredictable.

By noon everyone at *Newstime* had heard of Chess Man's cryptic call. Most saw it as another point gained for the magazine. Few worried about the menacing implications.

During the morning hours Inspector Dimitri had listened again and again to Chess Man's voice speaking the few words of warning. He was up to something all right, but there were no clues in what he had said to Kenton. Nothing definite. Just like he knew he was being overheard.

Dimitri had ordered Kenton's phone at the St. Moritz tapped the minute he learned of the plan to make contact With Chess Man. Kenton's hotel was named in the newspaper interview, an unusual occurrence, and that plainly told what the reporter was up to. The tap had been connected just hours before the call, but Chess Man didn't speak long enough for a trace to be made.

Maybe the next time, said some of the task force members. If Kenton could keep him on long enough, they stood a good chance of getting him.

Dimitri wondered if they'd ever have him on long enough, or even if they'd have another chance. The voice sounded so—final.

Or was he just imagining things again?

Bishop got off at the tenth floor, not wanting the operator to know of his actual destination. In the elevator he had stared at a magazine he carried in order not to be engaged in conversation. As the elevator doors closed behind him, the young woman with the shoulder bag walked along the carpeted hall to the exit door. A gloved hand checked the outside knob to make sure it wasn't locked. The next moment she was racing up the fire stairs.

At the fourteenth floor Bishop slowly opened the door. There was no one in the hallway. He quietly walked to the end of the corridor and around the bend of the L-shaped floor design. He intended to work his way back to the other end of the hall room by room, then floor by floor, ripping downward until nothing remained of the ruined castle and death was its only lodger.

They would have their sign. And by it would he be known to all people and for all time.

He knocked on the door.

The woman was surprised to see her standing there. She could have sworn she knew all the female help in the hotel. And why the coat and bag just to bring a telegram upstairs? She frowned as she was given the pencil and pad to sign. Distracted, her eyes were not on the other as gloved hands came up swiftly to circle her throat . . .

A moment later Bishop closed the door and snapped the dead bolt in place. He put his bag on a chair and took out the portable radio and his knife. He removed his coat and gloves.

With the radio playing in the background and the dead woman's television set turned to an early afternoon movie, Thomas Bishop Chess Man slowly undressed and went to work on the body.

Long afterward he stretched out naked on the bed to await the eve of destruction.

Throughout the afternoon Adam Kenton stayed close to his office phone, hoping Bishop would call, knowing he wouldn't but thinking he might anyway. Like John Perrone, Kenton felt something fearful was coming. It wasn't only the fact of the call, itself no idle threat. But the very next day was the fifth anniversary of Bishop's escape, measured in months instead of years. He knew of the date of course; five months was a lifetime in such circumstances. He would want to celebrate, and what better time to work his latest feat of magic than at such a celebration? It was too perfect a piece of timing to let slip by.

Beyond all of that was the possibility that Bishop might be running down, losing energy. He had returned to New York. In almost four thousand miles of travel he had never gone back to any place, as far as was known. Granted that New York was uniquely suited to his needs, it was still backward motion and seemed to indicate a lessening of drive, a weakening of spirit. Or was it merely the fox doubling back?

Even so, wasn't that still the beginning of the end?

The hunter didn't know. He wondered if the fox ever thought in such terms. He tried to put himself in the other's position but he couldn't become the fox anymore. He had identified too closely in the chase with the hound and had lost his metaphoric abilities. He no longer knew what Bishop would do, and that worried him more than anything else.

At the special task force headquarters on East 21st Street, new information was being fitted into the factual profile on Chess Man. Fingerprints found in the dead Miami woman's apartment matched those known to belong to Thomas Bishop. He had been to Florida, which made it likely that he had been seen getting off the Miami bus. The description held: a man with dark hair and a goatee.

Also found was $21,000 belonging to Thomas Brewster. An assistant branch manager of a Jersey City bank had remembered the name, reading of Brewster over the weekend, and had checked the account that morning before calling local police, who had in turn notified New York.

The problem was determining how Bishop got that kind of money. None of his victims had been affluent. Most were bought women or lonely women of survival level to whom $21,000 would have seemed like a million. Even an aggregate figure probably would not reach that amount. And money was found afterward in many of the slain womens' homes, even on their bodies or in their bags.

Did such a vast sum of cash indicate yet another victim? A victim unknown to police, undiscovered, unreported? Or could the money have come from more than one such victim? How many?

How many more bodies were lying out there across the sweep of America?

It was a chilling question only Chess Man could answer. But no one on the task force expected him to live that long.

In the early evening Bishop watched a game show on television, fascinated by the antics of contestants.

Eventually he arranged his clothes carefully on the couch: the print dress with the floral design, a bit too large for him but not uncomfortably so, the gray wool sweater, the colorful scarves, the stockings and brown shoes. The green coat and black gloves were placed separately on a chair; he would not be needing them again until he had finished. His travel bag, now empty, was on another chair. On an end table next to the couch lay the blond wig and the telegram forms and pads and pencils.

All the makeup and the hair brush and earrings had

already been put in the bathroom. When the time came he intended to give himself an even finer face in the larger mirror and better lighting of his newest temporary residence.

Satisfied with his final preparations, Bishop returned to watching TV from a restful position on the bed. He anticipated a busy day for himself, a day to remember—at least for others to remember—and he wanted to be at his best. A stock phrase came to mind, "bright-eyed and bushy-tailed." Like a fox. He frowned, reminded of Adam Kenton, who no doubt saw him as the fox to be pursued. Except he was now once again the hunter; he had the power, and it was he who would be in pursuit.

For the fox there was nowhere new to run, and no place else to hide.

Thinking such thoughts, Bishop soon fell asleep in the middle of a war comedy about prison camps. He didn't understand how anybody could laugh at being locked up. He had been locked up all his life. It wasn't anything for laughter. No one laughed at being locked up. No one he ever knew laughed at it. No one he ever heard of either. Unless they were crazy.

He would never be locked up again. Never. He wasn't crazy. No matter what else came, he would never be locked away again.

In his dream the woman pursued him relentlessly. He had nowhere to run, no place to hide. She hounded him, followed him, dogged his footsteps. Wherever he went she came. In her hands was a box. She wanted to put him away in a box. He didn't want that. He kept running, she kept gaining in close pursuit—

He woke up in a cold sweat, his eyes closed, seeing the woman standing over the frightened boy. In her hand the great whip rose and fell endlessly. There were no sounds, never any sounds as the long lash cut into the boy's bare skin. And the whip hand rose and fell . . .

With frantic effort Bishop flung open his eyes.

On the TV screen Johnny Carson was smiling and mugging for the camera, expertly leading the beautiful people through their paces. Bishop looked at the clock by the bedside. It was after midnight and would soon be the dawn of a new day.

His day.

It had already begun.

Five months ago at this very hour he had walked out of the prison camp. Just walked away and started a new life.

Now he would do it again.

He reached out for the phone.

In the St. Moritz, Adam Kenton caught it on the first ring. He had been waiting all day for this call. Dreading it too. After a moment he announced himself, adrenaline shooting through his body.

The voice on the other end was distant, metallic, funereal.

"It has already begun."

He heard the soft click as the line went dead.

At the 13th Precinct the message was quickly relayed to a quiet home in Queens. A light switched on in an upstairs bedroom. Alex Dimitri, instantly alert, listened carefully and then ordered central command to be notified immediately. There was little else that could be done without more information. He cursed softly so that his wife wouldn't be disturbed.

Adam Kenton had been right about Bishop again. The lunatic planned something to celebrate his five months of freedom, something he apparently had already begun. But what was it?

What had he already begun?

Kenton didn't know either when Dimitri called him from the precinct an hour later. He was still a bit angry over the telephone taps, especially since he hadn't been told until almost noontime, but at least he got Bishop's words out of it. He regarded that as only fair.

It was obvious that Bishop intended to be cryptic, Kenton now told Dimitri, so they would have to wait for the first fearful reports.

Kenton also knew that Bishop was becoming even more conscious of his public image, more determined to have things set right. Maybe he really was preparing for his capture and triumphant acceptance into society, loved at last. All unconsciously of course.

Did he really think that—

Could anyone be that crazy? Even unconsciously?

Excited beyond endurance, convinced that his time was at hand, the man who loved women put on his dress and all the rest of his clothes, determined to continue his conquest immediately. He would stalk the hotel halls during the early morning hours, much as he had once stalked unseen down the California land on a dark and rainy night. A slight shift in plan perhaps but a necessary one. He would use the telegrams again during the day until his work was done. But for now he would patrol his preserve, picking off the stragglers and any who might have strayed too far from the fold.

With face fixed and wig in place, Bishop cautiously opened the door and stepped into the empty hallway. His knife was in the shoulder bag, as was the room key taken from the woman's purse. He would return in the morning for a fresh start.

The door closed softly behind him.

Alice Troop might have had one drink too many by her own count but she didn't really care at the moment. It had been a good party and she had enjoyed herself. Good people, good conversation and even a few indecent proposals politely refused. For a thirty-nine-year-old divorced woman just three months in New York out of a Midwestern mini-city, friendly and bright but not especially attractive, it wasn't a bad evening. She had looked forward to the convention party for weeks, and had not been disappointed. Now she looked only for a good night's sleep. Nine o'clock would be coming up soon.

For Alice Troop it would never arrive again.

Key in hand, she got off at the twelfth floor and started down the hall. She saw the woman coming out of a doorway up ahead of her. Wasn't that the fire exit? She mentally shook her head. Couldn't be. In front of her own room she stopped, smiled as the woman passed.

Her key was in the lock and she began to turn it. She heard nothing as hands reached out for her and something flashed in front of her eyes in the last second of life.

The door was pushed open and the body flung inward, squirting blood everywhere. Bishop quickly grabbed a sweater draped over a chair and wiped the blood from the door and sill. The next moment he locked himself in the room with the corpse.

Frank O'Gorman returned from his second tour of inspection at 2 A.M. The night security man, he had been with the hotel eight years and had a few stories to tell. He had often thought of writing a book about his adventures in a woman's world. Maybe someday when he retired.

Coffee in front of him, he sat in his small basement office and glanced up occasionally at the screen showing the various floors in the building. O'Gorman shook his head in disgust, a habit he was getting into whenever he looked at the newest security device. Something else for him to do. In between all his other duties he now had to watch a dozen damn floors on a silly screen. He turned the knob quickly, zipping through all of them. Nothing seemed amiss, as usual. The Ashley was a well-run building. Thanks mostly to himself, O'Gorman mumbled modestly, and went back to reading his *Daily News.*

At 2:55 Beth Danston came home to her ninth-floor single with private bath and was surprised by another resident, who engaged her in conversation at her door. She was dead at 2:57.

At 4:10 Cappy McDowell finally got back from a midnight supper with a special friend who had a 7 A.M. flight out of Kennedy. He was the pilot and had to be there at 5 A.M. By then Miss McDowell was dead.

At 6:40 Emma deVore got up and went out for two pumpernickel bagels and a pint of heavy cream from a nearby gourmet deli that opened at 6:30. It was her morning custom to combine a brisk walk with breakfast. Good for the digestion. She returned at 7:15 to the tenth floor and was never seen alive again.

Bishop had taken several brief catnaps during the night and now, back in his fourteenth-floor corner room, he felt as if he would never sleep again. Excitement amounting to frenzy was driving him on just as it had all those months ago when he left the prison camp.

He glanced at the television, the *Today Show* smiled back at him. They were interviewing somebody who had done something or not done anything. He wished he could get interviewed like that. He had plenty to tell them, tell everybody. Only nobody wanted to hear what he had to say. They'd read of him in the papers, but they wouldn't sit down with him and talk rationally about what he was trying to do. He had no one to talk to; in the whole world he had no one. His father was dead. So was his mother, whom he loved dearly. He was always and everywhere the outsider. No one wanted him or cared for him.

So what? He didn't need anyone. He was smarter than everybody. And they all knew it. Which was why they feared him.

It was after eight o'clock and he would soon be starting his rounds. Just like a doctor on TV. This was his hospital and he took care of people.

No, this was his prison camp and he took care of people.

He went into the bathroom to put on a fresh face.

This was his day.

Henry Field was starting his security shift in the basement office. He turned the TV control knob slowly; most of the floors had activity at this hour. When he got to the fourteenth floor he noticed a woman with something in her hand standing in front of a door, apparently waiting to gain entrance. No one else was in the hallway at the moment. The incident registered on his mind as he shifted to another floor.

Upstairs, Bishop had tried three rooms in a row, all unsuccessfully. He did not understand what women were doing at nine o'clock in the morning that they couldn't answer the door. As it was, he had to be careful of those waiting for the elevator. Several times he had been forced to walk by them and around the bend. He was sorry he would be missing those who left the hotel but someday he would catch up with them somewhere. He was certain of that. The world was only so big.

In the basement Henry Field again ran through the floors. He regarded the TV security system as an invaluable aid, one that freed him from unnecessary foot patrol and allowed for much greater surveillance.

On the fourteenth floor he saw the same woman in the hallway, this time pausing in front of different doors as though listening for sounds. He watched as she stood in front of one for some moments, then moved on to another.

Henry Field was a good security man, and experienced. He knew all the signs. His hand automatically went out for the phone.

The first report of a 10-31 possible burglary in progress came in to the 19th Precinct on East 67th Street at 9:12 A.M. Tuesday, December 4, 1973.

TWENTY-FIVE

The rain had begun shortly before dawn, a light drizzle that looked as if it might last all day. Black clouds hung overhead as the barometer dropped, bathing the city in harsh shadow. Everywhere darkness lingered long after daybreak, and by the morning rush hour it was obvious that New York was in for another dreary December day. Raincoats and umbrellas were the fashion as workers trooped to their jobs and schoolchildren sloshed along the curb or climbed into waiting buses that matched the yellow of their slickers. Though no one could have known of course, a raging inferno that had blazed out of control on another wet and weathered morning some five months earlier was about to come crashing down in final fury around the broken bodies of some of its victims.

Now, as the drizzle dampened people's spirits and turned traffic to a crawl, a police car whined its way into 61st Street between Park and Lexington and swerved to a stop in front of the Ashley. The hotel security man met them in the lobby and all hurried into a waiting elevator. They hoped to catch the suspect in the act, if indeed a burglary was taking place. The police had their doubts, based on past experience with security personnel. Still, a women's hotel like the Ashley was a good spot for a female thief. She would blend right into sheer invisibility.

Bishop was to do even better.

Bill Torolla didn't trust *anybody*, which was probably why he liked the security business. Coming out of the Marines at twenty-five, he had tried any number of peacetime jobs but they all seemed tame and unexciting to a man who had served in the secret intelligence branch of the Corps. At age twenty-nine he went to work for a small New York firm that specialized in premises protection. He liked the work and soon moved to a larger company where he found more challenge. After several years he left to form his own outfit but undercapitalization did him in and he lost whatever investment he had made in the try. It was back to a job, and the Ashley had looked good at the time.

Now, after four years as backup security man on the day shift, he wasn't so sure it had been a good move. He was thirty-seven years old and there was little chance for any advancement. Henry Field had the number-one spot and there wasn't anything else. What he needed, Torolla kept telling himself, was a bigger place, and lately he had been thinking of making the rounds. In January after the holidays he intended to do just that. But this was only early December and so Bill Torolla went through his normal duties, all second nature by now. Only Torolla's natural mistrust of everything kept him on his toes. While Field was upstairs with the cops he started on a credit check.

Bishop was back in his room, forced to retreat by women waiting for the elevator. He saw now that he had started his rounds too early. Either that or too late. This way he would miss all those who went to work or out sight-seeing, which seemed to be most of them. But at least it would make things a bit safer for him as he snared those others who remained. And after all, sooner or later he would get to everyone, every last one of them. So where in the world could they go to escape their doom?

Meanwhile he would wait until after ten o'clock before venturing out again. Then he'd have the rest of the day to himself to work undisturbed. In all likelihood he wouldn't be finished by evening so he would work all through the night, gradually descending until he had gutted the castle and stripped it of its demons. He already had made a good start and the blood lust was rising within him. He would not, could not, stop now, not before his vengeance was complete. At least for the moment.

Thomas Bishop was certain that the world would well note and long remember what he did here.

But even he in his infinite megalomaniacal wisdom did not expect monuments to be built to him. Not yet anyway. He knew it would take time for people to understand what he was trying to accomplish. And he had lots of time.

He looked at the clock by the bed: 9:25 A.M.

* * *

The police found nobody on the fourteenth floor, not in the hallway or on the fire stairs or even in the rooms that Henry Field checked with his passkey. They knocked on doors. Where the woman was home they apologized. Where no one answered they entered. Nothing seemed amiss.

Many were already gone at this hour, mostly to business, though tourists often preferred an early start in their attack on the city at large. The last room they investigated was at the end of the corridor and around the bend. A woman came to the door dressed in a bath towel, with a sweater hastily thrown over her shoulders. On her feet were fluffy white slippers. Her head was wrapped in a towel and her face smeared with cold cream. She had just taken a shower and was getting herself made up.

Field apologized for the annoyance; they were seeking a possible prowler. The woman rolled her eyes in fright and Field hastily explained he hadn't meant a male. They quickly left, one cop remarking that he wouldn't mind coming back for a taste of that. Terrific legs she had, and a damn good body. Yeah, said the other, but no tits. The first one scowled. Tits ain't everything, he said, getting into the elevator.

They checked out the thirteenth floor before leaving. When nothing turned up they told Field he probably just saw a hotel guest trying to borrow a belt from a neighbor. Either that or the suspect had been unable to gain entry and was already gone. Field glumly accepted the possibility.

In the corner room Bishop wiped the cold cream off his face. Luckily he had heard the police banging on a nearby door and so had been warned in time. But how did they know of a prowler? Was there another one, a woman after something at the same time and on the same floor? No, that was too much to believe. It had to be a woman at the elevator who had reported somebody in the hall apparently without a destination.

He wished people would mind their own business.

After removing all the cold cream he began putting on his makeup for the day. He had plenty of time and he wanted to look his very best for his public even though he would be seeing them one by one and they would be seeing him only the one time too.

* * *

In his basement office Henry Field too stared at the TV screen, only his was closed-circuit television and instead of monster movies he was watching the fourteenth floor. He saw nothing out of the ordinary. The 8:30 to 9:30 rush was over and the hallway had been virtually deserted for many minutes. A look at other floors produced the same negative results. It was certainly possible, Field had to admit, that he made a mistake. A percentage player, he knew the odds were against it, but mistakes did happen. Even to him.

Still, the thought bothered him. He had been so sure of his judgment. Sure enough to call the police, which meant he was positive. Otherwise a professional would never call them. Now they'd begin to wonder about him. He knew all the brass in the precinct and he didn't particularly like the idea of them laughing at him.

He went over the rooms again in his mind. First the empties, then the others. Everything was in order right down to the corner room with the bathing beauty wrapped in a towel.

What was there about—?

He stared at the mental image until he saw what was wrong. She was wearing earrings. In the shower? Some women do, if they have on the kind for pierced ears. But these didn't look like that kind; they were large gold hoops. But who could really tell?

Field thought he might just go up there again on some pretense and make sure. Probably nothing to the idea but he owed himself another look. Wasn't anything doing at the moment anyway, and he'd be right back.

Torolla was away from his desk as Field closed the office door and walked over to the bank of elevators.

Bishop heard the knock just as he was adjusting the blond wig. He was still in his underwear so he slipped into a cotton nightgown hanging on the bathroom door, glancing at himself in the mirror on the way out. When the hotel security man said his name, Bishop's eyes became diamond-hard before the mask quickly closed over them again.

Field saw the woman smile at him and he mumbled something about hotel security and how she could help. Just a few questions. He called her Miss Dunbar. Invited in, he sat on the couch and commented on her lovely earrings. For pierced ears, weren't they? He chuckled. His own wife was afraid to have her ears pierced. Claimed they could become infected. Surely that wasn't true, was it?

Bishop listened to him from the bathroom, as though getting dressed. Obviously the man suspected something. Through the crack of the slightly open door he watched Field look about the room until his gaze fell on the bed. He quietly walked over to it as Bishop's hand reached into the bag he had brought with him into the bathroom. He turned on the water tap, then silently pushed the door back and stepped out on soft-slippered feet.

Field heard nothing. His back to Bishop, he was on his knees and reaching under the bed when his peripheral vision caught a glimpse of something moving behind him. He instinctively turned his head around and upward just as the great knife was arcing down into the top of his skull, at the very center of the bald spot. Grasped with both hands by Bishop and driven downward with terrible force, the knife tore through bone and cartilage, almost to the hilt. There was a flash of incredible light, beyond anything Field had ever seen. The light quickly turned to red. His eyes rolled inward, the jaws slackened. He had no time to react or to recall anything. As his body began to sag toward the floor Henry Field was already dead.

Bishop returned to his final facial preparations. His hands shook. He was angry at the man for trying to trap him, to stop him from his work. Why were they like that? He was not the enemy. In the long run he was helping all of them. They should be praising him but instead they sought to lock him away again. Or even destroy him.

He became so enraged by the thought that he rushed back in the room and plunged the knife again and again into the lifeless body. The rug was soon wet with blood. When his passion was finally spent he shoved the body under the bed, where it came to rest next to that of the slain woman.

After washing the blood off himself, Bishop dressed in a leisurely manner. Then it was time to go. The hall would be empty and some women would be home. With thirteen more floors below!

By eleven o'clock Bill Torolla was wondering what had happened to his senior partner. He had been gone over an hour, which was not like the man. As a security precaution they usually kept each other informed of their location if they expected to be gone for more than a half hour. Torolla thought he might be with the manager upstairs. Or maybe chasing his phantom prowler again.

Had the closed-circuit TV been switched to the fourteenth floor, and had anyone been watching at the time, a young woman might have been seen knocking on a door in the middle of the hall. A door that was soon opened and through which the young woman rather quickly entered.

By noon Torolla was concerned. He learned that Field had asked about the person in 1438, Miss Dunbar. One of the elevator operators had taken him to her floor. No one had brought him down. Torolla called upstairs but got no answer. He decided that his partner was spending an amorous few hours with the woman in 1438. It was against hotel regulations of course, but both men had done it on occasion.

Frustrated, he returned to his work and then went out to lunch at 12:30 with a friend and promptly forgot all about it.

At about the same time in Berkeley, California, two parcels were being delivered to the home of Amos Finch. They had been sent to him by Adam Kenton in New York City and contained all the final possessions of Sara Bishop and her boy that had been saved. Almost all. Kenton had kept a few things for himself to help him in the search. Things that made him feel a closeness to Bishop, such as several childish drawings of monsters and copies of Caryl Chessman's books. And the worn leather strap—Kenton kept that too.

Finch was delighted with the new acquisitions. They would become part of the Thomas Bishop collection he was assembling. He had already acquired Bishop's meager possessions at Willows State Hospital: a few clothes, some books, the lockbox from under his bed, a blanket and sheet from the bed itself, other odds and ends. More important to the collection were the items given him just recently by Lieutenant Spanner. A very distinctive harmonica and an alligator comb, a little wallet with a picture of Sara Bishop, and the uniform that Vincent Mungo had worn on the night of the escape. Inside each garment was sewn the name of Thomas Bishop. Spanner did not expect Bishop ever to stand trial in his jurisdiction for the killing of Vincent Mungo. He would never, the lieutenant knew, stay alive that long.

Finch naturally hoped to get whatever he could of Bishop's things when he was finally killed. Like almost everyone, Finch had no doubts that Bishop would die swiftly. Already having resigned himself to it, he considered the loss a staggering one for criminology but nonetheless as certain as the ending of an epic Greek tragedy, with which Bishop's life had much in common.

Now, on this California Tuesday morning, Amos Finch dialed New York to thank Kenton, hoping the man would remember his promise to salvage everything he could that belonged to Bishop at the end.

In Sacramento, Roger Tompkins had just walked into Senator Stoner's office and announced his resignation. There were other offers, naturally. It had been a great time but it was just one of those things.

He returned several letters and copies taken earlier when he had feared he might become the victim of a forced resignation. That was in better times, of course. But no hard feelings. Politics is a rough game, as the senator well knew.

He smiled his warmest.

From behind his desk Stoner stared at the young man facing him. There was no doubt in his mind that Roger would go far in politics. He had the ruthlessness and hunger for power that were necessary, and he also had the insincerity and cynicism needed. He would make his mark.

Meanwhile he was making a mistake. A big one, but he was young and still had a lot to learn about politics. He was learning something right now, though he didn't realize it yet. Nothing was as it seemed in politics. Like snakes, politicians should never be counted out until after the death rattle.

Over the weekend Stoner had met with the state party leaders. Because of his new prominence he was considered a big asset to state Republican hopes, so they had given his present troubles special handling. Meaning a deal had been made. His questionable business maneuvers were actually honest errors of judgment rather than of illegal intent and had been stopped immediately when called to his attention. California Democrats had one of their own caught in a similar mess so neither party would press the issue. Without a storm of publicity the public would not regard the matter as serious. Californians were notoriously easy on their own, anyway.

Of even greater significance to Stoner was the reaction of the big power blocs in the Midwest and East. At first blush they had been ready to write him off. He had committed the unpardonable political sin of being caught. Yet his burgeoning popularity, his increasing national recognition, gave them second thought. They needed some new faces to take people's minds off some old ones. Even more, they needed some who could be shaped into winners in the coming dark season.

Stoner had captured the public's fancy with his imaginative campaign for capital punishment. It was a big issue and would get bigger as things like crime and urban terrorism got worse in the country. And the senator had capital punishment by the throat. As one New York Republican bigwig put it, "Stoner found it, he built it, and he's going to keep it."

The consensus was to back him, after a brief period to let the public forget the *Newstime* revelations. Much as an airline stops all newspaper advertising for several days following a crash.

None of this did Stoner mention to Roger Tompkins. Instead he accepted the young man's resignation with "profound regret" and wished him well. Fuck him! Let the little bastard learn on his own.

At noon he would call Tom Donaldson in Chicago. From now on he wanted big-time support in everything from press agents to fund raising.

He thought of the evening ahead, when he would be with his new mistress. She was big-time support too.

Senator Jonathan Stoner was not only a survivor, he was a winner. He would beat them all yet.

The other survivor sat in his New York hotel room and wondered if he would ever win again. He had been writing about the man for nearly four months and tracking him for almost two and still had not seen him or even come close. But at least he had heard the voice. Twice. For a few seconds.

It just wasn't enough.

Adam Kenton suddenly felt discouraged. He had spent the morning in his hotel thinking Bishop might call again. Here it was 1:30 in the afternoon and he had heard nothing. Nor would he again, he was sure of that now. And of something else too. Bishop was busy at that very moment, involved in an utterly mad grand design only he knew about. The man was capable of anything but pity. Kenton swore softly, fearful in spite of himself.

There had been some rings: from Fred Grimes, reporting his mob contacts, had no leads on the target; from John Perrone, who still had his premonition of disaster; from Inspector Dimitri, up all night waiting for the inevitable news; from George Homer, wondering if Bishop might be seeking to invade some unprotected preserve of women in the city, such as a nunnery or health club. Kenton passed the idea on to Dimitri, who ordered increased surveillance of those places.

At noontime Doris rang up to apologize. It wasn't easy to become physically involved and yet not be involved emotionally. Maybe she wasn't as grown up as she'd thought. Maybe she'd never be that grown up. But she hadn't meant to treat him unkindly or shout at him.

Kenton understood. It was as much his fault. They'd get together again, he told her. Until the next time anyway, or the time after that. What he didn't tell her was that he had been through it all before. More than once.

Amos Finch's call an hour later depressed Kenton further, reminding him that Thomas Bishop was not some evil monster from another world but a child who had been tortured so viciously that his mind finally took refuge in hopeless insanity.

There were thousands of adult children like him in mental hospitals all over the country, lost forever in the abyss of madness, the bottomless pit of hell. But not entirely like him. Thomas Bishop's torture had been so horrendous that he had touched bottom. He had turned on his own kind, seeing them as the enemy. In turning homicidal he had become a cancer.

Kenton couldn't even conceive of the incalculable suffering that could have done such a thing to another human being. His heart broke at the thought. He wanted to cry out for vengeance, but there was no one on whom to take revenge. No one was there. Except an army of police with infinite weapons trained on a single target, like a radiation machine focused on a malignant growth. When the moment came, the button would be pressed.

And he knew that was the right thing to do.

And he knew he would grieve for the dead.

It was 2:10 when Bill Torolla got back from lunch expecting to find Henry Field. The office was empty. He tried room 1438 again without luck. At 2:30 Torolla, still alone in the office, took his passkey to the fourteenth floor and entered the corner room. No one was home. He noticed dark stains on the rug by the bed, and he bent down for a closer look. . . .

By 3 P.M. the hotel on East 61st Street was an armed camp. Police vehicles were everywhere, precinct cars and division cars and forensic wagons and emergency trucks. Unmarked detective cars too. And, of course, those of the special task force under the command of Deputy Inspector Alex Dimitri. Network TV crews were arriving, setting up their equipment on the pavement since they were not allowed inside the hotel. Not yet anyway. The street itself was closed to traffic, and pedestrians were restricted to the opposite sidewalk for halfway down the block.

Inside, the confusion appeared even worse as seemingly endless police paraded through the lobby or gathered in ominous groups. The most frightful rumors were passed from one excited man to the next, all of which would eventually pale before the reality. One name was heard repeated over and over, often more as an improper epithet than a proper noun. *Chess Man.* The only certainty in those first hectic moments of arrival, during that first half hour as police brass set up field communications and priority missions, was that they had discovered, or stumbled into, the madman's latest outrage. It was not yet clear whether they had caught Chess Man in the act or arrived only after the final curtain.

Upstairs on the fourteenth floor every room was quickly searched with the help of a still dazed backup security man, but only the dead awaited the living. The count was five bodies, including that of Henry Field. Other units were beginning to check out the thirteenth floor in a more systematic approach as the nature of the gruesome task became evident. Still more police prepared for a search of lower floors. At ground level the entire building was sealed; men were stationed everywhere around the base, in every alley and passageway. If Chess Man were inside he would not escape again.

Soon after three o'clock the sensational news began to be broadcast on radio and television, special bulletins interrupting regular programming. TV showed the dramatic scene at the Ashley as network executives agonized over whether to scrap their regular schedule for the event. Either that or sandwich coverage between shows. Machine minds quickly began to calculate the cost.

Adam Kenton got the call at 2:50 from Fred Grimes. The police had just found Bishop's handiwork, and they might've found him as well.

No one was sure of anything yet. Except a lot of dead bodies.

The Ashley Hotel for women. Between Park and Lexington on 61st. About five blocks from the St. Moritz.

The crazy bastard was trying to knock off a whole building full of females!

Kenton was already gone.

A quick cab got him to Park Avenue and he was on the street in minutes. It was bedlam. His press card got him through police lines and Captain Olson, whom he spotted on the hotel steps, got him inside.

"Is he still here?" Kenton shouted into Olson's ear in the lobby.

"We don't know," Olson shouted back. "We've only been through the top floor so far. Five dead."

Kenton's face turned sick, the color draining out of him. "My God!" he mumbled. There were hundreds of rooms in the hotel and he didn't know how many floors. That meant hundreds of women. "My God!" he repeated to himself.

"The inspector's around somewhere," Olson yelled above the noise. "We've set up a command post in the manager's office. Over there." He pointed. "Only go easy on him right now."

"Why's that?"

"His daughter lives here," said Olson gravely, "and he hasn't heard from her yet."

In the crowded office Alex Dimitri sat barking out

orders and talking on phones, trying not to think of his eldest daughter. She was a fashion designer, often worked in her hotel room. Her office hadn't seen her since Monday noon when she left for some client meetings. She had taken a few things she intended to work on at home.

Dimitri said a silent prayer. He had already talked to his wife, assured her that Amy was safe and would call them any minute. Just as soon as she heard the news. Her room on the sixth floor had been looked into by one of his own men. She wasn't there.

Meanwhile he had work to do. . . .

It was a little past noon in California when the news broke. John Spanner heard about it as he returned from a briefing of a new homicide division he had started. He rushed to his office and snapped on the TV.

In Berkeley, Amos Finch was doing the same thing, having heard the announcement on the radio. As he pondered what lay ahead, Finch had the craziest urge to race for the airport and grab the next plane to New York.

By 3:30 the thirteenth floor had been gone over by special weapons units trained to deal with such emergencies. They had found seven more bodies. Only then did the full horror of the disaster become apparent to all. Hardened police officers were seen near tears, others turned to stone. A dozen bodies butchered beyond belief. And no one knew what lay below. There were still twelve floors to go.

As rapidly as possible the women were being evacuated from their rooms, at least those who answered. Police groups raced through the various hallways pounding on doors and herding emerging women into waiting elevators. They passed by those rooms whose doors remained shut. Chess Man could be in any one of them. Or another victim, beyond help. Their concern was to get the live ones out first. They would take care of him last, and forever.

At the lobby the frightened women, most wearing coats hastily donned, were told they wouldn't be able to return to their rooms for the moment. Perhaps by evening—they would have to wait and see. Then they were asked to leave the hotel so the police could get on with their work.

On the twelfth floor three more bodies were soon discovered, two in adjoining rooms at one end of the hall and the third several doors down. But a half dozen women were still alive, unaware of the slaughter around them.

To Dimitri's men it looked as if Chess Man had been forced to stop at that point by the arrival of police. When the eleventh floor yielded no new bodies the conviction grew that the madman had suddenly abandoned his plan on twelve. Which meant he was still somewhere in the building. Maybe. If he hadn't left through a basement exit as the police entered through the front door. Or flew away in an invisible spaceship parked on the roof.

Bishop had heard the sirens of course. Not having an invisible spaceship, he did the next best thing and blended into his surroundings. Scooping up his coat and bag, he raced down the fire stairs to Emma deVore's room on the tenth floor, letting himself in with the key taken from her body in the early morning. There he waited until police shepherded all the women into the elevators. In the lobby he walked silently through the confusion and out the front door with a dozen other women. Newsmen were waiting for them but Bishop managed to keep moving, saying nothing, and they quickly lost interest. He didn't linger on the block, walking rapidly to Park Avenue and around the corner. Eventually he slowed his pace and began to breathe easier.

He had done it again. Fooled them all.

At the Ashley the search went on, room by room. Over the next few hours police teams checked the entire building, including the top two stories again. Three more bodies were found, one each on the seventh, ninth and tenth floors.

But no Chess Man. Not in the rooms or halls or stairs, not on the roof or in the basement, not anywhere. He was gone. Like the wind, he was seen only by what he left behind.

What he left behind were eighteen dead. More than twice the number of Richard Speck's victims for a single night.

"We were lucky," said Dimitri privately to a few of his men. "It could've been a hundred."

No one disagreed.

In all the horror and confusion Bill Torolla never even thought of a possible tie-up between the infamous maniac and a female prowler whom Henry Field believed he had seen early that morning. By the time Inspector Dimitri finally heard of the incident it was too late to matter.

At the moment, though, Dimitri was happy for another

reason. His daughter was safe. She had called home at five o'clock when she learned of the Ashley siege, knowing her parents would worry. Where had she been? She was a bit hazy about that, something to do with working elsewhere for the day. To her father it sounded like she had been with a man, probably at his place. Damn kids today! Hell, she was twenty-five years old. It was her life. But the thought saddened him, he didn't know why.

Now at 7:30 P.M., he was ready to call it a day. The hotel had been gone over top to bottom. No one was hiding anywhere, the bodies had been removed, most of the police equipment was gone. The TV crews had left after the last of the bodies, when it was obvious that Chess Man was not in the building. Even the day-long drizzle had just about stopped.

The inspector wanted several men stationed in the lobby for the night, just in case. Would give the hotel guests a sense of security and keep away the overly curious. He told the manager they could start returning to their rooms —those who still wished to return. The manager knew what he meant. It would be a miracle if any hotel could survive such a blow.

For his part, Alex Dimitri was discouraged and suddenly resigned to the strong possibility that he would not get Chess Man. He snorted. Probability seemed more like it at the moment. There was something crazy about how the man was able to disappear like that. And he didn't mean mad crazy, he meant *weird*. What was that Adam Kenton had said about magic? Dimitri had a feeling this latest trick might cost him his career with the Department. He walked across the now quiet lobby on his way out. Wasn't a damn thing he could do about it either.

Kenton had left earlier, thinking Bishop might call him again at the St. Moritz to gloat over his latest triumph. By nine o'clock there had been no call and now as he sat in his room smoking cigarettes, the *Newstime* reporter began to think more clearly about the day's events. Maybe it hadn't been such a triumph after all. Bishop had obviously intended to go through the entire hotel, killing every woman in sight. An arrogantly impossible concept, too hideous even for contemplation. *Yet he could have done it*. If left alone, he might have literally committed the homicidal crime of the century. Without any exaggeration or hyperbole, it would have been exactly that. Nothing less than the absolute and irrevocable homicidal crime of the century, and would have assured him of a sinister immortality, far beyond even that of Jack the Ripper.

In that sense, then, Bishop had really failed in his own eyes.

But he was a sly fox.

A fox . . .

Without warning, as if by magic, Kenton was struck by a thought so bizarre, so hopelessly terrifying, that his whole frame shook in reaction. His eyes broke open in shock, his face tightened in a death mask. Moisture appeared almost instantly above his upper lip and across his brow. He sat there in stunned silence for a lifetime before fumbling for the phone. Two minutes later he was hurrying out of the St. Moritz.

Bishop's euphoria had left him. He sat in the darkened theater and absently watched the movie for the third time, his mind elsewhere. Even though he had demonstrated his superiority over all of them, his brilliant planning had largely failed.

He didn't like failure. His feet hurt from the shoes and his hands tightly gripped the shoulder bag on his lap. All he owned was inside; his knife and what was left of his money.

"Are you serious?"

"Let them all go. It's the only chance we have."

The inspector hesitated.

"If he spots them, we'll never get him," Kenton urged. "And we'll probably never get another crack at him."

"Who says we have one now?"

"He'll come," said Kenton with quick conviction.

Dimitri looked at him a long moment before walking across the lobby to the cops on duty, his mind made up. Then the two of them were in the elevator.

"Why the twelfth floor?"

"Bishop's methodical. He left on twelve and he'll pick up on twelve."

"You got the room number too?" asked a skeptical Dimitri.

"Almost," answered Kenton. "Only two possibilities."

He pulled out the diagram made earlier by the police. "He killed both women on this end over here. Then he got the other just two doors down, meaning he skipped this one." Pointed. "He'll either go for that door again or start on the other side of the third victim."

"You really think you know him that well?"

"I hope so."

A task force man in the basement would monitor the TV hall scanner, constantly turning to different floors. Anyone getting off at the twelfth floor would be immediately suspect. Other task force personnel would be in the manager's office waiting for any sign of trouble. The relief elevator operator was also a police officer.

"You sure he's dressed as a woman?" Dimitri asked when they got upstairs.

"Has to be," said Kenton. "That's how he got in and how he got out when he heard your men."

Dimitri found it hard to believe. "He should've been an actor instead of a nut," he growled.

"Maybe he could have, if things had been different for him."

It was 9:30 when they entered their respective rooms. Between them was the empty suite of the dead Alice Troop who had started a new life in New York.

By the end of the movie the young woman with the bruised feet and clutched bag was no longer in her seat. On the floor were a half dozen candy-bar wrappers and a popcorn container.

At 11:20 a slim blonde in a green coat bounced up the two steps and through the door of the Ashley. She crossed the dim lobby to the elevators, obviously knowing her way. In the elevator she smiled shyly at the operator and asked for the twelfth floor. Upon leaving she pleasantly bade the man good-night.

In the basement the detective looking at the TV already had her spotted.

She tiptoed down the hall until she came to the right door. She would continue her work as though there had been no interruption.

In her hand now was the passkey taken from the body of Henry Field. She would open all the doors with it.

Softly, gently, she would make her visits. There was no hurry, she had all night. And all day.

She had all the time in the world.

Bishop smiled happily.

At last he had all the keys he would ever need. How to think like them and how to talk like them, and now finally how to act like them.

He stuck the key in the lock.

Adam Kenton heard the door being opened. He knew who it was before he ever turned that way. From the window he stared at the other whom he had sought so very long. His blood suddenly froze, his heart stopped.

Their eyes met in combat.

Not a word was said. Bishop removed his shoulder bag and opened it. His hand came out with the knife as Kenton reached into his jacket pocket. The worn leather strap was rolled tightly and as Kenton unwound it, Bishop's eyes followed every movement. He drew closer as Kenton raised the strap over his head, and when Bishop was very near, the arm came down and struck Bishop with the strap. Bishop didn't move but stood there transfixed. Kenton's arm was raised again and lowered and raised again and the strap stung Bishop fiercely and still he did not move. Now Kenton's arm raised and lowered the strap again and again across Bishop's head, his neck and shoulders. There was no escape for the boy.

Down came the strap.

Bang!

In absolute terror now, hideous memory returning, Bishop screamed and dropped the knife. Screamed and ran to the window as Dimitri banged on the locked door. Shrieking in some monstrous private pain, Bishop flung his arms through the window and scurried onto the ledge amid the shattering of glass. Trying to escape what only his maddened mind could see. His hands bloody, his sobs those of a wounded animal, he straightened his body on the narrow ledge.

He looked down twelve stories deep into darkness. He was back on the top of Hoover Dam staring down, the dread feeling returned. He was getting sick, his knees buckled, his bladder began to empty. He felt himself slipping.

Kenton raised the broken window and grabbed Bishop by the arm as his legs gave out and he slipped below the window's edge. Kenton locked his hand into Bishop's and stopped his fall. He had a good grip and began pulling Bishop's limp body up just as Dimitri's men burst into the room, guns drawn.

Now Kenton looked into Bishop's pleading eyes and saw the incalculable pain and fright and madness and as Thomas Bishop's bloodied hand meshed with his, Adam Kenton slowly opened his fingers one by one and released the dying boy.

He knew there would be no more screams, and no more pain.

The madness was over.

That next morning Amos Finch did not go to his classes. He sat at home in meditative silence for much of those hours to commemorate the passing of a phenomenon, the like of which he did not expect to see again in his lifetime.

Afterward he organized his thoughts for the task ahead. *The Complete Thomas Bishop* would be written over a two-year period, under contract to his present publishers. He would immerse himself in Bishop's background; the history, the family, the life itself. He would visit every place Bishop lived or even stopped, see what he saw. He would of course have access to all official Bishop papers, from hospital records to police files. He would interview, talk with, listen to, everybody Bishop knew. He would learn of the man as well as the monster. Finally, he would draw with consummate skill the portrait of a man beset by demons, a man who looked like other men but who was yet apart, a man who killed not in cold blood but by reason of insanity. Bishop had stood hopelessly alone, yet in his towering isolation and megalomaniacal paranoia he had still tried to forge a bond with his fellow creatures. That the bond was one of total destruction was surely as much a reflection of his times as of his own unassailable madness.

Finch was certain that he would eventually acquire many of the artifacts having to do with the life and death of Thomas Bishop. He had already established himself as the scholar of note on the subject. With publication of the book he would be recognized as the authority of record, and would himself become an item in the Bishop canon.

It was now all a matter of persistence and hard work.

Had Amos Finch known what lay ahead of him in his quest for the greatest and most elusive individual mass murderer in American criminal history, a search that would rival that of Adam Kenton, he would not have been so sanguine in his projections on that early December morning.

Nor would he have then begun his initial outline with the words, "In the beginning, Thomas Bishop . . ."

By late afternoon Adam Kenton was reading the preliminary medical examiner's report on Bishop. He had been killed instantly in the twelve-story fall, of course. A white Caucasian male, approximately age twenty-five, height—. His eyes raced down the page: injuries, marks, body characteristics. He suddenly stopped, his face screwed into a quizzical frown.

The body had not been circumcised.

Not circumcised!

In California moments later John Spanner didn't believe it. Kenton assured him it was true, he had just made certain.

"Impossible," said Spanner. "Thomas Bishop was circumcised in Los Angeles County General hospital. The doctor's name was on the records and the file hadn't been touched in twenty-five years."

They immediately checked with Los Angeles. Bishop's file was again opened. No mistake. He was circumcised at birth. That was definite.

But the body of Thomas Bishop had not been circumcised. And that was definite too. Very definite.

Immediate investigation revealed that on April 30, 1948, forty babies had been born in the hospital. Twenty girls and twenty boys. At that time all the infants were kept in the same room the first few days, with name tags on the baskets and a paper bracelet on the baby's arm. That was in the days before footprints were recorded on the birth certificate.

"Anything could've happened," said Spanner.

"Something did," said Kenton.

Both men were shaken. Everything they knew to be substance had suddenly become shadow.

Adam Kenton felt Bishop's eyes on him, saw the maniacal stare, and he instinctively knew he would never really be rid of the man again. Not in his nightmares or in his memories, or even in the corners of his mind. He had run with the fox too long.

"If he wasn't Thomas Bishop," whispered Kenton helplessly, "who was he?"

EPILOGUE

Nowhere in Los Angeles police files is there mention of a woman named Sara Bishop being criminally assaulted on September 3, 1947. Sara Bishop never reported the rape, though she soon came to believe that the rapist was Caryl Chessman. She eventually imparted this belief to her son.

According to the official records of the California Department of Correction, Caryl Chessman was released on parole from Folsom Prison on December 8, 1947.

He was rearrested on January 23, 1948, in Los Angeles and executed on May 2, 1960, at San Quentin.

When the rape occurred, Caryl Chessman was in prison.

Sara Bishop never knew that.

Neither did her son, whoever he was.

Dell Bestsellers

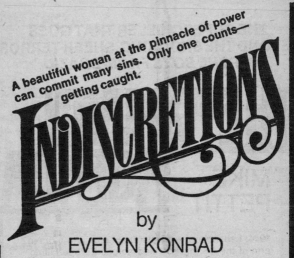

A beautiful woman at the pinnacle of power can commit many sins. Only one counts— getting caught.

INDISCRETIONS

by
EVELYN KONRAD

"Sizzling."—*Columbus Dispatch-Journal*

"The Street" is Wall Street—where brains and bodies are tradeable commodities and power brokers play big politics against bigger business. At stake is a $500 million deal, the careers of three men sworn to destroy each other, the future of an oil-rich desert kingdom—and the survival of beautiful Francesca Currey, a brilliant woman in a man's world of finance and power, whose only mistakes are her *Indiscretions*.

A Dell Book   **$2.50   (14079-X)**
At your local bookstore or use this handy coupon for ordering: